MUSIC IN JAVA

JAAP KUNST (1891–1960)

Photo: Thérèse Stern Le Prad

MUSIC IN JAVA

ITS HISTORY, ITS THEORY AND ITS TECHNIQUE

BY

J. KUNST †

THIRD, ENLARGED EDITION

edited by

E. L. HEINS

VOLUME I

THE HAGUE
MARTINUS NIJHOFF
1973

ISBN 90 247 1519 9 (Two Parts)
90 247 1520 2 (Volume One)

PRINTED IN THE NETHERLANDS

CONTENTS OF VOLUME I

DEDICATION VII

INTRODUCTION by Professor Dr. E. M. von Hornbostel IX

PREFACE to the first edition XI

PREFACE to the second edition XV

EDITOR'S NOTE to the third edition XVII

Chapter 1. GENERAL INTRODUCTION 1

Chapter 2. TONE- AND SCALE-SYSTEMS 11

Chapter 3. HISTORICAL SURVEY 105
- *a.* Before the advent of the Hindus 105
- *b.* Hindu-Java 106
- *c.* The post-Hindu period 113

Chapter 4. CENTRAL AND EAST JAVA 119
- *a.* Introduction 119
- *b.* Vocal music 122
- *c.* Instruments 135
  - I. Idiophones 136
  - II. Membranophones 202
  - III. Chordophones 220
  - IV. Aerophones 233
- *d.* Orchestras 243
- *e.* Structure, nature and use of the different compositions 295
- *f.* Notation 346

Chapter 5. WEST JAVA 356
- *a.* Introduction (a comparison of Sundanese with Javanese and Balinese music, both instrumental and vocal; the impression made on the Western mind; something about vocal music) 356
- *b.* Instruments 358
  - I. Idiophones 359
  - II. Membranophones 367
  - III. Chordophones 369
  - IV. Aerophones 375
- c. Orchestras 378
- *d.* Forms of composition, and their use 392

CONTENTS OF VOLUME II

Illustrations 1–165 413
Bibliography 457
Appendices 477
List of Grammophone Records mentioned in the Text 576
Supplement to the Second Edition 579
General Index 601

DEDICATION

This book — the result of twenty-eight years' listening, collecting and reflecting — is dedicated to His Highness Kangjeng Gusti Pangéran Adipati Aria Mangku Nagara VII.

The dedication in the first edition was inspired by sympathy and gratitude; this time it is also meant to be an expression of my profound veneration for the courage with which this prince faced a cruel and unscrupulous foe, and for his unshakable fidelity to his once given word. He was, indeed, a knight without fear or reproach, a real *Ksatriya.*

In him was embodied all that is best in the Javanese national character.

INTRODUCTION

One day in the summer of 1921 a postal delivery brought me a little packet of reprints from the periodical "Djawa": articles about Indonesian music by Dr. JAAP KUNST, which until that moment had not come to my notice. A cursory glance was enough to convince me that the author was a very gifted man, who had made a sound and absolutely scientific study of the subject, and thereby made a valuable contribution, by means of careful observation and actual tone-measurements, to the facts known from the older studies by GRONEMAN, LAND and ELLIS. These measurements were particularly satisfying to me personally, since they constituted an astonishing confirmation of a hypothesis concerning the genesis of tone-systems (through the "cycle of blown fifths"), which I had propounded two years previously, without, however, having published it. At the same time it was proved, through the perfect conformity existing between the measured and the theoretical absolute pitches (vibration frequencies), that Indonesian gamelan tuning, too, belongs to the radius of ancient Chinese culture — much the same as is the case with Pan-pipes and xylophones all over the world.

The first contact between Dr. KUNST and myself led to a regular correspondence, which especially contributed to a further development of the above-mentioned theory of tone-systems. KUNST generally communicated his numerous tone-measurements to me before they were printed, and from the exchange of our postal discussion the hypotheses concerning "Umschichtreihen" (alternating tone-series), origin and development of pélog and sléndro etc., arose.

However, tone-measurement and tone-systems are merely a part of a larger field, albeit one which is particularly important for ethnology and cultural history. One may say without exaggeration that KUNST has done more for the musicological exploration of Indonesia in every possible direction than anybody else; nay, more even than most authors together. Apart from a long series of larger and smaller articles we owe to him a thorough investigation into Hindu-Javanese instruments in which ancient artistic and literary works serve to illustrate and clarify musico-archaeological problems, and *vice-versa*, as well as a work in two volumes on the music of Bali—a standard book on this extraordinarily interesting field of music, which until then had been practically neglected. All these writings came into existence —truly a testimony of astonishing energy— during the brief hours of leisure of a very busy and frequently overworked Colonial Civil Servant. It was only during two years that KUNST was given an opportunity, as official musicologist to the "Oudheidkundige Dienst" (Netherlands Indies Archaeological Department), to devote himself entirely to his beloved profession, and to gather, on his own travels, a collection of musical instruments, phonograms, films and stills, thus laying the foundation for the archives, which, already in our days, guard the fast dying remains of the musical cultures of Indonesia with extraordinary completeness.

All these studies, journeys, and collections, to which should be added exhaustive discussions with native experts, form a preparation for this new work on Javanese music, so meticolous and many-sided as has been rarely obtained in the field of comparative musical science. This factual material of great wealth and presented with both clarity and simplicity, makes of this work a prodigious source of information, from which both the musical and the cultural-scientific explorer will be able to draw wisdom and encouragement for a long time to come.

The author, whose divining-rod has found the most likely spots, and whose borings have revealed so many new veins, may be certain of the gratitude of his readers.

E. M. VON HORNBOSTEL

PREFACE TO THE FIRST EDITION

The present work has grown from a treatise originally intended as an article in replacement of that by Mr. Joh. F. Snelleman, entitled "Muziek en Muziekinstrumenten", dated towards the end of 1917, and published in the second part of the "Encyclopaedie van Nederlandsch Oost-Indië". It soon became evident, however, that, owing to our increased knowledge, the size of the article would far exceed the ruling limits for lexicographical contributions, if written more or less in the style of Snelleman's generally informative treatise. It proved too difficult an undertaking to meet this objection by a greater condensation of the available material, since, on the one hand, the readability of the article would suffer considerably, whilst on the other hand there was still a lack of sufficiently reliable works of reference, not only in regard to the music in the "Buitengewesten" (Outer Provinces), but also, be it in a lesser degree, to that of Java. Taking everything into consideration, it seemed to me that a reasonable solution of this difficulty could be found by writing a book such as is here presented to the reader, and from which a summary might be drawn later on for the Encyclopaedia. The additional advantage of this procedure was that such matters as could not very well be explained by mere words could then be clarified by means of illustrations and musical examples.

I have thought best to limit myself for the time being to the music of Java. The music of other parts of the Archipelago will be dealt with later in a further work.

I am fully aware of my work being far from perfect, and not by any means complete. Further, the available material has not always been condensed in the same degree: wherever I was able, in connexion with a given subject, to refer to a more or less reliable source, I have not failed to do so, thereby saving space for those subjects which up to the present have received little or no attention.

I have done my best to give a definition or explanation of every word of Indonesian artistic terminology used in this book, the signification of each of which may be found quite easily by means of the General Register in Volume II.

The figures printed in bold type in the text refer to the publications mentioned in the second volume in the Bibliography.

With regard to the spelling used for native words, the following may suffice:

The lingual d and t are represented in Javanese words in het customary way by ḍ and ṭ; where no dot is printed under these letters—in Javanese words!—the dental d and t are meant. The Sundanese language has only the lingual d and the dental t. Since, therefore, there can be no misunderstanding as regards Sundanese words, we have refrained from printing dots under the d's occurring therein.

The mute e has been represented in the native words without accent; the short e as è, and the long one as é.

Finally, in the case of such words as awis, udan, arja, which are also found in literature as hawis, hudan, harja, the reader is advised, whenever he cannot find them in the Register under the letter h, to make sure by looking them up under the vowel following, in each particular case, on the "ceremonious" aspirate.

The photographs reproduced have partly been published before. As they were quite satisfactory, fresh photographs not throwing any new light on the objects in question, we have seen no objection to their re-publication here, the less so since the majority of them are hidden in publications which are either out of print or available only in very limited editions.

The reliability of my communications is considerably enhanced by the assistance which I was happy to receive from so many different quarters.

In the first place my warmest expressions of thanks are due to His Highness K. G. P. A. A. Mangku Nagara VII, who has, during the past fourteen years, honoured me on numerous occasions with his valuable collaboration and cordial hospitality; whose niyaga's and gamelans were ever standing in readiness; whose good advice and interest were my indispensable support during all those years, and who, notwithstanding the many cares and responsibilities that fall to the lot of ruling princes, has nevertheless been kind enough to go to the trouble of reading through critically the paragraphs dealing with Java Proper, and making marginal notes and corrections where necessary, principally, of course, with regard to the Solonese musical adat (tradition), based upon his own vast knowledge of Javanese music and that of his niyaga's.

I further received much valuable information from Dr. Purbacharaka and his brother Radèn Kodrat, both connoisseurs, the former of the old and new Javanese languages, the latter of gamelan, wayang and dance; amongst other things they introduced me to the secret beauties of the Chenṭini. On some occasions, too, Mr. Suhardha Sastrasuwignya was my guide through the sonorous labyrinth of this glorious poem. To them I owe, if not the form, then at any rate the entire content of the numerous quotations reproduced in the present treatise.

As regards Jogyanese music, my grateful remembrance goes out to His Highness K. G. P. A. A. Paku Alam VII, the prince whose guest I was in December 1919, when I received my first vivid impression of Central Javanese orchestral playing, and thanks to whose hospitality I was able *on many subsequent occasions to enjoy to the full Jogya gamelan playing of the highest order.*

I am also greatly indebted to Radèn Mas Jayadipura, a Jogya artist as versatile as he was modest and willing to help, and who, I hope, has found me, as a pupil, not too "slow in the uptake".

I was furthermore allowed to collect many precious data from the large Kraton-genḍing-collection, of which His Highness Hamangku Buwana VIII, Sultan of Jogyakarta, has presented a copy to the Royal Batavia Society of Arts and Sciences as an addition to its musicological collection. These data have greatly assisted me in my expositions of the structure and use of the different orchestral pieces. Many of the suluks *reproduced in the Appendices have been transcribed from this collection.*

The chapter dealing with the music of the Sunda-districts (the mountain-districts of West Java) largely owes its existence to Radèn Machyar Angga Kusumadinata, that talented musician and vigilant critic. I may be allowed once again to express my grateful thanks to him for his extremely valuable assistance.

My sincerest gratitude is also due to Professor Dr. B. J. O. Schrieke, the then Director of Education and Religion, for the liberal way in which he allowed me to make use of the results of a recently instituted inquiry among the Regents in Java and Madura concerning the numbers of gamelan and wayang outfits existing in their districts, and to the Java Institute for its permission to reprint part of the score Lebdapradangga-Jatiswara.

I also owe a debt of gratitude to my publishers, Messrs. Martinus Nijhoff, for having consented to take upon themselves, notwithstanding the present troublesome times, the risk of publishing this voluminous work with its many photographs and tables.

Finally, the fact that you, Professor Von Hornbostel, my "guru" *and friend, have been good enough to write a few introductory lines for my book, is for me a source of thankfulness and joy. It is, for me, one more incentive to continue to work to the best of my ability in the field of comparative musical science, whose great future possibilities are so largely due to the clarity of your intellect and intuition.*

Batavia, May 7th, 1933 *J. K.*

PREFACE TO THE SECOND EDITION

Since the first edition was published, Javanese music has received in ever increasing measure the attention of both fellow-countrymen and foreigners. During the past twelve years I have made careful notes of any new facts and points of view that I happened to hear of or see. In this second edition these data have accordingly been incorporated.

I was happy to receive numerous remarks and observations from various sides; in the first place from young Bernard IJzerdraat, to whom Javanese music, although he was never in the East at all, has become the heart's own natural speech, and who has given me many a welcome hint or correction derived from the practice of gamelan playing and from his vast knowledge of the music in the Principalities.

I further received, from Father P. Rozing, S.V.D., some important remarks concerning the genesis of pélog and sléndro from the hypothetical cycle of blown fifths; these will be found on p. 41 ff.

I have added several illustrations and replaced some by larger and clearer ones. The number of Appendices has also been increased.

The present edition is published in English, for the convenience of the many readers who are not familiar with the Dutch language. It should be pointed out in this connexion (in addition to what has been mentioned in the Preface to the First Edition concerning the spelling) that the sound which, in the Dutch transcription of native words, is represented by oe (more or less like the o and the u in to put) is usually represented by u, also in such words as sanḍung, kempul, keṭuk, plumpung etc. Further, the consonant j is represented by y; the double consonants dj and tj by j and by ch respectively. In order, however, to ensure agreement with the spelling of the names of authors and of the titles of their publications—which is necessary when referring to these works—the Netherlands spelling is retained in the Bibliography. The same applies for some of the Appendices.

The letter-combination eu in Sundanese words like cheurik sounds as the German ö.

In conclusion, a few words to express my warmest thanks to those who made possible the publication of this English edition: the Royal Institute for the Indies, which contributed largely by bearing the cost of the translation *fees and bij giving its much appreciated intermediary in obtaining the support of the "Prins Bernhard Fund", this Fund itself, whose generous subsidy enabled the publisher, Martinus Nijhoff, to defray the very high cost of printing, and to Mr. Nijhoff himself, for the kind interest he has once again shown in my work, and the great care he has given to its production.*

Amsterdam, February 3rd, 1948. *J. K.*

EDITOR'S NOTE TO THE THIRD EDITION

DR. JAAP KUNST's personal interleaved copy of *Music in Java* was the basis of the present re-edition of the book. After its publication in 1949 the author meticulously entered a considerable number of emendations and additions over a period of ten years, until death took him away in 1960. All these alterations have been included in the present edition.

To bring Jaap Kunst's original remarks further up to date, approximately, covering the past decade, the editor has added a number of entries to the bibliography (which therefore had to be reset) and compiled a discography of commercially available long playing records.

All these additions, i.e. the late author's personal remarks *and* the LP discography, have been grouped together in the *Supplement*, which is the newly added portion of the book at the end of Volume II.

References to newly added bibliographical entries have thus been put in their proper place within the original text: [**278A**] refers to that item in the bibliography.

References to all supplementary matter have been placed both in the text body *and* in the General Register in the following way: [*S10] means: *See also* (*vide*, *cf.*) entry nr. 10 in the Supplement. All new additional references, Kunst's own as well as the editor's, have been put between square brackets to mark them off from the original ones.

Jaap Kunst's personal (longer) additions are to be found in S2—S32. At his own responsibility the editor added S1, S27 and S31, as well as most discographical entries S33—S72. On the other hand, no words, terms, names of persons, regions and authors have been added to the General Register if they were not there originally. In this connection it should be pointed out, that, apart from a few obvious earlier printing errors, nothing has been changed in either the original text, the appendices, the illustrations or in Jaap Kunst's personal additional remarks, other than those emendations indicated as such by the author.

Due to the process of photographic reprint the original paging of the 1949 edition has remained the same. So has the numbering of the 'old' bibliographic entries, while new entries are recognizable as such by the capitals A, B, C etc. added to their reference numbers. Some of these new entries, however, had to be given a less orthodox number-letter combination (e.g. **336**AB) in order to preserve the alphabetical order. Due to the fact that the entire bibliography had to be reset, most entries underwent a change in typography to make them shorter as well as more informative.

In enlarging the bibliography the editor limited himself mainly to publications of direct Javanese, Sundanese and generally Indonesian musicological interest. Publications on *dance* have been included when possible. Publications on other art forms related to music, such as *wayang* and other dramatic representations, have been added only if they stress the musical and/or sociological aspects of Javanese theatre. With two monumental exceptions (**271**B and **336**B) mere text-editions of wayang-*lakons* or Javanese summaries (*lampahan*) thereof could not be incorporated. The choice, however, has been admittedly subjective.

In 1972 a new spelling was adopted in Indonesia, to which Kunst's own orthography of Indonesian words was remarkably close. The main difference is that 'ch' stands for (modern Indonesian) '***c***' and that Kunst also applied this spelling to proper names.

The editor, having studied in Indonesia in 1967/68 under a grant from the Netherlands Organization for the Advancement of Pure Research, acknowledges his debt to Mr. FRANS HARJADI who came to play such an important part in the compilation of the enlarged bibliography, that he virtually became its co-author, and to the librarians and staff of the KONSERVATORI KARAWITAN INDONESIA at Surakarta, the MUSEUM PUSAT at Djakarta and the LEMBAGA ILMU PENGETAHUAN INDONESIA, for their continuous assistance and support in obtaining data on recent Indonesian published material. The editor expresses his special gratitude to Mrs. C. KUNST-VAN WELY for the confidence she put in him. It was she who instigated the re-edition of *Music in Java*.

E. L. HEINS
Institute of Musicology,
Ethnomusicology Centre "Jaap Kunst"
University of Amsterdam

Chapter I

GENERAL INTRODUCTION

Difficulties in the way of a general characterization.

It is a well-nigh impossible task to formulate a characteristic of "the" music of the Indian Archipelago, and this for a variety of reasons. In the first place, it is inhabited by two utterly different races: the Malay (Indonesian) and the Papua-Australian. Not only do these two races differ strongly as regards outward appearance: spiritually, too, they are very little alike. In their music this difference is also markedly evident, although it is not an easy matter to indicate in a few words the nature of this difference. First and foremost the difference is one of atmosphere, the characteristic details wherein the discrepancy lies being observable only in the second place.

But even within the limits of one and the same race—and this applies chiefly to the Malay—one may notice differences so fundamental that a single general musical characterization becomes practically impossible; partly, too, in consequence of the great differences in the cultural level of the various component parts of the race. No such general characterization, therefore, will be attempted here. The method followed by the writer is that of regional treatment, combined with comparative indications—where possible, in view of our present knowledge of the available material—of differences and likenesses between the music under discussion and that of neighbouring or kindred population groups or musical expressions of other cultures or historical periods lending themselves to such comparison.

Influences from outside.

The music of these islands is not autochthonous in the (relatively) pure sense of the term, except to a very limited degree; in many respects it is closely akin to that of the surrounding territories, taking the adjective "surrounding" in a very wide sense.

That one cultural wave after another should have passed over this island-world might, even in the absence of concrete data, be readily assumed, for the Indian Archipelago is situated on the fringe of the great Asiatic continent, that aboriginal source of many, if not all great cultures; moreover it is desirable as a habitation, being fertile and having a generally favourable climate; finally, it is situated in the zone of the trade winds, which strongly favoured migration. The necessary data, however, for this assumption are not lacking by any means. Archaeology, ethnology, historical discoveries, linguistics, and during the last decades, comparative musical science have gradually succeeded in collecting a wealth of factual material from which it is evident that, in the course of the past *millennia*, successive races and peoples, each with their own characteristic culture —including music—have either driven away or subjected older, earlier arrivals in their search for fresh habitations, or introduced their own civilization by the more peaceful ways of trade and colonization, thereby inevitably affecting and reforming the existing native culture.

In a sense, we might speak of "cultural geology"; for on analyzing the music in a given territory, and on examination of the instruments in use, one is sometimes struck by the fact of a noticeable stratification. Some evidently very ancient cultural remnant may still linger on the surface, almost swamped by a younger stratum, which itself has not remained quite unaffected either (**202, 313**) [1]). It is possible in some cases to arrive at a reasonably documented relative chronology, *i.e.* at the conclusion that a given cultural phenomenon is younger than another; only in very rare cases, however, it is possible to give a definite date, the available facts being usually totally inadequate.

Before proceeding to a discussion of the native music of the various islands separately (in this book only as regards Java), we should bear in mind the fundamental fact that any outside cultural influences such as we referred to above can only be of a permanent and more or less intensive character providing the soil which is to nurture the seed blown upon it is a genuinely receptive one; in other words, that the population to be in-

---

[1]) Figures printed in bold type in the text refer to the publications contained in the list of literature in Vol. II.

fluenced is more or less attuned, and mentally equal, to the said outside influences; a society, therefore, which, tho', may be, not at the time on the same cultural level as the race which exercises the influence, is yet potentially able to come somewhere near that level; a community which, even when no longer in direct contact with the foreign civilization influencing it, is itself culturally potent enough to retain and guard what it has received, be it in modified form and after its own fashion, as if it were its own cultural possession. To summarize this argument in an extreme example: a Papua culture cannot be affected by the Kantian philosophy.

To give what is probably the most salient example within historical times of this condition of attunedness and similarity of mental direction, we may point to the case of part of the population of the Archipelago in its relation to the Hindu culture. The question of the extent to which this relation may have been caused by the more ancient Munda or Kôl culture, which, in pre-Aryan times, both on the Indian continent and in the Archipelago, exercised considerable influence [1]) (as a result of which one and the same cultural substratum is supposed to lie at the foundation of both the Hindu civilization and that of some of the Archipelago peoples), is outside the scope of our present argument. But the fact remains that the population of several of these islands—they are, by nature, musically very talented—has shown itself able to incorporate into their own culture the musical influences which came to it from other parts and to make them quite their own, nay, in some respects even to bring these cultural gifts to a distinctly higher stage of development. [**236**A]

Regression.

Now this native music, creation of many centuries and many races, is at the present time once more in a period of a turn of the tide. Once again foreign influences are affecting it, but this time the interloper is not a more or less kindred culture, not even one that could share with the civilizations of the Archipelago the collective appellation "eastern", but one of an utterly alien nature, one which not only modifies the existing cultural values without stimulating the organism it influences, but, like a corrosive acid, like a transfusion from a different blood-group, attacks and destroys it in

---

1) Cf. Suniti Kumar Chatterji, The foundations of civilisation in India (TBG LXVIII p. 65 *et seq.*), 1928; F. B. J. Kuiper, Munda and Indonesian („Orientalia Neerlandica", p. 372 *et seq.*), Leiden 1948.

its profoundest essence. European-American civilization is so utterly foreign to the Indonesian cultures that it cannot be assimilated by them; at best—and then only in its lower forms—it might be a substitute; whilst at the same time this civilization is, in the nature of its being, so aggressive and expansionist that it cannot be rejected or warded off either.

However this may be, and even allowing for the possibility of future recovery and a revival of much that seemed as lost, when the present time of transition and ferment will have passed: at the moment it does appear as if music, that most tender and intangible expression of a people's soul will have to share in paying the high price which many of the peoples of the Archipelago are charged for being allowed to take their place in world commerce. One can almost watch—or rather hear—native music degenerate day by day.

As one of the rare exceptions to this unfortunate tendency we may mention, in the first place, Central Java, which would appear to have become gradually, and just in time, conscious of its own cultural values; whilst also in Bali, which has, so far, escaped a too aggressive influence of Western culture, and whose population, moreover, is essentially healthy and of great creative strength, the native music seems to succeed in maintaining itself in its original purity, at any rate as far as its most important forms of expression are concerned. But in those regions where the ancient musical art is of an ingenuous and semi-conscious character, and consequently lacking in defensive power, it is, quite evidently, irrevocably doomed to die out. In some cases—this, too, is a consequence of Western economic expansion—it is Javanese music ousting that of South and East Sumatra; in other cases it is the monotonous and characterless wail going under the name of "Stambul" or "kronchong" music that causes Indonesians to become more and more estranged from their own art; sometimes—as, for example, in Nias—it is the influence of the Christian Mission; but in most cases it is European music, and then only in its lowest forms, that has proved too strong for the native art. In a fast and ever faster tempo it is either dying away or degenerating (**204**, **205**).

Regrettable as this state of things may be, it nevertheless appears impossible to avert it. The anxious and increasing anxiety, therefore, of musical authorities, both native and European, about the future of Indonesian music has not come a moment too soon.

History of musical investigation in the Archipelago.

It is understandable that this anxiety was, at first, chiefly directed towards the music—especially the musical instruments—of Java.

At the time of the "Netherlands East India Company" there was, apart from a few isolated cases, hardly any musical or scientific concern with native music. We have to content ourselves with a description here and there, such as, in "D'Eerste Boeck" (1597) (**257**), the terms *bedug, bonang, gendèr* and *gong* (the Dutch used to speak of "*gommetjes*", or the "*gomgoms*" of the Indians) [1]; "bommen, trommelen, fluyten ende andere spel" [2]; "tintamaar ofte bayaart" (**70** p. 648, 651); RIJCKLOF VAN GOENS' remarks on the music at the Mataram Court (1656) (**91**) [3]; a very brief description of a West-Javanese orchestra by CORNELIS DE BRUIN (1744) (**56**) [4], and a few anonymous notes, showing signs of a rather defective understanding, in a work dated 1782 (**20**) [5]. Only VALENTIJN (**385**) is a little more communicative, and gives brief descriptions of some of the musical instruments and *ensembles* found by him in the Moluccas, Java and Bali. [6]

The oldest European record of Javanese music is found in the logbook of Sir Francis Drake, who, in the course of his famous voyage round the world in "the Golden Hind" in 1580, visited the South coast of Java; he first gave a performance with his own musicians in honour of "Raia Donan, king of Java" and afterwards heard "his country-musick, which though it were of a very strange kind, yet the sound was pleasant and delightfull" [7].

It was once again the intermediate *English* government, in the beginning of the 19th century, which did the real pioneer work in this field as in so many others. We may mention three names: MARSDEN (1811) (**267**), RAFFLES (1817) (**303**) [**83B**] and CRAWFURD (1820) (**68, 69**).

Following the departure of the English, this fresh scientific wind ceased to blow for the time being, at any rate as far as music was concerned. Not

---

1) WOUTER SCHOUTEN, Oost-Indische Voyagie (1676).

2) From the report to the Governor-General HENDRIK BROUWER, on his journey to Bali ("Dagh-Register" 1631–'34, publ. by C. COLENBRANDER, p. 179 *et seq.*).

3) *Vide* below, p. 115 *et seq.*

4) *Vide* below, p. 391.

5) *Vide* below, p. 116 *et seq.*

6) *Vide* below, p. 114, 115.

7) Dr. H. TERPSTRA, De Nederlandsche Voorcompagnieën (in Dr. F. W. STAPEL, Geschiedenis van Nederlandsch-Indië vol. II p. 19), 1938.

until 1850 [1]) did WILKENS, in the commentary on his translation of the Javanese poem *Sewaka*, publish a fairly exhaustive description of the gamelan and its component instruments (**401**). In 1859 VAN BLOEMEN WAANDERS (**24**) brought the first communications about Balinese music—if we disregard a few sporadic remarks by AERNOUT LINTGENSZ (**256**) and VALENTIJN (**385**); SMEDING (1861) (**341**) and POENSEN (1872) (**301**) enlarged upon the Javanese orchestras; in 1874 F. W. WINTER published a collection of Javanese song-melodies in European notation [2]) (**402**), while in the same year an article appeared, by V. DE SERIÈRE, about the *angklung* (**337**); finally, VETH summarized what had up to then become known concerning Javanese music, in the first volume of his book "Java" (**388**).

It was once again an Englishman, the physiologist A. J. ELLIS, who made a beginning with the investigations on modern scientific lines. In 1884 he attempted, by means of tone-measurements recorded in a treatise entitled "Tonometrical observations on some existing non-harmonic scales", and written in collaboration with A. J. HIPKINS, to ascertain what intervals are formed by the tones of the two Javanese systems, *pélog* and *sléndro* (**82**). ELLIS's system of representing intervals by means of "cents" (one cent = 1/100 semitone of the equally-tempered European chromatic scale) has since been adopted by the majority of musicologists. This system is also used in the present work.

In 1890 Dr. GRONEMAN's book on "De gamelan te Jogjakarta" was published (**99**). GRONEMAN's communications, which testify to very close observation, chiefly contain the names and descriptions of instruments and orchestras found at the time in the Jogya kraton. This treatise was entrusted by the author to Professor LAND for publication; as is well known, the latter added to it an introduction entitled "Over onze kennis der Javaansche muziek" (About our knowledge of Javanese music) (**245**) and at the same time published an essay in the German (**243**) and—some years later—in the French language (**244**). Professor LAND had never been to the Indies, and the information on which he based his expositions was therefore restricted to what had been published up to that time; to what he had been able to cull from correspondence with Dr. GRONEMAN and others, and to measurements of intervals which he had taken from a few instruments in existence

[1]) Apart from brief communications by CORNETS DE GROOT (**66**) (not published until 1854). [and **86A**^{x}]

[2]) The first part of which, containing *sekar ageng*, was reprinted in 1883.

in Holland or sent to him. Nevertheless his writings on the subject are, no less than GRONEMAN's work, still worth reading even to-day [1]). The same cannot be said of a short article which Professor LAND published four years later, on "Muziek op Bali" (**246**), which is of merely historic interest.

In 1896 Javanese music once again became an object of serious investigation, be it, as is so often the case, from afar; in that year SERRURIER, in his "Wayang poerwo" (**338**), devoted an entire chapter to the gamelan, basing his assertions chiefly on replies which he had received to a questionnaire sent round to native civil servants. In the following year TH. MAYER, in "Een blik in het Javaansche volksleven" (= A look into Javanese life), gave some details concerning the music of Central Java (**270**), whilst in 1899 HANS VAN DE WALL published his "Impressies van den gamelan" (**392**).

A summary of all that was known up to 1900 concerning the entire field of Indonesian music is provided by SNELLEMAN's article "Muziek en Muziekinstrumenten" in the second volume of the first edition of the "Encyclopaedie van Nederlandsch Oost-Indië" (**342**). In 1901 the German psychologist and physiologist Professor STUMPF, in his treatise "Tonsystem und Musik der Siamesen" (**374**), discussed in passing the Javanese sléndro-scale. JASPER followed with a short article entitled "De gandroeng Bali" (1902) (**146**); in 1907 JACOBSON and VAN HASSELT published "De Gongfabrikatie te Semarang" (**145**); in 1910 appeared LINDA BANDARA's essay "Ueber javanische Musik" (**11**); in 1913 R. M. SUMITRA's lecture "Een en ander over den gamelan" (= A few facts about the gamelan) (**344**) and JAKUB and WIGNYARUMEKSA's "Over den gamelan" (**78**).

The above works set the ball rolling. In 1915 the first edition appeared of SACHS's excellent summary "Die Musikinstrumente Indiens und Indonesiens" (**311**). In 1918 SNELLEMAN, in the second edition of the Encyclopaedia, republished his article from the first edition, considerably extended and brought up to date down to the beginning of that year (**342**). This article was also published, with fresh additions and improvements, and co-signed by DANIEL DE LANGE, in the large French musical encyclopaedia of LAVIGNAC (**248A**). And then at last there begins a steady stream of publications, both European and Javanese, and continuing to-day. Of the authors of these publications we have already mentioned JAKUB and WIGNYA-

[1]) [*see also* **54A**]

RUMEKSA (**78**, **79**), and LINDA BANDARA (Mrs. L. HOFLAND-LEBER) (**11** to **18**A). In addition to these writers we should mention the following: J. S. and A. BRANDTS BUYS-VAN ZIJP (**30** to **54**A); KI HAJAR DÉWANTARA (**75-76**B); R. M. JAYADIPURA (**77**); R. M. A. KUSUMADINATA (**170** to **174**C and **200**); J. and C. J. A. KUNST-VAN WELY (**186** to **236**N); R. M. NATA SURATA (**280**, **349**); R. B. SULARDI (**343**); R. M. SURYAPUTRA (**348** to **359** incl.), and R. M. SURYAWINATA (**360**). Their articles appeared either as independent publications or in different periodicals, chief among which are "Koloniale Studiën" and "Indië Oud & Nieuw", and, later on, "Djawa", the "Tijdschrift van het Bataviaasch Genootschap" and "Cultureel Indie". It is these authors who have attempted to attain to a better understanding of the native music in its several forms of expression, and in this attempt penetrated gradually and more profoundly into the essential nature of its being.

Meanwhile musicological investigation had also begun to spread more to the so-called Outer Provinces. Although this did not immediately result in the appearance of any special publications, yet in the less accessible and more modest form of paragraphs and articles in works of a general ethnological nature, as well as in official reports and records of expeditions, a considerable amount of factual information—admittedly often of a rather superficial kind—was scattered about. It is only during the last few years that music outside Java has been explored more systematically and the results have been published in independent pamphlets or articles. These concern Bali (**189**, **192**, **193**, **259** to **262**H, **362** to **364** incl.); Celebes (**163**); Madura (**43**); Nias (**217**); Flores (**110**, **201**, **209**, **221**); the Kei-islands (**227**); New-Guinea (**202**, **203**, **226**), and, as regards the various instrumental and orchestral forms, the *kachapi's* (**137**); the *mokko's* ([**113**D], **138**, **283-7**); the slit drum (**274**, **275**, **368**); the gong (**145**, **223**, **340**); the Malay decoy-flute for pigeons (**219**); the Balinese *gendèr wayang* (**259**); the *gamelan angklung* (**260**) and musical instruments in general (**232**).

The labours of the above named investigators—to which should be added G. P. ROUFFAER with his beautiful article in the Encyclopaedie van Ned. Oost-Indië, entitled "Keteltrommen" (**308**)—have already rendered possible a provisional summary on a broader musico-ethnological basis. Treatises by LACHMANN (**240**, **241**) and SACHS (**313**, **316**) devoted considerable space to Indonesian music, whilst we owe it to VON HORNBOSTEL (**128**, **130**, **131**) that more light was shed on the origin of the Javanese and Balinese tone-systems, which, since the publication of Professor LAND's writings (**245**, p. 7) had been an object of mere conjecture. [Recent bibliography *S1]

Whereas, up to that time, the study of the music of the Archipelago had been exclusively a matter of private initiative, the Government has also, since 1930, officially recognized the importance and urgency of systematic research into this native art, which is evident from the fact that an official expert was placed at the disposal of the Chief of the Archaeological Department in January of that year, and commissioned to open the necessary investigations. Unfortunately, owing to the difficulties prevailing at the time, this appointment was temporarily cancelled, which is extremely regrettable if understandable. "Musical compositions, and especially musical instruments, because of their complicated construction and non-utilitarian character, afford particularly valuable criteria for tracing cultural connexions between peoples whose history is still, and probably will remain, to a great extent a matter of conjecture" [1]; —". . . . Das Wissen um Art und Schicksal der Tonzeuge ist keineswegs nur Sache der Musiker und Musikforscher" (**314**); —"On ne sait pas assez le rôle immense qu'a tenu la musique dans les civilisations anciennes comme un élément intégrant de la vie religieuse et politique" [2]. It is to be hoped that these and similar utterances may induce the authorities to take steps to prevent the precious musicological factual material which is still available, from being lost altogether, and to cause the investigation to be resumed as soon as circumstances permit. For it should not be forgotten that a systematic exploration of the native music ought, in fact, to have been commenced many years ago; the present moment is, indeed, the very last at which such an examination may be entered upon with any hope of fruitful results. As Professor J. HUIZINGA wrote twenty years ago in "De Gids" (**134**), the Indian Archipelago is yet able "to supply the richest territory of the entire world for the study of non-European music. Here is indeed a splendid field for the collaboration between the Netherlands and Javanese expert, the musicologist, the archaeologist, the linguist, the ethnologist and the historian. Here is a field where art and science enter upon their most intimate relationship, here is an art-form which can be preserved only with the assistance of science".

1) HELEN H. ROBERTS, Suggestions to field workers in collecting folk music and data about instruments ("The Journal of the Polynesian Society" Vol. XL p. 103), 1931.

2) From a letter of SYLVAIN LÉVI to the Director of the Kern Institute of the Leyden University d.d. November 25th, 1929.

This is still true to-day; but it will not be true much longer. Fortunately, thanks to the interest and munificence of a few Netherlands private persons, the foundations have meanwhile been laid for "the musicological archives", at present established at Batavia [1]). They seem to have survived the Japanese invasion and the subsequent political troubles. Here, musicologists, ethnologists, and other interested persons may gather information for their studies; literature, phonograms, photos and lantern slides are at their disposal, while, in addition, there is also a collection of many of the instrumental forms which we shall discuss later on in this work [2]).

---

[1]) [Now Museum Pusat, Djakarta]

[2]) At the time of the writer's departure from the East Indies (7th March 1934) these musicological archives, which had been handed over to the Royal Batavia Society a few months previously, contained the following: over 1100 musical instruments, 350 cylindrical phonograms, abt. 200 gramophone records, 800 photographic negatives, 500 lantern slides, a number of films showing orchestras, players and dances corresponding therewith (from Nias, Musi Ulu, Pasemah, Rejang, Flores, the Toraja-districts, the Atoni and Belu of Timor, the Kei-islands, Saparua, Northern New-Guinea; of a Jogya *garebeg*, and one of a *réog* performance and of a Solo *kuda képang*), as well as a small library of various manuals. To simplify their use by interested persons, all this has been card-indexed. An large amount of information was supplied, both in writing and personally, and hundreds of visitors from all parts of the world were conducted round the archives. For a few years after the writer's departure no expert guidance was available to direct the work; in 1937, however, the Austrian musicologist Dr KARL HALUSA was appointed custodian. *Vide* also **208**.

CHAPTER II

TONE- AND SCALE-SYSTEMS

(40, 43, 58, 82, 128, 130, 131, 190, 192, 193, 197, 199, 200, 202, 211, 212, 240, 314, 326, 351, 374) [**18**B, **59**A, **113**C, **123**I, M, **155**D, **254**A, **258**A, **316**A, **340**A, **395**A]

The music of any people not knowing the use of musical—at any rate, melody-producing—instruments, is, of course, purely vocal, and it appears that, in such cases, we cannot speak of "scales" in the ordinary sense of the word, let alone of tonal systems. Singing alone, uninfluenced by musical instruments, possesses no definitely fixed intervals; it knows only of higher or lower, the chief thing being the movement upwards or downwards, and not so much the absolute size of the intervals produced. As LACHMANN quite rightly remarks somewhere, the same may be said of dancing; there, too, stress is laid only on the direction and the order of sequence of the steps, whereas their length is relatively unimportant.

It is nevertheless evident that, also in purely vocal music, the melody is subjected to certain physiological and psychological "laws": the voice, in primitive music, has a natural tendency to move from high to low, correspondingly with the decrease in breathing energy of the singer, while the intervals into which the space between the essentially important tones ("Gerüsttöne") is divided, usually bear a definite quantitative ratio to one another, irrespective of the size of the interval to be bridged over (**202**, note 24). (These essential tones are nearly always clearly recognizable as such.)

It was not until man learned how to make musical instruments on which a sequence of tones could be produced that real tonal scales came into being, *i.e.* sequences of fixed intervals, and often, in such cases, vocal music would follow suit at least for the greater part. Only in the higher forms of culture was this stage of development reached; wherever lower types of civilization are found in possession of such instruments and such scale systems, they are always found to have been imported from some people with a higher culture.

In the Indian Archipelago we find cultures of practically every stage of development, and we may accordingly find there purely vocal music side-by-side with instrumentally-influenced vocal music, as well as purely instrumental music ranging from the most primitive to the highest forms.

It is too early yet to present our notions concerning the origin, mutual relation and development of these various forms of musical expression in one complete and consistent scheme. Only as regards Javanese and Balinese music do we have at our disposal a fairly large amount of material enabling us to design a sketch of the scales and systems in vogue in those islands, and of their supposed course of development.

* * *

In Java and Bali, as well in the islands, or parts of islands: Madura, Western Lombok, Banjermasin and South Sumatra, which were, and to some extent still are, under the formers' cultural influence, we have to deal with a "Hochkultur" (= high type of culture), or the remnants of it; in these regions, therefore, we find the above-mentioned fixed, or, to use another expression, "objectivated" tonal scales. This does not mean, of course, that no purely vocal music from former periods and uninfluenced by instrumental music can be found side-by-side with music built on scales.

These scales—if we may include some ancient pre-stages which are still found here and there—all belong to two different tonal systems (Sund.: *rakitan*), which are usually indicated by their Central Javanese names: *Pélog* (Sund.: *pèlog*) and *Sléndro* (Sund.: *salèndro*). In East-Java one sometimes hears, for the former system, when it occurs in its complete instrumental form of seven tones (originally, it seems, foreign to this part of the island [1]), but imported from Mataram), the term *mataraman* or *mentara-*

1) The ancient Eastern Javanese gamelans sounded either the bem-scale (called *pélog pengasih*) or the barang-scale (*pélog miring* or *laras slering*). Owing to the fact, however, that gamelans with exclusively the latter form of tuning are so few in number, the combination of both tunings—the complete instrumental pélog scale—is also called, after its rarest component, *pélog miring*. The regency of Pemalang (North Central Java) also knows these combined scales under the name of *miring* in those cases where the tone *pélog* is missing from the sequence (which then has only six tones). In case the pélog tone is present, however, the scale is simply denoted as pélog, as elsewhere in Central Java.

man (H. J. sometimes ***mentawis***) being used, and also, but only rarely (in Nganjuk), the term ***gamelan pégon*** [1]). In the large Jogya kraton gending-collection *"Pakem wirama"* [2]), sléndro is called *suréndro.*

In Bali these systems are called, respectively, ***saih pitu***, meaning "sequence of seven", and ***saih lima***, i.e. "sequence of five"; the latter name, however, is also used to indicate ***pélog*** sequences of five tones. Pélog is felt to be feminine, more or less humanly social, and frequently as somewhat sad, whereas sléndro is felt to be masculine, more severe, exalted, and festive.

Investigations have shown that both tonal systems have undergone various modifications in the course of time, which we shall discuss one by one in this chapter. In order, however, to give the reader some preliminary idea of the difference in structure of the principal scales of the two systems, we have set out schematically the places of the different tones within their respective "octaves" and in their average "modern" form, together—to facilitate comparison—with the European tempered chromatic scale. The tones that can be played on sarons (***vide*** below, p. 164 ***et seq.***) are, in this layout, indicated by black spots; the low ***nem***—which is occasionally added, especially in Solo—by a hatched dot, and the adjacent tones (only on the pélog-octave line) by open circles. In this, we have taken as starting point the tone ***nem***, which is the customary diapason (*laras*), and whose pitch, in the newer gamelans sléndro, generally coincides with, or at any rate very closely approaches, that of the tone *b'* (488 v.d.) in the European tonal system, but which, in most of the gamelans pélog, lies on a average about a semitone lower.

It should be noted that, taking the tone ***nem*** as *b* or *b♭*, not a single one of the remaining tones of both Javanese scales coincides with one of the other tones of the Western tonal sequence; therefore, the European ear is, at first, rather baffled on hearing them, and inclined to think of these scales as being "out of tune".

The size of the intervals is given in ***cents***.

---

[1]) ***Vide***, for ***pégon***—which here, as in some other cases, signifies "strange, different"—the article of the same name by ROUFFAER in the Encyclopaedie van Nederlandsch Oost-Indië, 2nd ed., vol. III, p. 271 ***et seq.*** For ***pégon*** as a term probably used in the Principalities for the purely ***equidistant*** sléndro, ***vide*** **198**, p. 79, Note 4.

[2]) In regard to this "Pakem Wirama" *vide* also PIGEAUD (**297**). [**123**M, **291**B, **402**B]

Pélog and Sléndro compared with the European tempered chromatic scale

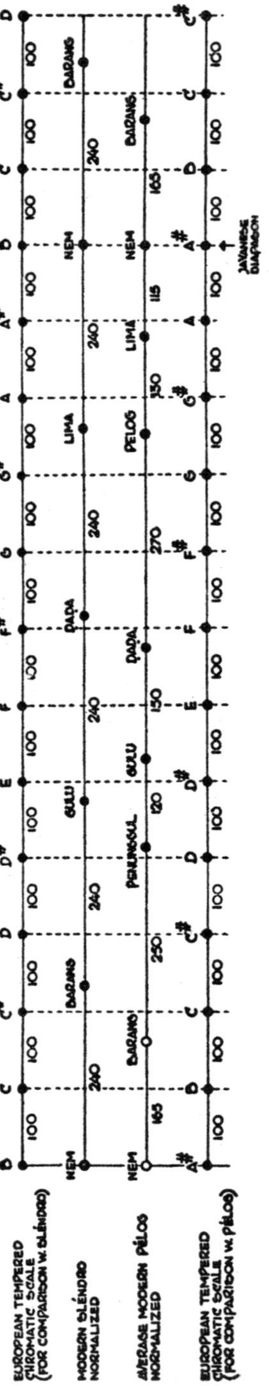

According to Javanese tradition, sléndro is much more ancient than pélog: it was presented to humanity, and in particular to Çri Maharaja Kano, alias Raden Pakukuan (also called Makukuan or Mikukuan), and by order of Giri Nata (*i.e.* Shiva), by the deity Baṭara Éndra; hence the derivation, customary among the Javanese people, of the word sléndro: *tabuhan* (*i.e.* gamelan) *Sura* (*i.e.* Déva) *Éndra* = *Suréndra* = *sléndro*. According to RANGGA WARSITA's "Pustaka Raja purwa" [1]) (vol. II, Chap. 4, p. 24/25) this is supposed to have happened in Çaka 326, i.e. A.D. 404; but the same author [2]), in another place (vol. I, Chap. 3, p. 224/5), gives another date,

[1]) *I.e.* the Chronicles of the Kings in the Purwa period, (*viz.* the period treated in the Mahābhārata.)

[2]) R. Ng. RANGGA WARSITA (d. 1873)—"the last of the pujongga's" (official chroniclers and maintainers of the adat in the Solonese kraton, at the same time poets and linguists)—also mentions here the instruments which are supposed to have formed part of these first orchestras, adding each time a modern Javanese "translation". We cannot trace the source from which he gathered the translation of these ancient Javanese names of instruments; these names, however, are also to be found in other writings. As far as can be judged with our present knowledge of the matter, the translation is not correct in every case. For the sake of completeness we give below the ancient Javanese names in question, together with the signification as given by RANGGA WARSITA, and as they are stated in the introduction to the large Jogya kraton genḍing collection:

1. genḍing	= rebab
2. kala	= kenḍang
3. songka	= gong
4. pamatut	= keṭuk
5. sahuran	= kenong
6. gubar	= benḍé without beating-knob
7. bahiri	= edged gong
8. puksur	= terbang
9. gurnang	= suspended gong in the form of a kenong, practically identical with the penontong
10. ṭong-ṭong	= bronze slit-drum
11. grit	= terbang
12. teteg	= beḍug
13. maguru gangsa	= a gong kemoḍong without sounding box, therefore a freely suspended bronze slab.

Out of the above translation that of *genḍing* (now = gamelan-composition, but formerly = gamelan (*vide* **194**, p, 9. note 4)) by *rebab* (N.B. a comparatively modern (Persian-Arab?) component of the Javanese orchestras) appears somewhat apocryphal. [*Cf.* **123**M].

Kala (*vide* **194**, p. 50 *et seq.*) may evidently stand for kenḍang in some cases (at any rate for some kind of drum or other); but *songka* should probably not be translated by gong, but by shell-trumpet (Skrt. *çangka*). True, ROORDA, in his dictionary, also translates *songka* by "a kind of gong" (actually mentioning that the word is

viz. Çaka 279, *i.e.* A.D. 357. Only the *gamelan* *Munggang* is supposed to be still more ancient (*vide* below, p. 260).

Pélog, on the contrary, is supposed to have been invented at a very much

---

derived from Skrt. çangka!), but in addition he nevertheless gives, for the combination *kalasongka*, the translation bazuin (trombone, straight trumpet) (cf. **194**, p. 34).

The translation *pamatut* = *keṭuk* may be correct. Taken literally, it means an instrument indicating that something is quite in order. This "something" might very well be, in this case, the time measure, the subdivision of the melodic phrases, in which case it would be quite a suitable appellation for the keṭuk, since (*vide* pp. 163 and 298) it divides up the kenongan into properly proportioned pieces.

Sahuran is not known to ROORDA as the name of an instrument; but *sahur* means "to answer verbally", and hence the word is also used to indicate sounds which, coming from different directions, as it were answer each other.

The translation of *gubar* by war-cymbal, *benḍe*, without beating-knob, is certainly correct (cf. **194**, p. 83), as is that of *bahiri*, which to this day, under the name of *bèri* is still in vogue as indicating a small sort of gong (*vide* p. 150), (but denoting in India Proper in ancient times, a species of drum (**194**, p. 79 *et seq.*)).

Puksur and *gurnang*, translated respectively by *terbang* and suspended broad, edged gong, are, both, according to ROORDA, species of gongs or war-cymbals. Gurnang is also supposed by him to mean "thundering noise". According to Dr. PURBACHARAKA, however, *gurnang* is not a musical instrument at all, but an adjective formed from the first three syllables of the phrase *ghurṇa ng mṛdangga*, *i.e.* "noisy were the drums".

The words *ṭong-ṭong* and *grit* are again conjoined by ROORDA, and translated by "heavy bells". Besides this, grit also means, according to him, the noise of weapons, rattling, or crackling. Dr. PURBACHARAKA, however, translates *grit* by squeaking, as of cartwheels. Thus, *geritan*, in the Atjèh language, still stands for a "squeaking wagon", *i.e.* a cart drawn by oxen and camouflaged with fresh green leaves and branches, in which hunters are hidden; when such a vehicle rides through the forest, squeaking and cracking on its way, the deer are moved by curiosity to come towards the sound and are then shot by the hunters from their hiding place.

The translation of *ṭong-ṭong* by bronze slit-drum is, of course, correct.

Finally, no particular kind of gong can possibly be meant by *maguru gangsa*. Neither is the translation given by ROORDA of the term *gong maguru gangsa* = the gong follows the gamelan, *i.e.* the subordinate complies with the wishes of his superior, correct—so Dr. PURBACHARAKA informed me—for the expression originally was—as became evident to him (Dr. P.) from an ancient Javanese *locus*—*maguruh gangsa*, meaning "the gamelan sounded noisily", or "the noisy gamelan".

Elsewhere in the Jogya kraton genḍing-collection the instrumental names *grantang* and *salunḍi* are to be found. They have there been rendered by the words *gambang* and *kempul* respectively. The first of these two translations is correct, providing one thinks of this gambang as a set of floating, suspended keys, more or less in the form of a *chalung* (*vide* p. 364 *et seq.*). For *grantang* = *garantang* = *garantung* is a frequentative form of *gantung*, which means *to suspend*. As a matter of fact, to this day this word means in the Batak districts, a kind of gambang with floating keys. In South-East Borneo, however, it occurs as the name of a gong (**310**, p. 153a; **311**, p. 175), also, of course, suspended. In ancient Javanese literature this instrumental name occurs repeatedly, for example in the Bhārata Yuddha (II

later date, by some more or less legendary Javanese prince, either Prabu Banjaran Sari, or Panji Hino Kertapati (who, in his quality of creator of the gamelan, is usually called Panji Sepuh) [1]; or, it may be, by king Jayabaya; the first *gamelan sekati* (still in the pélog system) is even supposed to have been made as late as Çaka 1441, i.e. A.D. 1519 (**99**) [2]. According to the tradition of the Jogya kraton, Panji merely added the tone pélog to the five sléndro tones, the tone *bem* being invented only in the sixteenth century, by the Panembahan of Demak, Sunan TUNGGUL (hence, in popular etymology, the other name for *bem*: *panunggul*). Thus the tradition of the Principalities.

In Cheribon, however, the *niyaga's* (musicians, Sund.: *nayaga's*) of the kratons believe that the creation of sléndro should be attributed to the Mohammedan saint Sunan KALIJAGA, and that of pélog to another saint, Sunan BONANG, whose instrumental name (cf. p. 153) is probably accountable for this belief. Quite apart, however, from the question of the paternity of the two scales, the notion that sléndro is older than pélog is consistently maintained. For, on the one hand all Javanese princes supposed to have created pélog lived long after the date at which the deity was said to have given sléndro to humanity, and on the other hand we were told that Sunan KALIJAGA was Sunan BONANG's tutor, and therefore older than the latter, from which it follows again that *sléndro* must be older

---

6), Sumanasāntaka (LII 2), Bhomakāvya (XCVI 16), Sutasoma (VII 1), and in an inscription (OJO CXVIII), dated about 1040. Cf. **194**, p. 82 and 86/7.

Salunḍi, however, is not a kempul, but a metallophone with floating suspended keys, in other words, a species of *gendèr* (*vide* p. 172), either with or without sound tubes. The musical instrument *salunḍing* (occasionally called *salunḍing wesi*) is found, in ancient Javanese and Balinese literature: in the Vṛtta Sañcaya (p. 53), the Bhārata Yuddha (L 5) and the Ghaṭotkacāçraya (VII 5), as well as in five Balinese charters, the three oldest of which date from 1181 (**194**, p. 90 et seq.; **196**, p. 351/2).—For the instrumental names mentioned by RANGGA WARSITA, we also refer to **43**, p. 16, note 6c.

In the Pakem Sastramiruda (**169**, p. 40/1), P. KUSUMADILAGA gives quite different significations for some of the Hindu-Javanese instrumental names enumerated above; thus, he translates *genḍing* by *kemanak*; *kala* by *kenong*; *songka* by *keṭuk*; *pamatut* by *kenḍang*, and *sahuran* by *gong*. He further mentions an instrument which, as far as I am aware, is not mentioned by RANGGA WARSITA, *i.e.* the *chaluri*, which he translates by *suling*. This translation, too, is incorrect (*vide* p. 182 *et seq.*).

[1]) This is, to this day, the name adopted by the principal gongsmith in the Jogya kraton. *Vide* also the names of gamelan smiths on p. 138 *et seq.*

[2]) According to P. KUSUMADILAGA (**169**, p. 43), the gamelan sekati did not make its appearance until Çaka 1477 = A.D. 1555, at the instigation of the Wali's of Demak.

than *pélog*, if only by a generation. (In reality, however, Sunan BONANG lived at an earlier period than Sunan KALIJAGA; he is supposed to have been his great-uncle).

There is also some relation between the native conception of the genesis of the pélog-scale and the explanation given by the Javanese of the limited use which is made of the pélog-*tone*. The relatively rare occurrence of this tone is attributed to the hesitancy of its mortal inventor, who, although he could not do without this new tone in his compositions, yet proceeded but reluctantly to its introduction, since he felt this modification of the existing scale bestowed on humanity by the gods to be a presumptious action towards the higher powers.

It has been explained elsewhere (**192** par. 13) why, notwithstanding all this, the priority of *pélog in Java* would seem to be more than likely. It is still my conviction that *pélog in Java* (*and in Bali*) is older than *sléndro*. I incline to the view that *pélog* was introduced in these islands by the ancestors of the present Javanese and Balinese people themselves, and that *sléndro* did not come until much later, probably as late as the 8th century A. D., *via* Sumatra, whose culture, thanks to the close contact existing between its princes and those of the Central Javanese states, was of considerable influence on Javanese civilization during that period [1]).

The new tonal system (*gamelan sléndro* = *gamelan Çailéndra*?) [2]) was pro-

---

[1]) It is not known with certainty what this relationship actually amounted to. Cf. Prof. N. J. KROM, De Sumatraansche periode der Javaansche geschiedenis (Inaugural lecture), Leyden 1919; id., Hindoe-Javaansche Geschiedenis, 2nd ed. (1931), p. 141 *et seq.*; id., Çriwijaya and the Çailéndra's (in Dr. F. W. STAPEL, "Geschiedenis van Nederlandsch-Indië" (1930), Vol. I, Chap. II. The Hindoe-Javaansche tijd. p. 69 *et seq.* (93 *et seq.*)); Dr. W. F. STUTTERHEIM, A Javanese period in Sumatran History (1929); GEORGES COEDÈS, Le Royaume de Çrivijaya (B.E.F.E.O. XVIII, Sixth section), 1918; id., On the Origin of the Sailéndras of Indonesia ("Journal of the Greater India Society" I no. 2, p. 61 *et seq.*), 1934; R. C. MAJUMDAR, M.A., Ph.D., The struggle between the Sailéndra's and the Chola's (ibid., p. 71 *et seq.*), 1934*); J. L. MOENS, Çriwijaya, Yāva en Kaṭāha (T.B.G., p. 317 *et seq.*), 1937; V. OBDEYN, Gegevens ter identificeering van oude Sumatraansche toponiemen (T.A.G., 2nd. series, Vol. LXI, p. 40 *et seq.*), 1944; F. H. VAN NAERSSEN, The Çailéndra Interregnum ("India Antiqua", p. 249 *et seq*). Leyden 1947; J. NORDEN, Inleiding tot de Oude Geschiedenis van den Indischen Archipel (1948), p. 37–65.

[2]) In addition to the arguments (**192**, p. 166 *et seq.*) and counter-arguments (**40**, p. 224 *et seq.*) we may also point to the curious fact that, in Sumedang (W. Java), the lagu pélog *Rènggong Sumedang*, and, similarly, in Indramayu (Res. of Cheribon) the lagu pélog *Sanga*, change their names to lagu *Jalèndra* when transposed to

*) [*vide also in* Feestbundel-Van Ronkel, 1950: 28ff]

bably limited in the beginning to the southern part of Central Java, where it has gradually ousted the original ancient pélog almost completely. We may further presume that as a result of certain political events in Central Java—perhaps only the removal of the kraton to the middle East—it very soon spread in an easterly direction, eventually reaching Bali by way of Eastern Java, being, as it was, the inseparable companion of the wayang purwa.

To my mind, the spread of instrumental sléndro in certain parts of Western Java (chiefly the Residency Batavia, and further south and south-east, Lebak, Buitenzorg, Sukabumi, Chianjur and Bandung, as well as southern Tasikmalaja), and the greater infiltration of this system in Eastern Java may be attributed chiefly to the expansion of Mataram in the 17th century. [1]) It seems to me that, at any rate as regards Western Java,

---

sléndro. In these cases, therefore, it would appear that the final *a* has maintained itself in a kindred form, which *a*, however, in the name of the tone system itself has turned into *o* (the Sundanese and Western Javanese, too, speak of salèndr*o* en nyalèndr*o*).

Dr. STUTTERHEIM has further called attention to the fact that the signification of the name *Giri Nata* (the divinity supposed to have endowed the Javanese with sléndro) and that of *Çailéndra* are identical, *i.e. Lord of the Mountains.* He also mentions (**375**, p. 113) two more data transmitted to him by Prof. BERG of Leyden, and which support the notion that Çailéndra and sléndro are identical: (a) that it is not at all surprising that in a word of three syllables like Çailéndra, the vowel *ai* (or *é*) of the first syllable should have disappeared, and (b) that there are more examples in the Javanese language of the transition from the final *a* to a pure *o*: thus, the word *gandharvv*a, which is also both Sanskrit and ancient Javanese, has been turned in modern Javanese into *gendruv*o. Dr. PURBACHARAKA, however, although not positively excluding the possibility of the transition of Çailéndra into sléndro, does not consider the last-named example as sufficient evidence in this respect. For, in *gandharv*(*v*)*a* the transition from the final *a* to *o* may be ascribed, linguistically speaking in quite a natural way, to the presence of the (double) *v* (which *v* at the same time had the effect of automatically turning the *a* preceding it into *u*). *Gandharv*(*v*)*a* should not, therefore, be put into the same class with a word like *Çailéndra*, in which there is no letter *v* to exercise its sound modifying influence. Dr. PURBACHARAKA, however, calls attention to another word that may serve as an argument in support of the possibility of the transition in question, namely the word *baka* (Sanskrit for heron) which has its equivalent in the modern Javanese word *bango*. (The transition from *k* to *ng* is in this connexion unimportant).

Cf. also: Malay *kud*a (horse), Toba-Batak *hod*a, Menangkabau *kud*o. Similarly, Sanskrit and ancient Javanese *ghanṭ*a (bell), Bal. and Jav. *genṭ*a, Menangk. *gant*o.

[1]) There exist in West-Java various Central- and Eastern-Javanese settlements, chiefly in the districts of Bekasi, Krawang, Chiasem and South-Tasikmalaya, South-Galuh and East-Sukapura)—a result of Sultan Ageng's war policy. Cf. Dr. F. DE HAAN, Priangan, Vol. I pp. 10*, 17*, 18*, 20*, 24*, Vol II pp. 38–41; Vol. III pp. 20, 21, 61–63, 70, 153, 154. The Javanese colonisation of Banten, however,

we have here to do with an attendant phenomenon of this domination, as should be clear from the fact that in the greater part of the territory mentioned the désa population has remained faithful to the ancient *pélog* as regards their vocal music [1]) (vide Appendix *58B*).

In the former sultanate of Banten, which has been subjected to fairly strong Javanese influences, *pélog* has been able to maintain itself only to a slight degree and with considerable difficulty; the sultanate Cheribon, on the contrary, which has always succeeded to a great extent in keeping culturally free from Mataram influences—notwithstanding a certain measure of political dependence—has been able to resist almost completely.the infiltration of *sléndro*. The Regencies Indramayu, Majalèngka, and, to a slightly lesser extent, Sumedang and Chiamis, which are situated around Cheribon, constitute, in fact, the only important Javanese territory to-day (apart from the Tengger- and the Bandawasa-Banyuwangi complex) where instrumental *pélog* has managed to retain an undeniable hegemony. Only Bali, where *sléndro* is found almost exclusively in vocal music and on the *gendèr wayang* (used to accompany a wayang depicting scenes from the

dates from as early as 1520, *i.e.* quite a century before Sultan Ageng. (Cf. Prof. HUSEIN JAYADININGRAT, Critische beschouwing van de Sadjarah Banten (1913), pp. 75, 80, 88, 111, 193.

[1]) It is less easy to explain the prevalence of sléndro *singing* in Indramayu, which, *instrumentally*, is one of the purest pélog territories if not the purest. True, its population consists for by far the greater part (95%) of Javanese; if this were the cause of the hegemony of vocal sléndro, how is the practically complete hegemony of pélog in the orchestral field to be explained? Partly, perhaps, by the fact—to which R. M. A. KUSUMADINATA called my attention—that the majority of the native officials in this district hail from the Sunda-districts (one of the exceptions was the former Regent, a Javanese).

There is another circumstance which may have contributed to this state of things, *i.e.* that the Central-Javanese emigrants, who must gradually have filled the sparsely populated Western Javanese lowlands, hailed from sléndro districts, and therefore practiced sléndro singing, but that they, as is usually the case with emigrants, did not belong to the possessing classes, and therefore did not bring any gamelans with them.

The same might perhaps apply to Krawang, where instrumental pélog and sléndro are represented about equally, whilst vocal music—as in Indramayu—is chiefly sléndro; with this difference, however, that the Javanese settlements in this fertile sawah-district, arrived at a higher level of well being, and were able gradually to acquire a fairly large number of sléndro orchestras.

The fact that, in Krawang, Sundanese (at least Western-Javanese) and Central-Javanese influences clashed with each other is quite evident from the compromise they made in the matter of the wayang; this regency is the land of the wayang golèk purwa *par excellence*, a typically Western Javanese kind of stage puppets with a typically Central Javanese repertoire. [**377**G]

Rāmāyaṇa)[1]), might be mentioned as *pélog* territory in the same breath with the former districts.

The Pasisir (districts on the northern shores of Central Java) are, as regards the western part, where cultural influences from Cheribon and Mataram clash, a typical mixture, *pélog* prevailing more or less in some places and *sléndro* in others. The eastern part of the Pasisir has doubtless been completely "sléndroized", and still is so, at least partly, to-day. In certain regencies around Semarang (especially in Kendal, Demak and Kudus), however, where, during the last few decades, there has been intensive recruiting of coolies by the large agricultural estate companies, hundreds of *sléndro* gamelans were bought up and sent to the Outer Provinces, in order to bring some joy into the lives of the labourers from Java working for these companies in territories outside their own homeland, and enable to celebrate their holidays as they are wont. As a result of this a considerable number of Javanese *sléndro* gamelans are found especially on the east coast of Sumatra. Since the number of orchestras manufactured and bought to-day is only very limited, the regencies mentioned have been simply drained of *sléndro*-gamelans, so that now there is hardly any question of a prevalence of the sléndro-system in these districts, at any rate in so far as it finds expression in the orchestral scales; whilst the actual number of gamelans there, as compared to that of the neighbouring regencies, has altogether grown very small.

It is also a remarkable fact that, in the mountain districts of the Regencies Purbalingga and Bajanagara, lying amidst sléndro territory since time immemorial, there still exists to this day a marked preference for pélog as regards vocal music.

The ancient pélog territory in the extreme East of Java, which, as may be assumed in view of its being backed by Bali, remained intact to a very large extent until after the Hindu-Javanese period, was badly affected and finally broken up in the first half of the 17th century as a result of the Mataram expansion. The removal or extermination of the original population by sultan Agung, and its gradual replacement by Central Javanese and Kediri colonists, which continues even to-day (although the vacuum

1) Two gamelans with sléndro—or, at least, sléndro-like—tuning were in 1930 seen by WALTER SPIES, *i.e.* a gamelan Gong at Mengwi and a gamelan Pelègongan (= Semar Pegulingan) in Kapal, whilst I myself discovered a gamelan Angklung with a sléndro scale at Sangsit in North-Bali (**193**, p. 479, Table III, No. 1).

created in the 17th century has now been practically filled) has probably caused *sléndro* to obtain a firm footing also here. Only in the less accessible mountain districts—in the first place the Tengger mountains, where Hindu-Javanism found a last refuge, and in the districts adjacent to it—has *pélog* succeeded in maintaining its preponderant position until today, thanks also to Madurese immigration as far as the coast is concerned. The same applies to the district of Besuki: notwithstanding the proximity of Bali it has grown little by little into a mixed, nay, a *sléndro*-territory; but in the mountainous centre (Bandawasa) and in the land of the Usingers (the eastern slopes of the Ijen mountain district and the adjacent coast) *pélog* has fully maintained itself, whilst in other places, owing to the immigration of pélog-Madurese, it has once again come to the fore, at any rate locally (Jember).

It should further be pointed out that the ancient seats of the princes themselves (Cheribon, Jogya, Solo) are, instrumentally, mixed territory, although they constitute centres of practically pure *pélog* or *sléndro* territories, respectively. This is probably to be attributed largely to the fact that, among the nobility and the rich who dwell in these centres, the habit prevails to cultivate both orchestral forms, in contrast to the country population, who give preference to either the one or the other system.

Pélog is latterly gaining ground again everywhere in Central Java, perhaps as a result of the recent popularity of the *keṭoprak* (*vide* below, p. 287 *et seq.*), which is always accompanied in *pélog*. In some places, *pélog* has pushed *sléndro* to the background—maybe only temporarily—even in vocal music (Temanggung, Demak, Japara, Rembang). This process, indeed, does not seem to be a mere by-product of the *keṭoprak* craze: SERRURIER, too, concluded as early as 1896, from certain facts placed at his disposal, that *pélog*, especially in eastern Java, was gaining ground at the expense of *sléndro* (**338** p. 228/9). It might be an interesting hypothesis that we have to do here with a phenomenon parallel to what we see in literature, and still more in architecture and the plastic arts, namely, a re-assumption of rights by the ancient Indonesian element—in this case long delayed—from the foreign Hindu, Hindu-Malay, and Hindu-Javanese cultural influences (vide also **298**, par. 98; [**28A**]).

A peculiar, "modern" reason why more *pélog* than *sléndro* is heard at Sundanese schools, is given by Radèn MACHYAR ANGGA KUSUMADINATA. I found the following in one of his quarterly reports of his activities as official charged with furthering native vocal music at the Sundanese schools: "With a few rare exceptions, the teachers seem to like *pélog* better than *sléndro*. Many of them allow their pupils only to sing in *pélog*. One may ask, why? The answer is, because the conditions under which the teachers live are beset with difficulties. They can hardly make ends meet on their scanty salaries. They always are in a melancholy mood, so that the bright, invigorating *sléndro* does not appeal to their feelings. I, who, for the last five years, have got to know these teachers intimately, realize their difficult circumstances. If we are to save *sléndro* from perdition, the position of these teachers must be considerably improved".

Thus far our summary exposition of the two Javanese tonal systems and their spread in the island. It is the result of a careful study of the results of an inquiry instituted, at my instigation, by the Department of Education and Religion (*vide* Appendices 57 and 58), combined with the knowledge of a small number of other facts relevant to the subject in question. For the sake of clarity I have framed my statement in fairly positive terms; it may be left to the reader to lard it with as many queries as he may think fit.

I would only point out the difference between the manner of "distribution" of *sléndro* as compared to that of *pélog*. The *sléndro* territory, apart from the Western Javanese "branch", forms a practically united field, whilst the *pélog* territory, on the contrary, is curiously broken up, and as a rule restricted to the less accessible mountain districts. This fact, too, would seem to support the theory of the greater age of *pélog* in Java.

With regard to the relative age of the two systems I might also mention that Dr Stutterheim (**375**) inclined to the opinion that *sléndro* should be regarded as the specifically *Javanese* tonal system, and *pélog* as that of the Sundanese—probably earlier arrivals in Java—and of the Balinese. Neither does the relative chronology change according to this notion; but the presence of *sléndro* in Java is antedated by many centuries by it. Thus, the derivation of the name *sléndro* from Çailéndra, which Dr Stutterheim also considers probable, would have its origin in the circumstance that the central *sléndro* territory was one and the same as that over which the Javanese Çailéndra's ruled during the period of its greatest prosperity and influence. It would, in that case, be only the *name* "sléndro" that arose in the eighth century.

I must also make mention here of the view of Dr Nyèssen concerning the racial composition of the population of Java, which, according to this ethnologist [1]), differs in the mountain districts from that in the plains. Dr NYÈSSEN comes to the conclusion, based on an examination of more than 10.000 men, that the population of Java (and also that of Bali and Sumbawa) consists of:

I. earlier arrivals: a mesocephalic, low browed, proto-Malay mountain population, also characterized by shorter stature, broader nose and light brown eyes, and

II. later arrivals: a brachicephalic, deutero-Malay lowland population, characterized by taller stature, higher brow, thinner nose and dark brown eyes.

The above division cuts across the other, usual division of the Javanese population into a Sundanese group, a Javanese proper and a Madurese one.

It would seem then, that *pélog*, which, as we saw, is chiefly limited to the mountain districts, having been pressed back by later arrivals, belonged originally to group I, and *sléndro* to group II.

According to this notion, too, the priority of *pélog* in Java is not affected *).

* * *

It is probable that both the *pélog* and the *sléndro* systems originated in the ancient Chinese series of successive fifths (the so-called blown fifths), derived from the harmonic tones of stopped bamboo flutes. These blown fifths are said to be slightly smaller than pure fifths (*702 C.*); they average only *678 C.* Whereas, as we know, a chain of pure fifths, after twelve fifths have been run through, comes to a tone (allowing for the difference in the octave) practically the same as that from which it started (*i.e.* the "Pythagorean" cycle) [2]), in the case of a cycle of blown fifths this happens only after 23 fifths have been run through [3]) (*vide* Appendix *59*).

---

*) [*S[2], **123**M]

[1]) In his letter addressed to the Governor-General and dated 18th Dec., 1933 (of which letter the Department of Education and Religion sent me an extract at the time).

[2]) $12 \times 702 = 8424$ C.
$7 \times 1200 = 8400$ C.
Difference: 24 C. = the comma of Pythagoras.

[3]) $23 \times 678 = 15594$ C.
$13 \times 1200 = 15600$ C.
Difference: 6 C. = ¼ comma of Pythagoras.

The full series of 23 blown fifths form the following steps when brought within the compass of a single octave:

0	I	II	III	IV	V	VI	VII	VIII	IX
366	541	400½	593	438	648½	480½	710	525	387½
X	XI	XII	XIII	XIV	XV	XVI	XVII	XVIII	XIX
574	425	628½	465	688	509	376½	557	412	609
XX	XXI	XXII	XXIII = 0.						
450½	667	493½	366						

The science of musicology owes this hypothesis of the "cycle of blown fifths" to the late Professor Dr E. M. VON HORNBOSTEL [1]). By means of an ingenious interpretation, supported by experiments, of the ancient legend of Ling-Lun, this musicologist put forward, in 1919, the hypothesis, generally accepted in subsequent years, that Chinese musical theorists produced this cycle on series of bamboo flutes as early as prehistoric times, and, from this, derived scales (first of five, later of seven tones to the octave) in some regular manner, combining them on Pan-pipes.

The starting point of this entire system was—and still is for the present-day Chinese tonal system—a tone of fixed pitch, the *huang chong* (= "yellow bell"), which more or less corresponds to the European *f♯'*, having 366 vibrations (v.d.) per second; it requires a tube about 230 mm long, at any rate, when this tube has the traditional diameter handed down to us in the writings of the 16th century Chinese musicologist prince CHAY YÜ, i.e.

---

1) The theory was expounded in various stages of its development, now concisely, now in greater detail, by its author in "Anthropos" 1919/'20 (p. 569 *et seq.*) and in Vol. VIII of GEIGER and SCHEEL's *Handbuch der Physik* (1927), and further by ROBERT LACHMANN in his *Musik des Orients* (1929); by CURT SACHS in his *Vergleichende Musikwissenschaft* (1930); by FRITZ BOSE in the „Atlantisbuch der Musik" (1934), p. 960 *et seq.*; by MARIUS SCHNEIDER in his article *Ethnologische Musikforschung* (in PREUSS, "Lehrbuch der Völkerkunde", p. 135 *et seq.*), 1937; by GEORG SCHÜNEMANN in the "Archiv für Musikforschung" Vol. I fasc. 3 and 4), 1936; by HEINRICH HUSMANN in his article *Marimba und Sansa der Sambesikultur* (in the "Zeitschrift für Ethnologie", Vol. 68, p. 197 *et seq.*), 1936, and by the present writer in *De Toonkunst van Bali*, Vol. II (1925), in the article *De l'origine des échelles musicales javano-balinaises* (in the "Journal of the Siam Society" Vol. XXIII, 1929), p. 111 *et seq.*, in *De Toonkunst van Java* Vol. I, p. 19 *et seq.* (1934), in *A musicological argument for cultural relationship between Indonesia—probably the isle of Java—and Central Africa* (in the "Proceedings of the Musical Association", Session LXII) (1936) and in the brochure *Around Von Hornbostel's theory of the cycle of blown fifths* (1948).

8.12 mm. [1]). It is this *huang chong*—blown, as stated above, on a stopped bamboo tube—and the cycle of fifths based upon it, from which the structure of a large number of tonal systems, spread over a great part of the world, may be explained: not only do the Javanese and Balinese scales seem to derive from it, but—as VON HORNBOSTEL was able to show—also the tuning of Central African, Siamese and Birmese xylophones and metallophones, and of Melanesian, Polynesian, Northwest Brazilian and ancient Peruvian Pan-pipes (**128**, **130**). At the same time, VON HORNBOSTEL made the curious discovery that this length of 230 ± 3 mm. had become in time the metrological standard measure, the sacred nucleus, as it were, of the entire system of length measurements, not only of the ancient Chinese, but so it seems, also of Sumeria at the time of the Lagash priest-king GUDÉA (abt. 2600 B. C.) and his Egyptian contemporaries (**131**).

According to VON HORNBOSTEL, the tone sequences that formed the beginning of this entire development of the scale, constituted a series of semi-fourths-intervals (therefore called by him "Halbquartenreihen"). He found them being produced a.o. on the Pan-pipes of the Northwest Brazilian Uitoto-tribe [2]). Later on I myself found them in other places, *viz.* on some of the Congo xylophones and on some gamelans from the Javanese Principalities.

The table on p. 27 contains a number of these semi fourths-scales, as found in Central-Java [3]).

It will be seen that the deviations from the theoretical pitches are extremely small. As far as the majority of the tones are concerned no differ-

---

[1]) Cf. MAURICE COURANT, Essai historique sur la musique classique des Chinois (in LAVIGNAC, Encyclopédie de la Musique, Vol. I, p. 77 *et seq.* (91)), 1912.

[2]) E. M. VON HORNBOSTEL, Ueber einige Panpfeifen aus Nordwestbrasilien (in KOCH-GRÜNBERG, Zwei Jahre unter den Indianern, Bd. II (Berlin 1910), p. 378 *et seq.*).

[3]) To enable the reader to form some idea of the sounds represented by the vibration figures given below, we here give the values of the tones of the European tempered scale from high to low:

c''	523	g'	392	d'	293½
b'	494	g flat'	370	d flat'	277
b flat'	466	f'	349	c'	261½
a'	440	e'	329½		
a flat'	415½	e flat'	311		

The tones of the next lower octave have, respectively, half the number of vibrations of the corresponding tones of the octave started from, and those of the next higher octave, double this number.

									huang chong								
Part of the cycle of blown fifths in semi-fourths-sequence	IV	XV	III	XIV	II	XIII	I	XII	0	XI	XXII	X	XXI	IX	XX	VIII	XIX
	438	509	296½	344	400½	465	541	314¼	366	425	493½	287	333½	387½	450½	525	304½
Gamelan *Kyahi Kanyut Mèsem* pélog (Mangkunagaran, Solo)	V	VII	I	III	IV	VI	—	II									
	439	512	295	345	399	465		317									
Gamelan *Kyahi Bremara* (kraton, Jogya).										V	VII	I	III	IV	VI	—	II
										425	496	290	332½	387½	450		308
Gamelan *Kyahi Pengasih* (kraton, Solo)										V	VII	I	III	IV	VI	—	II
										421	500	286	335½	392	450		313
Deviations from the norm in *cents*	+4	+10	—8	+5	—7	0	—	+15		0	+9	+18	— 6	0	—2	—	+20
										—17	+22	— 6	+10	+20	—2	—	+20

For the intervals of these three scales, expressed in *cents*, vide Appendix *61*, nos. 5, 11 and 2.

ence would probably be noticed if these gamelan scales and the corresponding theoretical sequences were to be played in succession.

Inasmuch as these semi-fourths-scales have been produced on Javanese instruments they should be regarded as scales which originated at some time before the splitting-up into the two groups of scales or tonal systems which are distinguished to-day under the names of *pélog* and *sléndro*. But the tone scales from the Principalities reproduced above deviate in practice so little from the other pélog scales (which, as a matter of fact, are not even all of the same construction themselves) that no Javanese would ever think of making a distinction between them and the other, authentic, pélog scales. That these scales are classed under the same heading with the pélog group and not with the sléndro group (which, as we shall see in a moment, also had its pre-stage, constructed on the semi-fourths succession principle) is purely and simply a matter of the number of steps: in the cases under discussion, seven tones have been brought together within the compass of the octave, whereas in the sléndro pre-stages there are never more than five.

It further appears that the three scales given in the table above have been derived from the cycle of blown fifths in quite a regular manner, with one exception: one of the tones skips a place. The tones of the gamelans measured follow upon each other, within the order of scale, as under:

Cycle steps:	X	XIX	XXI	IX	XI	XX	XXII	(VIII)	(X)
and	III	XII	XIV	II	IV	XIII	XV	(I)	(III)

which, expressed in *cents*, amounts to a scale of the following structure:

I *102* II *156* III *264* IV *156* V *102* VI *156* VII *264* I′

We have christened this scale "primitive pélog". Such scales, therefore, consist of a mixture of two groups of cycle steps, each of which forms a closed group in itself; in the examples given in the above table they are the groups XXII to XIX incl. and XI to VIII incl., on the one hand, and the groups XV to XII incl. and IV to I incl. on the other.

Another category of scales, which is also to be reckoned among the pélog group employs a series of *uneven* (*yang*, or masculine) or *even* (*yin*, feminine) fifths of that cycle. These scales have been called by von Hornbostel "Umschichtreihen", *i.e.* "alternating tone-series". It is probable that they did not in the beginning finish on the octave; for, as will be seen, the eighth interval goes beyond the octave by *48 cents*: 8 × *156* = *1248* C. It has not been possible to produce perfectly pure examples of this "Umschichtreihe" either in Java or in Bali. For these we have to look in other regions of the "blown fifths area", especially in the Southern part of the Belgian Congo territory. A remarkable specimen of this type—namely a combination of a "male" and a "female" alternating series—has been realized on a marimba of the Bayanzi-tribe:

Blown fifths	XIV	XVI	XVIII		VI		VIII	X			XII
female series								143½			
	172	188½	206								
	344	376½	412		480½		525	574			628½
Blown fifths				XIII		XV			XVII	XIX	
male series						127½				152½	
				232½		254½			278½	304½	
Marimba of the	I	II	III	IV	V	VI	VII	VIII	IX	X	XI
Bayanzi (Congo-						127		143½		151	
Mus. no. 31354)	171½	191	210	233		255			282½	306	
	346	381½	420		472		526	570			624
Deviations from						*—3*		*o*		*—14*	
the norm in *cents*	*—5*	*+25*	*+33*	*+4*		*+4*			*+24*	*+ 9*	
	+10	*+20*	*+33*		*—29*		*+3*	*—12*			*—12*

In Java and Bali a number of scales have been found to exist showing a transition from the "Umschichtreihe" to a "younger" form. The fact that these "Umschicht"-scales proved to be unable to maintain themselves is probably to be attributed to their inadequacy in the formation of melodies on a higher plane of development and based chiefly on fifths. As a matter of fact the scales mentioned consist of an equidistant sequence of intervals of *156* C. [1]) In playing either a Pan-pipe or a xylophone tuned to such a scale one did not have this important, and gradually indispensable fifth-interval at one's disposal. For, the intervals most closely approaching it, i.e. 4 × *156* = *624*, and 5 × *156* = *780* C. cannot replace the fifth (*702* C.). It is probable that, in order to obtain intervals of approximately that size, a "masculine" and a "feminine" instrument were used together. The fact that the Pan-pipe in Further India and in Western Java occurs exclusively in pairs might perhaps be regarded as the last glimmer of this kind of double-

[1]) *i.e.* two blown fifths diminished by one octave = (2 × *678*) — *1200* = *156* C.

instrument melody formation [1]). In later days the players saw how cumbersome, as well as avoidable, this manner of playing was. The next phase in this development—existing to this day in its pure form in both Java and Bali—simply consists in the exchange, between the two members of the instrumental couple, of three of their tones. In this way scales come into being of mixed gender, which, expressed in terms of *cents*, show the following aspect:

156 156 210 156 156 156 210,

or an inversion of this series.

This new scale actually leads to the goal aimed at, *i.e.* usuable fifths. For $(3 \times 156) + 210 = 678$ C., *i.e.* exactly the blown fifth required. When set out on the cycle of blown fifths, the tones of this younger, genuine pélog scale comprise an unbroken curve of that cycle [2]).

Good examples of this scale-formation are provided by the tuning of the following gamelans: [3])

1) With respect to this use of panpipes in pairs, VON HORNBOSTEL wrote to me (in the course of a letter dated 12th May 1935) as follows: "Paare von Bläsern: Reliefs aus den Han-Gräbern; Alt-Peru, Vasenbilder (die beiden Panpfeifen durch eine Schnur verbunden), plastische Totenfiguren auf einer Vase; Tukánò-Indianer am Rio Negro; Aymara; Cuna (Panama). Für die yang-yin-Verteilung ist auch die Form der Panpfeifen oft bezeichnend, die deutlich auf zusammengebundene (ursprüngliche) Paare weist: China 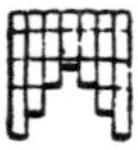 (alt), 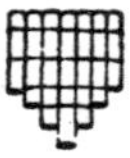 (jünger; auch Europa), Oberbirma (Shan) und Salomonen:  (also alle drei überhaupt möglichen Arten des aneinanderbindens kommen vor). Diese verbundenen Paare sind vielleicht noch starkere Beweise als die getrennten Paare, wenn man bedenkt, dass es so viele andere gepaarte Instrumente gibt (die aber vielleicht ihrerseits mit der yang-yin-Teilung zusammenhängen, wie die Posaunen in Tibet, die grossen Zeremonialflöten in Neu-Guinea und in Brasilien, usw.). Die grossen Flöten am Sepik werden, wie der hiesige Ethnologe BATESON mir mitteilt—er hat ein wunderschönes Paar mitgebracht—umschichtig geblasen: sie sind in der Stimmung um etwa einen Ganzton auseinander und man überbläst sie bis zum 7. und 8. Teilton. Das spricht sehr für eine ähnliche Praxis auf den Panpfeifen, und bei den „verteilten Panpfeifen" von Oberbirma, Ost-, Zentral- und Süd-Afrika ist es ja heute noch so."

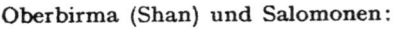

2) This applies to the *seven*-toned form of scale. In the case of the *five*-toned form (*vide* p. 49) it was naturally sufficient to interchange only *two* of the tones, thereby obtaining the blown fifth by combining the intervals *156*, *156*, and *366*.

3) The Roman figures represent the tones (of the cycle of blown fifths and of the gamelan-scales respectively); the Arabic ones, vibrationfigures, when placed either *under* or *above*, and Cents, when placed *between* the tone-figures or when printed in italics. This applies to all scale-measurements reproduced in the present work.

Series of blown fifths I–VII	II	IV	VI	I	III	V	VII	II
	200¼	219	240¼	270½	296½	324¼	355	400½
Gamelan Munggang pélog (Paku Alaman, Jogya)	I	II	III	IV	V	VI	VII	I′
	199½	217	237	273	298	326	357	399
	146	*153*	*245*	*151*	*155*	*158*	*192*	
Deviations in *cents*	*—7*	*—16*	*—23*	*+16*	*+9*	*+9*	*+10*	*—7*

Series of blown fifths VI–XII	XI	VI	VIII	X	XII	VII	IX	XI
	425	480½	525	574	628½	710	775	850
Hindu-Javanese demung, excavated in Banjarnegara, C. Java	I	II	III	IV	V	VI	VII	I′
	427	475	518	576	628½	710	768	(854)
	184	*150*	*184*	*151*	*211*	*136*	*184*	
Deviations in *cents*	*—8*	*—20*	*—24*	*+6*	*0*	*0*	*—16*	*—8*

A number of other examples are given in Appendix *59*.

Scales of the same type are found also, in beautiful examples, in Bali and Central-Africa, and with slight alterations, due to "temperature", in Siam and Birma.

* * *

Not only the pélog, but also the sléndro scale seems to have (as stated previously) its origin in the cycle of blown fifths, and similarly, too, in an "Umschichtreihe".

For some years we have had certain indications which seemed to support the theory that there has been an older form of sléndro, consisting of a regular sequence of notes obtained by missing out two "Umschicht"-tones each time:

I	III	V	VII	IX	XI	XIII	XV	XVII	XIX	XXI	0	II
1			2			3			4			5

As expressed in ELLIS' system, these would be sequences of intervals of *4068* C., which, if brought together within the boundaries of one and the same octave, anounts to a sequence of steps of *4068* — (3 × *1200*) = *468* C. In this way one obtains, when arranging them in scale-sequence, a series of alternating intervals of 264 and 204 C.:

I *264* II *204* III *264* IV *204* V *264* I′

Some sléndro scales had been found both in Java and in Bali, showing a transitional form between the scale constructed in the above manner and sléndro proper. There is yet another pointer in that direction: when one arranges the tones of the Balinese *gendèr wayang* scale (which belongs to the sléndro system) in the position given above (with steps of 468 C. each), then the vowels of the tone-names, as Professor VON HORNBOSTEL pointed out to me in one of his letters, arrange themselves "spectrally", i.e. *ḍing, ḍèng, ḍang, ḍong, ḍoong*. And this is significant of a race which is always trying to fix some connexion between the tonal pitch and the size of an instrument, or part of instrument (key, gong-kettle) on the one hand, and the vowel-sound of the name of that instrument, on the other hand [1]).

In fact, subsequent events proved that the above indication did not point to the wrong track, and the theoretical speculations set out above eventually proved to be quite well founded: it recently came to my knowledge, in quite an unexpected manner, that this hypothetical type of sléndro scales (afterwards called *medium* sléndro) had not only existed in the past, but that it had managed to maintain itself in a strikingly pure form. In one of the most "ancient" districts of Eastern Java, which until recently had not been subjected to strong outside influences, namely in the teakwood districts mentioned above (Bajanagara and the adjacent regencies, and also in some places in Surabaya and Bangil and further towards the East, but less frequent there, and often in less purer form) it appeared that there

[1]) As a matter of fact this does not apply to music only. In this connexion R. PURADIREJA and M. SURYADIRAJA, in their "Bijdrage tot de kennis der Soendaneesche taal" ("Handelingen van het Eerste Congres voor Taal-, land- en volkenkunde van Java, Solo 1919", p. 400 *et seq.* (405)), offer, for example, the following observations:

that a word finishing on (a syllable with) the vowel *i* indicates that which is small and more or less round;
,, ,, ,, ,, ,, (a syllable with) the vowel *è* indicates that which is thin and flat;
,, ,, ,, ,, ,, (a syllable with) the vowel *a* indicates that which is of ordinary size and shape;
,, ,, ,, ,, ,, (a syllabe with) the vowel *o* indicates that which is larger, globular and also that which is hollow;
,, ,, ,, ,, ,, (a syllable with) the vowel *u* indicates that which is largest of all and that which is piled up;
[,, ,, ,, ,, ,, (a syllable with) the vowel *e* indicates that which happens suddenly, and
,, ,, ,, ,, ,, (a syllable with) the vowel *eu* indicates that which happens gradually].

still existed a fairly large number of gamelans tuned in this way. Two examples may suffice:

Blown fifths	XIX	II	VIII	XIV	XX
	304½	400½	262½	344	450½
Gam. miring, ...	II	IV	I	III	V
Bajanegara	308	399	262	347	450
Deviations in *cents*. . . .	+*20*	—*7*	—*4*	+*15*	—*2*
Gam. miring, Ngumpak	II	IV	I	III	V
Bajanagara	310	405	266	348	455
Deviations in *cents*. . . .	+*32*	+*19*	+*22*	+*20*	+*17*

It will be seen that the entire pitch of the second of these two gamelans is about *20* C. higher than the most approximate steps of the cycle; it, however, excels the first in respect of its internal structure, its intervals showing hardly any deviation from the theoretical ones, so little, in fact, as to be completely indiscernable in practice:

Gam. miring,	I		II		III		IV		V		I′
Bajanagara	262		308		347		399		450		524
		280		*207*		*241*		*209*		*263*	
but											
	I		II		III		IV		V		I′
Gam. miring,	266		310		348		405		455		532
Ngumpak		*266*		*200*		*262*		*202*		*270*	
Theoretical scale		*264*		*204*		*264*		*204*		*264*	

In Bajanagara the orchestras using this scale are called gamelan *sléndro miring*, or, for short, gamelan *miring*, from which it will be seen that the modern sléndro scale (which is also quite well known in the regencies mentioned (*vide* Appendix *57D*)) is nowadays looked upon as the normal, whereas primitive sléndro is regarded as the peculiar, deviating (= *miring*) scale. In other places, *e.g.* in Prabalingga and Banyuwangi, orchestras using this tone-sequence bear the name of gamelan *sundarèn*.

Eastern Java, however, had one more surprise up its sleeve. It appeared that, among the measured miring- and sundarèn-scales, there were a few showing yet another, slightly different type, which bore the same relation to the other gamelans of that name as did, in its turn, "medium" sléndro itself to modern sléndro; and again, as, in pélog, the "Umschicht"-scales to modern pélog. This type of scale—which we have afterwards called "primitive" or "semi-fourth" *sléndro*—uses those tones out of the cycle of blown fifths which lie apart, each time, by 12 blown fifths, *i.e.* 12 × 678 = *8136* C., which, when brought together within the compass of one and the same octave, amounts to (7 × *1200* = *8400*) — *8136* = *264* C[1]). When calculated in this way, therefore, these scales, theoretically speaking, present the aspect (together with the finish on the octave, which in the beginning was probably missing, but is now always found to be present) of a sequence of four intervals of *264* C., supplemented, or interrupted somewhere, as the case may be, by a single interval of *1200* — (4 × *264* = *1056*) = *144* C.

In calculating the structure of this scale by the above method, however, we have left the "remnant-interval" out of consideration. For, this "primitive" sléndro is a sequence of tones brought together to a compressed position within the octave, but theoretically covering a range of 49 descending blown fifths, *i.e.* more than twice round the entire cycle. Now, as we said before, this cycle is not in reality completely closed (one might say that it is a spiral, just like the European one); therefore, the way in which it has been presented here, which is based upon the fictitious assumption that it is closed, is not quite correct, for it neglects an interval of *6* C., as should be clear from the above (p. 24, footnote 3). In the case of a scale, therefore, which, like the one under discussion, extends over more than twice the entire cycle, one should take an "error" of 2 × *6* = *12* C. into account.

Now, if one calculates, as we have just done, the large intervals without taking into account their share in this "error", one will finish by finding, for this "remnant-interval", an amount smaller by *12* C. than one would find if one had fixed it, in the first place, at an amount of two blown fifths (of *678* C.), reduced by the octave-interval (*1200* C.), *i.e.* *1356* — *1200* = *156* C.

Taking the "remnant-interval" at *156* C., this leaves, for the four re-

---

1) This may also be represented—since the scale *ascends* in the *descending* cycle of blown fifths, *i.e.*, in fact, in blown *fourths* (*522* C.)—by the calculation (12 × *522* = *6264*) — (5 × *1200* = *6000*) = *264* C.

maining, genuine intervals, *1044* C., *i.e. 261* C. per interval, that is exactly a semi-fourth (*522* : 2), t.w. the half of a "blown fourth".

A good example of this type of scale is found on the gamelan miring of MUSADIKRAMA from the désa Katur, district of Ngumpak, Regency Bajanegara:

Part of the cycle of blown fifths in semi-fourth sequence	IV 438	XV 509	III 593	XIV 688	II 801	(IV) 876
Intervals in cents:		*261*	*261*	*261*	*261*	*156*
Gamelan miring of Musadikrama désa Katur, Bajanegara	V 434	I 510	II 590	III 680	IV 791	V' 868
Intervals in *cents*:		*280*	*252*	*246*	*259*	*163*
Deviation in *cents* of each gamelan-tone	*—16*	*+4*	*—8*	*—20*	*—22*	*—16*

Certainly we have here to do again, like in the case of "primitive" or "semi-fourth" pélog (*vide* above p. 26) with a very ancient, nay, probably the most ancient form of blown-fifths scale. It has its origin in the application of the entire blown fifths cycle to a twin Pan-pipe (frequently, both in the past and at the present, combined into one double instrument), and has been dealt with in **130** (p. 431).

In this case as in others, Eastern Java joins hands with Bali and the Sunda districts, whereas in Central Java, whose cultural renewal is of longer date, this ancient stage appears to have become lost. It seems to me, however, that some indication of the fact that there, too, scales of this type existed at one time, is to be found in the Solo nomenclature for the structure of that sléndro scale of which the interval *barang-gulu* is larger than the remaining intervals, *i.e. laras sundari* or *nyendari* (*vide* below, p. 252/253). *Sundari* and *nyendari* are, indeed, different forms existing side by side with *sundarèn*, which, as stated before, is the name for the "medium" sléndro scale in Prabalingga and Banyuwangi. In both these cases, therefore, this term relates to a sléndro scale which is not quite equidistant.

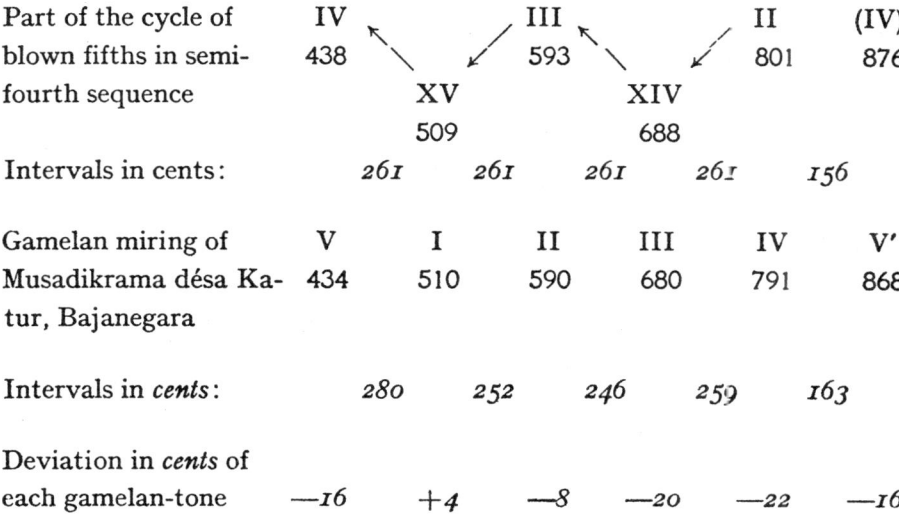

Nyundari (= *nyendari*) is also mentioned in the Chenṭini (**381**) as a kind of sléndro tuning (Chant 160, stanza 18 *et seq.*, Vol. V/VI p. 164):

18. ....
gamelan talu chumengkung
genḍingané *Titipati*
semada rempek nenaboh.

19. Jayèngraga Kulawirya sareng jumbul
nilingken gamelan muni
sami sasmitèng pendulu
arongèh dènira linggih
Jènraga tetanya alon:

20. man pengulu sinten kang natab gangsa gung
seḍeng rarasé nyundari
punapa tiang memantu
punapa kyahi petinggi
ingkang amochung seléndro.

The English rendering of this song would be something like this:

18. ....."Suddenly the sound of someone playing the gamelan came to them from somewhere; the genḍing *Titipati* sounded. The playing was even and regular.

19. Jayènraga and Kulawirya both started up and pricked up their ears, so as to catch the sound well. They exchanged knowing looks and could hardly keep their seats. Then Jayènraga asked softly:

20. "Penghulu, who it is playing the gamelan [1]) there? It is one of medium range [2]), with *nyendari* tuning. Might there be someone giving a wedding feast? Or would it be the *petinggi* (village chief) causing the gamelan sléndro to be played?" ....

In Bali and in the Sunda districts, however, small orchestras are to be found even to-day, whose scale is identical with the Eastern-Javanese sléndro miring/sundarèn in its oldest ("semi-fourth" sléndro-) form, except that their scales appear to have originated from the sequence of six

[1]) Literally: the (complete) gamelan (with bonangs, demungs and large) gong.

[2]) *seḍeng*; *vide* p. 186.

steps descending each time by 12 blown fifths, and not, as the Eastern-Javanese sequences mentioned, from a sequence of five such steps. Since, as we have seen, these scale-steps form intervals of 261 C, when brought together in scale sequence (as a result of which the corner tones of the hexatonic scale thus obtained would go beyond the limits of the octave, for $5 \times 261 = 1305 = 1200 + 105$ C.), these corner tones have been tempered, *i.e.* one is raised and the other lowered, until they reach octave distance. Of the tone sequences thus obtained—called in the Sunda districts *ringkung*—two examples are given below, one of which hails from Bali, and the other one from the Sunda districts.

Five-tone Angklungscale from	I	II	III	IV	V	I′
Sangsit (North-Bali) n° 1.	336	383	436½	501	588	(336)
Descending sequence of blown	V	XVI	IV	XV	III	XIV
fifths	324¼	376½	438	509	593	344
Tempered corner tones . . .	334					334

(**193**, Table III, No. 1)

Ringkung scale of the Angklung at Dayeuh Luhur, res. of	II	III	IV	V	I	II′
Bandung	374	422	494	576	336	(374)
Descending sequence of blown	0	XI	XXII	X	XXI	IX
fifths	366	425	493½	574	333½	387½
Tempered corner tones . . .	372½					372½

(**193**, Table XVIII, No. 10)

Without any doubt this method of temperament of the "corner" tones causes the scale to approach that of the modern sléndro scale, which we shall presently deal with. Thus, one might represent that Angklung-scale from Sangsit also in the following manner:

Modern sléndro sequence:	XVII/XIX	XXI	0/II	IV	VI/VIII	XVII/XIX
	291	333½	383	438	502	582
Gamelan Angklung Sangsit, N. Bali	V_1	I	II	III	IV	V
	294	336	383	436½	501	588
Intervals in *cents*.		*231*	*227*	*226*	*238*	*278*

I cannot refrain from making brief mention of a remark which Professor VON HORNBOSTEL made in connexion with the name *ringkung*, to the effect that the origin of this name, in common with, it seems, that of other Indonesian musical terms [1]), might quite well be Chinese, since after all, the entire system of blown fifths, and, therefore, also the Javanese and Balinese scales seem to have come to the Archipelago from the South-Eastern Asiatic continent.

Since the Chinese language does not possess the consonant *r*, *ringkung* must have been *lingkung* in China. Now, there exists a word *ling* (零), signifying: to be left over, to go beyond, to remain behind, to be superfluous. At present it is used chiefly in counting; *e.g.*, 103 = *i* (= one) *pé* (= 100) *ling* (surpassed by) *san* (= three). Assuming that *ling kung* is composed of this word *ling* and the word *kung*, signifying palace (宮) (the name of the tonic in the Chinese pentatonic scale), then its meaning would be: ***the*** (sixth) ***tone*** (of the semi-fourths sequence) ***which goes beyond*** (the octave of) ***the tone kung***, from which we might conclude that the system was called after the tone in the sequence which, before the tempering process, was the most conspicuous or disturbing [2]).

---

[1]) As VON HORNBOSTEL remarked to me in one of his letters, it is not altogether impossible that the Javanese instrumental name *kemanak* (*vide* p. 180) hails from the S.E. Asiatic continent; for, in Annam a wooden bell with a handle may be found, which, in Buddhistic ritual, is beaten alternately with small clocks made of metal and equally provided with a handle, which latter are also known to exist in China. The wooden clock is called *cai-mo-na-chua* (*cai* = objective prefix; *mo* = wood; *na* = house; and *chua* = pagoda). Further is *nac* = bell. For wooden bell, therefore, the Annam name ought to be *cai-mo-nac*. This name, whose composition would naturally not have been understood by the Javanese, might have been transferred from the wooden to a metal idiophone, which is quite a common thing.

One of the Dyak words for mouth organ, *keluri* (which instument as is well-known, hails from the northern part of Further India (Laos) or Southern China, would probably have been, in the original Chinese version: *ke-liu-li* (*ke* = prefix; *liu* = row, sequence, and *li* = shawm), meaning, therefore, a range of shawms, which is a perfectly correct description of the instrument in question.

Hatong, the Sundanese word for bamboo Pan-pipe, might have been derived from the Chinese *hsiao t'ung* (*hsiao* = panpipe; *t'ung* = bamboo).

[2]) Dr. PURBACHARAKA mentions the fact that *lingkung* is not only a Chinese, but also a purely Javanese word, meaning *to bend*, or *bending round*. It might just be possible, therefore, that *pélog* = *pa-ilog* = bending (cf. ancient Javanese *ilug*, which —*vide* Rāmāyaṇa XXV 115 —should be translated by "to bend to and fro", "to sway"), is synonymous with *lingkung*, and that both (as is the case with the term *miring*) stand for a form of "bent", *i.e.* deviating, scale.

This might not even be an isolated case. The sixth tone obtained by generating fifths is called by the Chinese: *pièn kung*. Now, this word *pièn* means: to change, to replace, and *pièn kung*—which tone is used to replace the tone *kung* in certain cases—means, therefore: altered, or replaced *kung*. *Pélog* would then be its direct translation, at any rate assuming this to have originated from the root *log* = *rog*, and translating *sorog* by "alternate" or "shifted" tone [1]). In other words, in this case, too, it would be the most conspicuous tone (*sorog gedè*!) that had given its name to the entire system.

But to return to the development of the sléndro system: the great majority of the measurements taken testify to the existence of another, younger, scale structure. In this structure, either the uneven or the even tones of the scale come together with the "Umschicht"-tones which remain when two are being missed each time, just as in the older "medium"-sléndro form. The remaining tones of the scale, however, are pitched in such a way as to keep exactly *between* those "Umschicht"-tones skipped. This halving of the "Umschicht"-intervals is often so strikingly precise that one is inclined to ask oneself in astonishment: "How on earth did they manage it?" No doubt this would have been VON HORNBOSTEL's ejaculation, too, were it not for the fact that, some years before, he happened to have made some experiments at the Berlin psychological institute in collaboration with Dr. OTTO ABRAHAM, which experiments formed part of an inquiry into the question whether, and, if so, to what exactitude, it was possible to split an interval into equal parts by the "unarmed" ear. The results were surprising: the average error amounted, in the case of intervals taken at random and not in use in music, to only 3½% of the interval so divided; whilst in the case of intervals musically in use—which included, for the ancient creators of sléndro, the blown fifth—the exactitude achieved was even much greater (**130** par. 2). There do not, therefore, seem to exist any objections, either psychological or physiological, against assuming such a course of development based upon the division of intervals. We are, moreover, faced by bare and undeniable facts: the degree of correspondence between the number of vibrations obtained by measurements and the

---

1) *Sorog* also means *key*: this, however, is, in Java, a more or less modern notion. How were doors shut in ancient time? Undoubtedly by means of a closing-bar (*slarak*, Mal.: *palang pintu*) or wooden bolt (*slorog*), both of which are objects which have to be *shifted* in order to open the door. Cf. also *sorogan* (or *lorogan*) = drawer, and *jorog* = to shove, to push.

theoretically calculated tone-pitch is so perfect in the case of numerous scales that there cannot be any question of accident whatsoever (cf. Appendix *60*). The tone sequences formed in the manner indicated above consist of chains of intervals of *234* C. [1]) It is probable that these scales did not originally finish on the octave, any more than the primitive pélog did; certain gendèr keyboards found during excavations seem to show signs of having belonged to that stage ($5 \times 234 = 1170 = 1200 - 30$ C.). There is no doubt that, later on, the scale was given an octave-finish, so that, theoretically, it ran as follows:

234 234 234 234 264

It appears, however, that the makers of the later gamelans aimed at a scale composed of perfectly equal steps (*i.e.* with five intervals of *240* C. in the octave); nevertheless several of the sléndro tone-sequences measured possess one slightly larger interval—in accordance with the scale development outlined above—which, however, is placed now here, now there in the scale (cf. below Appendix *62*), and has, therefore, no longer any functional importance.

From the following examples it will be seen how strikingly practice and theory sometimes tally, also in this "modern" sléndro:

theoretical tone sequence derived from the cycle of blown fifths	XVII/XIX 291	XXI 333½	XXIII/II 383	IV 438	VI/VIII 502	XVII/XIX 582
Kyahi *Kanyut Mèsem* Sl., Mangku Nagaran, Solo	I 291	II 331	III 383	IV 439	V 500	I' 582
Deviations in *cents*:	*0*	*—13*	*0*	*+4*	*—7*	*0*
theoretical tone s[illegible]ce derived from the cycle of blown fifths	I/III 283	V 324¼	VII/IX 371	XI 425	XIII/XV 486½	I/III 566
Gamelan sléndro from Ranchaiyuh, distr. Tanggerang res. Batavia	I 282½	II 323	III 371	IV 427½	V 486	I' 565
Deviations in *cents*:	*—4*	*—7*	*0*	*+10*	*—2*	*—5*
theoretical tone sequence derived from the cycle of blown fifths	III 296½	V/VII 339	IX 387½	XI/XIII 444½	XV 509	III 593

[1]) For then these tones lie at a distance of 1½ "Umschicht"-interval = $1\frac{1}{2} \times 156 = 234$ C. from each other.

Kyahi *Pengawé sari*, Paku Alaman, Jogya	I 295	II 341	III 390	IV 446	V 511	I 590
Deviations in *cents*:	—*8*	+*10*	+*11*	+*5*	+*7*	—*8*

theoretical tone sequence derived from the cycle of blown fifths	XV/XVII 266¼	XIX 304½	XXI/0 349¼	II 400½	XIII 465	XV/XVII 266¼ I
Gamelan Sléndro of R. M. Jayadipura, Jogya	266	304	349½	399	462	532 (266)
Deviations in *cents*:	—*2*	—*2*	+*2*	—*7*	—*12*	—*2*

For further examples we refer the reader to Appendix *60*.

* * *

Following what has been set out above, Father P. ROZING, S.V.D., whose studies of the problems relative to the cycle of blown fifths testify to profound interest as well as great ingenuity, has sketched out a somewhat different course of development which, among other things, has the great advantage of being less complicated, especially as regards the majority of sléndro scale forms.

Father ROZING's reasoning is as follows:

We may regard the existence of the octave-interval as a primary fact, since it arises in a natural way from the simultaneous singing by men and women, whose voices usually move at an octave's distance:

I	I'
0	*1200* C.

By overblowing a stopped flute one obtains the—too flat—twelfth of the tonic (*1878* C.), which, when brought back into the octave, yields the blown fifth of *678* C. We then obtain the following tone-sequence:

I	II		I'
0	*678*		*1200* C.
678		*522*	= *1200* C.

When applying the same process again, but starting, this time, from tone II, we get the blown fifth of the first blown fifth, and this, within the scale-compass, will be placed between tones I and II, at a distance of *156* C. from tone No. I (for, $678 + 678 - 1200 = 156$ C.):

I	II	III	I'	
0	*156*	*678*	*1200* C.	
156	*522*	*522*		= *1200* C.

So long as these tones were used only for the purpose of giving signals, or to accentuate dance-steps, they were quite adequate as such. For the purpose of melody-forming, however, the two distances of a blown fourth (*522* C.) are rather too great. There was every reason, therefore, to fill up these fourths by means of an intermediate tone. This filling up of structural intervals may still be observed to this day among primitive peoples, *e.g.* the North Papua tribes (**202**).

The smaller intervals aimed at may be obtained in two ways, *i.e.* either on the "consonance-principle" (the intervals already obtained came into being in this way) or on the "distance-principle"—in this case, by halving both fourths. Instances of the halving of fourths have also been found—as we saw above (p. 26)—among primitive peoples in our own time.

When halving the two fourths in question we obtain the following scale:

I		II		III		IV		V		I′	
0		*156*		*412*		*678*		*939*		*1200* C.	
	156		*261*		*261*		*261*		*261*		= *1200* C.

which is the very scale referred to above (p. 34) under the name of *primitive sléndro*, and which, as we have seen, is still found on certain *gamelans miring* in Bajanagara.

The heptatonic scale may also be explained by means of the course of development described above. We begin at the stage where the following tone-distances were available:

I		II		III		I′	
0		*156*		*678*		*1200* C.	
	156		*522*		*522*		= *1200* C.

Now instead of following, from this point, the "distance-principle", as we did in the case of sléndro, we adhere to the "consonance-principle". On overblowing a stopped tube with a pitch equal to tone No. II, we obtain a tone which, when lowered by an octave, yields a blown fifth lying *156* C. above step No. III (*678*). In the same way, another blown fifth may be derived from this newly-obtained tone (*834* C. above step No. I), whose position will be *312* C. (*i.e.* *834* + *678* — *1200* C.) above tone I. From the latter, in its turn, a blown fifth may be derived, which will take its place in the sequence at *990* C. above step No. I (for *312* + *678* = *990* C.); and finally, from the last-named blown fifth, a step whose position will be at a distance of 468 (= *990* + *678* — *1200* C.) from step No. I. In other words, in order to obtain this new tone-sequence we simply apply the overblowing process another four times, *i.e.* six times in all. The result, then, will be the following scale:

I	II	III	IV	V	VI	VII	I′
0	*156*	*312*	*468*	*678*	*834*	*990*	*1200* C.

156 *156* *156* *210* *156* *156* *210* = *1200* C.

i.e. the pélog-scale which, as we have seen, is constructed out of seven succeeding fifths of the cycle of blown fifths.

It is, of course, possible to carry on with this method of generating fifths, as has been done here six times, still further. The result will then be a series of intervals of *156* C. If we hold on to the principle of "limitation to the octave"—which was the initial idea in this line of thought—we shall get a series of seven steps of *156* C., followed by one of *108* C. And this is the "Umschichtreihe" (alternating series of tones) in the purest form which, therefore, in this line of reasoning, should be a younger scale-form than either real pélog or real sléndro (miring).

Modern sléndro may also be derived in a similarly simple manner, namely from the "Umschichtreihe" just mentioned:

156 156 156 | 156 156 156 | 156 108
468 | 468 | 264
234 234 | 234 234 | 264

which amounts, after all, to a halving of two intervals which are too large for melodic construction (distance-principle), in the same way as we supposed it to be the case in the construction of the *sléndro miring* scale.

The generation theory expounded above has the following advantages as compared to that given by ourselves:

(i) it is simpler, more feasible psychologically, and substantiated by examples from present-day musical practice;

(ii) both the fifth-interval and the octave are present from the start, and are not obtained, as in the case of the pélog-fifths, only afterwards by means of the interchange of male and female tones. Father Rozing is of opinion that one may well conceive the existence, in higher forms of culture, of tone-sequences constructed without the aid of these two fundamental intervals; but in the case of more or less primitive peoples this is less probable, and still less in this particular case in which the fifth-interval, according to our supposition, constitutes the foundation of the entire tonal system;

(iii) Finally there is the most important point that this presentation of the evolution of the scale does not require any previous acquaintance with a *cycle* of blown fifths, which is too complicated a structure to assume to have been present when the more primitive of these tonal systems were first generated. It is, however, quite possible that, later on, when all these different tonal sequences were available, the construction of such a cycle was proceeded to, just as the Chinese, and the Greeks, came to the construction and calculation of the "Pythagorean" cycle.

At the same time, however, we should remark that no explanation is given in Father ROZING's line of thought for the structure of "medium" sléndro, with the following steps:

264 204 264 204 264,

which, in our exposition of the matter, is the result of bringing together into a single octave five tones lying at distances of six blown fifths each time (*vide* above, p. 31).

We may draw attention to the fact that, both in the course of development described by Father ROZING and in our explanation, sléndro and pélog were correlated in the beginning, *i.e.* before they became individualized into the sequences indicated by their respective names. Sléndro—both in one of its pre-stages and its modern form—assumes its typical structure by transferring at a given moment from the consonance- to the distance-principle, whereas pélog (as well as the "Umschichtreihe") is typified by the fact that it remains true to the consonance-principle.

* * *

Now, if only in rare cases a passable correspondence could be ascertained between the different theoretical constructions of tone-sequences and the scales found in practical use, we might grant that it was reasonable to suppose that this correspondence was merely accidental. The regularity in the formation of these sequences in itself, however, as well as the uniformity of manner in which, both in pélog as in sléndro, a younger scale-form is developed each time from an older one, and, on the other hand the frequency of the cases, and the fact that the correspondence in question often amounts to complete identity, utterly exclude, to my mind, the possibility that we have here to do with any "accidental" concurrence.

It will no doubt be readily admitted that this theory of von Hornbostel revealing as it does the common structure and cultural kinship of scales used by peoples geographically, historically and ethnologically so divergent as those mentioned above, represents a culture-historical discovery of the first magnitude. A discovery, therefore, almost too grand to be accepted without scepticism or criticism. In effect, objections were duly raised to the theory; it is to be regretted that they were not put forward until after the death of him to whom we owe this hypothesis.

The chief critics who have published their objections to the theory of blown fifths, and who went so far as to reject it completely, are Miss Kathleen Schlesinger (**326** *passim*) and Dr. Manfred Bukofzer (**57, 58, 59**); while Curt Sachs, in his more recent writings, also gives the impression of discountenancing it.

Now it had already been remarked on previous occasions that it was rather difficult to imagine, that as early as 3000 B. C., people could have succeeded in creating such a very complicated theoretical structure as that embodied in a 23-degree cycle of blown fifths; nay, it was asserted that it was utterly impossible to achieve the construction of such a cycle by experimental means only. But is this view quite justified? I suggest that a structure such as that of the scales reproduced above on p. 27 and p. 40, and—more particularly still—that of a Pan-pipe from Equador to be found in the musicological section of the Musée de l'Homme, Paris, under no. 41. 39.1, would lead one to doubt it. The tonal sequence of the latter instrument which comprises 26 tubes, includes no less than 16 of the 23 steps of the cycle —16 consecutive ones, as a matter of fact—and corresponds to the latter with a degree of precision which is nothing short of remarkable:

[1]) One can find their arguments, together with my objections against them, in my brochure "Around Von Hornbostel's theory of the cycle of blown fifths", published by the Royal Institute for the Indies in 1948 (**235**).

Number of tube	Vibration-number	Interval in *cents*	Step of the cycle	Deviation in *cents*
1.	682		XIV 688	*—16*
2.	453	*708*	XX 450½	*+ 9*
3.	542	*311*	I 541	*+ 4*
4.	461	*287*	XIII 465	*—19*
5.	604	*469*	XIX 609	*—14*
6.	728	*323*	0 732	*—10*
7.	832	*231*	XVIII 824	*+17*
8.	690	*324*	XIV 688	*+ 4*
9.	932	*521*	XIII 930	*+ 4*
10.	746	*391*	XVI 753	*—16*
11.	1120	*704*	XVII 1114	*+ 9*
12.	940	*303*	XIII 930	*+18*
13.	1248 (624)	*491* (*709*)	XII 1257 (628½)	*—12*
14.	1034 (517)	*326*	XV 1018 (509)	*+27*
15.	1512	*657* (*1857*)	XVI 1506	*+ 6*
16.	1272	*298*	XII 1257	*+21*
17.	1700	*502*	XI 1700	*0*
18.	1472	*250*	0 1464	*+ 9*
19.	1992	*524*	XXII 1974	*+15*
20.	1584	*397*	II 1602	*—22*
21.	2368	*697*	III 2372	*— 2*
22.	1992	*300*	XXII 1974	*+15*
23.	2672	*508*	XXI 2668	*+ 2*
24.	1992	*508*	XXII 1974	*+15*
25.	2760	*686*	XIV 2752	*+ 4*
26.	2232	*489*	XVII 2228	*+ 3*

This panpipe, therefore, uses the following steps of the cycle:

XI	XII	XIII	XIV	XV	XVI	XVII	XVIII	XIX	XX	XXI	XXII	0	I	II	III
17	16	4	1	14	10	11	7	5	2	23	19	6	3	20	21
	13	9	8		15	26					22	18			
		12	25								24				

When confronted with tone-sequences such as these, one is surely entitled to ask whether it is not quite within the bounds of possibility that people, even in those remote times, did actually succeed in construing a complete cycle of fifths. [*S3]

Moreover, even granting that there may have been practical obstacles in the way of tuning by means of over-blowing because of the large number of steps to run through, there was still a second means at people's disposal to arrive at an equivalent result: we possess data which prove that, in addition to the method of constructing theoretically —and explaining—the scale by means of overblowing, there existed another method, namely with the aid of the measuring rod. Bij this method, each subsequent lü-tube was cut to a length of either 2/3 or 3/4 of its predecessor; in this way, too, a chain was obtained consisting of a sequence of slightly too small fifths. This possibility has been taken in consideration also by VON HORNBOSTEL, towards the end of his life. In a letter addressed to the present writer, dated May 12, 1935, we read: "Ich glaube jetzt eigentlich, dass es im alten China den in der Litteratur ausschliesslich beschriebenen *metrischen* Quintenzirkel auch in der Praxis gegeben hat. Wenn man nämlich Röhren (von konstantem Durchmesser) nach dem Rezept 1, × 3/4, × 4/3 usw. schneidet, so werden die Quinten ebenfalls zu eng und zwar (wie ich einmal durch einen flüchtigen Versuch überzeugt habe) etwa im gleichen Verhältnis wie beim überblasen. Für das Verhältnis des metrischen zum Blasquintenzirkel sind verschiedene Annahmen möglich: 1°. der BQZ ist älter, der metrische Zirkel erst von den Theoretikern eingeführt und dann neben oder statt den BQZ verwendet; 2°. der metrische Quintenzirkel ist älter, und erst in der Praxis durch den bequemeren BQZ ersetzt worden (dies könnte sogar erst ausserhalb Chinas bei Völkern geschehen sein, die keinen Maasstab und keine Längenmessung kannten); 3°. = 1°. plus 2°., d.h., der BQZ hat zu allen Zeiten bei den Praktikern vorgeherrscht, ist nur Zeitweise in den gelehrten Kreisen durch den metr. QZ ersetzt worden, ganz analog wie es mit den bequemen Körpermaassen (Fuss, Fingerbreite, Spanne usw.) und den normierten Maassen der Fall war. Diese letzte Hypothese ist mir persönlich die wahrscheinlichste."

* * *

It is really astonishing the way these scales have managed to hold their own in the course of thousands of years. There was one powerful motive, however, behind this consistency, and that was the force of magic inherent in musical tones and in the melodies constructed thereon. For, music is, originally, pure magic, "incantation"; a song is nothing but a magic formula in melody, whose effect, however, will be the exact opposite of what is intended, if it is not performed perfectly truly and on the right pitch [1]). This magical character of music is prominent even on the highest cultural levels; we need only remind the reader of the twofold meaning of the Latin word *carmen*, *i.e.* song and magic formula (hence the English and French word *charm(e)s* = amulets), and of the fact, that the French word *enchanter* and the English nouns *enchantment* and *incantation*, are derived from the Latin *incantatus*, that is: treated, fascinated, bewitched by a *cantus*, a song.

We may remark in this connection that one of the first things to which each succeeding Chinese dynasty always devoted especial care was to calculate, all over again and in the most meticulous manner, the length of the *huang-chong* tube, from which the basic note of the tonal system was derived (and upon which the metrological system was based, too), in order that music might henceforth become the saving grace of the ruling dynasty, instead of being the cause of its ruin, as had been the case with its predecessor [2]). In Bougainville, one of the Solomon-islands, the pitches of the sacred Pan-pipes are transferred each year, in solemn fashion, and to the accompaniment of a ceremonial dance, to a small number of newly-manufactured instruments (**128**, p. 614). The same in Java. There, too, the scale of certain gamelans was—and even is to this day—considered desirable and worthy of being imitated, above the others, as, for example, that of the very old gamelan sléndro *Layem* of the Regent of Tasikmalaya (**192**, p. 15, foot-note) [3]), and of one of the two three-toned gamelans *Munggang* of the Susuhunan of Solo, which are probably much older still (**191**, p. 28) [4]). [*S4]

* * *

[1]) J. Combarieu, La musique et la magie; id., Histoire de la musique, Vol. I, the first two chapters.

[2]) Maurice Courant, Essai historique sur la musique classique des Chinois (in Lavignac, Encyclopédie de la musique, Vol. I, p. 80.) — This is the cause—apart from the fact that the correct diameter was not always strictly adhered to—of the fluctuations in the length of the *huang chong* in the course of the centuries. Though admittedly remaining roundabout 230 mm, it generally varied by a few millimetres either more or less (cf. table in **131**, p. 307).

[3]) For the scale, *vide* Appendix 60, scale No. 13.

[4]) For the scale, *vide* p. 258.

Now both in the Sunda-districts and in Java-proper, as well as in Bali, complicated but very harmoniously constructed scale systems have arisen from those pélog and sléndro tone sequences.

We will commence with an exposition of the pélog system as found in the Sunda districts, since the less complete pélog systems in vogue in other places in Java (and Bali) are included in this Sundanese "systèma teleion".

Partly in view of our knowledge of present-day musical practice we may assume that, at one time, from the available 7 steps of the original pélog tone-sequence, musical practice selected as basic series a scale that comprised five tone-steps (Sund.: *hambalan, tahapan sora*, Jav.: *wilah*) [1]; that, perhaps following one or more pre-stages, it consisted in the end of five blown fifths brought together within the compass of an octave, and producing a sequence of the following structure:

I *156* II *156* III *366* IV *156* V *366* I'

and that, out of these tones, No. V was considered as the principal tone and starting point (*poko*, Jav.: *pokok*, *i.e.* stem).

Later on the two adjoining blown fifths were added to this basic scale. When added to the scale, they appear to split the large intervals of *366* C. into an interval of *156* and one of *210* C. We have noted this already (*vide* p. 30). In this way, therefore, we get a seven tone scale (Sund.: *naek turunna sora*) of the following structure:

I *156* II *156* III *210* IV *156* V *156* VI *156* VII *210* I'

It is probable that the addition of these tones ("exchange tones", Jav.: *sorogan*, Sund.: *sora geganti* [2]), or also *sorog*, Bal.: *penyorog*) was made in order to transpose, with their aid, the basic scale to a pitch lying a blown fifth (*678* C.) higher and to another, lying a blown fifth lower (*vide* table on p. 50).

In this way, therefore—since, in the first case the tones IV and VII, in the second the tones I and IV and in the third the tones VII and III drop out—we have at our disposal three scales, identical apart from absolute pitch, in other words, three different keys, different tonalities:

---

1) Literally, *wilah* means a key, or a slab of wood. The same term, therefore, is used for interval (of one step) and for the tonal points, which limit an interval—in the same way as is the case, in India proper, with the term *sruti*, which word, properly speaking, ought only to mean "interval", (which, for that matter, it usually does).

2) As against the principal tones, which are called *sora lelugu*.

THE SEVEN-TONE BASIC SCALE AND THE NUCLEAR TRIPLET

Intervals: 210 · 156 · 156 · 156 · 210 (156 + 210 = 366) · 156 · 156 · 210 · 156 (156 + 210 = 366; 210 + 156 = 366) · 156 · 156 · 210 · 156 (156 + 210 = 366; 210 + 156 = 366) · 156 · 210 · 156 (210 + 156 = 366)

SCALES	IV	V	VI	VII	I	II	III	IV	V	VI	VII	I	II	III	IV	V	SUNDANESE NAMES:
O					●	●	●	○	●	●	○						JAWAR
P									●	●	●	○	●	●	○		NYOROG
Q	●	●	●	○	●	●	○										LIWUNG

THE NUCLEAR TRIPLET REALIZED ON SINGLE-OCTAVE INSTRUMENTS

O	●	●	●	○	●	●	○
P	○	●	●	○	●	●	●
Q	●	●	○	●	●	●	○

● PRINCIPAL TONE
○ AUXILIARY TONE

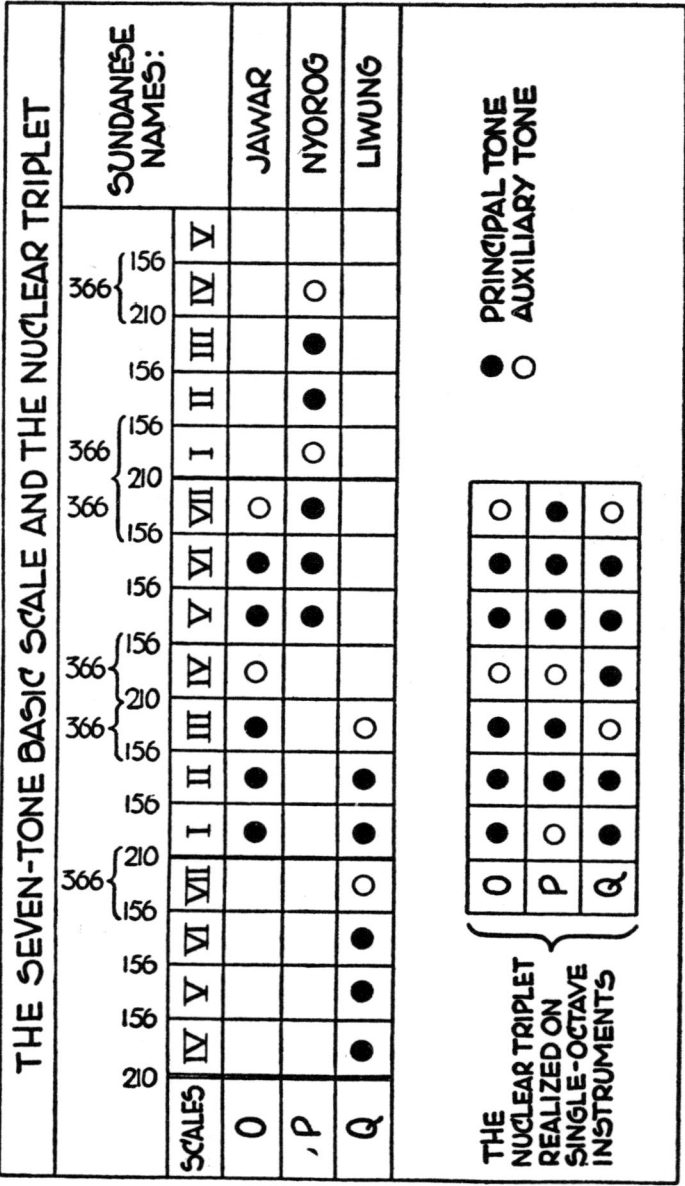

Complete pélog-sequence:	I	*156*	II	*156*	III	*210*	IV	*156*	V	*156*	VI	*156*	VII	*210* I'
Scale O:	I	*156*	II	*156*	III		*366*		V	*156*	VI		*366*	I'
Scale P:	V	*156*	VI	*156*	VII		*366*		II	*156*	III		*366*	V'
Scale Q:	IV	*156*	V	*156*	VI		*366*		I	*156*	II		*366*	IV'

It will be seen that these scales consist of one group of three and one group of two principal tones, separated by gaps of one tone. The tones that have been missed (they are represented in the diagram on p. 50 by a circle) are, as a matter of fact, not always completely eliminated; they may have a modest function as secondary tones (Sund.: *pamanis* [1]), *panyumbang* [2]), or *sènggol nyimpang* [3]), Bal.: *pemèro*) [4]).

The *poko*-position filled in the original scale by tone VI (originally V) is taken in the two new scales by the tones III and II respectively. Like the three scales taken as a whole, their respective *poko's* too, are, of course, placed theoretically at a distance of a blown fifth from each other:

II	*678*	VI	*678*	III
Q		O		P

Now this threefold scale-nucleus, to which we shall give the name of *nuclear triplet*, has grown, on instruments with alterable tone-pitches (*rebab*, *suling*), but in the first place in vocal music, into more complicated systems. This has led to distinctions being made between different tonal genders (*surupan*) [5]), which, as will be seen, owe their origin partly to the unchangability of the tone sequences such as are found on instruments with fixed pitches (metallophones, xylophones, etc.). In other words, these *surupan*,

---

[1]) From *manis* (sweet, harmonious).

[2]) From *sumbang* (out of tune, abnormal).

[3]) *Sènggol* means—according to COOLSMA's Dictionary of the Sundanese language—"the modulation of the voice, trills, turns, etc., with which the singer ornaments the tune (one might call them the "twiddlybits")"; *nyimpang* (from *simpang*) = to step aside, to evade, to deviate.

[4]) When they loose this secondary character it will be seen that modulation has, in effect, taken place, and that they can no longer be regarded as auxiliary tones of the initial scale, but have become principal tones of another one. (*Cf.* p. 91 *sub* A).

[5]) The term *surupan*—whose literal signification is supposed to be: *that which is pushed into something*, hence: *key*—has also several other musico-technical meanings, *e.g.* that of *key-note*, *tuning-tone*, *central tone* (*vide* p. 101). It also stands for the more general concept *tuning* (= Jav.: *laras*, from *nglaras*, to tune). For clarity's sake, however, we shall here use this term only to indicate the concept *tone-gender*.

each originated from another selection from the available instrumental pélog tone material, afterwards have started, so to speak, a life of their own. It is in this way the structure of the surupans *miring* and *ajéng* must be explained, which have gradually occupied a modest position side by side with the older scales, called *surupan mèlog* [1]). There is yet another—fourth—surupan, called *Malayu*, which has no direct relation to the others.

We shall now discuss, first of all, the *surupan mèlog*, this being the most ancient and by far the most important of the pélog tone genders.

* * *

All mèlog-scales in practical use tend to be imitations of the original scale, or, rather, of those scales of the nuclear triplet which are based upon this original scale—for, in certain cases, they may also have certain supplementary tones.

The seven toned pélog scale whose genesis we described above—we shall call it henceforth the "(seven toned) basic scale" or "fundamental (tone-) sequence"—creates, in the manner indicated, the possibility for the existence of three different scales of five principal notes, which scales satisfy the requirement of uniformity. The structure of this basic scale, however, is such, that only the tones VI, III or II can function as starting point (of the *descending* scale); should another tone be taken for this, then the scale proceeding from it would *not* have a structure (nearly) uniform to that of both original scale and the nuclear triplet. The cause of this is plainly the peculiar way in which the two different sizes of the intervals in the basic scale are mixed. If all intervals were equidistant, there would be no objection to taking any note of the scale as starting point.

Now, in the system under discussion something has been done towards achieving equidistance, *i.e.* by intercalating a tone halfway between each of the two large intervals of the basic scale [2]). These intercalated tones are called, in Sumedang, *panangis*, or wailing tone (between the tones III and IV) and *pamiring*, or deviating tone (between VII and I'). If the modern

---

1) *i.e. in* (the real, original) *pélog*.

2) These vocal tones, therefore, are not, like the other seven tones of the scale, derived from the hypothetical cycle of blown fifths. For, if they were respectively identical with the two fifths bordering upon the circle-arc used, they would not halve the large intervals in question, but split them up into an interval of *156* and one of *54* C.

pélog scale still contained the exact intervals of the blown fifth pélog, the splitting up of the two large intervals would not have effected an equidistant division of the octave by a long way, for in that case there would be four intervals of 105 C. against five of 156 C. The modern seven tone scale, or modified basic scale, however, deviates in some respects from the original structure—precisely, we may assume, as a result of the intercalation of *panangis* and *pamiring*, and the tendency to achieve equidistance: the smaller steps (originally 156 C.) are usually taken a little smaller nowadays, especially as regards the distances I–II and V–VI; the larger ones (originally 210 C.), on the contrary, a little larger, *i.e.* about 240 and 270 C. respectively [1]). This splitting of the large intervals by intercalation then yields a nine tone scale of something like the following structure:

I *120* II *150* III *120* *p* *120* IV *150* V *120* VI *150* VII *120* *p* *150* I′.

It will be seen that this scale much more closely approaches equidistance than the unmodified seven tone scale of blown fifths would have done if supplemented in this way.

It is surely worthy of note once again to see this tendency to equidistance at work in Malay music; the same tendency which once before, *i.e.* in Further India, had already turned the same basic scale into an equidistant sequence of tones. In the latter case, however, this was not done by inserting two new tones, but by dividing up the octave into *seven* equal intervals of approximately *171* C. each (**374**, p. 136 *et seq.*).

A third instance of this tendency to equidistance may be observed, as we saw before (p. 40), in a number of sléndro scales.

Now, it is this quasi-equidistant, nine toned scale that is the foundation, both of the scale system in *surupan mèlog*—which we shall expound here in the first place—and of that in *S. miring* and *S. ajèng*. This system, pliable unless bound to the unchangeable pitches of keyed instruments has grown into a rich tissue—one might even say, a multi-dimensional texture—of scales, in which the relation between the fifths is still the essential generating element (which is also true of the sléndro system). *Omnis comparatio claudicat*; one might, however, in order to characterize with a single term

---

[1]) It is just possible that we have here to do with an approach to half-fourths pélog (primitive pélog), whose tones, as we saw above (p. 28) yield the following sequence of intervals:

I 102 II 156 III 264 IV 156 V 102 VI 156 VII 264 I′

THE NINE TONALITIES IN SURUPAN MELOG

NUMBER IN THE SERIES OF TONALITIES IN FIFTH-SUCCESSION:		II GALIMER	III PANELU	* PANANGIS	IV LIWUNG	V KENONG	VI BARANG	VII SOROG	* PAMIRING	I SINGGUL	II GALIMER	III PANELU	* PANANGIS	IV LIWUNG	V KENONG	VI BARANG	VII SOROG
I	JAWAR									●	●	●		○	●	●	○
VIII									●	●	●		○	●	●	○	
VI								●	●	●		○	●	●	○		
IV	NYOROG HANDAP?						●	●	●		○	●	●	○			
II	NYOROG					●	●	●		○	●	●	○				
IX	LIWUNG				●	●	●		○	●	●	○					
VII				●	●	●		○	●	●	○						
V	(NYOROG HANDAP?)[1]		●	●	●		○	●	●	○							
III	MANANGIS	●	●	●		○	●	●	○								

● PRINCIPAL TONE
○ AUXILIARY TONE

[1]) *Cf.* p. 63.

the essential being of the surupan in both tonal systems, speak of *crystals of fifths.*

* * *

As stated above, the scales in question, inasmuch as they belong to surupan mèlog, imitate the original scale, albeit in the form assumed by the latter in the modified basic scale. Accordingly they all show more or less the following structure:

I *120* II *150* III *390* V *120* VI *420* I'

with a tendency to reduce interval I–II and augment interval II–III, to which are added sometimes, between tones III and V, and between VI and I', another two tones (IV and VII), and, at times, other supplementary tones as well.

Theoretically, these scales may start from any step in the basic sequence supplemented by the tones *panangis* and *pamiring* (*vide* table on p. 54).

Every one of these scales leave out two *other* couples of tones (occupying the same position within the scale), or, at least, degrade them to tones of secondary importance between their two groups of principal tones; they strive, moreover, to sound like one anothers transpositions. In other words, if the nine toned pélog sequence from which they are formed were perfectly equidistant, they might be called *tonalities*. In vocal music, indeed, they do become *pure* tonalities.

Not every one of these scales appears to have its own name; we were, at any rate, given the names of only five out of the nine classes of scales:

Jawar or *biasa* [1]) comprising the scales Nos. 2, 6, 35, 39, and 43 of Appendix *54*;

Nyorog [2]), comprising the scales Nos. 3, 7, 11, 40, and 44 of *do.*;

Manangis [3]), comprising the scales Nos. 4, 8, 12, 16, and 45 of *do*;

Nyorog handap [4]), comprising the scales Nos. 5, 9, 13, 17, and 21 or perhaps (see p. 63) the scales Nos. 10, 14, 18, 22, and 26 of *do.*;

---

[1]) *Biasa* = normal, *i.e.* in accordance with the tones of the (modified) primitive scale.

[2]) *i.e.* the tonality in whose scales one of the original principal tones (the *singgul* (I)) has been replaced by the alternative tone *sorog* (VII).

[3]) *i.e.* the tonality in whose scales (in addition to the *sorog* for the *singgul*) the "vocal" tone *panangis* has also taken the place of the original principal tone *kenong* (V).

[4]) *i.e.* the tonality whose scale-pitch (cf. scale No. 2 with scale No. 4 of Appendix

Liwung [1]), comprising the scales Nos. 1, 30, 34, 38, and 42 of *do.*

Out of these tonalities only *Jawar, Liwung* and *Nyorog* (as regards the latter two, moreover, only approximately) can be produced on the gamelan; the other six, as may be seen at a glance from the table on p. 54, have either one of the two, or both intercalated "vocal" tones, which cannot be played on the gamelan, as principal tones.

In each of these nine scales, each of the five principal tones may have to function as the melodic central point. The tone performing this function is called *dasar, i.e.* ground. In theory, therefore, the total number of scales in surupan mèlog is 9× 5 = 45.

Now, the two scale divisions mentioned are cut across by yet another one. For it is possible to arrange these 45 scales also according to the tone of the supplemented basic sequence which, in each of the scales, functions as *dasar,* "pivotal" tone. It then appears that each of the nine tones may act five times in that capacity. Such a set of five scales having the same dasar forms what is called a *paṭet* [2]), and consists each time of scales from five different—we might call them—"dasar-classes". These dasar-classes are characterized by the position of the dasar in the scale:

In class I the dasar is the highest tone in the group of 3 principal tones;
in class II it is the highest tone in the group of 2 principal tones;
in class III it is the central tone in the group of 3 principal tones;
in class IV it is the lowest tone in the group of 2 principal tones;
in class V it is the lowest tone in the group of 3 principal tones.

Melodies composed from the notes in class III are distinct from those using one of the other kind of scales inasmuch as they usually comprise, according to R. MACHYAR ANGGA KUSUMADINATA, instead of two, three supplementary tones.

One should not confound the notion "*dasar*" with that of *poko(k)*, which latter came up for discussion on p. 49. It should be clear from what was said there that *poko(k)* is purily a *scale* term, whilst *dasar*, on the contrary,

---

54) is related to that of the nyorog-tonality as one which starts one step *higher* (Sund.: *handap* = low, *i.e.* European *high*).

[1]) *i.e.* the tonality in whose scales one of the original principal tones—the *panelu* (III)—has been replaced by the alternating tone *liwung* (IV).

[2]) The concept "*paṭet*", which, especially in the wayang music of the Principalities, plays such an important part, will be discussed in greater detail further on (p. 71 *et seq.*).

is a *melodic* term. In those cases, however, where the dasar is the highest of the group of two principal tones (our dasar-class II), poko and dasar fall on one and the same tone, and as such is the case—amongst other instances—in one of the most frequently used scales, *i.e.* the principal scale of paṭet nem pélog (*vide* the lay-out on p. 95), it is clear that one might easily be inclined erroneously to identify the two notions.

In Appendix *54* the 45 mèlog scales are arranged according to the paṭet-division, that is to say, they are grouped into nine dasar groups; in Appendix *55* a concise summary will be found of those same scales, from which it will appear how the arrangement according to tonalities (diagonal sequences) cuts across that according to dasar-groups (horizontal sequences) and that according to dasar-classes (vertical sequences).

There is good reason to assume that, out of all these 45 scales, the music of the Principalities—from causes which will be explained fully on p. 94 *et seq.*—employs no more than ten, to wit: integrally, of dasar class I, the scales 1 and 6; of class II, the scales 2, 7 and 42; of class III, the scales 3 and 43; of class IV, only No. 44; and also—but not to the same perfect extent (*vide* p. 95)—of class I, scale 41, and of class III, scale 8.

As we said before, the complete realization in practice of the system outlined above is only possible vocally (and on the *suling* and the *rebab*); every now and then it requires, as a result of the fact that the (supplemented nine toned) fundamental sequence is not quite equidistant, certain small raisings and lowerings (theoretically about 30 C.) of some of the tones from this basic scale, functioning as principal tones (except, of course, in the case of the *jawar*-scales), as well as, in certain cases, the use of (one of) the two "vocal" tones, which split up the two large intervals of the seven-toned basic scale, and which cannot be played on instruments with fixed key- or gong-kettle-sequences.

The result of this is that, when the human voice or one of the instruments with alterable pitches are heard together with other instruments possessing fixed tone-pitches, the hearer is frequently struck by differences in intonation, which naturally are most prominent in those cases where one of those "vocal" tones is sung, bowed or blown, but which experienced ears will also notice as soon as one of the other tones is subjected to the small raising or lowering referred to above.

The raisings and lowerings of the tones of these mèlog scales, necessary to make them resemble the jawar-scale, are shown in the following table:

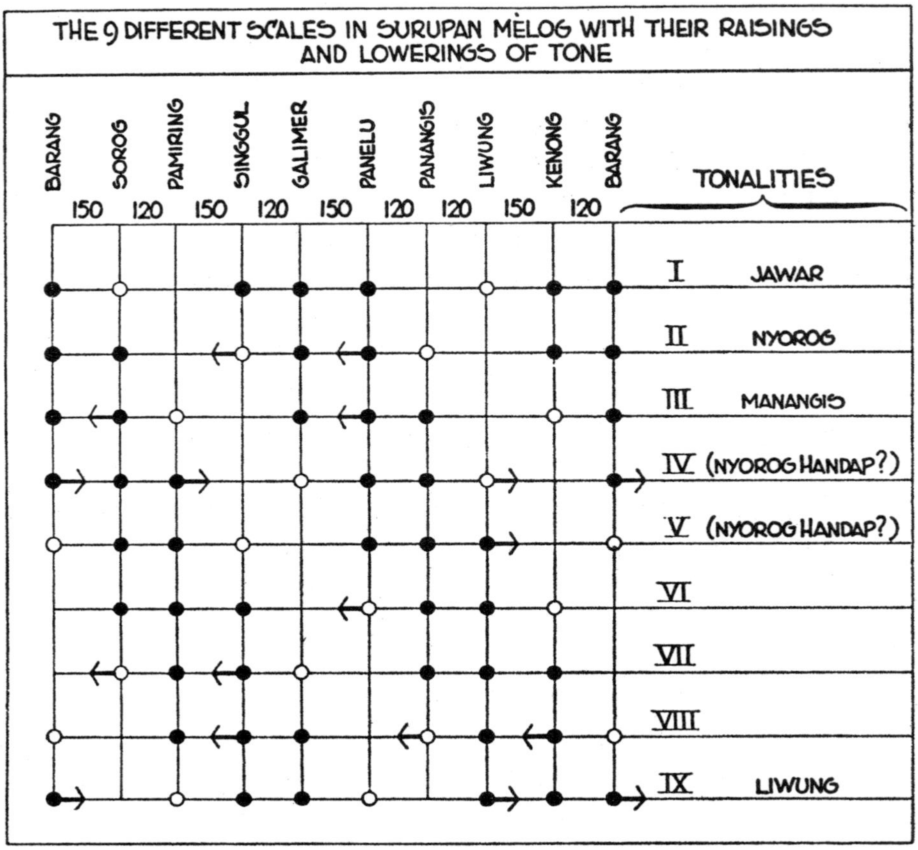

But of necessity a virtue was born: this partial discrepancy between vocally and instrumentally produced tones has developed unmistakably into an aesthetic element, of the same nature as is inherent in the pleasant sensation experienced when we hear two unequally ticking clocks "part company" in their respective rhythms and gradually approach each other again. This latter element, of course, is of a purely rhythmic nature, whereas the other pertains to the melodic, or rather, tonic field. One might say that the one is a kind of rhythmic, and the other a tonic "breathing", a play of tensions alternately arising and disappearing.

The fact that these discrepancies in intonation are to some extent satisfying to the Javanese ear may also be gathered from a passage in the 276th canto of the Chenṭini [1], referring to the playing of the *rebab* in the

[1]) Strophe 8 at the end.

following terms: "Every now and then there was a little deviation from the correct pitch so as to enhance the charm of the music".

Following this fairly exhaustive exposition of the surupan mèlog system, it will be sufficient briefly to discuss the other Sundanese pélog tone genders, the more so as they are of rare occurrence relatively to the mèlog gender as a whole.

The tone sequence produced by all scales in *surupan miring* [1]) differs from that of S. mèlog insofar as, counting from below upwards, the sizes of the first and second intervals respectively, as well as those of the two large intervals are interchanged: where as, as is shown above, the scales of S. mèlog, as far as the five principal tones are concerned, may be represented approximately by the following sequence (as we have seen already):

I *120* II *150* III *390* IV *120* V *420* I'

the scales of S. miring should, therefore, be represented as follows:

I *150* II *120* III *420* IV *120* V *390* I'

(Interval I/II is often taken slightly larger, and interval II/III a little smaller).

The basic sequence, as laid down on the ordinary gamelan pélog, produces a pure miring scale, without any raising or lowering, when we take the tone *galimer* (Jav.: *gulu*) as *poko* [2]). It corresponds therefore to the *liwung*-tonality in mèlog, providing the tones *barang* (Jav.: *nem*)and *liwung* (Jav.: *pélog*) are not raised.

When transposing this scale to one of the eight other theoretically possible pitches, it is necessary to either raise or lower one, two or three of the tones: (see p. 60).

Now, in order to have at one's disposal, also instrumentally, a *miring* scale in the "normal" pitch (*i.e.* that of the ordinary gamelan pélog, as produced, *e.g.* on the *sarons*), special miring gamelans have been constructed in West-Java. These gamelans are fitted with sarons possessing only five keys to the octave, as a result of which only five out of the, theoretically possible, 45 miring scales, forming a single tonality (one might call these *miring jawar*), can be realized (cf. p. 388 *et seq.*)

This limitation does not, of course, apply to vocal music.

---

[1]) *miring* = slanting, deviating (also: lying on one side, sideways).

[2]) *Vide* above, table on p. 54.

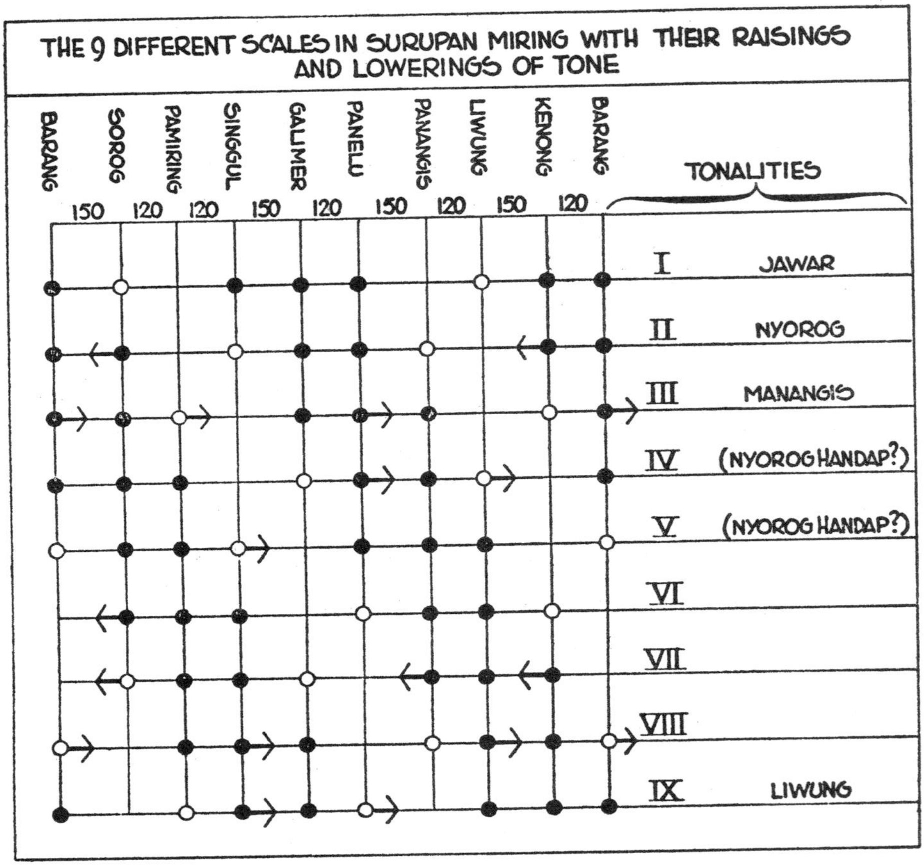

The structure of the *ajèng* gender, expressed in *cents*, and as far the intervals formed by the five principal tones are concerned, is approximately as follows:

I *150* II *120* III *390* IV *150* V *390* I'

The basic sequence, as laid down on the ordinary gamelan pélog and supplemented by the vocal tone *panangis*, without any raising on lowering produces a pure ajèng scale, when one takes the tone *sorog* (Jav.: *barang*) as *poko*. The ajèng scale, therefore, corresponds to the *manangis*-tonality in mèlog, providing the tones *panelu* (Jav.: *ḍaḍa*) and *sorog* (Jav.: *barang*) are not lowered.

The ajèng tone gender appears to be very rarely used; only very seldom does one come across any gamelans tuned according to it [1]).

---

1) *Vide* below, p. 386 *et seq.*

Similar to the mèlog- and miring-genera the ajèng scale as laid down on instruments possessing fixed tone pitches should be distinguished by the term *jawar*. The slight raisings and lowerings which the different tones of this jawar scale—augmented by the two supplementary tones and the two "vocal" tones—are subjected to in the eight remaining, theoretically possible, ajèng-tonalities, in order that all 45 scales shall then resemble this jawar scale, are shown in the following table:

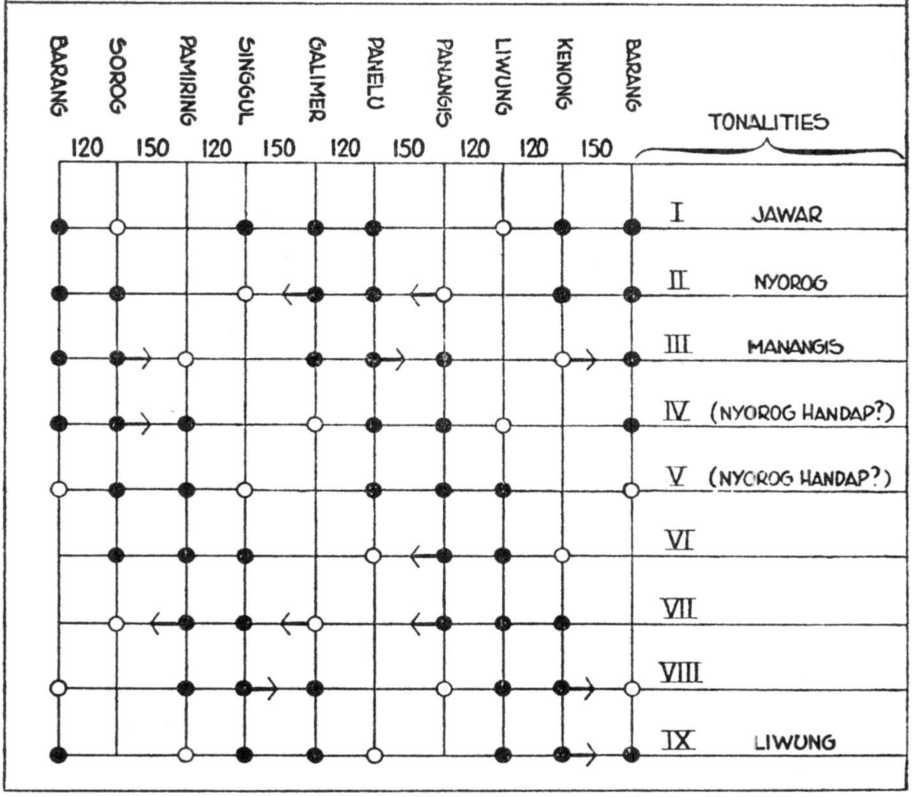

THE 9 DIFFERENT SCALES IN SURUPAN AJÈNG WITH THEIR RAISINGS AND LOWERINGS OF TONE

It will be observed that, in contradistinction to what we have seen in the mèlog- and miring-systems, there is, in S. ajèng, a second group of scales, in which neither raising nor lowering of tones occurs, *viz.* in the tonality V. Since, however, in addition to three jawar tones, both "vocal" tones function as principal tones in this tonality, it is impossible to realize it either upon a five- or seven-toned gamelan. It is probable that, out of this 45 ajèng scales existing theoretically, only the five jawar scales are in practical use.

* * *

We have now discussed three scale-genera which, broadly speaking, are constructed as under:

I. *Mèlog*:	*120*	*150*	*390*	*120*	*420*
II. *Miring*:	*150*	*120*	*420*	*120*	*390*
III. *Ajèng*:	*150*	*120*	*390*	*150*	*390*

It is natural that one should wonder whether there do not exist any other possibilities of scales, apart from these three, with the same features in common, *viz*, that (a) the sequence of principal intervals from the bottom upwards is:

small small large small large

and that (b) the large intervals are formed by adding three small ones from the complete (nine-toned) scale together.

One might think at first sight that, since the seven toned basic sequence, supplemented by two "vocal" tones, consists of nine tones, which, each in its turn, may function as poko, there should exist another six possibilities. This, however, does not appear to be the case. There are, in fact, only two more forms possible:

(a) tone-gender X (in accordance with the *unmodified* [1]) instrumental *nyorog*-tonality):

120 150 390 150 390

and (b) tone-gender Y:

120 120 420 120 420.

Tone-gender X is represented by the scales having, respectively, *panelu* (Jav.: *ḍaḍa*) and *singgul* (Jav.: *penunggul* or *bem*) as poko; tone-gender Y by the scale having *pamiring* as poko.

The remaining scales, with *kenong* (Jav.: *lima*), *liwung* (Jav.: *pélog*) and *panangis* (Jav.: *pangliring*?), respectively, as poko, possess, it appears, a structure respectively identical with that of the ajèng-, mèlog-, and miring-scales, and do not, therefore, present anything new.

---

[1]) Any modification of some of their tones by slight raising or lowering, such as we had occasion to mention before, would naturally deprive these tone-genders of their own peculiar character and make them identical with surupan mèlog.

This state of things would seem to point to an explanation of the curious fact that only five out of the nine possible scale pitches in the pélog-system supplemented with the two "vocal" tones appear to possess proper names: four of these, at any rate, differ, when instrumentally produced, to some extent as regards structure (vocally, however, they constitute as many tonalities); only *nyorog handap* forms an exception (unless Radèn MACHYAR is mistaken in attributing these scales to this rare, and instrumentally never realized tone-sequence), owing to the fact that it does not make use of the only remaining available scale-variety:

120 120 420 120 420

(which is reproduced in the tone-sequence V of the table on p. 54), but has been placed by him with tone-sequence IV, which corresponds to tone-sequence IX (liwung-scales).

If, however, nyorog handap ought to have been placed with the tone-sequence V, then all of the five possible scale-varieties would have proper names, whereas their "doubles" (VI = I, VII = II, VIII = III, IX = IV) would be nameless.

If the above exposition is correct, the explanation of the name nyorog handap, as given on p. 55, footnote 4, would have to be cancelled; and in that case the scales belonging to the nyorog handap-sequence would not be the Nos. 5, 9, 13, 17, and 21 of table *54*, but the Nos., 10, 14, 18, 22, and 26.

On the ground of the available data it is not yet possible to conclude which of these two possibilities conforms to the reality, but, if nyorog handap should rightly belong to the structure and pitch of scale V, then the five names by which at present the same number of different tone-sequences within the limits of a single *surupan* (tone-gender) are indicated will probably have stood originally for as many tone-genders; for, these genders are, in fact, nothing than the tone-sequences in question, *transposed* to the pitch of the "normal" gamelan (with a tone I of about 280 v.d. per sec.).

* * *

Finally, there is the *surupan Malayu*, which occupies a position more or less detached from that of the other pélog genera, and, by its peculiar structure, so free from any refinements, gives the impression of being younger as well as originating from outside Java. Its name, too, "Malay tone-gender", would lead one to suspect this.

Surupan Malayu uses seven tones of the (modified) basic tone-sequence, *i.e.* those, realized f.i. on the saron pélog; all seven of these are primary tones; it possesses neither auxiliary (secondary) tones, nor "vocal" intermediary ones, and, since each of them functions in its turn as *dasar*, this S. Malayu actually comprises seven scales, which are modally related to one another and form one single tonality.

* * *

The *sléndro*-system comprises fewer scales and possibilities, also theoretically, than the pélog-system.

In the first place there are only three tone-genders. One of these, which in West-Java bears the name of *salèndro biasa* [1]) = *salèndro jawar* = *jajawar* = *S. lempang* [2]) (Indram.) = *S. lanchar* [3]), is realized in practice on the keys and gong-kettles of the ordinary gamelan sléndro. However much this scale may have been, in certain phases of its development, composed of unequal steps—and still is in some places; *vide* above, p. 33 *et seq.*—in its *modern* form it is practically equidistant. True, in most of the modern gamelans one finds one (sometimes two) intervals slightly larger than the others (vide Appendix *62*), but these are not always the same two intervals out of the five existing ones, and these deviations from equidistance are therefore *functionally* of no consequence. Theoretically the *sléndro jawar* scale may accordingly be represented as follows:

I *240* II *240* III *240* IV *240* V *240* I′

In addition, however, there exist in West-Java two sléndro-genera with unequal steps, of which one is called *surupan madenda* = *nyorog malang* = *surupan cheurik* [4]) = *nyorog wisaya* [5]) = *nyorog rangu-rangu* [6]) and the other one, *surupan degung*.

Surupan madenda differs from S. jawar by the first and the third step of

[1]) *biasa* = normal.
[2]) *lempang* = straight.
[3]) *lanchar* = single.
[4]) *cheurik* = to weep.
[5]) *wisaya* = poison, magic influence, guna-guna.
[6]) *rangu* = hesitant, uncertain.

the sequence [1]) being lowered by about half a sléndro interval, as a result of which the scales belonging to this gender may be interpreted by the following scheme:

I *360* II *120* III *360* IV *240* V *120* I';

surupan degung, on the other hand, by the fact that, in addition, the fourth step [2]) is lowered in the manner indicated, so that we obtain scales of the following type:

I *360* II *120* III *240* IV *360* V *120* I' [3])

Now, each of the five scale-tones in each of the above three tone-genders may function as poko [4]). The result of this is that these lowered first, third and fourth steps come on or between other steps of the basic sequence each time; in other words, both these genera madenda and degung turn sléndro, which originally comprises only five steps, into a decatonic system.

Each of the five inserted steps has, in West-Java, its own name. By their intercalation the sléndro octave, from low to high, assumes the following aspect:

singgul (Jav.: *barang*)
120
sorog pamiring
120
bem (*galimer*) (Jav.: *gulu*)
120
sorog mangu
120
panelu (Jav.: *ḍaḍa*)
120

---

[1]) In paṭet barang (Jav.: P. nem), therefore, of the *singgul* (Jav.: *barang*) and the *panelu* (Jav.: *ḍaḍa*).

[2]) In paṭet barang (Jav.: P. nem), therefore, of the *kenong* (Jav.: *lima*).

[3]) S. degung is often confounded with the most generally used pélog scale (the jawar scale of S. mèlog), in which case the *bem* (*galimer*) sléndro (*i.e.* step II) is regarded as *singgul* pélog (step I):

S. Degung: II *120* III *240* IV *360* V *120* I *360* II'

Mèlog jawar: I *120* II *150* III *390* V *120* VI *420* I'

Cf. also the degung-scales reproduced on p. 388.

This also explains why one of the two kachapi-scales, which, according to the best nayaga's belongs to S. degung, bears the name of *mèlog*.

[4]) Naturally, in sléndro *jawar*—which may be considered, functionally, as being composed of equal tone-steps—there is no room for the notion "poko" ,whose signification is that of starting-point of the scale or, better, the "scale-melody".

sorog panangis
120
kenong (Jav.: *lima*)
120
sorog jawil
120
barang (Jav.: *nem*)
120
sorog samaran(g)
120
singgul leutik (Jav.: *barang alit*).

The lowering of the first and third, and the first, third and fourth step [1]), respectively, referred to above, is not taken by all singers and *rebab* players equally great in practice; neither are they at all times of the same size in the course of the same piece [2]). Some players, moreover, insist that the lowering should be slightly smaller than half a sléndro interval.

In the sléndro tone-sequence supplemented by intermediary tones, therefore, we are in reality dealing with a large number of different pitches, or, rather, with a scale of ten steps, whose tones are of a more or less uncertain, flexible pitch. Instrumentally, however, one may quite well content oneself—as Radèn MACHYAR ANGGA KUSUMADINATA has shown by means of his experimental instruments—with an equidistant scale of ten steps, in much the same way as European music manages to do with its equally tempered scale of twelve semitones. This temperament of an instrumental scale is called by Sundanese musicians *maling* (literally: to steal), which is a very appropriate name, since the operation amounts, as it were, to stealing small fractions from some intervals to add them to some others.

In each of the *surupan madenda* and *degung*, just as in the pélog system, it is possible, owing to the fact that both scales consist of unequal steps, to

---

[1]) Some nayaga's do not speak of *lowering* the first and third, or the first, third and fourth step, but of *raising* the second, fourth and fifth, or the second and fifth, which, as may easily be understood, leads to the same result, given an equidistant tonal sequence, when the raising or lowering in question amounts to half a sléndro interval (*120* C.).

[2]) Cf. also, in Appendices *24* and *36*, the several ways in which the tones *ḍaḍa* and *lima* have been reproduced, which is to be attributed to this.

distinguish a series of tone-sequences, to wit, ten, (*i.e.* as many as there are tones in the supplemented sléndro scale), which, however, in consequence of the equality of those halved sléndro-steps, in contradistinction to the pélog scales, constitute not only vocally, but *also instrumentally*, as many tonalities.

In each of these tonalities, again, each of the five principal tones may function as *dasar*. In this way we obtain, theoretically speaking, in each of these two surupans, a number of 50 scales. These, however, do not all seem to occur in practice, but chiefly those, which are included in Appendix *56*. These are the five scales with the fifth degree as dasar. For exceptions see p. 68/69.

In *surupan jawar* there are fewer possibilities. True, one might imagine the scales belonging to this surupan to exist in ten different pitches, and here, too, each tone might once again function as dasar. But owing to the fact that the scales of this tone gender are (practically) equidistant, and as the melodies extend over a range of more than one octave and through all the steps, it is clear that, in this case, the subdivision in "dasar-classes" does not apply; the number of scales in practical use is limited to a maximum of $2 \times 5 = 10$, *i.e.* the five jawar scales, as shown in Appendix *56* and those whose absolute pitch is to be thought of as lying $\frac{1}{2}$ sléndro interval higher or lower, as the case may be.

In the Sunda districts this extension of the surupans madenda and degung is known, as will be evident from Appendix *56*: the five madenda scales reproduced there—and the same applies to the degung scales—belong to as many different tonalities.

The same applies to the Principalities, as is evident from the structure of the *laras barang miring* [1]), in the way it is realized in the *suluk* bearing that name. It appears that three tones of the sléndro jawar scale in this suluk melody are lowered; it therefore belongs to the scale group which, in the Sunda districts, is called *surupan degung*. Since the laras barang miring is written in *paṭet manyura* (see below p. 84 *et seq.*), it is the tone III (Jav.: *ḍaḍa*, Sund.: *panelu* or *sanga*) which functions as dasar, as will be shown below. If surupan degung in paṭet panelu were limited to the one scale reproduced in Appendix *56*, the lowered tones would accordingly have to be: *barang* (Sund.: *singgul*), *gulu* (Sund.: *galimer* or *bem*) and *lima* (Sund.:

[1]) Cf. below, p. 327.

kenong). Actually, however, it is the following tones that have been lowered (*vide* Appendices **36–38** incl.): *ḍaḍa, lima* and *barang*:

	laras nem	*singgul barang*	*galimer gulu*	*panelu ḍaḍa*	*kenong lima*	*laras nem*	*singgul barang*
	V	I	II	III	IV	V	I
not:	●	←●	←●	◉	←●		
but:			●	←◉	←●	●	←●

in other words, compared to the panelu scale in degung (Appendix *56*), the scale has been shifted, as regards its structure, by two steps relatively to the dasar, and belongs, therefore, to another "dasar-class".

* * *

Just as the gamelan pélog does not contain all the tones of the pélog sequence—both the "vocal" tones *pamiring* and *panangis* being missing—the gamelan sléndro falls short as regards surupan madenda and S. degung. In sléndro music, too, therefore, differences in intonation are apt to occur when vocal (or rebab) music is performed together with the ordinary gamelan.

As a matter of fact the degung-scale has been realized in some places in West-Java on special gamelans, *i.e.* on those of the, fairly rare, Degung-orchestras [1]. The madenda-scale, on the other hand, has not achieved the same orchestral independence; but this tuning, according to R.M.A. Kusumadinata (cf. p. 370/371), is done full justice to—as is also the degung-tuning—on the Sundanese *kachapi*, whose *mèlog* scale, as we have seen above, corresponds to the degung-scale, whilst its *nyorog* scale corresponds to the madenda-sequence.

In Central-Java, sléndro with unequal steps is relatively so rare that —with one exception: the *laras barang miring* (*i.e.* the scale with the deviating *barang* tone)—it is not distinguished as an independent scale from the normal equidistant sléndro sequence. The musicians content themselves, it appears, with stating that the voice (and the rebab) are free now and then to depart from the tones of the accompanying gamelan, and that vocal melodies, and especially sléndro melodies, frequently make use of intermediary tones.

We may mention, as examples of Central Javanese sléndro songtunes with lowered tones—apart from the *suluk laras barang miring* (App. *36–38*

[1]) These will be described further on (p. 387 *et seq.*).

incl.), in which the vocal tones below the *barang*, *lima* and *ḍaḍa* are heard—: the *suluk tluṭur* paṭet 9 (App. *23* and *24*) and the song *Pangkur* paṭet 5, in which a lowered *ḍaḍa* and *nem* occur [1]); the song *Durma* [2]) paṭet 6 [3]) (App. *19*), and the *suluk tluṭur* paṭet manyura, in which the intermediate tone under the *barang* and the *lima* [4]) occur e.t.q.

It also happens sometimes that, although the voice generally moves within the scale of the accompanying gamelan, that it varies the melody by occasionally lowering some of the tones. This procedure may give rise to unexpected and splendid sound combinations. I remember hearing, at Solo, in the kepatihan Mangku Nagaran the *lagu Sinom* being sung to the accompaniment of *Srepegan* in paṭet 9 (*Sinom logonḍang*) [5]): on that occasion it was the tones *nem* and *ḍaḍa* that were sung a little lower every now and then. I also heard similar lowered intonations in the vocal part of the *genḍing Renyeb* (paṭet 9) and in its *munggah*, the *ladrangan Éling-éling kasmaran* [6]). The singers told me that, in such cases, they sing practically in pélog [7]).

Sundanese musicians call such incidentally lowered tones *samaran*, which word R. Machyar Angga Kusumadinata connects with *samar*, *i.e.* hesitant, uncertain, deviating [8]), but which appears to Dr. Purbacharaka to be rather a —linguistic very feasable—corruption of (*Éling-éling*) *kasmaran*, since it is especially this composition which is sung in this manner.

When melodies of this kind are played simultaneously with gamelan music, therefore, the result is that two different tonal genders are heard together, since the gamelan is, of course, bound up with the jawar genus. One might call such music bigeneric [9]).

Certain instrumentally realized sléndro scales with unequal steps from

---

1) Therefore with *gulu* functioning as *poko* and *dasar*.

2) An excellent reproduction of the Solonese (Mangku Nagara) version of *Durma* is given on the Columbia record G. J. 63 (fragment VIII of the lakon Ménakjingga Léna). In this reproduction, moreover, the *barang* itself may be heard as well as, and often immediately following upon, the intermediate tone below the *barang*. (This intermediate tone, for that matter, is not always sung at exactly the same pitch.)

3) Therefore with *ḍaḍa* functioning as *poko*, and *nem* as *dasar*.

4) Therefore with *ḍaḍa* functioning as *poko* and *dasar*.

5) Cf. Od. A 278028a (*Janturan Sinom logonḍang*).

6) *Éling-éling* = Memento; *kasmaran* = (to be) in love. [*S39-a1; S50]

7) Cf. above, p. 63, note 3.

8) In this connexion we remind the reader of the name of the intermediary sléndro-tone which Sundanese theory has intercalated between the fifth and the first step, *i.e. sorog samaran(g)*. It is just possible that the last letter of this name was added through contamination with the name of the town Samarang.

9) Cf. f.i. Col. G.J. 63 (fragment VIII of the lakon Ménakjingga léna).

East- and West-Java (*sléndro miring, laras sundarèn* and *ringkung*) have already been mentioned above (pp. 31–38).

* * *

In Bali, too, both the pélog- and the sléndro-system are to be found. The set of scales in practical use, which has developed there on the basis of the pélog-system resembles the Sundanese one in every particular insofar as we have been able to gather the necessary details (**192**, p. 16 *et seq.*; **193**, p. 379 *et seq.*; 413 *et seq.*, tables VI–X incl. and XII; **200**, p. 348 *et seq.*).

Just as in West-Java there are in Bali only five of the theoretically possible tonalities of the *saih pitu* system bearing their own names, and these are precisely the "corresponding" tonalities: they may be found in Appendix 55. There is one difference, however, as compared to the Sundanese scale-theory, *i.e.* that the names of these tonalities relate to the absolute pitch of the scale, *regardless of their structure* and their position within the system as a whole.

For the rest I will refrain from attempting a detailed exposition of the Balinese systems: partly because there are still numerous points concerning which the necessary data are incomplete, and partly because it will be more useful to deal with the systems in question together with the whole of Balinese music in a separate work. As regards Balinese sléndro I may refer to the remarks made in **193** (p. 369 and table II).

* * *

Sundanese music does not, anymore than European music, inevitably finish on one and the same tone of the scale, but, in common with Western music, there does exist a certain preference in this respect. As we know, the predominant majority of European folksongs finish on the fundamental tone (tonic) of the prevailing tonality; but it may also happen that the last note of the melody is the fifth (dominant) or the third (mediant). This also applies to the Gregorian chant, though to a lesser degree: there, in addition to the *finalis* we also have the *confinales*.

Something very similar characterizes Sundanese music. Preference is given, in each of the paṭets—at any rate in the Sumedang and Garut districts—to the tone lying either a pélog- or a sléndro-fifth under the *dasar*.

This tone is underlined three times in Appendices *54* and *56*, as well as below in the first table on p. 84. It also frequently happens (and the same may be said of the final tones of each long phrase, *i.e.* those, which, in gamelan music, coincide with a beat on the gong) that the final tone comes on the fifth below the fifth below the *dasar*. These tones are underlined twice in Appendix *54* and in the jawar- and madenda-scales of Appendix *56*. In the degung scales in Appendix *56* the fifth below the fifth below the *dasar* would come on an intermediate tone; hence, the *dasar* itself functions in these scales as second "gong-tone". In the pélog scales, however, as well in the jawar- and madenda-scales in sléndro, the *dasar* is to be considered as final tone only in the third place (underlined singly in Appendices *54* and *56*), whereas the former two scale tones are preferred by far [1]). This is undoubtedly with a view to the equilibrium which they create, from a point of view of musical feeling, as against the *dasar*. For in this case the melody rests upon two (or three) powerful pillars; the arch of the melodic bridge is well supported, as it were, across the river of time.

It will be seen from the above that, in Sundanese music, as in European music, musical logic has its foundation in what one might term fifth-consciousness, which appears to be an almost universal phenomenon.

As we have seen above (p. 50) the same applies to the relation between the "original" scale of the pélog system and the two scales which, together with this original scale, form the ancient "nuclear triplet". It also applies to modern *Javanese* music. This is evident again and again from the musical Appendices reproduced in volume II of this work, both as regards the melodic structure generally and as regards the relation of the final tones of the separate musical phrases in particular. We shall return to these fifth-relations in greater detail later on, when discussing the various types of modulation.

I should not be surprised to find that the limitation of the number of *paṭets* in the Principalities to *three* in each of the two tonal systems (although certain indications are also found to exist for the use of other, "not officially recognised" ones) has its original cause in these very fifth-relations and more particularly in the ancient nuclear triplet arisen from it. One

[1]) It appears that there are only very rare exceptions to these rules in Sundanese music. An example of such an exception is the lagu *Bayubud*, which, although in paṭet barang (Jav.: P. nem), finishes all the same on *singgul* (Jav.: *gulu*), or *kenong* (Jav.: *lima*). Cf. Od. A 39588a.

could not, indeed, explain the mutual relation between the paṭets of the Principalities in a more simple and logical manner by taking these fifth-relations as one's starting point.

This is not to say that the Javanese definitions of the conception "*paṭet*" (literally: to curb, to restrain, to limit) should directly lead us to taking this view. All these definitions, however, are either incomplete or too superficial. A genuine definition, *i.e.* one which would convey to us all essential characteristics of the conception, and, thereby, indirectly, the differences existing between the different kinds of paṭets, has not yet, as far as I am aware, been formulated.

R. M. JAYADIPURA's description: "paṭet is the couch or bed of a melody" and that of JAKUB and WIGNYARUMEKSA (**78**): "the paṭet serves to allow the genḍing to sit down (*nglunggguhaké*)" are couched in far too general terms; SURYAPUTRA's pronouncement (**359**): "paṭet is the harmonic relation between the pitch of a piece of music and the vibrations of the atmosphere at certain moments of the day or the night" is rather less musically technical than mystical; that of R. M. SARWAKA: "the distinction between a given paṭet and another one is based upon a difference in *chèngkok*" (which here means as much as melody or melodic line), takes into consideration only the form of the *paṭetan's* (*lagons*), by which the paṭet is usually expressed and maintained in wayang-music, and, moreover, does not take into account the fact that the melodies of the lagons paṭet 9 and those of the lagons paṭet manyura are the same [1]); SULARDI's description (**343**, p. 6): "what is called paṭet is really preluding (*grambyanganing*) on an instrument according to certain rules, from which the nature of the compositions to be performed shall become evident; this grambyangan is performed (instrumentally) only on the gendèr, rebab, gambang and suling" [2]) also relates merely to the manner in which the paṭet is intoned by means of a paṭetan (lagon); and the same is true of the definition given by SASTRASUWIGNYA and his collaborators (**323** No. 75, file 1931): "by paṭet is meant the singing of the ḍalang to the accompaniment of the rebab, gendèr, gambang, suling, kenḍang and (sometimes) the gong" [3]). [**302**c]

[1]) They therefore differ only in absolute pitch, which, in practice, differs by one step (theoretically, two fifths, therefore one octave + one tone). *Vide* below, p. 84.

[2]) "Ingkang dipun wastani paṭet punika grambyanganing gongsa ingkang mawi pugeran, saha anélakaken lenggahing genḍing-genḍing. Déné ingkang kaungelaken amung gendèr, rebab, gambang tuwin suling."

[3]) Cf., about the gong—and other colotomic instruments—in vocal suluk music, p. 323.

I sometimes incline to the view that the music of the Principalities, owing to its limited choice from the theoretically possible (and indeed, in the Sunda-districts, to a large extent practically living) scales, has lost its hold on the construction of the tonal systems in their entire complexity, and its insight into their inner correlation, as a result of which it is now impotent to find a satisfactory definition of a conception such as paṭet. We have here, as in so many other cases, an *intuitive* not an intellectual knowledge: a good niyaga from the Principalities immediately distinguishes one paṭet from another, without ever making a mistake; he is however, incapable of explaining how or why he does so [1]).

The reader will have gathered from what we have stated above concerning the Sundanese scale systems that to give a definition of *paṭet* is not, indeed, a simple matter. To my mind the nearest approach to the conception "paṭet" may be achieved by the formula: *"all scales possessing the same tone of the basic scale as central tone* (*dasar*) [2]) *form together one paṭet"*.

This, however, is not at all to say that this central tone—which, at any rate in the pélog-genera, and, as regards sléndro, possibly in the surupan madenda and degung, as we have seen (pp. 56 and 67) may be placed in five different positions in the scale—should be the tone to be most frequently or most conspicuously heard. Not a bit of it! As a matter of fact, even in European scales, the tonic, not withstanding the fact that it is far more in evidence [3]), is not usually the tone occurring most frequently in any composition: it often happens that, right up to the end, it is not much more than "the man in the back-ground". The other tones derive their melodic and tonal value from it, which is closely connected with their greater or smaller distance from the tonic; the latter, therefore, functions, one might say, as a "basis of melodic tension".

The *dasar*, too, fulfils a similar function, though undeniably in a much weaker form; the different tones, in the first place the gong-tones, derive

[1]) According to a communication from Radèn KODRAT, however, this musician determines the paṭet according to the kenong (which usually gives the tone *lima*). The first kenong-beat is, to him, the startingpoint or tonal point of reference, from which he determines—knowing as he does the "skeleton-tones" of each paṭet—in which paṭet shall be played.

[2]) I am using here—and also occasionally further on—when discussing the Central Javanese tonal systems, some of the Sundanese terms (such as *dasar, jawar, liwung, nyorog, panangis, pamiring*) because the equivalent Javanese terms are lacking or, at any rate, have not come to my knowledge.

[3]) We should definitely not conclude from this analogy that *dasar* and *tonic* are identical conceptions! Cf., in regard to this, p. 85 note 2.

from it their "tension-value" [1]), although probably not a single niyaga is conscious of this, however strongly they all *feel* it unconsciously.

But to come to the point: as is known, we distinguish in Central Java and the adjoining parts of East Java, as **paṭet pélog:** the paṭets *lima* (H. J. *gangsal*) (= 5), *nem* (= 6) and *barang*. Of these, the two first named are placed more or less in opposition to paṭet barang, under the name of *pélog bem* (Kudus: *pélog krawitan* [2]); East-Java: *pélog pengasih* [3])); paṭet barang being also called, in that case, *pélog barang* (East-Java: *pélog miring*; Malang and Nganjuk: *laras slering*). This is caused by the circumstance that the P. barang-scale, or, rather, -scales, although they belong to the same tone-system as that of pélog bem, nevertheless use a slightly different scale. For, whereas, in the majority of the bem-scales the tones *bem, gulu, ḍaḍa, lima* and *nem* function as principal tones, in the barang-scales this function is taken by the tones *lima, nem, barang, gulu* and *ḍaḍa.* *)

This distinction is apparent also to Western ears, even when no other differences between the various paṭets are consciously realized. The impression received is that both scales when played in the tone-sequences indicated above, are identical except for their absolute pitch; in other words, the western ear interpretes the distinction in question as a difference in tonality: pieces in *pélog bem* strike it as being written in *B flat major* or *d minor*; pieces in *pélog barang* sound to it as if they had been written in *F major* or *a minor*; the two tonalities, therefore, differing by a fifth. This is rendered possible by the "neutral" pitch of the tone *gulu* which, owing to its intermediate position, is "corrected" in *pélog bem* to *E flat*, and in *pélog barang* to *E natural*, as under:

pélog barang:					*lima*	*nem*	*barang*	*(bem)*	*gulu*	*ḍaḍa*
					A	B♭	C	—	E	F
Pélog bem:	*bem*	*gulu*	*ḍaḍa*	*(pélog)* [4])	*lima*	*nem*				
	D	E♭	F	—	A	B♭				

[1]) It is a curious thing that, in contradistinction to European folkmusic, which usually finishes on the tonic, and, therefore, with complete relief, most Javanese and Sundanese compositions—as we said before (p. 70/1)—finish on a tone at a distance of either one or two fifths from the central tone. It appears, therefore, that a harmonic tension (more or less comparable to a finish on the dominant) is preferred to a complete relief.

[2]) *i.e.* the pélog scale at the beginning (of the wayang performance); cf. also the genḍing *Krawitan*, with which practically every wayang kulit performance commences (*vide* below, p. 339).

[3]) *pengasih* = that with which love is awakened; instrument of love.

*) [See p. 102 for conversion of Javanese and Sundanese tone names]

[4]) The conspicuous position of the pélog-tone, which has such a peculiar sound

If, however, the pélog-scale had not (in order to render possible a transposition to any desired tone) deviated from the original blown fifth sequence in the direction of equidistance, (without, however, as we have seen, achieving this, not even by the intercalation of the two "vocal" tones in the two large intervals), then, in those cases where a genḍing in paṭet *lima* sounded the pélog tone as principal tone, the deviation from paṭet *nem* to paṭet *lima* would also convey the impression of a change in tonality, namely as a transition to the fifth below.

It may be confidently assumed, on the basis of what has been gathered from our inquiries into the development of the scale-systems that, in ancient times, paṭet 5 used to hold this position with respect to paṭet 6. The scale No. 42, Appendix *54*, *i.e.* a *liwung* scale with the tones *pélog*, *lima*, *nem*, *bem*, and *gulu* as principal tones, and *gulu* as *dasar*, should be regarded as the original paṭet lima scale.

This ancient *liwung* scale, however, has gradually been ousted by the *jawar* scale from the same paṭet, owing to the fact that the tone *pélog* has assumed such a prominent and peculiar position in the tone sequence in the course of time [1]), which, in its turn, is due to the slight modification of the intervals caused by the approach to equidistance. This *jawar* scale in question (App. *54*, No. 43) is characteristic of most of the paṭet *nem* compositions (App. *54*, scale No. 2), from which it differs only by a difference in *dasar* (which, for paṭet 5, is the *gulu*, and for paṭet 6, the *nem*). This is the only difference—apart from the difference in tones, on which the gong-phrases of a piece finish, which is correlated with the former difference, but which, owing to the many exceptions to the rule, is not always evident—which can still be observed to-day between the majority of the genḍings in paṭet lima and those in paṭet nem [2]). It would appear to me, however, that one is on safe ground in concluding from the whole of the history of scale

—usually a secondary or alternative tone—in the bem-scales, is taken, in the barang-scales, by the tone *bem*. This may be observed quite clearly in, for example, the genḍing (ladrangan) *Bima kurda*. (A very good rendering of this may be heard on the records Odeon A 39561b and A 278187b.) Our Appendix *3*b gives its nuclear theme without the embellishments. The tone *bem* is represented by *d*♯.

[1]) Also to Javanese ears. Javanese popular etymology accordingly connects the word *pélog* with *pélo* = deviating, prominent. The other six tones of the pélog-scale are thought to be *jejeg*, *i.e.* suitable, proper, correct, true, straight; the pélog-tone, on the contrary, is considered to be *miring*, *i.e.* on one side, deviating, out of harmony. (*Pélo* further means: to talk defectively, babytalk).

[2]) There are, however, supposed to be certain "ex-structural", "ethical" differences (*vide* p. 338).

development that, in the beginning, the difference between these two paṭets was in reality a pronounced difference in pitch, *i.e.* in *tonality*, between scales of identical structure, as is also the case, to this day, between paṭet nem and paṭet barang. There scale relations will be elucidated in further detail during the discussion of the modulation forms (p. 91 *et seq.*).

The problem of the **paṭet sléndro** in the Principalities may also be simplified considerably by looking at it in the same way.

As we know, the Central Javanese sléndro-paṭets—which are always played in *jawar* scales inasmuch as they are beaten on the gamelan—are differentiated under the names of *nem*, *sanga* and *manyura*.

When discussing the fact that, in both tonal systems, as regards Java proper, there are only three different paṭets in use, it was pointed out to me by a prominent native that this was only natural, since the human heart, too, knew only three great emotions, namely happiness, anger and sadness.

As far as the sléndro paṭets were concerned an analogy was also made with the three stages of life:

paṭet nem (= 6): infancy; the 6 (!) senses still slumbering and accordingly perfectly equivalent, so that ... the gong beats may coincide with all the tones of the scale. (But, as we shall see in a moment, the principal melodic points of support and final tones are *gulu*, thereafter *nem*, and then *lima*, whilst, in this paṭet, the genḍings whose gong-phrases finish on *ḍaḍa* are only few, and those with *barang* as final tone, very rare) [1].

paṭet sanga (= 9): life in full maturity: the nine apertures of the body functioning.

paṭet manyura (= peacock) [2]: old age; acceleration towards the end of life. P. manyura is similar in many respects to P. 6, just as very old people may have a period of second childhood. Hence, in many cases, the same final gong-tones as in P. 6!

Another Javanese musician who was asked by WALTER SPIES for a defi-

---

[1]) With *ḍaḍa* as finishing tone: the genḍings *Lagu*, *Damarkèli*, *Galagotang* and a few others; with *barang* as such (but in only one of its phrases): the ladrangan *Rajamanggala* (as appears from their notation in the Jogya-kraton-collection).

[2]) Cf. p. 338, note 5.

nition of the concept *paṭet*, replied that the paṭet of the genḍing was, as it were, its taste. Just as one might divide the different dishes into salt, bitter and sweet ones, one might distinguish Central Javanese compositions according to the paṭet. For this reason one could not say that one paṭet was more pleasant to the ear than another one; this depended, as with the dishes, entirely on the kind of appetite one had at a given moment. The charm lay in the first place in the variety and in the correct order of sequence. SPIES' interlocutor smilingly added: "buat orang blanda lebih terang kalu bilang: paṭet nem itu sup; paṭet sanga daging; paṭet manyura manisan rupa-rupa", *i.e.* "it will be more understandable to the white man if I say: P. 6 is the soup (of the musical dinner); P. 9 is the steak and P. manyura the dessert (literally: all kinds of sweets)."

D. VAN HINLOOPEN LABBERTON, in his edition of RADEN MARTA HARJANA's *Pepakem sapanti sakuntala*, makes the following remark about the paṭets (**239**, p. 64 *et seq.*): "...this music (...) must be in accordance with what is presented on the stage: struggle, love, anger or humility. But in addition to this it must be in harmony with the mood of the surrounding scenery.

In the silence of the night Nature has, for the Eastern mystic, its own peculiar sounds. Whoever is accustomed to hearken to these sounds needs no chronometer to tell him the time.

To the mystic poet there is a certain vibration in Nature at sundown, when all the forces appear to contract [1]); after this there is a sudden atmosphere of mysterious life until the hour of midnight. At that hour there is a new vibration again and a mystical restfulness between 12 and 3 o'clock. And at 3 o'clock Nature wakens from this tense silence. A strange rustling passes over the fields, as if—so Indonesian folklore says—the frogs are croaking with subdued voices in response to the call of the Naga-prince, who, every night, passes the review and count their numbers.

After this the sounds increase once more. The day is about to commence, and, as the morning begins to spread its wings, causing a vibration of light which passes over the darkness of the expanse long before the sun appears, the birds are awakened, the cocks raise their voices, the day awakens, with its restlessness filling the silence once more with its fascinating bustle; the play has ended, and the performance finishes on a confused mêlée.

---

[1]) This is the *talu* of the wayang orchestra (v.H.L.).

The three paṭets, *nem*, *sanga* and *manyura*, correspond to these three different phases of the night.

The voice of the (wayang-)performer should also be a reflection of these phenomena: during the early part of the night it should be full and heavy (*ageng*); after this it becomes moderate in volume (*tengahan*), and finishes thin and high pitched (*inggil*). I may point in passing—continues v. H. L—to the connexion between this mode of singing and the instructions given in the *Sanskreta Shiksa* (phonetics):

"In the *morning*, during the sacred recital, one should always speak with the *chest* tone, as the roaring of the tiger;

at *noon* one should speak from the *throat*, like the monotonous croaking of the *chakrawala* (= *meliwis*);

towards *evening*, the third period, the tone should rise up into the *head* [1]), like the sound of the peacock (*mayura*), goose or flamingo (*hangsa*) and cuckoo (*kokila*) appears to come, as it were, from these animals' heads."

It is curious to note that the paṭet *manyura*, which serves in the third period, actually derives its name from this very *Shiksa*-shloka (verses 36 and 37 of the Rig-Veda)! *Manyura*, indeed, is a later Javanese corruption of the word *mayura*, meaning peaçock".

Thus far VAN HINLOOPEN LABBERTON.

It will be clear from the commentary upon the paṭets 6 and manyura on p. 76 that the tones on which the melodic phrases finish—which are, in orchestral compositions, the tones with which a beat on the large gong coincides [2]),—have a certain significance, also in Central Java, relatively to the typical nature of the paṭet, at any rate in sléndro [3]). I may therefore be permitted to examine this question of the "gong-tones" a little more closely, which I propose to do with the aid of a few tables drawn from 53 genḍing paṭet 6, 98 genḍing paṭet 9 and 122 genḍing paṭet manyura; in total, therefore, 273 compositions, *i.e.* from more than half the number of all the sléndro orchestral pieces from the Principalities [4]).

The figures in the 2nd, 3rd and 4th colums represent the number of

---

[1]) Then the voice vibrates, as it were, between the eyebrows (v.H.L.).

[2]) For simplicity's sake we shall occasionally use the name "gong-tones" when referring to such phrase-ending tones.

[3]) In the pélog-paṭets of the Principalities, on the contrary, to only a very small extent. There is, indeed, a conspicuous difference in this respect with the Sundanese pélog-compositions, which almost without exception, adhere in practice to the theoretical gong-tones. I hardly think it necessary to record *in extenso* the negative

genḍings finishing their ***gongan*** (gong-phrases) on the scale-tones in the first column:

Final tones of the gongan	of 53 pieces in P. 6:	of 98 pieces in P. 9:	of 122 pieces in P. manyura:
1 = barang	—	4	1
2 = gulu	11	3	22
3 = ḍaḍa	1	1	12
5 = lima	4	29	3
6 = nem	9	1	29
1 2	—	2	—
1 3	—	1	3
1 5	—	33	1
1 6	—	3	2
2 3	1	—	5
2 5	4	7	1
2 6	12	—	15

---

result of the investigation concerning the Central-Javanese pélog-compositions. I shall merely give the following survey, drawn from 194 genḍing pélog:

one or more gongan finishing on:	out of 30 genḍings in P. 5.	out of 69 genḍings in P. 6.	out of 95 genḍings in P. bar.
1. bem	15 = 50 %	24 = 34.8%	—
2. gulu	12 = 40 %	32 = 46.4%	41 = 43.5%
3. ḍaḍa	16 = 53.3%	25 = 36.3%	21 = 22.1%
4. pélog	1 = 3.3%	—	1 = 1 %
5. lima	25 = 83.3%	44 = 63.8%	61 = 64.2%
6. nem	7 = 23.3%	31 = 45 %	28 = 40 %
7. barang	1 = 3.3%	2 = 2.9%	21 = 22 %

It may be deduced from this that, in all three paṭets, the tone *lima* is the most prominent "gong-tone"; that *gulu* occurs about equally often in all three paṭets; that the *nem*—although, as finishing tone, far from rare also in P. 5—yet is found to occur more frequently in that capacity in P. 6 and P. barang, whereas, on the other hand, *ḍaḍa* is more of a favourite in P. 5. Further, it is evident that, in the paṭets 5 and 6 (pélog bem), the tone *barang*, in P. barang the tone *bem*, and in all three paṭets the tone *pélog* are barred from the function of finishing tone.

[4]) In order to make the comparison as true as possible in this table I have not ncluded genḍings which modulate to another paṭet. (Cf. p. 98 *et seq.*).

Final tones of the gongan	of 53 pieces in P. 6:	of 98 pieces in P. 9:	of 122 pieces in P. manyura:
3 5	—	1	1
3 6	2	—	16
5 6	2	3	4
1 2 5	—	3	—
1 3 5	—	1	—
1 5 6	—	3	—
2 3 6	—	—	2
2 5 6	4	2	3
3 5 6	—	1	—
1 2 3 5	—	—	1
1 3 5 6	1	—	—
2 3 5 6	1	—	—
1 2 3 5 6	1	—	1

The above may be summarized as follows:

One or more gongan finishing on:	of 53 pieces in P. 6:	of 98 pieces in P. 9:	of 122 pieces in P. manyura:
1 = barang	2 = 3.8%	50 = 51%	9 = 7.4%
2 = gulu	34 = 64.2%	17 = 17.3%	50 = 41%
3 = ḍaḍa	7 = 13.2%	5 = 5.1%	41 = 33.6%
5 = lima	17 = 32%	83 = 84.7%	15 = 12.3%
6 = nem	32 = 61%	13 = 13.3%	72 = 59%

The *suluks* (*vide* below, p. 318 *et seq.*) show practically the same picture as regards the melodic points of support and finishing notes. Here, too, the tones *gulu* and *nem* in P. 6 sl., the tones *lima* and *barang* in P. 9 and the tones *nem*, *gulu* and *ḍaḍa* in P. manyura figure prominently as final tones in about the same relative frequency as in the orchestral compositions. True, now and then some of the phrases in the course of the melody may finish on other tones; but this does not usually happen to such an extent that the general impression of the suluk in question is thereby modified; the tones which determine the general atmosphere of the piece always predominate in sléndro. The only exceptions—inexplicable, or, at any rate, as yet unexplained—to this rule are the *ada-ada P. 6 wetah* and the *ada--ada galong* (P. manyura), at any rate in the way they are performed in the Jayadipuran at Jogya. Both of these, in their melodic structure, are identical to suluks P. 9: the seven phrases of the former finishing successively on *lima, barang, lima, lima, barang, gulu* and *barang*, whilst the three phrases of the latter all have the *barang* as final tone.

The following tables give a survey of the final tones of the phrases in 9 suluks P. 6, 11 suluks P. 9, and 13 suluks P. manyura, as they are sung in the Jayadipuran at Jogya. As in the preceding tables, 1 stands for *barang*, 2 for *gulu*, 5 for *lima* and 6 for *nem*:

Sléndro paṭet nem

Name of suluk	Final tones of phrases	Vide Appendix No.:
lagon wetah	3 5 2 2 5 5 6 2 2 6 5 2 [1])	*13*
lagon jugag	6 2 6 5 2	*13* (c.f p. 323)
lagon chekak	6 2 2	*13* (cf. p. 323)
irim-irim	1 3 5 2 6	*14*
plenchung	6 6 2 5 3 2 6 2 6	*15*
ada-ada wetah	5 1 5 5 1 2 1	*20*
ada-ada prang wetah	6 2 3 6 2 6 6	*21*
ada-ada prang jugag	6 2 3 6 6	*21* (cf. p. 326)
ada-ada prang chekak	2 3 6 6	*21* (cf. p. 326)

paṭet sanga

Name of suluk	Final tones of phrases	Vide Appendix No.:
lagon wetah	1 1 5 6 1 5 [2])	*22*
lagon jugag	6 1 5	*22* (cf. p. 324)
lagon Lasem sarabayan	1 1 5 6 1 5 1 5 2 5 1 5 6 1 5	*22* (cf. p. 324)
suluk tlutur wetah	5 3 1 1	*23*
suluk tlutur jugag	1 1	*24*

[1]) The version given by KI HAJAR DÉWANTARA (75, p. 120) differs from the one given here; its finishing tones being: 1 6 6 1 3 3 6 6 2 3 1 6.

[2]) In KI HAJAR DÉWANTARA's version (75, p. 122): 2 1 2 5 6 1 5.

Name of suluk	Final tones of phrases	Vide Appendix No.:
senḍon	1 6 3 5	*25*
jengking	1 1 1 2 5 1 2 5 6 1 5	*26*
ada-ada trenya	2 1 6 5 1 5 1	*27*
ada-ada wetah	5 1 5 1 1	*28*
ada-ada jugag	5 1 1	*28* (cf. p. 326)
ada-ada chekak	1 5 1	*28* (cf. p. 326)

paṭet manyura

Name of suluk	Final tones of phrases	Vide Appendix No.:
lagon wetah	2 2 6 1 2 6 3 [1])	*29*
lagon jugag	1 2 6 3	*30*
lagon Lasem sarabayan	2 2 6 1 2 6 6 2 3 6 2 2 6 1 2 6 3	*31*
senḍon	3 6 6 2 1 2 3 1 6 3 2	*32*
suluk galong wetah	1 1 3 6 1 6 6 3	*33*
suluk galong jugag	1 1 3 6 3	*33* (cf. p. 328)
ada-ada galong	1 1 1	*34*
ada-ada wetah	2 2 3 2	*35*
ada-ada jugag	2 2 2	*35* (cf. p. 326)
ada-ada chekak	2 3 2	*35* (cf. p. 326)
suluk laras barang miring wetah	6 2 2 2	*36*
suluk laras barang miring jugag	6 2 2	*37*
suluk laras barang miring chekak	2	*38*

It will be seen that, as far as the sléndro paṭets are concerned, there is, generally speaking, a pronounced tendency towards a particular manner of finishing a phrase, albeit there are a good many exceptions to the rule. We may say that, in P. 6, it is chiefly the tones *gulu*, *nem* and *lima* that

[1]) In Ki Hajar Déwantara's version (**75**, p. 122): 1 6 1 3 5 6 3.

serve to end a phrase; in P. 9 it is the tones *lima* and *barang*; in P. manyura more especially the tones *nem* and *gulu*, and, less often, *ḍaḍa* and *barang*, the tone *lima* being completely avoided. Precisely the same applies to the Solonese suluks.

Ki Hajar Déwantara, in his in 1930 published little work (**75**), from which we have already quoted several times, has published a schematic representation of the paṭets according to which, in P. 6, the *gulu* is the first, the *ḍaḍa* the second tone, etc.; in P. 9 the *lima* is the first, the *nem* the second, etc.; in P. manyura the *nem* is the first, the *barang* the second, etc.

	barang	*gulu*	*ḍaḍa*	*lima*	*nem*	*barang*	*gulu*	*ḍaḍa*	*lima*
P.6:		◉	●	●	●	●			
P. 9:				◉	●	●	●	●	
P. manyura:					◉	●	●	●	●

According to this the three sléndro paṭets, inasmuch as they are played on a (practically) equidistant gamelan would constitute as many different tonalities, differing in absolute pitch by two and one degree, respectively [1]).

The fact that the lagons P. manyura (Appendices *29/31*) are nothing but the lagons P. 9 (Appendix *22*) [2]) transposed one step higher, strongly supports the above manner of representation (cf. also **75**, p. 122). It seems to us, however, that preference should be given to another presentation of the matter, as shown below, above that given by Ki Hajar Déwantara, assuming, as we do, that the most frequent gong tones (underlined three times in the diagram below) in each of the three paṭets hold a "corresponding" position, and that, similarly to what is shown in Sundanese pélog-scales (vide Appendix *54*), a tone which is to be regarded as *dasar* lies a fifth —*i.e.*, in this case, a sléndro-fifth of three steps (about 720 C.)—higher than the principal gong-tone, and, furthermore, that the principle of the fifth-relation is realized not only in this respect, but also in the mutual relation between the paṭets themselves (as we saw it did in the pélog-

[1]) In his "Leidraad" (**76**), K. H. Déwantara gives yet another representation of this matter (p. 7/8): "paṭet nem = jolly as a child (*high* scale); paṭet manyura, or *medium* scale = bright and hopeful; paṭet sanga, or *low* scale = in a cheerful mood." I believe this interpretation to be incorrect. [*S5]

[2]) The same relation exists between the suluks *tlutur* in P. 9 and those in P. manyura.

paṭets as well as in the ancient relation liwung-jawar-nyorog) (*vide* App. 54, *e.g*, scales Nos. 1, 2 and 3, and p. 51 above), and, as we shall see in a moment, it also does in modulation, both to another paṭet and to another tonality):

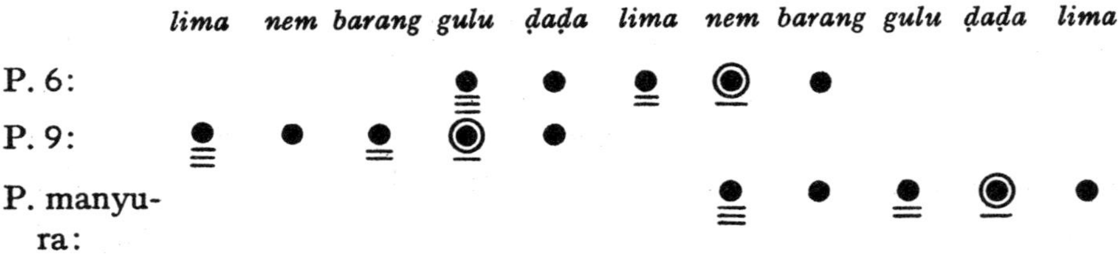

Thus it is, once again, the scale or group of scales with the original poko *nem* (*laras, surupan*: the pitch-tone) which takes the central place, also in this elaborate sléndro system, the two other scales, or scale groups, being placed around it, on either side at a distance of a (sléndro-)fifth. [1]) And in this case, too, as in the pélog system, we find the tones *gulu-nem-ḍaḍa*, lying at distances of a fifth from each other, fulfilling, in the respective paṭets, the function of *dasar*.

The fact that the structure of the paṭets is based upon the fifth may perhaps be made still clearer by placing the five tones of the sléndro scale in such a way that, between two successive tones, we get each time an interval of a (sléndro-)fifth, *i.e.* three steps. The nuclear tones of each paṭet, namely, the dasar (●) and the two other principal gong tones (*finales*) (×) will then be placed side by side, while, between the paṭets as such, there will be a fifth each time:

	barang	lima	gulu	nem	ḍaḍa
Paṭet manyura:			×——	×——	●
Paṭet nem:		×——	×——	●	
Paṭet sanga:	×——	×——	●		

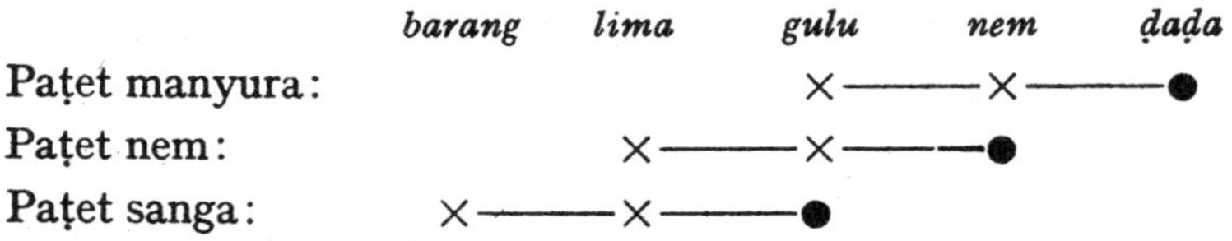

In addition, we may point out once more that, although the dasar may be recognised as such in any composition, even by European ears—especially in vocal music and when played on the rebab—it definitely does not

---

[1]) What would seem to be, in a case such as that of the lagons P. 9 and P. manyura, just mentioned, to be a transposition of a single step (which, in practice, it actually is) is naturally, theoretically, a transposition, back to the same octave, covering two fifths.

occupy the predominant position in the scale [1]) which, in Western music, has been acquired by the tonic [2]). In this connexion it is significant that, in the Principalities, there does not exist a special term to indicate this tone (the word *dasar*, in *this* musico-technical signification, is, it appears,

[1]) This applies especially to compositions in P. sanga, in which the tone *gulu* usually—in a manner to me inexplicable—keeps in the background, whereas the two principal gong-tones (*lima* and *barang*) come, proportionally, still more to the fore than the similarly-placed tones in the other paṭets. There exist, however, "normally" functioning genḍings P. 9, *e.g.* the ladrangan *Éling-éling*. It is, however, a curious fact that it is precisely these that are looked upon more or less as exceptions by the players. All the same, a composition of the structure of *Éling-éling* might very well be representative of the original paṭet-form that has now come to be at a discount. This case does not stand alone: the ancient sléndro-scales—now nearly extinct—with either one smaller interval or with alternating smaller and larger intervals (*vide* above, p. 31 *et seq.*) are now called sléndro *miring*, or deviating sléndro, although this name, in fairness, ought rather to be applied to the modern equidistant sléndro-scale.

[2]) One should be careful, however, when trying to discover the paṭet (via the dasar) of any sléndro-melody, not to interprete the latter according to the European tonal system. For, the sléndro-scale, as played iin the gamelan, is *practically* equidistant. The Western ear, however, hears it—with the aid of certain imperfections in the equidistance of the scale—as consisting of three steps of a whole tone and two of a minor third, which latter, however, do not on any occasion occur in immediate succession. In general, therefore, the European musician has the choice between five different possibilities of transcription and interpretation, *viz.* (barang = D):

	barang		*gulu*		*ḍaḍa*		*lima*		*nem*		*barang'*
1.	D	1	E	1½	G	1	A	1½	C	1	D'
2.	D	1	E	1	Fis	1½	A	1	B	1½	D'
3.	D	1½	F	1	G	1	A	1½	C	1	D'
4.	D	1	E	1½	G	1	A	1	B	1½	D'
5.	D	1½	F	1	G	1½	B♭	1	C	1	D'

out of which five possibilities he will naturally prefer one, for each particular case, to the other four. (Cf. the sléndro scales reproduced in App. *62*).

Now the European ear, owing to its tendency to "scale-correction", feels these five scales to be as many tonalities (although all scales derived from the equidistant sléndro tone-sequence—sléndro jawar—belong to the same, or, if you will, to no one particular tonality). It interpretes, in the absolute pitch given,

scale 1 as	(*a*) C-major,	(*b*) a-minor, or, more rarely,	(*c*) G-major
scale 2 as	D-major,	b-minor, or, more rarely,	A-major
scale 3 as	F-major,	d-minor, or, more rarely,	C-major
scale 4 as	G-major,	e-minor, or, more rarely,	D-major
scale 5 as	B♭-major,	g-minor, or, more,rarely,	F-major

However, as has been explained above, the tone functioning as *dasar* is:

in paṭet nem:	the *nem*
in paṭet sanga:	the *gulu*
in paṭet manyura:	the *ḍaḍa*

exclusively Sundanese), and that, both in Solo and in Jogya, during the many years covering my attempts to investigate the paṭet problem, nobody has ever drawn my attention to the central position of any particular tone in each of the paṭets as far as regards the melody; nay, it was evident from the fact that when I asked questions about the possibility of such a thing that people were of opinion that all the principal tones of the scale had perfectly equal melodic rights [1]).

It follows from this that, in sléndro, it is possible for the dasar to coincide with the tone which is heard as tonic, but that this is more often *not* the case. For, only if one regards the scale of a certain gamelan as being built up like the scales la, 2b or 3c, do the dasar and the tonic coincide in P. 6; in P. 9 this happens only if one takes that special scale to have the structure of the scales 3a, 4b or 5c, and, in P. manyura, if one hears it as being rendered in the scales 4a, 5b or 1c. In all other cases the dasar and the supposed tonic are not identical.

It, is therefore, safer not to seek the dasar by referring to the tonality-principle, at least in sléndro. Nay, one might even say that, the more completely one can inwardly shake off the tonal method of hearing, the better the true feeling for the dasar can develop.

In regard to pélog the matter is somewhat different. Pélog-compositions employ a scale which, as we stated before (p. 74), is heard—*i.e.* "corrected"—by the European ear as follows:

D E♭ F A B♭ in paṭets lima and nem
and A B♭ C E F in paṭet barang

Pieces in the first-named scale *may* be heard as being in *B* major—if not continuously, at any rate most of the time. One may therefore say that—*B♭* being here regarded as identical with *nem*—in paṭet nem the supposed tonic usually coincides with the dasar, since the latter is also the *nem*.

In paṭet lima, however, which has the *gulu* as dasar, the supposed tonic and the dasar never coincide.

What applies to the whole of the sléndro-system, therefore, also applies to pélog bem (*i.e.* paṭet 5 and 6 together): the European ear does not find in it any reliable guide for the determination of the paṭet.

In the case of paṭet barang, however, the matter is different. Compositions in this paṭet are commonly heard by the Westerner as being in *F* major (or *a* minor). Although it is possible that there are other scales (with other dasars, and actually, therefore, belonging to other paṭets) sailing under the flag of paṭet barang (with *ḍaḍa* as dasar)—it being therefore advisable not to speak of *paṭet* barang, but, instead, of *pélog* barang (cf. **200**, p. 346)—the same (supposed) tonality remains for all these scales. As regards pélog barang, therefore, the European ear does find a reliable point of reference in the tonality heard.

[1]) It was on these grounds that, in 1925, I made bold to make the following statement (**193**, p. 411): "– – – they (*i.e.* Javanese tone-sequences) altogether lack anything resembling a tonic or *amsa*, in other words, a melodic centre; apart from the two sorogan, *peméro's*, in the heptatonic scales, both pélog and sléndro constitute a community of tones having absolutely equal rights; both of them are, so to speak, democratic scale-types".

I have since learned—more especially from what R.M.A. Kusumadinata taught me—that this way of representing the matter was *incorrect*.

This however, is quite definitely not the case. A representation of the mutual relation between the three sléndro paṭets, as given by KI HAJAR DÉWANTARA, can, in the nature of things, be justified only when there exists, in each of those scales, a definite central point—since all three consist of the same five tones. A dasar, at any rate a central or principal tone is, one might say, *sous-entendu*. It seems to be such a *sine qua non* in a scale that, in Central Java, it is not generally accounted for (any longer) consciously. A man like KI HAJAR DÉWANTARA, however, must surely have felt the necessity for such a scale-centre quite *consciously*; for this reason he indicated the lowest in each of the three tone-sequences given by him, as *dasar*, or "the tone which serves to support the laras". He describes this tone (which is no other than the principal gong-tone, *i.e.* the tone lying a fifth below the actual dasar) more closely as "*babon ing laras*", *i.e.* the mother (*genetrix*) of the scale.

In this representation of the scale structure, therefore, the real, ancient Javanese dasar is dethroned by the principal gongtone, to which it has even ceded its name [1]). No doubt this is to be attributed to the influence of European musical theory. For, in the first place, KI H. D. regards the scales—in an un-Javanese manner—as running from the bottom upwards, and numbers their tones accordingly, and in the second place he actually states that the lowest tone of the scale is "in fact equivalent to the tone *do*, *i.e.* the tonic in European music" (**75**, p. 7).

Notwithstanding this it should be recognized that this principal gong-tone, a fifth below the dasar, is hardly secondary in importance to the dasar itself. They both (as well as the other, the secondary, gong-tone, which is another fifth lower again) function as melodic *foci*, as "bases of tension"; one might describe them, therefore—as we already did in the foregoing (p. 70/71)—as melodic "pillar-tones".

It is probably impossible to give an explanation of the fact that certain pillar-tones are felt to be, by the hearer, as the most properly suited at certain times in the space of 24 hours (*vide*, below, pp. 272, 338, 344 and 345). This will either have to be simply accepted as a psychological axiom or rejected. That this coupling of certain tones with certain periods

---

[1]) There is an—at any rate *verbal*—analogy to this in Western musical theory: although the tonic should undoubtedly be regarded as the most important tone in the scale, it is the fifth step that is called the *dominant*. The conception dominant is rendered by R. M. A. KUSUMADINATA by the term *patokaning laras*.

of day and night is something more than mere convention may perhaps be gathered from the fact that Westerners who have applied themselves to a study of the paṭet problem, have also observed this mystical correlation.

Further, since it seems to be a matter of no consequence in sléndro (jawar) whether the scale is perfectly equidistant or to some extent made of slightly unequal steps, and since, in the latter case, it does not matter where the larger or smaller steps are found in the scale, we may assume that in the system in question a paṭet is not, indeed, determined by the actual structure of the scale [1]), but rather by the absolute pitch of the "pillar-tones", and also possibly by the above-mentioned tension between the remaining three tones of the scale with respect to these pillar-tones.

One more remark about these melodic tensions: it might be quite possible for the satisfying or unsatisfying character of a melodic phrase—either of the nuclear melody or of the variations played around it—to depend upon whether or not these tensions relieve each other. According to a recent investigation into this question it would, indeed, appear feasable that melodic jumps or steps away from a pillar-tone are, in the end, compensated by as many jumps or steps in contrary sense. One should not, however, regard this too simplistically: both the fact that each paṭet possesses two or three pillar-tones, and factors of a rhythmic nature play an important and complicating part in this matter.

It should also be pointed out that, whenever a melodic phrase ends on a pillar-tone, this is not in itself a guarantee that equilibrium has been attained; neither does the fact that the melody has not finished on such a tone imply that equilibrium has not been achieved. Javanese melodics, therefore, is here seen to differ essentially from Western melodics, since, in the latter, a resolution on its chief pillar-tone, *i.e.* the tonic, usually causes complete melodic relief.

In the Principalities there is, in pélog, yet a fourth paṭet, distinct from and less frequently used than the others; it is felt as a kind of supplementary paṭet, related to paṭet barang, in which, however, the tone *barang* is replaced by the tone *bem* as principal tone. The name of this fourth paṭet is *paṭet manyura pélog*. It is supposed to have been introduced by that able musician and great dancer Radèn Mas Harya TANDAKUSUMA, the son-in-law of MANGKU NAGARA IV (cf. below, pp. 93, 129 and 258) (fig. 94*a*). In the

[1]) In pélog the situation is another, as we have seen above on p. 74 *et seq*.

Tatachara (**291**, p. 253 *et seq.*) we find, as compositions in pélog paṭet manyura, amongst others, the gendings *Ayoon-ayoon*, *Rèndèng*, *Randu kentir* [1]), *Rujak sentul*, *Kembang dara* [2]) and *Tunjung gunung*. We will meet this paṭet again, when discussing the different modulatory forms (cf. below p. 91 *et seq.*).

We may finally mention that SULARDI (**343**) has given to the pélog-paṭets the same names as to the sléndro-paṭets, *i.e. nem, sanga* and *manyura*.

With regard to the paṭet of the various compositions discussed in the course of this work—inasmuch as it has not been given in the text—we refer to the Index in the second volume, under the words *genḍing*, *ketawang* and *ladrang*.

There are several matters of detail which we have not, or hardly, touched upon so far. We will, however, pose some further questions, be it only in order to show that the last word has not yet been spoken with regard to the paṭet problem.

(a) Why does P. sanga bear this name, and why is it not—as P. nem (in pélog, as well in sléndro)—called after its dasar (*i.c. gulu*), or, as P. lima, after its principal gong-tone (*lima*)? *Sanga* is another name for the tone *ḍaḍa* (*vide* the nomenclature of the tones on p. 100). Since the dasar of P. manyura is the *ḍaḍa*, P. sanga, it would appear, would be a more fitting name for this highest of paṭet's in the Principalities [3]).

(b) If the representation given of the mutual relation between the paṭets is correct, why has P. 9 not been permanently regarded as the *lowest* of the three paṭets, but has in practice become the middle one (as it were through raising it by an octave), whereas the pélog patet 5, which is in the same position (also, *e.g.*, in the wayang-night subdivision), has retained its original place [4])?

(c) Why does, in P. 6 sléndro ,the tone *lima* not come in the *second* place as gong-tone, as regards frequency, as do the corresponding tones in the two other Central Javanese sléndro paṭets, but is put behind the tone *nem* in this respect (which, theoretically speaking, ought to have been satisfied with the third place)?

---

[1]) Usually, however, the genḍing *Randu kentir* is beaten in pélog paṭet nem.

[2]) Usually beaten in paṭet lima.

[3]) In the Sunda districts paṭet *sanga* is, indeed, identical with paṭet *panelu* (Jav. *ḍaḍa*).

[4]) It might just be possible that this is in some way related to the above-mentioned (p. 85, note 1) "modesty" on the part of the tone (*gulu*) theoretically functioning as dasar.

(d) How are we to explain the gong-tone "anarchy" in the pélog paṭets of the Principalities?

As a matter of fact there are certain indications that the essential being of the paṭets is not exclusively determined by the gong-tones and the pitch, but that other elements may possibly play some part. Thus it is not quite impossible that

(i) instrumental sléndro is, in fact, a combination or compromise between two or more slightly different sléndro scales which, however, are differentiated vocally (according to an oral communication from WALTER SPIES the sléndro scale was not intended to be equidistant; it is supposed to contain two larger intervals, one of which is stable whilst the other is slightly variable—which, of course, can only be expressed vocally);

(ii) there is a difference in the turn of the melody, especially in the manner in which the nuclear-melody reaches the finish of the gongphrases;

(iii) in the paraphrasing certain sound-combinations are correlated with certain paṭets (cf. below p. 176, note 4);

(iv) the factors mentioned under (i) to (iii) form part of an extremely refined and sensitive process by which the pitch of a melody is maintained as purily as possible, and which, after all, is to be explained psychologically rather than purely on the basis of scale technique. [**123**H *passim*; **76**A,C,D; **123**I; **167**B; **320**C; **340**A-B]

* * *

A few remarks concerning transposition:

A. Transposition of a genḍing from one tonal system to another occurs fairly frequently. Theoretically, every genḍing sléndro may be transposed to pélog; the result, however, would not be aesthetically pleasing in every case. According to SULARDI (**343**) the tones [1]) would then be replaced by the tones of the pélog scale bearing the same name, providing, however, that the *barang sléndro* is placed on a line with the *gulu pélog*, which means (at any rate as regards the names of tones) a shift of one step. In transposing a genḍing P. 9 to pélog, the tone *penunggul* (*bem*) would take the place of the sléndro tone *barang*, whilst the other four tones would be replaced by those bearing the same name, always providing that the tone *ḍaḍa* might now and then—if it so pleases the musicians—yield its place to the tone *pélog*. Again, a genḍing manyura would, when transposed, make use of pélog tones bearing the same name, with the exception, perhaps, of the *barang* which in some cases might also be replaced by the *penunggul*. For the rest,

[[1]) Viz. in Sl. pt. nem]

a transposition of this kind would be effected in the following way: a genḍing P. 6 sléndro would turn into a genḍing P. 5; a genḍing P. 9 into P. 5, 6 or barang, at the musician's discretion (but generally P. 6); manyura either in P. 5, 6, or barang, but usually into P. barang [1]).

B. Transposition from a genḍing pélog to the sléndro system is not possible in every case. From the particulars given above the manner of transposition, when possible, may be deduced to some extant.

C. Transposition of a genḍing to another paṭet of the same tone system is a fairly rare occurrence, which is probably to be attributed, among other things, to the character, or "vitality-content", of the piece to be transposed (*vide* below, p. 338). It happens most frequently in the case of the less complicated compositions of limited duration, such as, for example, the ladrangan *Pangkur*, which, according to R.M. JAYADIPURA, is occasionally beaten in pélog in all three paṭets; according to a communication from Solo in P. 6, P. barang, and by the way of exception occasionally in pélog manyura, and, in sléndro, in P. 9 and P. manyura. [**113**c]

Thus far as regards the possibilities of transposition.

* * *

In addition to transposition Javanese and Sundanese music also knows modulation, both in theory and in practice.

Whereas, in European music, there exist only one sort of modulation —the transition from one tonality to another (with or without a simultaneous change of tone-gender)—we distinguish, in the music of Java proper and the Sunda-districts, three forms of modulation (Sund.: *pindah*, literally: removal) [2]), which may be attributed to the existence of a feeling, not only for the *tonality* but also for the *paṭet* of a melody; and, as regards the third form of modulation, to the existence of two different tonal systems. Put briefly it amounts to the following distinctions being made:

A. Change of tonality with retention of the paṭet (only in pélog?)

B. Change of paṭet with retention of the tonality, and

C. Change of tonal system.

A. The attentive and musically-sensitive mind, when listening to a Central-Javanese composition, will often receive the impression that in the

[1]) For further detail regarding this, *vide* BRANDTS BUYS (**52**, p. 234/5).

[2]) Change in the tone-gender (Sund.: *pindah surupan*) is also known; European musical theory, however, does not bring this under the heading "modulation".

nuclear melody—although the players maintain they are still in the same paṭet—there has been a shifting of the melodic centre; a change, as it were, in tonality, which, however, after a period of longer or shorter duration, leads back to the original again. As a matter of fact this impression is well-founded. On closer investigation it appears that these changes are always deviations in tonality towards scales lying either a pélog fifth (4 steps) higher, or as much lower. These scales, however—which one might qualify as "auxiliary" scales—retain the dasar of the main scale as well as both its "pillar-tones" [1]), and actually remain, therefore, within the same paṭet. As a consequence of this they belong to different "dasar-classes"; for, the main scale belongs to the class which we have called (p. 56) class II, whilst the low auxiliary scale belongs to class I and the high one to class III.

In the paṭets lima and barang, however, there are a few complications, as a result of the seven-toned fundamental sequence, out of whose tone material all these scales are built up, not being equidistant.

In paṭet lima, deviation towards an auxiliary scale a fifth lower would result in a tone-sequence which, to the Javanese ear, differs too much from that of the original scale, because of the fact that, in that case, the tone *barang* would be too low, whilst an auxiliary tone to halve the interval *barang-bem* (which tone is known in the Sunda-district under the name *pamiring*—cf., above, p. 54) is not available. This is the reason why, in Central Java, this deviation in paṭet lima towards the fifth below is generally avoided. Nevertheless, its existence is recognized: Poensen (**301**, p. 59), and, following him and giving two further references, Groneman (**99**, p. 11) mention this scale built upon the fifth below which they call *pélog miring*, giving the names of the two tones of the complete fundamental sequence that are missing in this pélog miring scale, to wit, *ḍaḍa* and *nem*.

Another complication in paṭet lima we have already dealt with (*vide* p. 75), *i.e.* the customary replacement of the original main scale, a liwung-scale (because of its having the so conspicuous tone *pélog* among its principal tones), by the jawar-scale from the same paṭet, thus:

			bem	*gulu*	*ḍaḍa*	*lima*	*nem*
instead of:	*pélog*	*lima*	*nem*	*bem*	*gulu.*		

The original high auxiliary scale, therefore, has become main scale, and the main scale itself has been degraded to the position of low auxiliary

[1]) There is one exception to this, to be referred to anon.

scale. Nevertheless, compositions in the ancient main scale may occasionally be heard in the kratons. According to BRANDTS BUYS (**44**, p. 53) the genḍing *Glenḍeng* belongs to this oldfashioned group.

Now, owing to the fact that, generally speaking, this jawar scale has been substituted for the old liwung scale, a fresh—if somewhat incomplete—possibility of modulation has arisen, *i.e.* towards the scale of the fifth above the new main scale, a scale possessing the tone-material of a paṭet barang-(Sund.: nyorog-)scale, but, clearly, not with the tone *ḍaḍa*, but with the tone *gulu*—characteristic of paṭet lima—as dasar, whilst the original possibility of modulation to the fifth below (POENSEN's pélog miring scale) has become extremely rare. This new high auxiliary scale distinguishes itself from all other auxiliary scales by the fact that one of the two "pillar-tones" is missing, *viz.* the tone *bem*, which would be alien to the scale (German: leiterfremd) if included.

In paṭet barang, deviation towards the auxiliary scale lying a fifth higher meets with the same difficulty as, in paṭet lima, deviation towards the lower auxiliary scale, *viz.* the too incomplete realization of the interval-sequence of the fundamental scale; in this case owing to the tone *pélog* being too high for this purpose. If halving of the interval *ḍaḍa-pélog* by a tone *panangis* were known in Central Java as it is in the Sunda districts this difficulty would have been surmounted. This high auxiliary scale which, notwithstanding its less perfect structure, may nevertheless be heard now and then in practice, is given the name of *gulu miring* scale.

The low auxiliary scale in this paṭet barang is identical with the scale-form which R. M. A. TANDAKUSUMA has raised to the position of an independent scale, and to which, under the name of *pélog paṭet manyura*, he has given the place of a fourth paṭet in pélog. This paṭet we already discussed on p. 88.

Without any doubt modulation from this new main scale, which is built up from the tone material of the main scale of paṭet nem (the very same scale, therefore, as the five-toned primary scale, the germ of this entire pélog scale system) will be practised now and then to the scale of its upper fifth (a nyorog scale); but modulation to the fifth below will not take place, since the tone *ḍaḍa* is not to be found in the sequence built upon that tone (the tone *pélog*) and no scale in this paṭet, whether a main or an auxiliary one, can do without this tone *ḍaḍa*, it being the pivotal tone, dasar, of the main scale.

The circumstance that the music of Central Java—apart from paṭet pélog manyura which, for that matter, employs the tone material already covered by paṭet nem—is limited, as far as pélog is concerned, to the three paṭets here described, has its own compelling cause: the adjoining paṭets lying higher than paṭet barang and lower than paṭet lima*) would—since the music in the Principalities, at any rate the instrumental music, does not possess any intermediary tones such as the Sundanese tones *panangis* and *pamiring*—have a miring scale as principal scale; and this would clash too much with the fundamental principal of the entire system, namely, to create scales that are, either completely or very approximately, adumbrations of the central pentatonic primary scale; in other words, *to create tonalities* (and this through generation by means of fifths).

Modulation to auxiliary scales and back again to the main scale, such as are the object of the present discussion, invariably take place along the same way, *viz.*, in the paṭets lima and nem, *via* the tone *pélog* to the lower, and *via* the tone *barang* to the higher auxiliary scale; the return to the main scale, on the other hand, from the lower auxiliary scale *via* the tone *ḍaḍa* and from the higher one *via* the tone *bem*, respectively.

In paṭet barang the deviation to the lower auxiliary scale goes *via* the tone *bem*, and to the higher one *via* the tone *pelog*; the return to the main scale from the lower auxiliary scale *via* the tone *barang*, and from the higher one via the tone *lima*, respectively.

In paṭet pélog manyura modulation takes place *via* the tone *barang* to the higher auxiliary scale, and back again to the main scale *via* the tone *bem*.

It should be noted that these modulations cannot be done complete justice to unless compositions also make use. at the "critical" places, of tones *not* occurring in the tonal sequence of the scale to be reached.

The following lay-out will assist the reader in clarifying the whole situation, also as regards any deviations and complications. In each scale, the dasar is represented by an encircled dot, and the auxiliary tones (*sorogan*), functioning as principal tones in the high and low secundary scales, by open circles [1]:

*) [Resp. scales 12, 17, and 22 in the higher, and 36, 32, 27 in the lower direction]

[1]) **In the Principalities, the theoretical "pillar"- (*i.e.* gong-)tones in pélog are, in actual playing practice, adhered to only very imperfectly to-day, as may gathered from the schematic representation on p. 78, note 3. In sléndro, on the other hand, as we saw on p. 80, the theory is applied much more strictly in practice (except**

The paṭet-system in Central Javanese pélog

		BARANG	BEM	GULU	ḌAḌA	PÉLOG	LIMA	NEM	BARANG	BEM	GULU	ḌAḌA	PÉLOG	LIMA	NEM	BARANG	BEM	GULU	ḌAḌA	PÉLOG	LIMA	NEM	BARANG		SUNDANESE NAME OF TONALITY	DASAR-CLASS:	NUMBER OF SCALE ON THE TABLE OF APP. 54:
PAṬET BARANG	1																	●	◉	○		●	●	HIGH AUXILIARY SCALE (GULU MIRING SCALE)	IDENTICAL W. MANANGIS, SHOULD THE TONE PÉLOG HAVE BEEN REPLACED BY THE SLIGHTLY LOWER "VOCAL" TONE PANANGIS	III	8
	2													●	●	●		●	◉					PRINCIPAL SCALE (HIGH AUXILIARY SCALE OF PÉLOG MANYURA)	NYOROG	II	7
	3									○	●	◉		●	●									LOW AUXILIARY SCALE (TONDAKUSUMA'S PÉLOG MANYURA)	JAWAR	I	6
PAṬET NEM	4													●	◉	○		●	●					HIGH AUXILIARY SCALE	NYOROG	III	3
	5									●	●	●		●	◉									PRINCIPAL SCALE	JAWAR	II	2
	6					○	●	◉		●	●													LOW AUXILIARY SCALE	LIWUNG	I	1
PAṬET LIMA	7													●	●	○		◉	●					NEW HIGH AUXILIARY SCALE	NYOROG	IV	44
	8									●	◉	○		●	●									MODERN PRINCIPAL SCALE (FORMERLY HIGH AUXILIARY SCALE)	JAWAR	III	43
	9					●	●	●		●	◉													OBSOLETE PRINCIPAL SCALE (AT PRESENT LOW AUXILIARY SCALE)	LIWUNG	II	42
	10	○	●	◉		●	●																	OBSOLETE LOW AUXILIARY SCALE (POENSEN'S AND GRONEMAN'S PÉLOG MIRING SCALE)	MANANGIS, SHOULD THE TONE BARANG HAVE BEEN REPLACED BY THE SLIGHTLY HIGHER "VOCAL" TONE PAMIRING	I	41

Of the 10 scales composing the above lay-out, the Nos. 3, 5 and 8 belong to the jawar-, the Nos. 6 and 9 to the liwung-, and the Nos. 2, 4 and 7 to the nyorog-tonality. Owing to the absence from the gamelan-scales of tones that could take the place, respectively, of the *pamiring* and the *panangis* of the Sundanese system, the scales Nos. 1 and 10 stand, so to speak, alone and do not—as was shown above—quite fit in with the instrumental system of the Principalities. Vocally, however, a correction is effected, here, too, by actually singing the tone *pélog* a little bit "flat" (cf. **54**, p. 153, 2nd col.), resp. the tone *barang* a little bit "sharp".

Examples of the kind of modulation with which we are here dealing may be found in abundance in every collection of genḍing-notations. Our Appendix *7*, the genḍing *Golong* paṭet lima, gives—in its *bebuka* [1]) and, further, at the end, each time, of the last kenongan of the first three gongan, in the penultimate kenongan of the 6th gongan, and in the last kenongan of the last gongan—examples of modulation from the present main scale of this paṭet to its lower fifth, *i.e.* to the former main scale now degraded to auxiliary scale; and also, in the penultimate kenongan of the 4th gongan and in the first and 2nd kenongan of the 6th gongan, examples of deviation from the new main scale towards the scale of its upper fifth.

Our Appendix *8*, the genḍing *Nawungbrongta* paṭet nem pélog, shows a large number of deviations towards the lower fifth: in the bebuka, and, further, at the end of the first gongan until the 2nd kenongan following it, in the 2nd kenongan of the 3rd gongan until the 3rd gong beat; in the 2nd kenongan of the 3rd gongan until the 3rd gong beat; then in the *nḍawah*, first gongan, 4th kenongan. And finally, in addition to these, a very brief deviation to the upper fifth in the 4th kenongan of the 3rd gongan of the *mérong*.

The genḍing *Sudirah gambuh* paṭet barang (Appendix *9*) shows, each time in the beginning of the first, 2nd and last kenongan of the first gongan, as well as in the *pangkat* and in the beginning of the last kenongan of the nḍawah, examples of deviation from the main scale to the (in this case, as

---

in paṭet nem, where the gong-tone *lima* has been superseded, as such, by the dasar of the main scale: *nem*). In the Sunda districts ,which represent, generally speaking, an older phase of development, the ,,pillar"-tones are adhered to much more rigorously even today.

[1]) For the meaning of terms, with which the reader may not be quite familiar, we refer to the Index in Vol. II of this work.

we saw above, slightly defective) scale of the upper fifth (which is called *gulu miring* scale).

An extremely fine example of modulation to the scale of the lower fifth in paṭet lima is provided by the genḍing *Babar layar* [1]; one of modulation in paṭet nem, both to the scale of the upper, and that of the lower fifth, by the genḍing *Tropongan* [2].

Occasionally, the incidence of "critical" tones fails to lead to a complete modulation; this may be either because the melody at this point does not include certain tones from the scale to be left, or reached, as the case may be, (and does not, therefore, adequately represent these scales), or because the modulation is of too fleeting a character to be able to persevere and stabilize itself. In such cases the critical tones in question do not function as *main* tones of an *auxiliary* scale, but as *auxiliary* tones of the *main* scale. A fine example of this is given by the genḍing *Bima kurda* [3] (App. *3B*) paṭet barang. Here, on two occasions, the incidence of the critical tone *bem* befogs our realization of the tonality, but nevertheless no complete modulation to the scale of the lower fifth is achieved.

In the Sunda districts—thanks to the intercalation of the "vocal" tones *pamiring* and *panangis*—the difficulties of modulation here described do not obtain. In these parts, moreover, the melody often lingers in the new tonality for quite a long time, so that its scale, in fact, completely loses its character of *auxiliary* scale and now stands side by side and on a perfectly equal footing with the tonality just left. An example of this is provided by our Appendix *49* (lagu *Udan mas*). In this, the melody modulates from nyorog to manangis [4], maintaining itself in the latter to almost the end of the composition, when the return to the original nyorog tonality is anticipated again and rendered possible by the incidence of the "leiterfremde" tone *kenong* (Jav.: *lima*).

Finally it should be pointed out that the tone material of the main scale of paṭet nem, with its two satellites, is none other than that of the three scales which we mentioned before (p. 51) under the name of nuclear triplet, and that, in both other paṭets, the tone material of the main scale corresponds to that of one of the auxiliary scales in paṭet nem, around which,

1) Beka B 15007 II.
2) Odeon A 204324b.
3) Odeon A 39561b.
4) *i.e.*, therefore, from scale No. 2 to scale No. 3 of the Table on p. 54.

again—in imitation of the original triplet—two tonal sequences have grouped themselves at the distance of a fifth; in other words, that the three paṭets together form, as it were, in their turn a faithful reflection, in a higher power—to use a mathematical term—of this nuclear triplet.

On surveying once more the whole of this tonal system, set out in this way, one will probably be struck—even more forcibly than by the above argumentation—by the foundational rôle played in it by the fifth-interval.

Finally, I may point out once more, that modulations, as discussed in the preceeding lines, can be perfectly expressed only when produced either vocally or on the rebab; for only then can there be question of a complete change in *tonality*; on instruments with fixed tone pitches they take on the form of something like a change in tone-gender [1]).

B. The condition that, together with the change in the paṭet the tonality should be maintained, naturally limits the possibilities of modulation to those cases in which the paṭet to be left and the paṭet to be reached have a scale of the same tonality in common. Thus, to name a couple of instances, it is possible to pass from paṭet barang (Jav.: nem) only to the paṭets panelu, singgul, kenong and galimer, as far as the jawar-scale is concerned; in a lagu written in a nyorog-scale in paṭet kenong one can modulate only to the paṭets barang, panelu, sorog and galimer, etc. One might formulate this by the general rule that, in each special case, there exist only four possibilities of modulation, since each scale possesses only five principal tones able to function as *dasar* (**200**, p. 337 et seq.).

In the Principalities this form of modulation is, with rare exceptions, limited to the sléndro system. Some of the examples in sléndro are the genḍings *Bonḍèt* (J) [2]), *Prihatin* [3]) (J) and *Titipati* (J and S), which modulate from P. 6 to P. 9, and the genḍing *Renyep* (J and S), which modulates from P. 9 to P. manyura [4]). In these parts this form of modulating is called *panchadan* (= stepping stone; verbal form: *manchad*). In the Magelang

[1]) In these cases, however, the relation between the dasar-classes is neither a modal, nor a tonal one, but rather as that between (kindred) *genders*. Indeed, the liwung-scale played upon the ordinary gamelan pélog is actually a pure *miring*-scale (cf. also **173**, p. 342). *Vide*, too, **197**, p. 399 *et seq.*, where, for this very reason, the term "relation *sui generis*" is used.

[2]) In Solo, the genḍing *Bonḍet* is simply classified under paṭet 9. [*S[51]]

[3]) *Prihatin* = to be anxious, in serious mood.

[4]) The genḍing *Krawitan*, too, occasionally modulates from sléndro P. 6 to P. 9.

kabupatèn, the *mérong* of the genḍing *Genḍu* P. 6 Sl. is followed by the ladrangan *Kembang pépé* P. manyura as *munggah*; in the same way the mérong of the genḍing *Pari(a)nom* P. 6 Sl. is followed by the ladrangan *Liwung* P. manyura, while the genḍing *Kembang tiba* P. 6 Sl., after having played its "own" munggah in P. 6, follows it up with the ladrangan *Manis* P. manyura. In the Jogya kraton it is usual to follow up the normal nḍawah of the genḍing *Génjong* P. 9 by playing the ladrangan *Éling-éling* P. 6 Sl. (vide Appendix 5), together with the Solonese genḍing *Ludira genḍing* which modulates from P. barang to P. 6 pélog—the only cases of transition from a higher to a lower paṭet which have come to my notice from the music of the Principalities [1]).

According to Radèn KODRAT, all genḍings sléndro P. nem, whose gongan finish on *lima*, *might possibly* modulate to P. sanga, and those whose gongan finish on *nem*, to P. manyura.

Another example of pélog modulation in the Principalities may be found, apart from the *Ludira genḍing* already mentioned, in the genḍing *Sambul genḍing*, which passes from P. 6 to P. barang.

The lagu *Sungsang* (Appendix 47), which modulates from P. barang (Jav.: nem) to P. panelu, may serve as an example of Sundanese paṭet modulation.

Such paṭet changes, too, are usually anticipated. Thus, in the mérong of the genḍing *Génjong* (P. 9) [2]), the last two tones, *nem* and *lima*, are replaced by the tones *barang* and *nem*, respectively, when passing to the nḍawah (in P. 6). Other genḍings achieve a smooth transition by sounding, at the end of the mérong, and in a natural way, the tone common—as gong-tone—to both the paṭet to be left and that to be reached: examples of which are the genḍings *Prihatin* and *Titipati*, which possess the tones *gulu* and *lima* as gongan-finishing tones of their mérong; the *lima* ends the mérong, whereby the P. 9 atmosphere is adequately anticipated. Nay, the mérong of the genḍing *Bonḍet*, although being in P. 6, finishes its phrases exclusively on the tone *lima* (*i.e.*, as may be gathered from what is stated above, theoretically the second and practically the third gong-tone of P. 6). In the same way, the P. 9 composition *Renyep*—of which it might naturally be expected that it should finish its phrases on the tone *lima*—possesses, as *finales*, exclusively *gulu*-tones (*i.e.* again only the third gong-tone in that paṭet) in order to prepare for the transition to its munggah, which is in manyura.

[1]) In Solo, too, the ladrangan *Éling-éling* often follows the genḍing *Génjong*, in which case, however, it is normally in P. 9. *Vide* App. 5.

[2]) [**113c**]

Whereas, in the modulation form referred to above under A, it was the ***auxiliary*** tones of the scale about to be left that rendered possible that transition to another scale, in ***this*** modulation it is precisely the gong-tones of the scale, ***i.e.*** the "pillar-tones", which perform this function.

C. In the third place there still exists a very rare form of modulation, which, within the limits of one and the same genḍing, passes from the one to the other tone-system. An example of such a tone-system modulation is given by the genḍing *Beḍaya ketawang* (S). This genḍing, which starts in pélog P. 5, passes, after a few gongan, to sléndro P. 9, where it stays during four gongan, after which it returns once more to P. 5. 1)

* * *

The names of tones of the scales discussed so far differ locally. The following table shows the nomenclature of a number of tones. The tones have been arranged in such a way that their pitches rise according as one reads from left to right 2). We have already mentioned that the Javanese (and Sunda-

1) Apart from this transition the trained European ear imagines hearing still other transpositions in this genḍing. A few times, during the P. 5-period, one has the impression that the tonal centre changes its place; thus, some *wilet* sounded to me, at the start, unmistakably as if they were in P. barang; the players and singers, however, so they told me, had not left P. 5. It is possible that this should be attributed to the phenomenon that came up for discussion just now on p. 97, *viz.* the brief deviation to an auxiliary scale under maintainance of the paṭet (our modulation-form A). At another moment the pitch of the—continuously beaten—*kemanaks* appeared to have got lowered by a semitone, which impression could be given only if one felt the tonality of the melody as having been raised by a semitone. It will probably have to remain an impossibility to investigate these phenomena more closely, since the *Beḍaya ketawang* is so sacred that it is only very rarely performed in public, *i.e.* exclusively on the commemorationday of the Susuhunan's accession to the throne (cf. p. 280), and will probably never be allowed to be recorded on a phonogram. [**3**A, **113**C, **377**H, L]

2) I hesitated for a long time before employing this western representation for Javanese scales. On the one hand, the consideration that, as is evident from the placing of the tones *lima* (= 5) and *nem* (= 6) in the various tone-sequences, the enumeration of the tones starting from the lowest tone—in the European sense—would, after all, not appear totally strange and unacceptable to the Javanese musician (*vide* also **75**, p. 10), and, on the other hand, the fact that the numbering from high to low (starting, for instance, from the dasar) would create the utmost confusion in the minds of European readers, whilst this would, moreover, render any comparison with scales published elsewhere and comments thereon, if not utterly impossible, at any rate very objectionable, caused me in the end to give preference to an enumeration of the tones from low to high.

nese) enumeration—unless strongly under Western influence—runs from high pitch to low pitch [1]), whilst at the same time the tone which, according to European conceptions, is higher, is felt by the Javanese as being lower (Sund.: *handap* = low, *i.e.*, in Europe, high), and the tone which, according to Western feelings, is the lower one, is felt to be higher (Sund.: *luhur* = high, *i.e.*, in Europe, low). There are instances in which this is expressed in a system of notation, about which more later on (cf. pp. 350 and 354 and ill. 127). The Javanese and Sundanese musicians are in good company in this respect, namely in that of the ancient Hellenes, who, for example, indicated the tone of their scales which was in Western conception the lowest, by the word *hupatè, i.e.* the highest.

Further, the tones are, in every day language, not usually distinguished as high and low, but as great (*gedé*) and small (*alit*, Sund.: *leutik*), great being the equivalent to low in Europe.

* * *

We shall finish this chapter with a few remarks concerning the concept *interval.*

As we have seen above (p. 49) the interval of a single step is indicated in Java Proper by the word *wilah*, which means, literally, a flat piece of wood, slab (as found on the xylophone). SULARDI (**343**, p. 5) also uses, for the distance between two successive keys, the word *antawis* (L. J. and Skrt. *antara*).

For the concept *octave*, in the sense of the octave *tone*, the term *gembyangan* [2]) is used in Java Proper; in East-Java one also hears the term *chochokan*, derived from *chochok*, meaning "to correspond". The octave-*interval* is also called *gembyangan*, but, more frequently *sagembyangan*. As regards the octave in the sense of a tone series of the size of an octave, no

1) Although, as we said before, the order of sequence *lima-nem* and that of *penunggul-gulu-ḍaḍa* (= head-neck-chest)—one naturally starts with the head—points to a period in which the scale is regarded as running from low to high.

2) According to SURYAPUTRA (**357**, blz. 318/9) the signification of *gembyang* is: the harmonic relationship between two persons. Hence the fact that the term *gembyang* came into vogue, at first (according to this author) for harmonic intervals in general, and later on more particularly for the interval which is characterized by the highest degree of harmonic fusion, *i.e.* the octave. (The dictionaries of JANSZ, GERICKE-ROORDA and PIGEAUD do not contain the word. The first named does mention, however, a homonyme with the signification of abundance (as said of a fruit tree)).

Pélog

Degrees:	I	II	III	"Vocal" intermediate tone	IV	V	VI	VII	"Vocal" intermediate tone	I′
Central Java	bem, penung-gul	gulu (H. J. jongga)	ḍaḍa tengah		pélog	lima (H. J. gangsal)	nem	barang		bem alit
Sunda districts	Singgul, kuwing, papatet, panutup	galimer, bem, (singgul?)	panelu, sanga	panangis	bungur, liwung, sorog gedè	kenong, loloran	barang, laras, mamanis	sorog, sorog ku-wing	pamiring	singgul leutik
Cheribon	bem	sedasa, penggulu	sanga, panelu		bungur	lima, loloran	laras, nem, surupan, apik	barang		bem alit
Prabalingga	sorog pengasih	gulu, tenggok	ḍaḍa		pélog	lima	nem	barang		
Majakerta	sorog	tengah, tenggok	sanga		pélog	lima, gangsal	nem	barang		

Sléndro

Degrees:	I	inter-mediate tone	II	inter-mediate tone	III	inter-mediate tone	IV	inter-mediate tone	V	inter-mediate tone	I′
Central Java	barang		gulu, (H. J. jongga)		ḍaḍa, tengah		lima, (H. J. gangsal)		nem		barang
Sunda districts	singgul	pamiring	bem, galimer	mangu	panelu	panangis	kenong	jawil	barang	sorog	singgul leutik
Indramayu	panjang, panutup		kesekawan		panelu		pamindo		kesetunggil or kesetunggal		
Jombang, Prabalingga }	barang		tenggok gulu		ḍaḍa		lima		nem		barang alit
Banyuwangi, Majakerta }	sorog		tengah, tenggok		sanga		lima		nem		
Madura	bheng		tenggo'		lima		bharang		mèttèt		
Banjermasin	babon		tangah		lima		nam, bam		sanga, tanggo		

LITERAL MEANING OF THESE NAMES OF TONES

alit (J) = *leutik* (Sund.) = small.

apik	beautiful, melodious.
babon	mother, genetrix.
barang	starting point (?), literally = matter.
bem (*bam*)	(probably derived from the Persian-Arabian word *bam*) indicates a low tone.
bungur	the violet (tone).
ḍaḍa	breast.
galimer	great, low-sounding.
gangsal	five, (the) fifth (tone), L. J. *lima*.
gulu	neck, H. J. *jongga*.
jawil	(from Jav.: *anjawil* = Sund.: *towèl* = Fr.: *effleurer*): (the) softly and only incidentally intoned (sound).
jongga	neck, L. J. *gulu*.
kenong	the name of the well-known interpunctuating gamelan instrument which, when there is only one specimen of it in the orchestra, always sounds the tone *kenong* (Jav.: *lima*).
kesekawan	four, (the) fourth (tone).
kesetunggil	or *kesetunggal*, the first (tone).
kuwing	derived from *guwing*? If so, it means: (the) cleft (tone).
laras	tuning-tone, diapason.
leutik,	*vide alit*.
lima	(the) fifth (tone), H. J. *gangsal*.
liwung	dizzy, amorous, absorbed in thought.
lo(*r*)*loran*	(the) second (tone).
mamanis	(the) sweet, melodious (tone).
mangu	dull, absent-minded, in love, absorbed in thought.
mèttèt	?
miring	aslant, deviating, false.
nam	*vide nem*.
nem	(the) sixth (tone).
pamindo	(the) second (tone).
pamiring	substantive of miring.
panangis	weeping tone.
panelu	(the) third (tone).
panjang	(the) long(est) (tone-slab).
panutup	(the) closing (tone).
papatet	(the) limiting (tone).
pélog	(when $\sqrt{log}$ = $\sqrt{rog}$, the meaning will be: sliding or alternating tone) [1].
pengasih	love-instrument.
penggulu	= *gulu*.
penunggul	head, summit ($\sqrt{gul}$, from which also *tunggul* = chief, headman (cf. above p. 17), and *singgul*.
penyorog	= *sorog*.
sanga	nine, (the) ninth (tone).
sedasa	ten, (the) tenth (tone).
singgul	identical with Jav.: *penunggul*.
sorog	sliding or alternating tone.
sorog gedè	the great *sorog*.
sorog kuwing	the sorog of the tone *kuwing*.
surupan	key-tone, the "clou", the basis of the tone-system.
tangah	*vide tengah*.
tanggo	?
tengah	(the) middle (tone).

tenggok (*tenggo'*) throat.

---

[1]) Cf. p. 39, note.

Javanese name has, as yet, come to my knowledge; only a Sundanese one: *pangkon(an)*, *i.e.* womb. An octave in the sense of an octave-interval, is indicated in the Sundanese language by the word *beulit*.

The fifth-interval (*i.e.* three steps on the gendèr sléndro) is called, in the Principalities, *kempyung*; the "inversion" of it is not felt as being quite equivalent to it as regards consonance, which is evident from the fact that this "fourth"—as well as the interval covering *four* steps on the gendèr sléndro—is indicated by the name *salah gumun* which may be translated by "peculiar harmonic effect" [1]).

---

[1]) *salah* = agreement; *gumun* = astonishment, astounding, striking, out-of-the-way (cf. also p. 176).

CHAPTER III

HISTORICAL SURVEY

a. Before the advent of the Hindus.

(**19, 20C, 23A, 60, 62, 83, 87, 92–95A, 98, 101, 109, 111–113, 116–118, 120, 121, 124, 124A, 132A, 138, 143** vols. III, IV, V, VI, and VIII, **156A, 164, 182, 237, 268, 269, 272, 273, 281–287, 292, 306, 307–310, 313, 327–331, 367, 369, 389, 391**) [**84A, 109A, 113D, 125A, 241A, 255A**]

Whereas, in most islands of the Archipelago, the student of native music finds the available data to be limited almost exclusively to what is still being practised by the people to-day, in Java—and also in Bali—discoveries during excavations, temple-reliefs, documentary evidence in stone and bronze, as well as the ancient literature have enabled us to cast a glance into the past also, by revealing the existence of a manifold and highly-developed instrumentarium, namely in the Hindu-Javanese (and ancient-Balinese) period.

The oldest Javanese instruments known to us are (the remnants of) a few large bronze kettledrums (ill. 1) (**98, 109, 182, 273** Table I figs. 3 and 4, Table II figs. 1 and 2, **281**). It is thought, on fairly safe grounds, that these were imported into the Archipelago from Northern Further India and South China (**20B, 60, 62, 92, 93, 95, 112, 113** [1]), **132A, 156A, 164** [2]), **328**), some centuries before the beginning of the Christian era, and that they served, among other things, as "rain-makers" (**308**).

The territory in which they are to be found in this island world is not limited to Java, fragments of these instruments having also been found in Bali (**282, 283, 309**), Sumatra (**143** vol. IV pp. 103/4 and 141, vol. V pp. 66, 87 and 95), Borneo (**83**), Roté (**273** Table I figs. 1 and 2), Léti (**19, 237, 284, 306** p. 376 and Plate 35 fig. 3), Kur (**120, 143** vol. III pp. 146/7 and

[1]) [**125A**: Intr. p. XXXVII] [2]) [**255A**]

155/6, **369**), Luang (**306** p. 316), Sangia(ng) (**113**, **143** vol. V pp. 66 and 94/5, **331**), and Saleier (**121**, **330**, **331**), while, about 1930, VAN DER HOOP (**124**) and VONK (**389**) found pictures of them on some of the pre-Hindu images which are met with in such large numbers in the Pasemah district (**124** p. 81 et seq., and ill. 91–96) (ill. 2 and 3) [1].

When the first Hindu colonists, therefore, settled in the Archipelago—in Java probably during the fifth century A.D.—they must have found these instruments already here.

The extremely small kettledrum, no larger than a few centimeters—see ill. 4—which was recently dug up near Chibadak in the regency of Sukabumi, is probably also pre-Hindu. Very likely it was given to a dead person to take with him in the grave [2].

As is well known, kettledrums—but then in a rather different shape, more like an hour-glass—have been manufactured also in the Archipelago itself at later periods, even in post-Hindu times, and almost as late as our own times, *i.e.* at Grissee (Gresik) [3], from where they have been exported to Alor, where they still constitute a fixed part of the purchase-price of a bride (ill. 5) (**138**, **284–287**, **329**), while Father VROKLAGE (**391**) has come across a specimen akin to the Alorese ones, in Flores [4].

Most of the bamboo-instruments, too—although this cannot, owing to the perishable nature of the material, be proved by producing the instruments themselves—are to be regarded as of pre-Hindu origin.

b. Hindu-Java

(**97**, **147**, **184**, **194**, **196**, **222**, **223**, **224**, **263**, **377**)
[**236H**, **236N**, **303A**, **332B**]

The most ancient Hindu-Javanese instrumental piece of documentary evidence is, as far as I know, a relief originating from one of the *Dièng-*

[1]) Cf. also **313** and **369**.

[2]) **281**, file 1929, p. 40.

[3]) The large kettle-drum, also hourglass shaped, of Pèjèng (South Bali), might possibly have been cast in this island. Dr. CRUCQ found in 1933 some fragments of a mould of a similar drum—though of much smaller size—among a collection of *pusaka* (holy) images in a temple (the *pura puseh*, *i.e.* the temple of ancestors) of Manuaba in the district of Gianyar.

[4]) A *chronological* bibliography relating to the subject of kettle-drums may be found as an Appendix to my treatise "Een en ander over muziek en dans op de Kei-eilanden" (**227**). In *alphabetical* order it has been reproduced in Vol. II of the present work (*vide* Bibliography). Cf. the numbers printed at the head of this Chapter.

temples, and probably dating from the beginning of the 8th, or the end of the 7th century, on which small bronze bells are depicted. *Chanḍi Sari* (abt. 750 A.D.) adds to this: a three-stringed lute (ill. 6), a one-stringed bar-zither (ill. 7) and small cymbals, whilst *Chanḍi Nagasari*, dating from the same period, adds a pair of elephant bells. These, however, are merely a few from a superabundant wealth of musical instruments, as is proved by contemporary *Barabuḍur*. For, on the reliefs of that great *stupa*, we find depicted: many two-headed, conical or full-bellied or waisted kinds of drums with strap-tension (but always without sliding rings), beaten sometimes with the hand and sometimes with sticks (some of which are hook-shaped); drums of baked earthenware with a single skin; resonators for hand-clapping, made of earthenware ("sound-pots"); mouth-organs; a scraping-instrument; transverse flutes; shawms (or are they end-blown flutes?); a xylophone (something between a *gambang kayu* and a *cha-lung*); many kinds of two-, three- and four-stringed lutes, either played with a plectrum or with the bare fingers; many bar-zithers, some of which with a screw (or peg?) in front; small bow-shaped harps with loop-tension, and at least one such with tension by means of wooden plugs (or might they already be pegs?) and with 10 strings; shell-trumpets, blown at the apex; bronze bells of various dimensions, among them large bronze chimes, three-tongued temple-bells and large and small tinkling bells ("grelots"); a grelot-shaped wooden slitdrum with handle [1]); begging-cups with small tinkling rods; a *saron*; cymbals in all sizes, and sometimes tied together by a strap; tinkling-cups, often also tied in this manner; a *bonang-* or *kenong*-kettle [2]); straight trumpets (ill. 8 to 23 incl.).

---

[1]) Barabuḍur relief 0 39 (vide ill, 12 sub *b*). This grelot would actually appear to be identical with the wooden Anamitic *mo*, which is beaten like a gong in the temples (cf. KNOSP, "Histoire de la musique dans l'Indochine", in LAVIGNAC, "Histoire de la Musique", vol. V, p. 3100 *et seq.* (**319**, ill. 616).

[2]) The representation has become very indistinct. In any case, however, a gong-kettle of this description has been identified (under the name of *brekuk*) for the year 902 (inscription of Kembang arum), and as *kangsi* for about 1000 A.D. (Purwādhigama), whilst the Rāmāyaṇa also mentions it under the latter name.

And what are we to think of those remarkable bonang-shaped stones, which have been found here and there in the soil of Central- and East-Java? Should we really regard these as imitations of gong-kettles (and, if so, very likely put down in the forest for the comfort and recreation of demons and sylvan deities)? The Majapahit fieldmuseum at Trawulan possessed several of these, hailing from the North-western slope of the Anjasmara mountain (Residence of Majakerta); the Batavia Society has about a dozen of them, one of which (Cat. No. 449a) was

The *Prambanan* temple-complex, dating from a century later (ill. 24 to 31 incl.), and especially the great Shiva-temple, shows us—apart from proofs of the existence of some instruments known to us already from Barabuḍur (large and small cymbals, three-stringed lute, shell-trumpet, shawm, tinkling-cups, bells, bar-zither)—a number of other forms of drums deviating somewhat from those of the stupa, whilst the reliefs from the mausoleum-bathing resort *Jalatunḍa*, on the slopes of the Penanggungan [1]), dating from 977 A.D., show a small bow-shaped harp, which, however, has only three strings (ill. 32), together with—as was found in 1935 by STUTTERHEIM and GALL—pictures of the *bin* (*vina*) in its Northern Indian form (ill. 59) [2]).

From the Central Javanese soil there came to light a fairly large number of bronze playing instruments—not dated, and not datable, but very probably, at any rate partly, descended from the same period, namely series of *bonang*-kettles, series of *saron*- and *gendèr*-keys, bells (ill. 33), praying-bells, slit-drums, gongs (ill. 64), and *kakhara* top-pieces with tinkling rings (**135**, p. 61, **178**, fig. 8) [3]), as well as a few bronze statuettes playing, respectively, a three-stringed lute (ill. 34), a seven-stringed bowed harp [4]) (ill. 35), and a one-stringed bar-zither (ill. 36).

Contemporary *documents on bronze or stone* mention a number of names of instruments the majority of which it has been possible to ḍetermine. Central Javanese *literature* got lost, unless it might be that the Hindu-Javanese version of the Rāmāyaṇa—as Dr. PURBACHARAKA argued [5])—should be placed in the 9th century.

---

found in East-Semarang, and eleven (Cat. No. 449b) in the Klatèn district (ill. 165). The museum-catalogues, however, call these objects "neuten" (*i.e.* a kind of plinths) and MACLAINE PONT, the founder of the museum at Trawulan, also believes that, at any rate several of them, were intended as such. The knob on the top would then have served to prevent any beams or bamboo post erected upon them from sliding off.

Cf. also H. E. STEINMETZ in T.B.G. XL (1898), p. 29; H. R. VAN HEEKEREN in "Djawa" XI (1931), p. 14 and ill. 10; J. TH. à TH. VAN DER HOOP (**124**, p. 121 *et seq.*) and N.I. Oudheidkundig Verslag 1938, p. 10.

[1]) In Eastern Java; the style, however, is Central Javanese.

[2]) Relief IV; photo's GALL E 39 and D 74.

[3]) *Kakhara's* are jingling-staves used by begging monks. Cf. also TOBIAS NORLIND, "Beiträge zur chinesischen Instrumentengeschichte" ("Svensk Tidschrift för Musikforskning" 1933, p. 51 *et seq.*).

[4]) From Nganjuk in the regency of Madiun, *i.e.* on the border of Central- and East-Java; as regards its style, however, it belongs to the period called Old-(Central-) Javanese.

[5]) "De dateering van het Oud-Javaansche Rāmāyaṇa" ("Gedenkschrift Kon. Inst. v. T., L. en Vk.", p. 365 *et seq.*), 1926.

This Central-Javanese instrumentarium comprises, on the one hand, many instruments which do not, to-day, occur in Java any longer (earthenware drums and sound-pots, scraping-instruments, bow-shaped harps, lutes—the last named with the exception of the, not directly kindred, Arabian *gambus* (ill. 146 and 147)—barzithers, mouth-organs etc.), and, on the other hand, those which now constitute the gamelan, are, in fact, to be found, for the greater part, but neither the reliefs, nor the relevant bronze and stone inscriptions, nor the juxtaposition of the objects discovered during excavation, are sufficient evidence of their having been combined in ancient times into an *ensemble* at all resembling the present-day gamelan.

To these Central-Javanese instruments—some of which will probably have got into disuse very soon (especially the tinkling-cups, the bow-shaped harps, the bar-zithers and the mouth-organs), the Eastern-Javanese reliefs and excavation-finds do not add a great deal. A large number of instruments which are sculptured at any given moment for the first time are, moreover, sure to have existed already for a much longer time, and are, indeed, partly mentioned earlier in literature. A Bhairava statue found in the territory of *chanḍi Singasari* (about 1250 A.D.) holds, in one of its hind-hands, a waisted swing-drum—possibly, in view of the character of the godhead depicted, a skull-drum (as still found in Thibet to-day); a curiously shaped long-necked lute, influenced by the bar-zithers, in addition to a shawm (or is it an end-blown flute?), and a prototype of the *chelempung* is shown on a relief of the *chanḍi Jago* dating from about 1260 (ill. 37 and 38); *chanḍi Jawi* (about 1300 A.D.) reveals the existence of double wind-instruments, probably trumpets (ill. 39) [1]; either *chanḍi Ngrimbi* or a sculpture found in Keḍiri by the engineer MOENS [2] (ill. 40 and 41) gives the most ancient picture as well as the oldest proof of the existence of the dumb-bell-shaped *réyong* [3], now extinct in Java, but still occurring frequently in Bali; the main temple of *chanḍi Panataran,* dating from 1347, shows us the oldest known representation of a rather large gong [4] (ill. 43), besides pictures of a

[1]) Cf. GEORG BUSCHAN, Die Sitten der Völker II (without date), p. 96, fig. 118 at the left!

[2]) This also shows a full-bellied, two-headed drum.

[3]) In addition, one more image of a *réyong* has come to our knowledge, *i.e.* on a relief of a sacred shrine discovered by F. M. SCHNITGER, at Si Joreng Belangah in Padang Lawas (Tapanuli, N.W. Sumatra). Cf. SCHNITGER, "Oudheidkundige vondsten in Padang Lawas" (1936), plate VI, ill. bottom left, right-hand relief. The author himself took it to be a drum (ibid. p. 12, sub *a*).

[4]) There are indications, however, which render it feasible—and if the Old-Ja-

set of *kemanak* (ill. 42; cf. ill. 75 and 77), a probably one-headed drum beaten with a stick (ill. 44), a straight trumpet (or is it a shawm?) (ill. 45), small gongs (*bhèri*) beaten with a hook-shaped stick (ill. 42 and 45), and —on the so-called pendapa-terrace dating from 1375—a number of *réyongs* together with a set of small cymbals(?) (ill. 46), as well as a couple of bamboo *gambangs* [1]) with unequal keys and beaten with forked hammers such as are only to be found in Bali to-day—and of which yet another illustration has been preserved in one of the small terra-cotta statuettes (ill. 48) excavated in the Majapahit territory. Other Majapahit terra-cotta figurines give representations of a small drum, probably one-headed, as well as of two lutes deviating strongly from the forms known to us from the Central-Javanese period, and one of which leads us to presume a (Northern?-)Chinese, and the other, a Persian-Arabian influence (ill. 49). Whether some of the other terra-cotta finds represent fragments of waisted drums (with skin heads) is a debatable point. In 1935, on the slopes of the Penanggungan, A. GALL excavated a terra-cotta ocarina, supposedly of Hindu-Javanese origin, with three finger-holes (ill. 58). Finally, the small Naga-temple in the Panataran-precincts, dating from about 1300, shows us pictures of praying-bells (ill. 50); *chanḍi Tegawangi* (about 1358) that of a cylindrical two-headed drum with strap-tension (ill. 51), and both *chanḍi Keḍaton* (1370) [2]) and *chanḍi Sukuh* (15th century) that of a small gong (ill. 60 and 52 respectively), whilst the last-named temple also gives a picture of a shell-trumpet (ill. 53).

The Eastern-Javanese *bronze finds* (slit-drums (ill. 54); bells (ill. 55); *kemanaks* (ill. 57); pellet-bells; ranges of keys and beating-kettles, as well as a representation in bronze of a *ḍamaru* (swing-drum) (the latter from before 1287 A.D.)), do not add any new instrumental forms to those already mentioned. They prove, however, often in an imposing manner, the height of development to which the art of bronze-casting had risen in these lands, in the Kaḍiri period (1042–1222) and the Singasari period (1222–1292).

The contemporary *literature* yields quite a mass of instrumental names, a large proportion of which may be determined with satisfactory certainty. To the instruments which have come to our knowledge from the Central-

vanese version of the Rāmāyaṇa actually originated in the 9th century, it would even be certain—that the gong was known in Java already before 900 A.D. (**176**, p. 78/9).

1) Ill. 47.

2) *Vide* Dr. TH. GALESTIN, "Houtbouw op Oost-Javaansche tempelreliefs" (thesis 1936), p. 60/1.

Javanese period, and from the Eastern-Javanese excavations and reliefs, these literary sources have added some which are undoubtedly centuries older and certainly of pre-Hindu origin, *i.e.* the *sundari* (an Aeolus-bamboo) (Arjunavivaha, about 1040) (cf. **192**, p. 22 note 7); the *chalung* (1181 A.D., on one of the Buwahan inscriptions), still played nowadays chiefly in the Sunda districts (ill. 137, 138 and 154); the *damyadamyan*, the rice-clarinet (about 1188, Ghaṭotkacaçraya); the *guntang*, a bamboo zither (Kidung Sunda, not long after 1357 A.D.), which is to be found to this day in the entire archipelago, and is still called guntang in Bali; the *taluktak* or tilting-bamboo (to be dealt with further on, see p. 196) (about 1100 A.D.: Bhomakavya; 1157: Bhārata Yuddha), and the bamboo slit drum, which goes under the names of *kulkul* (Sudamala), *titir* (Smaradahana) and *kukulan* (Bhārata Yuddha). One may further find, in the literature, evidence of the existence—some centuries before the time of the Panataran-picture—of the *kemanak* (12th century, Vrrṭa Sañcaya). The existence of the *terbang* (ill. 121, 152, 153) is proved for the first time from the Smaradahana, dating from 1135; that of metallophones with floating suspended keys —of a gendèr-form, therefore (cf. ill. 72 and 73) —is proved, for the year 1157 A.D., by a passage in the Bhārata Yuddha, while the fact that its keys, at that time, were (often) made of iron—and usually not, as at present, of bronze [1])—is shown in various ancient Balinese inscriptions dating from 1181.

That during the Hindu-Javanese millennium, music was held in high honour, at any rate by the ruling castes, is proved, apart from the multiformity of the instruments and the abundance of images of instruments on temple-reliefs and of objects found during excavations, by different documentary inscriptions which repeatedly make mention of musical functionaries: chief drummer, orchestra-leader, chief lute-player, etc. In addition to this, Hindu-Javanese and ancient Chinese literature frequently testifies to the existence of a lively and versatile musical life, both at the courts of the princes and nobility and among the people: "...others accompanied on the *bangsi* (transverse flute), *tāla* (cymbals), *paṇawa* (a species of drum) and *muddhama* (? tinkling-cups). Some had brought a *wiṇārāwaṇahasta* (lute), and, to assist them they had girl dancers who were skilled in their work (?). According to each person's taste, there was a great variety in the

---

[1]) Gendèrs (without resonance-tubes) with *iron* keys are to be found in Bali to this day; they still bear the Hindu-Javanese name of *saluṇḍing* (**196**).

performances: the *bhèri* (here still meaning a drum, in later centuries it means a small gong) and *murawa* (a drum) sounded incessantly, mixing with the sound of the *çangka* (shell-trumpet) and *kālaha* (crooked trumpet)" (Virāṭaparvva 85). Or, if one prefers a quotation from later times (1365 A.D.) and from East-Java: "KṚTAVARDHANA (the king's father) started as an amateur to play the gamelan" (*i.e.* here, probably, the *gambang kayu*, or the *gendèr*). The queen sang a song, wearing a beautiful (wayang topèng-) wig. This manner of acting for fun exited merriment" (at a court festival at Majapahit) (Nāgarakṛtāgama XCL 5).

And from Chinese sources: (i) in MA HUAN's travel story of the journeys abroad made by CHENG HO (during the Ming period, about 1405 A.D.) (**263**, p. 164 *et seq.*), statements to the effect that "the gamelan instruments consisted of a set of copper drums (perhaps *bonangs*), and a large brass gong; the wind-instruments were made out of coconut shells" (p. 168), and that the tournaments took place to the sound of rolls on the drum (p. 167); and (ii) the communication (identical with the above?) in the Ying-yai-Shîng-lan [1]) about the occurrence, in Java, of brass drums and gongs, the blowing on coconut shells (ocarina's?; cf. the present-day Papuan ocarina's [2])), drums and bamboo drums (= bamboo zithers?; these are being often called drums, as, for instance, in Nias (*gŏndra hao* = bamboo drum)) [3]).

From the first—and most ancient— of the above two Hindu-Javanese quotations it also appears that, at the time of that prosa-redaction of the Mahābhārata-canto from which it is quoted (996), the instrumentarium of the ruling castes still bore a predominantly Hindu character. One may take it as certain, however, that in many respects the music played on it differed considerably, already at that time, from the music of the Indian home-land. Just like the architecture and the poetry of that period it probably possessed its own pronounced Hindu-*Javanese* character. But even tho' it had become remote from its continental sources, and became ever more typically Indonesian in the course of the centuries—again, like architecture and poetry—yet one should not imagine the music of this early Hindu-Javanese period as having already a strong resemblance to the music which is played in these lands at the present time. On the one hand, this is a necessary result of the totally different instrumentarium, but on the other hand it may

---

1) GROENEVELDT (**97**), p. 21.
2) **202**, p. 68 and plate X, ill. 37; also **226**.
3) SCHRÖDER, Nias, par. 711, sub I 5; KUNST, **217**, p. 39.

be deduced directly from the dance-reliefs on Barabuḍur, and also, more especially, from those of Prambanan. The music accompanying these dances must have been far more lively and passionate, and less stylized, if we are to judge by the unmistakably greater abandon of the dancers depicted in these images. Presumably present-day Balinese music and dance, charged, as they often are, with such demonic energy, are more closely akin to the old Hindu-Javanese arts than to the modern Javanese forms with their dignified and aristocratic manner.

c. *The post-Hindu period*

(19, 20, 56, 66, 68, 69, 91, 225, 256, 257, 303, 309, 381, 385)

During the last few centuries of the East (Hindu)-Javanese period the component parts of the gamelan, as we know them to-day, were practically all in existence. Actually there is only one important instrument of which there is no direct proof of its having existed in the Hindu-Javanese period, *i.e.* the *rebab* (ill. 97, under *b*). This may be merely accidental; the Hikayat Chèkèlwanèngpati—a Malay version of the tale of Panji—does mention the rebab. And it is supposed on good grounds that this Hikayat had its final edition as early as the Hindu-Javanese period.

But although all, or nearly all, gamelan instruments were known and played upon in Singasari and Majapahit, there is nothing to indicate that they were also combined into an *ensemble* such as the modern gamelans. We shall not be far from the truth if we hazard the supposition that in those later Hindu-Javanese centuries two chief instrumental groupings were known: one, as it were, feminine combination of soft-sounding instruments, intended in the first place for indoor use, such as the *gendèr*, *gambang* and *suling*; and another, typically masculine *ensemble* intended for male use, and consisting of large, loud-sounding instruments, such as drums, cymbals (now nearly extinct in Java, but still in full flourish in Bali), as well as different kinds of gongs, either suspended or placed flat, all of which were probably played in the open air, in the soldiers' camps, by way of war-music, and to introduce and accompany (temple-) festivities. This kind of "masculine" orchestras are still to be found in different parts of the archipelago, as, for instance, in Nias (**217**, p. 25 *et seq.* and ill. 8) and West-Flores (**221**, p. 111, and ill. 35 and 55). The most ancient of the Principality orchestras still in existence (the gamelans Munggang and Koḍok ngorèk, ill. 111 and 112) are, as a matter of fact, not much more than this either.

At all events, from PRAPANÇA's detailed description of the kraton of Majapahit (Nāgarakrṭāgama, Cantos 8–12), one receives, *e silentio*, the impression that in the 14th century orchestral music is, at least, very far from occupying the position which it still has to-day in the kratons of the Central Javanese Principalities. There, for some gamelans, a separate storeroom is set apart, and a special place assigned, bearing a special name of its own, where they are played, and many orchestras fulfil highly-specialized functions in the court-ceremonials (cf. p. 246, 259, 262, 265). STUTTERHEIM is of the opinion that for the kraton of Majapahit there is only evidence, and that only indirect, of the presence and ceremonial use of the gamelan Munggang (**377A**, pp. 40/1, 51 and 68, note).

Now, the "marriage" between the masculine and the feminine orchestras must, I believe, have been definitely arranged on a permanent basis at the earliest as late as the end of the Hindu-Javanese period. VALENTIJN, in his encyclopaedic work on the lands ruled over by the East-Indian Company (1723–'26) (**385**), evidently still keeps the two groups as separate entities. But the beginning of a combination nevertheless exists already—may be only incidentally. When staying at Semarang he heard "...some Javanese lasses singing to the sound of a gong and a *tifa* (*i.e.* drum) and of a native zither." As against this, however, there are several passages in which he mentions only vigorous loud music: "the horrible rumbling of a large number of gongs and *tifa's*"; "several sets of gongs and *tataboangs* (*i.e.* here probably *bonangs*) [1]", whilst in other places he mentions a soft *ensemble*: "...they (*i.e.* Balinese slavegirls) danced to a Javanese violin and another instrument, which was full of copper strings and was a kind of zither" (evidently a *chelempung*). Besides this, VALENTIJN also speaks of female voices accompanied by nothing but drums (*bodoc* = *beḍug*, and *rabana* = *terbang*).

VALENTIJN's appreciation of Javanese art is not yet very profound. This is already evident from some of the above quotations, but still more so from what follows the passage quoted first: "...some Javanese lasses, etc. ...but all their music merely consisted in bawling out the tones *re mi re* (just like the music of the Chinese) and in cadences in fourths, thirds and

[1]) The word, which derives from *tabuh*, *i.e. beating hammer*, may be used for any instrument made to sound by means of such a tool (also, therefore, for saron, gendèr, gambang, etc.).

fifths, in a most disagreeable manner, and with a drawl that irritated me beyond words." So we see that the Dutch of the 18th century—and even a man susceptible to impressions, as VALENTIJN undoubtedly was—had not got much further in this respect than their 16th- and 17th-century predecessors, one of whom—the first one, as it were, for he was the writer of "D'Eerste Boeck" of 1597 (**257**)—has nothing better to say about some Javanese girls—daughters of the high nobility—whom he saw dancing at the Banten court, than: "pulling their arms and legs about, and twisting their whole bodies, like dogs when they creep out of their nest." For the rest we do not find, in this oldest Dutch source of information about the archipelago, many data relative to Javanese art, as we may well understand. A few pictures, striking one as rather comic, of the girl- (and men-) dancers mentioned above, accompanied by a badly-drawn, but unmistakable *gendèr* (ill. 61), and of an orchestra under a penḍapa (and what a penḍapa!), consisting of large gongs, shaped like Brobdignac shaving-mugs ("with which they chimed"), and single-rowed *bonangs* looking like beef steaks (ill. 62), as well as a remark concerning the occurrence, everywhere in the town of Banten, of large drums, "of the size of a wine barrel of three hogsheads, on which they beat with a weaver's boat-hammer(?) (the which is hanging on to it), when in the case of some emergency (such as a fire, or a fight), early morning at break of day, and in the evening at sunset" (these drums, therefore, must be *beḍug's*)—this little is practically all that is to be found in this book with respect to music.

Out of all the servants of the East India Company it was RIJCKLOF VAN GOENS (1656) (**91**) who proved to be the keenest observer of, and most receptive to, Javanese music. True, in his wellknown colourful and well-written account of his voyage he mentions somewhere "the noise of goms (*i.e.* gongs) and drums", but we also find in it the following description of the opening of a *senènan* (tournament) at Mataram:

"On Saturdays, or, maybe, Mondays, it is customary for about 4, 5, 6, 7 or 8 thousand gentlemen on horseback to arrive in the large square to the north of the court, all of them, both the horses and the horsemen, most exquisitely adorned, collecting there at about 4 o'clock in the afternoon. Each of the high dignitaries has his own small open house in this square, and around this their horses and menfolk are posted to guard each of them. Beneath each little house the very highest dignitaries (such as the pangérans, radins, tomagons and nebeys) have their metal instruments at least

20 or 30 of them, small and large gongs, besides those of the king, which are spread over at least five or six places, up to as many as 200. These gongs are beaten very softly and sweetly before the arrival of the king (....) When the king has arrived in the outer square they start beating both large and small gongs with such violence that the noise would easily have drowned the sound of ten of our drums." (*Vide* also **385**, p. 159).

In a further passage, VAN GOENS relates something about the beḍaya's of MANGKU RAT: "Meanwhile a small open house was put down on the square (between that of the king and the lesser ones) in which the king's young dance-maidens come to dance, playing, for this purpose, on many small gongs, which, together with a number of flutes and violins, produce a sweet melody".

It is doubtful whether the author has represented quite correctly the instrumental combination of this dance-accompaniment (cf. p. 279). The flute (*suling*), although being played to-day invariably as a single instrument in the Javanese gamelan, was possibly blown in those days by two at a time, as is still the case in Bali to-day, and—as is evident from the Barabuḍur-reliefs—also in the Old-Javanese period; but we cannot assume that more than one rebab would have collaborated in the combination observed by VAN GOENS. This slip of the pen, however, must be cordially forgiven him. As an ambassador of the Company he had other things to do besides noting down musicological details in the presence of the mighty MANGKU RAT.

One swallow, however, does not make a summer. As late as the Company's latter days reports were made bearing striking testimony to the incapacity, on the part of the authors, to appreciate the native music [1]):

"The amusements of the night differ somewhat from those of the day, and consist largely of music and dance: usually, the musicians are a few of their slaves, some of whom play an instrument resembling more than anything an old-fashioned fiddle with three strings, commonly called "farmer's fiddle"; to this pretty instrument they add their large brass cymbals, on which a most irritating and sharp noise is produced, marking

[1]) In our own times, for that matter, we have much the same state of affairs, notwithstanding all the snobbery and affectation of profound interest in the matter, (and not to mention the well-founded admiration, based upon knowledge of the facts, on the part of a very few students). Even in the 2nd part of the 2nd edition of the "Encyclopaedie van Nederlandsch Oost-Indië", dated 1918, one may read, under the heading "Javanen" (p. 219a): Their music is on a fairly low level of development and deserves only partly the name of "tonal art".

only the time, without any change in the tones. Generally speaking one may remark upon this that music in the East is still in its cradle and is practised only upon very simple and monotonous instruments, which makes it most disgusting to European music-lovers; whilst the Easterlings, not being able to follow the quick succession of rhythm and melody in the European works of art, do not find the least pleasure in the same. In addition to all this it is a very remarkable fact that the Easterlings learn and practice only by ear, without using any written notes, which, to most of our musiclovers, appears almost impossible, and which, indeed, would be impossible when playing our own, much more complicated, pieces.

This abominable play on strings is accompanied by dancing....

The entire evening passes with these exercises, and at that time one hears, everywhere in the principal buildings, the sound of the aforementioned cymbals and further Eastern playing instruments." (**20**, vol. I, p. 35/6).

In the same publication (vol. I, p. 47) a remarkable utterance is to be found concerning the presence, at Mataram and elsewhere, of foreign girl dancers (slaves); we will reproduce it *in extenso*, if only for the sake of the mention, *in cauda*, of a kind of castagnettes unknown to me from any other source:

"Besides the usual native girl dancers, one finds here [1]), as in many other places in the East-Indies, yet another kind, maintained by the Princes, and also hired by special persons on the occasion of weddings or other excellent festivities. These females come from Babylon, where the art of dancing has been raised to a pitch of perfection as nowhere else, so that better ones cannot be found anywhere, and for which reason, too, they are extremely expensive, so that the Princes gladly spend two or three thousand guilders in order to acquire such a one, both here and in the countries of Bengal, Persia, etc. These women or girls are all very small of stature and slight of build, but at the same time so well-made and fair of complexion that they need not yield to the most lovable European beauties. In a word, when they dance with-another they resemble a host of angels rather than a crowd of females. Their natural beauties are not a little enhanced by their charming finery, for their clothes, arranged with most agreeable taste, are made from silk and cloths, richly woven through with gold; and their hair-locks, very artfully decorated, are adorned with the most beautiful pearls.

---

[1]) *i.e.* Mataram.

To their dances they often add lovely singing; for they are no less experienced in the art of singing than in the art of dancing, whilst at the same time they carry in their hands a row of small ivory balls strung on a cord, with which they know how to beat the time quite nicely."

With respect to the period of the East India Company we also refer to a few relevant remarks in Chapter I, as well as to pp. 155, 179, 221, 358, 384/385 and 391.

Finally, English authors from the beginning of last century (**68, 69, 303**) have brought to our knowledge a musical life which, in every respect, equals that of the present day—perhaps only in a purer form; indeed, it is probable that Javanese music in those days was at the zenith of its development. This, at any rate, might be concluded from the fact that such an important place was reserved for music in that remarkable and beautiful poem, the Chenṭini, written at that very time, and encyclopaedic in its all-comprehensive description of Javanese life in all its stages and outward detail. Only a period of the greatest devotion and love for music, and in which this art had been raised to the highest level of refinement could have inspired a poet to such masterly stanzas dealing with the gamelan as may be found, for example, in the 44th and the 276th canto of his poem [1]).

---

[1]) For a historical survey of the various written utterances known to us, concerning Indonesian music, we refer to **225**.

CHAPTER 4

CENTRAL AND EAST JAVA [1]

> "Art is here a function of the social order, not an ambition.... The themes of art are provided by general necessities inherent in racial mentality."
> (Dr A. COOMARASWAMY, "Introduction to the art of eastern Asia", p. 38)

> ".... habe ich gelernt, dass die Mehrheit, die Gesamtheit das Heil ist. Sie ist eine tiefere, eine magischere Grösse als das Individuum...."
> (FRANZ WERFEL, "Verdi", p. 390)

> "Un art d'un caractère universel par sa puissance d'évocation de la vie, sous une forme de beauté compréhensible et émouvante pour tous."
> (GABRIELLE FERRAND, "Le théatre et la danse à Java" (79))

a. Introduction

Anyone coming into contact with a form of music hitherto unknown to himself is confronted by considerable difficulties, even though he may be musically receptive and full of goodwill: he has to eliminate his own theoretical conceptions, his own aesthetics and axioms—if he has any—as well as his own conventional ideas— which he is sure to have. He will nevertheless find that he is, at first, inclined to criticize, in the art of the foreign race, that in which this art, which is strange to him, is backward as compared to his own; whereas those elements which in his own art have been more or less neglected, and for which he accordingly has a less sensitive—or, at any rate, a less developed—organ, are not, as a rule, esteemed at their proper value in the foreign art. Thus, many Europeans will reproach Javanese

[1]) In this chapter the abbreviation S. stands for Solo; J. for Jogya; L.J. for Low Javanese (*ngoko*), and H.J. for High Javanese (*krama*). The indication J. or S. does *not* imply that the technical term, or name of composition preceeding it, is limited exclusively to Jogya or Solo, but merely that the author himself has either come across it there, or had it brought to his knowledge through some document or oral communication referring to the district in question.

music with a certain primitiveness of melody and a lack of "development", of climax in its form; but the subtle refinements of rhythm and melodic ornament, as well as the delightful shades of the *kendangan*—drum-playing—will elude him. *Vice versa*, the Javanese deprecates in Western music its arbitrary application of tonalities, not bound to any particular time of the day (**359**, p. 120); the uniform use of drums, and the paucity of the percussion-instruments; but he will not, at first, have an ear for the wonderful spans of melody, the tremendous climaxes, in a word, the actual psychic content of our great orchestral and chamber music works. It is in these latter elements of Western music that one of the most essential differences lies between it and Javanese music. In European music there is action, tension; the great compositions for orchestra are representations, in sound, of a crisis, a conflict, a psychic process in course of development; there is an element of striving and attainment in them. Javanese music, on the other hand, may best be characterised as "time become sound"; it is "aimless" in the better sense of the word; it renders a state or condition; it is not *becoming*, but *being*. If we wished to describe this difference by means of a single adjective, we might say that Javanese music is *static*, and modern-European, *dynamic* (**195**, **214**).

SURYAPUTRA feels this distinction in a different way (**359**, p. 119): "... Eastern music amounts to the expression of one or a few sentiments, whereas Western music usually means a multiplicity of emotions. Eastern music is concentration-music, and is, in essence, contemplative; Western music, barring exceptions, is essentially emotional."

Another difference is that modern Western music is strongly individually-coloured, and that often there is only a relatively small esoteric group to which it has anything to say. Javanese music, however—and this applies to all Indonesian music—constitutes the greatest possible contrast to this, inasmuch as it is still entirely a communal form of art (also the music at the Princes' courts). It is music of, and for, the people in all its social strata. The origin of most compositions is very much like that of Western folk-songs and mediaeval art: is the author perhaps known in some cases, he was still only the creative organ of the masses [1]). In Java, high and low

---

[1]) No doubt many compositions owe their existence to some already existing piece being remembered by ear, or to their being written under the impression of some piece heard and found beautiful, but whose nuclear melody one did not have in one's possession.

listen with the same attention to the same songs and orchestral pieces; one should, for that matter, have assisted at a *wayang wong* performance in the palace of one of the ruling princes, in order to realize completely how both, the Prince and his people, are entirely absorbed in it, equally and collectively; the Prince with his following and his guests on the marble dais of the penḍapa; the people, brown and silent, in a dense crowd all around them (**195**).

The space at my disposal does not allow of my going more deeply into this difference in character and the relation between Eastern and Western music. I must confine myself to referring to what has been written upon the subject elsewhere, in the first place to the expositions by BRANDTS BUYS (**33**), FELBER (**84**) and SŪRYAPUTRA (**349**, **356**, **359**).

With regard to the relation of Javanese music to that of the surrounding civilizations, present-day Javanese music—and the same applies also to Balinese music—does not, in contradistinction to the literary forms of expression and the dance (**254**), and as far as I have been able to trace, show the slightest essential likeness (any more) [1]) to that of India proper, which latter, with its "drone", its raga-system and its preference for plucked string-instruments, reveals quite a different atmosphere altogether. To find the next-of-kin of Javanese music we have to go to Further India, where, more especially, Siamese music shows all sorts of features corresponding to Javanese music (**129**, **132**, pl. 16; **198** *passim*; **240**, p. 109; **325**; **374**). Chinese influences, which no doubt are noticeable here and there in the instrumentarium and in the structure of the orchestral compositions, and which, as we saw in Chapter 2, are also to be held finally responsible for the structure of the Javanese tonal systems, may have had some slight effect on Javanese (and Balinese) music; but on the essence of its melodic structure and its manner of interpretation, in brief, its whole psychic nature this influence has surely been almost neglegible. One might perhaps say that the greatest differences between, for example, Siamese and Javano-Balinese music precisely lie in the fact that the latter, in its profoundest being, hardly, if all, shows any affinity with Chinese music, whereas the former, on the contrary, shows this affinity fairly strongly.

Finally, with regard to the relation between the art of the Javanese courts and that of the people, the gradual transitionary forms between the

---

[1]) Cf. above, p. 112/113.

two and the interaction upon each other we refer to an essay by PIGEAUD **(296)** and to his (unsigned) contribution in the "Indisch Verslag" of 1931 **(142)**. [**29**A, **81**D, **123**B–E, **276**B, **303**A, **342**F, **346**A, **362**M].

b. Vocal music

The ideal which Javanese vocal music strives after is different from that of the Western manner of singing. As all Eastern singing, the Javanese variety, too, is more or less nasal. This gives it, to Western ears, a somewhat instrumental timbre, akin to that of the shawm and the rebab. The European way of singing, in an erect position, with open mouth and facing the audience, seems strange to the men—and still more so, to the women—of Java. To the Westerner, on the other hand, it seems a curious thing to see and hear a woman vocalist singing in sitting position, her head bent or turned aside. At times, decency is still further guarded by partly covering the mouth with a sléndang or a handkerchief (see woman singer, ill. 163). Most Europeans do not like Javanese singing, especially by females; but whoever has taken the trouble to settle down to listen to it with an unprejudiced mind and without allowing himself to be discouraged by an initial lack of appreciation, will find that this vocal music will gradually reveal to him unsuspected beauties.

To the Javanese, singing and poetry are one and the same thing; poems are always recited in song-form.

Purely vocal compositions (*tembang*; High-Javanese: *sekar*) are grouped into three distinct kinds, which also differ as to age. The most sacred are the classical, lyrical-epic *sekar ageng* (L.J.: *tembang gedé*), or "great" songs, which came into being under Hindu influences. Next to these come the *sekar madya* (L. J. *tembang tengahan*), "middle"-songs, and, finally, there are the simplest songs, the *tembang machapat*, which, according to earlier views, are the youngest of the three, but which, according to modern opinion, are, on the contrary, the most ancient, being of pre-Hindu origin.

The strophes which are sung comply with strict rules of poetic construction. [**157**A, **302**A]

The ancient Javanese forms of *sekar ageng* are completely identical with different metres in India proper [1]) and obey, therefore, certain definite

[1]) *Vide*, in regard to these Hindu metra, *e.g.*, H. T. COLEBROOKE, "Miscellaneous Essays", vol. II, p. 62, *et seq.*

instructions regarding the number of lines in a stanza and syllables in a line, the quantity of syllables, and the caesura [1]).

The same applies to the modern-Javanese sekar ageng (**336**, **351**), with the exception that each strophe numbers only *four* lines ,whose *lampah* (*i.e.* their length expressed in numbers of syllables) [2]) has to be the same for each and that the quantity-principle is no longer applied to the syllables themselves. But all four lines must be split up into parts (*peḍotan*) by one or more caesurae. It is usual to indicate these details when mentioning a sekar ageng, *e.g.* sekar ageng *Bongsa patra*, lampah 17, peḍotan 4, 6, 7; sekar ageng *Wohingrat*, lampah 24, peḍotan 6, 6, 6, 6; sekar *Maduretna*, lampah 12, peḍotan 5, 7. According to PADMASUSASTRA, 44 different sekar ageng metres may be distinguished in Solo. They are enumerated in **291**, p. 249 *et seq*. The Chenṭini (**381**, Vol. III p. 13) also gives, in Canto 48, an extensive survey of the sekar ageng metres. *Vide* also **380**, p. 243. [**302**N, **377**K]

Such a sekar ageng, discretely supported by gendèr-tones, frequently serves as a vocal introduction (*bawa*) to a genḍing [3]). An example of this is given in our Appendix *3* (genḍing *Génjong guling*, with the bawa *Chondra wilasita*). Less frequently, sekar madya and tembang machapat are also employed by way of bawa. [*S40,44]

In contrast to the (modern Javanese) sekar ageng, the lines of the *sekar madya* (*tembang tengahan*) and those of the *tembang machapat* are of varying number and moreover, often of unequal length. For the rest, the number of lines in a single strophe, and the number of syllables in each line, but in addition also the vowels of the final syllables, are laid down in definite rules, for the different kinds of poems belonging to these two groups. PADMASUSASTRA distinguishes, in Solo, 11 different forms of the tengahan metra (**291**, p. 251). The Chenṭini gives a survey of the tengahan metra in the above-mentioned 48th Canto, strophes 180 *et seq*.

There is no general agreement as to the position of the borderline between the tengahan- and the machapat-metres.

---

1) What this ancient Javanese sekar ageng chants must have sounded like is impossible to say; perhaps one may imagine their character to be something between the modern Indian and the Balinese style of rendering.—According to Dr. PURBACHARAKA, the modern rendering of sekar ageng is far too much under the influence of the gamelan to allow of any conclusions being drawn as to the manner of interpretation of the ancient sekar ageng.

2) *Lampah* literally means: walk, gait, the space covered in walking; further also: course of affairs (as, for example, in the expression *sinḍènan lampah genḍing*—cf. below, p. 303).

3) *Vide* also below, p. 311.

We give below the structure-formulae of the machapat metra that came to our knowledge. The figures indicate the number of syllables, in each line; the vowel below each figure refers to the final sound prescribed for the line in question. These two indications are distinguished under the names of *guru wilangan, guru pètungan* or *guru wichalan*, and *ḍongḍing* or *guru lagu*.

1. *Ḍangḍang gula*: $\frac{10}{\text{i}}\ \frac{10}{\text{a}}\ \frac{8}{\text{é(o)}}\ \frac{7}{\text{u}}\ \frac{9}{\text{i}}\ \frac{7}{\text{a}}\ \frac{6}{\text{u}}\ \frac{8}{\text{a}}\ \frac{12}{\text{i}}\ \frac{7}{\text{a}}$

2 *Sinom*: $\frac{8}{\text{a}}\ \frac{8}{\text{i}}\ \frac{8}{\text{a}}\ \frac{8}{\text{i}}\ \frac{7}{\text{i}}\ \frac{8}{\text{u}}\ \frac{7}{\text{a}}\ \frac{8}{\text{i}}\ \frac{12}{\text{a}}$ (cf. the strophe on p. 277).

3. *Asmarandana*: $\frac{8}{\text{i}}\ \frac{8}{\text{a}}\ \frac{8}{\text{o(é)}}\ \frac{8}{\text{a}}\ \frac{7}{\text{a}}\ \frac{8}{\text{u}}\ \frac{8}{\text{a}}$

4. *Kinanṭi* [1]): $\frac{8}{\text{u}}\ \frac{8}{\text{i}}\ \frac{8}{\text{a}}\ \frac{8}{\text{i}}\ \frac{8}{\text{a}}\ \frac{8}{\text{i}}$ (cf. the strophes on p. 224 *et seq*. and App. *44*).

5. *Pangkur* [2]): $\frac{8}{\text{a}}\ \frac{11}{\text{i}}\ \frac{8}{\text{u}}\ \frac{7}{\text{a}}\ \frac{12}{\text{u}}\ \frac{8}{\text{a}}\ \frac{8}{\text{i}}$

6. *Durma* [3]): $\frac{12}{\text{a}}\ \frac{7}{\text{i}}\ \frac{6}{\text{a}}\ \frac{7}{\text{a}}\ \frac{8}{\text{i}}\ \frac{5}{\text{a}}\ \frac{7}{\text{i}}$

7. *Mijil*: [4]) $\frac{10}{\text{i}}\ \frac{6}{\text{o}}\ \frac{10}{\text{é}}\ \frac{10}{\text{i}}\ \frac{6}{\text{i}}\ \frac{6}{\text{u}}$

8. *Mas kumambang*: $\frac{12}{\text{i}}\ \frac{6}{\text{a}}\ \frac{8}{\text{i}}\ \frac{8}{\text{a}}$

9. *Puchung*: $\frac{12}{\text{u}}\ \frac{6}{\text{a}}\ \frac{8}{\text{i}}\ \frac{12}{\text{a}}$ (cf. the strophes on pp. 177, 211, 223 and 275/276).

For some reason unknown to me, the metra

---

[1]) Cf. Od. 1936b (*Kinanṭi madumurti*); Col. G.J. 130 (*Kinanṭi sandung*). [**87A**]

[2]) Cf. Col. G.J.X. 22 (*Pangkur*). [*S[39, 40, 54, 55]]

[3]) **In *Durma*, for example, the text is sung of the *langendriyan*** (Singspiel, opera) *Ménakjingga léna* (Col. G.J. 60 *et seq*.).

[4]) Cf. Od. 39562a (with *keṭoprak* accompaniment).

Megatruh (= *Duduk wuluh*) [1]: $\frac{12}{u}\ \frac{8}{i}\ \frac{8}{u}\ \frac{8}{i}\ \frac{8}{o}$

and *Gambuh* [2]: $\frac{7}{u}\ \frac{10}{u}\ \frac{12}{i}\ \frac{8}{u}\ \frac{8}{o}$,

included in the first edition of this work among the machapat-metres, are nowadays usually (**4A**) being classed among the tengahan-group, together with

Juru demung: $\frac{8}{a}\ \frac{8}{u}\ \frac{8}{u}\ \frac{8}{a}\ \frac{8}{u}\ \frac{8}{a}\ \frac{8}{u}$

Wirangrong: $\frac{8}{i}\ \frac{8}{o}\ \frac{10}{u}\ \frac{6}{i}\ \frac{7}{a}\ \frac{8}{a}$

Balabak: $\frac{12}{a}\ \frac{3}{\acute{e}}\ \frac{12}{a}\ \frac{3}{\acute{e}}\ \frac{12}{a}\ \frac{3}{\acute{e}}$

and some others [3].

Each of these poetic forms belongs to one particular mood. Thus, (parts of) love-poems are sung on *Kinanṭi*, *Asmarandana* or *Mijil*; *Sinom* has a didactical character; *Pangkur* and *Durma* may be heard where violent passions or fighting are the subject of the song; in *Mas kumambang* expression is given to feelings of longing or homesickness. The *Puchung* metre has a more neutral character, and is often used, among other things, for posing riddles in song-form. Neither does *Ḍangḍang gula* have a pronounced ethos; since the *pujangga* ("master of letters", "chroniqueur") Yasadipura I (the grandfather of the pujangga Rangga Warsita), this metre is used for preference by way of introductory song to a poem.

For further detail concerning the different metra, *vide* Nos. **4A**, **75**, **106**, **324** [**105AB**, **157A**, **302A**, **302G**, **302N–D**, **324A**, **377K**, **402D**] and **381** (Vol. III/IV, p. 13, str. 135 *et seq.*) of the bibliography.

[1]) Cf. the strophes on p. 36, and the record Col. G. J. 57.

[2]) The Chenṭini distinguishes no less than 7 variants of the Gambuh-metre. The structure as given above is that which is customary in the Chenṭini itself (cf., *e.g.* the Canto's 51, 60, 72, and 79).

[3]) For an extensive list of Javanese and Balinese *machapat-* and *tengahan-* metres, vide also **192**, Table XVI.—In Java, however, many of them are no longer in use. As a matter of fact, in modern poetry one meets only the metres mentioned above.

No two Javanese vocalists sing their songs in exactly the same way. The nucleus is definitely fixed and is always recognisable in every performance; the ornamentation, however, is added by every singer according his or her own personal taste. The different interpretations—although bound down by tradition—may nevertheless vary considerably: but they are often more or less in the same style within the limits of a given region. Thus, to the initiated, the difference between the Solonese and the Jogya styles seems to be unmistakably noticeable in vocal music, as in so many other forms of art [1]).

Differences in tempo, too, influence the form of a melody when sung (although it naturally adheres strictly to the essential tones, in whatever way the song may be performed) to such an extent that the non-initiated often imagine that they are listening to quite a different melody when it is sung in another tempo: for the manner of ornamentation alters considerably with any change in tempo. To give an example: the vocal introduction (*bawa*) to the genḍing *Kinanṭi madumurti*, as rendered on the Odeon record No. A 39603b, is essentially the same as the melody appearing further on in the actual genḍing, but only those who are thoroughly familiar with this song will be able to appreciate this. [**87**A]

When the singing forms part of a gamelan composition the voice has not the same freedom of movement, for then it has generally to take into account the structure of the genḍing, which, being the result of the playing together of several persons, rather than the performance of a single artist, is naturally bound to certain fixed rules. (*Vide* also, with regard to this point, **44**, p. 57/8). In those cases where a choir sings (always in unison) (*gérongan*), whether or no with instrumental accompaniment, the singers' fancy is, of course, still more firmly restricted. The melody is then rendered practically without any ornaments. A good example of this is given in our Appendix *3D* [2]).

[1]) A peculiar and rare form of machapat singing should be mentioned here, if only briefly: this is called *tembang penḍapa* or *tembang pringgitan*. Every evening in the Solonese kraton, an official, belonging to the prajurit corps of the *Tamtama*, places himself at the foot of, and with his back to, the large central penḍapa, turns his face in the direction of the large door behind which, in olden times, the Susuhunans were wont to sleep, and proceeds to sing, all night long, various machapat songs. The style of rendering in this performance, however, is such that only a perfectly trained ear is able to discern that it is indeed machapat melodies that are being sung, the execution being extremely surcharged with variations and fioriturі prescribed by tradition.

[2]) Reproduced from Col. G.J. 175 (*Ayak-ayakan kaloran* (P. manyura)).

This *gérongan*, performed by two or three, or sometimes more, persons, has been, since time immemorial, male choir singing [1]). To-day, however, gérong for women is also known in Jogya, *i.e.* when, in the *wayang wong*, a man has to sing a part for solo voice. This, according to R. M. JAYADIPURA, is for the sake of the effect of contrast.

The singing intoned by men and women together, as accompaniment to the *beḍaya-* and *serimpi*-dances (*), however, is not called gérongan, but *sinḍèn*, the male and female singers forming the choir being called *pasinḍèn*.

The solo voice (also called *sinḍèn*), whilst collaborating with the gamelan, has nevertheless still kept a large measure of independence, although, usually, it takes into account the *ḍongḍing genḍing* [2]), or musical joints of the melody [3]).

Four kinds of *sinḍènan* may be distinguished in the Jogya kraton, namely:

a. *Sinḍènan lampah genḍing*, in which the singing takes care to remain in harmony with the nuclear melody and the parts playing around it, and follows the general course of the genḍing. In this type, the orchestra starts by itself, the voices join in later, and, owing to the fact that they adapt themselves to the genḍing, and that their phrases are usually shorter than those of the latter, the singing has more or less intermittent character. The tempo is generally *wirama lomba*, (see p. 335 hereafter). For this kind of

---

[1]) Some excellent examples of gérongan are given in the Columbia records G.J.X. 1 (genḍing *Langengita*); G.J.X. 2 (G. *Walagita*); G.J.X. 5 (G. *Tarupala*); G.J.X. 6 (G. *Puspawarna*), and G. J. 57 (G. *Megatruh*). [**6**A, **105**C-D, **113**C, **291**E, **302**G, **302**K, **302**N, **344**A, **377**K] [S39]

[2]) Dr. PURBACHARAKA would rather call this ḍongḍing genḍing: *singgetan* (litt: partition, insertion), in order to reserve the term ḍongḍing exclusively for poetry (cf. above, p. 124). *Singgetan*, however, already has quite another musico-technical signification: this term stands for a musical fragment, usually of the size of either a whole or half a kenongan, played in the place of the music actually belonging to the genḍing being played. In Jogya, they usually speak, not of singgetan, but of *santun wilet* (= change of wilet); in Solo, of *santun chèngkok* (as a matter of fact, *wilet* is, in Solo, a vocal, not an instrumental term). These fragmental changes usually take place, in genḍings with 4 kenongan to the gongan, after the third kenong beat— *i.e.*, for example, in the part called *pangkat*, or, maybe, in the *nḍauah* (vide Appendix 5, continuation, 4th column); in genḍings with 2 kenongan in the gongan, halfway down the second kenongan, *i.e.* in both cases when 3/4 of the gongan has been got through. In a restricted sense, the term *santun wilet* there stands for a very special change of wilet, i.e. for the transition, by means of a modified nuclear theme, to the second part of the genḍing. Since, then, the term *singgetan* is already in use to indicate a definite musico-technical notion, it is, to my mind, advisable to continue to denote the whole of the colotomic beats exclusively by the term *ḍongḍing genḍing*. Any confusion with the literary conception of the word is, moreover, practically out of the question, the more so when the word genḍing is added.

[3]) *Vide*, however, below, p. 132 and 222, under *ganḍul*.

(*) [S39]

accompanied singing the *Kinanṭi*-metre is very often used, on account of its regular structure. Examples: *Surung ḍayung* (Od. A 39595a); *Pohak bem* (Od. A 39531b), and our Appendix *3* (*Génjong guling*); in the latter the *Kinanṭi*-metre is followed.

b. *Sinḍènan lampah sekar genḍing*, in which the singing is accompanied by the complete gamelan, whilst the balungan-tones follow the melody sung. In this, the singing and the accompaniment start together; the vocal part is much more of a continuous whole than in the case of the sekar lampah genḍing. The characteristic tempo is *wirama rangkep* (App. *44*). Therefore, in this case also the saron-part forms the accompaniment to the vocal music. A good example of this is provided by Col. GJ 157 (*Ilir-ilir gunanṭi*), as well as by many other children's songs, as recorded some years ago by the Columbia Coy. in the Mangku Nagaran (*). Also: *Pangkur* (*e.g.* Ultraphone A 61013)(**), and *Kinanṭi madumurti* (Od. A 39603b, or Musik des Orients, O 1936b).

c. *Sinḍénan lampah sekar*. In this, the singing is accompanied only by the colotomic instruments (*i.e.* keṭuk, kenong, and gong); a purely rhythm-instrument (kemanak); a few paraphrasing instruments (gambang, gendèr), and an agogic instrument (the ketipung). The cantus firmus instruments, however, (sarons etc.) remain silent [1]). This is the customary form of the music accompanying the beḍaya- and serimpi-dances.

d. *Sinḍènan lampah lagon*. Here, the vocal music is accompanied only by the rebab, the gambang, the gendèr, and occasionally, the suling. It is the usual manner of interpreting the *paṭetan* or *lagon* [2]).

There is further a fifth, apparently independent kind, *i.e.* the *sinḍènan lampah jineman*.

Jineman is the term by which is indicated the soft music [3]), either instrumental or vocal or both, by means of which two genḍings are, as it were, connected with each other. Concerning the vocal music which forms part of it, the Introduction to the large Jogya kraton-collection states that it actually is *lampah genḍing*, but that it is performed as if it were *lampah sekar*; on the understanding, however, that both the rebab and the kempul

---

[1]) As example we may mention the genḍing P. barang *Anglir menḍung* (Col. D 33001). [**3**A, **113**C, **377**L]

[2]) In regard to these concepts, *vide* below, p 319 *et seq.*

[3]) In JANZS' dictionary, the term *jinem* is rendered by: quiet, modest, demure, sedate, "the silence that is golden". For *jineman* it gives only the other, non-musical signification, *i.e.* gaoler, police officer, leader of a thieves' gang.

(*) [S39]

(**) [S40, 54–5]

are also played with it. The idea is that it should give the impression of being lampah sekar, since the balungan-instruments do not join in the playing. The rebab, however, is mostly the instrument that carries the principal melody; in other words, the genḍing—*i.e.* the instrumental parts—give the lead; the voices see to it that they adapt themselves to their lead; the singing does not join in at once when the instruments start, but only there, where it can do so with the most harmonious effect. It is, therefore, definitely a form of lampah genḍing.

The first words of the text of this *jineman*, as used invariably at Jogya, are "*uler kambang*" (litt. "the floating caterpillar") [1]. Accordingly the whole of the interlude is sometimes called by that name; similarly, another jineman (*Jineman Kawispita* = *Glaṭik glinding*) [2] is called by the name of *Chérémèndé* [3].

Certain vocal melodies may be sung together with some genḍing or other, as, for example, *Kinanṭi sanḍung* (Od. A 278001b). With regards to this we also refer to pp. 317 and 318, where mention is made of *Puchung*, accompanied by *Ayak-ayakan*, and of *Pangkur*, accompanied by *Sampak*.

With the exception of the suling none of the instruments within the gamelan-ensemble has so much freedom as the human voice. If we may use the terms "counterpoint" and "polyphony" at all, in connexion with gamelan-music, then it should be the vocal parts and the suling, as well as—if in a lesser degree—the rebab, and—in rare cases—the gambang, which should justify us in doing so. The polyphonous effects produced, more or less accidentally, by the other instruments in the ornamentation of the nuclear theme, have been termed (for the first time by STUMPF) "heterophony". This distinction, however, does not apply in all cases with equal strictness; for in the parts played by the gendèrs and bonangs, too, polyphonous passages occur from time to time.

Many genḍings possess both a gérongan- and a sinḍèn-part, whose respective melodic lines may sometimes be woven into each other and with the orchestral parts. In this case the female soloist never starts together with

---

1) We have here to do with a *wangsalan* (*vide* below, p. 320); the words stand for *lintah* (= leech). — Solonese versions: Beka 27883; Col. G.J. 161 ("*Jineman*").

2) Recorded in the Solonese version by Columbia (G.J. 161), and in the Jogya version by Odeon (A 39630a) and Col. G.J. 233. [*S41]

3) The jinemans in question are said to have been composed by R. M. TANDAKUSUMA (cf. above, p. 88 and 93, and below, p. 258).

the choir, but always intones her phrases either before or afterwards [1]). Sometimes her initial phrases are the same as those of the choir, so that the listener hears a kind of antiphony, more or less overlapping, between the solo voice and the choir, and may occasionally pick up some fine bits of canonic imitations.

Apart from timbre and pitch, *sinḍén* and *gérongan*, when singing together, are also to be distinguished rhythmically. The choir, closely adhering to the gamelan accompaniment, sings, most unanimously, strictly in time, the sinḍèn floats above it, apparently quite detached from the dark and severe regularity of the gérongan melody, overlapping the main beats by syncopation, often using triplets of various values and with an almost total lack of accentuation, an un-material, ethereal *cantilène*.

The opening of the *Gandrung manis* (paṭet barang) may serve as a—for that matter, quite simple—example of the mutual relation between gérongan and sinḍèn [2]):

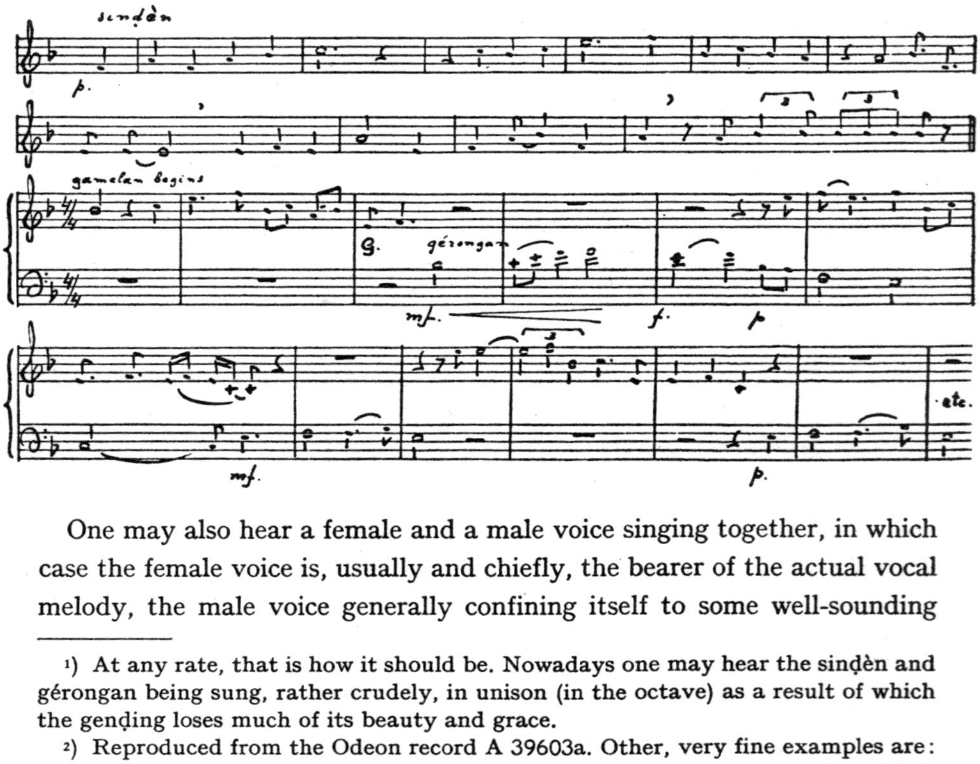

One may also hear a female and a male voice singing together, in which case the female voice is, usually and chiefly, the bearer of the actual vocal melody, the male voice generally confining itself to some well-sounding

[1]) At any rate, that is how it should be. Nowadays one may hear the sinḍèn and gérongan being sung, rather crudely, in unison (in the octave) as a result of which the genḍing loses much of its beauty and grace.

[2]) Reproduced from the Odeon record A 39603a. Other, very fine examples are: Od. A 39561a and Col. G.J.X. 6 (the ketawang *Puspawarna*, P. manyura) and Col. D 33001 (the ladrang *Srikaton*, P. barang). [*S[39, 51, 55]]

interjections and brief melodic phrases. To this type of singing belongs also the so-called *sengg(r)akan*, which will be dealt with a little further on. An example of this is recorded on a record which I bought some years ago in the toko Yo Kim Chan at Solo; the tune is the genḍing *Bambang manah*.

That great enchantment goes out from the semi-polyphonous, semi-heterophonous tissue of sound of a good gamelan, also to European ears, is clear from the unsollicited testimony given by the guitar-virtuoso ANDRÈS SEGOVIA, who made a tour on Java in July, 1933. When this musician was a little boy he used to hear the priest depict the glories of Heaven, in which the chants of the blessed souls were an important element, and the way he used to imagine it was, that each of the souls would sing as his heart moved him, and without giving heed to the song of the other souls. But, since in Heaven everything is perfect, all these separate voices, without wanting to, as it were, joined together into one wonderful and glorious hymn. Now that was the very thing that SEGOVIA was reminded of on hearing for the first time the Paku Alam gamelan, with sinḍèn and gérongan: to his hearing, none of the parties seemed to trouble about the other voices, and yet everything flowed together in the highest form of harmonic unity, into one fascinating whole; truly, "le ciel sur la terre".

What, too, is beautiful sometimes is the sudden silence of the gamelan, immediately followed by the solo voice of the singer, accompanied only by a discreet gendèr, the singer, in his turn, being succeeded again—*attacca*—by the gamelan. It may also happen that the gamelan is silent after the third kenong-beat, allowing the voice to finish the genḍing by itself. [*S6]

Besides gérongan and sinḍèn there exist a number of other vocal forms of expression in collaboration with the gamelan. In the first place the *sengg(r)-akan*.

By this term—derived from *sengg(r)ak* (= to incite, to fire the enthusiasm) —are meant those peculiar stimulating shouts which, intoned softly at first, rapidly get louder and louder as well as—often in a glissando—higher in pitch; when they have arrived at their dynamic and tonic climax, they suddenly halt, and, after a "pause in the air", subside just as gradually, going down both in pitch and in strength. The term also applies to musical exclamations, sung to a few meaningless syllables as text, such as *hik-hik-ha*, *halok-halok-hé*, *hik-o-lo-lo-lo-lo*, *duwa-lolo*, *lo-lo-hing*, *a-u-wa*, and suchlike [1]).

---

[1]) Examples: Ultraphone 61013 (genḍing *Pangkur Palaran*) and Col. G.J.X. 6 (*Puspawarna*). [*S39, 72]

This *sengg(r)akan* is somethimes distinguished into (i) *senggrakan* in a restricted sense, in which the singer takes care to remain in unison with the gamelan or with the vocal melody, and also to adhere strictly to their rhythm; (ii) *chenguk* (S.)—a single exclamation, frequently accompanied by handclapping and emitted immediately after a kenong-beat (especially in the baḍaya- and serimpi-music) and (iii) *salahan* (S.) or *nyalai* (J.), an exclamation going counter to the instrumental rhythm or the pitch, sung on some syllables such as we just mentioned [1]).

This latter term *salahan* or *nyalai*, whose actual signification is "wrong, unusual, going counter-to", is also used, as a matter of fact, for the peculiar against-the-grain rhythm of the *keprak*; further, the particular kind of *suling*-playing within the scope of gamelan-music is indicated by it: this, too, often removes itself, both rhythmically and as to pitch, from the music of the instruments playing or praphrasing the nuclear theme.

Again the same word serves as the name of one of the colotomic *kenḍang chiblon* figures (cf. below, p. 213). and, fifthly, it is the term used for those peculiar rhythmic "condensations" which may be heard in certain cases in the *beḍug-*, *ketipung-* and *keṭuk*-parts (cf. p. 215, 260 and 263).

The term *ganḍul* (litt. hanging, dragging) means a break in the gamelan-quadrature by the *sinḍèn*, which, in that case, does not seem to trouble about the *ḍongḍing*-tones, more especially the gong- and kenong-beats, but allows its phrases now and then to overlap them, and affecting, as it were, to reach the end of a given melodic period too late [2]).

There is also the term *uran-uran* [3]), which has the general signification of "song", or "singing", without any specification as to the particular kind of singing that is meant.

Finally, mention should be made of that suddenly-broken-off crescendo-bawl of the ḍalang or dance-leader, with which he warns the nyaga's (invariably at Jogya, but very seldom, and, if at all, less conspicuously at Solo) to soften their playing and that is called *kajantur* [4]) (S.) or *rep* (*sirep*)

---

[1]) About these and similar exclamations during gamelan playing, *vide* also **33**, p. 18 *et seq.*

[2]) According to connoisseurs, it is desirable, in *klenéngan*, for the gong-beat not to synchronize exactly with the last kenong-beat, but to come either very slightly behind or before. This is also called *ganḍul.*

[3]) The verb is *ura-ura.*

[4]) The word *jantur* is also used to denote, amongst other things, the trick of letting a grasshopper dangle by one of its *palpi* so as to infuriate it, and make it

(S. and J.). When this happens, the sarons and bonangs usually stop playing [1]), to allow the dialogue of the dancers, or the voice of the ḍalang, as the cases may be, to become audible [2]). In Solo, this vocal warning is usually replaced by a signal on the *koṭak* or the *keprak* with the following rhythm: 

When the dialogue of the dancers, or the recital of the ḍalang, comes to an end, the dance-leader or the ḍalang notifies the fact by means of *ngombang* or *ngumbang, i.e.* a brief spell of vocalising [3]), which anticipates the tones of the genḍing that is being played at that moment, whilst at the same time the genḍing usually goes on to its second movement (*munggah, linggih, nḍawah*) and continues again at its normal strength of sound (*mari dijantur*) (S.) (**380**, p. 194).

In modern Javanese writings it is usual to denote orchestra playing including a vocal part by the term *genḍing-genḍèng*. [**302**G, N, **377**K]

For the sake of completeness we should also, be it briefly, make mention of the vocal music for and by children (*dolanan laré*), about which nothing, or next to nothing has been published up to now.

It is not at all unlikely that future investigations might show Javanese children's play-songs (like the Sundanese, *vide* Appendix *51* D) to make use of intervals and tone-sequences that can be traced back to the extremely ancient, primitive *miring*- and *ringkung*-scales discussed above; at any rate that they should not, without further consideration, be incorporated with modern sléndro or pélog (**295**). (Cf. also p. 406). It is not possible, on the basis of the few collections published up to the present (**149, 175, 181**)[4]),

---

fight well afterwards. The melody sung is felt to be "dangling" too, *i.e.* when the safe supports of the *balunganing genḍing* are lacking (S.). The Rijksbestuurder (Prime Minister) of Jogya wanted to place the greater emphasis on the dependance of that which is "hanging"—in this case the orchestral accompaniment— upon that from which it is suspended, *i.e.* the ḍalang's singing.—It is said that the chant of the ḍalang at the first appearance of Semar, in the wayang, is more especially indicated for preference by this term (*janturan Semar*) (Regent of Magelang). In JANSZ' dictionary, the signification of *janturan* is given as "The ḍalang's own words of historical elucidation, accompanied by soft music".

[1]) According to **380**, p. 194, also the gambang, slenṭem and gendèr panerus.

[2]) Example: Od. A 39562b (*Gangsaran nḍawah kagok Liwung*). [*S^{39}-a1]

[3]) Literally: humming, like the *kombang* (*kumbang*), a species of bee (*Xylocopa latipes*).

[4]) [**264**B, **302**G,R, **342**A,C, **377**K Vol. II]

to come to any definite decision with respect to this. The majority of these notations appears to be in sléndro ("corrected" as regards No. **149**), whilst in addition there are also a very few pélog-like little melodies (*vide*, in regard to these, more especially **30**, p. 512). A few Javanese children's songs reproduced by K. H. DÉWANTARA (**75**) are all in sléndro; those collected by R. D. DARMAÄTMAJA and M. SURATMAN SASTRADIHARJA (**72**) are mainly in sléndro, the rest being in pélog. The majority of those recorded by the Columbia Grammophone Coy. in the Mangku Nagaran, Solo (f.i. the records Nos. GJ 59, 156, 157, 158 and 160) are in sléndro (*vide* Appendix *51* sub C), only one or two being in pélog. Of three children's songs, given by Mrs. VOLKERS-SCHIPPERS (**388A**) two are in sléndro and one in pélog. Even in East-Java the children sing more often in sléndro than in pélog, as is evident from an investigation instituted, by order of the then Governor of East-Java, Mr. Ch. O. VAN DER PLAS, by the Taman Siswa teacher SASTRASUKACHA, into the children's vocal music in that province (*vide* **73**). In any case all children's vocal music in the districts visited (Trawas, near Majasari; Bulumedura, near Tuban; Kedungwaru, near Jatiroto) appeared to be sléndro *). Again, Dr. KARL HALUSA, who, in 1939, made a study tour through East-Java, Madura and the Kangean-archipelago, chiefly for the purpose of collecting children's songs [1]), did not find any in pélog, although he frequently worked in remote parts; they were always in sléndro. And before this—in 1927—J. S. BRANDTS BUYS had the same experience [2]). It is evident, or at least possible, that pélog children's songs are to-day limited exclusively to the mountain districts [3]).

Closely akin to the children's songs are the *dongèng*-songs; they are very ancient ditties, usually containing only a few tones, and intoned every now and then during *dongèng* (*i.e.* the telling of fairy-tales). The best known Solonese dongèng-melodies are reproduced in Appendix *51* sub A and B. According to Radèn KODRAT, the first one of these (which occurs in a story that strongly reminds one of "Hop o' me thumb"), is neither sléndro nor pélog—although perhaps tending towards the latter— the second being pure sléndro.

When speaking of children's songs, one involuntarily thinks also of the

*) [*S7]

[1]) Cf. his letter to the author, dated Dec. 7, 1939, No. 1158/S (Royal Inst. for the Indies No. 2960/39).

[2]) **43**, p. 228 *et seq.*, in which notations of several melodies may also be found.

[3]) *Vide* above, p. 22. [**340G**, **264B**]

various collections of school-songs published during the last few decades; but these, of course, have nothing whatever to do with real children's vocal music, consisting, as they do, of texts that are kept by the authors more or less in accordance with the children's mentality, and set either to existing native "grown-up" song-melodies (*e.g.* **170**, **173**, **402**), or—at least partly—to brand-new simple little melodies, composed in a child-like style (*e.g.* **161**). [**377**E]

* * *

c. *Instruments*

Many different orchestral combinations are known in Java, as well as a large number of instruments which are also—and, in some cases, exclusively—used as solo-instruments. The gamelan proper is nothing but the most highly-developed orchestral form; the other, smaller combinations are usually, at the same time, more primitive. Some of the instruments used separately approach (and, according to some writers, exceed) the limit of the concept "musical instrument". Personally, I would, however, extend this conception and define it as *an object manufactured—or, at any rate, intended—for the purpose of producing sound*. This definition excludes all objects which, although producing sound, and even in some cases rhythm, have not been constructed with that end in view (*e.g.* a squeaking wheelbarrow or a piledriving block), while it covers such primitive noise-instruments as a beaten hollow tree-trunk, rattles made of dried fruits, etc.

A description of the principal Javanese instruments will now be given. In all cases where a given instrument forms part of an orchestra this will be stated in the description, together with its function within the combination.

The different forms have been arranged into the four main instrumental groups usually distinguished in musicological science since MAHILLON [1]), SACHS and VON HORNBOSTEL [2]), namely into:

I. *idiophones*: *i.e.* "self-sounders": instruments whose body-material itself produces the sound without being kept taut in any way;

[1]) V. C. MAHILLON, Catalogue descriptif et analytique du Museé Instrumental du Conservatoire Royal de Musique de Bruxelles, I. II, III (1893–1900, 2nd ed. 1900–1909), IV (1909–1910), V (1922).

[2]) E. M. VON HORNBOSTEL and CURT SACHS, Systematik der Musikinstrumente ("Zeitschrift für Ethnologie" 1914, p. 553 *et seq.*).

II. *membranophones*: *i.e.* all kinds of drums, etc.;
III. *chordophones*: *i.e.* stringed instruments (both plucking- and bowing-, as well as "Aeolus"-instruments), and
IV. *aerophones*: *i.e.* instruments, whose body-material itself does not sound, but where in some way or other the air (usually the aircolumn contained within their walls) is made to sound (all blowing-instruments, but also others, such as the bullroarer). [*S8]

I. Idiophones.

Proper gongs, by which is meant vertically-placed soundbowls, usually hung up on a stand (*gayor*), with an edge which is narrow in proportion to the diameter of the instrument, are known in Java in various dimensions. The largest of all is the **gong ageng** (H.J.)or **gong geḍé** (L.J.) (ill. **64,69, 111, 112** and **163**). Its diameter may be up to one metre, but does not as a rule exceed 60 to 70 cm. Its weight amounts in most cases from 30 to 50 *katti*, *i.e.* between 19 and 31 kg. There are, however, a few gongs in existence of 100, nay, even of 130 *katti*, or, expressed in our own weight, 62½ to 80 kg. A nyaga of the old school expresses the weight of a gong in "reales" (*réyal*), of which there are 20 to one *katti*.

Like many other metal mušical instruments in Java, gongs are usually from *gangsa* or *prunggu*, which is an alloy of 10 parts copper (*tembaga*) to 3 parts tin (*rejasa*), *i.e.* a kind of bronze [1]).

Nowadays the majority of large bronze gongs are made at Semarang [2]), both as regards Java, as the Outer Provinces; it is —or might be—quite possible to manufacture them also in other parts of Java, especially in Solo [3]), Magetan [4]), Blora [5]), Keḍiri [6]), Cheribon [7]), Sukabumi [8]), and Bui-

[1]) On the subject of Javanese copper alloys, we may refer especially to J. G. HUYSER (**139**).

[2]) *i.e.* by SARASA and by PAH ALIYAH, both in the kampong Genḍingan (= Gamelan-kampong), whereas PAH LADINAH is nowadays only a dealer in gamelan-instruments. [*S34]

[3]) In the Susuhunan's territory, by Mas Ngabéhi GUNAPRADONGGA, in the kampong Sangkraknyayan, désa Jajéngan, sub-district Seréngan, and KARTAPANDAYA in the kampong Jatiteken, désa Laban, sub-district Bekonang (the latter not making any gongs ageng), and in the Mangku Nagaran territory by ATMAWIGUNA, in the kampong Genḍingan. [*S31] [**113B**]

[4]) By SASTRADIHARJA and by SASTRADIHARJA alias SIPIN, both in the désa Ka'uman, district of Maospati.

[5]) Kota Blora: DASIYA, kampong Kedungjenar; JAJASARMAN, PADISANA and

tenzorg [1]), but in these districts the demand is mainly for smaller instrumental forms, which we shall discuss further on: the gong suwukan, kempul, kenong, bonang, keṭuk, saron, gendèr and suchlike. In Jogya [2]), Pachitan [3]) and Krawang [4]), as a matter of fact, only the smaller forms are fabricated.

The ancient centre for the forging of gongs, Gresik (in RAFFLES' time still the most important; *vide* **303**, p. 471) has, therefore, completely disappeared as such.

In some places in the Archipelago outside Java metal keys and beating-kettles are also manufactured; the only place in the Outer Provinces, however—as far as I am aware—where large bronze gongs are being cast and/or forged, are the Karo-districts in North-Sumatra, where, in the kampong Kuta tengah (in the sub-district of Lingga) excellent specimens are being manufactured. These Karo-Batak gongs may be distinguished at first sight from the Semarang ones; they are of a somewhat lighter structure and of less sensitive profile, if I may judge from the only specimen that has come to my notice (at Kabanjahé) [5]). It had a beautiful, dark-sonorous sound.

Just as was the case in mediaeval Europe, the Javanese smiths are not mere craftsmen like the others; an atmosphere of mystery surrounds their labours—more especially those of the gamelan smiths—and their activities can flourish only under the special patronage of the higher powers. More than all other mortals they are exposed, during their work, to the cunning artifices of evil spirits.

In order to ward off any disasters the gamelan smiths, therefore, adopt

---

MARTASAIMIN in the kampong Bangkle; MARJANI, kampong Jetis, in the district of Chepu, sub-district Panolan; SARDAN, désa Ledok; KARSA, désa Kendilan, and KIMPUL, désa Pojokwatu.

[6]) By MARTASENTANA, désa Tugureja, and PARAN, désa Sambiresik, both in the district of Keḍiri.

[7]) By AMA, désa Pagongan (= Gong-désa), and TALKA, désa Kedungdawa, both in the district of Cheribon, and by WINDRIK, désa Pabuaṇlor, and TIRTAWANGSA, désa Jatiseëng, both in the district of Chiledug.

[8]) By Haji HUSEIN, kampong Chikarèt, désa Chikarèt, sub-district of Baros, district Sukabumi.

[1]) By JAKIM, kampong Pasirkuda, sub-district of Chiomas, and by NETIN, RAIN and ALI, all three residents in the private estate of Gunungsindur in the kampong Chibinong, district Parung.

[2]) By PADMASUKARTA, dèsa Rejawinangun, district Kotageḍé, regency of Bantul, and WANGSAKARIYA, Dipawinatan, Jogyakarta.

[3]) By SAMASUKARTA, désa and sub-district Tulakan, district Lorok.

[4]) By MAJA, désa Krawangwètan.

[5]) Cf. also **95**, p. 179/180, and the illustrations facing p. 169 (relating to a specimen excavated in the Karo district).

other names during their labour than those they bear in daily life. These names they borrow from various personages from the Panji-stories. One may wonder why it should be precisely from this cycle of stories that they choose their adopted names. In regard to this, RASSERS (**305**) arrived at some remarkable conclusions. He discovered, in fact, that the identification of the prince or tribal hero (for that is what Panji, after all, appears to be) with the smith has been carried to such an extent that the two are, at times, almost indistinguishable. The art of gong-forging is thereby elevated to a sacred act, heavily charged with magic, on the part of the king-priest.

His Highness MANGKU NAGARA VII gave me the following names with respect to Solo: the chief smith, *i.e.* the real gamelan-smith (*empu*), uses as his professional name that of the principal character in the cycle mentioned: Panji Hinokertapati or Panji Tuwa (H.J.: Panji Sepuh) [1]). The first of his *panjaks* (fellows, journeymen) [2]), the *malu ngarep*, bears the name of Charangwaspa or Panji nom (H.J. Panji (he)nèm) [3]), *i.e.* the half-brother of Panji sepuh, and a son of a younger sister of the former's mother. After these two come, in order of importance:

3. Handaga 4. Wirun 5. Kartala	half-brothers of Panji sepuh, out of secondary wives of the Prince of Jenggala,
6. Banchak 7. Doyok	inseparable servants (*panakawan*) of Panji sepuh,
8. Sebul 9. Palèt	panakawan of Panji henèm,
10. Ragilkuning,	the youngest sister of Panji sepuh, and full sister of Panji henèm,
11. Jangkung,	the learned jester of Panji sepuh.

Their tasks are divided as follows:

Panji sepuh manipulates the staves (*penyukat*) with which, during the heating process, the gong is turned round uniformly in the fire, as well

1) Further names are: Panji Wanèngpati and Panji Asmarabangun. Cf. also above, p. 17.

2) Apart from its signification "blacksmith's man", the term *panjak*, at any rate in Central Java, also denotes the lurah genḍing's subordinate players. Cf. also, below, p. 381. The leader of the Banyuwangi *gandrung* orchestra is also called panjak kenḍang (**372**).

3) Further names are: Panji Sinomberdapa and Radèn Harsingtilam.

as the tongs (*supit, sapit, nyapit*), with which the job is held during forging and brought into the right position. He also pours the fluid material from the melting-pot (*kowi*) into the mould (*penyingen*).

Charangwaspa operates the anvil (*paron*), in which duty he is assisted by Handaga, Wirun and Kartala.

Banchak and Doyok handle the bellows (*nglamus*).

Sebul and Palèt hand the material from the fireplace to the anvil.

Ragilkuning holds a light for the workers to see by, when it should be necessary to work during the night.

Jangkung's duties consist only in keeping the smithy clean.

The large Jogya kraton collection mentions the same names, with the exception of the last four; in addition, however, it also gives Panji Wulung, alias Radèn Jayapuspita, and Radèn Kalangbapang, alias Brajanata, the latter being an elder brother of Panji sepuh.

These persons' respective activities are described, in the collection mentioned, to be as follows:

1. Panji sepuh manipulates the *supit*, places the job on the anvil, gives shape to the *penchu* (beating knob) and the *wot* (part of the gong-edge, what time he swings the *gemblok alit* (the smallest of smith's hammers of the gemblok type);

2. Panji henèm handles the *penyukats*, smelts the gong-material and takes the lead in hammering-out the gong-to-be, which at first has a basin-like shape;

3. Jayapuspita, 4. Kartala, 5. Handaga and 6. Brajanata perform the forging-work proper, beating in turn, one at a time. Jayapuspita always gives the first beat; the others follow in order of sequence of their rank, as indicated above. Each of these four smiths works with a different format of *palu* (*i.e.* an iron hammer with a very long-drawn-out head), Jayapuspita swinging the smallest and Brajanata the largest one.

7. Semat (= Doyok) and 8. Turas (= Banchak) keep bringing the job each time from the fire to the anvil.

9. Wirun operates the bellows.

It will be seen that, here again, there is some difference—although much likeness, too—between the Solonese and the Jogya adat.

It is indeed a great pity that this industry, which, although carried on in an incomparably primitive manner, achieves the highest results in its own fields, is now on the verge of ruin. The demand for good instruments is getting steadily smaller. The principal—*i.e.* the Semarang—gong-smithies, for example, which, in 1907, still numbered seven, and at present, as we saw above, only two, hardly, if at all, train any pupils now, so that it is probable that this beautiful craft, so full of ancient tradition, will die with the present generation, unless, in some way or other, a helping hand is offered in the nick of time. [*S[31, 34]]

The manufacture of iron instruments, on the other hand, is being cultivated much more generally to-day (cf. also p. 278). It appears from the inquiry instituted by order of the Department of Education and Religion into the spread of the various kinds of gamelan and wayang in Java (some results of which are given in Appendix 57), that iron keys, and also some kinds of iron cymbals, are to-day being manufactured in more than 50 places in Java, by no less than 146 smiths.

Brass and zinc keys and cymbals are of least frequent occurrence; the former were recorded only for Malang [1]), Tegal [2]), Jogya [3]) and Sukabumi [4]); the latter exclusively for Chilachap [5]).

The large gongs are distinguished and graded—apart, of course, from their beauty of sound, their size [6]) and weight—also according to the number and nature of their sound-beats (*ombak* = wave). A gong is most beautiful to the taste of the people of the Principalities when, on being beaten, it sounds 12 or 13 of these ombaks. They distinguish gongs without any beats, called *gong ba'ung*; gongs with a relatively small number of rather slow beats, in which case they speak of *Bima gumuyu* (the deep, slow laugh of the wayang-hero Bima), and gongs with a larger number of beats in quick succession, which sound is given the name *Bima ngguguk*,

---

1) Smiths: PAH BUN and WONDA, both in the désa Kendalpayak, district Malang.

2) Smith: TARMAH, kampong Pèpèdan, district Adiwerna.

3) Smiths: WANGSAPREWITA, Tamanan, regency Jogyakarta, and three smiths in the district of Semanu in the regency of Gunungkidul, i.e. PAWIRASENTANA in the désa Kalangbangi, MANGUNSEMITA in the désa Gunungsari, and GONDAPUSPITA in the désa Ngebrak.

4) Smith: AWAL, kampong Pintuhèk, désa Parungseah, sub-district and district of Sukabumi.

5) Smith: SUTADIWIRYA, désa Sidakaya.

6) This on the understanding that a gong is held to be deserving of greater esteem according as its smaller volume still allows of its producing a sound of the desired depth and darkness. This type of sound is called *ulem*.

i.e. Bima's "burst of laughter". Gongs with a strong, fast-vibrating sound are called *ganjur* [1]). In the Sunda districts they often use, instead of Bima gumuyu, the term *ombak banyu*, *i.e.* undulating water. Each region seem to have its own preference in regard to these beats; thus, Samarinda (East-Borneo) demands gongs with three, and Makassar with as many beats as possible.

It is possible to make the sound of a gong slightly heavier and deeper by pouring a few litres of water into the bottom. One has to take care, of course, to remove the water again soon after playing, in order to avoid the gong rusting.

Tuning (*nglaras*) of a gong is done by cold-hammering the gong-wall both inside and outside. It is said that the tone changes slightly during the first years of the instrument's life; some say that the gong-tone is not completely stabilized until after 30 years (**145**).

Each part of the gong (and the same applies to the kenong, about which more later) has its own name. Thus, the top of the beating-knob or boss (*penchu*; the gong-smiths call it *endas*, *i.e.* head) is called *ucheng*; the rounding of the boss, *kumba*; the sunk part around it (when present), *wideng*(*an*); the outer ridge of this wideng, *tikel*; the flat part of the surface adjoining it, *rai*; the outer edge of the latter, where the said surface begins to incline a little, *pasu*; this incline itself, *rechep*, and the extreme outer edge of the instrument, bordering on the rechep, *dudu*; the edge which turns inward: towards the top, *para*, in the centre, *bau*, and lower down, *wot*; the bottom edge, *lambé* (= lip), and the opening itself, *lolohan*.

Of the gong ageng it is customary to polish only the boss, and even this is sometimes omitted. The smaller kinds of gongs are usually polished all over.

In the larger *ensembles* in the Principalities there is at least one gong ageng, and often there are two, in which case they are tuned approximately to *gulu* (sometimes *ḍaḍa*), and *lima*. When there is only one it nearly always sounds the tone *lima*. It is only on very rare occasions that one comes across a gong tuned to the tone *nem*. (This more especially in the Sunda districts).

The same gong ageng is played in both pělog and sléndro, from which it follows that, although—as we have seen above—it has a definable tone-pitch, its esthetic value consists exclusively in the deep, dark nature

[1]) Cf. below, p. 149.

of its sound, whose actual pitch cannot exactly be realized by the hearer within the totality of gamelan-sounds. As a matter of fact, its pitch is usually somewhere in the neighbourhood of the limit of the sound-spectrum, comprising frequencies between about 40 and 50 vibrations, *i.e.* not much more than an octave above the said limit (16 v.d.).

In the gamelan the gong ageng serves chiefly to mark the close of the longest melody-periods, which, for that reason, are called *gongan*.

The instrument is made to sound—as is the case with all other kinds of gongs with central bosses—by beating against that boss with a hammer (*tabuh*), which, so far as the larger kinds of gongs are concerned, is provided with a round, toughly-resiliant woollen ball-head. In the kampong the tabuh sometimes consists of a large *jeruk* (grape-fruit) stuck on to a short stick: this combination gives an excellent substitute for the real tabuh, some consumate music-lovers even preferring this *tabuh jeruk*. A better tabuh than this, however, is the bare, stiffly-clenched fist, with the outer side of which the player then beats the boss.

In Europe one may search in vain for any gongs with a beauty of sound as those of the best orchestras of the ruling princes, the nobility and some of the Chinese music-lovers in Central Java. These gongs possess a sound that grips one through the splendour that emanates from them, spreading an atmosphere of truly lofty restfulness and power. Whoever has been fortunate enough, be it only once, to hear the benefaction of this timeless booming tone, dominating the teeming sounds of the gamelan, and to hear it, as it were, come out of the silence of eternity, will forever carry it with him as a most precious memory:

Gong jumeglug mandul-mandul
Gumulung obaking waréh.

i.e. "The sound of the gong, beaten heavily, rolls on its ponderous beats like the ocean tide" (**176,** 7th stanza).

In ancient Javanese literature this noblest of instruments is occasionally referred to as *gong*; the first time in the *Rāmāyaṇa* (XXV 66); probably it is also referred to by the name of *mahasara* (ibid. *e.g.* XIX 13; Virāṭaparvva (A.D. 996) p. 52), whilst, for the smaller types of gong, the names *gubar* and *munda* used to be customary (**194**).

It may be asked: where does the gong actually come from? SIMBRIGER, in a voluminous treatise (**340**), has collected everything that had come to his knowledge concerning the gong; but in his summary he comes to the conclusion that, in fact, nothing can be stated with certainty concerning its origin. It appears that the most ancient —and, for that matter, not completely incontestable—mention of gongs hails from China, in the 6th century. The Chinese are supposed to have adopted the instrument from a "barbarian" people living further west.

Now the gong is undoubtedly a product of a high culture, and further —although the title "barbarian", as used by the Chinese of that period, any more than by the ancient Greeks, need not be taken too literally, conveying, as it does, only the slightly contemptuous meaning of "alien", or "being different"—yet we do not suppose that the gong originated with the people through whom China made its acquaintance. According to SIMBRIGER the origin of the gong is most probably to be found in N.W. Further India, or in a territory situated south-west of China.

Personally, however, I am of opinion that the cradle of the first gongs may not have stood in S.E. Asia at all, but in quite a different place, namely in the Near East, in, what we should call, the Aegean civilization.

There are many cultural forms—including several kinds of musical instruments—of which it is known with either relative or absolute certainty that they originate from some very early West-Asiatic (or from the, in many respects kindred, ancient-Egyptian or ancient Greek) culture, and have found their way, either along the coast or by an inland way through Central Asia, to the Far East. This applies, for example—to confine ourselves to musical instruments—to the bow-shaped harp and the long-necked lute.

Now it appears to me not at all impossible that the origin of the gong—*i.e.* the special form without central boss—should be looked for in this very birthplace of the most ancient civilizations, even though the gong is nowadays to be found exclusively in India proper, and East- and Southeast-Asia.

For, some Greek authors make mention of an instrument which they call ἠχεῖον (ècheion), and which is used, according to their communications, both for the interpretation of thunder-effects on the stage and, in the Eleusinian mysteries, at a climax of the ritual. This term, related to ἦχος (echo), stands for a sound-instrument which (*a*) is made from metal, and (*b*) sounds long after it is beaten. This is evident from the—unfortunately not very numerous—*loci*, as well as from the fact that one part of the lyre, the well-known Greek plucking-instrument, is also called ἠχεῖον, and is then identified with χαλκῶμα, which word derives from χαλκός, *i.e.* copper, or, more often, bronze. We cannot gather from the text handed down to us (a passage in HESICHIOS) which part of the lyre is meant by it. SACHS (**310**, p. 125b) supposes that a resonator is meant by it, whilst the Greek-English dictionary of LIDDELL and SCOTT translates it by *metallic sounding plate.*

But this is not all. W.F. OTTO, through whose publication „Der Sinn der Eleusinischen Mysterien" [1]) the existence of this ancient Greek instrument came to my notice, says, on p. 105 of his treatise: "At the moment when Korè was called, so he (APOLLODOR of Athens) reports, the hierophant beat the so-called ἠχεῖον, a kind of gong made of ore (Schol. Theokr. 2, 36). The context in which this fact is communicated leaves no room for doubt that at that moment the Realm of the Dead had been opened, since, immediately following upon this, it is stated that a cymbal of this description was also sounded at the death of the Spartan kings. We are here in the region of extremely ancient rituals, such as have maintained themselves also in other forms in Eleusis and Sparta; and many of those who have experienced oriental, and especially Chinese death-ceremonies, must have been vividly reminded of them by this beating on gongs".

Here, therefore, we may see the close connection which exists between the instrument ἠχεῖον and death, and OTTO quite rightly reminds us that, in South-East Asia, the gong plays a similarly important part in the death ritual among many peoples. There are passages galore in SIMBRIGER's book which go to prove this (**340**, pp. 96 to 100 and 102 to 104). With the aid of the mighty sound of this regal instrument it is attempted to safeguard the deceased against the influence of evil spirits, or—as is done by the Dyak in Central Borneo—one accompanies death-dances with it (which, after all, also serve to ward off the spirits), whilst the gong-sound is also used to call the attention of the divine powers, as, for instance, in the Buddhist convents in China [2]).

There exists, therefore, a threefold correspondence between ἠχεῖον and gong, namely, as regards a) material, b) sound, and c) function.

Now, assuming that we may indeed identify ἠχεῖον and knob-less gong (disque sonore)—and it would seem to me that we are more or less en-

---

[1]) Eranos Jahrbuch, 1939, p. 83 *et seq.*
[2]) VAN AALST, Chinese Music (1884), p. 57.

titled to do this—then the question arises: when, and along what road, did the Aegean instrument penetrate so far towards the East?

It is very doubtful, in view of the scarcity of the ancient Greek sources, and the insufficiency of our knowledge concerning the contact of ancient China with the Western world and the history of the Central-Asiatic trade routes, whether we shall ever succeed in obtaining any more certainty in this matter. I may, however, be permitted to venture a cautious suggestion as to the most probable road which the ἠχεῖον might perhaps have taken.

However rarely, and relatively late, the gong has been either mentioned or depicted in sources of information from India proper, still, the disque sonore may be found mentioned as early as the eight century, and is still used there, to this day, as a temple-instrument [1]).

The fact that older sources let us down in regard to this does not prove that the gong did not exist there long before the eighth century. I may remind the reader of the fact that another musical instrument, the pellet-bell (grelot), cannot be proved to have existed in India proper before the end of the 13th century [2]), whilst it may be safely assumed, from the fact that they are to be found on heavenly trees on the Central Javanese Barabuḍur-reliefs [3]), that this same grelot was known in Buddhist ritual, and used as a "religious" instrument, at least five centuries previously.

All this inclines me to the theory that the supposed eastward spread of the ἠχεῖον might be sketched as follows: having penetrated, along with Greek (Hellenistic) cultural influences, as a result of ALEXANDER's expedition, as far as N.W. India and the country, now called Afghanistan—probably still in its function of religious instrument—it might, in the beginning of our era [4]), with the expansion of Buddhism (with which the Hellenistic princes in Bactria and India—the Euthydemids—had already been in intimate contact some centuries before [5])), have come to China in the beginning of the sixth century [6]), still as an attribute of Buddhist ritual.

---

[1]) Cf. CLAUDIE MARCEL DUBOIS, Les instruments de musique de l'Inde ancienne (1941), p. 32/33, 147, and plate XXVI.

[2]) id. ibid. p. 37.

[3]) KROM-VAN ERP, Barabuḍur, relief III 21.

[4]) J. PH. VOGEL, De Buddhistische kunst van Voor-Indië (1932), p. 26.

[5]) W. W. TARN, The Greeks in Bactria and India (Cambridge 1938), p. 268.

[6]) Where it has had considerable influence ever since the middle of the 4th century (cf. J. WITTE, Der Buddhismus in Geschichte und Gegenwart (1930), p. 110). We already mentioned above that the gong (without beating knob) is still being used in the ritual in Chinese Buddhist monasteries. [*S[9]]

As the sinologists Mr. KENNETH ROBINSON from Oxford and Dr. R. P. KRAMERS from Leyde pointed out to me, this last supposition finds corroboration in a passage from the Chinese encyclopedia Ku Chin T'u Shu Chi Ch'êng, reading: "In the [time of the] Later Wei, from [emperor] HSÜAN-WU (abt. 500 A.D.) on, [people] for the first time liked music (lit.: tones) from the border [regions]. [The instruments which] arrived at the transferred capital [1]), [were] the *ch'u-tz'u p'i-p'a* (the five-stringed p'i-p'a), the five-stringed *k'ung-hou* (guitar), and the bronze gong (*t'ung lo*). When beating the gong (*ta sha-lo*), its sound generally was rather restrained and slow at first, but changed to agitated and quick. Probably this music originated in the Western regions and (?) from there it extended to the Middle and East regions" [2]).

The ethnologist professor ALFRED STEINMANN of Zürich recently called my attention to yet another indication that the gong must have reached Eastern Asia from more westerly regions: H. A. BERNATZIK, in his latest work "Akha und Meau" (**20**D p. 147), mentions the use of small bronze gongs (judging from the pen-drawing reproduced here, probably of the type without beating knob) by the mountain tribes, now living in Southern China and Further India. This author states—more particularly in reference to the Meau (Miao) of Northern Siam—that these tribes hail from "Steppenhaften Räumen, wo Tibet, Mongolei und Alt-China zusammenstossen"—*i.e.* from more westerly regions, precisely there, where, according to our hypothesis, the gong must have found its way to the Far East—and did not emigrate to their present places of settlement until relatively late.

These Meau, again, use their gongs—together with rattles and mouth-organs—first and foremost as religious instruments at funereal and sacrificial ceremonies, when consulting good, and exorcising evil spirits.

Unfortunately, as I said before, the necessary iconographic and literary

---

[1]) This must be Lo-Yang. In 496 A.D. the Wei emperor removed his residence to this place.

[2]) Category XXIX, Chapter 136: "Variegated musical Instruments" 2; quoting the Yo Shu (Book of Music) by CH'EN YANG (Sung dynasty).

This foreign music had a strong and not altogether favourable influence on the Chinese mind, as we may conclude from the words with which the passage cited goes on: "Thus, of those who experienced its sound, there were none who were not extravagant and wanton, excitable and fearful, and (their) rising up and coming to a stop (was) unstable. Now leaping or jumping, now active and now at rest, walking on tiptoe, snapping their fingers, shaking their heads, rolling their eyes, their emotions burst forth in the middle (of the dance) and they could not restrain themselves".

data to support our hypothesis also in other details are still lacking, *unless*, that is, we should interpret the curious disc-formed instruments that may be seen on a relief of Mathurā (50 B.C. to abt. 200 A.D.) [1]) as such "disques sonores" (*vide* ill. 64*a*). These, however, are generally regarded as large frame-drums (Rahmentrommel, tambours sur cadre) [2]).

I am wondering, however, on what grounds. The players are carrying the instrument, whose diameter may be estimated at about 90 cm., on their left shoulder on a strap fixed to the edge at two places, and play on it by means of a slightly crooked stick held in the right hand. This manner of playing a frame-drum is not, as far as I am aware, known in any part of the world. The—smaller—West-Javanese: *terbang besar* (diameter up to abt. 75 cm) is already so heavy that it has to be carried by two men on a carrying-pole and played by a third (ill. 153). The Lappic drums [3]), which were usually smaller, but sometimes as high as 85 cm, were mostly placed on the player's knees [4]), but also—unless they were too big—held in the left hand by means of a wooden handle at the back [5]). Again, other kinds of frame-drums, such as the ordinary present-day Javanese *terbang*, are generally rested on the ground when played (ill. 152 and 158). In other places, they are sometimes carried on the shoulder [6]), or the instrument is held pressed against the chest, either with or without the aid of a strap [7]); or it is held tight under the crooked left arm [8]). I do not know the manner of playing the very large present-day South-Indian and Bengalese frame-drums (diameter up to 150 cm) [9]), but it stands to reason that it cannot possibly be that of Ma-

---

[1]) J. Ph. Vogel, La Sculpture de Mathura ("Ars Asiatica" XV) (1930), planche XXIII, fig. a.

[2]) Op. cit., p. 34; Cl. Marcel Dubois, op. cit., p. 41/42.

[3]) Ernst Manker, Die Lappische Zaubertrommel (Nordiska Museet: Acta Lapponica I) (Stockholm, 1938), p. 144.

[4]) Op. cit., p. 417, ill. 614.

[5]) **313**, Table 29, ill. 205 and 208; Ernst Manker, op cit., p. 49, ill. 26.

[6]) **311**, p. 62, ill. 37; V. Loret, Note sur les instruments de musique de l'Egypte ancienne (in: Lavignac, Histoire de la Musique, lre partie, vol. I, p. 1 *et seq.*), p. 13, ill. 37.

[7]) Cl. Marcel Dubois, op. cit., p. 42.

[8]) Thus, on one of the balustrade-reliefs of the Bharhut temple (abt. 150 B.C.), at any rate assuming that the instrument represented there is not actually a drum (cf. the identical method of playing an undoubtedly one-headed drum of Panataran (East-Java, 14th century) as shown in our ill. no. 44).

[9]) Cl. Marcel Dubois, op cit., p. 43.

thurā, since these instruments, if carried along in a procession in that way, would drag along the ground.

Looking at the matter from all angles, therefore, it seems to me that some doubt is permissible as to whether these Mathurā instruments, *mounted*, moreover, *as gongs*, as they are, are actually frame-drums.

But then the only other possibility is that what is depicted here is thin metal sound discs, disques sonores, or ἠχεῖα. They must have had thin walls, of course, otherwise they would be much too heavy to carry in the manner depicted. But if we bear in mind the ancient Greek use of the ἠχεῖον, *e.g.* for thunder-effects on the stage, we may assume that they were, indeed, thin-walled.

It is, of course, questionable whether it will ever be possible to fill up the above speculations with sufficient data to form an incontestable proof of their correctness. It may be, however, that, as time goes on, surprise finds in Eastern Turkestan, that source of unexpected discoveries in the cultural-historical field, will provide us with more facts. [**223**, **236**G, *S10]

When the gong-beats have to come relatively in quick succession, as in the *gending lampah* (used to accompany the wayang), as well as, generally, in the smaller wayang kulit orchestra *klenéngan tengahan* (*vide* below, p. 274 *et seq.*), the gong ageng is replaced [1]) in Central Java by the **gong suwukan** or *gong siyem* [2]) (ill. 65, sub *a*), an instrument of the same shape as the gong ageng, but of smaller dimensions and with an edge which is often turned slightly more inward. The tone of the gong suwukan is between one and two octaves higher than that of the gong ageng, so that in the ensemble its pitch may be clearly distinguished by the hearer, in contradistinction to the gong ageng sound. It is for that reason that, in a "double" gamelan, the pélog- and the sléndro-half of the orchestra each possesses its own gong(s) suwukan, whilst, in the largest combinations, there may sometimes be found a number (*e.g.* three) of these instruments for each

---

[1]) In the case of the *gending lampah*, all but the final gong beat, which is nowadays always beaten on the gong ageng.

[2]) Originally, the name of *gong siyem* used to be given to the instrument referred to here, when, instead of being manufactured —as were the majority of gongs— from a slightly convex, circular bronze plate by repeated heating and hammering-out (*vide* **145**, plate XI), it had been cast straightaway into the required shape.

The precise signification of the term *siyem*, it appears, is not known. There do not seem to be any reasonable grounds, as far as I am aware, to assume its derivation from *Siam*, as has occasionally been suggested.

tonal system. In this case, a gong suwukan *bem*, if present, is not used in a gending pélog barang. When there is only one gong suwukan present for both tonal systems, then it is tuned to *gulu*.

The gong suwukan derives its name from the fact that, in olden times, it used to be beaten at the end—reached, as always, after a ritardando (*suwuk*)—of the above-mentioned genḍing lampah, which occurs so frequently in wayang music (cf. App. *4* and p. 306 *et seq.*).

The **kempul** (ill. 65 sub *b*) is a size smaller again, and about an octave higher than the gong suwukan-group. Another, probably older name for it, which is still used sporadically (*e.g.* in Grobogan), is *genjur* or *ganjur*. As we remarked before (p. 141), this name applies, in fact, only to gongs (and kempuls) having a strongly vibrating tone.

Originally each gamelan pélog or sléndro used to possess one only of these kempuls; later on the number was gradually increased until they had one specimen for each of the tones of both systems (with the exception of the tone *pélog*). The same applies, by the way, to the kenong, which we shall discuss further on. The strong esthetic objection which some have against such a large number of kenongs [1]) also applies to some extent to the kempuls, for the latter, too, fulfil a colotomic function; *i.e.* to help the gong, the kenong and the keṭuk with the subdivision of the nuclear theme into regular periods. In view of the fact, however, that its tone is an octave lower and much less conspicuous than that of the kenong, which sounds as clearly as a bell, and since, moreover, the kempul is used practically exclusively in compositions of the *ladrangan-* and *ketawang*-type, those critics who share the objection mentioned in respect of a complete set of kenongs will probably have little or no qualms against the presence and use of a large number of kempuls in one and the same orchestra.

When there is only one kempul in a gamelan it is tuned either to *nem* or to *lima*.

In the *genḍing lampah* and the *genḍing talèḍèk*, already mentioned, and sometimes also in small pieces of the ladrang-type (as, for example, in rapidly beaten "welcoming"-compositions), the kempuls are also used in another way, namely closer together, thereby forming a more or less driving, rhythmic element.

[1]) *Vide* below, p. 162.

The **penontong** (ill. 111 sub *c*, and 112 in the background left)—also called *kenong penontong*—is a gong with a strikingly broad rim, and somewhat smaller than the kempul. It may be found in some Central-Javanese ensembles with three- and four-toned scales, especially (in two specimens) in many gamelans *Munggang, Koḍok ngorèk* and *charabalèn*, and, further, because of its far-carrying sound, as a signalling-instrument on fishermen's proa's in the Java sea.

A little smaller still is the **benḍé** (ill. 124 sub *f*). This small species of gong is not used in Java in the gamelan proper. The Jogya kraton, however, possess four *pusaka* (*i.e.* sacred) benḍé's, three of which are carried along by the *prajurit* (*i.e.* the kraton-troops) in the procession at Garebeg Dal, and decorated with wreaths and festoons of melati-flowers. These three are the Kyahis *Bichak* 1), *Udan Arum* (= Rain of scent) and *Tunḍung mungsuh* (= He who drives away the foe). The fourth sacred benḍé, *Kyahi Sima* (= Lord Tiger), which—so the story goes—is supposed to have belonged to the last prince of Majapahit, but which—nothwithstanding its frightful name—did not succeed in saving the said prince from ruin, is, for that reason, not carried around by the prajurits with the other three. For the rest, the benḍé chiefly serves as a signalling-instrument. In this function, for example, it sounds its sad and monotonous tones at auction-sales. It is further to be found in the music of the Jogya prajurit-corps, called Dahèng (= Buginese), as well in some small primitive rural orchestras (*vide* below, pp. 284, 287 and 293).

Whereas the instrumental name *bèri* (*bhèri, bhairi, bahiri*), during the first Hindu-Javanese centuries, as well as in its continental country of origin, stood for drum (**194,** p. 79 *et seq.*), it has been used during a later period to indicate a small species of gong. The present-day Javanese **gong bèri**, too, is a small, often knobless gong. It is never found in any gamelan, but serves exclusively as a signalling- and war-cymbal.

The names *benḍé* and *bèri* are sometimes substituted for each other, so that one cannot say with certainty, without having seen the instrument in question, what it looks like.

Mention must finally be made of the very smallest hanging gongs, which are used exclusively—and not always even then—in the gamelan sléndro:

1) [*S11]

the **engkuk** [1]) and the **kemong** (ill. 65, sub *c* and *d* resp.). This couple of small cymbals belong inseparably to each other, and, like proper twins, resemble each other in every detail. They may on rare occasions be found in gendèr-form. The engkuk (E) is tuned to *barang*, and the kemong (K) to *nem*: usually both in the slenṭem-octave, but sometimes the kenong is tuned in the demung-octave, *i.e.* one octave higher. The couple is beaten alternately in a calm rhythm and fulfil a colotomic function of a lower order. Together with the keṭuk (T) and the kenong (N) they form the following colotomic pattern:

E K E T
E K E N

In the Jogja kepatihan these small cymbals have been replaced by a single, horizontally-placed gong-kettle, the shape of a bonang-kettle, which is tuned to *barang* and called *kempyang sléndro*.

The engkuk and kemong, as well as their substitute, the kempyang sléndro, are played by a single player, by means of a tabuh, such as is used with the bonang, and used only in dance-accompaniment; in the groups of compositions, called genḍing ageng and genḍing tengahan, they are not heard until after the genḍing has "fallen", *i.e.* only in the second part of the composition. In the gamelan pélog their task is taken over by the kempyang (cf. p. 163). An example of the playing of engkuk and kemong is given in the ladrang *Ular kambang*, as recorded by Odeon (A 278001a) and in the Mangku Nagaran langendriya-record (Col. G.J. 61, Ménakjingga léna, parts 3 and 4).

Hindu-Javanese specimens of most of the "hanging" gongs with which we have dealt so far, have been found either burried in the soil or in river-beds. These foundlings, inasmuch as they are in the hands of the Javanese, are guarded with the utmost care and reverence, and reckoned among the most precious *pusaka*.

I should also mention in this connexion the sacred gong of Loḍaya, in South-Keḍiri (**346, 396**). Once a year this instrument is stripped of the seven tissues in which it is enveloped, after which it is washed, as a result of which the *borèh* (yellow *curcuma* powder, the same with which the serim-

---

[1]) *Engkuk* is also the name of the *Bucco philippensis*, a green bird with a red head. Its cry resembles that of the cuckoo (**380**, p. 199).

pi's and beḍaya's, as well as a bride and bridegroom at their wedding, cover the upper part of their bodies), which has been smeared on it the year before, is washed off. The washing-water is then caught in small flasks and basins and sold as salvation-bringing medicine. After this the gong is smeared with *borèh* once more and wrapped up in its seven swathings again. This whole procedure takes place in the presence of a large crowd of people. Once, the Susuhunan of Solo took the gong with him to his place of residence—or, as some will have it, it was stolen by a Solonese. All the tigers from South-Kaḍiri then flocked after the gong, and the district of Surakarta suffered from a veritable plague of tigers. The gong was thereupon brought back to Loḍaya in great haste, and the plague of tigers immediately ceased.

No European is allowed to touch this gong. One civil servant, who ventured nevertheless to touch it, died soon afterwards.

Some of the gong ageng bear proper names. Thus, the venerable great gong of the Jogya gamelan Munggang is called *Kangjeng Kyahi Linḍu* (= the Venerable Sir Earthquake) and the couple of pusaka gongs of the gamelan Koḍok ngorèk, in the same place, *K.K. Mahésa ganggang* [1]) and K.K. *Sima* (= Tiger) [2]). One of the gongs of the Regent of Banjarnegara is called *Kyahi Kumbang* (= Venerable Sir Wood-bee) on account of its humming sound [3]). We already mentioned, on p. 150, the names of four pusaka benḍé. [*S12]

We shall now proceed to deal with the "horizontal" gong-forms.

---

1) *Mahésa* (L. J. *kebo*) = buffalo; *ganggang* = fighting.

2) Cf. p. 262, note 2.

3) About the last-named gong, the following traditional, but reliable story has been handed down through the ages: When the mighty sultan AGENG of Mataram (1613–1646) began to feel that his end was near, he caused six gongs (partly *benḍe's*) to be made by his best smiths. Hardly were they completed when he died. The gongs, together with the other treasures belonging to the State, then came in possession of his successor, his oldest son, the cruel sultan MANGKU RAT I. Thirty years afterwards MANGKU RAT, who, by this time, was a doting old man, saw himself compelled by the great rebel, TRUNUJAYA, to leave Plèrèd, his residence, and fled to Banyumas, to the town of Panjer, where one of the ancestors of my informant (the present Regent of Banjarnegara, KOLOPAKING VIII) was the then Regent. The place was put in order and beautified, and its name became Kotawinangun, i.e. "the beautified city" .The Regent took the ejected Sultan in, looked after him well, and as a reward, got one of his daughters in marriage, with, by way of dowry, one of the six gongs. Thus the gong *Kyahi Kumbang* came into the family of the Banjarnegara Regents. This was in 1677.

Two of the remaining five gongs are to-day among the State treasures in the

The **bonang** (ill. 66), in Java proper, usually consists nowadays of a double range of bronze beating-kettles, which are shaped like small gongs with relatively broad rims, and placed with the open side downward.

In pélog, the instrument generally comprises $2 \times 7 = 14$, in sléndro generally $2 \times 5 = 10$, but sometimes $2 \times 6 = 12$ of such small kettles. They lie upon an under-frame (*ranchakan*), consisting of a wooden grating mounted on feet. In the squares formed by this grating two cords are fixed taut, either parallel or crosswise, and on these cords (*pluntur, janget*) the kettles are placed. At Jogya a folded piece of banana-leaf is often placed between the pluntur and the kettle, which causes the tone to resound slightly longer; this is thought desirable in Jogya, where a full and powerful orchestral tone is appreciated more than in Solo. It is perhaps for the same reason that the Jogya kraton-gamelan (sekati) *Kyahi Guntur madu* possesses, underneath its bonang-kettles, earthenware sound-pots (*kenḍil grabah*) [1]).

The bonang-kettles have a—for their size—fairly heavy boss. They are made to sound by beating this boss with a stick provided with a cylindrical head wound round with either wool or cord. The player holds one of these sticks in each hand.

The range of the bonang, in pélog, is always two unfinished octaves; in sléndro only when there are 2×5 kettles. Only the sléndro-bonangs with 2×6 kettles have a range of two *closed* octaves.

The player, who sits at the long side of the instrument, has the lowest of the two octaves immediately in front of him, the higher of the two octaves being placed in the row behind that. The kettles of this higher octave have a slightly higher rim and ditto *penchu* than that of the lower octave (they are *brunjung*): they are regarded as "male" (*lanangan*), and distinct from the latter, which are regarded as "female" (*wèdokan*) and are of lower

Solonese kraton. One of them is the benḍé *Kyahi Bichak*, which has been mentioned already on p. 150. The other three seem to have disappeared.

At the end of the 18th century, a hundred and twenty years after the death of Mangku Rat, the great-grandfather of my informant, then Regent of Ambal, south of Kebumèn, residency of Banyumas, caused a gamelan pélog to be made to the gong *Kyahi Kumbang*, in such a way that the tone *lima* was made identical with the pitch of the gong. The scale which thus came into existence may be found in Appendix *61*, under No. 36.

1) Earthenware sound-pots, for that matter, may often be found inside the sound-box of the *gong kemoḍong*, especially in East- and West-Java; often, this gong even derives its name from this fact: *vide* below, p. 180. Cf. also **194**, p. 102/3, note 3.

build (they are *dempok*). Since the bonang is very often beaten in octaves, the kettles do not—at any rate as regards at least one of the rows—lie in the usual order of sequence corresponding to the pitch of the tones, but are arranged, to facilitate playing, in such a way that the player, when beating in octaves, needs never play on two kettles lying immediately behind each other. Thus, the bonangs of a gamelan hailing from Jogya, and, at that time, in the possession of the Regent of Bandung showed the following arrangement in pélog [1]:

3′ 5′ 4′ 2′ 1′ 6′ 7′
7 1 2 6 4 5 3

and in sléndro:

4′ 3′ 2′ 1′ 5′
1 2 5 3 4

GRONEMAN gives, for the Jogya arrangement in sléndro:

′1 5′ 4′ 3′ 2′
2 3 4 5 1

The arrangement of the—not very numerous—Sundanese bonangs differ according as they are played in *laras gedè*, *laras biasa* or *laras leutik*. In laras gedè (= great, *i.e.* low pitch) it is as follows:

4′ 3′ 2′ 1′ 5′
1 2 5 3 4

in laras biasa (= usual pitch):

5′ 4′ 3′ 2′ 1′
2 3 1 4 5

and in laras leutik (= small, *i.e.* high pitch):

1′ 5′ 4′ 3′ 2′
3 4 2 5 1

As may be gathered from the above, it is usual to take care that, in pélog, the tone pélog (tone 4), and either the tone *barang* (tone 7) in *pélog bem*) or the tone *bem* (tone 1) in (*pélog barang*) are placed at the corners. In this way, the two beats for which the player has to stretch his arms out furthest, and which, therefore, take most time and effort, are reserved for the tones occurring only rarely in the composition to be rendered. In *pélog bem*, the arrangement most frequently followed in the Principalities is, accordingly, this one:

---

1) The numbering is from low to high, the tone *penunggul* in pélog, and the tone *barang* in sléndro being taken as No. 1.

4′ 6′ 5′ 3′ 2′ 1′ 7′
7 1 2 3 5 6 4

The arrangement in *pélog barang* is the same, with the exception, that the kettles 1 and 7 change places.

The same applies to the Sunda districts, except that there, in the *liwung*-tonality, the kettles 3 and 4 change places.

It is nothing unusual, however, to find that the arrangement varies here and there [1]).

Some gamelans, *i.e.* those which are (or used to be) carried along and played in processions, carry the ranchakan bonang provided with iron carrying-clasps fixed to the narrow sides (ill. **115**, rather indistinctly in the background; *vide* also **100**, plate XXIII). This fact is also mentioned in the "Historische Beschrijving der Reizen" (*i.e.* Historical description of Travels), in which the following passages occur, relative to the life-guards of the king of Banten (1602): "Their drums are high-pitched pans of some metal called Tombaga, and which generally make a hellish noise"... "This music consisted of ten or twelve Tombaga pans, carried upon a hand-pole, between two men. Each was tuned a note higher than the other, and two persons kept time, beating upon them with sticks" (**119**, vol. II, p. 63 and 64).

The tuning of the bonang-kettles higher or lower is done by filing off from the knob or the upper kettle-rim, respectively. In the désa tuning is sometimes done by sticking lime into the inside of the knob; the more lime, the lower the sound.

Details concerning the manufacture of bonang-kettles may be found in **147**, p. 28/9, and in **81**.

In Java proper, three kinds of these double-range bonangs are known in all. From low to high pitch their names are: *bonang panembung, bonang barung* and *bonang panerus* [2]). Of these three, the latter two may be found anywhere; the bonang panembung is confined to Jogya.

Their scales are related in such a way, that the lower octave of the next higher instrument equals the higher octave of the one immediately below it.

The smaller combinations, which evidently represent an older period, do not possess the double-range bonangs dealt with above. Their beating-kettles—which are also of more powerful build—are ranged in a single

---

1) *Vide*, for other arrangements, Brandts Buys (**43**, p. 30 *et seq.*).
2) From *nerusi* = "drawing through" (*i.e.* of the melodic line).

row (*rènthèng*). They usually comprise an incomplete pélog-scale: the gamelans Munggang (ill. 111), patalon, Koḍok ngorèk (ill. 112) a three toned, and the Charabalèn (ill. 115) a four-, five- or six-toned one.

The Koḍok ngorèk-ensembles often have bonang-ranges of 8 kettles; in this case they give, alternately, the lowest and the medium, or exclusively the highest tone. Each of these instruments has, as a rule, four players, each of whom operates two kettles.

The bonang sets of the Charabalèn consist, in every ensemble, of two octave-ranges: a higher one—again distinguished as "male", and called *klènang*,—and a lower one, "female", called *gambyong*.

In some Eastern-Javanese Regent's gamelans one may find a bonang instrument of one octave—in a single row—with kettles of a large format and slenṭem-function; this instrument is called either *monggang* (as, for example, in Jombang) or *ponggang* (*e.g.* in Malang and Prabalingga).

The kettles of all these one-row bonangs may be distinguished from those of the two-row ones, apart from their larger size, also by their colour, which is very dark; this is because they have been left unpolished, whereas the double-row instruments usually have brightly shining kettles.

The shape of the Solonese bonangs is slightly flatter than that of the Jogya ones.

In former times, when they were probably all single-row, the bonangs are said to have been mounted on a half-circular ranchakan. It appears, from a photograph to be found in the N.I. Musicological Archives (ill. 108), that this was also the case, not so very long ago, with at least one of the Jogya kraton gamelans, the pélog *Kyahi Bremara*. According to R. M. JAYADIPURA its ranchakan, as well as that of its sléndro counterpart, the *Kyahi Marikangen*, were bent because it was customary in those days for the instrument to be played by women, the short-armed sex [1]). The only bonangs mounted on a bent ranchakan at the present time are—so far as I am aware—those of the *ponggang* in the kabupatèn at Prabalingga, and those of the instruments of the same name belonging to the *gamelan talu*, from the Malang kabupatèn (ill. 114), as well as those of a similar instrument in the Sriwedari museum at Solo.

Now as regards the function of the bonangs in the Javanese gamelan. The single-row instruments are, in the first place, the bearers of the

---

[1]) These female niyaga's used to form the corps *Prajurit Langenkusuma*.

nuclear theme (*balunganing* [1]) *genḍing*); at most, one may occasionally hear them add to this nuclear melody some simple ornamentation.

The task allotted in the *ensemble* to the double-row bonangs, however, cannot be described in a few words. Admittedly, they sometimes assist—in the more vigorously-beaten pieces (*genḍing sabetan*)(S), *genḍing gagah* or *gagahan* (J))—in carrying the cantus firmus. This, however, is not their most prominent task. For, this cantus firmus, as we shall see more plainly further on, is beaten in the first place on certain instruments of the saron-group. Far more than in the more primitive orchestras, the bonangs in the modern ensembles—at any rate the *bonang barung* and the *bonang panerus* —devote themselves to the paraphrasing of that main theme. Now they anticipate it, now they analyse it into smaller values or imitate it in the octave. Then again, they syncopate it—with the aid of the highest of the saron-instruments—and, when the balungan-tones come with longer inter-spacing, they fill up the melodic gaps with their penetrating tinkling sound (cf. Appendix *3*). In short, their task varies with the character of the pieces rendered.

A typical form of this "playing around" the theme is that in which ample use is made of series of small groups of three tones each, separated by a rest, in binary rhythm. These are usually beaten in such a way that the first and third tones of such a set of three are the same, whilst the placing of these sets within the melodic framework is such as to ensure one of the main theme tones coming each time exactly in the short pause between two such groups of three. This applies both to the bonang barung as—in a still higher degree—to the bonang panerus.

It is probably to this that Ko Mo An's description of the playing method of the bonang barung (called by him bonang (a)geng) and the bonang panerus (**176**, 3rd and 4th stanzas) refers:

"bonang geng pating talening
i(m)balan bonang panerus rinaras rinachik rachik",

i.e., "the bonang geng repeatedly produces small groups of tones. It is alternated by the bonang panerus whose sound brings harmonious order (into the music), whilst splitting the bonang ageng figures into smaller time-values".

---

1) derived from *balungan* = bones, skeleton. The word balungan itself is also used as a name for the nuclear theme, as is also the term *baku*, meaning "the principal, real thing".

In both types of bonang mentioned one may also frequently hear triplets being played (cf. Appendix *3*, bonang panerus part). [*S13, **113F**, **248D**, **291E**, **319C**]

The introduction to a genḍing is also often rendered on the bonang (barung) (*bebuka bonang*) [1]. [**113G**]

The orchestral function of the *bonang panembung* differs according as it joins in the playing of ordinary genḍings or in *gending lampah* and in *Gangsaran*, and according as the tempo is faster or slower. In ordinary genḍings, and in fast tempo, it is beaten together with the kenong and—if in use—the kempul; in normal tempo together with the keṭuk, kenong and kempul; in slow tempo the same as in normal tempo, but, in addition, also half-way between the different keṭuk-, kenong- and kempul-beats, whilst in very lively orchestral pieces falling outside the range of the actual genḍings—such as the genḍing lampah and Gangsaran just mentioned—the panembung is beaten exclusively together with the kenongs and gongs. The pitch of the tones played is not always the same as that of (the lower octave of) the balungan-tones played at the same time (cf. Appendices *5* to *9*, *jo.* p. 353). [**107B**]

One might perhaps say that the bonang panembung plays a melody which is simpler still than the nuclear melody, giving, as it were, its essence. Its function, therefore, is not quite the same as that of the *gendèr panembung* (*slenṭem gantung*), which—as we shall see in a moment—simply stresses the nuclear melody, by "weighting" it with its lower octave, at regular intervals, *e.g.* one tone out of four each time.

In the *gamelan klenéngan* the bonangs are conspicuous by their absence. To distinguish the klenéngan, therefore, the gamelan with bonangs is sometimes called *gamelan bonangan*. [**113E**; *S67]

A large number of bonang-kettles have been left us from former times; in some cases complete, or almost complete sets. Most of them do not differ in appearance from present-day instruments, with this exception that, in the rim, four (in some cases only two) small holes have been bored in a "diagonal" position. The presence of these small holes is to be explained by the different, older methods of mounting the kettles, all of which methods correspond in this respect that the kettles did not, as at present in Java, lie loose upon their *pluntur*, but were either kept floating in some way or

[1]) Cf. below, p. 310 *et seq.*

other by means of those holes, above their underframe, or fixed—as is the case of the Balinese *réyongs* (ill. 67) and the instruments, identical with these, on the Panataran-reliefs (ill. 46, sub *a*; vide also ill. 40 and 41)—two-by-two in a vertical position, onto the ends of a stick-shaped centre-piece [1]).

The bonangs of Further India—they are also to be found there (Siam: *khong vong yai* and *khong vong lèk*; Cambodga: *khong toc(h)* and *khong thom*; Birma: *krewaing, krewong* (**198**))—also show these small holes, which there, too, are needed in mounting them, either horizontally or vertically, in 3/4 circle-setting.

Some of these excavated kettles also differ from the present-day bonangs in that the upper part around the boss is not, as in the modern ones, practically flat, but slightly convex, or bonnet-shaped (ill. 56, sub *c*). When this is the case the alloy, too, appears not to correspond quite to the material used to-day, whilst the instruments themselves are also considerably more solid of construction [2]). Further, they have been *cast* in a bonang mould,

1) This fixing method, for that matter, has persisted in Java until the end of last century, i.e. in the Regency of Banjarnegara; the present Regent remembers seeing beating-kettles, mounted in this way, being carried around hanging on a string round the neck of the players, on the occasion of the so-called Javanese New Year (*lebaran*). When, however, after many years' sojourn in Europe, he returned to his native place, these réyongs had disappeared. All the same, it appears that there are still Javanese réyongs in existence, be it not in Java itself: they were seen at Padang in 1925, forming part of a small Javanese orchestra accompanying a *talèḍèk* troupe.

2) Dr. PURBACHARAKA recently suggested that these heavy, cap-shaped bonang-kettles might be instruments *in statu nascendi*, which ought to have been further wrought into thinner-walled, larger cymbals. Arguments in favour of such a probability are: the seemingly useless solidity of these kettles; the bad, and, moreover, unusably high sound of the majority of them, and the fact that they hardly, if at all, show any traces of having been forged, but are evidently still in the same state in which they came out of the casting mould.

Counter-arguments, however, are by no means lacking either: (*a*) it does not seem possible that, by means of heating and forging, this unwieldy and relatively cery high-edged form could be altered into the other, "normaly"-profiled and usually lower-edged form of bonang-kettles (a large number of specimens of which have been dug up from the soil); (*b*) in accordance with this, no cymbals have been dug up, as far as I am aware, which might be said to form a transitional type, and (*c*) these cap-shaped bonang-kettles, alleged to have remained in the un-forged state, are invariably provided with holes in their edges, for mounting purposes, which holes, at any rate to-day, are never pierced until the very last, when the instrument is otherwise completed (cf. **145**, p. 36).

Further, two gong-smiths, from Solo and Buitenzorg respectively, after examining these cap-shaped kettles, which, as they said, were completely unknown to them, expressed the opinion that these kettles, in the state in which they had been discovered, were quite "finished", and that it would, moreover, be impossible to

in contrast to the present-day kettles and to most of those found buried in the soil, which have been made by repeated heating and forging of a small disc of cast bronze, slightly spherical in shape at first, and which took on its bonang-shape after long and elaborate operations. The bonnet-shaped kettles, therefore, are amongst the bonangs, what the old gongs *siyem* (vide above, p. 148, note 2) are among the hanging gongs.

At the present time, bonang-shaped instruments, usually consisting of a series of (generally 5, or 2×5) beating kettles, are found in the archipelago, outside Java, in the following places: Madura (**43**), Bali and Lombok (*trompong, babarangan, réyong*) (**192**); in the district of Nagé in the middle-western part of Flores (in the *laba-go* ensemble) (**221**); in Muna [1]); Banda (*gong sembilan*: nine kettles, placed in three rows of three); Ambon (*gong duwabelas*: twelve kettles, placed in four rows of three); further—usually under the name of *chalempung*—in a large part of Sumatra, namely in Siak, Jambi, Palembang, Menangkabau, Rejang, Benkulen and the Lampong districts; and, finally, in the parts of Borneo that once have been under Javanese political and cultural influence, especially in the surroundings of Banjermasin (*kromong*).

With regard to Hindu-Javanese forms of gong-kettles, *vide* also **194**.

Kenong (ill. 68, sub *a*) is the name of a single sound-kettle with a very high rim. It has a high-pitched, clear sound.

Kenong galong gegolongan,
Serengé ngalangut tebih,

meaning: The kenong divides the music into phrases by means of piercing tones, which penetrate to a far distance (**176**, 7th stanza).

It is placed upon crossed cords on top of a wooden, bottomless box, and is used, in the gamelan, chiefly for the purpose of subdividing the large gong-periods into medium-sized phrases. These "kenong-cuts" are called *kenongan*. In the *gending lampah* and *gending taledek*, and occasionally in the "smaller" pieces, the kenong-beats are heard in much quicker succession, so that the instrument then actually performs a rhythmical function.

---

obtain from this form, by further forging operations, a "normal" bonang kettle as final form.

It would seem, therefore, that these completely cast, unforged, cap-shaped beating-kettles should be regarded as the representatives of an extinct branch of the bonang family.

[1]) Musicolog. Arch. Batavia, Nos 234a-f.

According to GRONEMAN (**99**, p. 41) the kenong is, in the latter case, invariably tuned to *nem*, and known by the names of *kenong wayangan*, (H.J.: *kenong ringgitan*) or *kenong playon*.

The kenong-stick resembles that of the bonangs, but often has a somewhat shorter and thicker head, which is barrel-shaped rather than cylindrical.

In the older gamelans only one kenong is found for each of both tonal systems; it is tuned to *lima*. Besides this—only in Jogya and the Javanese districts under Jogya influence—another, the *kenong jàpan*, may be found, which sounds one octave lower and is beaten chiefly in the *genḍing gagah*, *i.e.*, as stated above, the more powerfully-sounding pieces. This kenong jàpan is probably unknown in Solo. Its name is supposed to derive from a Regent of Jàpan (= ?Majakerta), who introduced it into Jogya on his appointment to Rijksbestuurder (Prime Minister of the Sultan). In contradistinction to the kenong jàpan, which is thought of as "female", because it is larger and its sound lower, the ordinary kenong is also distinguished as *lanang*, *i.e.* "male".

In the large ensembles more kenongs have gradually been added. So long as this amounted to nothing more than the addition of a kenong *nem* and a kenong *barang*, it might be regarded as an enrichment and ennoblement of the sound-palette as well as an addition to the possibilities of expression. Each of the kenongs had its own task. Thus, the kenong *barang* was beaten when a melodic phrase intoned on a high register (*ngelik*) was to follow, whereas the kenong *nem* was beaten only in *Ayak-ayakan* and *Srepegan*. As time went by, however, kenongs with other pitches were added as well, until, in the end, in the largest orchestras (first in Solo, but later on, especially, in Jogya, *e.g.* in the double gamelan made in 1907 for the Crown Prince, under the supervision of the musical expert, R. M. JAYADIPURA), there was a kenong for every tone of the sléndro-, and (with the exception of the tone *pélog*) for every tone of the pélog-scale; this, therefore—the two kenong *jàpan* included—amounted altogether to no less than 13 of these instruments [1]).

---

[1]) When a double gamelan is either *tumbuk nem* or *tumbuk jongga*, i.e. when the tones *nem pélog* and *nem sléndro*, resp. both *jongga* tones have exactly the same pitch, then a single kenong for the *nem*, resp. the *jongga* suffices, which reduces the number to 12; whilst, when the gamelan is *tumbuk lima*, even 11 kenongs are sufficient for a complete combination, owing to the fact that, in that case, both the kenongs *lanang lima* and both the kenongs *japan*—which, as we have said, are also tuned to *lima*—may be conveniently represented by one and the same instrument.

From that time it became the custom in these large orchestras to beat the particular kenong, each time, whose pitch corresponded to the tone in the nuclear theme that happened to sound at the same moment. And with this, according to the judgement of some musicians (and also of P. A. A. Mangku Nagara VII) gamelan music had made a step backward. For, in this way, a unison of kenong- and balungan-tones had arisen, where formerly there had nearly always been a difference in tone. In the older practice —which always avoided as far as possible the coincidence in pitch of the said tones—the feeling was kept alive that the genḍing was not yet finished, and that the melody was about to unfold itself still further. Henceforth, however, each kenongan obtained, in these large orchestras, its emphatic full stop, owing to which the melody no longer conveyed the impression of striving further onwards.

This state of things gradually began to be felt as unsatisfactory; since some twenty years ago, therefore, another method of playing has been introduced in Jogya (where, more than in Solo, these kenong-"batteries" had struck root), and this new method of playing, which is called *nyegat* (= to await, anticipate) prescribes that the pitch of the kenong-beat must be the same as that of the first balungan-tone of the following kenongan.

In the playing of the so-called *srepegan rambangan* (J), however, the (numerous) kenong-beats, to this day, invariably sound in unison with the tones of the (vocal) melody, also in Jogya; but in this case the kenong does not have a colotomic function, but becomes a pure melody-instrument.

A peculiarity of certain genḍings is, that some of their kenong-beats may be trebled, in such a way that the first beat coincides with the finish of the kenongan, the two others following at distances of $1^1/_2$ or 3 *keteg*. This is done, in the Mangku Nagaran, in the genḍings *Sobrang barang* (P. barang) and *Surung ḍayung* (P. 6 pélog) (Appendix *3*, bars 158/161 and 166/169) [1]), and in the Jogya kraton, in the genḍing *Gandrung-gandrung* (P. manyura). [*S14]

In Hindu-Javanese literature the kenong is probably mentioned under the names of *brekuk* (the earliest record being a document dated 902 A.D.), and *bungkuk* (in a document dating from 943) (cf. **194,** p. 101).

---

1) In this case they appear to lie apart $1^1/_2$ "bar" of 4 keteg. This, however, is only appearance, and the result of the manner of notation: on account of the very slow tempo in which the genḍing-part in question is beaten, a common time bar has been made, in the transcription, out of each set of 2 keteg.

The **keṭuk** (ill. 68, sub *c*) is a sound-kettle which stands on its own, is much flatter and lower than the kenong, and has not such a bright sound:

Keṭuk mantuk ing tutukan

i.e.: "the keṭuk gives dull, sleepy sounds", says Ko Mo An (**176,** verse 7).

The keṭuk, too, is mounted by means of crossed cords above a wooden box or grating, on short legs (*ranchakan*). In a few cases a calabash is placed underneath it by way of sound-box (cf. **311**, p. 34), and one may also find some keṭuks here and there provided with a sound-box of baked earthenware (*keṇḍil grabah*) underneath, *e.g.* under the bonangs of the Jogya gamelan *Kyahi Guntur madu* [1]).

The beating-stick has the same shape as that of the bonangs.

Both the gamelans pélog and sléndro comprise one each and never more than one keṭuk, which is usually tuned to *gulu* (*keṭuk kintel*) (J) [2]), but occasionally (in sléndro) to *barang* (*keṭuk kungkang*) (J) [3]), or, in pélog, to *nem* (S). Its chief duty in the orchestra is to subdivide the kenongan into smaller periods. Besides this, it also has a practically rhythmic function in the *genḍing lampah* and *genḍing talèḍèk*.

The **kempyang** (ill. 68, sub *b*), originally exclusively a pélog-instrument, consists of two sound-kettles, either both tuned in *nem* (S), or in *nem* and *barang*—nowadays also occasionally in *lima* and *nem*—respectively (J). They are beaten simultaneously.

The kempyang is used in all ordinary compositions, but in pieces with a *munggah* (*nḍawah*) only during this second part. It is not played in the *genḍing lampah* and the *genḍing parikan*.

That, in some places in Jogya, the tuning *nem/barang* has been replaced by *lima/nem* is caused by the fact that some critics (amongst whom was also the late P. A. A. Danureja VII [4]), Prime Minister of the Sultanate and highly gifted musically) objected to the beating of the tone *barang*—as alien to the scale—in *laras bem* (= paṭet lima and nem).

The division of the keṭuk-section by (generally) two kempyang-beats takes place in the same way as that of the kenongan by the keṭuk-beats, *i.e.* according to the principle $1/2 + (n \times 1) + 1/2$ (cf. p. 298 and Appendix *3*).

1) *Vide* above, p. 153.
2) = toad.
3) = giant-frog.
4) died 1933.

The **rojèh** (ill. 111 sub a and 112, on the far right, at the back), is a knob-less, thin-walled beating cymbal shaped like a pan-lid, and is supposed to sound either the tone *barang* or the tone *nem*. It is generally used in duplicate, hung up by its centre and beaten with a hammer-shaped tabuh with a head made of horn. This instrument is found in some Central-Javanese gamelans *Munggang* and *Koḍok ngorèk*. It is also mentioned in Hindu-Javanese literature, for the first time, as far as I am aware, in the poem Sumanasāntaka (CXIII 3), which originates from the Kaḍiri period (1042–1222).

The instruments of the **saron** group (ill. 69, 70, 71) consist of a number of, usually fairly heavy, bronze (or iron) [1]) keys; the largest of these keys are sometimes provided with a boss. They are called *untu* [2]), or *wilah(an)* [3]), are slightly arched on top (at any rate the bronze ones are), and rest upon a low, wooden, trough-shaped underframe (*pangkon, tlapakan*) [4]). The form of this underframe, again, differs for Solo and Jogya; in Solo it has nowadays the appearance of a somewhat long-drawn volute, with the keys lying on top of it, whereas in Jogya the horizontal centre piece of this volute drops down by about the width of a hand, causing the scrolls to the right and left to be correspondingly raised (cf. *e.g.* the sarons of ill. 69 with those of ill. 112).

The keys are kept in place by metal pins fixed into the rim of the underframe (*trachak*; literally: hoof, claw; or, in Jogya, also *planchak*), which stick through two small holes bored at a few cm's distance from their ends. The keys do not touch the wooden underframe directly: if they did they could produce only a dull, hard-hollow sound; for this reason the pins just mentioned have been wrapped up at the foot with plaited ratan, cork or woollen material, so that the keys have only two narrow supporting points. The tiny supporting cushions thus obtained are called *sumpilan* or *tawonan*; they refine the tone of the keys and prevent the incidence of by-sounds. Nevertheless, in fortissimo passages one may occasionally hear a sharp-

---

1) Cf. below, s.v. *gamelan wesi, kempling, mondrèng(an), gamelan barut*, and also **40**, p. 208/9.

2) *Untu*, literally: 1° tand (also of a saw or a harrow); 2° rung of a ladder; 3° beam pierced by nails; 4° grain on a maize-ear.

3) *Wilah*, literally: *key*, or *lath*; it sometimes also denotes the interval between two successive tones of a scale (*i.e.* of the size of one step).

4) According to MAHILLON (vol. III, p. 288) also: *banchik*, at any rate for *kenḍang*-underframes.

sounding alien tone, caused by the keys' jumping up and touching each other.

The sarons comprising a single octave are beaten with one *tabuh*, usually in the shape of an ordinary wooden mallet, but also sometimes—in the case of the smallest, high-pitched variety—with one made from the end of a buffalo-horn, provided with a handle fixed to it at right angles. We may mention in this connexion that in Solo preference is given to tabuh's with softwooden head, whereas in Jogya tabuh's with a very hard wooden head is preferred—one of the reasons why the Jogya gamelan-playing usually sounds so much more vigorous than that in Solo. That head of the mallet is not beaten against the keys with the entire width of its side, but with the edge only, so that the player's technique is sometimes half-way between beating and "chopping". The gambang gangsa is beaten, both in Solo and in Jogya, with two tabuh's, with long handles and a small, round, hard-wooden head.

Sometimes—*e.g.* in the restricted ensemble which accompanies the wayang kulit play—the two or three largest forms are beaten by two players sitting opposite each other; this is done when it is necessary to play both very strongly and very fast, and when there are not two instruments of the same kind available. When these are available, then the players beat alternately, but each on his own instrument (cf. also p. 273).

The pitch of the keys is raised when they are filed down (underneath) at the ends, and lowered when they are filed down in the middle. Raising the pitch is also sometimes done by slightly bending the keys round their longitudinal axis (so that a cross-section would show a curve). This process, however, is more often applied to the iron than to the bronze metallophones.

The saron-group comprises five members, one multi-octave, and four single-octave ones.

The highest (single-octave) form is called **saron panerus**, *saron panachah, peking, selo(u)kat* (J.), *penitil, chenṭé* (S.) or *tété lilé* (S.) (ill. 69, sub *c*); the next lower one in pitch: *saron barung* (ill. 69, sub *b*); then follows the *(saron) demung* (ill. 69, sub *a*) [1]), and finally the lowest, and now somewhat antiquated, *saron slenṭem*, which has probably always been provided with

---

[1]) In the *gamelan klenéngan* this is the name for the single-octave species of gendèr, which, in the large gamelan, bears the name of *slenṭem gantung* (S.) or *gendèr panembung* (J.); it may also denote the gendèr sounding one octave higher.

bosses (ill. 70). The one multi-octave form, which, so far as Java is concerned, is also antiquated, is called *gambang gangsa* or *gambang selukat* (in the Solo kraton also called *chelepita*) [1] (ill. 71); when provided with bosses it may also be called *panṭu.*

The single-octave forms have, in pélog, practically always 7, in sléndro either 6, 7 or 9 keys. On only one occasion did I see a gamelan pélog whose sarons had 8 keys, *i.e.* the *gamelan sekati* which hails from the Sumenep kraton and is now to be found at Kedawung near Pasuruan. Sarons sléndro with 9 keys are chiefly to be found outside the Principalities, and, in that case, especially in those orchestras which are used to accompany wayang kulit performances; often, therefore, in gamelans owned by the ḍalangs. Otherwise, the saron key-range comprises, in pélog, an unfinished octave; in sléndro, on the other hand, it closes on the octave of the lowest tone, whilst, added to this—at any rate in Solo and East-Java—there is often yet another tone, *i.e.* the octave of the highest tone but one of the tone sequence. In Jombang, a gamelan sléndro with these seven-keyed sarons is called *gamelan sekar gaḍung.* Such a seventh key is added in order that the players may have at their disposal both a high and a low tuning (*laras alit* as against *laras geḍé*). The lowest tone may then function either as *nem* or as *barang,* at the players' discretion; in both cases one still has a completely rounded-off octave at one's disposal, supplemented, in *laras alit,* by a low *nem,* and in *laras geḍé,* by a high *gulu* [2]. [*Vide* **83**B, pl. 10, 11]

Sorogan—exchange keys—(Sund.: *sora geganti*) are never, as far as I am aware, found on any of the sarons, neither for changing *pélog bem* into *pélog barang* (which is unnecessary, since all the tones of the pélog-octave are present on these instruments) nor for a change from pélog to sléndro—a method which, to my knowledge, is never practised on any Javanese instrument having a fixed range of keys [3].

In the large orchestras of the nobility in the Principalities and of the Chinese music-lovers the sarons, especially the sarons *barung* and *demung,* are often present in remarkably large—and always even—number: *e.g.* four demungs and eight S. barung, which enables a truly imposing unison

---

1) Cf. below, p. 171, 180, 191, and 217.

2) In regard to the absolute pitch of the various gamelan-tunings *vide* also, below, p. 251 *et seq.* and 390.

3) It is highly probable that the communication relating to this method in **342**, p. 814b, repeated in **248**A, p. 3151a, and reproduced again in **311**, p. 28, is based either upon an error, or upon an isolated case or experiment incidentally observed.

melody-effect to be obtained (*Gangsaran*!). The following combination may be considered as normal: 2 demung, 2 or 4 saron barung, and in addition one, or sometimes two saron panerus. When the saron *slenṭem* is present, it is usually in duplicate. In the event of a greater number of sarons barung and demung being used, the number of S. panerus and S. slenṭem is not increased.

In slow pieces, the keys are often left to sound freely after being struck; when muting (*piṭet, pekak*) is thought desirable, (*e.g.* in quick succession of tones) it is done with the thumb and forefinger of the left hand, at the same time the next is beaten, except when this next tone falls on the same key, in which case the first tone is not muted.

Another method of muting is practised in the *ngenchot* (cf. p. 353): a melodic anapaest, the first two beats of which are given on a key which has been muted just before with the left hand. As may be imagined, this involves a radical change in the character of the sound produced. The third beat of such a ngenchot-anapaest is then left to sound away quite freely again. Examples: Odeon A 39563b (*Lunggaḍung*) and Beka B 15007 II (*Babar layar*).

The function of the saron-family is a versatile one. The *saron panerus* plays a syncopating or duplicating rôle with respect to the *balunganing genḍing* or nuclear theme. Often, too, it plays, with its keen, brilliant sound, around the balungan-tones, somewhat stiffly in fourths-figures (*vide* Appendix *3*).

Hence, KO MO AN (**176,** 4th stanza) says:

saron panerus kumrichik
chinachah chochog irama

i.e. "the saron panerus chops up the nuclear tones (*irama*) by tinkling sounds in the higher octave". [*S17, **113**E, **248**D, **319**C]

The nuclear theme itself, in its most severely strict form, is usually beaten upon the **demung** and/or the **saron barung**. Appendix *3b* contains such a nuclear theme without any embellishments. In Appendix *3* the *saron barung*, the *demung* and the (*gendèr*) *slenṭem* are collectively the bearers of the nuclear theme. It is this theme (called, for short, the saron-part, although, as is evident from what we said above, other instrumental forms may also be the bearers of this cantus firmus) [1]), whose clear and

---

[1]) Cf. also, below, p. 222, note 3. In sabetan-compositions, the bonang barung —*vide* p. 156/157— does not do so very much more than render the balungan-tones, either.

distinct rendering is the main purpose of all forms of Javanese music-notation (cf. Appendices *4* to *9* and *11*).

We must also mention one particular method of beating, characteristic of Jogya — the Solonese play-adat hardly ever practises it (any longer) [1] —: it happens sometimes—in the real genḍings always, after they have "fallen" (*tiba*, H.J. *nḍawah*), *i.e.* in the second part of these compositions—that the *saron barung* does not only sound the cantus firmus, but, in addition, each time between the tones of this nuclear theme, another tone, always the same one for quite a long time, whereby the impression is created that this nuclear theme is, as it were, curled like a festoon around a fixed pivot, or, to put it another way, hanging upon a straight line. This continually recurring tone is called *pancher*, meaning literally: pole used to mark out part of a field, another meaning being: tap-root [2]. A pancher is beaten only when the nuclear theme-tones lie far apart, as is the case in *wirama rangkep*; it saves the playing from losing some of its equilibrium and firmness owing to the time-intervals between the tones of the cantus firmus being too long.

Compositions with pancher—either or not accompanied by *imbal* (which we shall describe further on)—are much more numerous in sléndro than in pélog. In sléndro the most customary pancher-tone is the *barang*, *i.e.* the *barang alit*, when the genḍing in question is played softly (*lirih*), and the barang *ageng*, when it is played loud (*sora*). Other pancher-tones occur only very rarely in sléndro, as, for example, the *gulu* (= *jongga*) in the genḍing *Jongméru* (P. manyurá), and the ladrangans *Konḍa* and *Sumiyar* (also both in P. manyura); the *ḍaḍa* in the genḍing *Chondra* (P. 9) and the ladrangans *Gagak sétra* (P. 9) and *Liwung* [3] (P. manyura); the *lima* in the genḍings P. manyura: *Gonjang anom*, *Kopiya bedah*, *Montro* and *Pechowan*.

In pélog, on the contrary, it is precisely the panchers *ḍaḍa* and *lima* that predominate. *Ḍaḍa*, for instance, is found, as pancher, in the genḍings P. 6: *Buḍeng-buḍeng* [4], *Hela-hela* and *Songgaléwang*; the ladrangan *Hèndèl*

---

[1]) It is only in the kraton that the pancher is still beaten in the munggah of some genḍings, *e.g.* in the *G. Gambir sawit pacharchina.*

[2]) It also has the signification of (genealogical) *lineage*; e,g,. *pancher lanang* = male, *pancher wadon*, or *wèdok* = female lineage.

[3]) = to spin round like mad.

[4]) Said to be a composition by the Susuhunan PAKU BUWANA IX. The piece was played to me in paṭet 5, in the kabupatèn at Magelang, and on that occasion struck

pengantèn (P. 6) and the gendings P. barang: *Munchar* and *Suralaya*; *lima*, as pancher, in the gending P. 6: *Maraséba* and the gendings P. barang: *Gandrung manis*, *Kinasih* and *Lempunggunung*. The only gending pélog with pancher *barang*, known to me, is *Pandil ori* (P. barang) [1].

Sometimes two different panchers occur in one and the same piece. Thus, in sléndro P. 9, the ladrang *Uluk-uluk*, with panchers *barang* and *dada*; in pélog, with panchers *dada* and *lima*: the gendings *Ranumenggala* (P. 5)(*), *Mégamendung* (P. 6)(**), *Heneng-heneng* (P. barang) and *Harum-harum* (P. barang).

The tones *nem*, in sléndro, and *bem*, *gulu*, *pélog* and *nem*, in pélog, are never used as pancher, at any rate in the Jogya kraton [2].

Now, this manner of playing with pancher on the saron barung is nearly always accompanied with what is called *imbal* (literally: to repeat) on the demung. This imbal is a method of playing in which the nuclear theme is played by two nyagas and "broken up" into smaller values: two crotchets resp. four quavers to a minim according to the tempo being either wirama I (*seseg*, quick) or II (*alon*, slow). They play *imbal* by alternating one-step patterns in *hocket*style. For practical reasons this imbal is, if possible, divided over two demungs; if only one such instrument is available, the two players sit facing each other. The player who anticipates the next following nuclear theme tone is said playing the *gawé* (H. J. *damel*) [3]; the other one, whose beats coincide with the nuclear theme (*balungan*) plays the *ngintil* (*i.e.* inseparable, following like a shadow; Sund.: *ngikintil*, nutur) [4].

The following fragment, an extract from the gending *Génjong* (P. 9), provides an example of *pancher* and *imbal*. The transcription follows the Jogya kraton notation [5]. On the upper line the minims following each bar-

---

me by the large number of the tones *pélog*, *barang* and *barang miring* sung by the woman singer assisting in the performance. [*S52]

[1]) Solo: *Bandil ori*.

[2]) According to Radèn KODRAT, one may occasionally hear, in the Solonese kraton, a pancher *nem* in certain gendings P. sanga.

[3]) = to make something.

[4]) PIGEAUD (Pocket dictionary) gives: to follow, hang after, a person.

[5]) Without any notation, therefore, of the variations played by the gendèrs, bonangs and the gambang kayu, or of the counterpoint by the rebab, the suling and the voice. [The originial transcription has been replaced by a revised version. *Vide* S15 for acknowledgement. – E.H.]

(*) [*S52]

(**) [*S50, 57]

line represent the nuclear theme (*balungan*). Each nuclear theme note, however, alternates with a high *barang*, notated as c''', called *pancher barang*. In the imbal-part (both middle lines), the notes with the upward stems represent the *ngintil*, and those with the stem downwards the *gawé*. Further, *T* stands for keṭuk-beat; *W* = *wela*, for the missing of a colotomic beat [1]); *N* for kenong-beat; *b*, *d* and *t*, respectively, for the drum-beats *bem*, *ḍunḍung* and *tepak*. Our transcription shows the softly-beaten form (*lirih*), with *barang alit*. [The two versions of *imbal* correspond with quick tempo (wirama I) and slow tempo (wirama II) resp. *Vide* remarks S15]

It is the custom, at any rate in Jogya, to beat the lower octave of the nuclear theme tones on the *saron slenṭem*—when present—in those parts of a genḍing in which the said tones lie far apart (*e.g.* four *keteg* in a slow tempo), in *keteg*-values, but with the omission of the beat on the fourth keteg each time. [*S17]

In addition to this the saron slenṭem occasionally performs the same function as that of the *gendèr panembung* (ill. 73), inasmuch as it consists in the playing of the nuclear theme tones. It would be possible that the cause of the saron slenṭem becoming antiquated should be sought in this fact; there being only a very modest place available, in the gamelan-ensemble,

1) PIGEAUD (op. cit). gives the signification: to skip or miss out, and: space left open.

for the saron slenṭem by the side of the gendèr panembung, with its incontestably preferable tone-quality. Notwithstanding this, however, it has managed firmly to maintain itself in the Balinese gamelans, side by side with the *jègogan*, an instrument similar, in both form and function, to the gendèr panembung.

This may be a convenient place to say a few words about a method of performing certain compositions, which is characterized by the omission of the nuclear melody which would otherwise be rendered on the saron group. This manner of playing is indicated by the name of *janturan*, a term also used in slightly different, if more or less related, significations [1]). The *tertium comparationis*, here, again, is the „hanging", or "floating" of the music, which, in these cases, of course, lacks the customary, solidly audible realisation of its balungan-tones.

A good example of *janturan*, in the sense referred to here, is provided by Col. GJX 22 (*Pangkur kajantur*).

Finally, the **gambang gangsa** may be regarded as a representative of an older period, during which the now existing demung, saron barung and saron panerus, whose pitches connect up with one another, did not yet exist as separate instruments. This triad, indeed, form so to speak, between them, a gambang gangsa "fallen apart". In Sumedang, as a matter of fact, I found in the kabupatèn, such a bronze gambang, each of whose octaves bore the name of one of the sarons, *i.e. saron* and *panerus*. We may assume that the gambang gangsa began to become antiquated from the moment the single-octave sarons came into general use. Instrumental forms, however, seem to offer a tough resistance to being superseded, especially when they are made of durable material. And so specimens of the bronze gambang are still met with in Java to this day. They usually possess 14 or 15 keys—as we said before, generally without bosses. Both in sléndro and in pélog the gambang gangsa sounds all the tones of the scale; this is in contradistinction to the gambang kayu, which, in pélog, never sounds the tone *pélog*, and, further, leaves out either the *bem* or the *barang*.

In the Solonese kraton the gambang gangsa is nowadays played only in the genḍing *Hundur-hundur kajongan* = *Chelepita* [2]), *i.e.* the genḍing played when the Susuhunan raises himself from his seat to retire to his

[1]) Cf. above, p. 132 and 133, and below, p. 188, 276, 310, and 318.
[2]) Cf. also, above, p. 166, and below, p. 180, 191, and 217.

apartments, or after a dinner, when His Princely Highness gets up to repair to another hall, and, finally, outside the kraton, when he rises to depart.

Whereas the sarons, in the complete gamelan, constitute such an important component, they do not occur at all in the *gamelan klenéngan* in its purest form. Their part is taken there by a few instruments of the gendèr-type.

It should finally be mentioned here that, in some orchestras in the Regencies Pachitan and Panaraga, one single saron-key, laid loosely on the ground, is beaten with a hammer as an accompaniment to the dance. This solitary saron-key is called *kenut*, after the sound it produces, which is, as it were, "smothered", and does not sing out freely. It serves, therefore, actually as a substitute for the kemanak (cf. p. 180 *et seq.*). I found such playing of a single, or, at most, two saron-keys also in South-Sumatra in Musi ulu (1931), in the *dusuns* along the rivers Musi and Lakitan. There, they were placed upside-down on the ground and struck with a small iron stave, as a result of which their sound, with a shrill tinkle, was able to mark the rhythm of the gamelan-playing and the dance of the *gadi's*.

Certain instruments in other parts of the Archipelago show close kinship with the gambang gangsa, and the same applies to the Siamese *ranat thum lèk* and *R. èk lèk*, and the Cambodgian *ronéat dèc* (**198**).

Saron-key-ranges have also been recovered from the Hindu-Javanese period, partly completely identical with the existing single-octave forms, and partly of multi-octave range, with keys of the demung-format. The most ancient illustration of a (single-octave) saron may be seen on one of the Barabuḍur-reliefs (Ib 98) (ill. 22).

We shall now pass on to the instruments with freely-suspended metal keys.

The **gendèr** (ill. 72, 73, cf. also 83) is a metallophone whose thin bronze keys are hung up by means of cords (*pluntur*) on prominences sticking out of the underframe (*sanggan, trachak, angkring*), usually above tubular resonators. These sound-tubes are generally made of bamboo, in which case they are cut in such a way that a node is left somewhere in the tube. When the key suspended above the resonator is beaten, the air-column above the node vibrates in sympathy and so reinforces the sound; according as the pitch of the key is higher, the resounding air-column in the corresponding resonator should, therefore, be shorter. The nodes may accordingly be seen to climb up by regular degrees, diagonally, on the plane formed by the resonators. In the newer instruments the sound-tubes are sometimes made of zinc or glass. In such cases artificial nodes (*tumbengan* (J)) have been made in them.

In former times the Javanese gendèrs are supposed to have been of much higher build, which caused them to look like the Balinese gendèr wayang and those of Banjermasin, more than they do to-day [1]. Thanks to an invention attributed to Pangéran BUMINATA [2], however, by which the resonators were covered (*suweg*) at the top but for a small opening in the centre, it was henceforth possible to manage with shorter tubes than before, also for the lower tones. Since then the lower-built gendèrs have come into general use in Java. This made it unnecessary for the players' position to be raised, as they were obliged to do before, and they could henceforth refrain from this breach of court-etiquette and squat on the ground the same as their colleagues.

It is probable that—as is the case with "covered" organpipes—only the *uneven* harmonics of the resounding air-column make their influence felt in the sound of the keys, and that it is to this that the softness and luxuriousness of the gendèr-sound is to be attributed.

Fine-tuning is done in the same way as in the case of the sarons.

With regard to the manufacture of gendèr-keys, *vide* **147**, p. 28/9.

Of gendèrs—as of instruments of the saron-type—quite a "family" may be found both in Java and in Bali. The orchestral music in the Principalities, however, knows—apart from the morphologically kindred *gong kemoḍong*, which we shall describe a little further on—only four forms: the multi-octave **gendèr panerus** [3] and **gendèr barung** (ill. 72)—the latter sounding an octave lower than the former—and two single-octaves forms, the lowest-sounding of which—at any rate in the complete great gamelan—is called in Solo **slenṭem** (really *slenṭem gantung* = Sl. with hanging keys; Pasuruan: *slenṭem ganḍul*) [4], and in Jogya *gendèr panembung* (ill. 75). Its pitch is the

---

[1]) Banjermasin instruments probably descend from the period of the Majapahit expansion.—Regarding Javanese influences on music (and the dance) in South Borneo, *vide* also Radèn Mas GANDAWINATA's article "Borneo en Java", in the Triwindu Memorial Book "Mangku Nagara VII" (Surakarta, 1939), p. 270 *et seq.*

[2]) A brother of the Susuhunan PAKU BUWANA IV (1786–1820).

[3]) It is said that the Pangéran BUMINATA was the first to add this instrument, and also the *slenṭem gantung*, to the gamelan ensemble.

[4]) This in contrast to the *saron* slenṭem, which, as we said before, has lying keys.

same as that of the lowest octave of the gendèr barung. The other single-octave form bears the name of **demung (gantung)**; it is pitched one octave higher than the slenṭem, and is found only in the *gamelan klenéngan*.

The gamelan sléndro possesses one of each of the two multi-octave instruments. The gamelan pélog, on the other hand, has two specimens of each type, *i.e.* one for the *pélog bem* scales (= P. lima and nem), which, in each octave, have at their disposal the tones *bem, gulu, ḍaḍa, lima* and *nem,* and another one for *pélog barang* (the P. barang scales), which, in each octave, sound the tones *gulu, ḍaḍa, lima, nem* and *barang* (better: *lima, nem, barang, gulu* and *ḍaḍa*). (The practical method of changing keys by means of *sorogan* (exchange-keys), possible on an instrument with loose-lying keys, such as the gambang kayu, cannot, of course, be applied to an instrument such as the gendèr with its floating, but fixed keys) [1]). Here and there in the middle-east of Java—especially in the Regencies Tuban, Rembang, Grobogan and Kudus, and also more to the west, in the Regency Pemalang—one may sometimes come across gamelans sléndro without any gendèrs at all. Such orchestras are called *gamelan seḍit, nyeḍit, cheḍit* or *amèn* [2]); in Pemalang: *klenéngan kaplok.*

It will be seen that the tone pélog does not figure on these multi-octave gendèrs at all. As a result, the gendèr pélog octave, both in *laras bem* and in *laras barang,* has only five tones. Since both the pélog gendérs in question, like the sléndro ones, carry 11 or 13 keys, they accordingly comprise invariably either two closed octaves, or two octaves + three tones [3]). Gendèrs of earlier date—and this is proved by key-ranges found during excavations—are supposed to have had only 10 keys, just like the instruments of the Balinese *gendèr wayang* to this day.

In a "double" gamelan the three gendèrs panerus, as well as the three gendèrs barung are placed in such a way as to form a square closed in from three sides, within which the player sits down.

Only one specimen of the single-octave form is found both in the normal gamelan pélog and the gamelan sléndro. They comprise, in pélog, a complete

---

Such instruments are called, in Bali, *jongkok* (= squatting, lying low). I do not know of any equivalent Javanese musical term.

1) I only once came across a gendèr with sorogan. One of the keys is removed by talling away the small transverse bit of wood (*bremara*) which prevents the *pluntur*-loop pushed through the key-holes from sliding back.

2) In regard to *amèn, vide* also below, p. 380, note 3.

3) Gendèrs with 14 or 15 keys are very rarely met with.

octave, not closed, therefore seven tones; in sléndro either six keys, sounding the closed octave, or seven keys sounding that octave plus one tone. If—only in the large, complete orchestras—the keys of the slenṭem are provided with knobs, then this instrument is sometimes called *slenṭo* [1]).

The function of the multi-octave gendèrs in the gamelan is, in the first place, that of playing around and paraphrasing the principal melody, the cantus firmus; together with the *gambang kayu* and the *chelempung* they belong to what is called the *panerusan*. The gendèr barung generally moves, cautiously, in crochets (either or not in two parts); the gendèr panerus in running quaver-figures (*vide* Appendix *3*). In addition to this the gendèr barung sometimes discretely supports such solo singing voices as are otherwise unaccompanied (*e.g.* the *bawa*, *i.e.* the vocal introduction to certain genḍings). Many genḍings also possess a *bebuka gendèr* [2]).

The soft playing on the gendèr, which assists the ḍalang to hit on the right pitch before intoning the different *suluk's* and to keep to it during the recital prior to intoning the next suluk, is called *grambyang(an)* or sometimes *griming(an)*.

The task of the gendèr panembung or slenṭem gantung consists, in the large orchestras, in the first place, in marking or emphasizing the cantus firmus tones which are placed at regular distances from each other (thus, usually he doubles, each time, the fourth tone in the lower octave), in which case, therefore, it should be classed among the interpunctuating instruments; but occasionally, too, it sounds the nuclear theme in its entirety, especially in vigorously-played pieces (*sabetan*, *gagah*); in such cases it is purely a cantus firmus instrument. The latter function is always allotted to the slenṭem when it is beaten—in the absence of a real *demung gantung*—in *klenéngan* under the name of *demung*; at any rate in the pure form of klenéngan, because then the instruments of the saron-group are not present. Whenever such a demung gantung is present in the *ensemble*, it is the latter that carries the main theme, whilst the task of the slenṭem, in that case, is the same as that which it fulfils in the great gamelan.

We distinguish two methods of beating the gendèr—and the same applies to the gambang kayu and the bonang. They are called, respect-

---

1) Communicated by R. LURAH JAYENGGUTARA, Jogya, in his competition-essay (not published).

2) Cf., below, p. 311 *et seq.*

ively, *ṭuṭukan lomba* (sometimes *T. kuna*, H. J. *kina*) [1]) and *ṭuṭukan rangkep* [2]).

Certain frequently-occurring figurations within the latter form of playing are indicated by special names; they are the following beating-methods:

puṭut gelut (= the struggling disciples of the heremit), in which both hands, in turn, beat the same tone in quick tempo;

Semar nyampar (= Semar pushing something forward with his foot), in which the right hand each time touches three successive keys in the following rhythm:  [3]);

Pétruk ngandul (= Pétruk hanging, or floating), in which both hands, beating alternately, sound the same tone (but each a different one) a few times in succession, as for example:

salah gumun (= queer, extraordinary harmony) [4]), in which both hands go parallel to and fro, in "fourth"-intervals:

[**113**F, **167**B, **291**E, **381**D] [*S39]

The gendèrs are beaten with short-handled, disc-headed *tabuh's*, held loosely by the player between index and middle finger. Unless muted, the tones resound for a long time, and, since the gendèr-part—at any rate that of the multi-octave forms—generally consists of tones following in quick succession, and is, moreover, often two-voiced, the total sound would grow into an inextricable chaos of noise unless the player immediately muted each tone beaten—*i.e.*, of course, only when another tone is to follow at once. This muting is done, on the multi-octave forms, with the same hand with which the tone was beaten: on the *left* side with the back

[1]) *i.e.* the oldfashioned style of beating.

[2]) *i.e.* the double, lively, modern style of beating.

[3]) The springing, irregular rhythm suggests the peculiar gait of Semar, who has a club-foot.

[4]) Cf. also above, p. 104. This last style of beating is said to be customary only in P. nem sléndro.

of the hand, the tip of the little finger, and, for low tones, when one has to play on the middle register immediately after, with the elbow; on the *right* side with the thumb and with the side of the crooked little finger. This inequality in the technique of muting the tones is the result of the inequal handling of the left- and the right tabuh. Illustration 74 shows the way the beating sticks are held.

The technique of playing the gendèr in the perfection can be learnt only by persons with very supple wrist-joints. This is the reason, according to some, why women are occasionally found as gendèr-players [1]. According to others, however, this is simply caused by the circumstance that this instrument, which is so important in the accompaniment of the wayang, is usually played by one of the nearest relations of the ḍalang himself, and, therefore, in many cases, by his wife, as a result of the understandable desire, based upon economic considerations, to have as many members as possible of one's family playing in the orchestra.

The Chenṭini (Canto 44, verse 78 *et seq.*—vol. I/II, p. 245) gives the following masterly description of the playing on the gendèr:

78. ....
Gondasana
anggendèr grenengan ririh
angatimil kumrining srengé nyalupak

79. ngenuk-enuk bebengkakané ulem mpuk
chèngkoké chlempungan
pancher sanḍungan minchachi
angepinjal jejel nyelani irama,

i.e. (with apologies for the inadequacy of the translation):

"Gondasana played the gendèr in a mumbling, heaving, rocking manner; but when the music became more passionate the tones sounded deep and penetrating. The rippling gendèr-sounds were chubbily-round; the *chèngkok* [2] he played sounded like that of the chelempung [3]. Now he played the *pancher* [4] (with one hand) and (with the other one) a frisky rhythm [5],

[1] Cf. ill. 74a from an old Javanese drawing (top row centre).
[2] *Vide* below, p. 334.
[3] *Vide* below, p. 229 *et seq.*
[4] *Vide* above, p. 168 *et seq.*
[5] Literally: jumping like a flea (*pinjal*).

now he beat (with both hands) alternately, thus filling up the spaces in the *wirama* [1]) with tones in quick succession".

Ko Mo An (**176**, str. 4) says, about the sound of the *slenṭem*, *i.e.*, the one-octave gendèr-type, that it "ulem ngalèbi", *i.e.* "saturates (the orchestral ensemble) with sonorous tones", and of the *gendèr* (**176**, 2nd stanza):

„gendèr gumlendeng gumrining
nyupak sumruwung bumbungnya",

i.e. "it meanders along in its immaculate beauty; as its keys are beaten the buzz of the bamboo tubes responds".

In the case of those single-octave forms, which are played with only one tabuh, muting is done with the thumb and index of the left hand.

Besides in Java, instruments of the gendèr-type are also found in the archipelago: in Madura, Bali, Lombok, and, in Borneo, roundabout Banjermasin.

Outside the archipelago, the only near relatives of the gendèr that have come to our knowledge are some instruments found in Central Africa, and, via that continent and the slave trade, in Central America. In these cases, however, the resonators are usually made of long-drawn gourds, and the keys of wood. Curiously enough, the tone-sequences on these African *marimba's* and *balafons* are in many cases identical, both as regards the intervals, as the absolute pitch of the tones, to those of the Indonesian ones (*vide* **212** and **235**) [2]). [**113**EE, **155**D]

In addition to this spread "in space", there is also a considerable spread "in time": the instrument—in spite of its intricacy—is fairly ancient.

---

1) *Vide* below, p. 333 *et seq.*

2) There are illustrations of African marimba's a.o. in the "National Geographic Magazine", 1922, p. 432, and 1926, p. 697; in **313**, Table 14, fig. 104, and, in large numbers, in Dr. Olga Boone's important treatise "Les xylophones du Congo belge" (1936), in the "Annales du Musée du Congo belge".—In Guatemala, the marimba managed to become the national instrument (illustration in **313**, Table 15, fig. 111). The North-Americans there made the acquaintance of the instrument; they tuned it European fashion—in so far as this had not yet been done in Guatemala—, replaced the long drawn calebashes by brass sound-tubes and the wooden keys by aluminium keys, fixed a muting gadget to it which is worked by the players foot, and introduced *vox humana* effects by means of a small electro-motor. Thus modernized the ancient gendèr, under the name of "Vibra-harp" took the music-halls of the Western continent by storm. A Vibra-harp of this description, but with its ranges of keys once more tuned to Javanese scales, was ordered from Chicago in 1932 by His Highness Mangku Nagara VII, and has now been incorporated into his oldest and most beautiful gamelan, the *Kyahi Kanyut Mèsem.* Thus the gendèr, after many vicissitudes, has completed its tour round the world.

This is evident, in the first place, from its presence in Central Africa. As regards the archipelago, I already mentioned (p. 111) that its existence as early as 1157 has been proved (**194**, p. 90 *et seq.*). Its Hindu-Javanese (and modern Balinese name) is *saluṇḍing* (*wesi*). It is not probable, however, that it has always been provided with resonators underneath the keys, for there are still gendèrs in existence to-day that lack these, *i.e.* the Pemalang and the Pekalongan *gendèr lemprak* from the *gamelan jiring* [1]), as well as here and there in Bali, *e.g.* in the three Tenganan and the Trunyan *gamelan saluṇḍing* (**196**, p. 352). In "D'Eerste Boeck" (1597), too, a description of the gendèr may be found: ".... a few reeds upon which is placed a small steel plate as on an organ, similar to a clavecymbal" (**257**, under plate 25, between pp. 128 and 129) (*vide* ill. 61).

Finally, we must describe another instrument of the gendèr-type, *i.e.* the **gong kemoḍong** (S.) or *gong kemaḍa* (J.) [2]) (East-Java: *gong jun* or *gong jemblok*; Kebumen: *gong genṭong*; Banyumas: *gong anggang-anggang* [3]); Panarukan and Bandawasa: *gòng guchi*, or sometimes *gong panggang*; West-Java: *goöng buyung*) (ill. 83); an instrument which, for cheapness' sake, often serves as a substitute for the more expensive *gong ageng*, and which, in the *gamelan klenéngan*, actually replaces it.

The *gong kemoḍong* usually consists, in Java proper, of two large bronze (occasionally iron) [4]) keys with beating knobs, suspended above a sound-

---

[1]) *jiring* = sharp edge (standing up).

[2]) According to the Pangéran NATANINGRAT, a native of Solo, the original word-form was *gong kemoḍong*. He maintains that the word kemoḍong is derived from *kumloḍong*, which, in its turn, is related to *teloḍong*, or *loḍong*. The latter word, whose main signification today is "stop-flask", used to mean, in former times, (chiefly) bamboo water-tube; hence also vessel, or pot. In other words, *kemoḍong* should be of the same order as *jun*, *jemblok* and *buyung*.

The form *gong kemaḍa*, then, would have arisen, through popular etymological influences, from gong kemoḍong. For kemaḍa (or *kumaḍa*) is said to have been derived from *paḍa* = like, resembling. Kemaḍa would accordingly have to be translated by *behaving as similar to*, or *being a substitute for* —a most appropriate term for an instrument which, as we have seen, serves to replace the gong ageng.

The late "Rijksbestuurder" of Jogya, P. A. DANUREJA VII, as well as R. M. JAYADIPURA, on the contrary, consider *gong kemaḍa* (and its explanation) the original and correct, and *gong kemoḍong* a later term, the derivation and meaning of which, they say, were invented afterwards.

[3]) = floating.—In Solo, *anggang-anggang* means: to touch rather gently. It is also used for the movement of a spider, which, moving *on* the water keeps jumping upstreams after having floated a certain distance downstreams.

[4]) In this case the instrument—which then usually belongs to the smaller village

box (*grobogan*). They are tuned either to *lima* or to *nem*. Frequently two earthenware pots may be found inside the sound-box (*jun, jemblok, genṭong, buyung, guchi*). One may occasionally come across a gong kemoḍong with only one key; in West-Java, where the instrument is also known (*vide* ill. 152, sub *d*), this is, indeed, the general rule.

Whenever there are two keys, there is always a slight difference in pitch. In this case they are beaten, in the gamelan, in immediate succession, almost simultaneously, the slight difference in pitch causing beats which sound most deceptively like those of the ordinary suspended gongs.

The pitch of the gong kemoḍong is between that of the gong ageng and that of the gong suwukan.

The shape of the **kemanak** [1]) (ill. 75 and 77, sub *b*)—at any rate that of the modern Javanese instrument bearing this name—is usually, and rightly, compared to that of a banana with a stalk, opened up along its convex side and with the pulp taken out. In Jogya it is also likened to the form of a kuwuk-shell (kéyong kuwuk, *i.e. Melo vulgaris*). The instrument itself is not (any longer) in general use, and occurs in Java only in fairly limited numbers. Most of them are found in possession of the Cheribon kratons and the ruling princes and lesser nobility in the Principalities, as well as here and there in the Middle-East of Java (chiefly in the Residence of Keḍiri). In East-Java they are also called *kenawak, nawek, tèwek, keṭé* or *chelepita* [2]). Under this last name, for instance, Radèn Panji Chakradiputra, the assistent-wedana of Maja ageng, possesses a set of kemanaks [3]). In West-Java—apart from Cheribon—they may also be found in possession of the Tasikmalaya *tukang saté domba* (sellers of sheep-flesh *saté*), where they go by the name of *kolèndang* [4]).

In Java the kemanaks are usually made of bronze, but in Tasik of iron; in Bali—where they are in more general use—the material used is either bronze or iron. On looking at them closely it appears that there exist a number of varieties: the principal ones being a stout, more straight

ensembles made from iron and bamboo (a kind of klenéngan-orchestra's) often called *gamelan ringgeng*—may also have the name of *gong ringgeng*.

[1]) Ind. Inst. No. 1090/1a, b; Mus. Arch. Btv., No. 556.

[2]) Cf. also, above, p. 166 and 171, and below, p. 190 and 217.

[3]) These are probably excavated, and may be even Hindu-Javanese specimens. They are said to have been in the family's possession for many generations; any beating on them is supposed to be unlucky and cause disasters.

[4]) Ind. Inst. No. 1055/6; Mus. Arch. Btv. No. 473.

and cylindrical form, and a more slender and curved one. They occur exclusively in pairs—except in Tasikmalaya. In Cheribon and East-Java such a set is handled by a single player, and beaten crosswise in such a way that the back of one of the kemanaks each time touches the convex (slit) side of the other one, and *vice versa*. In the Principalities, two players hold one each of the instruments in the left hand and make it sound by beating against it with a *tabuh* in the shape of those used with the bonangs (ill. 85). This is also the method of playing the single (very stout) iron specimens of the Tasik saté-sellers.

Both the absolute pitch of the kemanak-tones and the interval between them vary with each different set. The pitches of the specimens we measured fluctuated between 350 and 600 vibrations per sec., and their intervals between a minor second and a fourth. The instrument accordingly has no melodic function, its task being confined to marking the rhythm.

In Keḍiri the kemanaks are only beaten in the gamelan accompanying the wayang kulit; in the kratons in the Principalities their use is limited to the small orchestra accompanying the beḍaya- and serimpi-dances. They accentuate, being beaten in turn, the first three "beats" of each common time bar, in the following manner: 1 2 1 rest, 1 2 1 rest, etc. 1) A fine example of this serimpi-accompaniment-music may be heard on Col. D 33001 (genḍing P. bar. *Anglir menḍung*).

"Kemanak ngénaki nala
Lir walang angkup merpeki"

says Ko Mo An (**176** stanza 6):

i.e. "The kemanak creates a cheerful mood,
As that of (its namesake) the locust,
making for a young green leaf".

The word kemanak occurs repeatedly in ancient Javanese literature. The oldest *locus* in which there is undoubtedly question of this instrument dates from Keḍiri in the 12th century (Vṛtta Sañcaya 93); the oldest, and perhaps only existing relief-picture may be found on one of the Panataran-reliefs dating from the 14th century (also Keḍiri) (ill. 42, sub *b*). Kemanak (-sets) are also found occasionally buried in the soil; as recently as a few years ago such a set was dug up—also in the Keḍiri region—together with, amongst other things, a bronze ornamental quiver bearing the date 1185 Çaka = A. D. 1263.

These Hindu-Javanese kemanaks are generally of the stout, cylindrical

1) [**113**c]

type (ill. 57, sub *b*), although representatives of the more slender and curved form (ill. 57, sub *a*) have also been discovered. They are generally much heavier than the modern specimens; their weight is sometimes as much as treble that of their descendants, but occasionally, *e.g.* in Wanagiri in 1931, a set has been dug up halve the size of the modern variety [1]).

The kemanak represents an instrumental form of great antiquity. This may be assumed, apart from any excavated specimens, from the literature or from images seen on reliefs. Its genesis goes back far into the past. This is evident from the fact that it has spread over such a large area. Instruments morphologically akin to the kemanak (which may be gathered from typical, formal similarities, perfectly arbitrary and not at all essential) may be found—in addition to Bali—amongst the N.E. Siberian Chukches, and in the Congo basin (**313,** p. 126/7) [2]). Such extremely peripheric spreading points to great antiquity. [**236**M]

Whilst the kemanak is already relatively scarce, the **cheluring** is definitely rare. Only very few specimens of this instrument are now to be found in Java.

The cheluring consists of a number of small bronze cups nailed side by side on to a wooden underframe. It is made to sound by ticking upon the edge of these cups with a small iron rod. A specimen with two of these small cups is in the possession of H. H. PAKU ALAM (ill. 77, sub *a*); another one, with seven cups (ill. 76), is found in the Jogya kraton, where there must be also one other with two cups.

The function of the two-toned Paku Alam cheluring is (or, rather, was: it is not used any longer to-day) the same as that of the kemanaks, *i.e.* a rhythmic one; that of the seven-toned instrument in the possession of the Sultan, on the contrary, is a melodic one. It is beaten, in the kraton, in the gamelan *Kyahi Kanchil belik* (= Venerable Sir Bleating of the Pygmy deer[3])),

---

[1]) This is also the case with the two "fossile" kemanaks (not belonging together) in the collections of the Royal Institute for the Indies, Amsterdam (Ind. Inst. Nos. 1637/1 and 2).

[2]) In 1930 PAUL SEELIG found, in North-Siam, a set of kemanak-like instruments shaped like crocodiles (oral communication).

[3]) Apart from *bleating*, *belik* also means *source*, or *brook*. To this fact the following legend—so R. M. SUJANA TIRTAKUSUMA told me—owes its existence: one day, when Pangéran MANGKUBUMI, later Sultan HAMANGKU BUWANA I, had retired for meditation to the mountain Dlepih, belonging to the Lawu-range, he happened to notice a peculiar kind of kanchil (pigmy deer, *Tragulus kanchil*). The pangéran

in the softer parts of the genḍing, when it has a function approximately corresponding to that of the *saron panerus* (*peking*).

However rare the cheluring may be to-day, in the Middle-Javanese period it was a dance-accompaniment instrument in general use. The cups, however, were not, at that time, mounted upon an underframe and neither were they beaten with a rod, but held loose in the hand and ticked one against the other. It is thus that they are found depicted in great number in different dance-scenes of the Barabuḍur reliefs (*e.g.* 0 72, 0 149, Ib 19, IBa 300) (ill. 10, 11, 17) and of the Prambanan (ill. 28). The probable Hindu-Javanese names were *tuwung* and *churing* (tho' the latter term also frequently stands for different kinds of bells). It may be pointed out in this connexion that *cheluring* signifies: a number of churings (**194**, p. 58 *et seq.*).

In regard to the manner of playing, therefore, the same process of modification has taken place as in the case of the kemanak: the older manner, in which the instruments were beaten one against the other, was succeeded by another in which each instrument was beaten separately with a *tabuh*.

Apart from Java, the instrument is, or has been, known to exist in the south of India proper, Siam, Birma (*ye gwin*), Northern China (*sing*), some parts of West-Africa (as in Benin), and also, from small terra cotta images, in 7th century Eastern Turkestan. The later form (*i.e.* series of cups made to sound by means of iron rods)—practically identical with the cheluring in the Jogya kraton, although the cups were not yet mounted upon an underframe—may be found in India proper under the name *sabdaghantika* (cf. **313**, Table 48, ill. 325).

Another bronze gamelan instrument found relatively rarely in Java but all the more in Bali is the **ke(chi)chèr** (in East Java also called *kenchèr*; in Grobogan *chiyeyèk*) (ill. 78, sub *a*), consisting of two small cymbals, one of which is often found mounted on a wooden underframe. The player

---

followed the little animal to a brook, where it suddenly vanished from his sight. Who could describe the pangéran's astonishment on finding a gamelan in that very place! This gamelan (no doubt nothing but a number of keys or of beating-kettles that had been hidden there by their owner in those times of unrest and warlike action) was afterwards added and completed by MANGKUBUMI, once he had ascended the throne; it was given the name of *Kangjeng Kyahi Kanchil belik* after the place and circumstances of origin.

beats the loose cymbal flat upon the one fixed to the frame, *i.e.* not in the way European cymbals are beaten, which are "grazed" or slid one against the other, nor in the manner of the Indian and Further-Indian beating cups, which are merely ticked carefully together at the edges. In some cases the kechichèr is double, in which two small cymbals are mounted side by side, and touched simultaneously with the two loose ones.

The kechichèr is practically limited in Java proper to a few gamelans Munggang, Koḍok ngorèk, Charabalèn and some large princely *ensembles*. Only in the extreme Eastern part of the island, which once has been under Balinese domination, are they to be found fairly frequently (*vide* below, s.v. *tèng-tèng*). The Balinese names for this instrument are, in order of sequence from large to small: *chèng-chèng*, *ke*(*n*)*chèk* and *richik* (**192**, p. 82).

At this point we should also make brief mention of another bronze instrument occurring in Java: viz. the "schelleboom", **"bell-tree"**, a contraption consisting of a central wooden spindle upon which series of small bells are suspended in some way, at different heights or "storeys", usually on wooden or metal crosses or wheels fixed at right angles to this spindle and decreasing in size towards its top.

Three specimens of this instrument have come to my knowledge in Java, *i.e.* two in the Solonese kraton, called, respectively, *genṭa* (the customary Hindu-Javanese name for bell) and *klinṭing*. Of the two, the former sounds lower than the latter. The third specimen I found in the Jogya kraton (ill. 112, right, background); it is called *byong* [1]) or *kembang delima* (= pomegranate blossom).

These instruments form part of the archaic three-toned gamelan *Koḍok ngorèk*.

Outside Java they exist in fairly large number in Bali under the name of *gentorag*.

Loose **bells** are not found any longer in the Javanese gamelans. I remember, however, a rack full of small bells, belonging to the former Banten Sultan's gamelan *Suka ramé* and which may now be seen in the Museum of the Royal Batavia Society of Arts and Sciences. And another specimen I saw among the instruments of the large gamelan pélog in the Leiden Ethnographical Museum.

From former centuries, on the contrary, *e.g.* from the Hindu-Javanese

[1]) Perhaps from *rombyong* = something provided with appendages.

period, many relief images of clocks and bells, as well as many specimens found in the soil are still in existence (ill. 14, sub *b*; 18, sub *b*; 19, 20, 23, sub *f*, 29, sub *b*, and 55). They, moreover, were often used in combination with an orchestra, as may be deduced from some of the Barabuḍur-reliefs (*e.g.* IBb 89, II 1, IV 7 and others).

Pellet- or tinkling-bells, too, were known in all shapes and sizes (ill. 21 and 33).

The Javanese name for these bells is *klinṭingan.*

Many different sorts of bells are to be seen and heard in Java to this day, albeit not in the gamelan. When made of metal they are indicated simply by the general name for bell: *genṭa*; if made of wood (as they frequently are in the Jogya regency of Gunung-kidul) they are called *kloṭak* or *klonṭang.*

The supersession in Java of Hinduism by Mohammedanism was also the direct cause of the disappearance of the "priest's bells", so familiar to every visitor of Bali. It is only in the mountain range of Tengger, where much of the old faith has been preserved, that one may come across them, be it in limited number.

Numerous illustrations of both ancient and modern Javanese bells may be found in **147**, p. 123–130.

Having thus dealt with the metal instruments—all but a few, which we shall presently describe—let us proceed to the wooden and bamboo ones.

As the chief representative of this group one may safely mention the **gambang kayu** (ill. 89 and 163). It is composed of a wooden trough (*grobogan*) across which lie, on small cushions made either of twined ratan or of cloth (*sumpilan, tawonan*), some 16 to 21 keys (*wilahan*), generally made of teak-, but, according to R. M. JAYADIPURA, also sometimes of either rawan-, sembir-, nangka- or slanking [1])-wood [2]) or of bamboo, and which are held in place by means of pins fixed into the edge of the grobogan. Gambangs

1) GRONEMAN (**99**, p. 37) gives for this—perhaps erroneously—*langking.*

2) *rawan* = nutmeg tree (*Eugenia aromatica*);
sembir = *Artocarpus glauca* (with white sapwood, and a red, coarsefibred heart); GRONEMAN (*op. cit.*) gives, for this species of wood, the name *jembir*; the wood of this tree, in GERICKE-ROORDA's dictionary, is given the name of *gambar*;
nangka = *Artocarpus integra* (with lemon-yellow wood which afterwards turns brown);
slangking = probably given here erroneously, since it is the name of a herb (*Anisomeles indica*, and two more species of the same family).

whose keys are made of rawan-wood (which does not grow in Java; it is imported from Borneo) are deemed in Solo to be the most beautiful of all; next come those with keys made of sembir-wood. In Jogya preference is given to wilahan of slangking-wood.

Gambangs with bamboo keys are found relatively seldom in Java; more than anywhere else in the Keḍiri *gamelan bumbung* (ill. 116, sub *h*), and in more primitive village-orchestras. [*S18]

Here and there, in small rustic ensembles, bamboo key-instruments are found with a range of a single octave. Judging from the material from which they are made one might feel inclined to discuss them under the same heading as this gambang kayu; but if one takes into special consideration their function within the orchestras of which they form part, one might rather regard them as bambu sarons. We may mention here the "saron" of the Sumpiuh *gamelan jemblung* (ill. 122, sub *h*) and the *tèngtèng* in the Besuki orchestra of the same name (**40**, p. 212/3).

The instrument is played with two *tabuh* consisting of a somewhat resiliant, soft-wooden disc, occasionally edged with rubber or cloth, and mounted on a fairly long, slightly flexible stick, which the player holds very loosely in his hand between forefinger and thumb. A good gambang-player should make an impression of making the sticks dance across the keys. The sound has a mellow quality: it entirely lacks the macabre sound of the European xylophones.

The gambang comprises from just over three to more than four octaves, also in pélog, since this has, in this case, in common with sléndro, five-toned octaves, owing to the fact that, just as in the case of the multi-octave gendèrs pélog, the tone *pélog* always, and either the tone *bem* or the tone *barang* are lacking.

The niyaga's distinguish three registers on the gambang, *i.e.* the middle register, which is most generally used, and called either *seḍeng* or *tengah*; the low register (*ngisor*; H. J. *nganḍap*), and the high register or *ngelik*. The Jogya kraton musical notation, which will be discussed later on (p. 350 *et seq.*), comprises certain signs serving to indicate that the play of the gambang around the melody is to move within either the high, the middle or the low register. In the Sunda districts (West-Java) four registers exist on the gambang (*pangkonan*, *i.e.* octaves); these are termed, from high to low: *petit*, *manis*, *galimer* and *gedé* (**171**, p. 12).

As in the case of the gendèrs barung and panerus of the gamelan pélog, distinction is made in the gambang tone-series between the *bem* and the *barang* tuning. Here, however—since the keys are not, as with the gendèrs, held in a floating position by means of cords, but lie loose upon their underframe—there is no need for two different instruments to ensure the presence of both forms of tuning (although, in the Solonese districts, for the sake of convenience, there are several orchestras having separate bem- and barang-gambangs). When it is desired to play in pélog barang, the bem keys are replaced by an equal number of barang keys. The unused keys (*sorogan*, or exchange keys) are kept inside the grobogan.

In **171** (pp. 11 and 12) R. M. A. KUSUMADINATA gives a list showing the order of sequence of the tone-names in the various Sundanese *laras* (Jav.: *paṭet*) in both pélog and sléndro.

The keys sounding the lowest tones are flat, and, naturally, longest; the higher their sound, the rounder and shorter they get; sometimes the the highest keys are, in fact, perfectly round, small rods.

Since moisture in the air causes the gambang keys to expand and their pitch to drop, two of these instruments may be found in the orchestras of some of the more sensitive lovers of music; of these two, the one intended for the wet monsoon sounds a few vibrations sharp in the dry season, but has the required pitch during the wet monsoon, whilst the other one, out of use during the wet season, is in the dry monsoon in perfect harmony with the other, bronze, instruments, whose pitch is not subject to the influence of moisture.

In common with the gendèrs the gambangs belong to the order of the *panerusan*, *i.e.* paraphrasing instruments. They play around the nuclear theme in semiquaver- or quaver-figures, and also frequently in triplets, occasionally doubling in octaves, and at other times in such a way that the left and the right hand each go their own way, be it only temporarily (*vide* App. *3*). [**291**E]

As in the case of gendèr-playing—and, for that matter, bonang-playing, too—a distinction is made between an old-fashioned, simple method of beating, called *ṭuṭukan kuna* (H. J. *ṭuṭukan kina*), or *T. lomba*, and a more modern, "double", more richly ornamented method, called *ṭuṭukan rangkep*.

In T. rangkep, again, there are two playing methods, termed *toyamili* and *keter* or *grontolan*, respectively.

The name *toyamili* (= running water) is used to indicate the type of playing in which both sticks either touch the keys simultaneously in a regular rhythm; by *keter* (= strongly mobile) (J.) or *grontolan* (= like a roll on the drum) (S.) [1]) is meant the kind of playing in which the right-hand *tabuh* touches the keys slightly later each time than the lefthand one, and, moreover, often touches one and the same key a few times in quick succession, which tends to give the sound picture a somewhat restless, fussy or shaggy character, compared to which the toyamili playing is tranquil, smooth and serene.

Within the scope of these two styles of playing distinction is further made between a number of frequent-occurring figures each bearing their own name, as follows:

by *ngrachik* or *ngranchak* is meant an anapaest formed from three successively ascending tones;

by *nyaruk*, an anapaest formed from three successively descending tones;

by *gantung* (= to hang, to suspend, to float), also *jantur* (= to lift up, to drift), the halting of a tone, for a few moments, on a single tone (and its octave), frequently in triplets [2]);

by *ngepinjal*, or *pinjalan* [3]), the type of playing in which the right hand, as compared to the left hand, beats tones of half the duration, for instance semiquavers, against quavers in the left hand.

There is a single case in which the gambang kayu has a more or less independent, rudimentarily-polyphonous function, *i.e.* when, in the *langendriya*—a Mangku Nagaran wayang-wong play in which the male parts are also taken by women [4]), and in which scenes are staged from the Damar Wulan cycle—it just anticipates the melody in order to warn the woman singer on what tone she is to start her part and how the melody goes afterwards (S.). Besides this the gambang is a favourite solo-instrument, especially in Jogya.

The Chenṭini describes gambang playing as follows (Canto 44, stanza 81 *et seq.*—vol. I/II, p. 245):

81. . . . .
Jèngraga anggambang

---

[1]) from *grontol* = cooked grains of maize; when poured out, they make a kind of drumming noise, with which any Javanese is familiar from childhood.

[2]) One occasionally hears this term also being applied to bonang-playing.

[3]) One sometimes hears this term also being used to denote kenḍangan. Literally, it means: to play like a flea ((*ke*)*pinjal*), *i.e.* in a jumping, hopping manner.

[4]) chiefly for the sake of the vocal music, as there is no *parlando* but only singing in this type of play.

neriṭil asta kumitir
tan selaya kiwa tengené arikat
82. kumalunṭung nareṭek geter glebeg ṭur,

i.e.: "Jayèngraga's hands bestirred themselves in quick motion, left and right in the same tempo. The sounds moved smoothly in a rapid, hasty succession, closing together to a final drum-roll."

All Ko Mo An has to say about the gambang-playing is:

"glebek gumalinḍing"

i.e. "like a wagon on wheels it rolls on without stopping".

(**176**, 2nd. stanza).

No evidence of the existence of perfectly identical xylophones has come to us from the Hindu-Javanese period. The most ancient image of a xylophone is to be found on the Barabuḍur (relief IB 89) (ill. 14, sub *a*). This has the appearance of a modern gambang cut in half, the player sitting at one of the narrow sides of the instrument. An instrument of this kind is still supposed to exist in a few Sundanese désa's, namely in the Tasikmalaya district, and be called *gagambangan* (meaning as much as "substitute for gambang" or "gambang-like") [1]).

There is also mention from a Chinese source about the music in the Kaḍiri empire at the time of Jayabaya, in which, besides transverse flutes and drums, small wooden boards are mentioned as instruments (**97**, p. 17).

Further, as previously stated (p. 110), there have been found, on the site of the former town of Majapahit, a terracotta image (ill. 48), and on the penḍapaterrace of Panataran (1375 A. D.) some representations in relief, of bamboo gambangs with unequal keys played with forked beating hammers (ill. 47)—an instrument still subsisting in Bali to this day, in the gamelan gambang (**30**, p. 34; **189**, **192**, p. 96 *et seq.*, **193**, p. 413 *et seq.*).

Again, in Hindu-Javanese and Hindu-Balinese literature and on ancient documents, gambang-like instruments are repeatedly met with, under various names (**194**, p. 85 *et seq.*): *calung* [2]), *galunggang petung* [3]), and probably also *garantung* [4]).

[1]) Notwithstanding repeated efforts in that direction, I never succeeded in setting eyes on one of these Tasik *gagambangan*, let alone acquire one on behalf of the Musicological Archives.

[2]) Sumanasāntaka XXVII 8; further on an ancient Balinese document dating from 1181 (*vide* van Stein Callenfels, Epigrafica balica I, p. 41, pl. IIIa, 3) and on another dating from 1204 (ibid., p. 57, pl. IIb, 3)'

[3]) Ancient Balinese charter of Çri Maharaja Haji Jayapangus (A.D. 1181).

[4]) Bhārata Yuddha II 6; Sumanasāntaka LII 2; Bhomakavya XCVI 16; Sutasoma VII 1; Brandes-Krom, Oud-Javaansche Oorkonden CXVIII 17.

Instruments related to the Javanese wooden gambang are also found to-day, besides in different places in the archipelago, in Further India, more especially in Birma (*patala*) and Siam (*ranat èk mai, ranat thum mai*) (**198**), and in Central Africa [1]).

The **kechrèk**, or *kepyak* [2]) is a rattle-instrument consisting of two or more small rectangular iron slabs, of either the same or unequal length, and loose bundled together. During the fighting episodes in a wayang play—at any rate in Solo, not in Jogya—the noise of battle and rattling of weapons is imitated with this instrument by the ḍalang. To this end, it is suspended to the wall of the *koṭak* (*i.e.* the chest containing the wayang requisites) facing the ḍalang, the koṭak being placed on his left side. He plays it in a sitting position with the toes of his right foot, often in anapaests or triplets, and finally, when the fight is nearing its climax, in fast semiquavers. In Solo the custom is for the ḍalang to sound the kechrèk for the first time during a wayang kulit performance on the appearance of the *jaranan, i.e.* the wayang steed, simultaneously, that is, with the first advance of the army (at about half past ten at night). [**113G**]

The kechrèk—the name kepyak is more specially reserved for it in its function of wayang-instrument—is, further, the typical professional instrument of the "tukang soldeer" (itinerant tinker), who announces his arrival from afar, by means of it, as he wanders along past the houses.

The same name, **kepyak**, is also applied to the quadruple clapper which STUTTERHEIM has shown (**376**) to be an extremely ancient tantric instrument made from buffalo bones—used by those most remarkable functionaries in the Solonese kraton called *kriḍastama* or *abdi dalem baḍut* [3]). One usually hears these clappers being called *chanṭang balung*.

From the combination of the fact that the genḍing to which these kridastama execute a dance during the *garebegs, viz.* the genḍing *Hundur-hundur kajongan* [4]), is also occasionally called genḍing *Chelepita*, and the other fact that, in Bali, until a short time ago (in the *gamelan gambuh,*

[1]) Cf. OLGA BOONE, Les xylophones du Congo belge (1936).

[2]) Ind. Inst. No. 1056/1; Mus. Arch. Btv. No. 490. [*S43, 44]

[3]) Their colleagues in the Jogya kraton—the *lurah talèḍèk, lurah pasinḍèn* or *lurah prayalata* (cf. below, p. 246 and 266)—do not (any longer) handle this kind of clapper.

[4]) Cf., for the occasions on which this genḍing is also played, above, p. 171/172.

which accompanies the gambuh-dance) a similar clapper —though in this case consisting of four small wooden, longdrawn egg-shaped slabs of nangka-wood, and called *chelepita* [1])—was being played, we may conclude that the chanṭang balung, too, used to bear this far from specific name [2]).

From a communication by Mr. P. F. DAHLER, it is evident that, about 50 years ago, such a clapper—according to this informant, often made from buffalo bones, but only in two instead of four parts—was used in Madura during the burning of incense and the mumbling of magic formulae in the calling up of spirits, and during incantations. Here, therefore, the tantric character of this little instrument had been preserved intact until our time.

About this chanṭang balung *vide* also **44**, in which an illustration this instrument will be found.

In the Chenṭini (Canto 4, stanza 13) a chelepita (or chalapita) made of ivory (*gaḍing*) is beaten in the *singir*-ensemble [3]). It is clear from the description given that this *singir* also contains tantric elements, in which full justice is done both to the spiritistic [4]) and to the obscene side of the affair.

It is probable that, in addition to the kechrèk (kepyak), another instrument served to imitate the noises of battle in the wayang, *viz.* a bronze **scraping-instrument** of which I came across a single specimen in the museum of musical instruments of the Brussels Conservatoire. It was evident that the instrument formed part of a gamelan brought back by a Belgian medical man about 1870, and subsequently presented by him to the Conservatoire. Investigations made in Java failed to bring to light any further specimens; the Brussels one, therefore, is a unicum, "the last of the Mohicans". Some wooden predecessors of it, not mounted on a plinth, have come to our knowledge from Hindu-Java (*vide* above, p. 107 and ill. 12 at *d*) (**216**).

The Brussels instrument in question consists of a strip of bronze with ridges across it, fixed to an underframe shaped something like a parrot or a shrimp; the player scrapes across those ridges with a small stick (ill.

---

[1]) Another, more popular Balinese name is *krepyak*.

[2]) Cf. above, p. 166, 171 and 180.

[3]) *Vide* below, p. 217.

[4]) Cf. below, p. 195, where it is stated that, on the occasion of these *singir*-parties, a kind of rice-block "table-dance" is conjured up.

81). There is no such scraping stick with the Brussels specimen. The name given in MAHILLON'S catalogue, *viz. slenṭem*, is certainly wrong [1]).

The **keprak** (ill. 82), as a dance-accompanying instrument, has the shape of either a parallelopiped or a short horizontal wooden tube, closed at both ends, and with a slit in the top lengthways; in other words, it is nothing but a small slit drum placed horizontally. It is played with a wooden hammer (*chempala, tabuh keprak*; in Banyumas also *ganḍèn*), with which the leader of the dance (who has taken up a position in front of the accompanying gamelan) touches the right longitudinal side. The knocking sound produced in this way gives to the *wayang-wong* and the *wirèng-* (S.) or *beksan-* (J.) dancers the required indications and warnings [2]) and may, further, be beaten in all other kinds of dance-accompanying music—generally in the rhythm

In the wayang kulit, the ḍalang uses, in stead of the keprak, the *koṭak* to the same end. He plays on this chest—which, as stated before, stands to the left of him—with the *chempala*, holding it either in the left hand or between the toes of his right foot [3]).

The sound of the keprak is heard, during a wayang kulit performance, chiefly at the end of a genḍing and during the *ada-ada*.

More ancient and also more numerous, because less costly than the different metal instruments, are the slit drums or alarum-blocks, which, when made of wood, are called **kenṭongan** (ill. 116, sub *i*), and, when made of bamboo, *tètèkan*. The customary Dutch name of *ṭongṭong* is, I believe, seldom used to-day by Javanese people, although this term used to be in vogue during the Hindu-Javanese period to indicate (? bronze) slit drums [4]).

These instruments consist either of a stout bamboo segment, closed on both sides by a node, and into which a slit has been cut longitudinally (or, in a few cases, two slits (ill. 133; *vide* also **39**, p. 92/3)), or of a scooped-out

1) *Vide* above, p. 165, note, 172, and 178 s.v. *slenṭem*.

2) *Vide* p. 133 and 308.

3) the latter method when he needs both hands to move the puppets. [**113**G; *S 39, 43–4]

4) Cf. above, p. 15, note 2 sub 10.

piece of tree-trunk, left closed at both ends, between one and two yards in length and also provided with a longitudinal slit. The sound produced is called *kenṭong*.

The instrument which not unfrequently has the shape of a man or animal (fish, *gendruvo*, tiger, monkey, etc.) is provided at the top with a kind of prominence or handle, which is pierced, and in some cases ornamented with carved figures. On this handle the instrument is suspended freely floating from a cross-bar, *e.g.* in a watchman's shed, or penthouse. Very large specimens are also found set up in a horizontal position. The smaller bamboo specimens are beaten while held loose in the hand, for example at night by the supervising désa police. A club serves as *tabuh*.

These kenṭongans are to be found in every kampong. Various signals are given on them [1], *e.g.*, in Solo, one consisting of a series of groups of two beats (*kenṭong loro*) in cases of theft; one of groups of three beats ((*K. telu*) in cases of fire; one of groups of four beats (*K. pat*) during a *banjir*; a fast series of beats not subdivided into rhythmic groups (*K. titir*) when a murder has been committed, and so forth. A peculiar manner of beating was mentioned to me as being customary in Jombang. It is called *kenṭong pinchang* (*i.e.* the limping kenṭong), and—hence its name—is characterized by the following rhythm:

It is beaten in cases of manslaughter.

The kenṭongan is also played to call the people together or to their work. This curious rhythm is called *gobyog* (= drum-roll) and consists of a uniformly accelerated series of beats (they bear much resemblance to the beats of a rubber ball falling from a height and freely rebouncing), and finally wound up, after slowing down again, with a couple of vigorous beats.

---

1) Cf. about signals elsewhere (in Austronesia and Africa): R. PARKINSON, Dreissig Jahre in der Südsee (1911), p. 133 *et seq.* (New-Britain = Neu-Pommern, especially the Gazelle peninsula); JOSEPH SCHMIDT S.V.D., Die Ethnographie der Nor-Papua ("Anthropos" XVIII/XIX (1923/4), p. 729 *et seq.* and XXVIII (1933), p. 330 *et seq.*; ROBERT HEINE-GELDERN, Trommelsprachen ohne Trommeln ("Anthropos" XXVIII, (1933), p. 485 *et seq.*; P. WIRZ, Het eiland Sabiroet en zijn bewoners ("Ned.-Indië Oud & Nieuw" XIV, p. 345 *et seq.*); ED. HERMANN, Schallsignalsprachen in Melanesien und Afrika (1943). **[63A]**

This peculiar gobyog would seem to be an ancient Indonesian rhythm. It is also found, used as an aesthetic element, in the ancient imperial Bugaku music at the Japanese court, as I found out from a gramophone record played during a lecture on Japanese music by HENRY GIL MARCHEX. This Bugaku music is of Cambodgian origin (cf. PAUL DEMIÉVILLE, La musique Čame au Japon) [1] .The gobyog rhythm is also found among the Indonesian Naga tribes, on the border of Assam and Birma (cf. CHRISTOPH VON FÜRER-HAIMENDORF, Die nackten Nagas (1939), p. 85).

The police slit-drums are the subject of special articles by D. H. MEYER (**274**, **275**, **275A**), whilst Dr. ALFRED STEINMANN has described (**368**) the anthropomorphic slit-drums, which, it appears— as far as the archipelago is concerned—are limited to Java, Madura, Bali and Lombok. [**293A**]

The parts of the Javanese slit-drum bear names corresponding to those of parts of the human body. The top-part is called *sirah* (head); this is followed by the *gulu*, or *jongga* (neck); the slit is called *chlèwèkan*, or *changkem* (= mouth) and its side edges *lambé* (lips). The sides of the drum are called *lambung* (flank) (**275**, p. 423).

The instrument is mentioned in the Hindu-Javanese poem Sudamala under the name of *kulkul* (this is still the modern Balinese name, and slightly modified, *i.e.* to *kohkol*—ill. 132—the Sundanese one, the Madurese name being *gulgul*), and in other places, *e.g.* in the Smaradahana, under that of *titir* (already mentioned above), which name is still in vogue to indicate one of the Central-Javanese rice-block stamping musical parties—*vide* **37**. A third Hindu-Javanese name is *kukulan gantang* (Bhārata yuddha L, stanza 6).

As is evident from discoveries in the soil, splendidly worked bronze kenṭongans also used to exist in Java during the Hindu period (ill. **54**).

Outside Java, the slit drum is known throughout the entire archipelago. Morphologically and socially, however, it reaches its culminating point elsewhere, *i.e.* in Central Africa and Melanesia (**313**, p. 44 *et seq.* and **325**, p. 72 *et seq.*) [2]. [**20B**, **63A**, **96A**, **113H**, **239A**]

At this point we should also say a few words about the riceblock stamping music mentioned above (*koṭèkan*, *géjongan*, **béndrong** or *genḍong*) (ill. 84).

This is performed by a number of women, who—especially during moon-

[1] "Etudes asiatiques" I, p. 199 *et seq.* (1925). [*S19]

[2] *Vide*, about slit-drums and related instrumental forms, also BRANDTS BUYS in "Djawa" XIII p. 341 *et seq.* (**36**).

lit nights, and also at times of eclipses of the sun or moon [1])—stamp in, and against the edges of an empty rice stampingblock (*lesung*; Sund.: *lisung*) in such a way that, from their interplay, there arises a texture of sounds which is sometimes very complicated and polyrhythmical. Various of these stamping compositions are known under distinct names in Central- and East-Java. Each of the women players stamps or beats the riceblock at a definite point and in a certain way, so that the ensemble gets at its disposal a fairly large number of different sounds. The parts from which such a stamping-composition is built up are each indicated by a separate name (**37**, p. 26, and **43**, p. 96). Here follows a rice-block score, as noted down by Mr J. S. Brandts Buys:

The Chenṭini (Canto 3, stanza 18 *et seq.*) speaks of a remarkable, spiritualist (magic-tantric) rice-block stamping musical party. In this, Mas Chabolang, who wields higher powers, "addresses" two rice-blocks, which thereupon, without being touched by human hands, start moving, knocking against each other and shifting to and fro together, being played upon lustily all the while by eight stamping sticks each, which also move about entirely without the aid of any human agent [2]). The poet renders the sound produced as follows:

ṭung prong ṭung prong tuk prek tuk prek ḍong ḍong brag brag.

Similar music, though of more simple structure, may also be met with in other parts, both in and outside the archipelago, *e.g.* in Siam, where it is termed *kung long* (**188**, p. 252, and **198**, p. 96). *Vide* also below (p. 287 *et seq.*) *s.v.* *keṭoprak*.

---

1) In the Sunda districts—according to R. M. A. Kusumadinata—this rice-block stamping music is performed not only during moonlit nights and during eclipses of the moon and/or the sun, but also on the occasion of circumcision festivals.

2) Hidding (**114**, p. 98) mentions a Sundanese equivalent, called *ngadu lisung* (= rice-block fight).

The bamboo **shake-angklung** (frame-rattle) (ill. 121, 136, 149, 150 and 151) occurs in the major part of Java. In view of the fact, however, that it is, nowadays, chiefly a Sundanese instrument, we shall not discuss it here but in the next chapter (p. 361 *et seq.*).

We should mention here in a few words, too, the **jinontra** (also called *kinchir bamboo*), *i.e.* the water-wheel, sometimes provided with protruding parts which, one after the other, tick against bamboo segments of different pitch suspended above the wheel; this contraption, therefore, might be called a mechanical water-*gambang*.

Another instrument which is made to sound by means of running water is the **taluktak** or *bluntak*, the bamboo water-clatterer or tilting-bamboo, consisting of a bamboo tube which, much like the barrel of an oldfashioned gun, turns in such a way that its "muzzle" points upwards on the slant. This position is obtained by fixing the pivot just above the middle of the tube. The end of the tube directed downward rests upon a stone; there is a node in the tube just above the pivot. Now, when this bamboo gun is put into place in such a way that its mouth catches a spurt of water, the upper part of the tube is filled each time, which causes the equilibrium to be deplaced, so that the barrel turns round the pivot, shedding the water previously taken in, and resuming its original position with a wrench, when the other end of the tube comes down with a bang upon the stone underneath. In this way, an intermittent beating sound is produced, having the character of a stamping-drum beat.

This instrument, for that matter, does not primarily aspire to achieving any musical purposes, but serves to inform the owner of the sawah, at the higher side of which it is erected, of the fact that he is still getting water, and that the landowners living higher up have not cut off the supply.

Secundarily, however, there has been, in this case, too, the desire to serve Beauty, for, with that innate sense of melody and "Spielerei" so typical of the Javanese, whole series of these taluktaks are often erected quite superfluously. In doing so care is taken to make the tilting bamboos of different dimensions, so that their respective pitches differ and they tilt at different moments, with the result that, together, they produce an amusingly capricious, and at the same time very melodious sound-sequence.

The instrument is mentioned in the Hindu-Javanese period, namely in the Bhomakāvya (dating, according to van der Tuuk, from abt. 1100 A. D., according to Kern from the 14th century) [1]) in the XLth canto, verse 2, and in the Bhārata Yuddha (1157 A. D., canto L, verse 4), but certainly it may be classed with the pre-Hindu instrumentarium.

In those Javanese districts which now lie outside the Principalities, and which are sometimes called by the ancient names of *Monchanegara* [2]) and *Pasisir* [3]), several instrumental forms have managed to maintain themselves which, in the centres of culture, have been superseded by instruments of later date, or, at any rate, have become very rare. In this category, for example, a number of instruments should be classed that have held their ground in part of the former residence of Banyumas, and are played in the *gamelan jemblung*, about which more will be said further on (p. 291).

In the first place, the **kenḍang jemblung** (ill. 122, sub *g*) [4]). This instrument is made out of a stout bamboo segment, of the species called *pring tali*; about a yard long, open at the extremities, and with a node just above the middle. This segment is planed down at one side both above and below the node, enough to ensure the wall being very thin at this point. This thinned-out wall is beaten with a tabuh both above and below the node. Owing to the fact that the node is not exactly in the middle, the instrument produces two different tones, with an interval of a fifth. At the back of the spot where the lower of the two tones is produced a small bamboo rod is often found tied flat against the tube, which, so the players say, makes the sound "firmer". Apart from the two tones played by beating, which are produced with the right hand, other, ornamental tones may be played on the instrument with the fingers of the hand holding it.

There are further, in the same jemblung-ensemble, a number of instruments consisting of a bamboo tube of the species called *pring wulu*, cut off on the slant like a "goose-quill" from about half way down to the end. These tubes are fixed rigidly together by means of a small cross-lath, which serves at the same time as a kind of yoke, and upon which they are suspended from a *gayor* (stand). They are distinguished, respectively, by the names of *gong suwukan*, *kempul*, *kenong*, and *keṭuk* (ill. 122, sub *b*,

[1]) Cf. A. Teeuw, Het Bhomakāwya (1946), p. 59, note 8.
[2]) *i.e.* the Regencies bordering on the Mataram central districts.
[3]) *i.e.* the northern coastal Regencies.
[4]) Mus. Arch. Btv. No. 500.

c, *d* and *e*); within the ensemble they have, in common with their namesakes from the bronze gamelan, an interpunctuating function.

The *demung* (ill. 122, sub *f*) is constructed entirely on the same lines as the four preceding instruments; it possesses, however, not two, but five such tubes tied firmly together which form a single range.

Finally, there is the *saron* (ill. 122, sub *h*), consisting of six bamboo keys (species: *pring petung*), lying side by side upon a small "trough". On this instrument the melody, whose nuclear tones only are produced on the just mentioned *demung*, is beaten out to its full extent.

In some parts of East-Java there exists a type of xylophone made from between 12 to 14 bamboo segments, cut down on the slant either at the top or at the bottom-half and closed by a node at the other side, which segments—the keys of the instrument —are fixed in scale-sequence on to a wooden frame by means of cords passed through small holes. This frame, whose vertical sides protude both at the top and at the bottom, is set up in a slanting position against some wall or other, by means of the protuberances in question. The player beats the keys with two small hammers, shaped more or less like those used for the gambang kayu; the handles, however, are considerably shorter, whilst, in the case of this type of xylophone, the heads of the tabuh's are made of small discs of soft wood. In Banyuwangi this instrument is called **angklung** (ill. 86 and 87) [1]; it is customary there to play on two specimens, of equal pitch and tuning, simultaneously. In Majakerta it is said to be known also under the name of *kechruk*.

The tuning of this instrument is—or, at any rate, tends to—sléndro, as is evident from the intervals of the specimen in the musicological archives at Batavia, which originates from Banyuwangi (Mus. Arch. No. 557) [2]:

298		350		414		457		544		596
I	279	II	290	III	172	IV	301	V	158	I′

Instruments closely akin to this type of angklung, but usually of far superior finish, are found in Bali; their name is *grantang*.

For the East-Javanese form, *vide* also **40**, p. 209 and 211; for the Balinese, **192**, p. 104 and **194**, p. 463, 471 and 472.

[1]) Ind. Inst. Nos. 1046/1 and 2.

[2]) The Roman figures represent the tones; the Arabic ones in between, the intervals in terms of *cents*, and those above, the numbers of vibrations per sec. (v.d.) of the tones.

An instrument akin to the preceding one—as it were, a "hardened" form of it—is also found in East-Java, although of Madurese origin; this is the **chontang** (**40**, p. 212 *et seq*.). Its five bamboo keys—perfectly identical, for that matter, to those of the angklung—do not hang in a more or less mobile position on their frames, but are placed upon a wooden underframe. It might therefore be described as a five-toned bamboo saron with tube-shaped keys cut on the slant. The instrument forms part of a small orchestra called *Balibalian*.

A very popular instrument is the **rinḍing**, a small Jew's harp. This is found all over Java, as well as in numerous other places in the archipelago (**217**, p. 27 *et seq*.), in two main types, namely one made from either bamboo or arèn-wood, and a metal one (ill. 131 and 88). The latter, *rinḍing wesi* [1]) by name, which is found in different formats varying, in their greatest length, between about 5 and 11 cm, consists of a, usually more or less circular, but sometimes (ill. 88, sub *a*) rather angular [2]), wrought iron brace, shaped something like the section-circumference of a rather long-necked vase (*kenḍi*) and to the bottom part of which a small, resilient, brass or steel tongue has been soldered, which, lying within the flat plane of the brace, protudes just a little above its "neck", finishing in a short continuation-piece which is bent down at right angles. The player carefully takes the brace between the lips at the point where its narrows down, and moves the little instrumental tongue to and fro, choosing certain harmonics of the tone thus produced by that tongue, by making the cavity of his mouth greater or smaller. In this way he is able to produce simple, as it were large-meshed, melodies. The sound is a weak, somewhat humming one and quite agreeable to listen to.

Evidently—from a description of it by a Chinese musicologist at the end of the 11th century—this metal Jew's harp already existed in China at that time; it was said to be of Mongolian origin [3]).

---

[1]) Ind. Inst. Nos. H 746a and 1031/4a and b; Mus. Arch. Btv. Nos. 520, 521 and 555.

[2]) This angular form is said to be of German manufacture, imported into Chilachap roundabout 1920.

[3]) COURANT, "La Musique en Chine", in LAVIGNAC's Histoire de la Musique, Ire partie, vol. I, p. 147.

The rinḍing made of bamboo or arèn-wood [1]), which is, of course, a much more ancient instrument, is, in Java proper, a small oblong rectangular lath of about 8 cm in length and one cm wide, into which a small tongue, something in the shape of a tiny red wine-bottle or a slender tower with a single battlement, has been cut in such a way that it is closed in on all sides—also at the top, therefore—by the frame to which its foot is organically attached. The player gets hold of the instrument with the left hand on the side where the foot of the tongue is, places it in front of his half-opened mouth, and either ticks with one of the fingers of the right hand against the other extremity of the instrument, or pulls, in a certain rhythm, at a small cord fixed to it. Change of tone (harmonics only) are, again, produced by increasing or decreasing the cavity of the mouth.

A curious and remarkable instrumental form belonging at once to the idiophones and to the chordophones, and which has gradually become very rare—being now, apparently, limited to a few, chiefly mountainous, districts of Central- and East-Java—is the **kowangan** (*gowangan* (J.), *chelempungan* or *chaping buyuk* (S.), or *tuḍung punḍuk* (Bayalali) (ill. 89–92) [2]). It has been found so far in the district of Ampel (regency of Bayalali), Sukareja (regency of Kenḍal), the regencies of Wanasaba and Banjarnagara, and in the district of Chermé in the regency of Gresik.

One might form a picture of this instrument by imagining a more or less shield-like construction (one might also compare it to a part of the peel of an enormous melon cut into quarters and again laterally into half, but with a curious broad head finishing in a hump at the back), made from bamboo leaves lying on top of one-another like the scales of a fish and kept in place by means of string made from arèn (= *ḍuk*) fibres stretched across them, and given a certain firmness on the inside by means of a kind of letticework of small bamboo laths (ill. 92). Now, at various heights, one underneath the other and between two vertical laths of the trellis-work in question, fibre strings have been stretched in horizontal position like so many bow-strings; further, between a few horizontal laths of the trellis-work, and with the aid of a small cross lath pushed underneath by way of "bridge", two small flat bamboo rods have been pinched in, whose unequally long top-parts protude freely.

[1]) Ind. Inst. Nos. H 1155 and 1031/3a and b; Mus. Arch. Btv. Nos. 492, 503, 504, 505 and 549.

[2]) Ind. Inst. Nos. 1044/1–3; Mus. Arch. Btv. Nos. 545–548 incl.

The six or seven strings producing the highest tones, when plucked, function together as either *saron* or as *demung*, whilst the two lowest ones function as either *kempul* or *kenong*, and as *gong*. On the two pieces of bamboo sticking up, which, owing to the unequal length of their protuberances, produce different tones, the *kenḍang* is imitated surprisingly well by plucking those protuberances. The "hood" itself functions as a sounding-board.

These kowangans also serve the cowherds as a combination of hat and hood for protection against the rain (ill. 91), and, too, placed in threes or fours in a close circle with the openings turned towards each other, as a small house or shelter. In complete serenity and peace of mind, squatting, dry and cosy, underneath this contraption, and with music and song, they wait until the shower is over (ill. 89 and 90).

The tuning is said to be in sléndro; in reality, however, it resembled sléndro only remotely, whilst considerable discrepancies could be heard between the different tuḍungs playing together.

Sometimes small bamboo "markers" (*banḍulan*) (after the type used in card index files) are fixed about the middle of the strings serving to produce the interpunctuating sounds; these are cut from the wood of the *sidaguri*-bush (Sund.: *sadagori*). This makes the sound deeper and fuller and causes a certain unsteadiness in the strength of the sound, which is reminiscent of the *ombak* of the gong-sound. These markers are also placed upon the lowest saron- and demung-strings; in this case, however, not about the middle, but close to the extremity of the strings and they do not cause these ombak's.

On the tuḍungs of which the photographs 89–92 were taken, seven genḍing were played to me, *i.e. genḍing Jaṭilan* (a piece, therefore—*vide* below, p. 284—which serves as accompaniment to réog, sranḍul, jaran képang, etc.), *G. srepegan*, or *ringgitan* (*i.e.* accompaniment to wayang, since *ringgit* = wayang, and *srepegan*—*vide* below, p. 308 *et seq.*—an orchestral piece occurring repeatedly in the wayang), *G. Samiran*, *G. Kembang jeruk*, *G. Ela-elo*, *G. Godril*, and *G. Waleson* (called after a wood merchant of that name, well known all over the Bayalali district, and dead long since) [1]).

We should finally mention that the term *chaping* = *tuḍung* means

[1]) It was sung by Mr. WALESON's coolies, when carrying and lifting—with a lever—loads of wood.

"hat", and *buyuk* = *punḍuk* = *kowangan*, a species of beetle to whose wing-shells the instrument is compared. *Kowangan* (? *gowangan*) however, was also related by some of my informants with *gowang*, which means "rough-edged", scooped out, partly broken, which term also occurs in the name of that typical, ancient Javanese headgear called *topi pachul gowang*, *i.e.* the hat in the shape of a rough-edged *pachul* (hoe) [1]. The name *chelempungan*, meaning *chelempung*-like, points to the presence of strings (two more kinds of stringed instruments bearing the name of chelempung will be dealt with further on).

About these kowangan *vide* also **36**, vol. XI, p. 133 *et seq.* and XII, p. 50 *et seq.*, where a few more varieties are described.

Java possesses in this instrument—inasmuch as these bamboo protuberances imitating the kenḍang are concerned—the only known equivalent (apart from the oldfashioned musical box of that famous African instrument usually called *sansa*); in fact the manner of fixing the pinched bamboo-pieces of the kowangan is entirely identical with that of the keys of the *sansa* [2].

II. Membranophones.

The **kenḍang genḍing** (ill. 93, sub *c*, 94, [3]) 109, 111, sub *f*, 112, and 115) [*S20] is the principal one of those drum-forms which are part of the large Central-Javanese gamelan. It occurs in two types: an older one, shaped like a truncated cone, and a younger one, which is full-bellied, in which case its longitudinal section is asymmetrical. The body of the drum is made either of wood—usually *nangka*-wood—or of *glugu* (coconut trunk). In

[1]) In the Jogya kraton there exists also a genḍing of that name.

[2]) *Vide, e.g.*, the "National Geographic Magazine" of 1926, p. 709; also BAGLIONI, Ein Beitrag zur Kenntniss der natürlichen Musik ("Globus" XCVIII (1910), p. 250), and **313**, Table 47, fig. 233.

[3]) The niyaga depicted here is the late MAS RANGGA WIGNYAPRADANGGA, the able *lurah genḍing* of the Mangku Nagaran orchestras, as is also indicated by his name, chosen and borne in his official capacity. For, *praḍangga*, derived from the Sanskrit word *mṛḍangga*, or drum (from *mṛḍ* = earthenware; drums in India proper consisted, and often consist today, of an earthenware body with one or two skins stretched across it) "is a hyper-correct form, which has arisen from a language-sense attributing to the nasalisation of the initial consonant an activity-indicating value, and conceiving non-nasalized forms, on the contrary, as neutral or passive words, and which accordingly changes the initial nasal sound of foreign words possessing a neutral or passive character, into the corresponding *tenuis* (voiced consonant)" (C. C. BERG, Inleiding tot de studie van het Oud-Javaansch (= Introduction to the study of Ancient Javanese) (1938), p. 109, note 1)).

every case there are two drumheads (*tébokan*), the larger one of which the niyaga is supposed to play with the right hand, and the smaller one with the left. Notwithstanding this one may frequently notice, in the désa, the kendang being beaten the other way round, *i.e.* with the larger drumhead to the left; this is evidently in imitation of the arrangement of the keys of the saron, gambang and gendèr, which instruments have their largest keys on the left and their smaller on the right. This arrangement is called *ngédé* (derived from *kédé*, to be left-handed). During playing the niyaga either holds the drum in his lap or has it in front of him on a low wooden footstool (*ranchakan* = *banchik* = trestle, *tlapakan* = sole of the foot). [*S21]

Sometimes, in the Jogya kraton, one may see, in so called *kendangan loro*, double drumming, the large drumhead being beaten with a short, bare wooden *tabuh*; this is in order that the drum-playing may be audible to the wayang-dancers above the robust sound of the sarons and demungs. This, however, is an exception; a beating-stick is used also, during *topèng* (mask-dance)-performances [1]), and in the *wayang golèk*, when either Dasamuka or Ménakjingga appears on the stage.

In the West-Javanese (Sundanese) districts, too, the kendang is usually played with the bare hand.

With respect to this kendang, again, some difference exists between Solo and Jogya: in the former place the smaller drumhead is, proportionately smaller than in the latter. Further, in Solo, the large drumhead is made from the skin of a she-goat, and the small one of that of the male of the species. The Jogya adat, on the other hand, prescribes for the larger drumhead the hide of a young buffalo, and for the small one that of a *kidang* or *munchak* (*Cervulus muntjac*), or, when this is not available, also that of a young buffalo. One of the most famous kendang-makers, in the third quarter of last century, was PAH SONGYAN, in Bayalali.

The drumheads are stretched by means of ratan hoops, which are interconnected by either ratan or leather cords (*ulur-ulur*) after which they are drawn tighter still by ratan sliding rings (*suh*). This is what is called "Y-stretching", in contradistinction to that without such rings, which may be indicated, for short, by the name of "V-stretching".

[1]) About *topèng*, *vide* **156**; further B. P. A. SURYADININGRAT, De wajang orang topèng in het heden en verleden ("Djawa" XV, p. 194 *et seq.*), 1935, and TH. PIGEAUD (**298**, plates III–XVI and XXIII). There are also some good illustrations in "Djawa" III, pp. 190 and 191.

"Y-stretching" is, in Java, relatively modern; none of the Hindu-Javanese relief-drums possess these sliding rings.

The older, truncated-conical form is found to-day, as far as the Central- and East-Javanese kratons, dalems and kabupatèns are concerned, only in a number of rather primitive ensembles (Munggang, Koḍok ngorèk, Charabalèn), and, further, frequently in the désa.

Tuning of the drumheads to a certain pitch is done (to-day) only rarely; in former times, however, it appears to have been the rule. Only in the large orchestras of the nobility in the Principalities is it still being practised fairly frequently, especially in the case of the *ketipung*, a smaller drum which will presently be discussed. In these cases the drumheads are tuned to the tonal "pillar-tones" (German "Gerüsttöne", Dutch: pijler-tonen) *e.g.* that of the ketipung, in paṭet sanga, to *lima* and *barang*, and in paṭet manyura, to *nem* and *gulu*.

In any case modern Java does not, as Birma and the Toba-Batak-districts, know any series of drums specially tuned for melodic purposes. Usually, attention is paid merely to whether the tone of the kenḍang is dull (*kenḍo*, Mal.: *kendor*, literally: slack, flabby) or bright (*kemrampyang*, *kencheng*). For stately, slowly-played pieces the drumheads are stretched slightly less tight (hence the term *kenḍo*) than for quick, exiting music (*kencheng* = tense). Occasionally one finds a kind of tuning paste being used (often of *gambir*), which—in accordance with what we said just now—does not (? generally) serve to give the tone any particular pitch, but only to improve its quality or timbre (ill. 95). Small tears in the drumhead caused by constant use are also sometimes closed up by means of this paste.

Javanese drum-playing, which, at first sight, looks hopelessly difficult to learn, nevertheless employs only a relatively small number of primary varieties of beating.[1]) In the Mangku Nagaran (S.) these were enumerated to me under the following names:

1. *ḍeng, beng, bem,* or *bah, i.e.* the beat with four closed fingers on the edge of the large drumhead;
2. *ḍung*, or *genḍung, i.e.* the beat with three outspread fingers simultaneously on the middle of the large head, what time the hand rests with the ball of the thumb on the skin;
3. *tak*, or *tang, i.e.* the beat with closed fingers on the middle of the small head;

[1]) [**89**B-C, **107**A, **248**D, **291**B, **302**B, **377**G]

4. *tek, i.e.* the beat with either the index or the middle finger on the large head;
5. *tong*, or *kempyang* (= bright), *i.e.* the beat with the index on the edge of the small head. This is the most neutral of the sounds, and chiefly serves to "count the time", *i.e.* indicate the time-measure of the rhythm.

The following beats are distinguished in Jogya:

1. *bem, i.e.* the beat with the closed middle-, ring- and little finger on the large head, slightly towards the edge. The sound itself is termed *ḍeng*;
2. *ḍunḍung, i.e.* the beat with the closed index, middle- and ringfinger in the centre of the large head; the sound is called *ḍung*;
3. *tepak, i.e.* the beat with four or five closed fingers on the centre of the small head, these fingers not being lifted up again immediately after the beat. The sound is called *tak*;
4. *(ke)ketek, i.e.* the beat with either the middle finger or the index on the edge of the small head; this is more a "counting" than a "sounding" beat; the sound is called *tong*, or *pen*;
5. *kempyang, i.e.* a quick, ticking-grazing beat with the middle finger and index along the top of the edge of the small head (executed more especially just before a beat on the gong ageng).

These five elementary types of beat are indicated in the Jogya kraton notation by means of special signs (*vide* below, p. 352); Nos. 4 and 5, however, have to share one sign between them. As against this there are, for each of the beats *bem* and *ḍunḍung*, two extra signs, serving, respectively, to indicate accelerando and ritardando [1]).

---

[1]) I do not quite see how, in the Jogya kraton notation, there can be room for these accelerando- and ritardando-signs for the kenḍangan, in addition to the general sign for changes in tempo, unless the former should only (or also) represent brief, intermittent accelerandi and ritardandi (which, however, I cannot remember from auditions of gamelan playing in the Principalities, and neither do any of the notations known to me adduce any proof of this), as against the *general* sign, which would then represent a general, permanent transition to another tempo, as well as the known, traditional acceleration, followed by slowing down of the tempo towards and at the end of a movement. It is a fact however, that in the great kraton collection these kenḍangan signs and those indicating the change in the general tempo coincide in very many cases, or, at any rate, occur during the same wilet, especially in places where such transitions to a subsequent part of the genḍing is being prepared, and in the final "bars"; but that, on the other hand, in the same genḍing collection—in other genḍings, but also during such transitional and final phrases—either the kenḍang signs in question or those indicating the general change of tempo are lacking. All this points to identity, or, at any rate, to mutual

It will be seen that there exists considerable correspondence between the kenḍang-beats of Solo and Jogya; there are, however, also some small differences (notable in the cases of the beats Nos. 4 and 5).

As we said before, a large part of the tone-figures played on the drum by an experienced niyaga are combinations of the above-mentioned foundational beats. In the Jogya kraton some tens of these different drum-beat patterns are known in sléndro, and as many in pélog, each of which is in itself typical of certain compositions or groups of compositions, and bears its own name. These names are mostly derived from those of certain genḍings or groups of genḍings of which the drum-patterns in question are characteristic.

In the Jogya kraton the following patterns are played in the genuine *genḍing ageng*:

in sléndro: ***kenḍangan Mawur*** [1]; in pélog: ***K. Mawur keṭuk 8,*** or ***K. Mawur keṭuk 4*** (***hawis***) [2], as well as *K. Semang keṭuk 8* [3]. In K. Mawur pélog there are a number of variants (*M.* ***tungkakan keṭuk*** *8* [4]), *M.* ***tungkakan glenḍeng*** [5]), *M.* ***tungkakan weḍikèngser*** [6]), M. *Kinasih* [7])) and, of Semang keṭuk 8, the variety *S. beḍaya* [8]).

For the ***genḍing ageng tengahan,*** *K. Jongga* [9]) is beaten in sléndro [10]), and *K. Semang keṭuk 4* (*kerep*) [11]) in pélog (*vide* App. 9). Of K. Jongga, too, there exists a variant, namely *K. Jongga larachiblon* [12]).

---

replaceability. In other genḍing collections contained in this kraton notation *both* forms of indicating tempo-changes are lacking. Neither are these signs absolutely indispensable: both *sesegan* and *suwuk*—often indicated, moreover, in letter script above the relative wilet bars as well—have been sufficiently laid down by playing tradition, as well as the moment at which they are to set in. [*S22–24]

[1]) Genḍing *Mas kumambang* and *Marasonja* (P. 6 sl.); G. *Mawur* and *Renyep* (P. 9); G. *Montrokenḍo* and *Blabar* (P. manyura), etc. [*S50]

[2]) G. *Lunṭang* (P. 6), *Babarlayar* (P. barang).

[3]) G. *Agul-agul* (P. 5); *Semang* (P. 6); *Bonḍèt* (P. barang).

[4]) G. *Pangrawit* (P. 5).

[5]) G. *Glenḍeng* (P. 5).

[6]) G. *Pengawé*; *Klenṭung, Taliwangsa* (P. 5).

[7]) G. *Kinasih* (P. barang).

[8]) G. *Semang beḍaya* I and II (P. 6 pélog).

[9]) The only exception to this is the G. *Kinanṭi Mataraman*, which, although in sléndro (P. manyura), nevertheless uses K. *Semang keṭuk 4*.

[10]) G. *Jongga* and *Peksibayak* (P. 6), *Kembang soré* and *Glompong* (P. 9), *Lambangsari* and *Chondra Madura* (P. manyura), and many others.

[11]) G. *Panḍan binèṭot* and *Chondra sari* (P. 5), *Rebeng* and *Mongkok* (P. 6), *Gendréh, Sudira gambuh* (App. 9), *Siring* (P. barang), and many others.

[12]) G. *Galagoṭang* (P. 6 sl.).

In the Mangku Nagaran there are, in addition to the above, a few other kenḍangan-names in vogue for the genḍing ageng pélog; I do not know, however, to what extent these cover the above-mentioned Jogya names. They are, amongst others, *K. Rebeng* 1), *K. Pasang* 2), *K. Mawur sungsun* 3), *K. Semang rangkep* 4), and *K. Laranjala* 5).

For those genḍings which, in Jogya, are reckoned to belong to the *genḍing alit*, but which, in Solo, are still classed with the *genḍing tengahan, i.e.* those with two keṭuk beats per kenongan but with four kenongan per gongan, the customary drum-beat pattern is, in sléndro: *K. chondra* 6) (*vide* App. *5*), with its variant *K. chondra larachiblon* 7), as well as *K. Gandrung-gandrung* 8) and (but this only for the genḍing *Krawitan* (P. 6 sl.), which belongs to this group) *K. Krawitan*; in pélog *K. Sarayuda* 9) (*vide* App. *8*) and *K. Gandrung-gandrung* 10) are beaten for compositions of this structure.

In addition to the above there also is, in the Mangku Nagaran, for the same category, *K. Myanggong* 11).

For the genuine *genḍing alit* (alias *ketawang genḍing, ketawang ageng*) *K. Lahela* or *Lala* 12) is used in Jogya both in sléndro and in pélog, and in sléndro, on rare occasions, also a variant of it: *K. Lahela gandrung-gandrung* 13).

---

1) G. *Pasang* and *Muntab* (P. 5), *Pengawé* and *Menyan kasilir* (P. 6), *Siring* and *Jenṭar* (P. barang), etc.

2) G. *Lunṭang* and *Lagu* (P. 6).

3) G. *Jalaga* (P. 5) and *Gonjang anom* (P. 6).

4) G. *Laranjala* (P. 5).

5) G. *Rara pamular* (P. manyura).

6) G. *Titipati* (in Solo, with K. jongga), *Hudan soré, Prihatin, Bonḍèt* (P. 6), *Renyep, Gambir sawit, Gègèr soré, Génjong* (App. *5*), *Keḍaton bentar* (App. *11*) (P. 9), *Gonjang anom, Kuwung-kuwung, Gurisa* (P. manyura), etc. etc.

7) G. *Chèngbarong* (P. 9).

8) G. *Danḍun* (P. 6), G. *Gandrung* (P. 9), and many others.

9) G. *Kumbang mara* (P. 5), *Sarayuda, Hela-hela, Nawungbron(g)ta* (App. *8*) (P. 6); *Munchar* and *Gandrung manis* (P. barang), and many others. For yet another signification of *sarayuda*, *vide* below, p. 323.

10) G. *Doradisah* (P. 5), *Mas kumambang* (P. 6 pélog), and *Suralaya* (P. barang), etc.

11) G. *Wiḍang* (P. 9).

12) G. *Hela-hela alit* (S.) (P. 6 sléndro), *Lahela, Dempel, Tlutur laranangis* (P. 9), *Boyong, Halaspadang* (S.) (P. manyura), etc. (especially in P. 9); *Tlutur* (P. 5), *Tlutur sangubron(g)ta, Randu kéntir* (S.) (P. 6 pélog), *Hangun-hangun* (S.), and *Basuki* (S.) (P. barang). *Vide* also, below, p. 297 and 299. [*S50]

13) G. *Merak kasimpir* (P. manyura) (in the Mangku Nagaran, this genḍing has the ordinary K. Lahela).

The following are typical of *ladrang*-compositions, both in sléndro and in pélog: *K. ladrang kenḍang setunggal* (= one) [1]) (with, as subsidiary forms, *K. ladrang kenḍ. setunggal sekar* [2]) and *K. ladr. kenḍ. setunggal Dempel* [3])), *K. landr. kenḍ. kalih* (= two) [4]) (with, as variant in both sléndro and pélog, *K. ladr. kenḍ. kalih raja* [5])), and, in addition, in pélog: *K. ladr. kenḍ. kalih sabrangan* [6]), as well as *K. Bibaran*. Further, in sléndro, *K. Jangkrik génggong larachiblon* [7]) and—exclusively for the genḍing of the same name—*K. Gangsaran kagok Liwung kenḍ. kalih, K. Gangsaran kagok Dirada meta kenḍ. kalih*, and, in pélog, *K. Gangsaran Ronèng tawang kenḍ. kalih, K. Gangsaran Bima kurda kenḍ. kalih*, and *K. Gangsaran Hembat-hembat penjalin*.

In addition to the above, the Mangku Nagaran also knows, as kenḍangan ladrang, *K. chiblon chak Pangkur* [8]) and *K. chiblon nikel* [9]).

Of all these ladrangan drumming patterns, the *K. raja, bibaran* and *sekar* do not belong to any particular genḍings, but may, if desired, at any time be used for pieces of the suitable type.

K. raja can be played to every genḍing ladrang kenḍang kalih; but this is done only in wayang accompaniment, when some powerful prince appears on the stage.

K. bibaran is heard only during the winding-up of a wayang performance or festival meeting (*bibar*, L. J. *bubar* = finish, all over) or when the chief personage departs from a ceremony [10]).

---

1) G. *Sekar gaḍung pupuletan* (P. 6 sléndro), *Gandasuli, Peksikuwung* (P. 9), *Sumiyar, Ladrang manis, Kutut manggung* (S.) (P manyura), *Puspakanṭi, Teḍak sa(ng)king* and *Rangu-rangu* (P. barang).

2) G. *Hènḍèl pengantèn* (P. 6 pélog).

3) G. *Ladrang sinom* (P. barang), *Dempel* (P. 9).

4) G. *Dirada meta* and *Wirangrong* (P. 6 sléndro), *Uluk-uluk* and *Surung ḍayung* (P. 9), *Richik-richik* and *Liwung* (P. manyura), *Riyemriyem, Golong* (App. 3) and N*yekarsih* (P. 5), *Laras ati, Langen asmara* and *Surung ḍayung* (App. 7) (P. 6 pélog), *Jongkèli* and *Widasari* (P. barang), and a great many more. [*S60]

5) G. *Lunggaḍung Madura* (P. 6 pélog).

6) all marches ("mares"), *e.g.* G. *Mares bron(g)ta, Mares Raja* (P. 6), *Mares "inpantri", Mares Kinanṭi, Mares pengantèn, Mares "Prasman"* (P. barang), etc. (most of them are in P. barang), and further *Bima kurda, Arjuna mangsah, Arjuna asmara* (P. barang).

7) G. *Jangkrik génggong* and *Bawangsebungkul* (P. 9).

8) G. *Wéya-wéya jurangjero* (P. 9), *Ledok asmara* (P. 6 sléndro).

9) G. *Ringa siwul* (P. barang).

10) Some well-known genḍings, for which K. Bibaran is customary, are: G. *Gagaksétra* and *Kebogiro* (P. 9), *Bibaran* and *Béndrong* (P. manyura), *Tropongan* and *Udan mas* (P. 6 pélog).

K. ladr. sekar should actually be beaten only in serimpi- and beḍaya-accompaniment, although it may also be heard to-day in ordinary *nguyu-uyu* (J.) = *klenéngan* (S.).

For the *ketawang alit* compositions there is a lesser variation of drum-beat-patterns; they have, for both sléndro and pélog, only *K. ketawang setunggal* [1]) and *K. ketawang kalih* [2]).

The general principle, both for ladrang and for ketawang, is that, in softly-beaten pieces, kenḍangan *kenḍang setunggal* is used, and in the more vigorously-played ones, *K. kenḍang kalih.* In this connexion, K. ladr. setunggal is also occasionally called *K. ladrang alus* [3]).

It should be pointed out that, although both in sléndro and pélog the names K. setunggal and K. kalih are used without further distinction, this does not mean that these drumbeat-patterns are perfectly identical in both tonal systems. In Jogya, at any rate, slight discrepancies may be noticed, especially towards the moment the gong-beat is due.

Those compositions which deviate either in form or in the particular manner of instrumental rendering, owing to which they could not be classed with any of the foregoing forms of composition—such as the genḍings *Munggang, Koḍok ngorèk, Nalaganjur, Charabalèn, Ayak-ayakan,* and *Srepegan*—have each their own kenḍangan, which, in those cases, often bear the same name as the genḍing of which it is typical. The peculiar nature of the kenḍangan for Ayak-ayakan and Srepegan, however, is generally indicated by the term *kenḍangan patut, i.e.*: the kind of kenḍangan suitable to it (cf. App. 3).

In Solo it is not the custom to use terms for the kenḍangan such as the above Jogya ones [4]), apart, that is, from the distinction in K. setunggal and K. kalih, in ladrang and ketawang. In Solo it is the custom to state, after the name of a piece, and in addition to mentioning the particular

---

[1]) G. *Chlunṭang* (= "waggishness") and *Gaḍung melati* (= melati-flower) (P. manyura), *Gunungsari* (mountain of perfumes) (P. manyura), *Ketawang Sinom, Ketawang Gandrung manis* (P. barang).

[2]) G. *Subakastawa, Rajaswala* (P. 9), *Panji ketawang* (P. manyura), *Srimaléla* (P. barang).

[3]) *alus* = gentle, refined.

[4]) An exception to this should be made for the Mangku Nagaran, where, in this respect—as was already evident from the review given above of the various sorts of kenḍangan—the Jogya adat is followed, be it with a few deviations (possibly owing to the fact that the wife of his Highness MANGKU NAGARA VII, Ratu TIMUR, a sister of the eighth Sultan, hailed from Jogya.)

composition-group and the paṭet to which it belongs, whether the keṭuk-beats come close together (*kerep*) or lie far apart (*arang*, (*h*)*awis*), as well as the number of keṭuk-beats per *kenongan* and the number of kenong-beats per *gongan*—all of which is sufficient indication of the kind of drum-beat pattern required [1]).

Besides the classical type of kenḍangan, bound to strict rules—but of which, for that matter, there also exists a slightly more ornamental and playful form called *kosèkan* [2]), whose use is limited to the *munggah* of the longer genḍings and to ladrang-compositions [3])—there are other, freeer, forms. A certain measure of freedom in playing is also allowed the *kenḍangan kalih* (L. J. *K. loro*), in which the beats are divided between two drums, *i.e.* the *kenḍang genḍing* and the *ketipung* or *penunṭung* (App. *6* and *7*).

The *banḍolan* (derived from *banḍol* = naughty, skittish, frolicsome) leaves the player still more freedom in his performance, although this style, too, can be represented by the notation in vogue for the classical kenḍangan. Banḍolan is proceeded to during *nguyu-uyu*, after the players have first treated their audience to a number of pieces of a more serious kind, and to some ladrangan.

In the end, the freedom allowed the players culminates in what is called *gembyakan* (= banter)—in Solo, it appears, also called *ḍagelan* = clownish. This freedom is so great, and so completely left to the *bon plaisir* and inspiration of the players, that it would be impossible to represent it by any notation at all. This gembyakan is often coupled with keṭuk-anapaests, such as are shown further down when the *genḍing talèḍèkan* are dealt with. Some genḍings have classic kenḍangan and gembyakan alternately. An example of this is the ladrangan *Sumedang kebar* (P. 9) (J.).

As may be seen from the above remarks, Javanese drum-playing is something extremely complicated and many-sided. The Western ear, unadapted as it is to such auditive refinements, is, indeed, inclined to underrate its value. For those, however, who have learned to understand this art of drum-playing, be it only summarily and incompletely, there is fresh joy to be got each time out of hearing these richly-shaded sounds,

---

1) Cf. also below, p. 296.

2) from *kosèk* = stirring peeled rice (*bras*) by hand in a basket.

3) *Kosèkan*—although still belonging to classical kenḍangan—tends towards what is called *kenḍangan chiblon*, to be discussed directly. This, again, is explicitly stated in the Chenṭini (Canto 276, stanza 27; vol. VII/VIII, p. 203): kosèkan raras siblonan, *i.e.* "in kosèkan-style, inclining to kenḍangan chiblon".

a joy almost amounting to physical pleasure, that of imagining them to be produced by one's own supple fingers.

In the Chenṭini the playing of the kenḍang is described as follows (Canto 44, stanza 84 *et seq.*—vol. I/II, p. 246):

84. kenḍangipun ajeg jejeg lomba kukuh
ulet wilet samya
rebut yatmakaning genḍing
— — dangu dènya nges-nges chènkokira

85. genḍingipun niba kenḍangé angguguk
kipat akosèkan
bem sebah kempyang nelampit
ambiantu tan selaya wiletira.

An aproximate translation of this would be:

84. "The kenḍangan was regular, as it should be, not artificial, and kept strictly to the time-measure. The weaving together of the sounds (*ulet*) [1]) and the meandering of the melody (*wilet*) [2]) vied which each other within the soul of the genḍing. For a long time melodies were rendered which moved the hearer's heart.

85. As soon as the genḍing "fell" (*niba*) [3]) the kenḍang barked in quickened tempo after the manner of *kosèkan* [4]); the *bem* [5]) moaned; the *kempyang* [6]) slipped in between and went along with the *bem*, without disturbing the harmony of the *wilet*"."

Ko Mo An (**176**, stanza 2) says of the kenḍang: "tétéhana runṭung, swarané salin sumalin jejek ajek iramanya" *i.e.* "should be plainly audible, driving on (the ensemble) with ever-varying sounds, but setting the tempo (*irama*) firmly and inperturbably".

The function of the kenḍang in the gamelan is, in the first place, an agogic one, that is, it leads, slows down, accelerates and maintains the tempo, either or not at some indication from the rebab. In addition it

[1]) *Ulet* refers to the heterophony (c.q. polyphony) of the different orchestral parts.

[2]) *Wilet* relates to the structure of each individual part. *Vide* also, below, p. 333 *et seq.*

[3]) *Vide* below, p. 313 *et seq.*

[4]) *Vide* p. 210.

[5]) *Vide* p. 205.

[6]) *Vide* p. 205.

fills in, with its play-pattern, the *ḍongḍing*-framework, and functions, therefore, at the same time more or less as an instrument producing melodic ornamentation. In this manner, the kenḍang keeps in the closest touch with, and leads—be it often according to hints given it by the rebab—all the important elements in gamelan playing: in the first place, tempo and interpunctuation. For this reason it is the instrument *par excellence* of the *lurah genḍing*, the leader of the orchestra. [**377**K, **402**F]

The introduction to certain genḍings is also played on the kenḍang genḍing (*bebuka kenḍang*) [1]).

In common with some *pusaka* gongs, some of the kenḍangs enjoy the special reverence of the population, and bear their own proper names. Thus, in the Jogya kraton, one may see the *Kanjèng Kyahi Mèyèk*, on the occasion of the *Garebeg Dal* [2]), held once every eight years, being carried around in a stately procession, wound round with *melati* festoons, and under the burning of incense (**100**, p. 49).

The **kenḍang chiblon** (ill. 93, sub *b*), has exactly the same structure as the kenḍang genḍing, but is of smaller dimensions and does not seem to occur in the truncated conical shape. It is supposed to have been incorporated into the gamelan as late as 1870, when the need was felt for a somewhat lighter and brighter drum-sound, especially as accompaniment of the dance, and for the "smaller" kinds of genḍing (*ladrang* and *ketawang*) that have gradually come to the fore, at the expense of the genḍing *ageng* and *tengahan*. The kenḍang chiblon is also used for preference during *nguyu-uyu* (*uyon-uyon*) (in the Solonese sense), *i.e.* the performance of *genḍing sabetan* on the day or the evening before some festivity, and—but, it appears, for the present only in Solo—nowadays also fairly frequently during the second part (the *munggah*) of the genḍing ageng and tengahan. Finally, in wayang-accompaniment, one may hear, alternately, the so-called *K. batangan* on the kenḍang chiblon and *K. loro* (*kalih*) on the kenḍang genḍing and the ketipung; the former, that is, when the wayang figures are dancing, and the latter when they stand still (J.). [**377**G]

We may mention also that the function of the chiblon was, in the beginning, a far more limited one than it is now. Only very few pieces (*e.g.*,

---

1) Cf. below, p. 311 *et seq.*
2) *i.e.* the Garebeg Mulud, celebrated with very special pomp and circumstance.

in Jogya, the ladrangan *Bawang sebungkul*) used to have a kenḍangan chiblon in former times.

Chiblon playing is much less tied to rules than that of the kenḍang genḍing. Such freeer form of playing is called *chiblonan*, or *jamplakan* (S.); it forms, in its turn, part of *kenḍangan gembyakan*, which we mentioned above [1]). Kenḍangan chiblon is also the typical drum-play for what is called *genḍing banyolan*, those somewhat burlesquely-tinted compositions in which a more or less comic unisono choral singing (*gérongan*) plays an important part.

Another peculiarity of chiblon-playing is that the actual kenḍangan-phrases are separated from each other by short, stereotyped beaten figures which, in this case, fulfil a function in drum-playing comparable to that of the keṭuk, the kenong and the gong in full-orchestra playing, *i.e.* a colotomic one. Four of such "phrasing" chiblon-beats may be distinguished in Solo; they are called, respectively, *salahan*, *ngaplak*, *magak* and *ngenḍelong*.

Although no separate signs exist in the Jogya kraton-notation for the different gembyakan-beats, they each have their own name, at any rate in Solo. Of these names I noted the following when I was there:

1. *ḍangḍang*, *i.e.* the beat with the flat of the hand on both drumheads simultaneously;
2. *tulung*, *i.e.* a rapid alternation of a beat with the four fingers, spread out, on the large head, and with the index on the small one;
3. *ṭungṭung*, *i.e.* a beat, given simultaneously on the large head with four stretched-out fingers and with the index on the small head;
4. *ḍootḍoot*, *i.e.* a figure in which the hand, resting on the little finger, touches the large head with the other, spread-out, fingers (minus the thumb), whilst at the same time the small head is rubbed over with the middle finger of the other hand;
5. *ḍet*, *i.e.* the sliding, or rubbing, over the large drumhead, with four closed fingers.

The **penunṭung**, or **ketipuṇg** (ill. 93, sub *a*) is a drum of very small format, of which both a round-bellied and a truncated-conical shape are in existence, and which, when in use, is invariably beaten together with the kenḍang genḍing. We have already mentioned this *kenḍangan loro* (H. J.

[1]) Hence the fact that, in Jogya, the chiblon is also called *kenḍang gembyakan*.

K. kalih)—used exclusively in the composition-groups *ladrang* and *ketawang* and in some other special compositions, not belonging to such a group. Often, both drums are beaten by one and the same niyaga. To this end, he either places the penunṭung upright on its large drumhead and therefore plays only on the small head (this is often done in West-Java), or he has both drums lying horizontally in front of him, so that he has all four heads at his disposal; this is customary in the Principalities.

In very rare cases the introduction to a gamelan piece is beaten on the ketipung; in Jogya only in the genḍings *Gangsaran* and *Munggang*.

Already during the Hindu-Javanese period many different kinds of drums were known in Java. No other instrument has been more frequently represented on temple reliefs (vide ill. 8, 9, 10, 23, 29, 30, 31, 44 and 51). Besides these, some drum-images in terracotta have been found in the ruins of Majapahit (**194**, fig. 54, sub 4). Further, ancient literature mentions drums under manifold names, as, for instance, *mrḍangga, paḍahi, murawa* (*muraba*), *mardala, paṭaha,* and *paṇawa*. The name *kenḍang,* too, already occurs at an early date (Rāmayaṇā; Virāṭaparvva 996 A. D.). Cf. also **194**, p. 42 *et seq.*

Stretching by means of straps is not the only method in which the required tension may be given to a drum-head, another way being by means of nails, usually with large round heads on them, or of wooden pins. The Javanese instrumentarium possesses two forms of drums employing this manner of stretching the head, namely the two-headed **beḍug** or **teteg** (ill. 82, sub *d*), and, occasionally, the one-headed *jeḍor* (*jiḍor*).

The former may be found in some of the Central-Javanese princely orchestras in a relatively small size. It forms an essential part of the gamelan sekatèn, which has no other drum-forms besides this one. It is also beaten in the genḍings which accompany the so-called "toilet-dance" (*kiprah* (S.) or *nglana* (J.)) and in the ladrangan *Kebo giro* [1]). And finally, at culminating points in the wayang wong, it sounds its muffled, heavy, rhythmical drone to the obsessional syncopation of the gamelan *Koḍok ngorèk*. I particularly remember a moment during the wayang wong performance, lasting four days, held in the Jogya kraton in commemoration of the 25 years' jubilee of the reign of Queen Wilhelmina, in 1923. Whilst

1) Col. No. G.J.X. 18. [*S45]

the chief personage in the play, Janaka (= Arjuna in his youth), was liberated from prison, the gamelan Koḍok ngorèk was playing, now softly, now oppressively loud, and in unflinching rhythm, a figure of two tones, for a long time on end. In this figure the beḍug accentuated each time the third crotchet of the "bars"; but every now and then this regular against-the-grain rhythm condensed, as it were, under a strong crescendo, resulting in a curious, driving impulse, suggestive of unbridled power:

This is a rhythmical figure of the same kind as that which, in Jogya, is usually formed by the keṭuk-beats in the last bars of the *pangkat nḍawah* (this is the winding-up of the first part of a genḍing, which anticipates, and urges towards, the second part; *vide* below, p. 313), altogether it is a synthetic-rhythmic formula occurring fairly frequently in Javanese music (cf. **36**, III, p. 65). It is called *salahan*; hence the terms *salahan beḍug*, S. *keṭuk*, S. *ketipung*, etc. (cf. above, p. 132).

Outside the princely courts the beḍug is lacking in the gamelan. As a matter of fact its chief function does not lie in the orchestral, but in the religious field: by beating on a beḍug of very large dimensions—usually in the uniformly accelerated rhythm already mentioned on p. 193—the faithful are called to the missigit. In orthodox Mohammedan parts, and more especially in the fasting month, the air is often filled with the dull booming of these large barrel-shaped drums. They are usually suspended on a yoke or cross-beam by means of a chain fixed to the middle of the body of the drum; sometimes they lie on a underframe.

For kindred instruments we must go to Further India and China. The Siamese *klong tad* (**198**, p. 86) and the Chinese *ying ku* and *puo fu* [1]) c.s. resemble the beḍug in every detail. It is also depicted several times on the reliefs of the Bayon temple at Angkor Thom, in the former Khmer country [2]).

[1]) *Vide e.g.* SOULIÉ, La Musique en Chine, p. 81.

[2]) H. DUFOUR et CH. CARPEAUX, Le Bayon d'Angkor Thom (Paris, 1913), plates 34, 40 and 126. Although the instruments depicted there are taken by GROSLIER ("Recherches sur les Cambodgiens", p. 126) to be gongs, one can hardly imagine the "pearl-edging", with which the sculptor has so noticeably provided them, to be

The large, one-headed **jéḍor,** it would seem to me, is more general in the Sundanese districts—where it is usually called *bajidor* (or, sometimes, just *jidor*)—than in Java proper, where, however, it also occurs fairly frequently.

Besides instruments of this name with nailed-down drumheads there also exist others in which a different method of stretching is employed, *i.e.* that using a ratan hoop combined with wooden wedges. The skin is caught tight between the body of the drum and the hoop, the latter being tightened by beating the wedges with a hammer until the skin is sufficiently stretched. As compared to the Hindu method of stretching by means of straps, and the Chinese (-Assyrian) method by means of nails, this hoop-and wedges-tightening may be regarded as typical Malayan.

The jédor ḍiffers from the beḍug in that it is not symmetrical and pot-bellied, but truncated-conical in shape. The drumhead is fixed to the larger of the two openings. There are, for that matter, a fair number of varieties in shape, which may be either larger or smaller, more thick-set or long drawn-out.

A type just like the jéḍor, only much smaller and invariably with the stretching by means of ratan-tape and plugs, is that of the different specimens of **ḍogḍog** (East-Java also *réog*) (ill. 44), identical with the Sundanese instruments of that name (ill. 143, 149, sub *b*, 154, sub *d*), which are in more general use and therefore it might be better to discuss them in the next chapter.

Finally, we have, in Java proper, as well in the Sunda districts, the **terbang** (ill. 121, sub *b*), a membranophone constructed on the same structural principle as the ḍogḍog. As regards its form, however, it is not a real drum, but a transitory form between a drum and a tambourine. To get an idea of what it is like one might imagine an old-fashioned wash-

properly belonging to a gong, whereas, on the other hand, such an edging would very correctly represent the wreath of thick-headed nails on a Chinese drum. Another argument in favour of the view that this picture represents drums is the circumstance that the instrument depicted is beaten with *two* sticks; quite a normal thing in the case of a drum, but—as far as I am aware—never and nowhere done with a gong, either now or in the past. This is not contradicted by the fact that the part beaten is ornamented (c.q. painted); a drum, decorated with evidently similar *motifs*, may be found *e.g.* in Paul Wirz, Exorkismus und Heilkunde auf Ceylon (Bern 1941), fig. 2.

basin (one whose walls gradually fade into the bottom of the basin), but from which the inner circular plane—the actual bottom—is missing. Now if one imagines this object to be made of heavy wood, and provided with a goat's skin stretched across the top, one will have a fairly accurate picture of this terbang. Sometimes a piece of ratan is wrung in between the skin and the wooden edge of the instrument, on the inside, in order to increase the tension of the skin. The terbang is not, in Java, a gamelan instrument, but may be seen in the hands of beggars [1]), itinerant songsters reciting tales full of wise counsel, moral advice and depicting the punishments of hell (cf. also, below, p. 293 under the heading of *kentrung*); and, further, in the hands of religious individuals who play on it as accompaniment to their hymns of praise, resembling our psalms. These songs of praise (Jav.: *slawatan*, *terbangan* or *jédoran* [2]), Sund.: *nyalawat*) may be heard more particularly on the Prophet's birth-day (the same as the day of his death).

One may also hear the terbang being played in schools, to indicate the time-beat in otherwise unaccompanied unisono choral singing (*tembang terbang*).

Round about the year 1800, this instrument played a much more important rôle in Central Java, at any rate judging from the place it occupies in the Chenṭini. There, it is said to be played frequently in several specimens varying in size, and together with the angklung and the kenḍang. In Canto 37, stanza 223, a large terbang occurs bearing its own proper name: *Machan garongan*, *i.e.* Tiger's Roar; the smaller forms are called *kempyang* (= bright); the sound of the latter is represented (ibid. stanza 226) by the word *kipyah*; that of the former is said that it "*angguguk imbal geḍug*", *i.e.* "repeatedly barked with a heavy sound". The angklungs "*angentir*", *i.e.* "made a sound like a *jangkrik* (cricket). The ensemble is called *singir*. In some cases a *chalapita gaḍing*, an ivory clapper, is also beaten with this combination [3]). Its repertoire appears to have consisted of typical, more or less Arabianlike *genḍing terbang*, with, in addition, some compositions borrowed from the gamelan (a.o. *Gambir sawit*, *Gonjang ganjing*, *Lahela*, *Sinom pangrawit*, *Lompong kèli*, *Sekar gaḍung*, etc.).

---

[1]) The general Central-Javanese name for the very numerous "instrumental" beggars (usually blind men) is *chokèkan*.

[2]) The latter name because there is usually a *jéḍor* in the ensemble as well.

[3]) *Vide* also, above, p. 166, 171 and p. 180.

Frequently, too, the poet of the Chenṭini renders the play of the terbang in onomatopoea, as, for instance, in Canto 2, stanza 16, where we read:

"The story is about Mas Chabolang, who played capably and skilfully on the terbang. His playing was full of rolls, trills and rapid tone-sequences:

ketungtung pyek tong ting tong grig
prung prèng grung pang pang pong ping
klong klung chrik chrik bah bah gur
ṭungklek ṭungplek ṭung ṭing brang
pap pep bah bah ter nal nil nil
nguk nguk breng brung pung pak pung pyak
nguk nguk breng brung pung pak pung pyak ḍung ḍeng ḍung brang".

It is evident that, in Mas Chabolang's instrument, small tinkling plates had been fixed to the side-wall, since the sounds *chrik chrik nal nil nil* are unmistakably imitations of these small metal discs.

In one of his articles in "Djawa" (**36**, vol. XIII p. 205 *et seq.*), J. S. BRANDTS BUYS has dealt exhaustively with the modern Javanese terbang.

In our day, the terbang is more in vogue in the western, than in the eastern part of the island. It is also met with—usually under the name of *rebana* (*rabana, robana*)—in various other islands in the archipelago.

The orientalist Dr. PIJPER has pointed out to me the possibility of the name *rabana* being derived from the opening word of so many Arabian hymns of praise sung to the accompaniment of these tambourines, *i.e.* "rabbana", being the vocative of "Our Lord". [*S25]

Terbang might well be nothing but the translation of one of the names given to the instrument in question by the Arabs in Java: *ṭairān*, a word which is a popular by-form of *ṭarayān*. As a matter of fact, this latter word, in common with the Indonesian word *terbang*, means *to fly*.

In Hindu-Javanese literature we find the terbang mentioned under the names of *tabang-tabang* (as, for instance, in the Ghaṭotkacāçraya XXXVI 7, Smaradahana IV 10, Sumanasāntaka IX 1), and *redep* (as, for instance, in the Harivangça XX 17 and the Vangbang vidéha III 69). The latter name is still met with here and there in our own time, as, for example, in Bengkulen (S. W. Sumatra).

The **klontong** (or *klonṭong*) (ill. 96) is a very small-sized drum, placed upon a stem, and usually barrel-shaped. It is covered on either side with a head of snake-skin. On both sides, fixed exactly to the middle of the body of the drum, a small ball of wax hangs on a cord. By moving the handle to and fro the player imparts a swinging movement to the waxen balls, causing them to hit each of the two skins in turn, the length of the cords being taken so as to ensure this happening.

In Java, this little instrument is seen being manipulated exclusively by itinerant Chinese shantung pedlars; and indeed, it is of genuinely Chinese origin. Nevertheless, it has been incorporated in Bali with the native instrumentarium (*ketipluk*), as one of the instruments used by the helpers of the *sengguhu*, a sudra priest, to exorcise ghosts. In this case, however, it is not barrel-shaped, but truncated conical (**192**, pp. 125 and 233).

It is probable that the Bhairava statue found near Singasari (East-Java) and dating from the middle of the 13th century, also holds in one of his back-hands a drum of this description (cf. **194**, p. 157), be it without a handle, and, moreover, "waisted" [1]; whilst a twenty years ago, in the désa Salumbung, district of Gandusari (Keḍiri), a specimen was dug up about 15 cm in length, made of bronze and of truncated conical shape, and which, as appeared from a hollow handle attached to it, was intended to be carried on a stick [2]. There are, further, another two images—also in the collection of the Royal Batavia Society (catalogued under Nos. 126 and 200a)—hailing from Keḍiri and representing Pārvatī and Shiva guru and both showing such a swing-drum of, respectively, cylindrical and truncated conical shape.

It is probable that the name for these Hindu-Javanese swing-drums was, in common with their kinsmen from India proper, *ḍamaru*, for this word still exists in the Javanese language, be it more or less hidden away as a technical term in architecture. Dr. PURBACHARAKA is of opinion that we may recognise it in the word *gondomaru*, the term current in Java, both in wood- and stone-technique, for a dovetailing joint. According to him it was formed from *adon ḍamaru, i.e.* ḍamaru-joint. As a matter of fact the double dovetail, as applied in Central-Javanese temple-building in the 8th and 9th centuries, especially in stone joints, looks remarkably like the small drum of that name, at any rate as far as the "waisted" type is concerned.

---

[1]) and probably manufactured from a couple of human skulls, as is done in Thibet to this day.

[2]) Oudheidkundig verslag ("Archeological Report") 1928, p. 97/8.

III. Chordophones.

The **rebab** [1]) (ill. 97, sub *b*, 155, sub *a*, 161, foreground right), probably of Persian-Arabic origin (the name, at any rate, is Arabic) is a two-stringed bowing lute. The body of the instrument is more or less heart-shaped, and in Jogya usually slightly more broad-shouldered than in Solo. The back (*pentat*) is generally pierced by a small rosette of little holes (*nawa*); back and sides are made either from the half of a coconut (*baṭok*) [2]) or (but this more generally in West-Java) from a single piece of wood; the belly (*babad, kenḍangan* or *tilam*) is made from buffalo-intestine or -bladder parchment. The instrument possesses a "pen" (*sikil* = foot) at the bottom like that of a violoncello, and finishing in a somewhat widened foot (*palemahan* [3]) or *songgabuwana* [4]); extreme point: *tunjung*), serving as a support on the ground when it is being played. The neck (*jeneng* or *watangan*; upper part also *daga* or *sirah* = head), whose top is called *menur* — in the case of precious instruments either wholly or partly made of beautifully-turned ivory—is proportionately long. It widens out towards the bottom; this widening is called *popor kangduwur*, or upper popor, and also *umpak ngingil*, in contradistinction to the *popor kangngisor* (*umpak nganḍap*), *i.e.* the widened part of the *sikil*.

The strings (*kawat*), of copper wire, are tuned to *gulu* and *nem* by means of two gracefully-shaped transverse pegs (*mangol*) provided with a knob (*kupingan* = ear), made of the same material as the neck. In paṭet lima only, preference is given—at any rate in Solo—to the tuning in *penunggul* (*bem*) and *lima*.

The bridge (*santen* or *srenten*) which is narrow at the top and very broad at the bottom and preferably cut from teakwood, rests on the parchment belly, rather high above the middle. Before playing, the niyaga fixes a small folded piece of banana leaf (*ening, sumping* or *srawing*) immediately underneath the bridge between the two strings, which takes away a certain sharpness from the tone. The two strings are distinguished by the name of *jindra* (or *jaler* = male) and *laranangis* (weeping virgin) or *istri* (= female). Both together they are sometimes called—at any rate as regards the part immediately above the bridge—*pengantèn anyar* (*i.e.*

---

[1]) Ind. Inst. Nos. H 742, 500/5, 854/26 and 27; Mus. Arch. Btv. No. 534.

[2]) The best, largest, and most regularly formed baṭoks are said to come from Blora.

[3]) From *lemah* = foot.

[4]) From *songga* = standard, and *buwana* = world.

the new bridal couple). The part of the string from the bridge to the bottom of the instrument is called *lepet*; the place where it is actually fixed, *senting*.

The bow (*kosok* or *chèngkok*), which is similar in shape to the European bow from the 17th century (MERSENNE 1620), but built a little higher, is held in the right hand in such a way that the fingers, and especially the ring- and little finger, keep the hair stretched. The wooden part of the bow is called *rangkung*; the hair, *yoga*. Putting resin on the bow is sometimes done—as I was able to observe on several occasions—in a very economical, and, as it were, automatic way, namely by sticking a quantity of resin on to the body of the instrument, at the point where the neck emerges from it; during the playing the hair keeps rubbing along this little lump of stuff.

It will already be clear from this that the strings are bowed just above the body of the instrument. The player presses the inner part of the upper phalanx of the fingers fairly softly upon the string [1]); he chiefly plays on the *nem*-string. There is no fingerboard, such as one finds on the European string-instruments; all the same, the sounds produced do not have the quality of the harmonics on the violin; rather do they remind one of a somewhat nasal and melancholy Javanese voice, either a woman's or high-pitched man's. Even the reverend VALENTYN (see herefore p. 114) could appreciate rebab playing to some extent, however averse he was to the "appalling boredom" of Javanese music. He, at least, talks somewhere about "a Javanese playing quite nicely with a long bow upon an instrument that looked almost like a bellows, but was in itself a small harp with two or three strings" (**385**).

As a further detail we may mention that, when there are two rebabs (one for each of the two tonal systems) in the double orchestras of the nobility in the Principalities—as is generally the case—the pélog-rebab is usually provided with a neck made entirely from ivory, whereas the sléndro-rebab possesses a neck whose top and bottom are made of ivory but whose middle part is turned out of buffalo horn. A rebab of the latter manufacture is said to be *pontang*, whilst those with all-ivory necks are described as being *blongsong* or *byur*.

When the neck is turned out of wood, the nuclear wood (*galih*) of the

---

1) In the Sunda districts, the *tarawangsa* is played in this way, whilst the strings of the *rebab* are pressed down more with the finger tops (communicated by R. M. A. KUSUMADINATA).

tamarind-tree is often used for this. A rebab with a wooden neck is generally supposed not to sound so well as one with an ivory or ivory-and-bone neck.

Finally, the body of the rebab is frequently clothed in a small velvet "coatee", called *jamangan* or *dodot* and sometimes richly embroidered with gold- or silver thread.

When the rebab is not being played, it is placed upon a wooden standard, which is often decorated with fine carving and is called *plangkan* (ill. 97, sub *c*; and 161, extreme right in the foreground).

One often hears the rebab being played as a solo instrument. The European ear, too, is peculiarly affected by the sound of the rebab: "jamais voix humaine n'a chanté plus plaintivement sa vie, de façon plus vibrante, plus chaude, que le rebab, dont le son erre seul et mince sur les flots impétueux qui jaillissent de la batterie" [1]).

Within the orchestral combination a melodic function is naturally allotted to it. In the softly (*alus*) sounding pieces it produces a fully elaborated melody, which, however, does not depart from the cantus firmus to the same extent as does the melody of the solo voice or the suling (*vide* App. *3*). It does, however—at any rate in Solo, not in Jogya—anticipate the other orchestral voices now and then, betraying, as it were, the further course of the melody [2]); on other occasions it may lag behind (*gaṇḍul*); in both cases it tends to give to the Western ear the impression of canonic imitation. The Jogya method of playing, which follows more closely the cantus firmus [3]), is given the name of *ngeḍasih* (derived from *keḍasih*, a singing bird also called *emprit ganṭil*), whilst the freeer and more modern Solo method is called *nyendari* (from *sendari* or *sundari*, the Aeolus bamboo). The more or less passionate way of playing the rebab, with somewhat spasmodic strokes and strong crescendi, called *nyenḍal*, is often heard in Solo, but rarely in Jogya. Further, playing in the higher registers

---

1) Mrs. C. DE GRUYTER, Kabar anghinn (Paris, 1922), p. 113.

2) The poet of the Chenṭini observed this, too (Canto 276, stanza 36—Vol. VII/VIII, p. 203):

chèngkoking rebab ngentengi
misah ngumpul ing irama,

i.e. the rebab part was characterized by the peculiarity that it now anticipated the melody, now coincided again with the other instruments."

3) In the Jogya gamelan, the rebab keeps to the balunganing genḍing to such an extent that the former Regent of Magelang, R. A. A. DANUSUGANDA, was even in favour of classifying it with the nuclear theme instruments (the demung, etc).

is indicated by the usual term of *ngelik*; that in the middle register by *ngungkung*, short and pointed martelé-playing by *ngechek*, and the glissando to the higher register by *ngekik*.

The introductions of several pieces are played on the rebab (*bebuka rebab*) [1].

Although, as we said before, the orchestral leader usually plays the kenḍang, yet it may also happen that he prefers the rebab. According to a Javanese conception the rebab may be called the *raja*, and the kenḍang the *patih* (prime minister) of the gamelan community (the gong, which subdivides the composition according to fixed laws, may be called the *jaksa* (here = judge)); in other words, according to this view the rebab is admittedly the principal instrument, but it has delegated the real work, *i.e.* the leading of the orchestral society, to the kenḍang, which, as it were, translates the former's instructions into a form easily understood by the community, whilst the gong sees to it that all melodic phrases are equitably allowed the same length [2]. [*S26]

In strongly-sounding pieces (*genḍing sabetan* (S.), *genḍing gagah* (J.)) the rebab is silent, in common with some other softly-sounding instruments.

The Chenṭini renders the playing of the rebab in masterly fashion, as in Canto 44, stanza 75 *et seq.* (Vol. I/II, p. 245):

75. ....
tutupan geter amiwil
nguler kèkèt panuduhé ngembat kawat

76. chumenṭeng mpuk angatonggèng masang antup
jariji pat nganggang
lir sikiling laler kesit
jriji manis jenṭik ting chengkenuk rikat

77. anglir sunguting kupu angingsep madu
kosokané lomba
muput sègegan lestari
walikané rangkep ngechek rikat rata.

---

1) Cf. below, p. 311 *et seq.*

2) Javanese mysticism compares the rebab with breathing, and the kenḍang with the heart-beat.

This is, in English translation approximately:

"The strings were pressed down with a vibration of the vingers. The index caused the strings to move like a looper raising itself up resiliently every now and then, as a scorpion does its sting. The four fingers touched the strings gently, like the legs of a timorous fly, the ringfinger and the little finger bent themselves quickly and continuously like the sucking tongue of a butterfly gathering honey. The way of bowing was quite natural: with long, uninterrupted strokes, with a sforzando (*sègegan*) each time the bowing changed, and varied by short martelé (*ngechek*) playing in twice as fast a time; everything in the right tempo, and with steady, even tone".

And elsewhere in the same poem (Canto 276, stanza 5 *et seq.*—Vol. VII/VIII, p. 201):

5. Ki Jayèngraga agupuh
anggamel rebab respati
rebabé langkung prayoga
watangan pinonṭang gaḍing
kosok pinatra pinrada
batok jamangan balenggin

6. kawat ṭinenṭeng nemipun
sinenggrèng ngèk wus pekolih
lan neming gendèr myang gambang
eneming suling nyamlengi
Jèngraga miragèng rebab
pachak jatmika amanjing

7. angangkang kinosèr muput
santené karjuni
kengkeng wewangkisanira
sedayanipun sarwapik
gya sesenḍon paṭet sanga
jaridja geter awiwil

8. lir ketunggèng masang antup
tumèmbel tutupanèki

anging gyat ngembat kawat
mèt wilet chèngkok pinipil
angentul pangelusira
mégo raras nges mrih manis

9. angléla penunggulipun
penuduh amupus pakis
jentik nyikiling gang-anggang
klilinganira terampil
kosok muput angler lomba
jèn rangkep alus lestari

10. ngechek ngekik ngelik ngungkung
barung gendèr gambang suling
tapis rarasing yakmaka
wileté anglutut ati
tutupé awiwilahan
achéta rata amatis

11. ingapti pangrebabipun
ameses besus awasis
wentisé akalesedan
sad-ingsed saradanèki
laminé tan lir punika
tinuntungaken angenting

12. entong atiné kang nabuh
sitong tan ana maoni
anjomblong para niyaga
mlompong mulat ing Jèngragi
andungong pan kegawokan
ngetonggong mitenggeng mèksi

13. dènira sesendon nutug
wali lih-ulihanèki
gya *sarayuda* sabeman
egong nglegakaken ati

sawusira pepaṭetan
rebabé dèn-ling-ilingi

14. Ki Kidang Wirachapèku
suka gumuyu sarya ngling
dubilah déné kepénak
amarasaken wong gering....
....

which, translated, means approximately:

5. "Jayènraga, with an elegant gesture, took up the rebab. It was well-shaped. The neck was *ponṭang* [1]); the bow was ornamented with carving and gilded; the sound-box provided with an embroidered covering (*jamangan*).

6. The *nem*-string was plucked; when bowed, its tone was evidently quite in accordance with the *nem* of both gendèr and gambang. The *nem* of the suling, too, harmonized. Jayèngraga settled himself; his attitude was humble, as was his nature.

7. He bowed a few times up and down, to test the instrument. The bridge was cut from teakwood; the tension of the skin was firm; in short, everything was perfectly well-finished. He then intoned *paṭet sanga*. His fingers vibrated, touching the strings now and then,

8. like the scorpion getting ready its sting. Pressing down the string was done accurately; the tips of the fingers pressed the resilient string down, searching for a *wilet* and a *chèngkok*, in rapid tone-figures. The sliding to and fro of the hand caused the strings to bend through. Every now and then the exact pitch of the tone was deviated from, so as to heighten the charm.

9. The middle finger was conspicuous in its movements; the index was like the sprig of a young fern; the little and ring-finger looked very much like spider's feet. The fingers were placed skilfully on the strings, each in its turn. The bow was used in quite a natural manner, from the nut to the point; whenever the tempo accelerated, the bowing adjusted itself to this without any hesitation.

10. *Ngechek, ngekik, ngelik* and *ngungkung* [2]) were done in accordance

[1]) *Vide* p. 220.
[2]) Cf., for these terms, above, p. 222.

with gendèr, gambang and suling. The enchantment was perfect. Garlands of tones twirled round the (hearer's) heart. The play of the strings harmonized with the tones of the nuclear melody; it was distinct, regular and suitable.

11. On close examination of Jayèngraga's rebab playing one had to acknowledge that it was full of devotion, well-finished and clever. Sometimes he slightly moved his thighs: that was a habit of his and is, after all, not annoying. It was not the same this time as on previous occasions; the playing this day excelled everything.

12. The other players were in ecstasy (lit.: had no heart left); not a single niyaga had any remark to make; they all sat dumbfounded while watching Jayèngraga; they simply sat perplexed, looking at him in dumb admiration.

13. The *senḍon* was finished; *sarayuda* [1]) followed immediately after and was wound up with a drumbeat *bem* and a beat on the gong that gave one a feeling of satisfaction. After the *paṭetan*, Jayèngraga gave a critical look at the rebab.

14. The host, Kidang Wirachapa, laughed heartely and said: "Bless me, wasn't it lovely. It would cure a sick man!"....

A delightful contrast to the description of this courtly playing is provided by that of a simple désa-dweller's playing of the rebab (Canto 135, stanza 5 *et seq.*,—Vol. V/VI, p. 116):

5. ....
Ki Suradigdaya gupuh
rebab pinatut nemnèki
lan gambang klèng klèng klong klong klong.

6. Jayèngraga angling lah sewawi talu
nang-onang kéwala bechik
wusnya paṭet nulya talu
nga nga ngi ngi nga nga ngi ngi
chekèngèng chekèngèng ngèngngong.

7. Kulawirya Yèngraga samya guguyu
mring pachaké ki petinggi

[1]) Cf. p. 323.

ibut badané sakojur
wilet désa ambesusi
tutuping tangan ngejojor.

8. pangrebabé sarwi begènggèng abesus
sikutẹ ngembyak ṇut genḍing
yèn ngelik gulu tumungkul
yèn mring ageng gulu tangi
awaké mèlu gak-ènggok.

The approximate meaning of which is as follows:

5. ".... Suradigdaya quickly tuned the rebab to the *nem* of the gambang [1]): klèng klèng klong klong.

6. Jayèngraga then said: "Come, let us begin with the genḍing *Onang-onang*; that will be fine". (They started playing a paṭetan in the customary way). After the paṭet he (*i.e.* the petinggi) started with: nga nga ngi ngi nga nga ngi ngi chekèngèng chekèngèng ngèngngong [2]).

7. Kulawirya and Jayèngraga smilingly exchanged a look of understanding because of the petinggi's attitude. He was trying to play a real désa-*wilet* as nicely as possible, but he pressed the strings down with stiff fingers.

8. He bowed on the rebab and adopted a somewhat striking and affected attitude the while. With this, his elbows moved up and down like a bird's wings, with the movement of the genḍing; whilst, when playing in the higher positions, he bent his neck down; when bowing in the lower register he threw his head backwards. His body was swaying to and fro ceaselessly".

Ko Mo An (**176**, stanza 1) says about the rebab:

Rabab anyendari ngakang
pamaṭeté ḍèmes maṭis
ngaleler nges wilettira
lakuné kasok lestari,

---

[1]) From this, too, the rustic quality of this kind of gamelan playing is at once evident. In the Principalities, the rebab is tuned to the *nem* of the gendèr; but the petinggi is not likely to possess this refined instrument.

[2]) an imitation of unadorned, honest-to-goodness, bald, village-style of rebab playing.

i.e. "The rebab is as a beautiful woman, an elder sister. When tuned to the (desired) paṭet, it sounds distinguished, in accordance with its position. Slowly and without interruption the melody (*wilet*) flows on in a long garland of sounds, stirring the listerner's heart".

Vide, for attemps to "improve" the rebab, the "Taak"-article by the violin-maker Dr. van Leeuwen (**251**).

That the last word about the rebab and rebab playing has not been spoken by a long way, should be clear from the article "Omtrent de rebab" ("About the rebab") by J. S. and A. Brandts Buys-van Zijp (**53**). As a matter of fact, nothing is known with certainty concerning the essential nature of its tone. [**123**G]

The **chelempung** [1]) (ill. 78, sub *b*, and 79), a kind of zither, possesses a sound-box usually made of teakwood, standing on four barocq-shaped little legs, and shaped like a trapezium. During playing, the base of this trapezium is turned away from the player. Owing to the fact that the feet underneath the base are longer, and as, moreover, the sound-box at this point is higher, the player has the strings before him on a plane slanting upward. Occasionally there is some sort of opening in the belly of the instrument; in the back of the sound-box there is always a—usually round—hole; the 13 double strings, attached on the player's side to tiny hooks, are stretched and kept on the right pitch by means of metal pins, on the high side of the instrument, which pins are fixed on to a faintly S-shaped tuning stick, and turnable by means of a tuning key. The strings are stretched across a fairly high bridge placed on the bias across the width of the sound-box. The tuning is the same as that of the gendèr: in sléndro, comprising all the tones of the scale; in pélog, either the bem- or the barang-sequence, in both cases without the tone pélog. For the octaves, covered by its tones, *vide* Appendices *1* and *2*.

The structure of the chelempung gives the impression of having been subject to European influences. Evidently, indeed, the instrument did not acquire its present form until during the course of the 19th century: an illustration in Crawfurd (1820) (**68**) (ill. 98) does not yet show either a sound-box or feet, nor a tuning stick or tuning pins, and looks still quite closely akin to the only relief-image that we know of a Hindu-Java-

1) Ind. Inst. Nos. 474/1 and 500/10.

nese zither (on chanḍi Jago, about 1260; ill. 37, sub *b*), whilst even MAYER (**270**) gives pictures of two deviating forms as late as 1897 [1]). Moreover, the style of the present-day chelempung, with its typically barocq, dachshund legs, points to stylistic influences under whose charm Western civilization was living two generations ago.

The chelempung is plucked with the nails of the thumbs, whilst the strings sounded are muted each time with the inner side of one or more fingers held underneath the strings. CRAWFURD's drawing of his chelempung shows two plectra; MAYER, too, mentions their use, but it appears that these plectra are not used with the chelempung nowadays.

The function of the chelempung in the gamelan is that of playing around the melody. In softly-sounding pieces, its single-toned sounds harmoniously fill up, with fairly rapid figurations, the framework of the cantus firmus beaten upon the instruments of the saron-group. In addition to this, it sometimes keeps closer to that nuclear melody itself, whose tones, in that case, it resolves into smaller values, more or les in the manner of the saron panerus.

A very good rendering of gamelan playing with the chelempung is given by the Odeon record A 278001 (the ladrangs *Ular kambang* (P. 9) and *Kinanṭi sanḍung* (P. manyura)); another by H. M. V. No. 9037 (*Uluk-uluk*) (P. 9) and *Puspawarna* (P. manyura), and a third by Columbia No. G. J. 228 (*Megatruh kembang kachang*) (P. barang)).

KO MO AN (**176**, 6th stanza) quite correctly characterizes the playing of the chelempung as follows:

"chalempung umyung ngempyungi
chetạné lamun prijangga; chinorak charuk kumenching",

i.e. "the buzzing of the chelempung fuses into the ensemble; when playing solo, its plucked tones, plainly audible, dominate the total effect".

The instrument is not so widespread as the two other paraphrasing instruments: gambang kayu and gendèr, and is said to be manufactured exclusively in Solo. In the double orchestras of the Central-Javanese nobility, however, it regularly has its place; in this case there usually

---

[1]) The drawings given by MAYER (**270**), for that matter, should be viewed and accepted with a certain amount of caution; thus, his suling has 7 stops instead of either 4, 5 or 6; his gendèr has a double row of sound-tubes, and, as tabuh, a tabuh peking; in his gambang kayu the keys do not protude outside the grobogan, whilst some of his other figures, too, seem to be more or less defectively drawn.

is one chelempung for the sléndro-, and one for the pélog-orchestra; occasionally there are two for each of them. The re-tuning of the 26 strings, would, of course, involve far too much time and trouble. Sometimes, too, a kind of klenéngan or house-music is met with, comprising a large number of chelempungs (frequently replaced to-day by ordinary European zithers) (cf. ill. 110).

The **gumbeng** (ill. 116, sub *a/f*, and 117), a bamboo-idiochord (German: stammsaitige Röhrenzither), consists of a bamboo segment closed on both sides by a node (one of which, however, is often pierced). Part of the wall of this tube is loosened by means of two parallel, longitudinal shallow incisions. Underneath the "string" (*senṭeng*) thus obtained two small bridges (more rarely only one, but then in the centre) (*ganjel* = support; East-Java: *tlapakan* = foot-sole) are placed in such a way, that the string produces the tone required, when plucked or beaten. The string itself is protected from tearing out further, by means of bamboo or ratan fibres (*suh*). In many cases a kind of small vibrating bridge (*siwil* = small tuber, protuberance; Majakerta: *bindingan*), more or less in the shape of a tiny ladle, is fixed half way down this string, and underneath this siwil the thinned-out bamboo wall is completely pierced. The siwil vibrates when the string is touched (with a small bamboo stick), and makes the tone of the string more vigorous, durable and also lower in pitch. When this siwil is present, SACHS classifies the instrument with the group "Trommelzither" (drum zithers) (**313**, p. 203).

In the Principalities, and frequently also in East-Java, the name of the instrument is *gumbeng*; in the regency of Keḍiri, however, one also hears it called *bumbung* (meaning simply bamboo lid).

In the regencies of Tulungagung and Madiun, several of these instruments are placed side by side upon an underframe, in which case they are collectively called (a) bonang, (b) saron, and (c) gong + kempul + kenongs + keṭuk; this nomenclature relates to the function of such series of idiochords within the ensemble, *gamelan gumbeng* or *gamelan bumbung*, of which they form part.

Instruments of this or kindred structure are known throughout the archipelago. Frequently, however, the above-described small bridge is lacking, whilst often, too, each instrument carries more than one string (up to 7 or 8); and in some cases the bamboo tube is not left round, but—

wholly or partly—halved longitudinally (Flores [1]), Timor [2]), Alor [3])). As we said before, bamboo idiochords are also found here and there with the bridge somewhere half-way, so that a tone may be produced on either side (ill. 99).

The one- and two-stringed, and some of the three-stringed specimens are beaten with a small stick; the remainder of the three-stringed, as well as the four- and more-stringed ones are plucked like a zither, with the thumb-nails.

The instrument is also known to us from the Hindu-Javanese literature, in which it is mentioned a few times, in 14th century documents, as *guntang* (Kidung Sunda III, 40; Rangga Lawé VII, 149), under which name it is still found to this day in Bali.

Outside the archipelago kindred instruments are known from Further India, Madagascar, the Philippines, S.E. Europe (Carpathians, Yugoslavia)—all "Röhrenzither"—and from French Camerun ("Halbröhrenzither") (**313**).

A kind of one-stringed "Aeolus-harp" exists in Java under the name—also used, for that matter, to indicate an "Aeolus-flute"—of **sundarèn**, *sendarèn, sundari, sendari*, or *sawangan layangan* [4]). Its form is that of a bamboo bow, held tight by a string of either horsehair or extremely thin ratan fibre tape. This bow is attached by its curved side to a kite (*layangan*), in such a way that the bow and the cross-lath of the kite lie in the same plane, which plane is at right angles with the plane of the kite itself. When the kite is up in the air the string of the sundarèn is made to sound by the wind.

This instrument is also known elsewhere in the archipelago, as in the Sunda districts (*vide* below, p. 369, sub *b*), and in Bali (**192**, p. 22).

An instrumental form quite identical, morphologically, with this sundarèn is the **bajang** [5]) **kerèk**, to whose existence my attention was called

[1]) Mus. Arch. Btv. Nos. 658 and 659; Ind. Inst. Nos. 893/93 and 1148/129; Leyden Nos. 804/149 and 1710/9. *Vide* also **221**, p. 129 *et seq.* and ill. 23, sub *c.*

[2]) Mus. Arch. Btv. No. 763.

[3]) ibid. Nos. 725–727 incl.

[4]) To distinguish it from the pigeon-tail flute, called *sawangan dara*; cf. Ind. Inst. No. 1029/13a–d.

[5]) About the concept *bajang*, *vide* P. V. VAN STEIN CALLENFELS, Javanese Folklore (B.K.I. vol. 81, p. 538 *et seq.*), 1925.

by the Government official Mr. HOLWERDA. This latter instrument, however, is much smaller because of the manner of playing it; for the bajang kerèk is played by holding it in the mouth and causing the string to vibrate by breathing against it. Personally I have never had a chance to see this little instrument, for it is one of the secret requisites of certain oldfashioned *dukuns* (in the Regency of Demak, that is, and, maybe, also elsewhere). They use it to imitate the sound which, so they say, is made by the ghosts of unborn children that were unable to come into the world owing to abortion. It is, for that matter, at the same time the sound produced by a certain kind of insect, whose name accordingly is *walang kerèk*.

And finally mention must be made of the **tiḍuran**, a so-called "earth-zither"; an instrument consisting of a ratan string whose ends are nailed to the ground by means of small bamboo pins, and which is lifted and held tight in the centre by a "bridge" in the form of a small, erect, round bit of stick. The foot of this bridge rests upon a reversed half-coconut, which, in its turn, rests upon bamboo wicker-work covering a cavity dug into the ground; in this cavity there may either be an earthenware pot, or an opening is made in the bamboo wickerwork covering the cavity, ensuring communication between the air underneath the covering and the outside air. The instrument thus produced is played with two beatingsticks.

For further particulars, *vide* **36**, XII, p. 57 *et seq.*, where a simpler and smaller form may also be found described and illustrated.

IV. Aerophones.

The Javanese **suling** most generally in use (ill. 97, sub *a*, and 100, sub *b*) is an endblown flute, manufactured from a bamboo tube about 45 cm in length, and a little over $1\frac{1}{2}$ cm in diameter. The kind of bamboo usually taken for this purpose is the one called *pring wuluh*; according to JAKUB and WIGNYARUMEKSA, either *wuluh wawratsari* or *wuluh bobotsari* [1]).

This bamboo tube is open at the bottom, whilst there is a node (*ros*) at the top. Out of this node and the part of the tube immediately adjacent to it, however, a small, wedge-shaped scale has been cut away, below which a tiny opening is then made. After this a flat, narrow bamboo or ratan

[1]) After the place and the district of that name, in the Residency North-Banyumas?—*Bobot* (H. J. *wawrat*) = weight; *sari* = flower.

ring (*suh, sumber, karah* or *jamangan*) is placed around the extremity thus treated, and this ring guides the player's breath, along the slit formed by the partly-cut-away node and the ring itself, to the sharp bottom edge of the opening just mentioned. The peculiar construction of this mouthpiece justifies the suling being classified with the category of ring-flutes (German: "Bandflöten").

In sléndro the instrument has only four finger-holes; in pélog either five (as is generally the case in the princedom Solo and to the east thereof) or six (as is usual in Jogya and further west) [1]. The finger-holes are of the size of a "chicken's eye" (which apparently is larger in Jogya than in Solo) and are distributed over the lower part of the tube. By closing up the 2nd and 5th holes of a six-holed pélog flute one obtains, approximately, a suling sléndro, which, in the absence of a real sléndro instrument, may serve as a substitute in the hands of an experienced player. The sléndro scale obtained in this way is actually the same as sléndro *miring*, "deviating" sléndro, indicated above (p. 34) by the terms primitive or semi-fourth sléndro. In the Sunda-districts—where the people are not unduly particular, at any rate instrumentally speaking, and where ancient forms and customs are blessed with a longer life than elsewhere in Java, notably in Central Java with its much greater cultural creativeness—this type of sléndro scale, played on a suling pélog is taken more seriously to-day; nevertheless it is admitted there, too, that only an *approximation* to the now customary sléndro scale is thereby obtained [2].

The fingering of the suling is as follows. (One should imagine the mouthpiece to be above; the open circles represent open finger-holes, the black dots the closed ones):

---

[1]) Thus in *modern* Jogya practice. About fifty years ago, five-holed pélog flutes could be heard also there. *Vide* **99**, p. 33.

[2]) For, as R. T. Jayadipura has observed, the *gulu* is then too high. True, this might be remedied by a slightly different manner of blowing, or by not quite closing the stop in question (= *plèsèdan*; —*vide* below, p. 236), but that would be rather a lot of trouble. This kind of quasi-sléndro executed on pélog-instruments, however, is occasionally used to accompany comic situations in the wayang purwa, especially during the appearance of the panakawan Semar and his sons.

A. Principalities.

I. *Pélog-flutes with five stops*

○	●	●	●	●	●
○	○	●	●	●	●
○	○	○	●	●	●
○	○	○	○	●	●
○	○	○	○	○	●
barang	*nem*	*lima*	*ḍaḍa*	*gulu*	*bem*

II. *Pélog-flutes with six stops*

○	●	●	●	●	●	●
○	○	●	●	●	●	●
○	○	○	●	●	●	●
○	○	○	○	●	●	●
○	○	○	○	○	●	●
○	○	○	○	○	○	●
barang	*nem*	*lima*	*pélog*	*ḍaḍa*	*gulu*	*bem*

III. *Sléndro-flutes*

○	●	●	●	●
○	○	●	●	●
○	○	○	●	●
○	○	○	○	●
barang	*nem*	*lima*	*ḍaḍa*	*gulu*

B. Sunda-districts

(according to R. M. A. Kusumadinata (**171**, p. 9/10)):

I. *Pélog-flutes with six stops*

	○	●	●	●	●	●	●	●	●
	○	○	●	●	●	●	●	●	●
	○	○	○	◉ 1)	●	●	●	●	●
	○	○	○	○	○	●	●	●	●
	○	○	○	○	○	○	●	●	●
	○	○	○	○	○	○	○	◉ 1)	●
Jav.:	*gulu*	*bem*	—	*barang*	*nem*	*lima*	*pélog*	—	*ḍaḍa*
Sund.:	*galimer*	*singgul*	*pamiring*	*sorog*	*laras*	*kenong*	*liwung*	*panangis*	*panelu*

1) = partly closed finger-hole.

II. *Sléndro-flutes*

○	●	●	●	●
○	○	●	●	●
○	○	○	●	●
○	○	○	○	●
galimer	*singgul*	*barang*	*kenong*	*panelu*

III. *Sléndro* (*as blown on a six-holed pélog-flute*):

○	●	●	●	●
●	●	●	●	●
○	○	●	●	●
○	○	○	●	●
●	●	●	●	●
○	○	○	○	●
galimer	*singgul*	*barang*	*kenong*	*panelu*

The softly-rounded, guilelessly-melancholy sound of the suling is one of the most precious elements in the consonance of the gamelan. In combination with the orchestra the suling is heard exclusively in the softer type of pieces, in which case it plays a richly-ornamented part, which, occasionally, with remarkable independence, goes a long way away from the cantus firmus of the saron-group. Owing to this it introduces, more than any other instrument, and about in the same degree as the solo voice (*sinḍèn*), a polyphonous element into the gamelan music (vide App. *3*). Its intonation, too—as that of the rebab and the singing voice—occasionally deviates from that of instruments with fixed pitch, as we remarked and explained above (pp. 57 and 68/69). Such tones, which are obtained by only partly covering a finger-hole, are called *plèsèdan*, meaning "tones that have slid down". About this plèsèdan, *vide* also **43**, pp. 53 and 170, and **44**, p. 61/2.

The Chenṭini, again, describes (Canto 44, stanza 80 *et seq.*—Vol. I/II, p. 246) suling-playing in its inimitable—and well-nigh untranslatable—manner, in the following words:

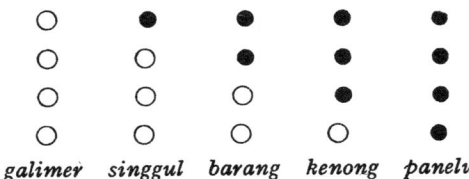

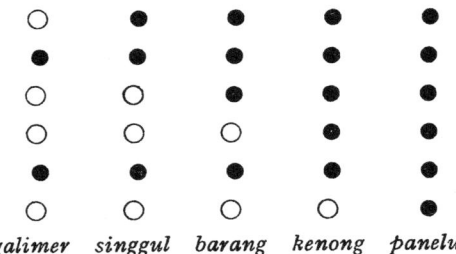

80. ....
anyuling bening chumlering
anyaririt tutupané atilepan

81. ngelong tutup papélon aliu-liu,

i.e., approximately:

"the sound of the suling was bright, clear and pointed. The finger-holes were now completely closed, now only half-covered, as a result of which the warbling of the flute would sound *pélo* (miring, deviating, alien to the scale)".

And Ko Mo An (**176**, 3rd stanza), with his keen gift of observation, says of the suling:

"pepet tutupan ning ngraras lir keḍasih ngasih-asih"
i.e. "it impresses one as tending to retard the melody by sounds resembling the plaintive cry of the keḍasih (*Cuculus flavus*, "Piet van Vliet").

Owing to its simplicity of manufacture and lovely sound, moreover, the suling is definitely the most popular solo-instrument. One may often hear, in the evening, its lonely, plaintive voice in the native villages (*vide* also **41**).

A third type of end-blown flute known in Central-Java is the **suling réog**, which is found in the small orchestras accompanying the réog-play in the Principalities. It has only three finger-holes, and is shorter and slightly thicker than the other Javanese forms of suling.

Flutes of a similar structure to that of the Javanese end-blown sulings hitherto described are also found elsewhere in the archipelago, as in Celebes, Bali (ill. 100, sub *d*), Lombok, Madura (*ibid.*, sub *c*), and in the Sunda districts (*ibid.*, sub *a*). In Java itself they are without doubt very ancient; it is, however, doubtful—to say the least—whether they are depicted on the Barabuḍur (reliefs 24 and 117 of the buried base) (ill. 13). In any case considerable preference was given during the Middle-Javanese period to the transverse flute (*wangsi*, *bangsi*, *wenu*, (?) *tudung*(*an*)), which is evident from the numerous relief images (ill. 8, 10, 11, 16), as well as passages in the literature. True, the word *suling* also occurs a few times on inscriptions and in literature (the earliest evidence dates from 923 (Brandes' charter II 9b)), but it cannot be shown with certainty whether the word refers here to an end-blown flute or to a transverse one.

The **selomprèt** (*seromprèt, somprèt*; East-Java and Madura: *saronèn* or *serunèn* (ill. 102) [1]); Banyumas: *tètèprèt*; Hindu-Java: *pèrèrèt, plèrèt, gem(p)rèt*; Sunda districts: *tarompèt*; Bali: *pèrèrèt*) is, in Central- and East-Java, as well as in Madura, a wooden shawm about 45 cm in length, narrow in diameter, slightly conically bored, and finishing in a wide, circular—or, much more rarely *kalamakara*-head shaped—bell. The instrument has a double blowing reed (Mad.: *sober*) made of lontar-leaf; it is, therefore, a kind of oboe. Generally it possesses six stops on the side directed towards the listener, and one stop on the opposite side. The selomprèt, with its shrill, jaunty sound ("it sings like a lark, but with the voice of a shrill peacock" (**33**)), is never found in the actual gamelan, but frequently in the smaller orchestras. More especially does it fill an important place when the music demands the creation of some state of (say, sexual) excitement, hypnosis or frenzy, for instance, during *kuda képang* dances, whip duels, and often also during *ronggèng* dances.

Such shawms, and instruments closely akin to them, are found in a large part of the archipelago. The selomprèt originated from the Persian-Arabian culture (*surnai*, turned in the archipelago into *serunai*, as in Sumatra, or *saronèn*, as in Madura and East-Java), but, as is evident from its occurrence in Java in the Hindu-Javanese period, in Bali and in the Batak country, was adopted also by the non-islamized groups of the population. The same also happened, for that matter, to the *rebab*; whilst, as regards the *terbang* (*rebana*), described above, and the *gambus*, which will be described further on, the archipelago has apparently shown itself rather more conservative.

The **puwi-puwi** (ill. 101, sub *b*) is a glottophone, a tongue-instrument, with a conically-bored, wooden sound-funnel, and a single reed made of ratan (species: *plumpung*, said to exist exclusively east of Prambanan). The puwi-puwi, therefore, is a kind of clarinet.

In contradistinction to that of many other Indonesian forms of clarinet, its tongue is cut out in such a way that the freely-vibrating part is directed *towards* the player: the tongue is "subjacent". For the rest, the same applies to the puwi-puwi as to nearly all other Indonesian clarinets [2]), namely

---

1) Ind. Inst. No. 629/37; Mus. Arch. Btv. No. 559.

2) An exception to this are the Bima (Sumbawa) clarinets, which are provided with a mouth-funnel.

that, when played, its tongue is held full length in the player's mouth. In this it differs from European clarinets.

The puwi-puwi has six stops in front and one at the back. With these, seven different tones can be produced; actually, however, I never heard more than six being played, but this may be merely an accident.

I found the following scale on a Jogya instrument:

294		337		359		392		419		425		(588)
I	236	II	110	III	152	IV	115	V	25	VI	562	(I');

and for the specimen in the N.I. Musicological Archives (Cat. No. 539):

306		315		341		355		367		405		427		(612)
I	53	II	138	III	69	IV	58	V	170	VI	92	VII	620	(I').

On measuring the instrument in the archives, however, it appeared that, by blowing either harder or less hard, one is able to vary the pitch of the tones—without their blowing over into a harmonic—within the limite of about a minor third. The intervals I recorded represent the scale-sequence on blowing with medium force, as I suppose would be the case in the general practice of playing. Notwithstanding this, one should not attach too much value either to the above interval measurements or to the great differences between the two sequences.

The puwi-puwi is now used exclusively in the small orchestras of the Jogya *prajurit*-corps [1]) called Dahèng and Bugis—both names meaning Buginese—which in olden days were composed of Buginese hireling soldiers. The wind-instrument, however, which is now called, in South-Celebes, *puwi-puwi* is, as far as I am aware, not a clarinet at all, but an oboe, identical in practically every detail with the *selomprèt* described above (cf. also **163**, p. 249 *et seq.*). True, small bamboo clarinets are also found there, but invariably under other names, *i.e. sikunru* and *basing-basing*.

Another wind-instrument, which does, it seems, not exist in Central- and East-Java outside of the *prajurit*-music of the Principalities, is the **transverse flute**, which, in common with the ordinary end-blown flute, is now called *suling* (ill. 101, sub *a*). It has six stops, is closed at the extremity nearest the blowing hole, and open at the other end. The extremities are silver-mounted; it is a beautifully finished instrument. Although it

---

[1]) In former times also in the Solonese prajurit corps *Talangpati*. For that reason this prajurit music was sometimes called *gamelan serunèn*.

seems that this instrument came into vogue at the same time as the roll-drum—probably to imitate the drum-and-fife music of the East India Company's troops—it is also quite possible that we have to do here with a native descendant of the Hindu-Javanese transverse flutes, since flutes of this type are known also in West-Java (*vide* p. 377), and are called, in Batavia, by the ancient Hindu-Javanese name of *bangsi(ng)*.

The tuning of this *"prajurit"* transverse flute does not in the least correspond to that of the puwi-puwi; nevertheless, both instruments are blown cheerfully and at the same time in the Dahèng orchestra. The oriental ear—and the western ear, too, once it gets used to these sound-mixtures—evidently finds pleasure in the sharp dissonants and the brusque crossing-lines of this kind of double melodics.

The *bumbung*, or **gumbang** (East-Java and Madura: *serbung*) [1], which forms part of some of the more primitive bamboo-ensembles such as the gamelans *jemblung* and *chalung* (ill. 122, sub *a*, 154, sub *c*, 155, sub *d*), is a wind-gong, consisting of an extremely stout bamboo segment closed at the bottom by a node, and open at the top. The player blows into a much thinner bamboo tube, open at both ends, whilst holding the latter inside the first, thicker tube. The sound is deep and sonorous. The instrument is probably capable of producing three different tones: one very deep one; the fifth above it, and the octave higher. It is the same instrument that constitutes the bass in the Amboinese flute-orchestras—although in that case the large bamboo is often replaced by a zinc tube. In Banyumas, and probably also in other places, a long-drawn calebash is sometimes used instead of the large tube. The Institute for the Indies at Amsterdam possesses a tube of this description (No. 1029/9).

The **bull-roarer** (Jav.: *(o)wèr-(o)wèr*, or *èrèg-èrèg*; German: *Schwirrholz*; French: *rhombe ronflante*; Dutch: *snorrebot*) occurs in Java in various forms. One of these (ill. 103, left) consists of a narrow, thin bamboo lath, in whose one extremity a small hole has been pierced by means of which the lath is attached to a piece of cord. When the lath is swung by the cord in a turning movement, a kind of humming sound is created. One may remember the procedure practised in one's jouth, when a flat wooden ruler had to serve as a bull-roarer (*vide* also **36**, IV, p. 18 *et seq.*).

[1]) Ind. Inst. No. 629/38.

Another form (ill. 103, right) consists of a strip of coconut leaf folded double, which holds in place the extremities of the nerve of a coconut leaf bent to resemble a bow. One might call it a "roaring- or whizzing-bow". It is turned round by means of a long leaf-nerve functioning as a cord, which operation produces a softly-clattering sound (*vide* also **36**, IV, p. 27 *et seq.*).

Both these forms also occur elsewhere in the Archipelago; among other places—and in exactly the same guises—in Nias (**217**, p. 72 *et seq.*); Timor; Alor, and Flores (**221**, p. 158 *et seq.*). They have been degraded to the rank of toys in these places, as well in Java; evidently nothing is left of their original magic function (ghosts' voices), as may be met with in other parts of the world, *e.g.*, New-Guinea and South-America (**226**, **313**, p. 10 *et seq.*).

The **susurilitan** (ill. 104) is a small ocarina made of terracotta and shaped like a cockerel or pigeon without either legs or wings. The blowing hole, a mere slit, is in the tail-piece, whilst there is a second, slightly larger, hole in the "belly", at the point where the blowing-slit finishes and the "bird" becomes hollow. Two stops enable the player to produce a sequence of four different tones, *e.g.*, *f''*, *g''*, *g#''* and *a''*.

There exist at least two kinds of rice-stalk aerophones. One of them, called **de(r)mén(an)**, consists of a segment closed at one end by a node. Closely underneath this closed extremity, the wall has been slit, so as to make a "beating" tongue, whose fixed end is at the side of the node: a "suprajacent" tongue, therefore [1]). The player takes the instrument far enough into his mouth to allow the instrumental tongue to vibrate quite freely inside the cavity of the mouth.

This *de(r)mén(an)* may be provided with stops (either two or three) and/or with a sound-amplifying bell made of strips of coconut leaf wound together (cf. ill. 134, taken from a Sundanese specimen). In the latter case the instrument often bears a different name. In the regency of Tegal it is called *ilo-ilo-goto* [2]) (cf. the Sundanese name, *olè-olèan*); the Hindu-Javanese spoke of *damyadamyan* (Ghatotkacāçraya XXXVI, 7) (cf. Sund.: *dami*, or *jarami*).

In the other form of rice-stalk aerophone the stalk is bruised just

[1]) About the rhymes and other ditties recited by East-Javanese children whilst cutting these dermènan, *vide* especially **36**, VI, p. 323 *et seq.*

[2]) This is, in Solo, the name of the *sound* of the de(r)mèn(an).

underneath the closed extremity, after which it is pushed in a little in the direction of the longitudinal axis, which creates a somewhat basket-shaped, *à jour* slit-open thickening. During playing this thickening completely disappears into the cavity of the mouth. When blown upon, the small slits of the thickened part in question close together intermittently, as a result of which the air-column inside the rice-stalk vibrates, causing a sound which, for such a delicate instrument, is remarkably powerful.

Both forms described above—the former of which is a clarinet, and the latter an oboe—are also met with elsewhere in the archipelago; I came across both types in Nias (*lai waghé*) (**217**, p. 56) and in Flores (Manggaray: (*ra'us woja*) (**221**, p. 155), in the Menangkabau, and among the Toraja's (*om-om*). In the Toba-districts I found only the clarinet form (*oli-oli, alal*). J. KREEMER ("Atjèh" I, p. 391 *et seq.*) mentions them as existing in Achin (*wa*), in the Gayo district (*pepéon*) and the Alas district (*iyup-iyup*), and J. ELBERT ("Die Insel Sumbawa" (1912) I, "Das Sultanat Bima", p. 70 *et seq.*) as being found in Donggo, East-Sumbawa (*kafoa*).

In addition to the instruments described above, the number of other, small noise-instruments found in Java is legion; to name and describe them all in a book such as this would be nearly impossible, however curious and intriguing some of them may be. The majority of them are aerophones (both flutes and glottophones), manufactured from simple materials such as coconut leaf, hollow stalks, wood: *e.g.* the pithy, graceful ocarina-like little **pigeon-tail flutes** (*sawangan dara*) [1] (ill. 105) cut either wholly or partly out of the thorn of the changkring tree [2]; they are tied to the tail of the owner's doves and made to sound, as soon as the birds start flying, by the fast air-deplacement [3]. Then the bamboo ones, such as

---

[1] This to distinguish them from the Aeolus-bow attached to kites (*sawangan layangan*).

[2] *Erythrina fusca, Lour.*, or *E. indica, Lam.*

[3] There exist various forms of this *sawangan dara*, e.g.,

a) a cylinder-shaped one, of thin bamboo, with a changkring lid with one slit (*Sawangan dudan*);

b) an "ant's head"-shaped one, medium size, either with two slits side-by-side, or with a single slit (*S. randan*);

c) also an "ant's head" shaped one, small model, with one slit (*S. gejilan*);

d) ditto, a twin-form, one above the other (*S. gandok* or *S. rènteng*); (*gandok* = connected; *rènteng* = in a row);

e) ditto, very small model;

These four types are made entirely from changkring-thorn, except the protuberance with which the instrument is attached to the tail-feathers—which is usually made of bamboo.

the *sundari* (*sendari*) or *sundarèn* (*sendarèn*), played upon by the wind, an **Aeolus-flute**, therefore; a small **piston-flute** (German: *Stempelpfeife*), provided with an inside slide, regulating the length of the air-column (*sempritan, sosowitan*); a **spinning top** (*gangsingan, panggalan*) [1]) (ill. 106); the *titituit, i.e.* the small **slit-stop flute** of the "bird-man" (**141**) (ill. 107); the *ṭoroṭok*, which are a pair of bamboo **clappers** [2]); the *kitiran*, a small **humming bamboo windmill**, serving as a scarecrow [3]); the **kokoprak**, *i.e.* a series of bamboo tubes that fall up against a bamboo cross-bar and is set in motion by means of lengths of string (used as scarecrow at the watch-houses in the rice-fields) [4]), etc. etc. For particulars of many of these small instruments, which we have not, or only incidentally dealt with, we refer to the Nos. **36**, **38** and **270** (pp. 65 and 448/450) of the Bibliography in Volume II.

d. Orchestras.

> ,,.... une musique de rêve, lointaine et douce....
> On se demande avec inquiétude pour quoi l'on a parfois parlé de porter la "civilisation" a des races qui savent si divinement comprendre et exalter la beauté."
> (SUZANNE LAROCHE in ,,L'art vivant", Aug. 1931, p. 427).

> ,,La perfection d'ensemble d'un tel orchestre, la fusion de ses instruments si divers est la plus étrange surprise; et, quand, par une de ces nuits claires d'Orient, dans la demi-obscurité fantastique d'une cour de palais, commence à s'elever en sourdine une melodie de gending qui fait songer à un frôlement d'ailes, à des soupirs d'insectes, ou à un ruissellement d'eau, on reste saisi et comme envoûté par cette musique éminemment distinguée qui fait pressentir et qui éveille une qualité d'émotions si supérieures, qui exprime, même dans la plus intense expression de joie, la melancolie sourde et lointaine—éternel accompagnement dont l'essence est la même partout—et qui scande, triste et funèbre, les plus splendides joies de nos vies."
> (GABRIELLE, FERRAND, "Le théatre et la danse à Java" (**86**)).

> ".... shall we ever forget those evenings and nights when the opportunity came our way to taste the timeless joys of a wayang

---

f) ditto, small model, either triplet, quadruplet or quintuplet, made of a species of wood unknown to me (this type being Madurese) (*sabhangan*).

[1]) Ind, Inst. Nos. 1029/12a–f, 1031/1a; Mus. Arch. Btv. Nos. 493, 526 and 540.

[2]) Ind. Inst. Nos. 1031/2a and b; Mus. Arch. Btv. Nos. 529 and 530.

[3]) About the musical bamboo windmill, *vide* also H. BALFOUR, Musical instruments from the Malay Peninsula (Fasc. Mal. Anthropology, II, 1904), p. 7/8.

[4]) Cf. *e.g.* the identical Malgassic instrument in SCHAEFFNER (**325** plate IV opposite p. 49, fig. 1). A model of such a *kokoprak* may be found in the Colonial Agricultural Museum, Deventer, Neth.

performance in the Astana (Mangku Nagaran). Then the golden sounds of the Kyahi Kanyut Mèsem (The Lord tempted to smile) sing through the night, at times flaring up wildly into an orgy of sound and rhythm, when the fight of the dancers causes the blood to throb faster in the veins, and then again falling back into an unspeakably lovely twilight of sound in the finest possible shadings. Oh, the soft play of the Solonese gamelans! .... Whereas Jogyakarta's greatest charm is the mighty sound of its festive fortissimi, the glory of Solo lies in the gentle musings of the klenéngan, the almost immaterial meditations of the rebab, coupling themselves with the serene interplay of the voices of the gendèr and the gambang and the softly-humming singing of women. (**191**).

The number of orchestras (*gamelan*, noun, derived from *gaməl* = to handle [1]); H. J. *gangsa* = bronze; also, in the language of the kraton, *pradangga*) is still very large in Java, but probably decreasing little by little. Appendix *57* gives the definite figures per regency, and in many cases per district; Appendix *58c* a survey of the "density" of gamelan possession per regency expressed in figures representing the number of inhabitants per orchestra [**113**B, **123**G–H, **142**A, **236**F, **302**T, **340**B]

The wealth of gamelans culminates in East-Solo and West-Madiun, or, in other words, in the plains around the volcano Lawu. Ngawi bears the palm, with one orchestra for every 590 inhabitants which may almost be called a Balinese state of things [2]). The poorest territory, from an orchestral point of view, is Garut, where one gamelan may be found for every 22.000 souls, which, however, is compensated to some extent by the large number of angklung ensembles to be found scattered about this regency.

The best orchestras are in the possession of the ruling princes of the Principalities, some members of the nobility, some of the regents, a few ḍalangs, and also in that of some wealthy Chinese music lovers [3]). The gamelans in the désa are generally simpler in their composition, less nicely finished and tuned, and very often not made of bronze, but of iron (cf. pp. 140 and 278).

---

1) and, as Dr. PURBACHARAKA informed me, not = tool, more especially hammer (as is usually said). Cf. *e.g.* the Chenṭini, Canto 277, stanza 8 (Vol. VII/VIII, p. 264): *tegesing gamel nyekeli*, *i.e.* the signification of gamel is: to handle, to manipulate.

2) The South-Balinese district of Ubud, with 38.000 inhabitants, possesses 138 orchestras, *i.e.* one gamelan to every 275 souls; the—also South-Balinese—district of Tegallalang, with 25.000 inhabitants, about 100 orchestras, *i.e.* one to every 250 souls!

3) About Chinese gamelan players, *vide* KWEE KEK BENG (**238**, p. 87).

The gamelan-property of the ruling princes, which is largely owned by the State, but partly privately owned, is very remarkable in quality and very considerable in quantity. If for simplicity's sake one counts an orchestra consisting of a pélog- and a sléndro-half, as two, then the total gamelan property of the Paku Alam state comprises 6 [1]), that of the Sultanate Jogya at least 19 [2]), that of Mangku Nagara 27 [3]) and that of the Susuhunan of Solo at least 29 orchestras [4]). All of these without exception must be reckoned either among the very good, the exceptionally good, or the most excellent gamelans. Many of them have special functions allotted them in the scheme of the year's festivities. They are tended and looked after by a special functionary, the *panéwu genḍing*, who, in Jogya, bears the hereditary official name of KARYADIMÉJA (**100**, p. 9).

---

[1]) *i.e.* a gamelan marked *P*(AKU) *B*(UWANA) *X* (sléndro and pélog) (ill. 109); *K. Pengawé sari* (sl.) and *Telaga munchar* (pél.), as well as a gamelan *Munggang* with complete, respectively five- and seven-tone scales (sl. and pél.). [*S⁷²]

[2]) *i.e.*, besides the Munggang *K. Guntur laut* (ill. 111) and the Koḍok ngorèk *K. Mahésaganggang* (ill. 112), the gamelans pélog *K.K. Guntur madu* and *Naga ilaga* (both gamelans sekati), *Kanchil belih, Guntur sari, Panji, Bremara* (ill. 108), *Puspanadi, Tumenggung* (or (*H*)*arjamulia*), *Pawook,* and *Sirat madu,* and the gamelans sléndro *K.K. Surak, Medarsih,* (*H*)*arjanagara, Marikangen, Pusparana, Riya* and *Madukénṭir.* [**89**C, **155**C, **291**B]

In addition to the above there are, further, a gamelan sléndro, a gamelan pélog (*K. Mikatsih*) and a *Koḍok ngorèk* in the Kadipatèn, as well as the *K. Mangunsih* (sl.), *Mangungkung* (pél.) and a *Koḍok ngorèk* in the Kapatihan.

[3]) *i.e.,* besides the gamelans Munggang *K.K. Segara windu* and *Sengkan turunan,* the Koḍok ngorèk *K. Pamedarsih,* and the gamelans charabalèn *K.K. Berama* (with a four-tone scale) and *Baswara* (with a six-tone scale), also the gamelans *K.K. Kanyut Mèsem* (sl. and pél.) (ill. 66, 69, and 72)(*), *Lipur tomba neng* (sl. and pél.), *Udan asih* (pél.) and its counterpart *Udan arum* (sl.), *Jaka larassih* (pél.) and its counterpart *Jaka larasrum* (sl.), *Pamiwalkung* (sl. and pél.), *Riris manis* (pél.) and its counterpart *Riris arum* (sl.); *Sekar sih* (pél.) and its counterpart *Sekar rum* (sl.), *Prèchèt* (sl. and pél.), as well as another large gamelan sl. and pél. in the kabupatèn at Karanganyar. Then there is, in the private possession of the prince, a gamelan klenéngan (sl. and pél.), and a complete orchestra (sl. and pél.).—For a detailed description of the gamelans in the Mangku Nagaran, *vide* **191**.

[4]) *i.e.,* besides the Munggang *K. Udan arum,* 2 gamelans *Koḍok ngorèk,* the gamelan *Patalon,* and a gamelan *Charabalèn*: the *gamelans* sekati *K. Sepuh* and *K. Henèm,* as well as *K. Pengasih* (pél.) and its counterpart *K. Laras ati* (sl.); *K. Semar Ngigel* (pél.) and its counterpart *K. Lokanonta* (sl.); *K. Kanchil belih* (pél.) and its counterpart *K. Guntur madu* (sl.); *K. Udan asih* (pél.). and its counterpart *K. Udan arum* (sl.); *K. Kuta windu* (pél.), and its counterpart *K. Windu sana* (sl.); *K. Kadook manis* (pél.)(**), and its counterpart *K. Manis rengga* (sl.); *K. Suka sih* (pél.), and its counterpart, *K. Pamedarsih* (sl.); *K. Jimat* (pél.), and its counterpart, *K. Déva katong* (sl.); *K. Mangung harja* (pél.). and its counterpart *K. Harja winangung* (sl.); *K. Swara harja* (pél.), and its counterpart, *K. Harja swara* (sl.); *K. Raras rum* (pél.), and its counterpart, K. *Ruming raras* (sl.) [**3**B, **395**A]

(*) [*S³⁹];   (**) [*S⁶⁷].

The great Jogya kraton genḍing-collection, which also contains an inventory of the orchestras present in the kraton, the kadipaten (*i.e.* the abode of the crown prince) and the kapatihan (the abode of the prime minister)—in sofar as they are the property of the kraton—gives particulars of almost every gamelan regarding the occasions on which it is to be played. The Solonese kraton, and, to some extent, the Mangku Nagaran and the Paku Alaman, also know this manner of using certain gamelans for specific purposes.

As far as the gamelans *Munggang*, *Koḍok ngorèk* and *Sekati* are concerned, some particulars may be found further on pp. 259, 262 and 265/266. Of the other orchestras existing in the Jogya kraton the task of the *Kyahi Surak* [1]) —to give an instance—is to accompany the Mounting of the guard by the prajurit-corps *Panyutra*, on the occasion of the *garebeg Ḍal*, which takes place once every 8 years; during *garebeg besar* and *garebeg Puasa*, on the other hand, it accompanies the *lurah's Prayalata* [2]). It further adds lustre (installed in the southern gamelan pavilion) to the Sultan's birthday with *nguyu-uyu*, and may also be heard on the occasion of his circumcision and that of the crown-prince. In olden times, moreover, it used to be beaten during fights between tiger and buffalo (then a public amusement), when the fighters, tired or exhausted by loss of blood, let go of each other (during the fight itself the *Kyahi Koḍok ngorèk* is sounded), and—also alternated by the last-named orchestra—during *rampok machan*, *i.e.* the impaling of tigers which are let loose in the aloon-aloon in front of the Pagelaran [3]), surrounded by lance-bearers forming square. Finally, the *Kyahi Surak* is heard (in common with every other kraton-gamelan, this is emphatically stated with the description of each of them separately) "*sekarsa Dalem*", *i.e.* at the Prince's pleasure; for, in many respects, the prince's position is superior to the adat.

It would lead us too far to state, of each of the princely gamelans, the functions *in extenso*. For many details regarding this matter we refer to GRONEMAN (**99**, p. 45 *et seq.*), who, with respect to the Jogya orchestras, deals with this point fairly exhaustively. [3B]

The money values of gamelans diverge considerably [4]). Whereas a simple

[1]) *Vide*, for the signification of *surak*, below, p. 252, note.

[2]) Cf. above, p. 190, note 3 and below, p. 266.

[3]) *i.e.* the fore-court in front of, and below the *Setinggil* (raised penḍapa, from where the prince surveys the aloon-aloon).

[4]) The prices following here are those ruling before the slump which began to make itself felt towards the end of 1929.

"estate gamelan" (invariably sléndro, since it is intended for the accompaniment of the wayang purwa) is supplied by the Semarang *tukang gong* MAT LÉMAN, alias PAH LADINAH, for 950 guilders, the same manufacturer charges, for an equivalent gamelan pélog, comprising some valuable bronze instruments and some sound-kettles and keys more than the gamelan sléndro, and is also sometimes slightly stouter of dimensions, as much as 1500 guilders. For a gamelan intended for a music lover or for a native civil servant in Java itself he asks, respectively, fl. 1500.— if a sléndro, and fl. 2500.—, if a pélog orchestra.

Old, good orchestras, consisting of a sléndro and a pélog half, vary in price between about f. 3000.— and fl. 10.000.—. There are orchestras, however, *e.g.* the one that was the property of the now deceased Jogya Chinese music lover LI JING KIM, which are said to have cost a multiple of the lastnamed figure.

Among the various Javanese orchestral forms, the large ensemble that, among other things, accompanies the wayang-wong performances, adds lustre to the great festivities in the kratons and dalems, and is used for the *nguyu-uyu* (which has to reverberate wide and far during princely celebrations), occupies the principal place (ill. 68, 72, 108, 109) [1].

Such a great princely gamelan is apt to confound the listener who hears and sees it for the first time: the grouping of the orchestra and the manner of playing the instruments appear completely arbitrary, and only gradually does one become aware that each instrument actually performs its own fixed task within the ensemble. Little by little, one learns to distinguish:

a. cantus firmus (nuclear theme)-instruments;
b. interpunctuating (colotomic) instruments;
c. instruments playing a more or less independent counter-melody;
d. paraphrasing instruments, and
e. agogic instruments.

Those under *d*, the so called *panerusan*, may, again, be subdivided into instruments that keep fairly closely to the nuclear theme, and those which, more especially, supply the variations to the theme, and are responsible for the actual filling and ornamentation ((*sa*)*sekaran*; L. J.: (*ka*)*kembangan*) of the framework of the said nuclear theme (*balunganing genḍing* (S.), *mlampah* (J.)). The latter of the two types of instruments are

[1]) The Odeon records A 39638a–d (lakon *Pujawati Nilawati*) give a good impression of wayang-wong music and the singing of the ḍalang. [*S43, 44]

generally indicated by the name of *(h)isènan* (= "filling-in" instruments).

It is not, in all compositions, invariably the same instruments that come under the different categories enumerated above; but it is nevertheless possible to associate some principal function with nearly every instrument. This should also be sufficiently clear from the discussion of each of the instruments separately.

The former Regent of Temanggung, R. A. A. CHAKRAHADIKUSUMA, in an unpublished treatise written in competition for a prize for the best monograph on Javanese music, attempted to elucidate the peculiar nature of the various instrumental groups by a graphic simile. He compares a gamelan composition (*genḍing*)with a batiked cloth, and subdivides the instruments—apart from the, so much more independent, rebab, suling and kenḍang—into three groups, corresponding, respectively, to the *kalowongan* (*i.e.* the outlines of the batik pattern); the *plataran* (lit.: open field; what the writer probably means is the more or less neutral background), and the *(h)isèn-(h)isèn, i.e.* the filling-in with ornament, with decorative drawing. The gong, the kenong, the keṭuk and the kempul he counts, in this subdivision, amongst the kalowongan, as well as the demung (a nuclear-theme instrument), from which it is clear that he does not feel any essential difference—quite a defensible view, too—between colotomy (*ḍongḍing genḍing*) and the nuclear theme (*balunganing genḍing*). The remaining instruments he then divides (methinks rather arbitrarily) over the background and the decorative filling.

But, in whatever way one would like to subdivide the instruments of the gamelan according to their function within the ensemble, one should firmly keep in mind the fact that it is far from the player's intention, consciously to make them fulfil their function in this manner; rather do they intend to create, nay—for even this still sounds too purposeful—they together form, the intermediary, which produces, tho' hardly conscious of doing so, by means of a tradition sanctified and purified through the centuries, that incomparable, both saturated and yet so remarkably transparent orchestral sound which distinguishes the gamelan of the Javanese Principalities from all other orchestral forms existing in the world; a sound so vital and richly shaded, so fascinating in the delicate grace of its beauty, that, whoever has experienced the effect of its miraculous wealth of tone will henceforth cherish it as one of the most precious possessions of his memory. Many Western artists, visitors to Java, have had this experience. Among them the great piano virtuoso, LEOPOLD GODOWSKY, who, later, gave testimony of his impression in the following words: "The sonority of the gamelan is so weird, fantastic and bewitching, the native music so elusive, vague, shimmering and singular, that on listening to this new world of sound I lost my sense of reality, imagining myself in a realm of enchantment". [1])

Some years ago, J. S. BRANDTS BUYS published his impressions in the following—very happily chosen, and therefore already frequently quoted—terms: "An evening in the Pakualaman. The gamelan gilds the time. The hours forget their usual course. The quarters shrink to golden minutes; minutes seem like blissful hours. Now in its softer moments, the music sounds as if I heard angels sing, now, when at half strength, as if I heard all the chimes in heaven. And then again, in the fullness of its mighty power, it is as if a storm of bronze thunders through my temples.

I believe I think this mezzo-forte loveliest of all. But the pianissimo has more tenderness. And it is also the greatest surprise to my ears. The most singular things happen there. There are moments in which, close to me, the softer instruments, the lithe gendèr, with its voice of young, silvery gold, and the wooden gambang wave a silky substratum of sound, and then, suddenly, the sweet song of the suling arises from afar". [2])

LEONHARD HUIZINGA describes the peculiar quality of sound of gamelan music no less suggestively: "There are only two things one can compare it with: moonlight, and running water. It is pure and mysterious like moonlight; it is always the same and yet always changing, like running water. This music does not create a song for our ears; it is a "state", such as moonlight poured over the fields. It runs and flows, clucking, tinkling and gurgling, as the water coming down from the mountains. Yet it is never monotonous. Now its sounds flow quicker and louder, just as the running water may suddenly speak louder in the night, and then again they fade into silence". [3])

For a few more similar descriptions we refer to the quotations at the head of this chapter, and to the writer's own pamphlet, "The appreciation of exotic music in the course of the centuries" (**225**).

It is undeniable that the primarily important thing is precisely this

[1]) In the Introduction to the first volume of "Phonoramas, Tonal Journeys for the Pianoforte" (New York, 1925).

[2]) Mail-edition of the Nieuwe Rotterdamsche Courant of May 4, 1920.

[3]) Algemeen Handelsblad of October 31, 1937.

experience of the orchestral sound heard as one single, pure entirety; intellectual analysis should come later, at any rate for those who like to make themselves, as far as possible, conscious of the phenomena coming under their notice, so that intuitive apprehension and intellectual probing may supplement each other, and, together, provide an enjoyment of a higher order than either function could provide unaided.

It is worthy of note that most large gamelans belonging to princes and regents are *double* ones; *i.e.* that they consist of a pélog- and a sléndro-half. These two halves share between them only the large gongs, the drums, and —when present—the *ke(chi)chèr* (and also the *keprak* and *kechrèk,* if one wishes to count these among the orchestral instruments), as well as, frequently, the *rebab,* since its pitch can easily be changed. Sometimes, too, they have a few *kenongs* and *kempuls* in common, that is, when the double gamelan is *tumbuk nem* or *tumbuk lima*; and, in the case of *tumbuk jongga,* also occasionally the *keṭuk.* About the signification of this term *tumbuk* (literally: to coincide) *vide* above, p. 161, note.

Needless to say the sléndro- and pélog-halves are never played simultaneously. There is, in fact, only a single curious exception to this rule, *viz.* the gamelan Koḍok Ngorèk in the Solonese kraton, in which—although it plays in an (incomplete) pélog scale—a few sléndro instruments occasionally join in (*vide* below, p. 262). (In the Jogya kraton this also happens, but there the Koḍok ngorèk—in common with that of the Regent of Demak—is more or less sléndro in character, (although, in the Introduction to the kraton genḍing-collection, it is classed with the pélog orchestras). Transitions from one tonal system to the other—and therefore from one orchestral half to the other—in one and the same composition, are also of extremely rare occurrence (cf. above, p. 100, sub C.).

The whole of the gamelan sound-spectrum comprises 6 à 7 octaves (*gembyangan*) (*vide* Appendix *I*). In the upper four of these lie the scales of the instruments playing the melody and those playing the ornamental variations around the melody, as well as those of the interpunctuating instruments: kenongs, kempuls and keṭuk. In the lowest octave are only the large gongs and the gong kemoḍong, and in the lowest but one, the gongs suwukan.

Two of the instruments cover no less than fully four octaves: the gambang and the rebab; the remainder cover at most 2½, comprising, therefore, tones out of three octaves. These three octaves are distinguished, on each of the instruments—from high to low—by the names of *chilik* (*chenik*, *alit*), *sedeng* (*tengah*), and *ageng* (*gedé*). In the Sunda districts a four-part octave-subdivision exists, *i.e.*—from high to low—*peking*, *saron*, *kedemung* and *jengglong*. This corresponds to the nomenclature of the single-octave instruments, which, respectively, cover the octave of the same name. There is yet another subdivision of the range of multi-octave instruments, which does not take into account the octaves, but the registers, of which there are also three, distinguished as *ngelik*, *tengah* and *ngisor* (H. J. *ngandap*).

In vol. II, in the tables of Appendices *61* and *62*, the intervals of a number of Javanese and a few Sundanese and Madurese gamelan scales, as measured by means of the monochord, will be found. As usual, the Roman figures represent the tones; the Arabic figures in between, the intervals, expressed in "cents", and the figures above them, the vibration-numbers of the tones. Most of the measurements were taken from one of the sarons *demung* of the orchestras in question. [**18**B, **395**A]

Of these gamelan scales, Nos. 8 shows an example of *tumbuk nem*; the Nos. 1, 5 and 14, one of *tumbuk lima*, and Nos. 10, of *tumbuk jongga*.

It should be noted that, in olden times, some tones (? only the *barang* tones) were not tuned exactly alike through all the octaves, but slightly sharper for each higher octave. The sound of the gamelan thereby became what is called *silir* (= out of tune), but gained in penetration. Any unintentional, more marked or irregular falseness in a gamelan is called *gèsèh* (J.) or *bléro* (S.). At present the corresponding intervals are tuned perfectly alike through all octaves (*i.e. mleng* (J.) = true; *pleng* or *resik* (S.) (**77**, p. 95) [1]).

The gamelans of the Principalities are classed into different species both according to their absolute pitch and according to the mutual relation between the intervals.

In Solo, two groups might be distinguished according to their *general tone-register*; their respective scales are indicated by the names of *ageng* (*gedé*) and *chilik* (*alit*). In the same way, in East-Java, (Pasuruan, Jom-

[1]) In Bali, this intentional unequal tuning is still in vogue. The beats caused by it are called *pengèjèr* (**192**, p. 77). This is said to occur chiefly in the tuning of the *babarangan* relatively to the *trompong* (one-rowed bonang), which is tuned an octave lower, and in that of the two forms of *gendèr-wayang*, *pengisep* and *pengumbang* (**193**, p. 376/7).

bang), there is a lower scale called *laras kenḍo*, and a higher one, *laras kencheng*. In Jogya, three gradations are known, whose names, from low (great) to high (small) are *ranté, sumyang* and *surak* [1]); in Purbalingga—also from low to high—*laras udan arum, laras sikumpul* and *laras banuwati*; in Blora, for pélog, *pélog* (or *laras*) *sekar delima, pélog* (? *seḍeng*) and *pélog pengasih*, and, for sléndro, *sléndro* (*laras*) *jatimuliya, sléndro* (? *seḍeng*) and *sléndro larasati* or *maraséba*. It might, for that matter, be possible to infer from the Chenṭini (Canto 160, stanza 20) that in Solo, too, *three* pitches are occasionally to be distinguished. How, indeed, would it be possible otherwise to speak of *laras seḍeng, i.e.* "medium pitch"?

The criterion upon which orchestras are distinguished *according to the size of the intervals* lies chiefly in the interval *barang-gulu* in sléndro, and *penunggul* (*bem*)-*gulu* in pélog. If this interval is very large (*i.e.*, in sléndro, appreciably larger than 1/5 of an octave = 240 C.; in pélog about 140 C., and sometimes even a little larger), then the scale as a whole makes the impression of striving upwards, rapidly and energetically; in that case one refers to the scale as being *srigak* (= bright, cheerful, smart). If the interval in question, on the other hand, is small (in sléndro, appreciably less than 240 C.; in pélog, round about 100 C.) one senses something oppressive and indolent in the scale, which, in this case is called *luruh* (= soft, gentle). When the distance between the tones mentioned is of average size (in sléndro, round about 240 C.; in pélog, 120 C.) the scale is called *rata* (= even, medium).

In Solo, too—according to SULARDI (**343**, pp. 4 and 5), only in sléndro—three such scales are known, called respectively *laras sundari* (*nyendari*), *laras larasati* and *laras lugu*. This author refers to the two scales deviating from equidistance as having *embat*. Now, embat means, literally, to *stretch, to make taut, e.g.* of a bowstring. SULARDI, therefore, looks upon the equidistant scale (*laras lugu*) as being the normal (he says, in fact, that L. lugu has not "embat"), and feels some of the tones of the two other scales as having been pushed, or wrenched, from their places. Being evidently strongly visual in his conception of the matter, he views the L. *nyendari* as a pointed figure:

[1]) One of the gamelans sléndro in the Jogya kraton is, it appears, even called after this particular quality: the *Kyahi Surak*. It has a barang with 278 vibrations per second, which for a sléndro-orchestra is rather high; at any rate for the older emsembles; the newer ones are generally tuned a little higher (with a *barang* which, in some cases—vide Appendix *62*—even goes up to 293 v.d.).

barang ↑
gulu — mangingil (= upwards)
dada
lima — mangandap (= downwards),
nem ↓

L. larasati as the inverse of this, and *L. lugu* as two parallel lines. Further, according to him, *L. nyendari* creates a feeling that may be interpreted by the term *sereng* (vigorous, energetic, but also: disturbed); *L. larasati*, on the contrary, one that might be rendered by the word *seneng* (harmonic, inwardly free, untroubled).

There is a great reverence for a fine old gamelan. The most important orchestras of the ruling princes bear—as we have already seen in the notes to p. 245—the title of *Kyahi* (Venerable Sir), either preceded or not by the predicate *Kangjeng*), followed by some poetic and sweetly-flowing name or other, such as *Kanyut Mèsem* ("Tempted to smile"); *Guntur madu* ("Torrent of honey"); *Lipur tomba neng* ("Consoling remedy giving mental peace"); *Udan asih* ("Shower of love"); *Pamiwalkung* ("He who makes us forget even amorousness"); *(H)arjanagara* ("The welfare of the country"); *Mangunsih* ("Practising Love") [1], etc. etc. Sometimes, too, the name is reminiscent of more agitated times and a corresponding use of the gamelan: *Kyahi Pusparana, i.e.* "Flower of the Battle". In one or two cases one may come across the proper name of *Semar ngigel, i.e.* "The dancing Semar". *Menyan* (incense) is burned for these Kyahi's every Thursday evening. It is remarkable that the most venerated orchestras, in nearly all cases, carry a pélog scale, either complete or incomplete (gamelan sekati, munggang, kodok ngorèk).

In the case of double gamelans the name, too, is often double, in which case the pélog-name invariably precedes: *Kadook manis Manis rengga, Udan asih Udan arum, Kuṭa windu Windu sana, Sirat madu Madu kenṭir, Raras rum Ruming raras*, and suchlike.

The composition of a large gamelan of this kind is as below [**155**c]:

[1]) The third Regent of Banyumas, named YUDANAGARA, faithfully had supported Pangéran MANGKUBUMI in his fight against the Susuhunan, and as a reward he was appointed—after the division of the territory under the Treaty of Gianṭi, in 1755, and the elevation of MANGKUBUMI to the position of first Sultan of Jogya—as the latter's prime minister. P. YUDANAGARA took his gamelan with him when he removed from Banyumas to Jogya. It is this orchestra, *Kyahi Kéré* (= Venerable Sir Beggar) which, in commemoration of the above-mentioned events, was re-christened *Kyahi Mangunsih*.

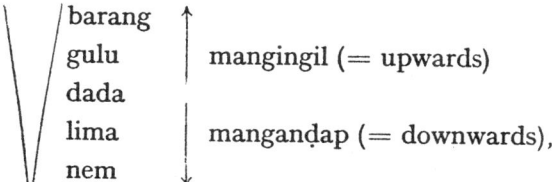

Pélog	Together	Sléndro
1. saron panerus		1. saron panerus
2. saron barung (usually two or four)		2. saron barung (usually two or four)
3. saron demung (often two)		3. saron demung (often two)
4. (saron slenṭem)		4. (saron slenṭem)
5. (gambang gangsa)		5. (gambang gangsa)
6. bonang panerus		6. bonang panerus
7. bonang barung		7. bonang barung
8. bonang panembung (J.)		8. bonang panembung (J.)
9. gambang kayu bem		9. gambang kayu
10. gambang kayu barang		
11. gendèr panerus bem		10. gendèr panerus
12. gendèr panerus barang		
13. gendèr barung bem		11. gendèr barung
14. gendèr barung barang		
15. gendèr panembung (J.) or slenṭem (gantung) (S.)		12. gendèr panembung (J.) or slenṭem (gantung) (S.)
16. kempyang		
		13. engkuk
		14. kemong
17. keṭuk		15. keṭuk
18. kenong lanang (one or more)		16. kenong lanang (one ore more)
19. kenong japan (J.)		17. kenong japan (J.)
20. kempul (one or more)		18. kempul (one or more)
21. gong suwukan (one or more)		19. gong suwukan (one or more)
22. suling		20. suling
23. rebab	(rebab)	21. rebab

Pélog	Together	Slendro
24. chelempung		22. chelempung
25.	gong kemoḍong	23.
26.	gong ageng (one or two)	24.
27.	kenḍang genḍing	25.
28.	kenḍang chiblon	26.
29.	ketipung	27.
30.	beḍug	28.
31.	ke(chi)chèr	29.
32.	keprak	30.
33.	kechrèk	31.
34.	kemanak	32.

Concerning the octave-position and range of these instruments—insofar as they lend themselves to precise determination—Appendices *1* and *2* give the necessary particulars; the former for sléndro and the latter for pélog.

Each of the two gamelans has its own special task. In as much as this consists in the accompaniment of stage performances, the *gamelan sléndro*—be it in a restricted combination (cf. p. 274)—is, amongst other things, the orchestra for the *wayang purwa* [1]), *i.e.* the shadow-play (*wayang kulit*), which depicts scenes from the epics of India proper (the Mahābhārata, Rāmāyaṇa, and Bhāratayuddha); the *gamelan pélog* provides the accompaniment to the *wayang geḍog*, *i.e.* the shadow-wayang presenting on the stage the Panji-tales, as well as to the *wayang golèk* [2]), which especially flourishes, at the present time, in West- and East-Java (*vide* Appendix *57 A* and *D*); this is the wayang with round wooden dolls, at any rate when there is no gamelan miring [3]) available for this purpose. For the accompaniment of the *wayang wong* (H. J. *ringgit tyang*), which came into exist-

---

[1]) Illustration, for example, in J. C. van Eerde, "De volken van Nederlandsch-Indië", vol. II, p. 292 *et seq.* (article by R. M. Nata Surata).

[2]) Some beautiful records of Sundanese wayang golèk are the Odeon Nos. A 203235 a–f (the lakon *Gurit Sagara*).

[3]) This applies to the original wayang golèk, which depicts the Panji tales, and sometimes also stories from the Amir Hamzah cycle. The *younger* form which, as *golèk purwa*, is to be distinguished from the older (*golèk ménak*), uses the purwa lakons as its repertoire, and is accordingly accompanied by the gamelan sléndro. There are exceptions to this rule on both sides; these, however, are invariably to be attributed to the circumstance that there happens to be no gamelan available of the required tonal system. [**101**B, **292**B, **317**A, **377**G]

ence much later—although interpreting, like the wayang purwa, scenes from the epics of India proper, for which, as a matter of fact, a sléndro accompaniment should be indicated—itinerant wayang wong troupes in Jogya and Solo employ both sléndro and pélog. *Vide* f.i. the Solonese record Col. G. J. 116. In Jogya, even the kraton and the Danurejan join in this deviation of the adat (cf. **318**, **319** and **365**) and, according to one of the latest programmes received from Java just before the outbreak of the second World-war, the Mangkunagaran at Solo also follows now and then this deviation from the old custom [1]). In the Solonese kratons and dalems, however, it is customary to adhere strictly to sléndro also for the wayang wong when it performs purwa-lakons. For the *wayang karuchil* or *kaliṭik*, *i.e.* the wayang with flat wooden dolls [2]), which is found especially in East-Java (*vide* Appendix 57 *D*), and which performs plays from the Damar Wulan cycle, the *gamelan pélog miring* is usually employed, but also sometimes a complete gamelan pélog (= *Mentaraman*), in which case, however, it is beaten exclusively in *pélog miring*, *i.e.* in *paṭet barang* [3]).

The play called *Langendriya*, which is performed by women only, and whose text, derived from the Damar Wulan and Ménakjingga cycle, is sung in machapat-metres [4]), is accompanied by the gamelan sléndro,

---

[1]) For, in this programme, *Ayak-ayakan P. 9 sl.* is mentioned as the frame between which the genḍing *Surung ḍayung P. 6 pél.* is sandwiched. This performance was also characterized by the peculiarity that—although comprising a piece, complete and self-contained as such—it nevertheless presented nothing but music in P. 6 and P. 9 sléndro (and once in P. 6 pélog). [**6**]

[2]) There are always, however, one or two *round* puppets among the *karuchil* requisites, among which always one representing Werkudara (= Bima) whose victorious dance ends every wayang-performance. [**360**A]

[3]) According to Pangéran Kusumadilaga (**169**, p. 24), the wayang kliṭik arose during the reign of Paku Buwana II (1727–1749), being known at first by the name of *Bèbèr pangomati*, and accompanied by a small ensemble called *Lokanonta* (cf. also, below, p. 260), which did not comprise a gong ageng(!), but was composed exclusively of a kenḍang, a keṭuk, a kenong, a kempul and a saron miring. What kind of miring-scale the author here refers to cannot be discovered from the passage in question. Further, only *playon* was beaten with this play (cf. below, p. 308); originally the kliṭik was never accompanied by any genḍings.

This information, however, is not correct—at any rate not as regards the "birth-date" of the wayang kliṭik. Dr. H. H. Juynboll (**156** p. 399b) points to the fact that this type of wayang is already mentioned in the older Javanese literature, *e.g.* in the prose-work Navaruci, and also in the Malat (about 1500) and in the Rama Sasak.

[4]) Of this, some excellent records were made some years before the war by Columbia, in the Mangku Nagaran (lakon *Ménakjingga léna* = the death of M. (G. J. 60/65, 162/167 and 168/173)). [**70**A; *S[39]]

as is also the *wayang topèng* [1]); the *Prana asmara*, on the other hand, which depicts tales from the Panji cycle, by the gamelan pélog.

It would lead us too far to examine here in more detail the use of the two large gamelans for each form of stage-play separately. Investigation in this direction, it would seem to me, should be a suitable task for one who has made a special study of the wayang in all its many aspects [2]). I might confine myself to referring the reader to Dr. JUYNBOLL's already mentioned article "Tooneel" in vol. V of the Encyclopaedia of the Dutch East Indies (**156**), and the sequel to it by Dr. RASSERS in vol. VIII, p. 1630 *et seq.*; to the programmes, with commentary, of some of the big wayang wong performances in recent times (**5**, **160**, **293**, **318**, **319**, **365** and several others); to a few brief treatises by KATS (**159**), KONING (**177**), VAN LEEUWEN (**250**), VAN HINLOOPEN LABBERTON (**239**), BEZEMER (**22A**,) KUNST (**229**) [**377H**], and to the extensive monographs by SERRURIER (**338**), HAZEU (**108**), KATS (**158**), VAN LELYVELD (**254**), RASSERS (**304**), GOSLINGS (**96**) and PIGEAUD (**298**). Only about the use of the various gendings in the wayang purwa and the wayang gedog will the reader find a few more particulars below (p. 338 *et seq.*). [*S[27]]

Besides the large ensembles discussed above there are a number of smaller orchestras. Of these, we may mention in the first place the gamelan **Munggang** (ill. 111 and 113), a three-toned [3]), primitive, or at any rate archaïc *ensemble*, in the Jogya kraton (from which ill. 111 and 113 were taken), consisting of the following instruments:

4 ranchakan, each with three very large *bonang*-kettles; two of these triplets are tuned an octave higher than the two others; the former, therefore, being distinguished again by the name of *jaler*, L. J. *lanang* = male, from the other two, which are felt as being *setrèn*, *istri*, L. J. *wèdokan* = female;

1 large, rather flat-shaped *kenong* (*kenong japan*), tuned to tone III, and beaten as a keṭuk;

[1]) Cf. B. P. A. SURYADININGRAT, De Wajang orang topèng ("Djawa" XV p. 195), 1935.

[2]) In regard to the wayang-forms themselves, Appendix *57* gives particulars of their spread and number.

[3]) Hence also called Gangsa *patigan* (from tiga = 3). There also exist some seven-toned orchestras of the name *Munggang*, *e.g.* in the Paku Alaman at Jogya, and in the kabupatèn at Tasikmalaya. These are, as far as their tuning is concerned, ordinary gamelan pélog.

2 (*kenong*) *penontong* (also called *bendé*), tuned to tones I and II;
2 *gong ageng*, one of which is called *Kanjèng Kyahi Lindu*;
1 pair of *rojèh* (tuned to tone III);
1 *kendang gending*;
1 (uncommonly large) *penuntung* (*ketipung*).

The three tones of the bonangs correspond in most cases approximately to the tones *lima—nem—penunggul* of a gamelan pélog:

Ky. *Udan Arum* [1] (kraton	192		206.5		262		(384)
Solo)	I	*126*	II	*412*	III	*662*	(I')
Ky. *Sèngkan turunan* (M.N.	192.5		204		255.5		(385)
Solo) [2]	I	*100*	II	*390*	III	*710*	(I')
Ky. *Segara windu* (M. N.	202		266		287		(404)
Solo)	I	*194*	II	*414*	III	*592*	(I')

The Munggang in the Jogya kraton, *Kangjeng Kyahi Guntur laut* [3]) however, forms an exception in that its three tones seem to tend somewhat towards sléndro:

159		191		211.5		(318)
I	*315*	II	*179*	III	*706*	(I')

1) It has been the custom for some time to fill in the large interval between tone III and the octave of tone I, with another 3 tones, which I found to be of respectively 296½, 314 and 350 v.d. Thereby the interval in question—of 662 C—was split into four intervals of, respectively, 214, 100, 188 and 160 C. Later on these tones came into disuse again.

2) The sacred tones of one of the gamelans Munggang in the Solonese kraton —highly revered, and anxiously guarded—were not permitted to be transferred to other gamelans. Therefore, the desire was accordingly strong, on the part of some of the nobility, to endow one of their own orchestras with the same pitch as that of that Munggang. And lo!—one of the Mangku Nagaran nobles, R. M. A. TANDAKUSUMA, son-in-law of MANGKU NAGARA IV (and the best known and cleverest dancer of his time, and the creator of the *Langendriya* and composer of several gendings) actually succeeded in "catching" the pitch; whilst the tones of the sacred orchestra set the air in vibration he produced three small bamboo laths which he had brought with him on purpose, and which were suspended by a cord, and cut them down, unnoticed by anyone, to the exact length required to make them produce the three Munggang tones, when tapped with a stick. After this, the tones of the M.N. gamelan, which had been selected for this purpose, were tuned to the three pieces of bamboo in question; and since then this orchestra is naively called *Kyahi Sèngkan turunan*, *i.e.* "Venerable Sir Attempt at Imitation". The fact that, shortly after this, R. M. A. TONDAKUSUMA went blind, was then, I am told, considered by some as a punishment from the divine powers for his audacity.

3) According to the Jogya kraton gending-collection, the *Guntur laut* was allotted to Jogya in the Javanese year 1682 = A.D. 1755, by the treaty of repartition of Gianti.

This is also said to be the case with the Munggang in the kabupatèn of Demak, which orchestra, moreover, distinguishes itself by having exceptionally large kenongs.

The Munggang is—or used to be—played exclusively on very solemn or festive occasions; for instance during the reception of very highly-placed visitors, and, formerly, to add lustre to the tournaments (held, in the principalities, as a rule on Saturdays, and in the "Gouvernements-landen"—the former Pasisir and Monchanagara—on Mondays; hence, respectively, the names *Gangsa setu* (Saturday-gamelan) and *Gangsa senèn* (Monday-gamelan), which names are also used occasionally for these ensembles) [1]).

They are (or used to be) played during the so-called *maleman, i.e.* the nocturnal sacrificial meals given at the kraton on the 21st, 23rd, 25th, 27th and 29th day of the month of fasting; further, during the first official meeting of a princely bridal couple; at the *garebegs* (the three great religious kraton celebrations, *vide* **378**); when the prince used to leave the kraton to go to the aloon-aloon for an audience, the administration of justice, or to witness the fight between a tiger and a buffalo; during the handing over of lettres from the Sunan to the Sultan (and vice-versa) of from the Governor-General to one of the princes, and, finally, again "*sakarsa Dalem*", *i.e.* at the Prince's pleasure.

The Munggang knows only one (naturally three-toned) melody, called, after the orchestra, *gending Munggang*, but also *gending Lokanonta*, and consisting of a well-nigh endless repetition of its three tones in this order of sequence: I III II III, etc. [2]):

[1]) Cf. above, p. 115/116, a description of the start of such a tournament, *i.e.* the awaiting, and arrival, of the Sultan (from RYCKLOF VAN GOENS' account of his travels).

[2]) Col. D 33003 gives a good rendering of Solonese munggang playing.

We have probably to do here with an old Indonesian *motif*; for I came across the very same Munggang melody amongst the East-Florinese tribe of the Lionese (**221** p. 121).

After a few bars of this, played rapidly at first, but gradually slowing down, the normal tempo is reached at the fourth gong-beat. The drive, or condensation, of the *beḍug*-beats (*salahan*) starting at *A* in the above fragment, is repeated a few times in the course of the piece, generally returning after 8 gong-beats. The *kenḍangan* is marked only as far as the change to normal tempo; it remains the same, however, after this. The tempo is quickened again (*sesegan*) towards the finish, and, at a sign from the *kenḍang* the piece is then brought to a close. The *rojèh* part, which is not printed in the above fragment, consists of the same rhythmic figure in every bar. Gamelans Munggang are found in possession only of the Central-Javanese ruling princes and Prime Ministers, and some of the Regents (the latter being often—either by descent or through marriage—amongst the highest nobility in the country). These gamelans usually form part of the State or family *pusaka*, since possession of them used to be a privilege attached to such a high—and generally hereditary—function.

Quite rightly Javanese tradition credits an orchestra like the Munggang with possessing great age. According to the Kitab Jitapsara, Baṭara Guru felt in need of an instrument with which he could call together the gods for consultations, or which he could use when going into battle. Having started with a single cymbal, he then added two more, both differing in sound from the first one and also from each other, and also caused this triplet of cymbals to be sounded on such occasions as, for instance, his entry into the council chamber. Hence arose the three-toned Munggang and its specialized use.

The first one of its kind was called Lokanonta [1]) and is said to have been put into service in Çaka 269 = 347 A. D. The position which it occupied in the kraton of Majapahit corresponded, it appears, to that which is reserved to-day for the gamelans sekati in the Mohammedan kratons in Central Java (cf. below, p. 265/266, and further **377A**, pp. 40/1, 51 and 68, note). *Vide* also, about the Munggang, **91** p. 42 *et seq.* [and **123M**]

Akin to the Munggang, and just as venerable, are the gamelans **Koḍok**

[1]) By Lokanonta, the Javanese actually means heavenly music played upon invisible instruments.

ngorèk (ill. 112 and 113). The Koḍok ngorèk ("Croaking Frog")[1]) also possesses a three-toned scale (although it is often thought that they are only two-toned, but this is because the genḍings played on them are two-toned)[2]), which scale, again, seems to be derived from the pélog system: it lies, however, much higher that than of the Munggangs:

kraton Solo I:	572		610		809		(1144)
	I	*111*	II	*489*	III	*600*	(I')
kraton Solo II:	396		427		567		(792)
	I	*130*	II	*491*	III	*579*	(I')
kepatihan Jogya:	625		672		844		(1250)
	I	*125*	II	*395*	III	*680*	(I')

The Koḍok ngorèk in the Jogya kraton[3]), the *Kyahi Mahésa ganggang*, again, forms an exception in that it tends towards sléndro[4]):

353		397		480		(706)
I	*204*	II	*328*	III	*668*	(I')

The composition of the Koḍok ngorèk is practically the same as that of the Munggang, except that its *bonangs* have not three, but 6 or 8 kettles each, which give either the tones I and II alternately, or only the tone III. The kettles of the last-named, highest-sounding bonang are called *ènèng-ènèng*, or *klènang*.

Further, the Koḍok ngorèk ensembles in the kratons include either one (in Jogya) or two (in Solo) "Turkish crescents" ("bell-trees" without

---

[1]) The frog plays a peculiar rôle in Indonesian music. Not to mention, for the time being, the koḍok figures depicted on various prehistoric kettledrums, or the chant, imitating the croaking of frogs, of the male choir singing, which accompanies the dance of the Balinese Sanghyang Dedari, we may point out that the koḍok has also found its way into a Jogya kraton genḍing, *i.e.* in the *Babar layar koḍokan*, (paṭet barang, kenḍangan Mawur keṭuk 4 hawis), which is characterized by its exceptional structure and which, after a normal *mérong* and a regular *nḍawah*, follows up this nḍawah with a *pangkat ngoḍok* (without the usual keṭuk-"drive", *vide* pp. 214/215 and 314), introducing a movement called *ngoḍok*, consisting of two gongan, and not differing in its style of rendering—to judge either by its structure or by the score—from an ordinary nḍawah or munggah, and, in its turn, is followed by a ladrang movement. —*Vide* also p. 163 s.v. *keṭuk*.

[2]) The third and highest tone has exclusively *pancher* function (cf. above, p. 168).

[3]) According to the Jogya kraton genḍing-collection this was allotted to Jogya by the repartition treaty of Gianṭi in the Javanese year 1682 = A.D. 1755, and somewhat added to and supplemented in 1757.

[4]) although, in the inventory of princely orchestras contained in the kraton genḍing-collection mentioned before, it is classed with the gamelans pélog.

crescent), whilst the second orchestra of that name in the Solonese kraton possesses a bunch of 6 tiny cymbals (called *kechichèr* or *rojèh*), which are suspended from an iron bar.

No less than 4 gongs ageng form part of the Jogya Koḍok ngorèk, *i.e.* two for normal use, and two pusaka gongs, called, respectively, *K. K. Mahésa ganggang* [1]) and *K. K. Sima* [2]).

On rare occasions in the kraton (*i.e.* in the genḍing *Koḍok ngorèk ayam sepenan*(g)) [3]) some instruments of the saron type (*demung* and *saron barung*) (*vide* ill. 112) are made to play together with the Koḍok ngorèk; sometimes, too, a *gendèr* and a *gambang gangsa*; this is done in order to have melody-playing instruments at one's disposal. Curiously enough, these are generally sléndro-instruments, although—at any rate in Solo—the Koḍok ngorèk itself comes fairly close to pélog. Possibly the idea was that, in this way, a closer imitation of the not always perfectly harmonious noise of the frogs' croaking [4]) might be achieved [5]).

The Koḍok ngorèk plays on the occasion of the first official meeting of a bride and bridegroom of the blood; further, on the prince's birthday; for the circumcision of a princely descendant; at *garebegs* upon the appearance of the *gunungan* (stacks of rice to be distributed among the Regents and the people), and, formerly, during *rampok machan* (the spearing of a tiger that has been caught, by way of popular entertainment) and fights between a tiger and a buffalo (*adu-adu machan*), also a popular entertainment [6]). It is also used sometimes in the wayang wong [7]).

Here follows the opening of the genḍing *Koḍok ngorèk*:

---

1) *Mahésa* (L. J. *kebo*) = buffalo; *ganggang* = fighting.

2) There exists a belief that, whenever those to whom the maintenance of this Jogya Koḍok ngorèk has been entrusted should fail to take all possible care, and more especially, neglect to bring incense and flowers on Jumahat-Kliwon (*i.e.* the day, on which the week-day Jumahat and the pasar-(market)day Kliwon fall together) for this gong, they shall suddenly come face to face with a tiger (= *sima*).

3) *ayam sepènan* = the isolated chicken.

4) To those who have heard the obstinate hooting, almost lowing, croak-concert of the bangkongs in the rainy period, the name of Koḍok ngorèk will be quite an understandable one for the ensemble described.

5) Another example of the mixing of pélog- and sléndro-instruments is the genḍing *Kombang mara*, which, although being in pélog paṭet lima, makes use, in Solo, of the kenong lima sléndro. [*S[67]]

6) A very good Koḍok ngorèk record, in which one hears bits of melody mysteriously bobbing up through the main thematic material, and the tinkling of bells, is Col. D 33002. [*S[34, 45]]

7) Cf. above, p. 214/215 and 246.

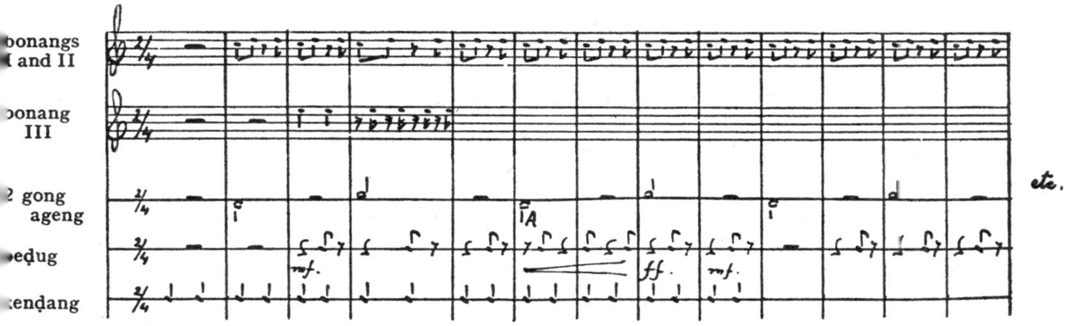

After a few bars of this, played rapidly at first, but gradually slowing-down, normal tempo is reached at the fourth gong-beat. The drive, or condensation, of the beḍug-beats (*salahan*) starting at *A* in the above fragment, is repeated a few times in the course of the piece, generally returning after 8 gong-beats. The rhythmic filling by the highest bonang III is also repeated after every 8 gong-beats, except in the quickened parts at the beginning and towards the finish. The first time, therefore, it is not beaten at all—although it is marked above for the sake of conciseness. The *kenḍangan* has been marked only as far as the change to normal tempo; it remains the same, however, after this. The tempo is accelerated towards the finish, and, at a sign from the *kenḍang*, the piece is wound up in the following manner:

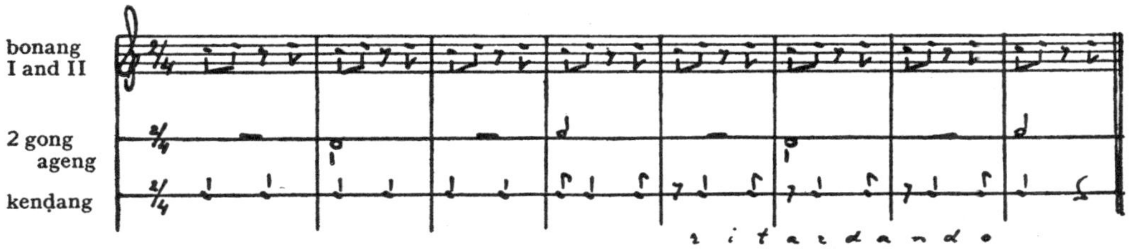

In addition to the genuine (two-toned) genḍing *Koḍok ngorèk* (either with or without *Ayam sepanan(g)*), another variant, also two-toned, is beaten on this gamelan; it is called genḍing *Nalanganjur* (J.). This genḍing however, is sometimes performed in a lower register (on *gulu* and *ḍaḍa* instead of ± *lima* and *nem*), and on an ordinary gamelan.

One other three-toned ensemble is to be found in the Solonese kraton; it is called *Kyahi* **Patalon** [1]). It consists of 1 ranchakan *bonang ageng* (*jaler*);

[1]) Derived from *talu*. About this word and its meaning, cf. below, p. 265.

2 ranchakan *bonang alit* (*istri*); 1 large *kenong*; 2 *gong ageng* (sounding the octaves of tones II and III), and 2 *kenḍang*.

Its scale resembles that of most gamelans Munggang and Koḍok ngorèk, *i.e.* a more or less incomplete pélog; its absolute pitch is high, like that of the Koḍok ngorèk orchestras:

420		457		564		840
I	*146*	II	*364*	III	*690*	I′

The Patalon is played every Saturday, and is, therefore, like the Munggang, a *Gangsa setu*. *Vide* also **403**, p. 159.

The gamelan **charabalèn**, or *charabali* (ill. 114 and 115), the signification of which names is uncertain (**192**, p. 178 *et seq.*), has sequences of either 4 or 6 tones in the octave, which usually constitute an incomplete "inversion" of the tonal sequence of one of the ordinary pélog gamelans belonging to the same owner. This tonal relation exists, for example, between the Mangku Nagaran gamelans charabalèn *Kyahi Berama* "(The Grandiose One") and *Kyahi Baswara* ('Great Sound") with respect to the gamelan *Kyahi Lipur tomba neng*:

Kyahi *Lipur tomba neng*	193 IV_1	*138*	209 V_1	*89*	220 VI_1	*182*	244½ VII_1	*222*	278 I	*126*	299 II	*150*	326 III	*292*	386 IV	*138*	418 V	*89*	440 VI	*182*	489 VII
Kyahi *Berama*					220 I	*182*	244½ II		*348*		299 III	*150*	326 IV			*519*			440 I¹		
Kyahi *Baswara*	193 I	*138*	209 II	89	220 III		*405*		278 IV	*126*	299 V	*150*	326 VI	292	386 I						

The composition of such a gamelan charabalèn is usually as follows: 1 ranchakan with either 4 or 6 "female" *bonang ageng* on one row, and called *gambyong*; 1 ranchakan with the same number of "male" kettles also in one row, and called *klènang*; 1 *gong ageng lima* or *barang*; 1 or 2 *penontong lima* and/or *nem*: 1 or 2 large *kenong lima* and/or *nem*, and 2 *kenḍang* of the truncated-conical model.

When the charabalèn has bonang-ranges with 6 kettles, it is played in two ways: in *laras alit*—high pitch—only the tones II, III, V and VI (from low to high) are beaten; in *laras geḍé*—low pitch—the tones I, II, IV and V. When, however, this 6-toned charabalèn joins in with the ordinary gamelan, then, naturally, all six kettles are in use.

When it is played independently, only one genḍing is commonly played on it, which is called *genḍing charabalèn.* It consists of a kind of incessant going to-and-fro, in two parts:

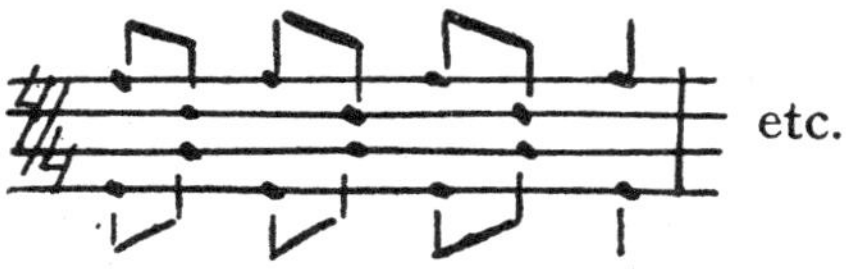

Quite possibly the name is derived from this continuous going apart and coming together again of the tones [1]).

In the Mangku Nagaran, however, one may distinguish no less than five genḍings charabalèn, namely, *Bali balèn, Pis(ah)an bali* [2]), *G(l)angsaran* [3]), *Klumpung*, and *Lung gaḍung*, all of them with *bebuka kendang*. These five can be played on the *four*-toned charabalèn; the six-toned one is naturally less restricted in its repertoire, and is, as we said above, often beaten in conjunction with the ordinary large gamelan, whose tuning corresponds to it.

The charabalèn may be heard at great festivities, at the entry of important guests; hence, it is also called, in East-Java, *gamelan talu* [4]) (ill. 114). Further, in bridal processions; for this reason the ranchakan of the gambyong and the klènang are often provided with iron braces to carry them by. Finally, the charabalèn is said to have served in olden times for accompaniment of wirèng dancers, and of the drill and lance-practice of the prajurits (**169**, p. 57).

The **gamelan sekati** (ill. in **100**, plate I) is that special orchestra of the native princes (both in Solo and Jogya, and in Cheribon, and also, formerly, in Madura and Banten) which, during the Sekatèn-week (*i.e.* from the

1) It might, for that matter, also mean: "in Balinese style" (*chara* = custom, manner, way, style, *balèn* = *balian* = *à la Bali*) which, in this case, would not refer to the orchestral combination, but to the style of playing characteristic of this ensemble, namely, the harsh, fierce way of playing the drum, as in Bali (moreover, as is customary in the latter island, on *two* drums). The name might also refer to the fact of the "inversion" of the scale (as compared to that of the gamelan to which it is usually tuned), in which case *bali* and *balèn* = *balian* should have to be traced to *balik* = reversed, back again.

2) Idiomatically, *Pisang-bali.* Both *Pisan* and *Pisahan bali* may be taken to mean to and fro.

3) The genḍing *Gangsaran* also serves as introduction to a number of other genḍings, as we shall see further on (p. 302 *et seq.*).

4) *talu* = signal, announcement, start (cf. below, p. 341). Hence, *gamelan talu* = introductory gamelan; an orchestra announcing the arrival, the first appearance of notable guests. Cf. above (p. 263), the gamelan *Patalon.*

evening before the 6th until the 12th of the month of Mulud), with the exception of the Thursday and Friday evening in that week, plays in the compound of the great *missigit*. [**276**A, **395**B (ch. 3), **402**C]

In its sounds the Javanese hears the plaints of "Dévi" Fatima on the death of the Prophet. More especially, the beats on the beḍug, as heard on the evening of Garebeg Mulud, are felt to interpret the way Dévi Fatima, in her grief, beat her breast.

The gamelan sekati is also played on the sitinggil, during great celebrations, such as were held at the time of the 40 years' jubilee of the rule of His Princely Highness PAKU BUWANA X; further, in Solo, as a rule on the eve of the *tingalan pawukon* of the Susuhunan and the Ratu, *i.e.* on the anniversaries according to the *wuku* (the astronomical year).

Of the two gamelans sekati [1]) in the Jogya kraton, the oldest, the *K.K. Guntur Madu* (Venerable Sir Torrent of Honey) [2]) is placed, during the sekatènweek, on the southern part of the compound of the great missigit; the other one—manufactured in 1757 during the reign of the first Sultan, and called *K. K. Naga ilaga* (Venerable Sir Fighting Snake)—on the northern part.

Both gamelans are also played on the occasions of the circumcision and the wedding of the crown prince, when the *Guntur madu* is lined up on the western, and the *Naga ilaga* on the eastern bangsal of the inner courtyard Srimenganṭi.

In addition to this the Naga ilaga is beaten on the occasion of the circumcision or the marriage of another child of one of the prince's chief wives, when it is lined up on the western bangsal Srimenganṭi; and, finally, its serves, during the Garebeg Mulud, to accompany the Mounting of the guard by the lurah's *Prayalata* [3]).

The gamelan, found by the Islam on arrival in Java as an indispensable element of all Hindu ceremonials, has never become (? for this reason) an integral part of Mohammedan religious rite. Accordingly, during the month of fasting, as well as on Fridays, all orchestras in the whole of the

[1]) In popular etymology, *sekati* is either considered as on par with *suka ati* (= heart's delight) or as meaning *one kati* (= 680 g) ,which weight is supposed to be about that of a saron key in this ensemble.

[2]) This gamelan dates from before 1755, the year in which it was allotted to the sultanate, by the repartition of Gianṭi, together with the *Munggang*, the *Koḍok ngorèk*, the *K. K. Kanchil belik* and the *K. K. Surak*.

[3]) Cf. above, pp. 190 and 246.

Javanese territory are expected to remain silent [1]). If, at the garebegs and during the Sekatèn-week, we hear the gamelan being played, then this is because it is the same population which, now converted to Mohammedanism, nevertheless neither could nor would forego the ancient *ramé-ramé* and the stately splendour of sound of its orchestras. Quite rightly—and wisely, from a psychological point of view—the great religious devotees of the 15th and 16th centuries [2]) have allowed the gamelan to retain its place in the new religious service [3]). And it would surely be a most desirable thing for the present Islamitic revival, embodied in the society Mohammadiyah, to abandon the unfriendly attitude it is taking up at present towards the ancient national music of its adherents, and to follow, also in that respect, in the footsteps of its great predecessors the Panembahans, Sunans and Pangérans, the Wali's from the time of the transition [4]).

It is once again the Chenṭini that has put into words both the severely orthodox and the more modern, tolerant point of view in a manner not to be bettered. I cannot deny myself the pleasure of rendering here the quintessence of both these considerations. First, the orthodox standpoint (Canto 276, stanza 41 *et seq.*—vol. VII/VIII, p. 203/4):

41. "But, Mr. Kulawirya, as far as occupying oņeself with music is concerned, that is forbidden by religion, since in the end it leads to poverty; poverty both in this world as later on in the hereafter. For these musicians are without any doctrinal conviction.

42. A musician, you know, deifies *music*; he hankers after nothing

[1]) This rule is not strictly adhered to in the kraton. All that is done there is to avoid beating the gong ageng, and to play the gong kemoḍong instead. The princes, for that matter, are regarded as above the adat. When, for example, one of their memorial days falls in the fasting month, then the prohibition of gamelan-playing, it seems, is raised entirely. Then, however, a sum of money is paid into the mosque cashbox as a compensation of this breach of the religious adat.

[2]) Cf. above, p. 17, note 2.

[3]) *Vide* also Dr. PURBACHARAKA, in „Bijdragen Taal- Land- en Volkenkunde", vol. 80 (1924), p. 253.

[4]) "According to some Mohammedans, gamelans belong to the *alatul malahi*, i.e. the absolute, estranged from God, order of things. If the gamelans actually excercise such evil influences, then they are reckoned amongst the forbidden things; if, however, they do not lead to evil, but, on the contrary, awaken the good in people, then they are not forbidden. The gamelans played during the sekatèn festivities in the missigit, never lead to dancing parties, etc.; for this reason most *ulama's* (religious authors) approve of the gamelans in question being played during these celebrations in the place mentioned." (L.G.K., in the daily journal "Darmo kondo", 18 Nov. 1925, No. 88 (translation by the Bureau voor Inlandsche Zaken (Native Affairs)).

except musical pleasure. As long as the gamelan is playing he cherishes music in his heart.

43. Confused, stubborn and conceited, he regards orchestral music and the bright sound of song as number one. If he were to make a comparison, he would not know a thing even remotely comparable to the gamelan. In addition to this he does not give the slightest attention to his appearance or to his surroundings.

44. He glorifies only music. He lives in a disorderly atmosphere; night and day he waits for people to call him to come and play. He has no religious inclination, owing to the power that music has over him.

45. He feels like a millionaire when he is playing. That is, Mr. Kulawirya, why music has a bad influence on man. For he does not then think of Him who commands both life and death,

46. endows and punishes, both in this world and in the next. For this reason the profession of a musician is the most contemptible of all professions.

All other workpeople earn their living under difficulty;

47. they pray to God for His blessing upon their labour; they are engrossed in their religious feelings, praying the Lord to lighten their efforts in gaining their livelihood.

48. Not so the *niyaga*. He looks upon music as number one. Therefore blind infatuation dwells within him. He is inseparable from buffoons, girl dancers and ḍalangs, and his thoughts are incessantly busy with music.

49. Indeed, it is the limit: he is completely loose of all religion. He regards it as a trifle to act in a way contrary to religious precept. He is damned and knows not good from evil; is morally corrupt, can never thrive, and is low and vulgar. He is indifferent to everything but music".

From the opposite argument: that the gamelan is quite compatible with religion, nay, that the latter may be furthered by the practice of music, we may quote the following (Canto 277, stanza 28 *et seq.*):

28. "Music is in harmony with *niat* (a striving after the sublime) in that, in both cases (*i.e.* in prayer as well as during the playing of music), the human heart tends towards inner peace and tranquillity, which we should strive after with all our energy.

29. We should however, not merely lose ourselves in the purely sensual sound of the genḍing; its enchantment be only the *means* to making the heart receptive,

30. and to cause a great longing for union with God. In this way, the genḍing itself disappears completely, and nothing is left of it", (*i.e.* then music does not exist any longer as an end in itself, but has wholly become an instrument, the road, the guide, towards the *Unio Mystica*).

31. This is the way one should go. The sound of the gamelan and the voice

32. one ought, as it were, to restore to Him from Whom all sound has come, and Who has endowed man with the faculty of hearing".

After this theological digression we will return to its concrete inducement, the gamelan sekati.

There is, firstly, its composition. This is fairly simple. The softly-sounding instruments (rebab, gendèr, chelempung, suling, etc.) are all lacking. There is, further, no kenḍang, but there is a beḍug. Thus, the principal gamelan sekati in the Solonese kraton—the already-mentioned *Kyahi Sepuh*—is composed of the following:

2 *gong ageng*, tuned respectively to *lima* and *nem*;
1 *beḍug*;
1 *kempyang*, both of whose kettles are tuned to *nem*;
2 *demung*;
4 *saron barung*;
2 *saron panerus*;
1 double-rowed *bonang*.

The last-named instrument, which is usually played by two niyaga's sitting opposite each other, turned out—when, in 1931, I heard the *Kyahi Sepuh* being played in Solo—to have the following disposition of its kettles:

2nd niyaga

x

4	6	5	3	2	1	7
7′	1′	2′	3′	5′	6′	7′

[7′] (x) [4′]

lurah genḍing

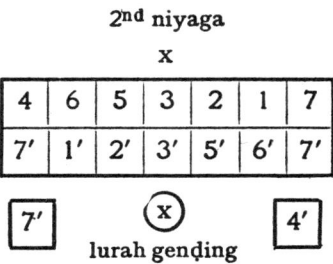

It included, therefore, no less than 3 *barang alit* kettles, one of which was, like the *pélog alit* kettle, placed separately by the side of the principal musician, the *lurah gending* (with the title of mantri) ¹). Those kettles are called *pangapit* = the flanking, or closing-in ones.

According to the Solonese musician RADÈN KODRAT, however, the disposition is generally as follows:

4	x	7

6	5	3	2	1
1	2	3	5	6

7	(x)	4

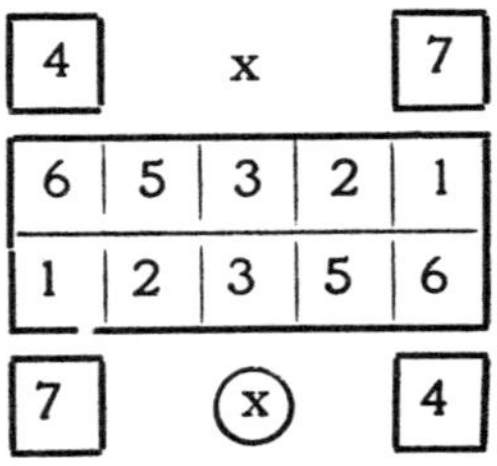

i.e. exactly symmetrical, and without this abundance of *barang alit* kettles.

The Jogya gamelans sekati *K. K. Guntur Madu* and *Naga ilaga* are of the same composition, except that they include another two bendé's (? penontong), but only 1 demung, 2 sarons and 1 saron panerus (peking).

The pitch is usually very low ²) (sometimes as much as a major sixth, or 900 C., lower than that of a normal gamelan; *vide* the scale of the *Kyahi Henèm*, on the table on page 271), and is invariably in pélog, although some of the intervals occasionally show fairly marked deviations. Whether this is caused by the fact that a gamelan sekati is actually not allowed to be tuned up to pitch (as still prescribed by the adat in the Kanoman at Cheribon) is not known; but since there is no relative difference in the tuning of the various instruments one would rather be inclined to suppose that the deviations in question have existed right from the beginning.

As is always the case, the large melodic periods are concluded by a beat on the gong ageng; further interpunctuation is left to the bedug, which performs about the same function that is allotted to the kempul in other gamelans. At the same time, however, its task bears some correspondence

---

¹) In Jogya, these *lurah gending* have the title of *demang*, while the leader of the Kyahi *Guntur Madu* bears the name—attached to his function—of MELAYA, and his colleague of the *Naga ilaga* that of MANGUN GENDING (= Creator of orchestral melodies).

²) The *Kyahi Sepuh* is tuned in such a way that the pieces played on it in the *patets lima* and *nem* definitely make the impression of being in *patet barang*; the key functioning as *nem* (*poko*) having precisely the pitch of the *dada* of the ordinary orchestras.

The scales of some gamelan sekati

	Degrees:	I pe-nung-gul or bem		II gulu or jongga		III ḍaḍa or tengah		IV pélog		V lima or gang-sal		VI nem		VII barang		I' pe-nung-gul or bem alit
Madura	1. gamelan from Sumenep (East-Madura); now in Kedawung (res. of Pasuruan)	244 I	*149*	266 II	*194*	297.5 III	*116*	318 IV	*204*	358 V	*175*	396 VI	*171*	437 VII	*191*	488 I'
Solo	2. *Kyahi Sepuh* (kraton Solo)	216 I	*171.5*	238.5 II	*162.5*	262 III	*205.5*	295 IV	*167.5*	325 V	*113.5*	347 VI	*191*	387.5 VII	*188*	432 I'
Solo	3. *Kyahi Henèm* (kraton Solo).	168.5 I	*189.5*	188 II	*94*	198.5 III	*314*	238 IV	*153*	260 V	*91*	274 VI	*191*	306 VII	*167*	337 I'
Jogya	4. *Kyahi Guntur madu* (kraton Jogya)	201.5 I	*63.5*	209 II	*108.5*	222.5 III	*293*	263.5 IV	*117.5*	292 V	*176*	316 VI	*79*	338.5 VII	*302*	403 I'
Jogya	5. *Kyahi Naga Ilaga* (kraton Jogya)	218.5 I	*85*	229.5 II	*216*	260 III	*230.5*	297 IV	*96.5*	314 V	*96.5*	332 VI	*149.5*	362 VII	*326*	437 I'
Jogya	6. *Kyahi Munggang* (Paku Alaman, Jogya)	199.5 I	*145.5*	217 II	*152.5*	237 III	*245*	273 IV	*651.5*	298 V	*155.5*	326 VI	*157*	367 VII	*192.5*	399 I'
Che-ribon	7. gamelan of Sultan Anom	282 I	*158*	309 II	*180.5*	343 III	*266*	400 IV	*88.5*	421 V	*134.5*	455 VI	*163.5*	500 VII	*208.5*	564 I'
Banten	8. The old Sultans-gamelan *Kyahi Suka ramé* (Royal Bat. Soc. cat. Nos. 1243–1256).	262.5 I	*160.5*	288 II	*166*	317 III	*181.5*	352 IV	*146*	383 V	*188*	427 VI	*87*	449 VII	*270.5*	525 I'
Cheribon	9. Gamelan Sekati (Ḳatjerbonan)	292 I	[*48*]	313 II	[*151*]	347 III	[*140*]	387 IV	[*141*]	420 V	[*158*]	460 VI	[*172*]	508 VII	[*241*]	584 I'

to that of the keṭuk, inasmuch as it subdivides the gongan according to the already-mentioned colotomic formula $^1/_2 + (n \times 1) + ^1/_2$, which, in ladrang compositions, with 32 *keteg* to the gongan, amounts to the following division:

$$4 + 8 + 8 + 8 + 4.$$

In this, however, the beḍug shares with the kempul the peculiarity that it is not played immediately after the gong beat, so that the subdivision becomes, in reality:

$$12 + 8 + 8 + 4.$$

A colotomic subdivision of a lower order is effected by the kempyang, which sounds with pauses, now of two, now of four *keteg*.

The gamelan sekati is played in all three paṭets, keeping strictly to the length of the playing period prescribed by the adat for each of them. It is customary in Solo to play it from half-past seven until 12 at night in *paṭet lima*, and from 12 to 2 a.m. in *paṭet nem*. After this the orchestra is silent until 7 a.m., when it starts again in *P. barang*; at 12 midday it changes again to *P. nem*, which, at 3 p.m. is left in favour of *P. barang*. This continues until 6 p.m., after which the gamelan is silent until it starts again at half-past seven.

The principal genḍings (ageng) sekati used to be the *G. Rambu* and *G. Rangkung*, both in *paṭet lima*. Nowadays these pieces are still being used to open a concert with, but, after this, other genḍings are also played, and especially, too, ladrang-compositions; generally a martial genḍing and a gentler, softer, genḍing rebab [1]), alternately. In the Solonese kraton I heard the *Kyahi Sepuh* play, amongst others, the ladrangans *Pangrawit*, *Sembawa*, *Peksi kuwung*, and the grandiose *Babar layar*—all in *paṭet lima*—as well as *Gliyeng* and *Rumung* in *paṭet nem*. The ladrangan *Barang miring* is said to present an example of *P. barang*.

GRONEMAN (**100**, p. 9) mentions, for the Jogya gamelan sekati, 12 compositions, *viz.* 4 genḍing ageng: *Rambu*, *Rangkung*, *Andong-andong* and

[1]) The genḍings are distinguished after the instrument which is most prominent in their bebuka, which, at the same time, determines their character (cf. below, p. 311). As far as their rendering by the gamelan sekati is concerned, the term *genḍing rebab* naturally refers exclusively to the character of the composition; the introduction is then, of necessity, beaten on the bonang, also in the case of these genḍings rebab, since, as we have said, the rebab is missing from the sekati ensemble.

Lungka [or *Lala* (*Lahela*)] *dempel*, and 8 genḍing alit: *Orang-aring*, *Atur-atur*, *Barung putih*, *Glèyong*, *Sulung ḍayung*, *Rènḍèng*, *Dénḍang sepinang* and *Songbah*.

Each of these compositions begins—after the *bebuka*—with an extremely slowly played *balungan*, beaten on the demungs and sarons, and led by the bonang beaten by the leader, the lurah genḍing. In addition, the bonang plays a very simple *wilet*-filling or variation, after this style:

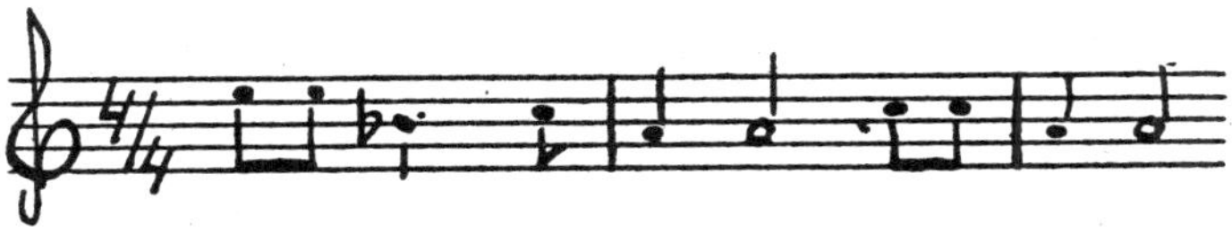

Then, suddenly, the tempo becomes livelier, a sign to which is given by a somewhat anticipated beat on the beḍug; at the same time the sound is driven up to the greatest *fortissimo* imaginable. In this, the two demungs are often beaten alternately [1]; it would, indeed, be above the power of a single niyaga to bring out to the full the balunganing genḍing with such rapidity and vigour. The tempo slows down towards the finish of the genḍing—at a sign given by a slightly retarded beḍug-beat—and the force of the sound gradually diminishes.

In the popular belief a niyaga who should succeed in breaking one of the keys of a saron sekati whilst playing on it is supposed to get a reward from the prince; thus the vigour of sekatèn playing is both explained and stimulated.

A remarkable thing is the frequency of occurrence of the tone *pélog*, especially in *P. lima*. The genḍing *Rangkung*—*mirabile dictu*—even finishes on this tone. Together with the tones *nem* and *gulu* this pélog tone—at any rate in the *Kyahi Sepuh*—forms a practically pure triad:

, which the European ear—especially in such places where it occurs in extended position—experiences as something surprisingly blissful when it emerges suddenly from the dominant-seventh atmosphere prevailing in this sekati-music.

With respect to the gamelan sekati in the Principalities, we also refer

[1]) that is, one niyaga the "even", and the other the "uneven" tones.

to BRANDTS BUYS, who has devoted a special treatise to this subject (**50**).

VAN DAPPEREN (**71**) gives a few data about the gamelan sekati from the Kanoman at Cheribon (it is called *gamelan sukati* there). The repertoire is said to consists of the genḍings *Chinṭing duwur*, *Kajongan*, *Parianom*, *Rambu geḍé*, *Rambu chilik* and *Rara buṭak*. During the ceremony of taking the *panjang* (sacred dishes) to the mosque, and during the return to the kraton on the 11th day of the month of Mulud, both in the evening and during the night, however, the genḍing *Rara buṭak* is beaten exclusively. The niyaga's must be ritually pure. For the determination of the periods of rest, a small wooden board is used, with 25 holes, called *chubleg*. After each set of 3 gongan a tiny stick belonging to the outfit is pushed into the next hole. After 75 gongan there is a period of rest.

A **gamelan klenéngan** (Pekalongan, Grobogan: *klonèngan*; Panaraga: (also) *gamelan klatan*; Tegal: (also) *gamelan moḍong*; Panarukan: *gamelan gendèr*; Jogya: (also) *gamelan klenyitan* (**76**)) is to a fully-equipped gamelan as a string orchestra is to a symphony orchestra. One might call it a "chamber-gamelan".

This combination never includes any bonangs. Neither does it contain the instruments of the saron group, at any rate not in the case of the genuine gamelan klenéngan; these instruments may, however, be found in the *tabuhan reprepan* (from *tabuhan* = orchestra of percussion instruments, and *rep* = soft) or *klenéngan tengahan*, medium sort of klenéngan. It is this last-named orchestra which usually serves to accompany the wayang purwa (wayang kulit). For this reason it is also occasionally indicated by the term *gamelan wayangan*. There is another instrumental form which is usually missing in the klenéngan orchestras, namely, the gong ageng. In its place—in the genuine klenéngan—the gong kemoḍong is beaten, and, in the klenéngan tengahan, either that or the gong suwukan. When, however, in the Solonese kraton, the orchestra is not used for the wayang kulit, the gong ageng may also be beaten in it.

Further, it also happens that the kenongs are replaced by a saron barung.

Here and there one may come across iron klenéngan from which the gendèrs, too, are missing (in such cases, however, a saron is usually included in the combination). In Pemalang such an orchestra is called *klenéngan kaplok*; the klenéngan orchestras with gendèrs are called there *klenéngan gendèr*. Kaplok orchestras are invariably tuned to sléndro; the klenéngan gendèr, either to sléndro or to pélog or miring [1]).

The nuclear theme, which, in the complete gamelan, is borne in most cases by different instruments of the saron family (in the first place the demung), and only in certain special cases by the gendèr panembung or the slenṭem gantung, is beaten, in the genuine klenéngan, exclusively on the last-named instrument (which is then, on account of its function, sometimes called *demung*), unless a real demung gantung is available, *i.e.* an instrument in the register of the demung but shaped like a gendèr. In that case this demung gantung is the bearer of the nuclear theme. If there is a slenṭem present as well, it may double every fourth tone of the theme on its lower octave, functioning, therefore, as a colotomic instrument of a lower order; or it is put in the place of the kempul(s), which can then drop out, thus causing the ensemble to become still a little more compact, as well as more accessible to modest purses.

The Chenṭini (Canto 44, stanza 104; vol. I/II, p. 247) reminds the reader of the fact that it is not "*ilok*", *i.e.* that it is taboo, to play klenéngan with the kenḍang but without the gong. This inadmissible manner of playing is condemned as being *kemaga*.

The same Canto in the Chenṭini also contains, in stanzas 110 *et seq.*, the following lively description of the playing of the klenéngan:

110. ....
...... lajeng buka
genḍing sanga *Gambir sawit*
ingegongan lega tyasé samya suka

111. kabèh baud paḍa rasané nenabuh
rereming irama
adu wileting malatsih
ukur jawil sajejanturaning ḍalang

112. langkung runtut rasaning genḍing pakantuk
dadya ngantak-antak
dangu dènira anggenḍing
tan antara aneseg genḍindé munggah

1) The Pemalang miring-tuning is the pélog-bem sequence (East-Java, *pengasih*), but without the tone *pélog*, and with the addition of the tone *barang*.

113. pan adangu saya gulet wiletipun
rebut nges kesaman
nabuhé samya birai
rahab bérag rasa-rasa yèn uwisa

114. sesegipun ngenḍelong anulya suwuk
nulya sesenḍonan
rebab lajeng ngechek ngelik
suluk suling gambang gendèr abarungan

115. nganyut arum nutug lih-ulihanipun
paṭet sarayuda
sabeman gong wisirèki.

Here follows an approximate English translation:

110. ". . . . then the *bebuka* [1]) of the genḍing (*paṭet*) *sanga Gambir sawit* was beaten. All those present had a feeling of liberation when the gong-beat fell.

111. The players were all experienced musicians, and attuned to one-another in their conceptions. The *wirama* [2]), which found its expression in the *wilet* [3]), strove after touching the heart. The manner of playing was light and supple, comparable to the *janturan* [4]) of the ḍalang.

112. It was exceedingly harmonious; the character of the genḍing was expressed in the right manner; thanks to this, one felt fascinated and moved. For a long time they played (the *mérong* of) this genḍing. After this the tempo was accelerated, and they proceeded to the munggah.

113. More and more opulently did the *wilet* entwine itself, striving after the awakening of emotion. The playing of all the musicians was perfect, full of devotion, joyful: they could almost have gone on for ever.

114. At a given moment, however, the *sesegan* [5]) was slowed down, and then came the finish. Following this, *senḍon* [6]) sounded; the rebab played some high vibrating tones; suling, gambang and gendèr played the suluk in concord with it.

---

[1]) *Vide* below, p. 311.
[2]) *Vide* below, p. 333 *et seq.*
[3]) *Vide* below, p. 333 *et seq.*
[4]) = kajantur-singing. Cf. above, p. 132/133.
[5]) *Vide* below, p. 316.
[6]) *Vide* below, p. 319.

115. The paṭet in its complete form [1]) was sweetly concluded, in a manner that carried the listeners away, by *sarayuda* [2]), ending on the drum-beat *bem*, and a beat on the gong".

And the following (45th) Canto of the same poem—which apparently cannot get tired of interpreting gamelan playing—contains in stanza 9 *et seq.* the following passage from which one may gather—if one did not know this already—what an extraordinarily exciting influence this seemingly restful, harmoniously meandering klenéngan-music can have upon the Javanese mind:

9. ....
seranchak ungelé kamot jroning kawat

10. nganyut-anyut langkung raras
kasmaran ingkang miarsi
lir mamresing karasikan
engesé ngekesi ati
wèh wileting malat sih
lir winulang ing wulangun
raosing tyas mengkana
saking nyenyeding kang genḍing
nguyu-uyu ngreranteg dènya gamelan,

the approximate English translation of which is:

9. The rebab-strings caused the klenéngan-sound to melt together into a single whole;

10. the sound carried the audience away, it was exceedingly lovely; all the listeners were fired with passion, as if driven to the most extreme erotic feelings. The power of emotion gripped the heart; the wilet intoxicated the senses. As when people are united in love: so was the emotion of the heart through the gripping power of the genḍing, which awakened a feeling of hankering expectation, as of one looking forward, full of longing. Thus it was that the gamelan played".

In Jogya, klenéngan-play is also called *nguyu-uyu*; a term which, in Solo, usually has a slightly different signification, which has already been

[1]) = *wetah*; *vide* below, p. 318 *et seq.* and 323.
[2]) *Vide* below, p. 323.

mentioned above: *i.e.* gamelan playing on the day preceding some festivity, and announcing the coming event to the population. This duality in the signification of the term nguyu-uyu has its origin in the fact that the literal translation is "softly warbling"; for however loudly the gamelan announcing a feast may be beaten in the kraton, the prince in his inner chambers as well as the people in the town nevertheless hear its sound as if it were soft and harmonious, on account of the distance.

There is a fairly close similarity between the klenéngan and the orchestras usually indicated by the names of **mondrèng** [1]) and **ringgeng**. These orchestras also use, for closing the longest melodic periods, the gong kemoḍong (G. kemuḍa), which, in that case, is called more specifically, either *gong ringgeng* or *gong anggang-anggang*. Further, in these ensembles, gendèr-shaped instruments also take a prominent part. There is this difference from the klenéngan, however, that instruments with a bonang-function are also used, all be it these latter have adopted the form of a gendèr.

The keys of the mondrèng- and ringgeng-combinations are generally made of iron. In that case the orchestra may be called *gamelan barut* (Jogya and Keḍu), *gamelan balas* [2]) (Sragèn and Magetan), *gumbeng wesi* (Demak), *gamelan timpleng* (Kudus), *gamelan jiring* [3]) (Tegal, Pemalang), *richikan* (Blora), and also, of course, *gamelan wesi* (wesi = iron). Even the term *gamelan sengganèn* [4]), which is usually reserved for gamelans with glass keys (*vide* below, p. 281), is occasionally heard in some places (*e.g.* in the Regencies Sragèn, Panaraga and Pachitan) as indicating these iron-keyed orchestras. In Madiun and Blitar they usually speak of *gamelan janggrung* [5]).

Although the names mondrèng and ringgeng are nowadays frequently used indiscriminately as meaning one and the same thing, there was formerly a difference between the two: the keys of the (gendèr-shaped) bonang, kempul and gong in a gamelan ringgeng are not provided with a beating

---

1) *mondrèng* = girl dancer.

2) *balas* = ballast.

3) Those orchestras which are called *gamelan jiring* are distinguished from other iron ensembles in that their gendèrs have no sound-tubes fitted underneath their keys. Such gendèrs without sound-tubes are called *gendèr lemprak*.

4) *senggani* = mixed (sound, brilliance).

5) *janggrung* = (strikingly) large, vigorous.

knob, whereas those of the same instruments in a gamelan mondrèng are. The latter, moreover, is intended rather for use out-of-doors, and the former for playing in a small private circle.

A very fine mondrèng—which, however, has keys made of bronze—is the *Kyahi Mardiswara* (consisting of the sléndro *Jaka Laras rum* and the pélog *Jaka Laras sih*) in the Mangku Nagaran [1]).

In some districts the number of mondrèng- and ringgeng-orchestras is considerably in excess of that of ordinary gamelans. And it appears that their number is getting steadily larger still, since these orchestras are very much cheaper than the bronze gamelans and require, moreover, a much smaller number of musicians. For this reason, too, the number of places where iron instruments are being manufactured (*vide* above, p. 140) is also correspondingly larger than that where bronze instruments are made (cf. Appendix 57).

The **beḍaya- and serimpi-orchestra**, in its most ancient form, is—at any rate in the Solonese kraton—like the gamelan klenéngan, a much-reduced ordinary gamelan. The only instruments retained in it, out of the ordinary combination, are the *kenḍang genḍing* [2]) and the *ketipung*, as well as three interpunctuating instruments: *gong*, *kenong* and *keṭuk*, with, in addition, a set of *kemanak*, whilst the melodic element is exclusively represented by unison choir singing, in former times only by women, but nowadays also by men. This is, therefore, a kind of *sinḍènan lampah sekar*, on the understanding, however, that, in the latter (cf. p. 128), both the gambang and the gendèr take part, but that there is, on the other hand, no kenḍang genḍing; whilst, moreover, the singing in the former is not by solo voices but by a choir. Later on more extensive orchestral combinations were added to this dance-accompanying vocal music.

In the Jogya kraton—according to the kraton genḍing-collection already mentioned—*sinḍènan lampah sekar genḍing* (*i.e.* vocal music accompanied by the complete gamelan) serves as beḍaya- and serimpi-accompaniment; buth with the wirama of *sinḍènan lampah genḍing*, *i.e. wirama lomba*. A probably fairly recent abuse has crept into this combination in the shape of certain European wind instruments (cornets),

---

[1]) A good record of this orchestra is Od. 114900 (genḍing *Kuswa Wirangrong*, pél. P. 5).

[2]) In **192**, p. 115, mention is erroneously made, in this case, of the *chiblon*.

which are occasionally found to be co-operating in these orchestras, as also in the orchestra accompanying the *Trunajaya*-dance performed on the occasion of princely marriages (**187**, p. 124) [1]).

The kemanaks have a purely rhythmic, time-dividing function. Their pitches do not usually harmonize with those of the tones of the gamelan in which they are beaten. That this is not felt to be irritating is probably due to the fact that in this orchestra there is not a single melody-carrying instrument. Cf. also, above, p. 181. [**113**c]

The pieces played used to be, in ancient times, exclusively genḍing ageng, but later also G. tengahan and alit. One of the beḍaya songs we will mention by name: the very ancient and most sacred song *Beḍaya ketawang*. The story goes that it was with this song and with the dance that goes with it that, in times gone by, Ratu Kidul, the Goddess of the South Sea [2]), who had fallen deeply in love with the great Sultan Ageng, revealed to him her feelings. This is the reason why this dance is allowed to be practiced only on special days, and to be performed only on the anniversaries of the Susuhunan's accession to the throne. Rehearsals for it must not be held on any day except the *anggara kasih, i.e.* the days on which a Thursday coincides with the pasar-day Kliwon (once every 35 days). Before these rehearsals—and also, only much more extensively, before the actual performance—an offering of food (*sajèn*) must be made; the girl dancers' bodies must be perfectly clean and they must be clad in bridal dress. During the dance, and even during the rehearsals, deputies sent by Ratu Kidul are supposed to dwell in their midst. Humming of the Beḍaya ketawang melody in daily life is taboo (nobody, in fact, would dare to do such a thing); in copying the text—incense being invariably burned the while—one or two intentional mistakes are made, because it would be presumption to copy such a sacred text *literally* (**102**, p. 88). [**3**a, **377**l]

Before we pass from the orchestras consisting predominantly of bronze instruments to those in which wood and bamboo are the main materials, we will consider a few irregular, partly experimental forms, of gamelan construction. More and more, as a matter of fact, traditional paths are

---

1) Exact particulars of the Trunajaya dance are given by B. P. H. Purubaya, Rondom de huwelijken in den kraton (About marriages in the Kraton at Jogyakarta) ("Djawa", XIX, p. 295 *et seq.* (**324**, sub 10), 1939.

2) Ratu Kidul is the goddess; Nyahi Lara (or Rara) Kidul, often erroneously identified with her, is her *patih*.

being left, and the finer, but more costly bronze replaced by either iron or glass, while in other instances the shape of the instruments is altered.

Thus, in the dalem of P. A. Kusumayuda in Solo, an orchestra may be found in which part of the instruments consist of metal rectangles on short legs, to which are attached some ranges of bells of the "grelot" type and immovable. These are beaten with a *tabuh* and are tuned in such a way that both pélog and sléndro, as well as the European scales, can be played on one and the same instrument.

Another gamelan, with instruments provided for the most part with keys of thick glass, was found in the possession of the former Prime minister of Jogya. As we said before, such an orchestra is called *gamelan sengganèn* (also G. *beling* or *geḍah*) [1].

We already mentioned above (p. 278) the gamelans *mondrèng* and *ringgeng* (also called *sengganèn*, and even *gumbeng*), which generally have iron keys and whose instruments are, more often than not, gendèr-shaped.

For a gamelan consisting chiefly of instruments with kenong-shaped beating kettles, we refer to p. 391 below (the gamelan Munggang of the Regent of Tasikmalaya).

It should finally be mentioned that an incomplete gamelan—a kind of improvised set of instruments collected together in a haphazard way, on which the essential parts of a genḍing or suluk can be played (the remainder, *e.g.* the interpunctuating tones, more especially the gong-tones, being imitated as well as may be with the mouth)—is called *gamelan gaḍon* (*vide*, *e.g.* the Chenṭini, Canto 44, stanza 70). In the instance described there, the ensemble consisted only of gambang, rebab, suling, gendèr and kenḍang.

The Keḍiri **Gamelan bumbung** (ill. 116) is composed mainly of bamboo idiochords, which are named, according to their respective functions, after the instruments fulfilling the same task in the ordinary gamelan. Its composition is as follows:

1 gong	together on one and the same ranchakan	all bamboo idiochords
3 kempul		
3 kenong		
1 keṭuk		
1 saron		
1 bonang		

[1]) = (made of) glass.

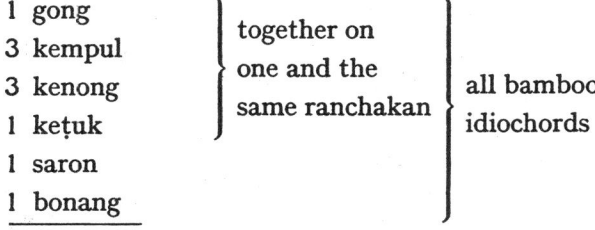

1 kenḍang
1 bamboo gambang

The tuning is in sléndro.

This combination is not of very ancient date, although its components have formed part of Java's cultural possessions for centuries.

These gamelan bumbung are also found, both in Solo and Jogya, in the possession of some of the nobility. There are one or more in the Solonese kraton, and I saw, in Jogya, an ensemble of this description in the house of P. ARJAKUSUMA (who has been holding the position of Prime minister of the Sultan, under the name P. A. DANUREJA VIII, since 1933).

The dance (*jogèd*) of the *talèḍèk* (girl dancers) [1]) is generally accompanied, in Central Java, by a complete if more or less abridged gamelan. The *genḍing talèḍèkan* found in the Jogya genḍing-collection are all in paṭet manyura. No doubt this talèḍèk accompaniment used to be played, in former centuries, by more primitive ensembles, as is still the case at the present time in West- and East-Java. In regard to West-Java, *vide* below, p. 380 *et seq*. In regard to East-Java, we should mention here, in the first place, the **gamelan gandrung**, in the Banyuwangi district (**40, 146, 298, 332, 372**) (ill. 102). Its composition is as follows:

2 violins, 2 keṭuk, 1 gong, 1 kenḍang, 1 klon(ch)èng or klun(ch)ing (triangle).

It may be assumed that the two violins (which, for that matter, as I found out, are tuned like *violas*, *i.e.* a fifth lower than normal) have formed part of this little orchestra since a relatively short time only, and that they have taken the places of two shawms (**43**, p. 161). This is analogous to what may be found, in the way of dance-accompanying music, further west (in the Madiun district); in the north (in Madura, *vide* **43**), and towards the east (in East-Sumbawa: Bima), as well as in West-Java. The (Banyuwangi) anklung also sometimes takes the place of the violin (**372**). The same orchestra accompanies (or, rather, used to accompany) the dance of the *seblang* (*i.e.* girl dancers in a trance, corresponding to the Balinese *sanghyangs*).

---

[1]) According to R. M. JAYADIPURA, four different kinds of *jogèd* are in the main to be distinguished, *i.e.* *J. pokok* (= principal dance, literally: trunk- or nuclear dance); *J. kubahan* (= secondary dance, literally: ornamentation); *J. gandrung* (= love-dance), and *tayub*, by which the free dances are meant. For an illustration

The East-Javanese **gamelan saronèn** (or *gamelan tètèt*), which shows traces of Madurese influence, also has such a shawm (*saronèn, tètèt*) as melody-playing instrument (ill. 102), and further consists—at any rate this was the composition of the orchestra which I heard and which is shown in ill. 120—of the following: 1 large gong, 1 kenḍang (ketipung) binè, 1 kenḍang (ketipung) lakè, 1 keṭuk binè and 1 keṭuk lakè.

The instruments called *lakè* (= male) are, as is usual, of smaller size and higher pitch than those called *binè*, or female.

Sometimes, however, the large keṭuk has been replaced by a kenong, there is only one kenḍang, and, in addition to the gong there is also a kempul. In some of the large saronèn orchestras there are, moreover, a bonang and two sarons.

Finally, BRANDTS BUYS gives, for the saronèn orchestra examined by him, the following composition: 2 Banyuwangi angklungs, 1 high saron with 10 keys, 1 lower saron with 10 keys, 1 saronèn, 1 rebab-like bowing instrument, 1 ordinary drum, 1 small drum, 1 rattling instrument and 1 large gong. It seemed, however, that the 2 angklungs did not properly belong to this ensemble (**40**, pag. 212).

Amongst other things, this little orchestra provides the accompanying music to the pranks and antics of the *ludruks* (**298**, pp. 322 and 335; **395**) and the jumps of dancers, seated upon (or, rather, *in*) the three-dimensional (!) [1] *kuda képang* (*"monèlan"*). [**101**D, **293**A]

A third ensemble in the Banyuwangi district is the **Balibalian** (*tabuhan Bali*), comprising a saron with 7 iron keys, 2 slenṭem with iron keys *lying flat* above sound-tubes hidden inside a high trough, such as are not found in any other part of java, although they do exist in Bali (**193**, p. 442), and 2 angklungs of the type described on p. 198 above (**40**, p. 208/9).

BRANDTS BUYS further reports (**40**, p. 212/3) the existence of a Madurese orchestra called, after its principal instrument, a small xylophone, **tèng-tèng**. In addition to a couple of these tèngtèng's this combination consists

---

we refer to J. C. VAN EERDE, "De volken van Nederlandsch Indië" (the peoples of the Netherlands East-Indies), vol. II, p. 290 (article by R. M. NATA SURATA).

[1]) An exception: in all other cases both the Javanese and Sundanese kuda képang are two-dimensional.

according to this author, of a kind of *kechrèk*, and a very peculiar sort of slit drum, provided, that is, with an X-shaped slit; further, a pair of one-stringed bamboo idiochords, and a *chontang* (*vide* above, p. 199). According to the facts as given by the Regent of Bandawasa, however, the 16 tèngtèng ensembles existing in the territory under his jurisdiction are composed as follows: 2 sarons (tèngtèng); 1 gambang; 1 kenḍang kechil; 1 kenḍang besar; 1 kenchèr, and 1 gong guchi.

The tuning of these combinations is called *pélog kagok*, *i.e.*, therefore, pélog-like, or approximately pélog. In Jember, where small orchestras of this name also occur in large numbers, their composition is somewhat different again: 1 saron besi, 4 gambang bamboo, 1 kenḍang, 2 tongtong of bamboo and 1 gong besi. In this regency, too, they are tuned to pélog.

What was mentioned above, in passing, under the name of **kuda képang** [1]) (L. J. *jaran képang*)—in Bayumas they speak of *èmbèg*, and in the Sunda districts, where the horses are made of leather, of *kuda lumping* [2])—is one of many forms of primitive dance-plays and musical shows known collectively as *jatilan* (**141**, **141**A, **298** p. 215, [**302**U]) (ill. 121).

The orchestras that go with these playlets are not quite the same in the whole of Java as regards composition. In the Madiun districts, where, especially in the Regency of Panaraga, the kuda képang play is still greatly favoured by the population (**366**), the accompaniment consists only of a selomprèt, a couple of angklungs, a terbang and a réog (ḍogḍog); in the Principalities it is the same, with the exception of the selomprèt (ill. 104); but in recent years it has often been added to in the direction of the gamelan-combination, namely with a kenḍang (instead of the ḍogḍog), saron, kechèr, and three benḍé (distinguished, respectively, either as *penitir*, *panengah* and *gong* or as *kemang*, *kemong* and *kempul*), as well as with an instrument not belonging to the sphere of the gamelan: the bamboo blowing gong (*gong bumbung* or *gumbang*) (**141**).

Often, in these hobby-horse dances, there comes on the stage, in addition to a couple of *ménaks* (knights) and their followers—the latter sometimes "on horseback", sometimes not—a *barongan* [3]), monster from the woods,

---

[1]) Malay and Sundanese *kuda* = H. J. *kuda* = J.L. *jaran* = horse; *képang* = basket work from strips of bamboo.

[2]) *Lumping* = leather.

[3]) from *barong*, whose actuel signification is *bear*.

a kind of fantastic tiger, with which the horsemen enter into combat. A fine description of this play is given by STAUGAARD (**366**). It is this form of jatilan which, in East Java, is indicated more especially by the name of *réog*. In Central Java, however, it appears that this distinction is not made; at any rate I witnessed a performance in the dessa Pakem, north of Jogya, in 1931, in which no barongan took part, and which was nevertheless called réog.

The procedure in this colourful, lively and extremely fascinating Pakem réog performance was a follows: one of the knights, Bagénda Ali, seated upon the (hobby) horse Mégà (= White Cloud), and the other one, Bagénda Amir, riding the horse Menḍung (= Black Cloud), meet somewhere in the forest, each at the head of a group of followers on foot (a master-of-arms called Mistir, a panakawan—the one, Pentul, with a white mask and the other, Tembem, with a black one—and a number of punggawa's carrying flags). These two groups enter into combat with each other. First—following an introductory dance in which everybody joins—a fight takes place between the two Mistir (ill. 125); after this between the knights themselves. The combat, however, remains undecided. The performance is accompanied by the music of 3 gongs (again called, from small to large, respectively, *penitir*, *panengah* and *gong*), a ḍogḍog, a kechèr, and a short, thick type of suling with three stops. Now and then, during the show, the panakawans sing. The accompanying music is—as is usual during this type of play—hauntingly monotonous, and rigidly rhythmical. I was able to note down pretty accurately, in European notation, what I heard there, in the désa Pakem; the result is given in the score-extract below.

The rhythm beaten in this by the gongs is identical with that of the Koḍok-ngorèk pattern. The melody seems to be of the pélog *genus*, —as might be expected of an artistic expression so very definitely of pre-Hindu origin and typically Indonesian:

1) During the fighting, on each beat.

Another rẹog performance which fascinated me strongly, I witnessed at Chimahi in 1923. I gave a description of this play in 1923 in "Jawa" III, p. 30 *et seq*. As this account was printed in a garbled version owing to two pages of the manuscript having dropped out, I reproduce it here in full:

"To the primitive but nevertheless most exciting music of terbangs and drums, and, surely, also stimulated by the hysterically yelling and frolicking tarompèt, two men, rather silly-looking *orang tani* (peasants), take up their position. Each of the men steps into an oval hoop, to which is fixed, in front, a horse's head made of leather, whilst at the opposite end a tail, also made of leather, is attached; the whole outfit is called *kuda lumping*. A white cloth is tied across their forehead.

Then, a third man arises; a vigorous, lean figure, with sharp features and a dominating air. He plants himself in between the two horse-men, and gets hold of each of them by his hoop.

The drums persist in their rhythm; their ever more penetrating sound becomes an obsession; the tarompèt yells like mad; we sense a growing tension in the atmosphere. But the horsemen, contained by their companion, still stand there motionless, hold their hoop-horses stiffly pressed against their bodies, and stare fixedly, with vacant eyes, straight in front of them. And then, all of a sudden, with such startling rapidity as to be inconceivable, the situation changes: the horse-men break loose, foaming at the mouth and with rolling eye-balls; they fling themselves on the ground, weltering round and round, and moaning and groaning as if in agony. The crowd surrounding them grows uneasy and looks on with tense expectation; several of the men rush forward and try to restrain the two crazy ones. Then the leader removes the white cloth from the head of the dancers, who are still wringing themselves, to the rhythm of the music, in the grip of the bystanders, blows into their nostrils and passes his fingers through their tousled long black hair and over their wild eyes. At first without apparent result; but after some minutes a noticeable relaxation and enervation sets in, and at last they are induced to sit down. Their limbs still tremble and shake convulsively now and then; with bowed heads and open mouths they gradually return to consciousness and reality.

It is said that the performance has no ill effect upon the dancers, but it is difficult to believe this when one has seen how it has them in its grip.

The wedana kota informed us that only very few men are suited as leader, while not every dancer is capable of participating in this transport of ecstasy. This probably means that only a few can exercise a hypnotic influence, and that only those can be used as "subjects" who possess the necessary aptitude for the state of trance required for this performance.

During garebegs, small réog-groups march behind the gamelan and the followers of the Regent concerned.

In the Solonese district they commonly move at the head of the procession accompanying a bridegroom, or, as the case may be, a youth to be circumcised, to the missigit, and—after the ceremony—back to his house; further also in the procession escorting a person who, in order to ward off some disaster, has made a vow, to the place where he is to redeem his promise (the so-called *paka'ulan* or *penadaran*) [1]—usually either a cemetery or a pasar.

The same instruments which are used to accompany the *kuda képang* also function as accompaniment to a peculiar form of popular dancing-play, called *sranḍul* (in Wanagiri: *sranḍil*); at any rate, "INGGRIS" (**141**) mentions the kenḍang, terbang, angklungs and benḍé as the instruments used for this purpose in Wanagiri (South Surakarta)—one of the last remaining places of refuge of this kind of show.

About the popular plays and dances described above, as well as a number of others, *vide* also PIGEAUD'S important work (**298**).

In 1923 a new form of art arose in the Principalities: the **keṭoprak.** Its birthplace seems to have been the dalem of the then Solonese kraton conductor R. T. WREKSADININGRAT; it was, however, taken before a larger public for the first time on the occasion of the celebrations held for the change of name of P. A. A. P. PRANGWEDANA, who then adopted the name of MANGKU NAGARA VII.

In the beginning the keṭoprak depicted Javanese fairy-tales and legends in which nothing but wooden instruments were used as accompaniment, namely, a rice-block (*lesung*), and some small horizontal slit drums (*keprak*). The actual creator of this new form of art was one of the dancers of the above-named R. T. WREKSADININGRAT: KI WISANGGÉNI [2]). The accompanying music he called *wreksatama* (= precious, or noble wood); which

[1]) *ka'ul* = *nadar* = a vow in order to avert some calamity.
[2]) died 1932.

name, however, was not able to maintain itself against the name of *keṭoprak,* this having, as an onomatopoea, a stronger appeal to the popular mentality.

After this, a suling was added to the combination. With this, the germ was laid of a typically popular form of art containing rich possibilities of development. Unfortunately this development has taken the wrong turning. Politics took possession of it; more and more the players started weaving critical sneers and allusions to the police and the authorities, thus unmistakably forcing the performances into a communistic direction.

At present the original form of keṭoprak theatre, with its repertoire of fairy tales, is kept alive exclusively by a society holding its performances in the Solonese Partini Garden. The form used for political ends was eventually compelled, in order to get the necessary police permits to hold its shows, to alter its character somewhat, and sought this change of direction in an adaptation to the Stambul comedy, or Malay opera. At the same time its rustic orchestra was replaced by a more or less hybrid ensemble. Its fixed components now appear to be the following: gong, kenḍang, terbang, suling, some stringed instrument or other (rebab, violin or mandoline), and a keprak. Many records have been made of keṭoprak music by Odeon; from a long series of these we may mention here the Nos. A 39544a and A 39562a.

The *lagu,* or melodies—always pélog-, never sléndro-compositions—which one usually hears in the keṭoprak, are for the most part good Javanese ones. Thus, for Banyumas, the following were mentioned to me: *Puchung, Gambuh, Megatruh.* The same are also performed in Solo, but later on other pieces were added to the repertoire, as, for instance, *Kinanṭi* and *Mijil.*

In latter times the popularity of the keṭoprak seems to be waning. This speaks well for the Javanese people; evidently they could not find permanent satisfaction in the not very refined dances and the coarsening of their music, which had gradually become characteristic of this form of art.

We may finally mention that POENSEN (**301**, p. 84) already recorded the existence of a *gamelan keṭoprak.* All he says about it, however, is "It is known to us only through the dictionary [1]), which states that it produces sound all by itself(?) without being played upon".

---

[1]) *i.e.,* according to his bibliography, the Jav.-Dutch dictionary by GERICKE-ROORDA (eventually the supplements thereto).

Naturally the keṭoprak here described is not the only expression-form of Javanese popular musical art that has sprung up suddenly in the course of time. The minutes of the Royal Batavia Society, vol. XXXI (1893), p. 46 sub 20, report a case comparable to the above in many respects, from the Banten district, in the year 1875. It is a pity that no attention was paid in this description to the form of the accompanying bamboo instruments, so that we remain in uncertainty regarding the structure of some of them:

"In 1875 a native "Komedie" was established by the Regent of Pandeglang, later Radèn Adipati SUTADININGRAT, Regent of Serang. Under his guidance the plays were put together, out of well-known tales, *e.g.* the 1001 nights, Abu Nawas, etc., by his younger brother, then his mantri kabupaten, and later Radèn Bagus JAYAWINATA, patih of Menes, and made to fit the end in view by interlarding them with popular witticisms. Boys from the native school, clerks, etc., appeared in them as actors. Some care was devoted to the costumes and décor, and the gamelan, occasionally alternated by European music, accompanied the play.

Very soon the public interest in coming to witness these comedy performances in the backyard of the kabupatèn grew very lively, the more so as the plays were written in the native tongue, *i.e.* Sundanese.

In 1878, when Chief Inspector VAN GORKOM was travelling in Banten, there was a general desire to show this so-called "Komedie Jawa" to him. Now it so happened that the very evening that had been fixed for the performance was that before a Friday, and since ancient times it was not allowed to play the gamelan, in Banten, (a) from Thursday afternoon to Friday afternoon; (b) from 1–15 Mulud, and (c) during the month of fasting, both on account of the sanctity of these days, as because, according to popular belief, the musical instruments would burst and go out of tune if the rule in question was transgressed.

In order not to scandalize people, therefore, the Regent replaced, this once, the gamelan by instruments with which South-Bantenners are wont to kill time, namely, the *chalung*, a few *angklungs*, a *suling* and a *beḍug*.

This more primitive orchestra turned out, by its softer sound, to be at least as suitable for the accompaniment of the stage plays as the metal gamelan; and so the regent conceived the idea to make an entire gamelan out of bamboo. This gamelan consisted of a *gambang*, a *karomong*, *saron*, *keṭuk* with *kempul*, a large and a small *gong*, a (blowing-)*goông suling* and a *bedug*; and it was henceforth used with the "Komedie" as a regular thing.

There are certain classes of persons in Banten to whom listening to gamelan playing is forbidden; to whom it is *buyut*, as the expression goes. Thus, it is buyut to all people hailing from the désa Chimanuk; the reason for this being—so they say—reverence for the well-known saint Kyahi Haji MANGSUR, who, as all Moslem saints, hated music. In other désa's, such as Kasuniaten or the kampong Kupluk, in Menes, the "buyut-ness" of gamelan playing is limited to the place in question, so that popular belief raises no objection if inhabitants of such places enjoy the gamelan elsewhere; the reason for the latter prohibition, however, also lies in the presence of sacred tombs.

Many of these people have since been manufacturing bamboo gamelans after the model of the Pandeglang ones, persuaded as they were that playing, or listening to such instruments was not included in the buyut prohibition.

The "Komedie-Jawa", which made such a hit at first, and was already beginning to have many imitators in other parts of Banten, expired after 1878. I believe that the fear of certain European civil servants that the quips and witticisms of the Banten dramatists might have a damaging influence upon their notorious "prestige", was the cause of its death".

Several other small ensembles, usually spread over regions of limited extent, are to be found in the Javanese territority. They generally consist chiefly of bamboo instruments.

Thus, in the Regency of Banyumas, an ensemble exists which, after two of its component instruments, is called **Gumbeng** [1]). It is composed of:

a) a bamboo idiochord closed at one end by a node, the node at the other end being pierced. Three "strings" are cut out of the tube-wall, under each of which a "bridge" is pushed in such a way that each of the three strings can sound two different tones, so that, on the three strings together, either a sléndro scale finishing on its octave, or a five-toned pélog-bem or -barang scale can be played. This instrument represents, within the ensemble, the melodic element. The scale of the specimen present in the musicological archives at Batavia is as follows:

440		513		586		664		792		884
I	*266*	II	*230*	III	*216*	IV	*303*	V	*191*	I' ;

tending, therefore, towards sléndro;

[1]) Ind. Inst., Nos. 1029/4, 6 and 7; Mus. Arch. Bat., Nos. 501, 512 and 514.

b) a second idiochord, also closed at one end by a node, and with a pierced node at the other end, and three strings, two of which—provided in the customary way, at both extremities, with bridges which they share in common—are connected by a flat piece of bamboo, whilst the third is tightened by a bridge of its own, placed half-way the length of the string. The two interconnected strings, which are sounded simultaneously, function as kempul, the third string, whose inequal parts sound different tones, supplies the kenong-beats;

c) a third bamboo segment, with pierced nodes, functioning as kenḍang, the open nodes being beaten with the flat hand;

d) a blown gong.

Yet another small orchestra—limited, it seems, to West-Bagelén and the eastern part of the former residence of Banyumas (Sumpyuh and surroundings)—is the bamboo gamelan **Jemblung** [1]) (ill. 122), the instruments of which were discussed above (pp. 197 *et seq.* and 240). Its composition is as follows:

gong suwukan jemblung
kempul ,,
kenong ,,
keṭuk ,,
demung ,,
saron ,,
kenḍang ,,
blown gong (*gumbang, bumbung*).

Its scale, as measured on the saron, of two different sets is in sléndro, or at any rate tending towards sléndro:

590		674		762		876		1020		1180
I	*230*	II	*212*	III	*242*	IV	*264*	V	*252*	I'
504		578		684		754		870		1008
I	*237*	II	*292*	III	*168*	IV	*247*	V	*255*	I'

The first of these two series of intervals is that of a specimen heard at Sumpyuh, but hailing from Kalijering; the other was heard on a set manufactured in the same désa, and which is now in the musicological archives of the Royal Batavia Society [2]).

---

[1]) Ind. Inst., No. 1057.

[2]) Mus. Arch. Bat., Nos. 494 to 500 incl., and 513.

This combination serves to accompany the *wayang jemblung, i.e.* the wayang whose plots, derived from the Amir Hamzah cycle, are recited by the ḍalang without being represented in some way or other by pictures or puppets.

In Sumpyuh two quite distinct styles of playing could be noticed in the pieces performed, namely, genḍings for full orchestra and recitativo-accompaniment, chiefly on the saron alone. This accompaniment consisted of different, rather short, often repeated themes, amongst which the following *motif* occurred most frequently:

The accompanying orchestra was originally less complete than the combination described above, the ḍalang's recitation being formerly accompanied only on a few terbangs (= *jemblung*). Hence this wayang combination is known more eastward, *e.g.* in Solo, under the name of *wong* (= men) *barang jemblung.*

Wong (ba)barang, or *wong babakan* is the Central-Javanese name for itinerant street artists; they generally perform facetious and more or less drastic mask-plays (*topèng barangan* or *topèng babakan*), accompanied by a simple form of gamelan, usually provided with iron keys and kettles, which—at any rate in the middle-east of the island—more especially bears the name of **gamelan janggrung.**

We should further mention, for Banyumas, Purbalingga and Purwakerta, the **gamelan chalung** [1]). This combination consists in the first place of three *chalungs* (cf. below, p. 364 *et seq.*) mounted upon a sledge-shaped, resilient underframe of bent bamboo-laths, played like a gambang, similar as regards tuning and pitch, but having a different function, and distinguished by the names of *demung, pembabar* and *penitir.* Here we have, therefore, a second transitionary form from the chalung to the gambang, in addition to the one found on the Barabuḍur reliefs, which belongs to a different species (ill. 14, sub *a*). It may be that it is identical with the *gagambangan* of Tasik (*vide* above, p. 189).

[1]) Ind. Inst., Nos. 1029/8–11; Mus. Arch. Bat., Nos. 506 to 511 incl., and 515

Other instruments forming part of the chalung orchestra are a number of tubular bamboo keys, collected together on a single underframe, and also consisting of segments cut on the slant into a point, distinguished respectively by the names of *kempul, keṭuk* and *kenong* (of the latter there are three). Further, there is a *blown gong*, a *kenḍang*, asymmetrical and pot-bellied (with two skins), and a *ketipung*.

The scale of the chalung orchestra to be found in the musicological collection of the Royal Batavia Society (ill. 123)—a gift of the Regent of Banyumas—is purely sléndro, as might be expected of an ensemble hailing from this territory.

In the regency of Chilachap, there are unmistakable Sundanese influences. For in this part of the district of Banyumas we find—apart from the typically Sundanese "pantun"-singing, accompanied by the *kachapi*—the **lènggèr angklung**, which is identical with the Sundanese *bunchis*, or *badut* (*vide* below, p. 378), and the **dogèr**, which flourishes, under the same name, especially in the Tasik district (*vide* p. 381). For Chilachap there is, further, mention of the **angguk**, a play which would seem to have come into existence under Arabian influences, and whose accompaniment is formed by *kenḍang*, *terbang* and *jiḍor* [1]); then there are the **menoréh**, a kind of wayang wong, whose repertoire is borrowed from the Ménakjingga tales, and whose orchestra comprises: *jiḍor, terbang, kenḍang* and *keprak*; the **kentrung**, in which, by means of songs accompanied by *terbang* and *kenḍang*, and called *prawang kenya* [2]), a man addresses good advice to young virgins on the subject of cleanliness and order in the household, and warnings against the commitment of abortion (supported by drastic descriptions of death and scenes from hell); and, finally, the **gobyog**, a ronggèng-combination comprising the instruments *rebab, kenḍang, kempul, kenong* and *keṭuk*.

Mention was already made above (p. 239/240) of the **prajurit-music** (ill. 124 and 126) of the Sultan, when we discussed the clarinet *puwi-puwi* of the Dahéng- and Bugi-corps, and the transverse flute. These small orchestras consist, in addition to these two instruments, of metal trumpets of European manufacture; copies of the high, 17th century western roll-drums; gongs of two different sizes, distinguished as *gong* and *benḍé*; small cymbals

1) Demak, Kudus and Japara also know this *angguk*.
2) Modern Javanese *prawan* = Kawi *kenya* = virgin.

(*kechèr*); *kenḍang*, and *ketipung*; typically hybrid ensembles therefore.

The pieces played, which are of two kinds, namely ceremonial songs and "mares" (= marches), partly bear corrupted Dutch names (*Pandebruk* = VAN DEN BROEK; *Setok* = STOK etc.), and often remind one of the drum-and-fife marches of the Dutch marines (**378**, p. 94/6). [**180A**]

At this point we should also say a word or two about what is called *chiblon* (sometimes called *siblon*), or *ketimpung*, *i.e.* rhythmic beating with the hand in different ways (either with the crooked, or with the flat hand) on, and in the water, by bathing children (and sometimes by their elders), who, with the natural musicality peculiar to the Javanese race, succeed in producing, in this way, a surprisingly good ensemble-effect (**165**, **289**) [1]). The sound may be rendered onomatopoetically by *plung-plock*, *plung-blong*.

This chiblon has also given its name to a certain way of drum-playing, *i.e.* *rarachiblon* (or *rarasiblon*), meaning: the chiblon-playing girl, occurring, for example, in the Chenṭini (Canto 163, stanza 14, first line). (At the present time, however, this art-term is usually met with in its corrupt form *larachiblon*).

In this way chiblon afterwards became the name of one of the drum-forms themselves (*vide* p. 212).

It is as if, in the hands of an essentially musical race such as the Javanese, everything is turned into music. Thus, according to information supplied by Dr. H. H. NOOSTEN [2]), there may be found, in the limestone mountain-range near Punung (regency of Pachitan), a stalactitic cave, called the *Guwa tabuhan*, (*i.e.* Gamelan cave). Since time immemorial the population has cherished the custom of beating, with pieces of stone by way of beating hammers, upon a selected range of stalagmites and stalactites, from which they succeed in drawing surprisingly pure and harmonious sounds. They manage to imitate in this way every part of a gamelan, with the exception of the drum. For the kenḍangan, therefore, they use an ordinary instrument.

We conclude by just mentioning the curious art of imitating the gamelan

[1]) This style of playing is also mentioned in ancient Javanese literature, *i.e.* in the Smaradahana, canto IV, stanza 11 (edition PURBACHARAKA: Bibliotheca javanica III, p. 65, note 2).

[2]) In a letter addressed to the author, and dated 14th May 1938.

with the mouth, already in olden times a favourite pastime of the Javanese (and Balinese), the existence of which was already recorded, for example, in the Hikayat Chèkèlwanèngpati [1]), and is rendered onomatopoetically in the Chenṭini (Canto 4, Stanza 51) as follows:

pong pep em-em dah ketoté
eng eng ṭuk nang nang nong nang gung.

e. Structure, nature and use of the different compositions

(44, 78, 169, 195, 214, 228, 343)
[**54**A, **59**B, **77**A, **89**B–C, **113**C, E–F, **236**K, **248**C, **291**B, **302**K, L, **344**A, **381**B–C]

„Rules such as we speak of, having been involved by the organism for its own ends, are never arbitrary in their own environment; they may better be regarded as the form assumed by liberty, than as restrictions.
Themes are repeated from generation to generation, and pass from one country to another; neither is originality a virtue, nor „plagiarism" a crime, where all that counts is the necessity inherent in the theme. The artist, as maker, is a personality much greater than that of any conceivable individual; the names of even the greatest artists are unknown."
Dr ANANDA COOMARASWAMY, „Introduction to the Art of Eastern Asia" (pp. 21 and 40)

The many hundreds of Javanese orchestral compositions (*genḍing*) are classified according to their structure into different groups. These groups are:

a. genḍing ageng (in the more restricted sense);
b. genḍing tengahan or *genḍing madya*;
c. genḍing alit (in the more restricted sense),

which together form the group of genḍings in a more restricted sense (according to the view held in the Jogya kraton, the *genḍing ageng* in a wider sense); and, further,

d. ladrangan, and
e. ketawang (*ketawang alit*),

both of which are, as *genḍing alit* in the wider sense, or as *genḍing prenèsan* [2]) (S.) distinct from the genḍings proper.

The groups of genḍing proper differ from the *ladrang* and *ketawang alit*—among other things,—in that they possess an introductory movement, and at least one closing movement, whereas the *ladrang* and *ketawang alit* consist of a single movement only.

[1]) [Also in Ardjunawiwaha (IV v. 3, line d)].
[2]) From *prenès* = spruce, vivacious, charming, carefree, frolicsome, playful, voluptuous.

It is the colotomic structure of a composition (*i.e.* the interpunctuation by which the genḍing is subdivided into longer or shorter phrases and which is expressed by the *number* of keṭuk beats and *keteg* (= smallest unit of time, really: "heartbeat", Sund. also: *takol* and *dami*) per kenong-period (*kenongan*) and the number of kenong-beats per gong-period (*gongan*)) that gives the criterion for the classification of any composition into a given group. Apart from this criterion there is another—not quite infallible—one: often the groups are distinguished from one another according to their respective drum-beat patterns (*kenḍangan*; cf. above p. 204 *et seq.*).

Now, the boundary lines between the different groups are not laid in exactly the same place by all musicological experts. In Solo—and R. M. JAYADIPURA, tho' a Jogyanese, also uses this subdivision—all genḍings sounding 4 or more keṭuk beats per kenongan are classified with the group of the **genḍing ageng.**

These most stately and long-winded among Javanese orchestral compositions possess gong-periods (*gongan*) of 4 (very rarely 5) kenongan, generally of 64, but sometimes of as many as 128 keteg each; in each of these kenongan there usually occur 4, but in some pélog compositions, occasionally 8 keṭuk beats.

Examples of the most frequently occurring type of genḍing ageng—of compositions, therefore, with 4 keṭuk beats in kenongan of 64 keteg—are, apart from those already mentioned on p. 206 in notes 1 and 2, the following: in paṭet 6 sl.: *G. Godeg* (S.) and *Lobaningrat* (S.); in paṭet 9: *G. Klenḍung* (S.), and in paṭet manyura: *G. Miling* (*S*).

An example of a genḍing ageng with 5 kenong beats per gongan is provided by the Solonese genḍing *Mejemuk* (sl. P. 6); of one with 8 keṭuk beats *arang* (H. J. (*h*)*awis*) (*i.e.* lying far apart, namely, at distances of 16 keteg), and with 128 keteg per kenongan: the genḍing *Pangrawit* (J.) (P. 5); of one with 8 keṭuk beats *kerep* (*i.e.* lying close together, namely, at distances of 8 keteg): the Jogya genḍings *Agul-Agul* and *Semang*, and the Solo genḍing *Bonḍèt* (all three in P. 6 pélog) [1]).

According to the tradition of the Jogya kraton the first genḍing ageng is said to have been composed in Çaka 327 = A. D. 405, by Sri Maharaja Kano.

In the sultan's kraton the group of the genḍings ageng proper is taken in a more restricted sense; there are a number of pieces which, although

[1]) In Solo the genḍing *Agul-agul* is (?also) beaten in paṭet 5.

possessing 4 keṭuk beats in each kenongan, are called **genḍing ageng tengahan**, or, for short, **genḍing tengahan.** These are the compositions in which the keṭuk beats are *kerep*, close together, so that the kenong-period is only short, *i.e.* comprises not more than 32 *keteg*. Examples of this group are the genḍings *Jongga* [1] (sl. P. 6); *Sembung gilang* (P. 9); *Lambangsari* (*P. manyura*); *Chondrasari* (P. 5); *Unḍuk* (pélog P. 5); *Gendréh*, and *Sudira gambuh* (App. *9*) (P. barang).

To the genḍing tengahan belong further—according to the view held in Solo—the compositions with 4 kenongan of 16—sometimes 32—keteg per gongan, but with only 2 keṭuk beats per kenongan [2]. The Jogya kraton classifies these pieces with the **genḍing alit** (in the narrow sense), although their gongan comprise 4 kenongan. Examples of these (with kenongan of 16 keteg) are: in P. 5: the genḍing *Kumbangmara*; in P. 6 pél.: *Sarayuda* [3], and *Nawung-bron(g)ta* (App. *8*); in P. bar.: *Megatruh* (P. barang); in P. 6 sl.: *Krawitan, Keḍaton bentar* (App. *11*), and *Titipati*; in P. 9: *Layu-layu, Renyep, Génjong* (App. *5*), and *Gambir sawit*, and in P. manyura: *Pachul gowang*. An example with kenongan of 32 keteg (in which therefore, the keṭuk beats are placed *hawis*) is the genḍing *Gandrung madu* (P. manyura) (S.).

The remainder of the genḍings proper, *i.e.* the genḍings in the more restricted sense, are classified, both by Solo and by Jogya, with the genḍing alit group; they are the compositions characterized by kenongan of 16 keteg comprising only 2 keṭuk beats, and by gongan composed of only 2 kenongan. This group is also called **ketawang genḍing**. It is also distinguished from the other groups discussed so far in that the second movement of the compositions belonging to it appears to be of the ladrang-type, (which ladrang-like part is also frequently played separately as an independent composition). For the most part these compositions have—both

---

[1]) It is the genḍing which has given the kenḍangan, characteristic of this group in sléndro, its name. In pélog, the kenḍangan *Semang keṭuk* 4 is used for this group; at any rate in Jogya. Nevertheless, in exceptional cases the *K. Semang keṭuk* 4 may also be heard in a genḍing sléndro, for example in the genḍing *Kinanṭi Mataram* (P. manyura).

[2]) Some niyaga's also make a difference between the terms *genḍing ageng tengahan* and *genḍing tengahan*, the first of which, in that case, denotes tengahan compositions with 4, and the latter those with 2 keṭuk beats per kenongan.

[3]) This genḍing gave the kenḍangan, occurring most frequently in this group in pélog, its name. In sléndro, *kenḍangan chondra* is generally used for this group. For the rest, *kenḍangan gandrung-gandrung* also occurs frequently in this group.

in sléndro and in pélog—*kenḍangan Lahela* [1]). Examples will be found on p. 207, notes 12 and 13, and p. 299.

There are a few local exceptions, relatively to certain compositions, to the general rules given above. Thus, in Solo, in the genḍing *Mianggong* (sl. P. 6), and in Magelang, in the genḍing *Laler menggeng*, the first 3 out of the 4 kenongan of each gongan contain only 2, and the last kenongan 4 keṭuk beats each time. The length of the kenongan of the first-named genḍing is nevertheless the same, owing to the fact that the keṭuk beats in the first three are *hawis*, and in the last kenongan, *kerep*; in the last-named composition, however, the fourth kenongan is actually of double length. A similar structural deviation is seen in the Solonese genḍing ageng *Doradasih* (P. 5), of which the first kenongan consists of only 32 keteg, in which fall only two keṭuk beats, the remaining three kenongan, however, normally comprising 64 keteg with 4 keṭuk beats.

Another exception to the above general rules may be heard—according to a communication from the Mangku Nagaran—in some of the Solonese genḍings, namely, *Gendréh kemasan* (P. 9); *Bèlèk* (P. barang); *Glompong* (P. 9) [2]), and *Montro Madura* (P. manyura), which, although being ageng, yet contain only 2 keṭuk beats per kenongan. These keṭuk beats, however, are placed unusually far apart.

Both in the genḍings in the restricted sense as described above and in the ladrang- and ketawang-compositions which we shall presently discuss, it is the rule that the gongan are subdivided by the *kenong* beats into exactly equal parts [3]); in such a way that the last kenong beat synchronizes each time with the gong beat. Their first *keṭuk* beat, on the contrary, falls, after the gong beat, already after half a "keṭuk-period", so that all the keṭuk beats fall *within* the kenongan, no keṭuk beat, therefore, coinciding either with a kenong- or a gong-beat. On the "even" places of the colotomic structure, therefore, it may happen either three times (in genḍing ageng and ageng tengahan) or once only (in genḍing tengahan, alit and ketawang genḍing) that no interpunctuating beat falls within one and the same kenongan. This dropping-out—not being present, not sounding—is called *wela*, or *sela* (= space, vacuum). The

---

[1]) So named after a much-played genḍing using this type of kenḍangan.

[2]) A genḍing of this name is also known in Jogya; this one, however, is of a perfectly regular structure, and in P. 6 sl.

[3]) Apart from the rare exceptions just mentioned.

notation-system of the Jogya kraton has a separate character for this wela (*vide* below, p. 351, and Appendices *4–9*).

The number of keṭuk beats given relates, as regards the gendings consisting of two movements, to the introductory movement or *mérong*; the colotomic structure of the after-movement (Solo: usually *munggah*; Jogya: *nḍawah*) is the same, except that there are generally double the number of keṭuk beats in each kenongan, except for some pélog-compositions, in which the same number of keṭuk-beats, *i.e.* either 4 or 8, occur in both movements; as, for instance in the gendings *Bonḍan kinanṭi*, *Agul-agul*, *Ludira Madu*, *Layar Banten*, *Doradasih*, *Babarlayar*, and others. In such a case they speak, in Solo, of *munggah kenḍang*, because the difference between mérong and munggah is then especially noticeable in the drum-playing (which, in the munggah, is of a much more lively character). In the "keṭuk-formula" this peculiarity, of the number of beats in both mérong and munggah remaining equal, is indicated also by the term *poṭok* (= constant); as, for example, "*keṭuk kalih* (= 2) *poṭok*" (S.).

A second exception may be observed in the just-mentioned gendings *Bèlèk*, *Glompong*, *Montro Madura* and *Gendrèh kemasan*, as well as in a few others; they have—at any rate in the Mangku Nagaran (S.)—only *two* keṭuk beats in the mérong, but 8 in the munggah.

A third exception is formed—as we said before—by those gendings which have a ladrang composition as their second movement, and therefore sound only two keṭuk beats per kenongan in the second movement, *i.e.* either as many (in tengahan- and alit-compositions) or half as many (in genḍing ageng and ageng tengahan) as in the mérong. Examples of the former category (for the most part from the Jogya kraton) are: the genḍing *Glondong pring* (P. 6 sl.); a number of pieces in P. 9 with kenḍangan Lahela: *Lahela* (the name of the landrangan being *Wulangun*); *Dempel*; *Tlutur laranangis*; *Sumedang* (ladrangan: *Songgaléwang*) (*); *Penglaw-et gonda* (ladrangan: *Brontakingkin*); *Kabormanyarsih* (ladr. *Chlunṭang*); *Lalaling-kir*; *Gondakusuma* (ladr.: *Gondasuli*); further, in P. manyura: *Boyong* (with the ladrang *Rongé-rongé*), and *Merakkasimpir* (ladr. *Sekarpépé*), both with kenḍangan Lahela; and in pélog: the genḍings *Tlutur* (P. 5) with kenḍangan Lahela; *Yanjana* (P. 5) with kenḍangan *Sarayuda*; *Génjong-guling* (S.) (P. 6) (ladr.: *Surung ḍayung*), and finally, the P. barang compositions (with kenḍangan Sarayuda) *Gandrung manis*, *Lumpang bolong* (ladr.: *Teḍak (sang)king*) and *Megatruh* (ladr.: *Santi*); examples of the

(*) [*S59]

last-named category are: the gendings *Plaralaya* (ladr.: *Gléyong*) (P. 9); *Gonjanganom* (pélog, P. 6); *Buntit Surakarta* (pélog P. 6), and *Tunjung anom* (P. barang).

In addition to the above there are, further, those compositions in which a normal ndawah is followed by a ladrangan which, all according to the structure of the mérong and the ketuk-"formula" of the ndawah as determined by the said structure, sound either ¼ or ½ of the number of ketuk beats of the ndawah in question. Examples of the former case are *Peksibayak* (P. 6 sl.); *Jlagra* (P. 5), *Kinasih* (P. barang) and *Babarlayar ngodokan* (P. barang); of the latter case *Génjong* (P. 9) (App. *3*).

A fourth exception to the ketuk rule are, finally, those compositions which consist of a combination of *Gangsaran* and a ladrangan (cf. below p. 303); this in view of the fact that in Gangsaran there are no ketuk beats at all.

We see therefore, that in all gendings in the restricted sense, the colotomy is effected by three instruments: *gong ageng* (G), *kenong* (N) and *ketuk* (T) [1]).

Now, the ladrang- and ketawang-compositions add to these three instruments a fourth—except in extremely rare cases [2])—namely, the *kempul* (P), which is beaten in alternation with the ketuk, in such a way that, in ladrang, the first kempul beat after the gong-beat falls out. The dropping out of this kempul beat is also designated by the term and the sign *wela* (W).

The colotomy of the **ladrang** having gongan of 4 kenongan may, therefore, be represented as follows:

T W T N
T P T N
T P T N
T P T N }
G }

[1]) It is these three colotomic instruments that determine to which composition-group the gending in question belongs. There are also some colotomic instruments of a "lower" order: in pélog, the *kempyang*; in sléndro, the *engkuk* and the *kemong*; in both systems, in a certain sense, also the *slentem*, since it doubles on the lower octave, and reinforces, in many cases, every fourth tone of the nuclear theme; and often, too, in Jogya, the *bonang panembung*. These, however, need not detain us here, as they do not form part of the "iron frame" of elements forming an essential part of a composition.

[2]) In these cases the ladrang-character is determined exclusively by the kendangan.

A curious position is held by the ladrang pieces *Sinom* and *Hènḍèl* [1]), which, although they possess kenḍangan ladrangan (which is the final criterion), yet do not have any kempul beats, and therefore are, colotomically, *tengahan*. The same is true of the ladrang-movements serving as nḍawah to the genḍings *Gonjanganom* and *Buntit Surakarta* (both pélog P. 6), and of the ladrang following the nḍawah of the genḍing *Jlagra* (P. 5) (J.).

Examples of ladrang-compositions are: *Wirangrong* (sl. P. 6) (Od. A 39587b); *Uluk-uluk* [2]) (P. 9) (Od. A 39559b and H. M. V. N 9037); *Surung ḍayung* [3]) (P. 9) (Od. A 39595a) [4]); *Sekar gaḍung* (P. manyura) (Od. A 39585b [*S52]; *Golong* (App. 7), and *Ryem-ryem* (P. 5); *Laras ati* (Pél. P. 6) (Od. A 39585a); *Kapang-kapang* (pél. P. 6) (Col. G. J. 273); *Kebogiro* (pél. P. 6 or barang) (Col. G. J. X. 18 and H. M. V. N 9124 [*S45]); *Bima kurda* (P. barang) (Od. A 39561b and A 278187b), and *Arjuna Mangsa* (P. barang) (Od. A 39516b).

The *ketawang* colotomy, with gongan of 2 kenongan each, may be represented as follows:

T P T N
T P T N }
G }

Examples of **ketawang** compositions are: *Raja swala, Laras driya, Gajah Èndra* [5]) and *Gunungsari* [6]) (App. 6), all in P. 9; *Tarupala* [7]) (Col. G. J. X. 5), and *Puspawarna* [8]) (Col. G. J. X. 6, Od. A 39561a and H. M. V. N 9037), both in P. manyura, and further, *Langen gita* (Col. G. J. X. 1) and *Srimaléla* in P. barang. Ketawang compositions in pélog P. 5 and 6 are few in number, as are also those in sléndro P. 6. Examples: in P. 5: *Srigati* (S.); in pél. P. 6: *Walagita* [9]) (S.) (Col. G. J. X. 2), and *Puspanjala*

[1]) This piece is beaten exclusively as a continuation of the genḍing *Semang beḍaya*.

[2]) = the flying of a kite, or the firing of a warning shot; hence: announcement (of the arrival of guest).

[3]) = pushing with a paddle.

[4]) The Jogya version rendered by this Odeon record differs considerably from the Solo one given in Appendix *3*.

[5]) = Indra's elephant.

[6]) = mountain of fragrance.

[7]) = nutmeg tree.

[8]) = many-coloured flowers. [S39,72]

[9]) = hopping, skipping (song).

(S.); in sl. P. 6: *Keḍaton bentar* [1]) (S.) and *Pisan(g) bali* [2]). The *Semang ketawang* (pél. P. 6), with which, following the ladrang *Semang Hènḍèl*, the genḍing *Semang beḍaya* finishes, as well as the genḍing *Ronggajanur* (P. manyura) show the peculiarity again of not having any kempul beats. The only difference therefore between them and the compositions of the ketawang genḍing (genḍing alit) group—whose colotomy is entirely similar—lies in the kenḍangan and in the fact that they never include a second movement.

The following are outside the five groups of compositions already discussed:

I. *Gangsaran*;

II. *The genḍing parikan*,

both of which possess a colotomy deviating from that of the genḍings proper (including ladrang and ketawang).

The first-named, the genḍing **Gangsaran**, is almost entirely monotone. Right from the bebuka, or opening, this piece commences with the tone *gulu*, beaten in a powerful unisono of instruments. At the moment one has a feeling as if this tonal drive could not possibly be forced up any further still, the melodic current suddenly breaks through; after a few more lapidary phrases the genḍing—to which the Gangsaran was nothing but a kind of grand, expansive introduction—sets in *attacca*: either the stern and severe *Dirada meta* (= the raging elephant) (P. 9), the imposing *Bima kurda* (Bima (is) angry) (P. barang) [3]) or whatever the case may be.

The genḍing Gangsaran never occurs independently; it might therefore be called a sort of mérong in unison if it were not for the fact that it comes back again immediately after the final beat of the composition which it has introduced.

The number of pieces framed in this way by Gangsaran is only limited. In Jogya, as far as I am aware, they are—apart from the two already mentioned—the following: *Ronèng tawang* and *Arjuna semara* (both pélog P. 6); *Arjuna mangsah* (P. barang) [4]); *Agun-agun* and *Liwung* [5]) (both

---

[1]) = the split kraton(-gate).

[2]) This genḍing, in Jogya, also in pélog P. 6 (Odeon A 39559a).

[3]) Odeon A 39561b and A 278187b. Especially as accompaniment to parts of the Trunajaya dance. Cf. B. P. H. Purubaya, "Rondom de huwelijken in de kraton te Jogyakarta" (About the marriages in the kraton at Jogyakarta) ("Djawa" XIX, p. 295 *et seq.* (**324**B), 1939.

[4]) Odeon A 39516b. *Arjuna mangsah* = the attacking Arjuna.

[5]) Odeon A 39562b.

P. manyura). All seven of these are ladrang compositions. Some of these pieces show either slight or, sometimes, considerable deviations from the form they have when not preceded by Gangsaran. This is designated by the word *kagok*, meaning as much as "in the direction of, pseudo, tending towards, modified, quasi". For instance one may read in a catalogue of a genḍing collection: *Genḍing Gangsaran nḍawah* [1] *kagok* [2] *Liwung* [3].

It follows from what is said above that Gangsaran possesses its own kenḍangan, deviating from that of other pieces. [*S45]

Finally, its colotomy knows no keṭuk-beats—except that these may occasionally occur in the *pangkat* part, but there the customary brief drive in the colotomic pattern during the last bars is omitted. The colotomic structure of Gangsaran is a very simple one [4]:

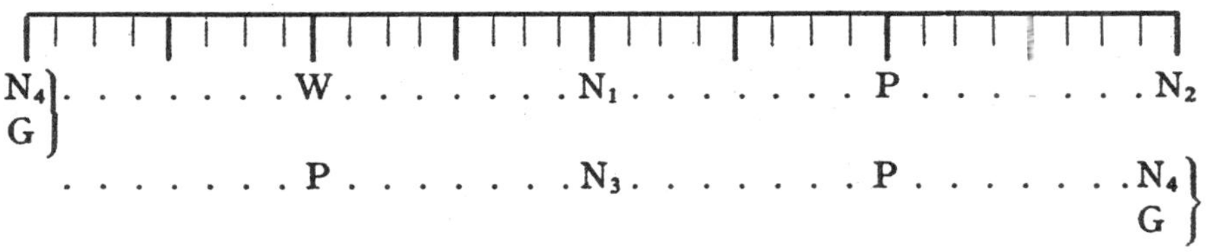

The following groups belong to the **genḍing parikan** mentioned under II:

a. those orchestral pieces which show a freeer kenḍangan (K. *gembyakan*) and a freeer tempo, so that they cannot be classified under a general group-heading [5], and

b. the *genḍing lampah* (S.), mentioned once or twice before [6].

The pieces belonging to group *a.* include those of the paṭet manyura compositions in the Jogya kraton collection that serve to accompany the

---

1) *Vide* below, p. 313 *et seq.*

2) Cf. also the ladrang-names *Kagok-Bali*, *Kagoklaras*, *Kagoklayar*, and *Kagok Madura* (all four of genḍings P. 9), and *Kagok ketanon* (P. manyura), as well as the tuning, called *pélog kagok*, of the Bandawasa gamelan tèngtèng.

3) Cf. Odeon A 39562b, in which, however, we hear a somewhat "abnormal" kenḍangan.

4) T = keṭuk; N = kenong; P = kempul; G = gong; W = Wela, and • = a "silent beat", on which no colotomic beat falls.

5) It might not be impossible that these pieces contain the germ for a further, more individualistic development of Javanese music in the future.

6) from *mlampah*, L. J. *mlaku* = to walk, to go. The genḍing lampah are, indeed, distinguished from other compositions as being livelier, more mobile. Or do the genḍing lampah derive their name from the fact, that their melodies constitute such an integrating part of the music accompanying the wayang-narratives (= *lampahan*, L. J. *lakon*)?

dance of the talèḍèks, and the midnight apparition of Semar, Petruk and Garèng during the *gara-gara* [1]). Here follow the colotomic patterns of some of them.

The genḍing ***Lambang sari talèḍèkan*** is composed of four gongan of unequal length, *i.e.* 64, 48, 32 and 80 keteg respectively.

Gongan A consists of 3 phrases of 16 keteg each, with the following pattern:

. T . . . T . N_1 . . . . . . T . N_2 / P

followed by a fourth phrase:

. T . . . T . N_7 . T . . . T . N_8 / G

Gongan B is the same as gongan A, with the exception that one of the first three kenongan is missing.

Gongan C is colotomized as follows:

. T . . . T . N . T . . . T . N_1
. T T T . T T P . T T T . T T N_2 / G

and gongan D:

. T T T . T T T . T T T . T T T
. T T T . T T T . T T T . T T N_1
(. T T T . T T P . T T T . T T $N_{2,3}$) twice
. T T T . T T P . T T T . T T N_4 / G

Another pattern is that of the genḍings *(H)ijo-(h)ijo tal.* and *Srun-*

---

1) "The name "*gara-gara*" signifies "ominous apparition"; in the wayang purwa especially, it has the meaning of a temporary disturbance of the prevailing world order as a consequence of the psychic power of some mighty personality, a man of exceptional character and ability, but who is going through a period of great grief, and invokes the aid of the gods in order to bring about a reversal of his state of mind. I suppose that the Jogyanese thereby wish to express the saintliness of the figure of Semar, often conceived as being the most significant of the entire *koṭak* (= box containing the wayang figures); a being, neither man nor woman, but the personification of the One and Indivisible, the divine mystery itself.

The Solonese does not let his *gara-gara* be shown except in those few cases where this scene is required by way of introduction to the appearance of a *ksatriya* who is roaming about in the midst of the woods and finds himself in the most desolate circumstances." (**264**, p. 12, 13).

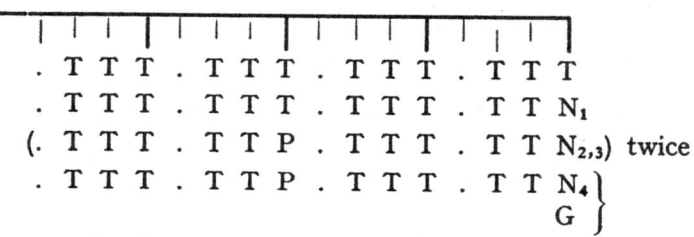

dènggosong tal. and of the nḍawah [1]) of the genḍings *Gambir sawit pachar-china tal.* and *Sulur kangkung tal.*:

. T T T . T T T . T T T . T T N_1
(. T T T . T T P . T T T . T T $N_{2,3}$) twice
. T T T . T T P . T T T . T T N_4 / G

The gongan of the genḍing *Kuduputri tal.* are constructed as follows:

. . . T . T . T . . . T . T . T
. . . T . T . T . . . T . T . N_1
. . . T . T . T . . . T . T . T
. . . T . T . T . . . T . T . N_2 / G

The same applies to the nḍawah [3]) of the genḍings *Dayungan* and *Hingkok tal.*

The genḍing *(H)onang-(h)onang panṭèng*, too, has a mérong with tengahan-colotomy (kenḍangan chondra; *i.e.* with two keṭuk beats per kenongan of 16 keteg), and a second movement with keṭuk-anapaests, after the style of those of gongan D of the genḍing *Lambangsari tal.*

Yet another division of the beats is that of the genḍing *Sènggreng tal.*, whose first and second gongan are constructed as follows:

a/b { . N . N . N . N . N . N . N . N / P P P P } twice
c . . . T . T . T . . . T . T . P
d . . . T . T . T . . . T . T . G

in such a way that the ketek-sequence *d* of the second gongan finishes on a kempul beat, and that the whole is followed by:

. T . N . T . N . T . N . T . N / P P
. T . N . T . N . T . N . T . N / P G

after which the genḍing finally closes on a short gongan of only 32 keteg of the following structure:

. N . N . N . N . N . N . N . N / P P P P
. N . N . N . N . N . N . N . N / P P P G

[1]) The mérong has a tengahan-structure, with kenḍangan Chondra.

And, finally, the genḍing *Janturan* shows a very complicated structure, owing to the fact that it starts on a ladrangan-colotomy (but with keṇḍangan chondra!), and proceeds, after a single gongan (of 64 keteg), to produce the following pattern (remarkable for its irregularly-falling gong-beat):

```
. . . T . T . T . T . T . T . N
. . . T . T . T T PTT PTT PTT N
. T T G . T T PTT PTT PTT PTT N
. T T T . T T P . T T T . T T N}
                              G}
```

In the second half of the second and third kenongan, therefore, the kempul and the keṭuk play in triplets, each of which fill in two keteg.

Of the **genḍing lampah** mentioned under *b.* both Jogya and Solo distinguish different forms, these being usually the following: (1) *ayak-ayakan* [1]), or *genḍing lampah sarèh* [2]); (2) *srepegan* [3]), *slepegan, kerepan* [4]); *playon* (J.) [5]) or *genḍing lampah madya* [6]), and (3) *sampak* [7]).

Of these, ayak-ayakan and srepegan are played in any of the 6 paṭets —and in more than one guise—with this exception that srepegan is said never to be beaten in paṭet 5. Sampak is heard only in paṭet manyura.

Ayak-ayakan (Appendix *3a*), of which two distinct forms are generally played, namely, a slower form, *A. tamban*, and a quicker one, *A. seseg*, serves as accompaniment to the start and the finish of a wayang performance (both purwa and geḍog); for instance when the prince retires to his appartments; it is further played when the wayang wong- (or, as the case may be, the wireng- (S.) or beksan- (J.)) dancers or the serimpi's and beḍaya's appear on the stage [8]) or leave the penḍapa, paringgitan

---

[1]) = to sieve, *e.g.* of sand. This is done by moving the sieve to and fro in a regular tempo, just as the melody of the genḍing *Ayak-ayakan* swings evenly to and fro. Examples of *Ayak-ayakan* (P. manyura): Col. G.J.X. 11, Col. G.J. 132 and Col. G.J. 175.

[2]) *Sarèh* = *tamban* = slow; for *lampah vide* above, p. 123, note 2.

[3]) *Srepeg*, from *nyerepeg* = not having much time; *slepeg* = *keslepeg* = lacking the necessary time. [*S39, 43, 62]

[4]) from *kerep* = close together (this refers to the kenong-, keṭuk- and kempul-beats).

[5]) *Playon* comes from *playu* = to run fast.

[6]) = average, medium sort.

[7]) = fight, struggle.

[8]) In Solo, the serimpi's and beḍaya's do not appear on the stage with *Ayak-*

or stage again after having finished their dance. In one particular case, too—*i.e.* when the prince appearing in scene 1, Act I of a wayang-kulit lakon does not belong to the class of the really mighty ones (as, for example, Kresna, Batara Guru, and others)—it is ayak-ayakan which, as introductory orchestral piece, must precede even the genḍing *Krawitan* (in the wayang purwa) and *Tlutur* (in the wayang geḍog).

A special form of ayak-ayakan (always beaten softly, or *sirep*), called *A. Anjang mas* [1]) is played in the jejer of a wayang-kulit performance at the moment the wayang-prince is supposed to be standing still in front of a beautiful kraton gate, while the ḍalang, in a lengthy recitation, is describing its splendour [2]).

This form also differs from the ordinary ayak-ayakan in that it must not be arbitrarily interrupted but should be performed in its complete length.

Then there are, in paṭet 6, the genḍings *ayak-ayakan Lasem*, which accompanies the entry of a prince; *ayak-ayakan tlutur*, which illustrates the appearance of a character in a sad scene, and *ayak-ayakan pinjalan*, which possesses a peculiar jumpy melodics, or, rather, style of execution (*pinjal* = flea; cf. above, p. 188, note 3), and which serves to add lustre to the departure of a *buta*-prince after his having held an audience (**169**, p. 63).

Ayak-ayakan paṭet 9 (= *A. jengking*) is the accompaniment to the ksatriya on his leaving the abode of a recluse (**264**, p. 15; **169**, p. 63); and, finally, two different forms of *ayak-ayakan manyura* may be distinguished, *i.e.* a *chilik*- and a *geḍé*-from, which are heard during the scenes of appearance and departure, respectively, at the beginning and the end of the manyura period (**169**, p. 63/4), as well as *A. sastradatan*, which accompanies the appearance of wayang figures whose entrance is announced by the *paṭetan* (*senḍon*) *sastradatan*.

The other varieties of genḍing lampah are music to accompany fighting.

---

ayakan, but solely to the accompaniment of the music of a lagon(paṭet), which, for this reason, is repeated and drawn out until the girl dancers have taken up their positions.

1) *Anjang*—usually *anjang-anjang*—, apart from denoting a species of freshwater fish, also means a "framework of bamboo twined widely apart, and on legs, used for carrying something on" (Mayer), or "a trellis-work for climbers or wall-trees and suchlike" (Roorda). *Mas* = *gold(en)*. The nearest approximation to *Anjang mas*, therefore, would seem to be "golden *berceau*".

2) Cf. also, below, p. 343.

They are beaten either very softly—during lulls in the battle—or very loud (*urip* = lively, alive) whilst fighting is going on.

Of *srepegan* [1]) two main forms are to be distinguished, which differ especially in their beginnings: *srepegan prang buta chakil* [2]) and *srepegan prang buta geḍé*. They may be recognized particularly by the start of the keprak-rhythm, which—at any rate in Solo—in the former case is:  , and in the latter: 

In both cases the melody is the same, except that, in Sr. prang buta chakil, it does "ngelik" a couple of times, *i.e.* it goes into a higher register. Further, the execution of Sr. prang buta geḍé—as it has to accompany the fight of a ksatriya with a big giant (*buta geḍé*)—is quicker and more violent than that of Sr. prang buta chakil.

Srepegan at the finish of the paṭet 9 period is called *srepegan tanggung*, *i.e.* "central srepegan".

According to some, *sampak* [3]) is simply synonymous with srepegan. Others, however, use the term sampak exclusively to designate the fastest and most violent form of srepegan [4]). The most embittered fights generally taking place in the paṭet manyura period, it is sometimes said, therefore, that sampak is another name for srepegan manyura (**264**, p. 93) [5]). In this case the colotomy—at any rate in Solo—also differs from that of srepegan, as will be seen further on.

The Jogya term *playon*—which, as far as I know, is never used in Solo nowadays [6])—stand for all srepegan-forms, and probably also for sampak. Notwithstanding this the final fight in a wayang kulit lakon bears, in Jogya, the name of *sampak galong* [7]).

The Sundanese equivalent for both srepegan and sampak is *karatagan*.

---

[1]) Odeon A 204406 (S.). [*S$^{39, 43-4}$]

[2]) *Vide* **264**, p. 86, and **380**, p. 27, note 122*a*. [**113**G]

[3]) Towards the finish, in Col. G.J. 57 (*ada-ada*). [*S$^{43-4}$]

[4]) The use of the term *genḍing lampah madya* (= *medium* G.L.) for "normal" srepegan probably has its origin in the latter conception.

[5]) *Vide*, in this connexion, also the description given below, p. 341, of the *talu*.

[6]) It was used in former times; *vide* **169**, p. 63.

[7]) This episode, together with that introducing this fight—the *suluk galong*, *vide* below, p. 328, and Appendices *30* and *31*—is denoted by the term *manyura geḍé*.

In all forms of genḍing lampah there occur many more kenong-, keṭuk- and (c.q.) kempul-beats than in ordinary genḍings.

The ayak-ayakan colotomy may be represented as follows:

```
T . N . T . . . T . N . T . . . T . N . T
    P               P               P     etc.,
```

and that of srepegan as follows:

```
T N T N T N T N T N T N T N T N T N T N
   P       P       P       P       P      etc.
```

The above applies to both ayak-ayakan and srepegan as beaten in the kraton. Outside the princely courts the kempul is usually omitted. This is the rule in *ayak-ayakan*, also in the Solonese kraton, in contradistinction to the Jogya kraton, which does expect the kempul to be used.

The colotomy of sampak is as under:

```
N N N N N N N N N N N N N N N N N N N N N N N
T P T P T P T P T P T P T P T P T P T P T P T etc.
```

The *gong suwukan* serves as gong, except at the finish, when it is replaced by the *gong ageng*. This is supposed to have been otherwise in olden times; as we had occasion to remark above (p. 149) no gong-beats were supposed to be heard during these genḍing lampah in former times, with the exception of a single beat on the gong suwukan at the finish.

According to the Introduction to the large genḍing collection already referred to more than once, and the notations contained in it, the Jogya kraton did not—and, for that matter, does not even now—make use of the gong ageng in the majority of cases, either in ayak-ayakan or in srepegan. The gong ageng is supposed to conclude ayak-ayakan only when, at the beginning of the *jejer*, it precedes the genḍing *Krawitan*, as well as, during the *gara-gara*, the srepegan P. manyura.

It is said that the gong ageng was applied in Jogya in the genḍing lampah for the first time in 1886, by Pangéran MANGKUBUMI, brother of the VIIth Sultan, on the occasion of a *langendriya* performance, at which he caused kraton dances to be performed in a squatting position.

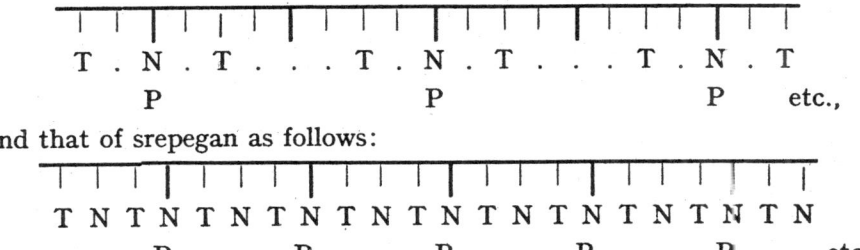

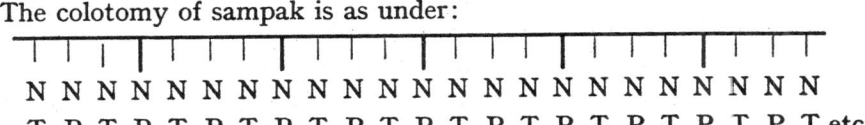

This modern form of genḍing lampah colotomy has since that time been adopted everywhere in the Jogya district; only in the kraton was the old method of beating preserved. There, however, gembyakan has gradually become in vogue as kenḍangan, although this, too, is said to be a modern touch that has crept in in recent times.

A special form of srepegan is further known, called *srepegan rambangan* [1]) (J.). This is adapted to a machapat melody sung simultaneously with it, and is beaten softly and without any sarons and demungs. Its kenong-beats always melt together in unison with the tones sung at any given moment. This method of execution is known in Solo both for *srepegan* and for *sampak*, albeit that the vocal part, in that case, is not sung by a choir but by a solo voice (often each successive stanza alternately by a man and a woman); it is then designated by that other, "cricket"-term already referred to above (pp. 132 and 171), *i.e. kajantur*—as came to my knowledge from and ancient Solonese collection of genḍing titles [2]). An excellent example of this kajantur is given by Col. G. J. 63 (varied by normal srepegan).

With regard to ayak-ayakan we should finally mention that, according to the Regent of Magelang, this form of art, when applied in the wayang kaliṭik and in the wayang geḍog, may also be termed *ayak-ayakan kemuda*, after Panji Nom's beloved Dévi Kemudaningrat [3]).

One should not confuse the genḍing lampah forms described above with the genḍing *Kalaganjur* (P. 9), which is deceptively similar to them, when listened to superficially. The colotomic structure of the latter is that of an ordinary ketawang composition, from which it differs only by its faster tempo and by a peculiar kenḍangan; it does, however, belong to the genḍing parikan).

* * *

A genḍing—whether it be a genḍing ageng, tengahan or alit, or a ladrangan, ketawang or genḍing parikan—commences, apart from a few rare exceptions, about which more later, with an introduction, called

[1]) from *rambang* = to lay down gently, said more especially of the placing of a fighting cricket upon the water, in order to refresh him and render him capable of recommencing the fight. The *tertium comparationis*, in this case, is evidently that the one should lie flat upon the other, that the one "covers" the other; here, the cricket and the water, there, the choral singing and the kenong part.

[2]) *Vide* below, p. 317.

[3]) *Kemuda—vide* below, p. 322—is also the name of one of the *Solonese paṭetan* 6 *pélog*. I was also given the name *paṭet kemuda* once as denoting the paṭet usually called *paṭet manyura pélog*.

bebuka (*buka*), *bukaning genḍing*, or *wiwitan* (Sund.: *pangkat* or *pamangkat*). During this introduction the players have an opportunity of getting into the atmosphere of the piece to be played and ensure proper "team-work". Frequently this buka contains some anticipatory fragments of the genḍing which is to follow it. At present the several types that may be heard in Java are: *bebuka swara* more especially called *bawa sekar* (*i.e.* a vocal introduction by means of a *sekar ageng*, or, at times, a *sekar tengahan* or *machapat*) (*vide* App. *3*, commencement), as well as several instrumental buka's: *B. rebab*, *B. bonang* (*barung*), *B. kenḍang*, *B. gendèr*, and—very rarely played—*B. beḍug* and *B. ketipung*; all according to the instrument which opens the introduction and fulfils the most important part in it. A great charm emanates from many of them, especially from the timidly-groping bebuka rebab and B. gendèr. The character of the bebuka is in agreement with that of the genḍing following it.

Thus, a bebuka bonang is followed by a strongly-beaten, martial genḍing gagah, without vocal music, and a B. rebab or B. gendèr by a soft, dreamy composition with a brooding rebab- and suling-melody, and often, too, a vocal part. Hence, to indicate the character of a genḍing, one hears also the names *genḍing bonang*, *genḍing rebab*, *genḍing gendèr*, etc. used. [**113**E]

The instrumental buka is usually no longer than a few "bars" of four keteg; the vocal introduction is sometimes rather long since a sekar is usually rather an extended affair. Often, however, only the first stanza-line of a sekar is used as bawa, the remaining lines coming in the gending itself. *Vide* f.i. Col. G. J. 60 *et seq*. In this case the bawa is not much longer than the instrumental bebuka. In cases where the entire sekar serves as bawa, its last phrase is often slightly changed in order that it may run better into the genḍing following it and anticipate its peculiar character (See also **44**, p. 57). [**302**K, **344**A, *S44]

One also sometimes hears—in lengthy bawa's— the gamelan joining in halfway down (without, of course, a nuclear melody, and therefore, without the instruments of the saron group). When this happens, a unison choir joins the soloist in singing the next few lines of the verse. Towards the end of the bawa, however, both the gamelan and choir singing stop altogether, and the finishing lines are sung again by the male or female soloist alone.

Both the instrumental and the vocal introductions are concluded by a beat on the gong, after which the genḍing proper follows *attacca*.

It is said that in former times only *B. barung*, *B. rebab* and *B. kenḍang* were known as instrumental introductions; this in accordance with the threefold use of the gamelan, *i.e.* (a) for *hormat* (ceremonial), (b) to add lustre to festivities (including the accompaniment of wayang), and (c) as martial music.

All, or nearly all genḍings *may* be preceded by a vocal introduction; but the joining together of sekar ageng and genḍing is not wholly arbitrary; in that case a given sekar is often used with a given genḍing. Thus, for example, I heard the sekar *Maduretna* sung as bawa to the genḍing *Lobong*; the S. *Juru demung* to the G. *Kembangdara*; the S. *Wohingrat* to the G. *Kuwung-kuwung*; the S. *Manggala gita* (App. *12*) to the G. *Onang-onang*; the S. *Rara* (*Lara*) *béndra* (J.) = S. *Rara* (*Lara*) *béntrok* (S.) [1]) to the G. *Gambirsawit*)(*) the S. *Tepi kawuri* to the G. *Montro-montro*; the S. *Chitramengeng* to the G. *Langengita* (Col. G. J. X. 1); the S. *Chondra Wilasita* to the G. *Génjongguling*; the S. *Mintajiwa* to the G. *Puspawarna* (Col. G. J. X. 6), and the S. *Prana asmara* to the G. *Tarupala* (Col. G. J. X. 5)[**344A**]

The following are examples of pieces with *bebuka rebab*: *Lambangsari*, *Marasonja*, *Titipati*, and *Gambir sawit*;(**) with *B. gendèr*: *Puspawarna* [2]) and *Babat kencheng*; with *B. kenḍang*: *Subakastawa* and *Pisan bali* [3]); with *B. bonang*: *Bima kurda* [4]), *Babar layar* [5]) and *Sembung gilang* [6]); with *B. ketipung*: *Munggang* and *Gangsaran* [7]) (App. *6a*), and with *B. beḍug*: *Nalaganjur* (J.) and *Koḍok ngorèk* [8]).

In playing compositions consisting of two movements (*angkat-angkatan*) it is customary first to repeat the introductory movement (*mérong*) a few times [9]). When it is desired to proceed to the second movement this is announced by the lurah genḍing on the kenḍang, after the penultimate

---

[1]) = sweet little girl.

[2]) Od. A 39561a; Col. G.J.X. 6, and H.M.V. N. 9037. [*S39]

[3]) Od. A 39559a.

[4]) Od. A 39561b, and A 278187b.

[5]) Beka B 15007(II) and Od. A 278187a.

[6]) Od. A 39531a. [*S56]

[7]) Od. A 39562b. N.B. The first three tones beaten on the saron still belong to the bebuka. [*S45]

[8]) *Koḍok ngorèk* also occasionally with *bebuka kenḍang* (cf. Col. D 33002, and the example given above, p. 263). [*S34, 45]

[9]) Often, at any rate in the Jogya kraton notation, it is indicated how many times the movement should be repeated (*e.g.*, rambah kaping 4); when the number of repeats is left to the players' discretion, this is indicated by the words *rambah saprayoginipun* = repeat at own pleasure.

(*) [*S40]. (**) [*S53, 56]

gong-beat of the mérong; the orchestral playing gradually accelerates (*seseg(an)*; *seseg arep* [1]) *munggah*); the nuclear theme, moreover, often takes a different turn starting from the penultimate kenong beat (*santun wilet* (J.); *santun chèngkok* (S.)). This altered balungan-part of the mérong, up to the gong-beat concluding it, is called *umpak-umpakan* (= plinth) (**40**) [2]). During this umpak-umpakan the movement is slowed down again. When the gong-beat falls the second movement of the composition sets in: the *munggah* (H. J. *minggah*) = to rise; *niba* (H. J. *nḍawah*) = to fall [3]), or, also, *linggih* (H. J. *lenggah*) = to sit down) [4]). The balungan tones of this second movement frequently lie twice as far apart as in the mérong; in the umpak-umpakan, too, this is sometimes the case.

Thus far the Solonese theory of form.

In Jogya a somewhat different terminology is generally used, while, moreover, a few more particulars are known to me from Jogya than from Solo.

In Jogya, when it is desired to proceed from the mérong to the second movement, this is also announced by means of a change in the kenḍangan, starting from the penultimate gong-beat (more rarely [5]) from the penultimate kenong-beat), and a different balungan in the last (sometimes in the last two) kenongan, called *pangkat nḍawah* (= preparation of the "dropping" (of the genḍing)). In addition to this the last 16 keteg of this pangkat nḍawah are usually [6]) distinct by a deviating colotomy. Instead of the steady:

---

[1]) *arep* = almost, just before, also: willing. About the meaning of *seseganipun*, *vide* below, in the discussion of the tempi (*wirama*) (p. 336).

[2]) In the Jogya kraton genḍing-collection I saw this term being used only to denote the bebuka of *Semang beḍaya* immediately following the genḍing *Semang pasowanan* ("the audience-Semang") and which precisely covers a period of 32 keteg.

[3]) In Solo, *niba* and *munggah* are generally used alternatively, and considered identical. Cf., *e.g.*, the Chenṭini, Canto 44, stanzas 85 and 112 (in vol. I/II, pp. 246 and 247). The Pakem Sastramiruda (**169**) on the other hand, makes a difference: by *niba* is meant the transition to a second part having as many keṭuk beats per kenongan as the mérong has (as is, for example, often the case with a transition to a ladrangan); by *munggah*, the transition to a second movement having double the number of keṭuk bèats per kenongan as the preceding mérong has. In Jogya, too, it appears, a difference is made.

[4]) As is evident from the literal meaning of *mérong*: passing to, transition, the second part of a genḍing is, therefore, looked upon as the nucleus of a composition.

[5]) Thus, for example, in the genḍing *Lagu* (P. 6 sléndro).

[6]) An exception to this is, for instance, the genḍing *Tunjung anom* (P. bar.) (J.).

W . . . . T . . . . N+G (in the genḍing ageng),
W . . . T . . . W . . . T . . . N+G (in the G. ageng tengahan),
or N . . . T . . . W . . . T . . . N+G (in the other genḍing tengahan and the G. alit)

one will hear the following colotomic sequence of beats, urging and driving, as it were, towards the second movement:

N . . . T . . T . . T . . . T . N+ G

a figure which we have already mentioned above when discussing the *beḍug* (p. 215) (examples in App. *5*, *8*, and *9*) [1].

After the gong-beat which concludes the *pangkat nḍawah* the second movement sets in; this, in Jogya, is usually called *niba* (H. J. *nḍawah*). When—as is frequently the case in sléndro—the balungan tones in this nḍawah lie far apart we often hear a *pancher*, either with or without *imbal*, being played (cf. above, p. 168 *et seq.*); usually starting just before the first kenong-beat. This is in contradistinction to Solo, where, as we said before, this pancher is hardly known (any longer).

It is in the manner sketched out above that, in the majority of cases, the transition from the first to the second movement proceeds.

But—at any rate in Jogya; I do not know whether such exceptions are known also in Solo—there exist a few compositions, almost exclusively in pélog, in which this transition has been elaborated on a broader basis. There, it already begins to make itself felt in the last kenongan of the *penultimate* gongan by means of a change in the balungan and a modification in the kenḍangan; the colotomy, however, does not yet join in this phase and remains normal. The kenongan in question is called *pangkat munggah* (H. J. *pangkat minggah*). After the gong-beat concluding this period the munggah commences, its length being that of a single gongan. The last kenongan of this munggah (which is still reckoned to belong to the mérong) then leads, under the name of *pangkat nḍawah*, to the second movement, the *nḍawah*.

The following are among the compositions possessing this elaborate

[1]) According to the highly expert Solonese musician and dancer Radèn Kodrat, this "condensation" of the keṭuk beats used to be practised in olden times—at any rate in Solo—before *each* gongbeat.

structure: in paṭet 5: *(H)agul-(h)agul*; *Panḍan binètot* [1]), *Bremara alit* [2]), and *Kumbangmara* [3]); in pélog paṭet 6: *Semang*; *Semang pasowanan* [4]); *Semang beḍaya, Rambu, Gonjanganom, Rebeng, Mongkok* [5]), *Hamenggita, Nawangsih,* and *Nawung-bron(g)ta* [6]) (App. *8*); in paṭet barang: *Kinasih* [7]), *Chachadiningrat, Sudira* [8]) *barang,* and *Pramugari* [9]). In sléndro I know of only one composition of this structure, *i.e.* the genḍing *Glompong* (P. 6).

As might be expected, most of these genḍings with munggah belong to the "greater" composition-forms (with kenḍangan Semang, Mawur and Jongga); there are, however, also a few which, according to the Jogya view, should be classified with the genḍing alit, albeit they are exclusively pieces with 4 kenongan per gongan (with kenḍangan Sarayuada); they are the genḍings *Bremara alit, Kumbangmara, Hamenggita, Nawangsih, Nawung-bron(g)ta* and *Pramugari* [10]).

After the second movement has been played once or twice the genḍing is, in fact, finished. Frequently, however, another genḍing, in this case usually of "smaller" construction, follows it immediately, *i.e.* without being preceded by an introductory *buka* of its own. Although this second piece is generally in the same paṭet as the first, it is not a rare occurrence to hear the paṭet changed (cf. above, p. 99). In Solo one often hears, after the munggah of the genḍing *Gambir Sawit,* a ladrangan being played, *e.g. Gonjang ganjing, Sekar tanjung,* or *Chondrahupa,* which is then followed in its turn by a ketawang alit composition such as *Raja swala* or *Langengita.* And in Jogya the enormously long and abnormally constructed, sacred genḍing *Semang* (pélog paṭet 6) (the composition of which is ascribed to Sultan AGENG), combined with *Semang pasowanan* and *S. beḍaya I* and *II,* is followed by the ladrang *Semang* and after this by *Semang ketawang,* whilst, also in Jogya, as we mentioned before (p. 300), the genḍings *Peksibayak* (sléndro P. 6), *Génjong* (P. 9) (App. *5*), *Jlagra* (P. 5) and *Kinasih*

---

1) = pulled-out pandan-leaves.
2) = the little bee.
3) = the approaching mason-, or stingless bee (*Melipona*).
4) = the genḍing *Semang,* as it is beaten in the place set apart for audiences.
5) = to start creeping.
6) = subject to falling in love.
7) = to be loved.
8) = courageous.
9) = chief, leader.
10) = *vide,* for the genḍing *Babar layar koḍokan,* with its exceptional structure —which, apart from *pangkat nḍawah,* also has a *pangkat ngoḍok* as well as a movement called *ngoḍok*—p. 260, note 2.

(P. bar.), amongst others, are followed, after a normal nḍawah, by a ladrangan.

Each time, towards the finish of each movement (in the genḍing ageng and tengahan from the first keṭuk-beat after the *penultimate* gong-beat, and in the genḍing alit from the first keṭuk beat after the gong-beat *before the penultimate*) the tempo is forced up (*seseg(an)*, *seseg arep suwuk*), and retarded again strongly right at the finish of the genḍing (*suwuk*), unless, that is, the players prefer to add piquancy to the performance by occasionally leaving out this stringendo and ritardando.

Often the same passages occur many times in the same genḍing, which adds a certain consistency and balance to the construction. If we represent each fresh kenongan by a different letter, the structure of, *e.g.*, the genḍing ageng ***Lungkèh*** (S.) appears as follows:

Bebuka					
Mérong:	*a*	*a*	*b*	*c*	
	a	*a*	*b*	*d*	(*d* here functions as *pangkat nḍawah*)
Nḍawah (J.) (*munggah* (S.)):	*e*	*f*	*f*	*d*	
	e	*f*	*f*	*d*	

The *ketegs* of the mérong are divided by the keṭuk-beats into the following groups:

Mérong, kenongan ***a***, ***b*** and ***c***:	8 + 16 + 16 + 16 + 8
,, ***d***:	4 + 8 + 8 + 8 + 4
Nḍawah, all kenongan:	2 + (7 × 4) + 2.

Kenongan *d*, therefore, is interpunctuated differently in the mérong from the way it is in the succeeding munggah.

It is further to be noted that the finish of the bebuka is identical to the finish of kenongan *d*, by which means a repetition of the mérong is anticipated in a natural manner.

The genḍing ageng ***Marasonja***, represented in the same way, shows the following picture:

Bebuka					
Mérong:	*a*	*b*	*c*	*d*	
	a	*b*	*c*	*e*	(*e* = *pangkat nḍawah*)
Nḍawah:	*f*	*g*	*h*	*i*	
	f	*g*	*h*	*i*	

The subdivision of the kenongan by the keṭuk-beats is the same as that of the genḍing *Lungkèh, i.e.*,

kenongan *a/d*: 8 + (3 × 16) + 8
,, *e*: 8 + 3 × 8) + 4
,, *f/i*: 2 + (7 × 4) + 2

And further:

in kenongan *a*,	keteg	1 to 16	incl.	=	keteg	17 to 32	incl.
,, ,,	*b*,	,,	9 ,, 24	,,	=	,,	25 ,, 40	,,
,, ,,	*c*,	,,	9 ,, 24	,,	=	,,	25 ,, 40	,,
,, ,,	*d*,	,,	1 ,, 16	,,	=	,,	17 ,, 32	,,

the first 12 keteg of the kenongan *f*, *g* and *h* being the same, whilst the kenongan *f* and *g* run parallel for another 4 keteg.

* * *

In the genḍings collection of the Javanese nobility the structure of a composition—more especially when it consists of several pieces strung together—may sometimes be found described in minute detail. I believe it is possible, with the aid of the data given in the preceding pages, to analyse such descriptions. Here follows an example taken from the list of names of genḍings composed by R. M. JAYASUDIRJA, *kliwon séwu*, and M. DEMANG WARSAPRADANGGA, *demang wiyaga* [1]) in the Solonese Kepatihan [2]), with its translation: [77A]

Sri Kastawa, ladrangan kenḍang kalih, kagérong kalajengaken *(H)ayak-(H)ayakan*, binarung sekar *Puchung* kalih pada kasesegaken dados *Sampak* kejanturaken mawi dipun (h)uran-(h)urani sekar *Pangkur* satunggal pada, lajeng kasesegaken malih, sasuwukipun *Sampak* dados genḍing *Boyong*, keṭuk kalih kerep minggah ladrangan kagérong kenḍanganipun chiblon, paṭet barang; *i.e.*

(the *genḍing*) [3]) *Sri Kastawa*, a *ladrang* composition [4]) (with) *kenḍangan kalih* [5]) and choral singing (*gérongan*) [6]), is followed by *Ayak-ayakan* [7]),

[1]) = chief of the gamelan players.
[2]) *i.e.* the dwelling of the "prime minister" (= Patih).
[3]) p. 295.
[4]) p. 300.
[5]) p. 208.
[6]) p. 126.
[7]) p. 306.

beaten *kajantur* [1]; simultaneously with it two stanzas (*pada*) of the *sekar* [2] *Puchung* [3] are recited, after which one goes on to a stretto (*seseg*)-passage [4], also beaten *kajantur* (and called) *Sampak* [5], together with which a single stanza of the *sekar Pangkur* [6] is sung. After this, following another stretto, this Sampak-period is concluded (in the customary manner) by a ritardando (*suwuk*) [7], when one proceeds to the genḍing *Boyong*, in which, (in its *mérong*) [8], two keṭuk beats (per kenongan) [9] are sounded close together (*kerep*) [10], and whose *minggah* [11] is a ladrang composition with choral singing and with *kenḍangan chiblon* [12]; (the whole being in) *paṭet barang* [13].

* * *

In addition to the musical forms described in this chapter—whose centre of gravity is on the instrumental side, although in many cases singing has an integrating part in the performance of it—there exist a number of other forms, which, though having accompaniments played by a few instruments, have primarily a vocal character. They form part of the wayang music—although some of them may be heard also on other occasions (*i.e.* the lagons and the (ka)kawins)—and are known under the collective name of **suluk**.

We shall briefly discuss the following in order of sequence:

a. the lagon (J. and S.)
b. the ada-ada (J. and S.)
c. the suluk plenchung (J.)
d. the suluk (h)irim-(h)irim (J.)
e. the suluk jenking (J.)

---

1) p. 132 and 310.
2) p. 122 *et seq*.
3) p. 124 and 125.
4) p. 313, 316 and p. 336.
5) p. 306, 308 and 310.
6) p. 68; with regard to the metre, also p. 124.
7) p. 316.
8) p. 312.
9) p. 296.
10) p. 296.
11) p. 313.
12) p. 213.
13) p. 74.

f. the suluk laras barang miring (J. and S.)
g. the suluk senḍon (J.)
h. the suluk tlutur (J.)
i. the suluk galong (J.)
j. (ka)kawin (J.)

For some of these suluks, more especially those under *a, c, d, e, g* and *h,* one may also—chiefly in Solo—hear the name *paṭetan* or *senḍon* (cf. p. 328, note 1) being used.

It would seem that, at a wayang performance or during *nguyu-uyu* (J.) (*klenéngan* (S.)) it is not considered sufficient that the paṭet is evident from the pieces themselves; the idea is evidently to imbue the listeners with the spirit of the prevailing paṭet and to saturate the atmosphere with it by letting, in addition, each genḍing be followed, and sometimes also preceded, by (usually fairly short) recitativo melodies, generally for vocal parts, and accompanied by the gendèr, the rebab and the gambang kayu, each of which melodies is characteristic of a given paṭet. (In klenéngan they may also be executed purely instrumentally.) Such melodies are called, more especially, **paṭetan** or **lagon**, and sometimes **senḍon**.

In each paṭet several of such melodies may be distinguished, each of which bears its own character, or rather—since they are generally akin to each other melodically, and often derived one from the other—to each of which a certain traditional "mood" attaches. As far as stage music is concerned they are selected in accordance with the emotional atmosphere, or the situation which is interpreted at that particular moment by the wayang or which dominates the dance that is being performed. Since they create the tonal atmosphere of the succeeding composition one may say that they announce, at any rate to some extent, the character of that composition.

The Chenṭini—which, indeed, seems to have fathomed even the smallest nuances of gamelan playing—does not fail to express this, too, in the 276th Canto, stanza 18 (Vol. VII/VIII, p. 202):

mungguh surasaning genḍing
wus telas nèng pepaṭetan
sesenḍon yakmakèng genḍing,

i.e. "as regards the essence of the genḍing, this is already contained in the paṭetan; the senḍon is actually the soul of the genḍing".

Generally speaking one may say that the *wetah* form of the lagons is sung *before* a genḍing, and the *jugag* form after it. (In connexion with this the beginning of the latter differs from that of the corresponding lagon wetah, since it follows *attacca* upon the genḍing just played.)

Notwithstanding this, in the wayang purwa in Jogya the ***lagon sléndro paṭet 6 wetah*** (*vide* App. *13*) is played *after* the genḍing ***Krawitan*** (that opens the first act of the wayang), and is then followed immediately by the ***kawin Gurisa*** (App. *18*).

The ***lagon sléndro paṭet 6 jugag*** is intoned when the wayang prince is being tormented by worry, and, in general, *after* a genḍing, ***ayak-ayakan*** and ***srepegan***; and further, when the prince receives a guest or an ambassador, or during his own entry into the kraton.

The ***lagon sléndro P. 6 chekak*** is heard when the wayang figure is in sorrow and grief. In such cases, however, the ***suluk tlutur*** (App. *23/4*), derived from P. 9, and transposed to P. 6, may also be used by way of a change.

The ***lagon P. 9 wetah*** and ***P. manyura wetah*** (App. *29*) are intoned by the ḍalang before he resumes his telling of the wayang story, and also when a genḍing is about to follow. [*S40]

With the ***lagon P. 9 jugag*** and ***P. manyura jugag*** (App. *30*) he introduces a visitor, or concludes the performance of a genḍing. [*S40]

The ***lagon P. 9 Lasem sarabayan*** (App. *22*) and ***P. Manyura Lasem sarabayan*** (App. *31*) is heard more particularly in ***nguyu-uyu*** (in the Jogya signification, *i.e.* = ***klenéngan***), and, more generally, during musical entertainments (***lelangen***).

The lagon *after* a genḍing or a genḍing lampah is usually followed by a recitation by the ḍalang, accompanied by ***jineman***; he gives a sign to start playing the next genḍing by a call on the keprak and a hint woven into his recitation and called ***wangsalan***, in this case in the form of a pun on the name of the genḍing which he desires to be played (at a pinch, this hint may simply consist of some emphatically pronounced word rhyming with the name of the said genḍing) [1]).

In the wayang geḍog, the ***lagon pélog P. 5 wetah*** (App. *39*), ***P. 6 wetah*** (App. *41*) and ***P. barang wetah*** precede a genḍing, whilst the *jugag* forms (*vide* App. *39* and *43*) serve as postlude to a genḍing.

---

[1]) About ***wangsalan*** and kindred literary forms, ***vide* 114**, p. 110 ***et seq.***, and **380**, p. 215, note 113. [**113**G]

The *lagon P. 5 gerjitawatang* (App. *40*) is used especially in the jejer "Panji henèm" (*i.e.* the younger half-brother of Panji sepuh) [1]).

The *lagons P. 6 Lasem* I (App. *42*) and II may be heard on the occasion of *nguyu-uyu*, as well as, respectively, at the start and the finish of a *beksan* performance; the *lagon P. barang Lasem* (App. *43*) also in nguyu-uyu and at the beginning of a beksan dance; for the finish of this dance the ordinary *lagon P. barang* is used in its *jugag* form.

Similar rules apply to Solo [2]). There, the wayang adat distinguishes the following:

in sléndro paṭet 6:

1. lagon (paṭet) wantah = paṭet(an) 6 ageng Mentaraman = P. 6 limrah (L. J. lumrah)
2. L. jugag
3. L. tloloran
4. L. lindur
5. L. Keḍu
6. L. Lasem
7. L. manyura ageng (L. J.: L. manyura geḍé)
8. L. manggalan (penanggalan)
9. L. sastradatan;

in paṭet 9:

1. L. wantah = L. lugu
2. L. jugag
3. L. ngelik
4. L. jengking (c.q. L. élayana [3]))
5. L. senḍon (? senḍon Bimanyu)
6. L. tlutur
7. L. renchasih (= sastradatan, according to **78**);

in paṭet manyura:

1. L. wantah = L. lugu
2. L. jugag
3. L. sastradatan,

---

[1]) Cf. above, p. 138.

[2]) Cf. **380**, p. 241 *et seq.*

[3]) *Elayana* is sung when the hero on the stage wears a full dress state costume (*dodot*) with "tail" (as, for example, Arjuna); for heroes without "tail" (as, for instance, Abimanyu), the ḍalang sings *jengking*.

to which, according to JAKUB and WIGNYARUMEKSA (**78**), there should be added:

4. L. ngelik,

according to SULARDI (**343**):

5. L. tlutur

and, according to the Sastramiruda (**169**):

6. L. jengking manyura.

In paṭet 5 the following may be distinguished in Solo:

1. L. 5 wantah = L. 5 lugu
2. L. 5 entèk = L. 5 telas
3. L. 5 ngelik = L. chilik;

in paṭet 6 pélog:

1. L. 6 geḍé
2. L. kemuda (kumuda) wantah
3. L. Lasem
4. L. 6 kagok,

and *in paṭet barang*:

1. L. wantah = L. lugu = L. limrah (L. J.: lumrah)
2. L. barang jugag
3. L. barang ngelik = L. barang chilik
4. L. entèk = L. telas.

Each of these paṭetan is closely connected with a given situation on the stage or wayang screen: thus, for instance, in paṭet 6 the lagon *tlororan* is sung by the ḍalang when the wayang prince retires to the inner sanctum of the kraton; *tlutur*, during sad scenes; *Keḍu*, following the march of the army to the attack; *Lasem*, during the *adegan sabrangan* (*i.e.* the scene occurring in well-nigh every wayang tale, "at the court of the foreign prince"); *lindur*, when approaching the change from paṭet 6 into paṭet 9, whilst the lagon s*astradatan* is played more especially after a *genḍing gendèr* (*vide* above, p. 311) (**169**, p. 59 *et seq.*), etc. etc.

Jogya does not, at first sight, seem to specify its lagons to the same extent as Solo; the niyaga's of the Sultan's city distinguish—as already shown above—only three forms *in paṭet 6 sléndro*, namely *wetah*, *jugag* and *chekak*, and in *paṭet sanga* and *manyura*: *wetah*, *jugag* and *Lasem Sarabayan*. Further, in *pélog*, in each of the three paṭets a *wetah*- and a *jugag*-form, as well, in *paṭet lima*, the *lagon gerjitawatang*, *in paṭet nem* two, and *in paṭet barang* one form of *lagon Lasem*. This greater simplicity is partly only apparently such, as various suluks which in Jogya are distinguished apart from the lagons proper (*vide* p. 318 and 319, sub *c*, *d*, *e*, *g* and *h*) are, in Solo, classed with the pateṭan.

It sometimes happens that, *at the end* of a paṭetan or senḍon, the colotomic instruments (gong, kenong, kempul, keṭuk) join in, so that this suluk-part thereby becomes "quadratized". An end-phrase which is "tamed" in this way is designated by the term *sarayuda* [1]).

When such "canalizing" of the melodic current takes place for a few moments *half-way down* a suluk (and the same applies to certain *bawa*'s) it is not called sarayuda but *jineman*—a term which, like sarayuda, has already been mentioned earlier in a slightly different signification (p. 128).

In regard to the several paṭetan- and lagon-names we may observe that some of them are derived from places or districts (e.g. *Lasem*, *Keḍu*, *Mentaraman* = *Ma(n)taraman* = à la Mataram); others from some special characteristic (*wetah* = full, complete; *wantah* = *lugu* = ordinary, unadorned; *jugag* = incomplete, stopped, ceasing suddenly, lopped off; *chekak* = brief, blunt; *kagok* [2]) = having an unusual character, "wouldbe", pseudo; *ngelik* = upwards, in the high register). One only paṭetan is called after a wayang figure (whose appearance it is supposed to announce or accompany), namely, the *P. senḍon Bimanyu*, after (A)bimanyu, a son of Arjuna. *Lumrah* (H. J. *limrah*) means general, common; *lindur* = to dream aloud; *ageng* (L. J. *geḍé*) = the great, the most important; *entèk* (H. J. *telas*) = "up", passed, out [3]). *Renchasih* is the name of a genḍing, and, finally, *sastradatan* is probably derived from the proper name Sastradata, which, it is said, was once borne by an influential niyaga, who either invented the paṭetan of that name or showed a special preference for it.

Some of the shorter lagons are simply fragments from the longer forms [4]). In Jogya the *lagon sléndro P. 6 chekak* is formed from the phrases 1, 2 and the second part of 5 of the *jugag* form consisting of 5 phrases; the phrases 2, 3, 4 and 5 of this *jugag* form are identical with phrases 9, 10 11, and 12

---

[1]) *Vide*, for another signification of this term, p. 207. Cf. also, above, p. 276 (stanza 115 from the 44th canto of the Chenṭini).

[2]) For the signification and use of the term kagok, *vide* also, above, p. 303.

[3]) This term, therefore, probably denotes those paṭetan, which are played as a postlude to a genḍing.

[4]) Hence the fact that shorter forms are denoted either by *jugag* or by *chekak*. They are such, in comparison and in proportion to the *wetah*-form.

of the *wetah* form; phrases 2 and 3 of the *lagon P. 9 jugag* are identical with phrases 5 and 6 of the *wetah* form. The *lagon P. 9 Lasem sarabayan*, on the other hand, is the same as the *lagon P. 9 wetah* augmented with a long end-piece. The *lagon P. barang Lasem* comprises, in its phrases 12a to 23 incl., the entire *lagon P. barang wetah* (with the exception of the latter's introductory phrase), and, in its phrases 19 to 23 incl., the entire *lagon P. barang jugag*. Further, the three *lagons P. manyura* are nothing more than the three *lagons P. 9* transposed a tone higher and provided with a short lengthening piece [1]).

Thus far as regards the notion "lagon". We shall now briefly discuss the other suluk forms enumerated on pp. 318 and 319.

The **ada-ada**, or *greget saut* [2]) are vocal recitations, each announcing some definite, violent (*sereng*) emotion on the part of the wayang figures [3]). They are sung by the ḍalang, who is accompanied and, if necessary, kept to the right pitch, by the *gendèr barung* and the *keprak* [4]) (sometimes also by the *kenḍang* and the *gong*) [5]). Each ada-ada used by the ḍalang has its own special place in the course of the story depicted by the wayang. Thus, the *ada-ada Girisa* may be heard, fore example, during the *jejer* [6]), the first scene of a wayang play, and also when the patih goes out to transmit a message to the warring hosts, and returns thence (**380**); the *A. astakuswala* introduces the marching on of an army; the *A.* (*budal*(*an*)) *Mataraman* announces someone's departure, etc.

An ada-ada is generally followed by *Srepegan*.

The Solonese musicians and ḍalangs distinguish, in sléndro, altogether

1) In the transcription, the identity of the lagons P. 9 and P. manyura is not done full justice to, owing to the fact that the practically equidistant sléndro scale is, of necessity, represented in the Appendices by a non-equidistant tonal sequence.

2) *Ada* = driving power, central support, stimulant, initiative. Further also = the main rib of a palm-leaf; spine; the longitudinal ridge on the flat part of a creese and the central back of a gendèr key. *Greget* = to clench ones teeth in fury; gnashing of teeth; sudden burst of temper; *saut* = to grasp quickly.

3) According to others, *greget saut* is not quite synonymous with *ada-ada*; it denotes the peculiar character of the emotional atmosphere, charged with passion and nervous tension, which the ḍalang creates by the ada-ada. Another term in vogue nowadays to indicate this, is *galak* (literally: aggressive).

4) In the Sunda districts, chiefly on the rebab.

5) *Vide*, p. 323 s.v. *sarayuda*.

6) *Jejer* = to stand erect (said of the wayang figures). The general term denoting a wayang scene is *adegan*; the *first* adegan, of a lakon, however, is never called by this name, but invariably by the name of *jejer*. (Actually, *adegan* means paragraph).

19 different ada-ada's (**323**, No. 75 of Vol. 1931); *i.e.* seven in *paṭet nem*:

1. A. Girisa (L. J.: A. Gurisa)
2. A. jugag
7, A. (budal(an)) Mataraman
4. A. astakuswala ageng
5. A. astakuswala alit
6. A. tengaran
7. A. tlutur;

also seven in *paṭet sanga*:

1. A. astakuswala sanga
2. A. wantah [1])
3. A. jugag
4. A. manggalan
5. A. palaran
6. A. sanga ageng
7. A. tlutur sanga

and five in *paṭet manyura*:

1. A. ageng
2. A. alit
3. A. jugag
4. A. wantah
5. A. tlutur.

The statements in regard to the ada-ada made by JAKUB and WIGNYARUMEKSA (**78**) are not quite, and those made by SULARDI (**343**) very far from, complete.

In Jogya four different forms of ada-ada are known for each paṭet, three of which, in P. sanga and P. manyura, are distinguished respectively (for the same reason as in the case of the lagons) as *wetah*, *jugag* and *chekak*. The *wetah* form (App. *20*, *28* and *35*)—which exists also in P. nem—accompanies the appearance of lords of the realm; the *jugag* form is played generally during a fight, and the *chekak* form at the moment when a fallen hero is about to raise himself afresh and continue the good fight.

Then there also are, in Jogya, in sléndro paṭet nem, the three *ada-ada prang* (*wetah*, *jugag* and *chekak*) (App. *21*) which are intoned before a fight; in P. sanga the *A. trenya* (App. *27*) which accompanies the meditations

[1]) Of this, a very fine record was made by Columbia, in the Mangku Nagaran (G.J. 57).

of the wayang prince; in P. manyura the *A. galong* (App. *34*) which precedes *sampak galong*, and together therewith embodies that part of the paṭet manyura period which is generally designated by the name of *manyura ageng*.

In a similar manner the *ada-ada pélog* are applied in the accompanying music of the *wayang geḍog*.

The use of the ada-ada according to the Solonese *adat* is described in the Pakem Sastramiruda (**169**, p. 61).

The three *ada-ada prang* are very closely akin to one another; apart from small, unessential differences, they are simply abbreviations of each other. The *chekak* form is composed from the *phrases* 2, 3, 6 and 7, and the *jugag* form from the phrases 1, 2, 3, 6 and 7 of the seven phrases-long *wetah* form. In the same way, the *A. P. 9 jugag* consists of the phrases 1, 2, 5 and 6 of the six phrases-long *A. P. 9 wetah*, and the *chekak*-form of an independent commencing phrase followed by the phrases 5 and 6 of the *wetah* form; the *A. P. manyura jugag* consists of the phrases 1, 2, 4 and 5 of the 5 phrases-long *A. P. manyura wetah*, and the *manyura chekak* form of a commencing phrase of its own followed by the phrases 3, 4 and 5 of the *wetah* form, whilst, finally, the *A. galong* is composed of the phrases 1, 2 and 3 of the *suluk galong wetah*, after which, however, there follows in conclusion the long-drawn final tone *barang*.

The suluk **plenchung** (J.) (App. *15*) is intoned by the ḍalang when, at the end of a scene, the army marches up [1]); the spectators will then know that the next scene is to be acted in another place. This all takes place in the paṭet nem period. In this, *plenchung wetah* is used exclusively in the first two *adegan*, the *jugag* form being used later on. The latter form is also sung by the ḍalang when the wayang prince deputes his servant on some mission or other.

As a curiosity it might be mentioned that the finish of *plenchung wetah* shows a remarkable similarity to the well known beautiful cello-theme in the last movement of the quartet op. 135 by Beethoven:

[1]) For this, Solo uses the *paṭetan* (*lagon*) *Keḍu*, the commencement of which is the same as that of *plenchung*, but which deviates as it goes on.

The suluk **(h)irim-(h)irim** (J.) (App. *14*) is heard at the moment when the wayang prince has set aside the affairs of state, and directs his steps towards the women's apartments. This suluk also comes within the paṭet nem period.

Jengking (J.) (App. *26*) is the name of a lengthening-piece of the lagon P. 9, which precedes the suluk *laras barang miring*. Of jengking, too, there exist a *wetah-* and a *jugag*-form. In Solo the paṭetan jengking together with its lengthening-piece is probably called *paṭetan* (or *lagon*) *jengking* (cf. above p. 321). It is heard on the appearance of a ksatriya in the company of a pandita (hermit sage). Solo, moreover, also knows a *paṭetan jengking manyura*, which is sung during love-scenes (**169**).

The suluk **laras barang miring** itself, in which the tones *barang*, *lima* and *ḍaḍa* are intoned slightly flat, which gives it a more or less pélog character [1]), is heard during the wayang night and played only by the rebab and the suling together with the voice, at the moment of Semar's first appearance; this is about midnight during the *gara-gara*, *i.e.* the interpretation in sound of the rise of the elements, which accompanies the appearance of Semar [2]). In this case the singing of the ḍalang serves to prepare the audience for a brief spell of playing in paṭet manyura, by which, on this appearance of Semar, the paṭet sanga period is temporarily broken [3]). (Cf. also, above, p. 132, note 4, and below, p. 340).

---

1) in which the *gulu* *sléndro* is felt as *bem* pélog;
,, *ḍaḍa* ,, ,, ,, ,, *gulu* ,,
,, *lima* ,, ,, ,, ,, *ḍaḍa* ,,
,, *nem* ,, ,, ,, ,, *lima* ,, , and
,, *barang* ,, ,, ,, ,, *nem* ,,

In that case, however, the interval *ḍaḍa-lima* is noticeably greater than the normal pélog interval *gulu-ḍaḍa*. In other words, the *laras barang miring* is identical with a scale of the Sundanese *surupan salèndro degung* (cf. above, p. 65).

2) No better evidence could be adduced of the divine power supposed to be embodied in the figure of Semar—notwithstanding his burlesque appearance and behaviour. Semar, for that matter, appears in some lakons (wayang-tales) as the *elder* brother of Batara Guru, the supreme god. Cf. also **158**, p. 40/41, and P.V. VAN STEIN CALLENFELS, "Pandji en Semar" ("Handelingen van het eerste Congres voor Taal-, Land- en Volkenkunde van Java, Solo 1919", p. 301 (304 *et seq.*), and H. H. P. A. A. MANGKU NAGARA VII, in his treatise "Over de wayang kulit enz." (**264**, p. 12–13) (*vide* above, p. 304 note 1).

3) so-called *nyilih* (= borrow), because the sanga period here borrows, as it were, manyura music (**264**, p. 19).

In Jogya, again, there exist a *wetah-*, a *jugag-* and a *chekak*-form of this suluk (App. *36*, *37* and *38*, respectively).

Senḍon (App. *25* and *32*) is the name of short dirges recited by the ḍalang about Semar and other panakawans of the "good" Panḍava party, when their lord—usually either Arjuna or one of his sons, *e.g.* Abimanyu (cf. the *lagon senḍon Bimanyu*), but maybe also somebody else—is stricken by grief [1]).

The suluk **tlutur** (App. *23* and *24*), which is heard both in the paṭet sanga- and in the paṭet manyura-period, is expressive of sadness. The manyura-form is identical with the sanga-form, with the exception that everything is sung one whole tone (*wilah*) higher. Further, the tones *ḍaḍa* and *nem* in P. 9, and the tones *lima* and *barang* in P. manyura are intoned flat [2]). The singers say that these lowerings give a sad character to the melody. On European ears, too, for that matter, such slight lowerings, against the background of non-flattened instrumental tones, produce a sad impression.

As mentioned before (p. 320), paṭet nem sometimes borrows an adaptation of this suluk tlutur from P. sanga, to substitute it, by way of a change, for the *lagon P. 6 chekak*.

The suluk **galong**, too (App. *33*), possesses a *wetah-* and a *jugag*-form. This suluk is heard especially (? exclusively) after the genḍings *Rina-rina*, *Sumirat*, *Maskumambang* and *Konda* (J.).

The jugag-form consists of the phrases 1 to 4 incl. and 8, of the wetah-form.

Finally, we must reckon among the suluk-group a form of art called, in Jogya (? not in Solo), **(ka)kawin**, and consisting of a melody with tembang geḍé, or with a machapat poem as text, which is intoned by the ḍalang when the wayang figure appearing at the time is a brave one and

---

1) In the Chenṭini, *senḍon* also occurs frequently in the wider signification of *paṭetan*. According to the Pakem Sastramiruda, too, (**169**, p. 57/8), *senḍon* and *paṭetan* are synonymous; it is said, however, that, in slendro, preference is usually given to the term paṭetan, and in pélog to that of senḍon.

2) In Sundanese terminology, therefore, the suluk tlutur are in *salèndro madenda*, at any rate according to R. Machyar Angga Kusumadinata.

full of fighting spirit. In Jogya—as fas ar the wayang purwa is concerned—only the tembang gedé *Gurisa* (App. *18*) and *Sikarini* (App. *17*), and the machapat songs *Asmarandana* (App. *16*), *Durma* (App. *19*) and *Pangkur* are used for this purpose. In Solo there is a far greater variety of choice in this respect; there, however, it is customary in this case to use sekar ageng, and only rarely tembang machapat. In Jogya, too, for that matter, one may hear, in the wayang wong, other tembang being used for *kawin* [1]). Of the songs named, *Durma* is sung for preference on the appearance of a *raksasa* (demon) [2]).

Many of the particulars given here concerning the suluks have been gathered from R. M. JAYADIPURA, and are derived from the Jogya play-adat. The customs prevailing in Solo are, of course, somewhat different again. The melody is also slightly different there, although never to such a degree that a Jogyanese could not recognize the Solonese version, or *vice versa*.

In regard to the suluks as they are distinguished in Solo we refer to **380** (especially p. 241 *et seq.*) [3]). Some data may further be found in PIGEAUD'S work **298** (p. 56, par. 32). [**23**B, **29**B, **156**AA, **167**B, **302**K–Q, **340**B, **377**DD]

All the suluks reproduced in the Appendices—and this applies equally to the others, whether Jogyanese or Solonese—are completely free in rhythm, as all tembang is. The instrumental accompaniment—not reproduced here—which is no more bound to any fixed ("quadratic") bar-division, influences the vocal part belonging to it exclusively as regards intonation (it keeps the singer "up to the mark"), and even that only inasmuch the voice uses the same tones that are played on the panerusan; rhythmically, both the voice and the accompaniment practically go each their own way, coming together at most on certain melodic points of juncture, and, of course, at the finish.

It may be better to avoid using, in this connexion, the term polyrhythmics, as the term polyphony was avoided, in favour of the term heterophony,

[1]) The term *(ka)kawin* is derived from *kawi* = poet, and therefore means *poem*; but, originally, only a poem in one of the ancient Hindu metra. In the case under discussion, however, it also evidently stands for poems in *machapat*-metre.—The Sundanese equivalent of *(ka)kawin* is *kakawèn* (cf. p. 398).

[2]) The syllable *dur* suggests evil; accordingly the bearers of the proper names *Durmagati, Dursasana, Duryudana, Dursilawati, Durna, Durnétra, Durjaya*, etc., all belong to the evil party in the wayang.

[3]) which also gives another subdivision, *i.e.* according to the composition of the accompanying ensemble.

in connexion with the interweaving of the different instrumental parts [1]). It seems to me proper to speak here of ***heterorhythmics***.

Now this very freedom of rhythm enables these suluks to be pressed into a quadratic straight-jacket without violence being done to their peculiar character. This has been done, for instance, with the Jogya lagons in the kraton genḍing-collection often mentioned previously. This quadratization, however, is not so stiff as would appear at first sight; the number of quasi-syncopated formations is legion. One should further bear in mind the "canalized" suluk-parts *sarayuda* and *jineman*, described above on p. 323. And then there is the *paṭetan beḍaya, i.e.* the paṭetan as sung on the appearance of the beḍaya's and the serimpi's, which has also lost much of its rhythmic freedom, in order better to serve as accompaniment to the stately stride of the girl dancers.

In regard to the execution of the suluks it should be pointed out that their tempo is a fairly slow one (Andante or Adagio), and that the final phrase—as a rule directed melodically downwards—usually fades out into a mysteriously sounding pianissimo. Further, the ḍalang is expected to sing the suluks *nges, i.e.* with emotional power, suggestively.

In a number of cases the quadratized kraton-version and the rhythmically free form phonographed in the Jayadipuran have, for the sake of comparison, been placed in the Appendices in volume II below each other. This serves to show what is, to a Javanese musician, the essence of a melody, and the extent to which the freedom of interpretation is allowed to go.

The reader will have observed that some of the suluk melodies are of quite an exceptional beauty. The *lagon manyura wetah* (App. *29*) in its rhythmically free guise is, in the author's opinion, a crowning example. It is a truly noble specimen of purely melodic vocal music uninfluenced by any harmony. The Chenṭini says about this lagon, in Canto 44, stanza 82 *et seq.*:

....
Widiguna suluk ngeliking manyura
83. nganyut-anyut loyop pantes suluk bangun,

---

[1]) *Vide* above, p. 129.

meaning: "Widiguna sang the suluk manyura in the high register (*ngelik*) and his voice dwelt indolently on the song that softly faded out [1]), as is proper for a suluk which is sung in the morning".

With regard to the form of the notations reproduced in the Appendices, they, of course, represent only an approximation—as near as possible, for that matter—to the real thing. On the whole one may say that the notations of the pélog-melodies come a little closer to the original than those in sléndro. For, the sléndro scale (without lowerings such as are heard in the *laras barang miring* and the *suluks tlutur*) is nowadays practically equidistant. The westerner involuntarily "corrects" certain of the tones in such a way as to make the intervals heard "understandable" to his hearing, *i.e.* so that they fit into his tonal system; the scale thereby becomes composed of seconds and minor thirds [2]). The same, if to a lesser extent, happens to some of the tones from the pélog system.

Failing a better method it is this conception which the author had in mind in drawing up the notations given here. Above each melody, or, as the case may be, above each group of melodies, however, the notation is accounted for by indicating each time which tones are meant by the various note-symbols.

It turned out that I myself was inclined to interpret (to "correct") a given tone differently according as it occurred in a different context: in the suluk-melodies, therefore, which employ the normal equidistant sléndro scale, the tone *nem* is accordingly rendered now by a *b*, now by a *c*; similarly, the tone *gulu* now by an *e*, now by an *f*.

In pélog, as was mentioned before (p. 74), the European ear hears the tone *gulu*, in the register used here, and as regards the paṭet's *lima* and *nem* (the *bem* scales), as an *e*♭; as regards paṭet *barang*, as an *e* (**200**, p. 346/7). Actually, this tone lies just in between; it is "neutral".

As far as the suluks with scales with two or three lowered tones are concerned, it is, however, not only the Western ear which is responsible for a certain unsteadiness in the notation; the singers themselves do not always intone these flattened tones in laras barang miring, in the suluks tlutur and in the kawin Durma exactly alike, so that I have been compelled in one particular case—*i.e.* in the *suluk laras barang miring wetah* (App. 36)—to represent the tone *lima* alternately by *g*, *g*♯, or (natural) *a*, and, in

[1]) *nganyut-anyut*, literally: to float away.

[2]) Cf. also, above, p. 85 note 2.

the *suluk tlutur jugag* P. sanga (App. *24*), the tone *ḍaḍa* alternately by *f* and by *f♯* [1]).

For the sake of legibility I have also placed here and there, in the Jayadipuran suluks, bar-lines in order to be able to give an occasional indication with respect to accentuation. On no account should one, however, take this accentuation to be at all heavy; it is, for example, far lighter than is usual in European music. Generally one can say, that rhythmic form, in European music partly expressed by accentuating some of the tones of the melody, in Javanese music is realized by the colotomic (phrasing) instruments (often by doubling those melody-tones in the lower octave), so that the melodic stream itself can quietly flow on, unhampered by periodical stresses. The colotomic instruments lacking, as is usually the case with the suluks here referred to (except *e.g. Sarayuda*), one frequently is at a loss to say which note of a phrase one should stress a little bit. [**156**AA, **269**B, **287**A, **302**O–Q, **377**DD, *S[43,44]].

Finally, in regard to the texts of these suluks, KERN has already observed (*vide* the Introduction to **271**) that they are derived from ancient Hindu-Javanese poems (Bhāratayuddha, Rāmāyaṇa, Arjunavivaha), but that these old stanzas have become very much corrupted in the course of time and their meaning not only to the audience completely, but even to the ḍalang himself [2]) partly, obscure. The content of these texts, moreover—insofar as it is still comprehensible—is sometimes totally irrelevant to the situations depicted on the wayang-screen [3]).

The suluk texts contained in the Jogya kraton collection also answer completely to the above description. Dr. PURBACHARAKA has recognized the text of the *lagon paṭet 5 gerjitawatang* and that of the *suluk galong paṭet manyura wetah* as having been borrowed from the Bhāratayuddha, whilst the text of the *suluk paṭet sanga tlutur wetah* proved to him to be a corruption of some verses from the Arjunavivaha. [**302**A]

As far as the texts are at all understandable their content is usually of an erotic nature, and sometimes—notably those of the ada-ada—heroic. Here follow a few specimens of translation, by Dr. PURBACHARAKA:

Lagon P. 9 wetah: (Thou art) the soul of my attachment, the lovable object of my enamoured heart. Thou art beautiful even to thy whims, supple and sweet. Thy charm arouses my love.

[1]) Cf. above, p. 66. [2]) *Vide* also **380**, p. 245/246.[**407**A] [3]) *ibid.* p. 246.

Lagon P. 9 jugag: I dream about thee in the night, and in the daytime I imagine sitting next to thee.

Lagon Lasem P. 9 sarabayan: A banana without spadix; a gateway without swinging doors. Do understand that I am sad. There is a most excellent woman, as fragrant as the flowers .... Her name is Dévi Wilutama, with overflowing sweetness .... Her face is like the moon. Her eyes resemble flames moved by the wind .... Even the honey is envious of her fragrance. Her body is a walking beauty.

Lagon P. manyura jugag: Pail (for fetching water from) the well; a crested bird with a splendid dress of feathers. Everywhere and at all time thou art captivating.

Suluk barang miring wetah: Ah, let me sing: a garden well; barren leaves floating away upon the water; already from infancy have I always done thy bidding.

According to CHAN CHU SIEM (**380**, p. 248 *et seq.*)—and, as far as I can see, he is right—the suluk's represent originally first and foremost a magic element in the wayang. [**29**B, **302**A, **360**C, **407**A]

* * *

Before concluding this discussion of the different musical forms we must say something about the way the tempi are indicated, and, finally, make a few observations with regard to the special functions of certain genḍings.

Javanese orchestral music distinguishes a number of different **(w)irama** (Sund.: *wirahma*). Probably the nearest translation of the notion *wirama* would be *tempo*; it also contains, however, something of the notions *measure*, or *bar* (in the significance of a defined, limited, duration of time), and *bar-division*. Thus, KI HAJAR DÉWANTARA (**75**) speaks of *wirama wutuh* (H. J. *W. wetah* = complete, whole), by which he understands a common time bar.

The Sanskrit word *wirama* means *rest*. But since, after all, the tempo of a genḍing is determined by the length of the time-intervals (*i.e.* the rest-pauses) between the different beats of the nuclear theme, the alteration in the signification of the term wirama is easily explained.

Sometimes one hears the word *wilet* being used, apparently as a perfect synonym of wirama. These two terms do not, however, completely cover each other.

Whereas, by wirama, as we said before, is meant the tempo as expressed in the time-intervals between the balungan-tones, ***wilet*** refers to those same time-intervals, as filled up by the melody sung, or played on the rebab. In the root ***let*** the notion ***to wind, to bend,*** is inherent; hence ***pulet*** = to wind round; ***ulet*** = to kneed, to entwine. ***Wilet,*** therefore, is the piece of melody, the melodic turn, between two given points. Wilet and wirama, therefore, are not identical; one might say that the wilet obeys, is determined by, the wirama.

Wilet, for that matter, does not serve only—and not even any more in the first place—to designate the fragment of melody between two balungan tones: it also stands at present for the piece of melody between two ***inter-punctuating*** tones, say two kenong- or two gong-beats, so that the best translation would actually be ***phrase***, or ***period***. This latter signification of the term ***wilet*** now predominates to such an extent that the fragment of melody covering a group of 4 ***keteg*** (in the Jogya kraton-notation, to be dealt with presently, such a group is closed in between two thick transverse lines) is known by the name of ***sa wilet alit, i.e. small*** wilet. This ***sa wilet alit***, therefore, might very well be translated by ***bar***—as meaning "a time-interval of 4 keteg, filled up in some way by tones".

In the Sunda-districts, ***wilet*** has retained the meaning of "(melodically filled) time-interval between two succeeding balungan-tones"; its signification has not been extended to that of a "melodic period". Besides wilet, however, the Sundanese use the term ***wiletan*** for the same notion.

A third notion, also more or less parallel with wilet, is that of ***chèngkok*** (cf. also above, p. 127 note 2). This ***chèngkok***, too, relates to melodics. But whereas wilet refers to the fragment of melody as it is being sung or played on the rebab at a given moment, *including all variations and fioriturі added by the player*, the meaning of chèngkok is exclusively the sequence of the essential, so to speak "compulsory" tones, ***i.e.*** those which give the melody its specific character. One might say, therefore: "Niyaga A plays a different ***wilet*** from that of niyaga B; but the ***chèngkok*** of both their performances is the same". [1])

[1]) The Pakem Sastramiruda (**169**) gives a slightly different use of the word ***chèng-kok***; there, a genḍing whose gongan all finish on the same tone in the scale is termed a ***genḍing chèngkok siji, i.e.*** an orchestral piece with a homogeneous chèngkok; a composition with 2, 3 or 4 different gongan finishing notes, as genḍing ***chèng-kok loro, telu,*** and ***papat***, respectively. [*chèngkok* = manner, variant, way, method].

After this digression, let us return to the conception *wirama*.

We distinguish a number of different kinds of wirama, each of which bears a different name. There is, however, little consistency in the nomenclature:

R. M. JAYADIPURA (Jogya) gave me the following names, arranged from fast to slow:

W. *kencheng* (= quick);

W. *seseg* (= narrow, close together) or *lomba* (= single, unadorned (this being because of the fast tempo);

W. *tanggung* (H. J. *tanggel*) or *dadi* (H. J. *dados*) = right, proper, the golden mean, tempo giusto;

W. *antal* = *kendo* (= slow) or *rangkep* (dual, double, folded in two; also: retarded).

SULARDI (**287**) (Solo) and also R. TIRTANATA (Temanggung), in a paper he wrote for a competition, distinguish the following:

W. *toyamili* (= running water);

W. *lomba, kalih* (= 2) or *lugu* (= ordinary, unadorned);

W. *rangkep* [1]);

the musicians in the Mangku Nagaran:

W. *kencheng, lomba* or *lamban*;

W. *sedeng* (= average) (H. J. *chekapan*), *loro* (= 2), or, very rarely, *rangkep kalih*;

W. *kendo* or *tembang* (*i.e.* the tempo most used for singing (*tembang*);

W. *telu* (= three), *rangkep* or *tikel* (= double).

R. LURAH JAYÈNGGUTARA (Jogya) mentions in his paper written for a competition:

W. *seseg*;

W. *chekapan*;

W. (*h*)*antal*,

while, finally, mention must be made of the custom, which is gradually gaining ground, as was already evident from some previous enumerations, namely that of simply *numbering* the various tempi from fast to slow. In this case we distinguish W. *siji* or *setunggal* (= 1); *karotugel* (= $1^1/_2$); *loro* or *kalih* (= 2); *telu* (= 3), and *papat* (H. J. *sekawan*) (= 4).

The slowest of these tempi (*sekawan, antal, telu*) are said to be used

[1]) For this, the Pakem Sastramiruda knows the term *wirama landung* (*landung* = roomy, wide).

especially in *klenéngan* when there is vocal music with it. It is unsuitable as accompaniment of the *dance*, which is generally beaten in W. *lomba*. W. *toyamili* is the tempo of the majority of *bebuka*'s.

Each tempo has its own panerusan-style. We already mentioned this when discussing gambang-playing. The same applies also to gendèr-playing.

Finally we may mention the term *wirama gobyog*, used to designate an extremely animated and lively style of playing. (*Gobyog* actually means "roll on the drum"; as has already been mentioned, it is the name for the fast drumming when a murder has been committed (*kenṭong titir*)).

Ngrèngrèngan refers to that part of a genḍing whose tempo is not yet quite stabilized, and which lies between the bebuka and the moment when the "normal" tempo (*wirama dadi*, *W. dados*) [1]) is reached.

A number of ladrang compositions have the peculiarity that, out of the usually 5 or 6 gongan of which they consist, there is one which is beaten in a much faster tempo than the others. This gongan, which, naturally, is heard as many times as the body of the genḍing is repeated, is termed *seseganipun* (L. J. *sesegané*), from *seseg* = fast, accelerated. This fast tempo is reached gradually in the last kenongan of the preceding part, which is played in normal tempo (*dados*), and passes again into this normal tempo just as gradually at the finish. Appendix 7 gives an example of a ladrangan constructed on this pattern.

With regard to the ritardandi (*suwuk*) and stringendi (*sesegan*) occurring in all compositions all relevant facts have already been given (*vide* pp. 313 and 316).

Cf. also, in regard to tempo, BRANDTS BUYS' exposition in **44**, p. 49 *et seq.* [**113**F–G]

* * *

We shall now deal briefly with the special function of certain genḍings.

Whoever has had the good fortune to attend a festivity or celebration at the residence of one of the nobles in the Principalities will no doubt

[1]) *Dadi* (H. J. *dados*), which we mentioned just now as the name for a medium tempo, means literally: to get ready; being plainly evident; to be effective; to be something in its full power or importance. As a musical term, therefore, it stands for the "normal" tempo, both in the meaning of "average" and "not under the influence of *ngrèngrèngan*, *sesegan*, *suwuk*, and suchlike"; there is also something in it of the force of "tempo giusto". (*Rèngrèng*, from which *ngrèngrèngan* is derived, is in contrast to *dadi*; it is, for example, also used as meaning "rough copy", as against which *dadi* is used to indicate the "fair copy").

recall the bright and cheerful gamelan-sounds with which the guests were welcomed and their entry added lustre to. The genḍing heard on that occasion was probably the ladrangan *Kebo giro* (= the skittish buffalo), [*S45] but it may also have been another composition lending itself to a vigorous style of execution and belonging either to the genḍings in a restricted sense or to the ladrangan. All *genḍing parikan* and *talèḍèkan*, however, are excluded from service in this homage to guests, "in order"—thus the Jogya kraton genḍing-collection—"that there may arise no misunderstanding, and that those present may not involuntarily be led to confound the entering guests with either Semar, Garèng or Pétruk". For welcoming princes and heirs apparent very special genḍings are to be beaten: for the Susuhunan, the ladrangan *Srikaton* 1); for the Sultan, the ketawang *Barangganjur*, or sometimes the ladrangan *Srikawuryan*;(*) for the Solonese successor to the throne, the ketawang *Rarasmaya* 2); for the Jogya successor to the throne, the ladrangan *Rajamanggala*, and for H. H. Mangku Nagara, the ketawang *Puspawarna* 3).

In the Sunda districts—we are here anticipating the next chapter—the lagu *Jipang*(**) is used, for preference, for welcoming guests, and, at their departure, the lagu *Kebojiro* (Sundanese for *Kebo giro*).

The genḍings *Munggang* and *Koḍok ngorèk*—as we saw when dealing with the orchestras of these names—are played only on certain very solemn and special occasions; the genḍing *Munggang* also after a toast to the prince, whilst a "conditie" (*i.e.* the customary Dutch word used in Java for "toast") proposed to the successor to the throne is followed by the ketawang *Barangganjur* just mentioned, and one to other prominent personages by one of the genḍings *Béndrong* 4), *Kebogiro* or *Ganjur*, beaten in quick tempo.

The ladrangan *Hundur-hundur kajongan* is heard in Solo exclusively in the kraton, *i.e.* at the moment when the Susuhunan retires or betakes himself to another part of the festive grounds, as well as, on the garebegs, during the dance of the *chanṭang balung*; the ladrangan *Teḍak sa(ng)king* and *Sembung gilang* 5), the genḍings sléndro *Gagak sétra* (= churchyard

1) Col. D 33001. [*S51]

2) Some say, erroneously, *Larasmaya*. [*S45]

3) Col. G.J.X. 6. [*S39,72]

4) = "collective rhythmic stamping in the rice-block". [*S44]

5) In Jogya, *Sembung gilang* occurs both in tengahan and in ladrang form; in Solo, it is said to belong exclusively to the group genḍing tengahan. [*S56]

(*) [*S60]. (**) [*S42]

crow), *Udan angin* (= rain and wind) and *Bibaran Klatèn* 1), as well as the genḍings pélog *(H)emprit néba* (= alighting flight of rice-birds), *Gambira* and *Suwéni* 2), are compositions beaten for preference during the departure of the guests 3) (J.); the ladrangan *Kapang-kapang* 4) (= being together) (S.) or the genḍing *Bindri* (J.), when the bridegroom arrives at the bride's abode; the ladrangan *Wilujeng*(*) (= hail), after the celebration of a wedding before the penghulu (Mohammedan priest) (S.); the ladrangan *Pengantèn* (=bridal couple), at the first (official) meeting between the bride and the bridegroom (when they are of princely blood either the genḍing *Munggang* or *Koḍok ngorèk* may serve in this case); the genḍing *Boyong* (=removal) (J.) when the newly-weds depart to the bridegroom's house. [S45]

Further, to almost every genḍing some special task in the wayang music is allotted; and as we said before, the genḍings sléndro are played in the wayang purwa, and the genḍings pélog in the wayang geḍog. They are then, again, subdivided into three main groups according to the paṭet.

Paṭet nem sléndro dominates the first part of the accompanying music of the wayang purwa to about midnight. The pieces in this paṭet are, generally speaking, quieter and less lively than those in paṭet sanga (which in their turn lag behind those in paṭet manyura in this respect), whilst the voice moves in the lower register more than in the two other paṭets.

At the end of the paṭet nem period either the genḍing *Prihatin* or *Bonḍèt* is sure to be played, because both these compositions—*vide* p. 98—possess the peculiarity of changing half-way down into paṭet sanga, and as a matter of fact are followed by the *lagon paṭet sanga* and *srepegan paṭet sanga*. In this way the gradual transition from paṭet nem to *paṭet sanga* is effected. [*S51]

From about 3 o'clock in the morning paṭet sanga, in its turn, makes way for *paṭet manyura* 5).

1) *Bibar*, L. J. *bubar*, = last, finish, to scatter, to go apart, finished with.

2) *Udan suwéni* (J.), or *sumawéni* (*samawéni*) (S.) means a kind of rain which may be heard in the air, but which does not fall on the ground.

3) All these departure-genḍings, as well as some of the arrival- and welcome-compositions (*e.g.* the *Kebogiro* already mentioned) have *kenḍangan Bibaran*.

4) Col. G.J. 273.

(*) [*S51]

5) *Manyura* is the Javanese corruption of *mayura*, the Sanskrit word for peacock. As was already pointed out above, the highest of the three styles of *Saman*-chant—this most ancient kind of Indian music—is compared to the sound of the peacock. (*Vide*, as regards this, also GROSSET, "Inde, Histoire de la musique depuis l'origine jusqu'à nos jours", in LAVIGNAC, vol. I, p. 279b). And it is not only this subdivision into three parts, according to the time of the day, which characterizes both Saman-

Further, within each paṭet, the pieces are again grouped—as far as the wayang purwa is concerned—into pieces for the "good" or Panḍava party (*golongan Panḍava* or *Ngamarta*) and those for the "evil" or Kurava party (*golongan Kurava* or *Ngastina*) [1]).

The genḍing *Krawitan* stands more or less apart from this classification, for it functions in nine out of ten cases as the traditional opening genḍing of the *jejer* of a purwa performance [2]). In case the play begins, however, with the appearance of a Ratu (prince) who does not belong to the very mighty ones (such as Batara Guru, Dvarawati (= Kresna), etc.), it is preceded by *Ayak-ayakan* [3]). When a guest appears who is *alus* (= refined, cultured), then, in the Jogya kraton, one of the ladrangans *Sekar pépé, Sekar gaḍung pupuletan, Gupuh*, or the genḍing *Ramiyang* is played; if the guest is *gagah* (fierce, unpolished, ferocious), one of the ladrangans *Girang-girang, (H)érang-(h)érang Kudus*, or the genḍing *Lungkèh*; when, however, the guest in question is the hero Baladéva, either the ladrang *Hèmeng* or the ladrang *Dirada meta* will be heard. When the Ratu retires to the kraton, then, if he belongs to the Panḍava side, one of the genḍings *Damarkéli, Mas kumambang* or *Titipati* is played; if he is a Kurava or an ally of the Kurava's, *Gendrèh rongèh, Lana* or *Marasonja*. And so on, and so on. Each wayang scene, each wayang figure has its own characteristic compositions: an audience, the marching of the army, the demon prince, the Ratu or ksatriya alus or the Ratu or ksatriya gagah, the lovesick Ratu, the aggrieved Ratu, the Ratu putri (princess), the pandita (hermit sage), etc. etc. Even Hanuman, the well-known leader of the apes, who belongs to the golongan Panḍava (and generally does not appear on the scene until the paṭet sanga period) has his very own tune, *i.e.* the genḍing *Hawun-awun* (P. 9).

The transition from paṭet 6 to paṭet 9 takes place, as we said before,

---

and wayang-music, but the mutual relation between the respective characteristics of the three groups is also the same: there is a climax in them, which causes the second melodic group to be more lively than the first, and the third more lively than the second (**193**, p. 408).

[1]) Ngastina is the capital of the Kurava's, as Ngamarta is that of the Pandava's.

[2]) It also serves as introduction to the *nguyu-uyu*. In the *wayang topèng*, on the contrary, although it is also accompanied by the gamelan sléndro, the genḍing *Kabor* (P. 6 pélog) is, at any rate in Jogya, always played as introduction. *Vide* B. P. A. Suryadiningrat, "De wayang orang topèng" ("Djawa" XV, p. 195), 1935. This latter genḍing also replaces the genḍing *Krawitan* in the wayang purwa, when the play starts with the appearance of the prince Suyadhana (cf. p. 341).

[3]) [89D]

at about midnight; the hour at which—at any rate in Jogya—to the sound of the elements in revolt (the *gara-gara*), Semar and his fellow-panakawans (Pétruk and Garèng) appear for the first time (cf. above, p. 327). [**23**B]

The genḍing *Gara-gara* is, further, heard sometimes (in Solo exclusively) 1) when Janaka (*i.e.* Arjuna) or some other hero belonging to the right side finds himself in the woods, in the company of his panakawans, among whom is Semar, and in difficult and grievous circumstances.

In addition, the genḍings characteristic of Semar are, in Jogya, *Kinanṭi rongé-rongé* and *Kaloran*, both talèḍèkan P. manyura, and the genḍing *Kuwung-kuwung* (P. manyura); for Garèng, the talèḍèkan *Sekar gaḍung* (P. manyura) and the genḍing *Sendéré*, which is actually taken over from the pélog-repertoire and transposed to P. manyura; for Pétruk, the talèḍèkan *Lembing kungking* and *Rinḍing putung*, both of them also P. manyura. The panakawan Bagong does not share in this manyura-privilege; his very own genḍing *Bibaran Klatèn* and the ladrang *Bujang daleman* being both in paṭet sanga.

Lastly we might mention that the genḍing *Rina-rina* 2) is performed exclusively at 5 o'clock in the morning and at 5 o'clock in the evening, and the ladrangan *Richik-richik* at 7 o'clock.

In the early morning *Rina-rina* rings in the last of the two scenes of the paṭet manyura period, just as the first was started on the ladrangan *Sumirat*. After the second scene, the Pandava's with their following—insofar as they have not been slain in battle in the course of the story—appear on the stage once more; but this does not constitute a fresh scene. This is the moment when Werkudara (= Bima) dances (a traditional and indispensable episode), to the accompaniment of one of the genḍings *Gonjanganom*, *Peksi pechowan*, *Giwanggonjing*, *Gurisa*, *Kopiahbedah* 3) or *Medarsi* (J.). And then, when at last the *gunungan* (or (*ke*)*kayon*), symbol both of the world and of life, is stuck for the last time into the middle of the banana-"stem" in front of the *kelir* (the wayang screen), which is done to the strains of the ladrang *Bibaran* (= the end, finish), the play

---

1) The Solonese causes this same *gara-gara* scene to be performed only in those rare cases when it is required by way of introduction to the appearance of a ksatriya wandering in the midst of a forest, in the most desolate circumstances" (Mangku Nagara VII, **264**, p. 13).

2) Rina = dawn.

3) = the torn bonnet.

has come to an end, and in the virgin morninglight the spectators return homeward fully satisfied.

The above is derived from the Jogya wayang-adat, as explained—far more extensively and completely, of course—in the Introduction to the great kraton genḍing-collection.

At Solo this play-adat is, if possible, still more richly shaded in its *nuances*. Here follows, for the sake of comparison, a summary of the music played before and during the first scene (*jejer*) of a Solonese wayang kulit performance, the details of which were communicated to me by the experienced ḍalang RADÈN KODRAT and his brother, the linguist Dr. PURBACHARAKA.

Solonese wayang kulit performances—with the exception of those in the kraton since the middle of last century—are preceded by an orchestral introduction called *talu* (literally: signal, announcement) [1]. Curiously enough, for this talu, *laras manyura* is used to the exclusion of all others. It starts with the genḍing *Chuchur bawook*, which passes into the munggah of the G. *Paré anom*, which, in its turn, is followed first by the ladrang *Srikaton* and after this by the ketawang *Suksma ilang*. This is followed—*attacca*—by *Ayak-ayakan*, *Srepegan*, and finally *Sampak*. In other words, the talu gets more and more lively towards the finish; in contrast with the greater part of Javanese music it shows a strong climax. (Quite rightly, indeed, ROORDA, in his dictionary, defines *talu* as "the music preceding a wayang- or topeng-performance, and finishing on a *furioso*".)

Not until the talu is finished does the ḍalang take his place in front of the screen, whereupon the actual play, the *lakon*, commences.

Just as in Jogya, it then depends upon the particular prince appearing on the stage in what way, musically, the first scene, or *jejer*, opens. For Batara Guru, or for Puntadéva (a prince from Ngamarta), the genḍing *Kawit* is used; for Kresna, and in general for princes, the genḍing *Krawitan*; for Suyadhana, the genḍing *Kabor*. The G. *Kawit* is followed by the ladrangan *Badranaya* as munggah; *Krawitan* has its own munggah, which also serves as munggah to the G. *Kabor*.

Outside the kraton the G. *Krawitan* is first preceded by *Ayak-ayakan*, without *ngelik*, *i.e.* without the melodic phrases in the high register customary in it at other times; in the kraton the performance starts straightaway with *Krawitan*.

[1]) Cf. above, p. 265.

The mérong of the genḍings mentioned is played for the most part softly (*sirep*) (and without either sarons or gambang), in order to give the ḍalang a chance to emphasize to his hearers, in his recital, the greatness of the prince appearing on the stage (*renggan* = ornament, decoration). When he has finished with this he gives the niyaga's a sign—by the so-called *ngombang* (cf. above p. 133)—to proceed again to the normal sound-amplitude and to the playing of the sarons and gambang, and, at the same moment the genḍing goes into the munggah. The ḍalang now has a moment's rest, which he employs in putting his puppets in readiness for the second scene. Meanwhile he sings now and then to accompany bits of the play; his singing, however, does not resemble either that of the ronggèngs or that of the gérongan or the ordinary *ura-ura*.

When the genḍing is finished the ḍalang follows it up immediately with the suluk *Lasem paṭet nem ageng*, and after this with the ada-ada *Gurisa*. Only then is the situation considered to have been adequately prepared for the stage-figures to start acting and for the dialogues to commence. Any particular emotions are stressed by the lagon *paṭet nem jugag*.

When a guest appears the ḍalang sings the *senḍon pananggalan*, which is followed by *Ayak-ayakan nem*, indicating the busy atmosphere created outside the assembly room by the arrival of the said guest. One of the punggawa's (officials of the prince) is detailed by the latter to go and see, and report upon, what is happening outside. On his return to the assembly-room the *Ayak-ayakan* is silenced, without a paṭetan following it.

To the tones of a ladrang-piece the guest now appears on the stage. If he is a refined, cultured character (*alus*), a corresponding genḍing is played, *e.g.* the G. *Ladrang mangu* for Puntadéva, or the G. *Srikaton* for *Arjuna*. If the guest is a vigorous, fierce ksatriya, for instance Baladéva, the G. *Dirada meta* or *Monchèr* is played. The appearance of Karna is accompanied either by the G. *Sobah* or by the G. *Peksi kuwung*; that of Sangkuni by the G. *Leré-leré*, and that of Kangsa by the G. *Remeng* or the G. *Sobrang*. For other visitors, if any, there are no special compositions, and the performers may play anything they fancy, providing the piece is a ladrangan.

At the moment the guest makes his appearance, the genḍing is "sirepped" in order to give the ḍalang a chance to enlarge upon the important visitor's qualities. The genḍing is again followed by a paṭetan (in jugag-form). During the conversation which now follows, any feelings of surprise are emphasized by the ḍalang by the recital of paṭet *nem jugag*; any emotions of an angry nature (not noticeable, for that matter, in the behaviour of the "actors"), by the performance of the ada-ada *Mataraman*.

When the visitor departs the paṭet *nem jugag* is sounded once more. The prince, after having conversed for a little time longer with his servitors, then retires to the keḍaton, all which is communicated to the audience by the ḍalang in his recital. The departure of the prince from the assembly-room is announced by a couple of beats with the *chempala* on the chest of requisites standing to the left of the ḍalang; after this follows *Ayak-ayakan nem*. All figures are then removed from before the *kelir*; the prince and his female servants *exeunt* to the right (*i.e.* towards the kraton), and the other figures to the left (*i.e.* outside).

On his way to the keḍaton the prince is supposed to come to a halt by a gateway. At this moment the *Ayak-ayakan* is beaten "sirep" after which it change into *Ayak-ayakan Anjang mas* (cf. p. 307). Meanwhile the ḍalang describes the splendour of the gate; in this he carefully regulates the length of his portrayal according to that of the accessory music, because, unlike the ordinary Ayak-ayakan, the *A. Anjang mas* cannot be arbitrarily broken off. After this interlude the ordinary Ayak-ayakan is played again, but this time strongly. The scene finishes at the moment the prince enters the keḍaton, to the tones of the *paṭetan nem jugag*.

The whole of the Solonese play-adat is to be found—"canonized", as it were—in a document drawn up by the Pangéran KUSUMADILAGA (who died about 1860) [1], written in the form of a dialogue and entitled "Pakem Sastramiruda", the first part of which appeared in print for the first time in 1930 (**169**). [**6**B, **23**B, **29**B, **63**B, **89**D, **113**G, **264**A, **277**A, **302**K, M, **340**C]

In exactly the same way as the sléndro repertoire has been put in the service of the wayang purwa, the pélog repertoire is distributed over the various phases of the wayang geḍog. Here, too, we find a division into two large groups (*golongan*), representing, respectively, the good party (the G. *Jenggala*) [2] and the evil one (the G. *Sabrangan*) [3], which division, as we said before, is crossed by another one according to the paṭets. And

[1]) He was at the head of the "wayang and gamelan department" in the Solonese kraton, under the VIIth and VIIIth Susuhunan.

[2]) Jenggala is the name of one of the two states (Kaḍiri was the name of the other one) into which Airlangga, on his abdication in 1043, divided his territory.

[3]) = the party of the shore opposite, the land on the other side.

here, too, we see a similar distribution of the gendings over the different characters and situations occurring in each lakon. [**185**A, **302**H, L, **340**C]

What the genḍing ***Krawitan*** is to the wayang purwa the genḍing ***Tlutur*** is to the wayang geḍog; also as regards the pecularity that only in case of the appearance of a mighty prince in the first scene (jejer) does the orchestra start straightaway on the said genḍing, but that in all other cases it is preceded by Ayak-ayakan.

Whilst, however, with respect to the wayang purwa, I already confined myself to giving a brief summary of the musical rules and regulations prevailing in this form of stage-play, with regard to the wayang geḍog, performed much less frequently as it is, (*vide* Appendix 57), it will suffice to make an even more modest selection from the available material, the more so as the instructions regarding the wayang geḍog are practically identical with those ruling the wayang purwa. The three pélog paṭets are divided in exactly the same way over the duration of the night as the sléndro paṭets in the wayang purwa; *i.e.* P. 5 up to midnight, P. 6 up to about 3 a.m., and after this P. barang until dawn. There is one deviation, however, in regard to the panakawans of the wayang geḍog (whose names are Banchak and Doyok), in that their first appearance, unlike that of three of their colleagues in the wayang purwa, is not attented by any temporary interruption of the prevailing paṭet (in this case P. 6 pélog) in favour of the paṭet coming to the fore in a later phase of the play (*i.e.* P. barang). Some of the ***senḍonan*** sung by the said panakawans in the P. nem period, however, are, in Solo, said to be in ***paṭet pélog manyura.***

It should further be noted that, in order to extend the relatively limited pélog repertoire, it has been necessary to resort in some cases to borrowing genḍings from the sléndro repertoire, a number of which have been transposed to this end to the corresponding pélog paṭets. This is the reason, for instance, why, during the last (P. barang) period of a geḍog-performance, the genḍings *Rina-rina* and *Sumirat* are also played. Similarly, in Jogya [**181**A–B, **381**B–C], the genḍing *Sarayuda seseg,* characteristic of Banchak, has been borrowed from the sléndro repertoire. [**269**B, **302**H, **360**B]

For the accompaniment of the wayang wong—at any rate in Jogya, and by itinerant troupes—both pélog and sléndro are made use of. Thus, we may hear, alternately with music in ***sléndro P. 6***, pieces in ***pélog P. lima***; side-by-side with *P. 9*, ***P. nem pélog*** may occur, and after (and sometimes before) ***paṭet manyura, P. barang***. In the Solonese princely abodes and dalems, however, this assimilation and blending of tonal systems and paṭets is unknown (cf. p. 256). [**5**, **6**, **20**C, **70**A, **100**A, **105**AA, **179**A, **181**AB, **248**BB, **279**, **293**, **365**, **381**B, **402**A. *S27]

Thus far as regards the use of the genḍings in the wayang.

* * *

In *nguyu-uyu* (J.) or *klenéngan* (J.) = music-making for its own sake (usually taking place in the day-time), too, it is, or, at any rate, was, customary to adhere to a definite order of sequence with respect to the different paṭets. In night-performances the order is the same as that which is observed in wayang-accompaniment. In the day-time it is usual, according to information obtained from the Jogya kraton, to play in P. manyura and P. barang up to midday; after this, until 3 p.m., in P. sanga and pélog P. nem, and from 3 to 6 p.m. in P. manyura and barang again. At 6 o'clock in the evening all music is silenced for some time. In the space of 24 hours, therefore there are two sanga/nem pélog and three manyura/barang periods but only one P. nem sléndro/P. lima period. [395B (ch. 5)]

The same applies to Solo, except that, in the day-time, it is usual to proceed from P. manyura and barang to P. sanga and pélog P. nem as early as 11 o'clock in the morning, reverting from the latter to P. manyura and barang as early as 2 o'clock in the afternoon.

As will be clear from what we mentioned above on p. 272, the times observed in the gamelan sekati show a slight difference.

* * *

This may be a suitable place to point to the interesting fact that certain genḍings—we already mentioned something to the same effect on p. 280—are regarded as being magically "charged", and therefore "pusaka". When it is intended to play a genḍing of this kind, it is customary first to burn *menyan* (incense), and to make a sacrificial offering of food (*sajèn*). Thus, for example, in Jogya, in the case of the genḍing *Semang* (played extremely rarely), and in Solo, in the case of the genḍings *Tanḍu* and *Beḍaya ketawang*, which are played during the dances of the beḍaya's in honour of Ratu Kidul, the mighty goddess of the Indian Ocean (Jav. South Sea) (**102**), as well as with the ketawang *Gaḍung melati*. At Cheribon, in the Kacherbonan, incense is burned before the genḍing *Kidung* is played, which, once upon a time, gave back speech to the wayang hero Gaṭutkacha (**190**, p. 36). This lagu *Kidung* is, in fact, a real magic melody; no one less than Baṭara Guru (= Shiva) himself, or Ḍalang Lunglungan (one of the forms in which Shiva appeared to the eyes of mortal man) sings it to hush his son, Baṭara Kala, to sleep and make him languorous and impotent.

f. Notation

(**15**, **16**, **29**, **33**, **35**, **49**, **52**, **54**, **75**, **78**, **79**, **99**, **105**, **170** to **174** incl., **192**, **297**, **343**, **350**, **351**, **353**, **357**, **358**)

[**54**A, **59**B, **76**A–D, **89**B–C, **101**A, **107**B, **113**C, F, **123**H, **167**B, **248**C–D, **291**B,C,E, **302**G, K, R, **319**A–C, **340**AB, **342**A–C, **377**K, **379**A, **381**C–D, **402**B, E–F]

To all appearances, no system of notation existed in Java prior to the middle of the 19th century [1]. This forms a contrast with Bali, which has possessed a concise form of notation for centuries (**29**; **192**, p. 47 *et seq.*).

In the course of the last 50 or 60 years, seven or eight different systems

[1] R. M. SURYAPUTRA, in his advisary report (**359**, p. 118), admittedly comes to the conclusion, on the grounds of a lontar in the Scheurleer collection at The Hague (now in the municipal museum), that a musical notation was already in use, in Java, before the fall of Majapahit, but it is not quite clear to us how he can have come to this conclusion. For, the lontar in question—of which we were able, thanks to the kindness of Dr. SCHEURLEER, to obtain an excellent photographic reproduction—is not an old-Javanese (as R. M. SURYAPUTRA supposes), but a *Balinese* lontar of modern times. The writing—according to the highly expert CHOKORDA GEDÉ RAKE SUKAWATI—appears to be that of a boy who, may be, practically masters the art of writing, but is still zealously studying it. With this, the content of the largest of the two sheets, of which this lontar consists, is fairly well in agreement; for it is formed by an enumeration of Balinese musical instruments, repeated four times with modifications:

rebab, saron, gendèr, trompong, chènchèng, kemong, keṭuk, gong, kenḍang, kempul, gambang;

rebab, saron, trompong, chènchèng, keṭuk, gong, kempul, kenḍang;

kenḍang, gong, kempul, kemong, gendèr, saron, rebab, chèngchèng;

gong titing (probably = Jav. gumbang), kenḍang, ... ? . . . . , suling, kempul, gupek.

The smallest of the two lontar sheets appears to contain a bit of melody, for on it one may read the words:

ning, nang, nung, ndèng, dong, ning, nang, ndung, ndèng, dong, nding, ndang, . . .

An approximation, in western notation, tho this tone-sequence, would be, as exactly as possible:

of notation have come to our knowledge from Java. In common with the Balinese system mentioned above, all of these aim at fixing the nuclear theme (*balunganing gen̩ding*) of a gamelan composition. The nuclear theme —one might also define it as the "cantus firmus"—is that part of a composition by which it is distinguished from all other ones; if, in the course of time, all knowledge of the nuclear theme of a gen̩ding should get lost, then that gen̩ding itself disappears from the repertoire for all time.

In order to prevent this from happening, collections of these nuclear themes have been formed in the kratons and in some of the dalems, as well as, in recent times, elsewhere. The collection of the ex-regent of Magelang, R. A. A. DANUSUGONDA [1]), comprises 126 gen̩ding sléndro (P. 6: 44; P. 9: 39; and P. manyura: 43); that of R. M. JAYADIPURA, 208 gen̩ding pélog; the gen̩ding alit collection of the Jogya kraton-regent R. T. WIRAGUNA, 60 ladrangan sléndro (P. 6: 17; P. 9: 23; and P. manyura: 20) and 40 ladrangan pélog (P. 5: 4; P. 6: 23; and P. barang: 13). The gen̩ding collection published by "Volkslectuur" *Serat enut gen̩ding sléndro*, by JAKUB and WIGNYARUMEKSA (**78**) comprises 123 gen̩ding sléndro; PAUL SEELIG'S collection *Gen̩ding Jawi* (**334**), 200 compositions, 136 of which are sléndro and 64 pélog [3]). These collections have not come into existence wholly independently of one-another; from the order of sequence of the pieces reproduced it is often noticeable either that one has been borrowing from the other, or that both have drawn from one and the same collection.

None of these collections, for that matter, aims at fixing the repertoire of the Principalities in its entirety; as far as the collections gathered by native persons and organizations are concerned, they should be regarded as anthologies, in which the best known gen̩dings and the favourite pieces of their publishers have been gathered together.

The collection of the Jogya kraton [2]), on the other hand, appears to aim at bringing together within its volumes all the classical gen̩dings from the Principalities. If it has succeeded in doing so, then the entire Central-Javanese (or, at any rate, Jogyanese) classical court-repertoire should

---

[1]) Himself one of the few composers of new gen̩dings.

[2]) As was already mentioned in the Foreword, His Highness the Sultan of Jogya, HAMENGKU BUWANA VIII, has been pleased to cause a copy of this collection to be made, and to present it to the Royal Batavia Society as an addition to its musicological collection. [**291**B, **402**B]

[3]) [**54**A, **59**B, **89**B, C, **291** B-C, **319**A, **402**B]

comprise rather more than 500 pieces, 200 of which are genḍing pélog, and 300 odd genḍing sléndro [1]).

In the existing genḍing collections we frequently find, in addition to the nuclear theme, also the interpunctuating beats (*ḍongḍing genḍing*) being indicated; sometimes the *bonang panembung* beats, and generally, in addition to this, the essential sounds of the *kenḍangan*. This is not strictly necessary, at any rate not as regards the colotomy, which is, of course, stereotyped, *i.e.* inherent to all compositions of the group to which the genḍing in question belongs. The same applies in most cases to the kenḍangan (only *not* in the case of the *genḍing parikan*). The necessity of fixing these elements of composition is, therefore, less urgent than is the case with the cantus firmus.

The official form of the Jogya kraton-notation also gives, so far as the instrumental parts are concerned, some additional indications with respect to tempo and to the pitch (whether high or low register) of the variations to be played around the nuclear theme.

Until a short time ago, when Western influences began to make themselves felt, the parts of the paraphrasing instruments were left without special notation (with the exception, that is, of the above-mentioned sparse summary indications concerning the register, in the Jogya notation). In a way, this was quite justified. Whereas, as we said before, the nuclear theme, the colotomy, and to a certain extent, also the kenḍangan in a given genḍing are "constants", the players of the panerusan are free to follow their own inspiration in shaping their paraphrases. All they have to do is to see to it that they sound the melody-tone whenever there is a balungan tone of a higher order—*i.e.* one of the principal tones of the nuclear theme; one might also call them interpunctuating tones of a lower order (generally, each fourth tone of the cantus firmus). For the rest they may give free rein to their fantasy. (But, as in so many expressions of Eastern art, so here, fancy has a powerful restraint in tradition). [**107**B–C, **167**B]

Now there have been serious objections against the fixing by notation of these panerusan parts, which was done for the first time by R. M. JAYADIPURA, in collaboration with LINDA BANDARA; and these objections

---

1) PADMASUSASTRA mentions in his work *Tatachara* (**291**), for Solo, the names of 413 genḍings (mainly in sléndro), which include—as is also the case with the Jogya kraton collection—a number of ladrangans.

came both from native as from European side. It is feared, in fact, that in this way the capacity to create beautiful paraphrases and ornaments will in the long run be lost, just as, ever since the figured bass made room for the complete parts written out by the composer himself, Western pianists generally have undoubtedly lost much of their capacity for creative improvisation owing to lack of practice. Again, the notation of the panerusan of a recognized, talented, and universally honoured musician might lead to a general imitation of his "manner" and thereby to the stereotyping of the ornamental figuration. True, the inclination thereto is sure to exist all the same; but it would then be indulged much more easily, and in a much wider field.

The use of written music by the players is, even to this day, among the exceptions [1]). The notation script serves almost exclusively as a kind of "file" for the conservation of the compositions; accordingly, none of the existing systems of notation is at all widely spread.

Of the Javanese music-scripts that have come to our knowledge those of the Jogya pangéran ADIWINATA (brother of the seventh Sultan) and of P. A. A. PAKU ALAM V are the oldest (**99**); the Jogya *"ruitjesschrift"* ("ruitje" is Dutch for "small square", or "check", "ruitjesschrift", therefore means as much as "checkered script") is the finest and most curious. It is supposed to have been designed in 1889 by P. A. PURWADININGRAT (died 1924), and further elaborated by R. T. WIRAGUNA (died 1936) (**33, 297**) [2]).

---

1) It is only since a short time ago that some notationscript or other is being used in several of the courses of instruction in gamelan playing. I witnessed playing from musical notation in 1932 in the kabupatèns of Magelang and Demak.

2) According to the title of the copy, just mentioned, of the Jogya "Pakem wirama" presented by His Highness HAMENGKU BUWANA VIII to the Royal Batavia Society, it might also be possible that R. T. KERTANAGARA was one of the inventors of the chequered notation. The whole of the title, translated into English, reads as follows:

By command of His Highness INGKANG SINUHUN KANJÈNG SULTAN AMENGKU BUWANA VIII (etc.), order has been given for the manufacture, for His Highness, of a book Pakem Wirama; the musical melodies of the gamelan, laras suréndro as well as pélog, *according to the work of* K. R. T. KERTANAGARA, Bupati Nayaka, Lurah Wedana Bumija, at Jogyakarta, started in the year Alip 1819 (A.D. 1889), for the purpose of saving the original and ancient musical melodies from being lost, and, further, collected by the Regent's younger brother, K. R. T. WIRAGUNA, Bupati-Pepatih to the court of Jogyakarta, with the assistance of the following lurah's and panéwu's of the gamelan players in the Kraton at Jogyakarta: M. L. BRANGTAMARA, R. L. PUSPAKANTI, M. P. DEMANG AGONGENDING and R. L. BABARLAYAR;

In P. ADIWINATA's system the names of the tones of the nuclear theme are written one below the other in vertical rows. The colotomic tones are noted at the side, with the words Gong, Keṭuk, etc. (**99**, plate I).

The system of the prince PAKU ALAM V [1]) (ill. 127) (**99**, plate II) is more like a notation in the European sense. The initial letters of the names of the tones are each written at a given height, on a (? fictitious) [2]) stave, (in which, in the proper Javanese manner, the high tones are placed below, and the low ones above), and are then connected by vertical lines.

The Jogya kraton-notation [3]) possesses *vertical* staves, of, respectively, 6 lines in sléndro and 7 in pélog. These staves are crossed by horizontal lines (*garis wirama*), at distances of one *keteg* each time (as stated before, *keteg* means rhythmic unit, actually: heart-beat). At the crossing-point of the stave- and keteg-lines—or, as the case may be, on the stave-lines just between two keteg-lines, *i.e.* when one keteg is filled by more than one balungan tone, which happens, among others things, in *ngenchot*, to be described presently)—the tones of the cantus firmus are noted by means or round dots; in such a way that the lowest tone of the scale (*i.e.* the *penunggul* in pélog, and the *barang* in sléndro) is placed upon the line farthest to the left, and the rest of the tones in order of sequence on the other lines. The sléndro-stave, possessing 6 lines, has room for the sléndro octave inclusing the closing octave-note (*barang alit*); the 7-lined pélog-stave, for the complete pélog octave *without* the octave-note. The colotomic beats are indicated to the left; the drum-signs to the right of the stave, by certain particular signs. One of the variants (ill. 128), for that matter, indicates the colotomic beats in another way, *i.e. in* the stave and by means of a change in the shape of the signs serving for the nuclear theme tones that are played at the same time. This is especially done when it is desired to reserve enough space by the side of the stave for the reproduction of any text to be sung to the music.

all with the approval of the Regent's Father, K.G.P.A. MANGKUBUMI, etc., First Prince of the Blood of Jogyakarta, Son of His Highness Sultan AMENGKU BUWANA VI, and by order of His Highness Sultan AMENGKU BUWANA VII at Jogyakarta.

Written at Jogyakarta, on Tuesday-Kliwon, the 24th of the month Muharram, in the year Dal 1863 (= the 31st of May, 1932) (**297**) [**291**B]

[1]) GRONEMAN attributes this notation to PAKU ALAM IV; but according to SURYAPUTRA (**350**, p. 383) this is based upon a misunderstanding.

[2]) In GRONEMAN's treatise, an example of this notation is depicted *without*, and in an essay by R. M. SURYAPUTRA (**358**, p. 382), one *with* a stave. Our own illustration 127 has been taken from the latter.

[3]) [**89**B-C, **291**B]

With regard to these staves, since a number of 6 or 7 lines presents some difficulty in analyzing the script at a glance, we often find, in sléndro, the 4th, and in pélog, the 4th and 5th lines being printed in heavy type.

Since the staves cover only a single octave, any vocal melody—which usually extends over more than two octaves—could, if the notation-system in question were to be used for the reproduction of such a melody, be represented only in a "folded-back" form, *i.e.* condensed into one octave; this is circumvented, however, by giving the notes, whenever the theme exceeds the limits of the middle octave, an appendix in the form of a tiny stroke directed downwards on the slant, and pointing to the left when the melody moves to the lower, and to the right when it moves to the higher octave, thus:  . The latter sign may also be found pointing upwards:  (cf. App. *4a*).

In instrumental scores these strokes appended to certain notes may also occur, although the nuclear theme, as beaten upon the saron or the demung, is limited to a single octave, and can therefore manage without those accessory lines. In this, however, the said lines signify that the gambang variation-play is expected to move towards and in the lower (*ngandap*) or the higher (*ngelik*) register; ornamental playing to nuclear tones without any appendix takes place in the middle register (*tengah*).

Further, a repetition of a passage is indicated by placing the part to be repeated between vertical lines, and stating above it the number of times the passage in question is to be played.

The signs used in the kraton notation script to represent the colotomic beats are the following:

A. when placed *by the side of* the stave:

 keṭuk (= pasangan [1]) *ṭa*);

 kenong (pasangan *na*);

 kempul (capital letter *Pa*);

 wela (pasangan *wa*);

[1]) A *pasangan* is an old form of a syllable-sign (*aksara*), which, when placed either behind or under the preceeding aksara, renders it vowel-less.

 gong + kenong (stylized combination of the pasangan ***na*** and the aksara *ga*);

 kenong + kempul (stylized combination of the pasangan ***na*** and the cap. *Pa*);

B. when incorporated ***in*** the stave, as,

 or  keṭuk;

 or  kenong;

 or  kempul;

 or  gong (+ kenong).

The signs for the principal drum beats are:

 bem;

 bem-beat starting a ***stringendo***;

 bem-beat starting a ***ritardando***;

 ḍunḍung;

 *of*  ḍunḍung-beat starting a ***stringendo***;

 ḍunḍung-beat starting a ***ritardando***;

 tepak;

 { ketek
kempyang.

Further, there are the following signs:

 which, when written on the crossings of stave- and

keteg-lines—either or not combined with a balungan-note—serve to indicate beats on the bonang panembung and suchlike (cf. App. 5 to 9 incl.). The variants given of the sign are equal in value; they exist side-by-side, in order that, when they are to be hooked on to a balungan-note already having an appendix, or altered in shape in any way, it may still be possible to apply the panembung sign in a distinctly visible manner.

Yet another kind of signs are the following:

 , serving sometimes to mark a change of tempo (both acceleration and retardation), the place in the gending being sufficient indication of whether a ritardando (*suwuk*) or a stringendo (*sesegan*) is intended [1]);

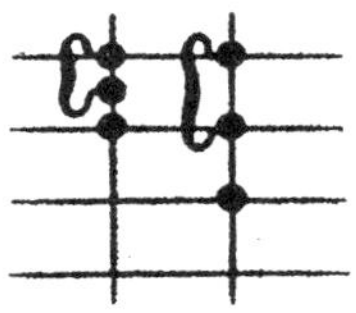

a sign for the muting of the first two of three tones of the same height, the first two of which each last a half, and the third a whole keteg; or the first two may last one, and the third, two keteg. This is called *ngenchot*, and may be represented as follows:  or  (cf. App. 5 to 9 incl.) [2]);

× (*chiri chawang*(*an*)), indicating that, from that moment onwards, a *pancher* may, or must, be beaten.

Finally, in combined orchestral and vocal notations, one sometimes sees the vocal part marked in red ink, and by means of the signs:

serving respectively to indicate whether the tone represented thereby should be sung in the lower (*tumedak* = downwards), the middle (*tengah*), or the higher (*minggah* = upwards) register. Occasionally, however, the mere sign × is used to render the vocal melody in a combined notation of this kind [3]).

1) Cf. p. 205, note. [*S23]

2) *Vide* also p. 167.

3) A fundamental discussion of musical notations of native vocal music may be found in HALUSA (**105**).

His article was written to comply with a request from the Neth.-Indies Government for the composition of a musical script suitable for the notation of native vocal music.

The author finally suggests a system of notation which closely follows the Kraton chequered script, that in his opinion fully satisfies the requirements of native singing. If the war had not intervened this new script would have been given a trial at the elementary schools for natives in the Province of East-Java.

This latter sign has yet another function: when, in a geṇḍing, a given passage is beaten twice in succession with only slight modifications, and the abbreviated notation by means of repeatlines is made use of, the sign × serves to mark those balungan-tones through which the nuclear melody deviates in the repetition.

It is sufficiently clear from the commentary given at the head of the geṇḍing-notation concerned which of the three functions the sign × performs in it.

This concludes our discussion of the Jogya "checquered" script.

The system of the late R. M. SURYAPUTRA (**358**) (ill. 129 and 130)—four-lined for sléndro and five-lined for pélog, preceded by a general four-lined draft (**351**, **353**), as well as that of JAYADIPURA-LINDA BANDARA—in its final form seven-lined for both tonal systems (the pélog tones being written *on*, and the sléndro tones *between* the lines) (App. *10*)—have been inspired by the European system of notation [1]). Both may be used, the latter having been applied by its designers, for complete orchestral scores. WALTER SPIES has shown that the just described Jogya kraton script, too—with slight modifications in the notation of some of the parts—is practicable for orchestral scores. His example has been followed by some of the Jogya niyaga's, a few amongst whom were able to write down their parts note-perfect, and to combine the different parts into a score.

The newest system of notation, which uses (horizontal) staves, was designed recently by R. M. A. KUSUMADINATA. His system is five-lined for sléndro and four-lined for pélog; upon these staves room has been reserved for the "vocal" tones *panangis* and *pamiring* in pélog and for the five intermediary tones in sléndro.

Mention should also be made of a number of cipher-scripts, all of them more or less after the manner of the Chevé-method, and one of which has struck root more especially in Solo (**54**, **78**, **79**, **343**, **402**A) [2]) and Magelang (App. *11*) as well as some others, applied in recent years in music primers designed by native teachers and intended for use in the schools (that by R. M. A. KUSUMADINATA (**170–173** incl.) being peculiar that a tone has a higher figure according as it sounds lower); and we may finally place on record that, in addition to the answers sent in to the Java Institute compe-

[1]) *Vide* also LINDA BANDARA's articles upon the same subject in "Weekblad van Nederlandsch-Indië", and "De Taak" (**15** and **16**).

[2]) [**248**C, **302**K-R, **319**B-C, **377**E]

tition already mentioned (**35**), one or two others were submitted to the jury; they, however, did not open any further perspectives.

During the last years of his life, R. M. JAYADIPURA designed yet another musical script, namely for the gamelan- society "Mardi Guna", which was under his direction. This script uses a kind of do-re-mi-fa-sol notation, the chosen tone-syllables *be, ja, ḍa, pe, gang, ne* and *ba* having been derived from the names of the tones, as shown by the table on p. 102. The interpunctuating tones are, as in the Jogya kraton-notation, indicated by the word *gong* in Javanese characters: ꦒꦺꦴꦁ, for the gong beat; the pasangan *ta*: ꧀ꦠ for the keṭuk beat; the pasangan *na*: ꧀ꦤ for the kenong beat; the pasangan *pa*: ꧀ꦥ for the kempul beat, and the pasangan *wa*: ꧀ꦮ for *wela*.

This system, therefore, is actually nothing than a simplification of the notation of P. ADIWINATA; the main reason why R. M. JAYADIPURA introduced it was that the players should not forget the names of the tones, which might otherwise be in danger of complete extinction owing to the exclusive use of ciphered systems [1]).

---

[1]) After the above was written I came across another, fairly complicated notation, done in red, blue and black and designed by RADÈN GUNADI, formerly dancing master at the Holland-Indian School for Teachers at Blitar. In this notation, the balungan- and ḍongḍings-tones, as well as two of the drum beats (*bem* and *gen-ḍung*), are represented by different dots and figures—partly in red and blue—on imaginary staves, and then connected by more or less wavy, vertical lines. This script might accordingly be characterized as "wave-line-degree" script. [**101A**]

It is probable that more of such notation systems, designed for the inventor's own use, may be found in Java. They are chiefly significant as being symptomatic for a widespread desire to attain to the formation of a clear and generally acceptable standard script. It would, in the writer's opinion, be a desirable thing if the Jogya chequered notation were generally adopted.

Chapter V

WEST-JAVA

a. Introduction

(a comparison of Sundanese with Javanese and Balinese music both instrumental and vocal; the impression made on the Western mind; something about vocal music)

Although music as cultivated in West Java differs in many respects from that of Central Java—a difference running parallel with the difference in national character (Central Java is purely Javanese; West Java largely Sundanese)—yet there is, so far as the instruments used are concerned, so much similarity between the two that the description of western-Javanese musical instruments, after all that has been said about those of Central Java, may be relatively concise. In the chapter dealing with Javanese music, moreover, we have often given particulars of Sundanese music (*vide* the General Register in vol. II, s.v. Sunda(nese)). There exist, after all, only few typically Sundanese instruments—if any at all—and the fact that, in addition to those, a number of instruments also known in Central and East Java are dealt with only in this chapter is due to the circumstance that they are found in so much greater numbers in western Java.

The Sundanese racial character is less complex, less stylized, more open and a little more rustic than the Javanese. In accordance with this, music in the Sunda districts is, generally speaking, simpler of construction, and the orchestras are less comprehensive. The vocal music, too (**170—173, 197, 324**), differs from that of Central Java: it would seem to me to be less nasal, and it makes a more robust impression on the western ear. This applies to the various vocal utterances with which I made acquaintance in West Java in the course of several years, and in the first place to what is called *alok* [1]), *i.e.* the after-piece, or closing chant following a song. An example of this is the alok *Ètok èyong* (App. *52*). Further, Sundanese singing seems to have been subject to a fairly strong influence from both Arabian and European singing; from the latter, through the schools, and from the former owing to the fact that so many from this thoroughly Mohammedan country have made the hadsj, the pilgrimage to Mecca.

For the rest, many of our general observations concerning the Javanese vocal music (p. 122 *et seq.*) also apply to that of the Sunda districts. Examples of Sundanese melodics for solo voice are reproduced at the end of this book (App. *46*, *50* and *53*). The reader will observe that these examples evince a strong "fifth-consciousness". For additional details concerning the scales used we refer to Chapter II, and to **197**, and **200**; for the various kinds of vocal music, to the description given below on p. 392 *et seq.*, the principal data of which I owe to the kindness and thorough knowledge of RADÈN MACHYAR ANGGA KUSUMADINATA [2]). A comprehensive survey of Sundanese versification may be found in the work by R. SACHADIBRATA (**324**), and an excellent disquisition about Sundanese poetry in that by HIDDING (**114**, p. 110 *et seq.*).

Taken as a whole, Sundanese music stands closer to the Balinese than to the Javanese art. Thus, when some Balinese songs were performed before the then Regent of Bandung, he was struck by the marked similarity in character and style of this music to that of his own people, whereas, during the hearing of Javanese tembang, and the Javanese manner of singing, it was precisely the differences that forced themselves upon this atention. In the same way, CHOKORDA SUKAWATI, the then South-Balinese member of the *Volksraad* (N. I. parliament), found very much more resemblance in the Sundanese songs heard by him, to those of his own island, than in Javanese vocal music.

To some small extent—chiefly as regards the districts around Batavia

[1]) The general signification of *alok* is scream, shout, call (*e.g.* "hela!", "murder!", etc.).

[2]) The only important exception to this are the descriptions and analyses of the *lagam kulon* and its scales, on p. 395 *et seq.*, taken from the study "Over Soendaneesche zangmuziek" (About Sundanese vocal music) (**197**), published before my meeting, and subsequent collaboration, with R. M. A. KUSUMADINATA.

—this closer kinship between Balinese and Sundanese music may, perhaps, be traced to direct influences; wealthy servants of the *Kompenie* would sometimes, in former centuries, keep orchestras whose players were Balinese slaves. This is shown, for example, in a passage from CORNELIS DE BRUIN's "Reizen" ("Travels") (1774) (**56**), where, in a description of the estate of Mr. Kasteleyn, at Meester Cornelis, he says: "this is the place where the Gomspelers (= gong-players) make themselves heard, who are Balinese slaves". We also refer to our remarks below (p. 382) relating to the gamelan *Lilingong*.

Westeners, too, are more accessible to Sundanese than to Javanese music, partly also because the former employs scales whose intervals (Sund.: ***raras***) deviate only very little from the western-diatonic ones, more especially as regards the mèlog- and nyorog-scales of the kachapi, which are frequently heard (**197**, **200**) (cf. below, pp. 396 and 397).

The uniformity in the nomenclature of scale-degrees (Sund.: ***hambalan, wilahan***), scales and instruments, so characteristic of the Javanese region proper, is largely lacking in West Java, probably owing to the fact that a strong central authority covering a large section of the country, such as Java proper has known for many centuries, was generally—may be even permanently—unknown in the Sunda districts. Small states such as Taruma, Galuh, and even Pajajaran, to name only the best known, covered only a limited territory; and the cultural influence emanating from the kraton has evidently not succeeded by a very long way in penetrating as deeply as that of the Central and Eastern Javanese kratons did in their own field.

b. Instruments

(188, 190, 197)

Practically all instruments described in Chapter IV under *c* (p. 135 *et seq.*) are also known to some extent in West Java. Some of them, however, occur only sporadically, for instance, it may be, only in the large gamelans owned by different Regents and wealthy persons; these gamelans invariably originate from Central Java, and are not used by the common people.

I. Idiophones

With respect to the forms already discussed above, the following remarks may suffice:

a. the *gong* is here called *goöng*;

b. the *kempul* is sometimes called either *katiwul* (*Chiamis*), *welèri* (Indramayu), or *goöng leutik* (= small gong);

c. the *bonang* is generally called *kolènang*; in Banten, *kromong* or (when, as is usually the case, it is one-rowed) *rèntèng* (= in one row); their beating-knobs (Jav.: *penchu*) are here called either *pihul* or *papenchelut*. The Sundanese nayaga's distinguish two ways of playing the kolènang, called respectively *dikemprang*—quiet playing, with beats at distances of one *keteg*—and *dicharuk*, the more lively, more richly ornamented, paraphrasing manner of playing;

d. the highest *bonang* (Jav.: *panerus*) is here and there called either *setukat* or *gembyang*, but, more frequently, *rinchik*, from which latter word is derived the term *rinchikan*, denoting both the preludes and the interludes on the kolènang;

e. in the Kasepuhan at Cheribon, *kepyak* is the name used for an instrument made of three bonang kettles, two of which are tuned unisono to *singgul* (Jav.: *bem*), and the third to *barang* (Jav.: *nem*);

f. in Indramayu and Cheribon, the *keṭuk* is sometimes called *chengkung*, and, if it is of a somewhat heavier type, *kebluk*;

g. the *saron demung* is called either *kedemung*, *panerus* [1]), or *penurung* (Indramayu);

h. the highest *saron* (Jav. *panerus*, *peking*, etc.) is usually called, in the more easterly parts of West Java (Cheribon, Indramayu), *titil*, but also *peking*;

i. the *gambang gangsa*, in Indramayu, is also called either *dempling* or *kedempling*;

j. the keys of the gambang kayu are manufactured, in the Sunda districts, either from *suanking*- or from *mangrawan*-wood (imported from Central Java), or else from *huru konèng*, *huru batu*, or bamboo (*e.g.* the striped variety: *awi surat* and *awi gombong*); of these, the suangking- and mangrawan-keys are held to be the finest, and after this come the ones made of huru (haur) konèng, which grows in West Java;

---

1) In contradistinction to the Javanese use of that name, which, as is known, denotes precisely the *highest* saron.

k. the *gendèr* is found only extremely rarely, *i.e.* exclusively in a few gamelans of the Regents, in which case it may also go under the name of *k(e)liningan* (*i.e.* Jav.: *klenéngan*), constituting, as it does—*vide* above, p. 175, 274 *et seq.*—one of the principal components of the *gamelan klenéngan*;

l. the *gong kemoḍong*, here invariably of the one-keyed type, is called *goöng buyung* (*buyung* = earthenware pot) (ill. 152, *sub* d); [*S65]

m. the *ke(chi)chèr* is known here under the name of *chechèmprès*;

n. the *kechrèk* [1]), known in West Java, in contrast to Central and East Java, as a regular orchestral element (serving to mark the time, together with the kenḍangan) is called *kekechrèk* when consisting of more than two tinkling plates;

o. the metal cattle-bell is called, as in Java proper, *genta*, but the wooden variety, *kolotok*;

p. the slit drum bears the name of *kohkol* (ill. 132), and a combination of a few of these instruments—in that case always made of bamboo, and small in size—that of *keplèk*;

q. rice-block stamping (Java, amongst other names: *koṭèkan*) is here called either *gondang* or *tutunggulan*; [*S34, 65]

r. musical beating on the water (Jav.: *chiblon* [2]) or *ketimpung*) is here called (*i*)*chikibung* [2]) or *dèngdo*; the low sounds either *blung* or *indung*, and the high ones either *bling* or *anak*;

s. the *rinḍing* (jew's harp) is here called *karinding* [3]), and the small tongue of the bamboo- or arènwood form usually finishes into *two*, and sometimes even *three* protuberances [4]), so that it reminds one of a fork, between whose teeth the frame—which, also in the Sundanese instrument, encloses the said tongue all round—penetrates with one or two teeth. Another difference between the Sundanese and the Javanese instruments consists in the presence of a bamboo tube open at both ends, whose upper end is brought to the mouth when playing (in a squatting position), and whose bottom end is rested on the ground, for the purpose of slightly strengthening the rather weak sound of the karinding (ill. 131). In the

---

[1]) Mus. Arch. Bat. Nos. 432 and 444.

[2]) As Dr. PURBACHARAKA informs me, *chiblon* comes from *chiblu*, which, in its turn, derives from the ancient Javanese word *si-bu* = "to plunge oneself". *Ichikibung* is, ethymologically, i + chi = ki (= si) + bu(ng) = to plunge into the water.

[3]) Ind. Inst. No. A 4483; Mus. Arch. Bat. Nos 440 and 441. [*S65]

[4]) Ind. Inst. No. 1603/1 and Mus. Arch. Bat. No. 431.

Tasik district the jew's harp is called *karinding* only when cut from arèn-wood; when made from bamboo it is there called *karèng*.

Thus far as regards the forms already discussed. We will now give some particulars about a few species of idiophones which are not, or less often, met with in the Javanese territory proper, *i.e.*, in the first place, the shake-**angklung** (ill. 121, 136, 149, 150 and 151).

Although this well-known instrument was, and/or is, spread over the whole of Java, Madura and Bali, as well as part of Sumatra and Borneo, it is not, at present, found anywhere so generally as in the Sundanese mountain districts, for which reason it is often wrongly taken to be a typically Sundanese instrument. In recent times, however, it is still reported as having been seen in the territory of Banyumas, Cheribon, Brebes, Purbalingga, Wanasaba, Bagelén (ill. 121), Jogya, Solo; in the regencies Panaraga, Trenggalèk, Tulungagung (ill. 136), Majakerta, Sidaärja, Grissee, Surabaya, and Prabalingga; as well as in Madura [1]), Bali [2]), South-Sumatra [3]) and S.W. Borneo [4]), whilst it is probable—although I am not at present able to state this for certain—that these instruments also occur, if only sporadically, in the majority of the other Javanese regencies.

As we know, the shake-angklung consists of two or three bamboo segments, usually tuned to as many octaves (Sund.: *beulit*). Their upper part has been partly removed to about half their lengths so as to form a sort of tongue, and they are closed at the bottom by a node. They are suspended vertically and mobile inside a bamboo frame. Their bottom ends are hampered in their movements by means of small protuberances, which can slide to and fro for a short distance inside a slit made into the bottom frame-tube. The bamboo tubes are made to sound through the shocks caused by shaking the instrument to and fro. The sound is curiously bright; a kind of "mellow clucking." [5]).

It should be noted that the air-column in the tubular part of the mobile bamboo segments produces, when being blown, the same tone-pitch as the entire segments (*i.e.* tubular part plus tongue), when being beaten or shaken.

1) Illustration in VAN EERDE, "De volken van Nederlandsch-Indië", vol. II, p. 192.

2) Mr. P. GEDIKING there came across one or two specimens. Cf. also "Djawa" XI, Nijverheidsrapport (Report on Industry), I, pp. 86 to 89 incl., and **260**, in which there are also some illustrations.

3) Musicological Archives, Photograph No. 603; Leyden Cat. No. 40/58.

4) Ind. Inst. No. 1297/1, 2. Their presence in Borneo was first revealed by a communication to the author from the mining engineer KROL.

5) Good records of angklung music are those made by Beka, No. B 15723.

A number—usually either 9 or 14 —of such instruments, all of different format, and therefore of different pitch, belong together, and form a pentatonic tone-sequence extending either over one octave + 4 tones or over 2 octaves + 4 tones, in either two- or threefold octave-doubling, sometimes, seemingly, *ringkung* (*vide* pp. 37 *et seq.*, and 406), but mostly sléndro (or, at any rate "slendroïd"), as under:

Scale of an angklung set from Tasikmalaya (N. I. Musicological Archives, No. 470) [1].

174		196		217		247½		280		355		392		447		504
I	*104*	II	*176*	III	*228*	IV	*213*	V	*411*	VI	*172*	VII	*227*	VIII	*208*	IX
2		3		4		5		1′		2′		3′		4′		5′

When played, the angklungs are either held in the hand (ill. 127), in which case a single player can naturally handle only two instruments at most, or suspended, in scale-sequence, on to a long-drawn bamboo yoke (*kakancho*) (ill. 150), with the result that two or three players will then suffice.

The angklung—at any rate the variety tuned in octaves—is, in the first place, a paraphrasing instrument. But, as each instrument separately can only sound one tone (doubling on the octave) we get a kind of mosaic-melodics: the players between them build up the, usually very simple and "asthmatic", paraphrasing *motifs*, which serve as a background to the melody, generally blown on the *tarompet*.

Here follows, in a transcription by BERNARD YZERDRAAT, one of these angklung melody-textures, borrowed from the record Odeon 91413:

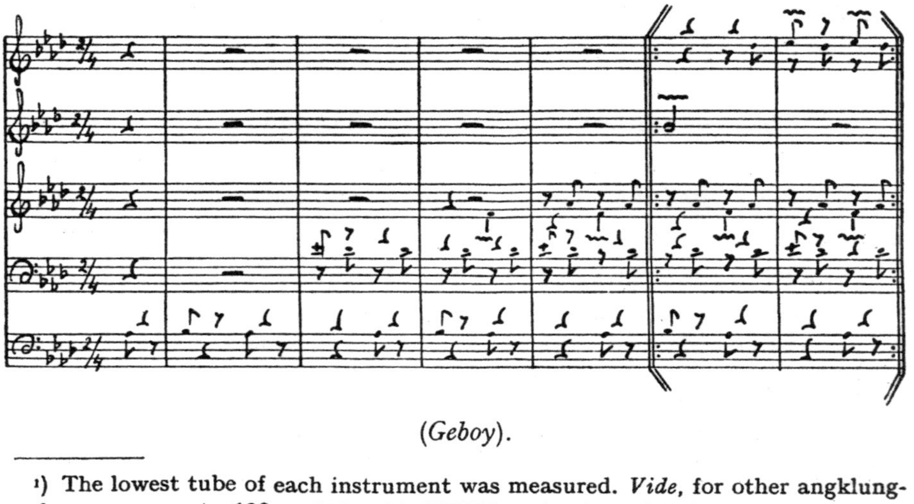

(*Geboy*).

[1]) The lowest tube of each instrument was measured. *Vide*, for other angklung-scale measurements, **193**, p. 500, table XVIII, scales 6 to 12 incl.

One may sometimes come across gamelans—both in the Sunda districts and further east in Javanese territory, especially in Bagelén—in which the sarons, bonangs, jengglong (the latter only in West Java) and gambang have been replaced by ranges of 5, or 7 angklungs, suspended on a yoke.

Further, one occasionally comes across an angklung in the hands of men on guard in a kampong, although the *kentongan* is, for such men, a more customary signalling instrument.

Among the South-Banten Baduy's, it is said to be the custom to shake three or four angklungs at the finish of the work upon the *huma sérang*, *i.e.* the sacred arable land, on the occasion of the *kawalu* feast.

In Bagelén (*i.e.* the regencies Purwareja, Kutaärja and Kebumèn, west of Jogya), another, different type of angklung may be met with in addition to the ordinary octave-angklung. True, in outside appearance they resemble the Sundanese and other Javanese angklungs, but they are often made of another kind of bamboo, namely of the spotted kind (*bamboo tutul*, or panther-bamboo), and their (invariably three) sound-tubes are *not* tuned in octaves, but form some chord or other, as each of them produces a different tone.

Measurement of the three Bagelén instruments belonging to the N. I. Musicological Archives yielded the following result:

No. 517:	397	(349) [1]			608		734
	I	(I)	*738*	(*961*)	II	*326*	III
No. 518:	370	(416) [1]			552		740
	I	(I)	*692*	(*489*)	II	*508*	III
No. 519:	489				700		828
	I		*621*		II	*290*	III

These chord-angklungs also occur in some of the kampongs in the Residency of West-Borneo [2]) and in the districts round Martapura in South-Borneo [3]) (where the population, as a matter of fact, is held to be of, at least partly, Javanese origin).

The same can be said of South-Sumatra, from which territory the Leyden Museum acquired a specimen [4]).

In Bagelén they may be found in the small orchestras accompanying the so-called *jatilan* (ill. 121) (**141, 141A**).

---

1) a strong partial tone, almost as powerful as the sound here taken as fundamental tone. 2) Ind. Inst. Cat. Nos. 1297/1–2.

3) Ind. Inst. Cat. Nos. 1767/1–3 4) Leyden Cat. No. 40/58.

Angklungs combined together into a small orchestra—either or not in conjunction with yet other instruments (dogdog, tarompèt, goöng buyung, etc.) usually bear, in the Sunda districts, a special proper name as well. The two largest and deepest-sounding instruments are called either *indung, jong-jrong,* or *genjung*; the two following them in pitch: *ambruk* (= shake together); No. 5: *èngklok* (onomatopoea for an instrument sounding short intermediary tones, like drops, as it were); Nos. 6 and 7: *panchèr* (literally: main root, stem of a root; this refers to the function of these tones in the melody; *vide* above p. 168); Nos. 8 and 9, *roèl* (= to flounder), or *anak.* MAYER (**270**) mentions, for Central Java, as bridal music, an ensemble of three angklungs, called, respectively, *byang, èngklok* or *ganchang,* and *tangklit.*

Another instrument, also making use of bamboo tubes cut off on the slant at one end in the way of a goose-quill, and closed by a node at the other end, is the **chalung** [1]) (ill. 137 and 138). It is mainly limited to-day to the West-Javanese mountain districts; formerly, however, it was spread over a larger region, being found, for example, in Panaraga (East Java) as recently as 25 years ago. [*S[34,65]]

It consists of either twelve, fourteen or sixteen such tubes, tied together with cords, in a horizontal position, much like a rope-ladder; from above downwards these tubes get lower in pitch, and therefore increase in dimensions. During playing the instrument is hung by its upper end somewhere on to the wall of a house or against a tree, the lower end being tied either to the left knee of the sitting, or round the waist of the standing player. It is beaten with two faintly sickle-shaped wooden sticks of slightly different size (*panakol*), whose beating part is wrapped round with cotton material. The instrument is always tuned to some five-toned scale, usually in sléndro, or, at any rate, "sléndroid":

Chalung from Tasikmalaya, (Musicological Archives, No. 469) [2]).

185		232		256		276		339		373		458		515	
I	*392*	II	*170*	III	*130*	IV	*356*	V	*166*	VI	*356*	VII	*202*	VIII	*212*
582		680		746		920.									
IX	*270*	X	*160*	XI	*363*	XII.									

1) Ind. Inst., Nos. 1030/4, 1035/1, 1045/1, 1045/5, 1055/1; Mus. Arch. Bat., No. 469.

2) For other chalung-scale measurements *vide* **193**, p. 500, Table XVIII, scales 1 to 5 incl.

In the case of instruments comprising more than one octave, such as this chalung and the "yoke" of angklungs described above (p. 362), the octaves are distinguished from one-another by special names. In the Sunda districts, three succeeding octaves bear the following names from high to low: *petit* (= tail, extremity) or *leutik* (= small); *tong* or *tengah* (= middle), and *galimer* or *gedè* (= great) (**170**). KUSUMADINATA (**171** p. 12), however, also mentions a division into four, at any rate on the gambang; this was referred to on p. 186.

We may further note that chalung-players do not usually refer to the tones of the highest octave of their instrument by the ordinary names, but designate them collectively by the term *petit(an)*.

We have already made mention (p. 189) of transitional form towards the gambang, *i.e.* the *gagambangan*, which, it is said, occurs in the Tasik territory, as well as (p. 292) of the Banyumas chalungs, mounted and assembled into a small orchestra (ill. 123).

Another variety of the chalung possesses only a few tubes (from two to five), cut down on the slant to half their length, which, firmly bound together at short distances by means of cross-laths, are suspended side by side. They are identical in shape with some of the instruments of the Sumpyuh *gamelan jemblung* described above (p. 197 *et seq.*).

Such tubes are sometimes played separately, as shown in ill. 154 (third man from right).

As in Madura, Bali, Flores, New Guinea, and probably other islands in the Indian Archipelago, we also find in the Preanger mountain country the so-called **stamping drums**, consisting of a bamboo internodium open at the top and closed by a node at the bottom, which tube is made to vibrate and produce sound by letting it drop perpendicularly from a moderate height on to a hard surface (stone). Each of the players—in the Preanger, usually, little goat-herds—manipulates two of such little instruments, of unequal size, and, therefore, pitch. In Tasikmalaya the instrument bears the name of *kẹndang awi*, and in the Bandung district, it appears, that of *kinchir* (which, for that matter, also means *reel*). Water-carrying women, too, often use their water-bamboos (*lodong*) as musical instruments in the way described above.

A curious, rustic instrument is the **rengkong** (ill. 140), or grating bamboo [1]). During the harvest festival in honour of Dèvi Sri, Goddess of the Rice, sheaves of *padi* (*i.e.* cut rice) are suspended, by means of loops made out of a narrow bamboo strip and coconut string, loosely hung across the slits cut length-ways into the side of a number of heavy bamboo internodia, carried on the harvesters' shoulders. When the men begin to march along, these bunches of padi start to swing to the rhythm of the walkers' steps, and, by their friction against the bamboo, draw therefrom some not quite unpleasant sounds.

The rengkong invariably occurs in pairs; when more than one pair is used, the whole collection is designated by the name of *saäleutan*. They usually serve as accompanying instruments to the *hatong* music, about which more later.

The territory where the rengkong may be found appears to be: Banten, South Batavia, the whole of the Preanger, South-Cheribon, West- and South-Pekalongan, and Banyumas.

Brandts Buys (**42**) mentions, for Banjarnagara—and gives an illustration of—yet another form of grating pikulan, called *rungkut*, and whose sound-producing part is located centrally (on the carrier's shoulder). Another name for this rungkut is *oṭot* [2]). According to Dr. Purbacharaka, this latter form of grating bamboo is also known among the population of the Solo valley. The sound is rendered, *e.g.* in wayang-tales, by *engkèt-engkèt*.

An instrument which, apparently, is also limited to Western Java, is the **degung** (ill. 159, *sub a*); it consists of a range of six fairly small gongs, suspended, in a row in the same plane, from a common stand. This instrument has bestowed its name on a small gamelan of which it forms an indispensable element, and outside which it is never found: the *gamelan degung*.

The tuning of the 6 small gongs is not always the same; they sound some, but not always the same, tones of the lower two or three octaves. The gong with the lowest sound serves as *goöng gedè*, in case this should not be available itself. The other five—and, if a separate large gong is present, al six of them—fulfil the rôle played in the Javanese gamelan by the *gendèr panembung* or *slenṭem gantung*; they double on the octave, and accentuate, at regular brief intervals, the tones of the nuclear theme, *e.g.*

[1]) Ind. Inst., No. 1029/14 a–e; Mus. Arch. Bat., Nos. 472.

[2]) Mus. Arch. Bat. no. 502.

each time the fourth tone; in other words, it is a colotomic instrument of a "lower" order.

The same function is taken, in the "ordinary" West-Javanese gamelan, which generally lacks an instrument like the gendèr panembung, by the **jengglong** (ill. 139), composed of a number (in pélog, seven; in sléndro, six) of beating kettles lying on an underframe, and of a format that is something between the *keṭuk* and the *kenong*, both as regards diameter and as regards height. These beating kettles are arranged thus:

in pélog:

2	3	4	5	6
1				7

in sléndro:

1	2	3	4
5_1			5

Something has already been said of the **rèntèng** (ill. 158, *sub d*), the largest of the Sundanese one-row bonang-instruments. It usually consists of two rows of beating kettles forming two adjacent sides of a rectangle. The short row—with the lowest-sounding kettles—is called, in Tasikmalaya, *kachibong*, and in Sumedang, *indung*; the longer one more especially *rèntèng*, and in Sumedang occasionally *anak*. Sometimes this instrument occupies three sides of a rectangle, *i.e.* one short, and two long sides. This is a kind of partial doubling; for in this case the two long sides carry identically-tuned ranges of beating kettles. The instrument is too large to allow of its being mastered by a single nayaga, and is therefore beaten by a number of players together.

II. Membranophones

Concerning the membraphones already discussed we may give the following additional details:

a. the *penunṭung*, or *ketipung* is here generally called *kendang leutik* (= little K.) or *kolantèr* (ill. 152, *sub b*, and 161);

b. the Sundanese *kendangs* (ill. 152, *sub a*; 153, *sub c*; 160, and 161) are all truncated conical in shape (the "full-bellied" specimens occurring exclusively in the Regents' gamelans mentioned before, and being imported from Central Java) [1]); there tightening straps are called *rarawat*; their sliding rings, *gelang*, and the low wooden trestle on which the instrument sometimes rests, also when being played upon, *kuda-kuda*.

[1]) The "full-bellied" kenḍang depicted in ill. 159 as joining in the playing, was borrowed from another large gamelan belonging to the Regent, and hailing from Jogya.

For the rest only two forms of drum need be described here, *i.e.* the *dogdog* and the *terbang*.

The Sundanese equivalent of the Javanese *réog* is called **dogdog** (ill. 143, 149 *sub b*, 154 *sub d*). It occurs in various sizes, and is now more compact, now more long-drawn in shape. The largest specimens would be about 80 cm in length, and have a head of 20 diameter; or, when only 35 cm long, the skin would have a diameter of 30 cm; the measurements of the smallest specimens are, respectively, about 24 and 18 cm.

In the various small rustic orchestras one sometimes comes across two, but usually four, unequally large specimens. In this case these drums have each their own name, whose vowel is darker in sound according as the instrument denoted by it is larger in size: *tilingting*(*-tik*), *tong*, *bangbrang* or *ambrang*, and *brung*. In addition to these names we sometimes come across the—evidently inevitable—*indung* and *anak*, and, further, *tèmpas*, or *panèmpas*, which may be translated by "joiner-in", and *èngklok*, the signification of which we gave above (p. 364) when discussing the angklung.

Usually the largest and the smallest dog-dogs in a set are beaten with the bare hand, and the two medium-sized ones with a stick. The players hold their instrument either under the left arm or carry it before them in a sléndang.

Of the **terbang**, as already described on p. 216 *et seq.*, several forms are known in West-Java (ill. 152 *sub e* and 153, *sub a*). We mention here the *terbang besar*, the largest of all, sometimes between 60 and 75 cm in diameter, and having a nailed-down skin (ill. 153, *sub a*); the *terbang gembrung*, about 25–30 cm in diameter, and whose skin is kept tightened by means of a ratan hoop and wooden plugs, as is also the case with the other terbang-forms to be mentioned hereafter; then there is the much flatter *terbang ketimpring*, diameter 25–35 cm; it has two or three small tinkling plates fitted into the side-wall, at equal distances fron one another (ill. 153, *sub b*). The above names are those current in the Regency of Lebak. Elsewhere, especially in the Sumedang district, the terbang is also called *gembyung*, *i.e.* when there are no tinkling plates fixed in the side-wall. A small-sized terbang is distinguished, in this district, by the name of *kempyang* (= having a bright sound). In Sukabumi I came across five terbangs bearing the following names, from large to small, respectively:

indung, tojocharang, tèmpas, kempyang and *anak*. The name *kitimplik*, too, may be met with there as denoting a very small form of terbang. In Tasikmalaya the terbang besar is called *T. benjangan*; the terbang with tinkling plates, *T. genjring*, and a very small species, whose "bowl" is not made of wood but of coconut shell (*batok*), *T. batok* 1).

III. Chordophones

After what has been said about string instruments, the following additional details may suffice:

a. the *chelempung* with metal strings is, in West-Java, an instrument imported from Central Java. Along with this, however, there are also either one- or two-stringed bamboo idiochords denoted by the same name. The bridges of these bamboo chelempungs are called *pahul*; the central vibrating "bridge"—when present at all—is called *sumbi*. The ensemble of which a couple of such instruments form part—respectively in the functions of keṭuk and kenḍang (hence: *ketuk awi* and *kendang awi*)—is also called *chelempung* (ill. 155).

b. the one-string aeolus-bow (Jav. *sundari*), which is tied to a kite and made to sound while up in the air, is called, in the Sunda districts, *petèng*; the combination of kite and string, *langlayangan petèng* or *pepetèngan*.

c. the Sundanese *rebab* is distinguished from the Javanese in that the soundbox is not made of coconut shell but of wood—usually *nangka* wood—and by its slightly broader "shoulders" (cf. ill. 97, *sub b*, and ill. 155, *sub a*). Its component parts are naturally called here by different, Sundanese, names: the neck becomes *tihang*; the upper piece, *puchuk*; the body, *bobokon*; the buffalo-bladder from which the sounding board is made, *wangkis*; the bridge, *inang* (= breast); the keys, *peureut* (= to wring), and the bow, *pangèsèt*. Generally *jeruk* wood is used for the making of the tihang, puchuk and peureut.

The old-fashioned, very simple style of playing the rebab is known in Sundanese by the term *dèngdo* (cf. above, p. 360, *sub r*), the modern, more ornamental style is denoted by the term *lèlol*, and "glissando" or "portamento" is called *lèotan* 2).

1) See further about terbangs the important article by Brandts Buys in "Djawa" XIII, p. 205 *et seq.* (**36**).

2) *Lèotan* is not exclusively the manner of sliding tonal transition peculiar to rebab playing; both in vocal music and in playing the suling, too, two tones are often bound by a portamento, in which case the term *lèotan* is also used.

During the last few years the rebab has practically ousted the other, venerable and specifically Sundanese bowing-instrument, the *tarawangsa*—about which more later—but is now, in its turn, giving more and more place to the Western violin.

That which Central and East-Java possess in the *chelempung* with metal strings (ill. 78, *sub b*, and 79) and the *rebab*, West Java, or, rather, the Sunda districts, possess in the *kachapi* and the *tarawangsa*.

The **kachapi** (ill. 144 and 157, *sub a*) consists of a long-drawn, box-shaped wooden sound-body (*raraga*), which stands upon four short legs, and whose sides go in a little from above downwards, so that the upper plane is considerably larger than the base. Both the narrow sides rise above, and curl round, the sounding board, after the manner of breakers on the beach (this is called the *gelung* = haircurl). The bottom of the sound-body is for the greater part left open. From 6 to 18 strings (*gandar* = long) run along the sounding-board of the instrument, each of which strings is fixed to a wooden or metal pin; at the other end they disappear somewhere into the sounding-board and are wound round pegs ((*peureut* = to wring) on the inside. These pegs stick through one of the side-walls of the instrument, and, inside, through a wooden bar (*ilat* = tongue) lying lengthways against the inside of the sounding-board.

The strings are kept tightened by a common fixed high bridge spanning the entire width of the kachapi, as well as by separate, small, four-sided pyramidal, mobile bridges (*inang* = breast) pushed underneath; tuning may be done both by moving these inang and by turning the pegs. The strings are plucked with index and thumb.

The general form of the instrument reminds one more or less of a proa. Popular fancy, however, rather sees in it a resemblance to the *kunti*, or *pontianak*—an evil female spirit—and has, as may be seen from the above-mentioned terms, named various component parts of the instrument in accordance with this train of thought (**188**, p. 237). The fact that the kachapi has, at the bottom, a longitudinal opening, gives still more point to this comparison: the kunti is imagined to be enchantingly beautiful in front, but having a hideous, oblong cavity in the back.

The kachapi is, in East-Priangan, and especially in the Chiawi district, frequently tuned in sléndro (*nyalèndro*); for the rest, they are, both there and in the rest of the Sundanese territory, generally tuned in scales that are usually called *mèlog* and *nyorog*. One obtains the nyorog scale by raising the tone *panelu* of the mèlog-scale [1]) (which, according to some, is identical with the scale *salendro degung*—cf. p. 65) by about three-quarters of a tone (**197**, **200**). The result is a pure *madenda*-scale (cf. above, p. 64).[*S28] In addition to this, kachapi-scales are occasionally come across which, without any doubt, have come into existence under Western influences.

More and more one comes across kachapi's nowadays whose sound-body has cast off the elegant proa-like shape in favour of that of a parallelepiped, one of whose longitudinal sides, however, partly runs slightly on the slant; an intermediary form, therefore, between the classic kachapi and the European zither. In this new form, moreover, the oblong opening underneath has been replaced by a slit running diagonally. This more modern instrument is generally denoted by the term *siter* (ill. 145). [*S33: 37–8, 42, 63–5, 70]

The Sanskrit name *kachapi* is that of several plucked string instruments in the archipelago; they, however, are generally instruments after the model of a lute [2]). It would seem that this name does not, as was formerly assumed, derive from the species of tortoise of the same name (whose carapace, it was said, originally served as resonator), but from the tree kachapi (*Cedrela Toona*), from whose wood the Indian instrument, which has given its name to the Indonesian forms, was made (**311**, p. 125/6). Hence the fact that the name is not bound to any fixed instrumental form, but may be, and is, borne by stringed instruments of very diverse nature, providing only they are made of wood.

After the suling and the angklung, the kachapi is, among the Sundanese, the most widely-distributed instrument. It is also one of the few instruments known to the Baduy's. Their *tukang pantun* accompany themselves on it when reciting the heroic sagas from the ancient realm of Pajajaran [3]). (The content of such a pantun provided, some 30 years ago, the necessary data for the symbolic-historic stage play *Lutung kasarung*, which was performed for the first time during the Congress of the Java

---

[1]) It is, of course, only the kachapi-scale of that name which is referred to here; the mèlog-scale of, *e.g.*, the ordinary gamelan is purely a pélog-scale.

[2]) Borneo: *kechapi*; Toba-Batak: *kachapi*; *hapetan*; Karo-Batak: *kulchapi*, *hasapi*; South-Celebes: *kachapi*; Mindanao (Maranao): *kuchapi* (Philippine Magazine XXXVI, July 1939, p. 296 and 298).

[3]) In contradistinction to the *Malay* pantun—a quatrain built up according to definite rules—the *Sundanese* pantun is a partly recited and partly sung epic. Cf. **300**. [**82**A, **167**A, **179**B, **300**A, **402**D] [*S42]

Institute in 1921). During ***ngaroronda***, *i.e.* the collective singing of love-songs by unmarried young Baduy's in the "house of youth", there are often 10 or 12 singers present, with as many kachapi's (**384**, p. 88).

If one may judge from the only Baduy-specimen in the Musicological Archives, which is only 66 cm long, these kachapi's are much smaller in size than the Priangan instruments, which sometimes reach a length of 150 cm (vide also **144**, p. 163).

The kachapi is played with both hands and, as a rule, in two parts. The upper part either consists of a genuine complete melody or contains a more or less rigid paraphrasing. The lower part comprises either rhythmic figuration, or a skeletal melody (against the rigth hand melody) or a more elaborate melody (against the melodic figurations of the upper part) [1]).

Outside the Baduy territory the kachapi usually shares the accompaniment of the voice with the suling, as well as with the **tarawangsa** (ill. 157 *sub c*), a melody-playing stringed instrument. It might just be possible, that it is a descendent of the kachapi; for its shape is practically the same as that of a small kachapi to one of whose narrow sides a neck has been fixed. The head of this neck is often ornamented with fine *à jour* carving. Generally the tarawangsa has two strings, but sometimes three, in which case one of the strings does not run over the bridge, which is fairly high, very narrow at the top, and has two feet. The strings disappear half-way down the sounding-board into the interior of the sound-body, *i.e.* resembling the way in which the kachapi is strung, but in contrast to all other plucked and bowed string-instruments, known to me in the archipelago, whose strings either run along the entire length of the sound-box, being attached in some way right at the bottom, or are fixed to a more or less knob-shaped ,,bridge" which, in these cases, forms an organic whole with the "belly", or flat top, of the instrument. (This is the way the Celebes and Sumbanese boat-lutes are strung).

The bow of the tarawangsa, like that of the rebab, is kept tightened by the player's hand.

It is a great pity that the tarawangsa is becoming more and more rare; in large areas it has already been ousted by the rebab and the western violin. Nevertheless one often comes across it in more remote districts;

---

[1]) For records of kachapi playing, *vide* the numbers given below, and p. 402. [*S 33, 37, 38, 42, 63–65, 70]

it is, for instance, still a favourite instrument among the Outer Baduy's (the so-called Panamping, or Keluaran) (**384**).

Col. G. J. 222 (lagu *Chatrik* and lagu *Rènggong Malang*) gives two good examples of a vocal part accompanied by a combination of two (!) kachapi's, suling and a bowed instrument (tarawangsa or rebab). [*S[42,65]]

Five members of a group of "alien Easterlings" deserve to be mentioned here; they are four Chinamen, and one Arab.

The Arab is the **gambus** (ill. 146 and 147). The name derives from the Arabic name for this instrument, *i.e. qopuz* (*via* the East-African form, *gabbus*) [1]). The instrument has the form of a long-drawn, pear-shaped lute with a wooden sound-box which is only very slightly arched; a sounding-board made—at any rate as regards the specimens found in West-Java—of wood in the narrow part, and of parchment in the wide part; a beautifully carved, big "scroll", and—at any rate in Java—seven strings, the 6 higher-sounding of which are made of silk, and tuned, like those of a mandoline, two-by-two on the same tone, only the lowest being single and made of metal.

In the narrow wooden part of the sounding-board, half-way down, and underneath the strings, there is a small hole. The strings, which run over a flat bridge placed close to the bottom edge of the instrument, are tuned by means of seven pegs, three of which are fixed to one side of the scroll, and the other four to the other side. At the bottom end the strings are fixed to a stout button sticking out as much as 5 or 6 cm.

Elsewhere in the Archipelago we also find *gambus* possessing a sounding-board made entirely of wood. There are, too, different formats in this instrument. We should, it seems, distinguish two main forms: a slender one, the Hedzyas type, and a stouter form, the Hadramauth type, which, however, is said to be descended originally from Egypt.

The gambus is, in West Java, usually played in conjunction with a shawm and a kendang; it may also serve as accompaniment to vocal music, which, in that case, bears an unmistakably Arabian character.

[1]) In Europe, too, the *qopuz* became known, *viz.* in the beginning of the 14th century at the latest. SACHS ("Handbuch der Instrumentenkunde", p. 211), quotes in this connexion a line of verse by HEINRICH VON DER NEUEN STADT, reading, "*Die Kobus mit der luten*", and he further points to the Hungarian and Russian word *kobuz*; the Russian *kobza*; the Rumanian *cobuz* and *cobza*, all of which words stand for instruments to be plucked with the fingers.

Some good gramophone records of this are the Ultraphone Nos. A 60020 and A 60039.

The four Chinese instruments which should be briefly described here are also chordophones. Two of them are completely identical in shape, only differing in their respective sizes. They are the **ohyan**, or *rebab batok kechil*, and the **gihyan**, or *rebab batok besar* (ill. 148, *sub b*), the latter—the Malay name already conveys as much—being the largest. These instruments are two-stringed bowing instruments, with a relatively, fairly long neck provided with two pegs at the back, and a sound body consisting of a half-coconut, in the back of which there are a few small holes usually forming an *à jour* rosette, and to the front of which is fixed a thin wooden sounding-board. The tiny bridge is cut from arèn-wood. The bow moves *between* the two strings, being thus inseparable from the instrument; as a result, one of the strings is stroked with the top-, and the other one with the bottom-part of the hair. According to COURANT the instrument was brought into China by the Mongols, and is called there *hou khin* [1]). This ohyan and this gihyan are sometimes found in small orchestras in Batavia.

The same manner of playing as is described above is practised on the small bamboo violin, also of Mongolian origin, and also two-stringed, which one may find in Batavia, usually in the possession of Chinese, but sometimes in that of Malay owners [2]). The sound-box of this violin consists of a fairly stout, but short piece of bamboo, open at the back, and closed in front by a piece of parchment, bladder, or snake-skin. The rather short neck, in which there are two pegs—at the back—, continues, close behind the sounding-board, through the sound-body, protuding a few cm at the other end. I failed to get to know the native term for this instrument: according to COURANT the Chinese name for it is **eul hyen**, or **hwo khin**. It belongs, for that matter, in common with the preceding instrument, also to the Further-Indian, more especially the Siamese instrumentarium.

Finally, there is the instrument which is usually designated by the name of "moon-guitar", but which, in Batavia, is simply called *kachapi*, or sometimes **china sampan**, and, in China itself in common with a few other forms of plucked instruments, *yue khin*. [1])(ill. 156, *sub a*). Its resonance-body is a flat cylindrical disc, to which is attached a very short neck.

1) [*S29]. 2) [ill. 148-a]

There are four strings, whose pegs are fixed, two on either side, in the neck [1]). Although the china sampan is usually seen in the hands of Chinamen, one may also hear it played by real Batavians; it even seems to form a regular component of the small orchestra accompanying the, purely Malay, *Lenggo*.

About the instruments proper to the type of music called **kronchong**—in so far as we have not already dealth with them—and about kronchong-music itself we shall content ourselves with stating that they originated in South-European folk-music which came to the Archipelago in the 16th century with the advent of the Portuguese, and that they are still being played, especially among the Indo-European population, with enthusiasm and unmistakable musicality, be it without the slightest rea musical culture. The instruments, in so far as they are chordophones, are all modern, imported ones (mandoline, guitar, violin, ukelele, etc.), except, in some cases, the actual *kronchong* itself, which has been copied by skilful native hands, in the kampong Tugu near Batavia, after the Portuguese model; it has the shape of a small, very narrow, five-stringed guitar with pegs at the back of its neck. To the ensemble belong, further, an occasional *bangsing* (transverse flute), with which we shall deal in a moment, and on rare occasions a *terbang* with tinkling plates. The text sung—invariably in pantun-form—is Malay (**33**, pp. 5 and 53; **80**, **89**, **265**, **361**, and **407**). [**83**A, **121**B, **278**B]

IV. Aerophones

About the aerophones already dealt with, we give here the following additional particulars:

a. The West-Javanese form of the *selomprèt*, called *taromprèt*, differs from the Javanese instrument by having large coconut "wings" attached to the mouthpiece, into which the blownout cheeks of the player fit exactly (ill. 135, 152 *sub c*, 154 *sub b*) [2]);

b. the earthenware, bird-shaped ocarina (jav.: *susurilitan*) is called, in the Priangan mountain districts, *surilit*, or *talèot*; the former name, for that matter, is also used to indicate the small whistles used by coachmen, and the latter name, in Banten, to denote a bamboo transverse flute; [S65]

[1]) Mus. Arch. Bat., No. 1028. [*S42, 65]
[2]) Ind. Inst., No. H 3201; Mus. Arch. Bat. No. 459.

c. in Tasikmalaya the bull-roarer, when made of coconut leaf, is called *hohoang* (ill. 103, right); when made of other material, *kekinchiran*;

d. the "pigeon-flute" (Jav. *sawangan*) is here called *sosoangan* (from *soang* = goose);

e. the bamboo spinning-top (ill. 106), *panggal awi*, or *papanggalan*;

f. the rice-stalk shawm, *i.e.* both the clarinet- and the oboe-form, is sometimes called *empèt-empètan*, but more generally either *dami* or *jarami*; when it has a coconut-leaf "bell" attached it, the name is *olè-olèan* (ill. 134).

As I mentioned on p. 366, the sounds produced by the *rengkong* form an accompanying background to the **hatong** music. This hatong (ill. 141) is a bamboo Pan-pipe, usually occurring in pairs, namely a larger specimen, with either 2 or 3, and a smaller one with from 10 to 14 small tubes. These are—needless to say—distinguished once again by the respective names of *indung* and *anak*. The tuning is either sléndro, pélog, or "miring".

In the district of Charingin (regency of Pandeglang, residency of Banten) the population has three different kinds of hatongs in use when stag-hunting. These hatongs are made from *bamboo tepus*, on the same day the hunt is to take place. One of these three forms, with a single pipe, bears the name of *hatong ijen*, or *hatong honghong*; this type is reserved for the exclusive use of the drivers. The two other kinds, *i.e.* the double-piped *hatong sekaran* and the three-piped *hatong pan(g)ajak* are blown by the hunters themselves.

Outside the Sunda districts Pan-pipes are rare in the Archipelago. As far as is known, the only other places where they are still to be found are Flores (in an incomplete, *i.e.* unconnected, form) [1], Timor [2] and in the eastern part of the central mountains and the South coast of New Guinea [3]. The instrument seems to be of Central-Asiatic origin, and to have spread over part of Austronesia (and of South-America) during the Han period (206 B.C.–220 A.D.), as a consequence either of migrations or commercial traffic [4].

---

1) *Vide* **221** (p. 152 *et seq.*, and ill. 49).

2) **311**, p. 146; **232**, pl. XII fig. 27, and Ind. Inst., No. H 2059.

3) **202**, plate XIII, fig. 57, and **226**.

4) Possibly *hatong* is an originally Chinese word (*vide* p. 38, note 1). Cf. the name for the Chinese funeral trumpet(?) *fa-(ta-?) haotong* (MAHILLON III, p. 329, No. 1872). Think also of the correspondence, in form, between another Sundanese instrument, the *kachapi*, and the Chinese *tseng* (remark by MAHILLON, in III, p. 346).

Another instrument called *hatong, hatong manuk, i.e.* bird-hatong, is a short bamboo slit-stop flute (German: Kernspaltflöte) [1], or, maybe, ring-flute (German: Bandflöte) [2], both of which are used as bird-calls.

In addition to the endblown forms of flutes dealt with above (p. 233 *et seq.*) (*suling pélog* and *suling sléndro*), which are also known in the Sunda districts, and about which nothing further need be mentioned except that the pélog-instrument here has 6 stops, as in Jogya, there is also in West Java, the *suling degung* (ill. 142), with only 4 stops, and in the typical degung scale [3]. The second stop from above is invariably much larger than the three others.

At first hearing, this degung-scale seems to be a kind of europeanized pentatonic pélog; according to some, however (amongst them KUSUMADINATA, *vide* **170**, 3rd vol., p. 5), it is a sléndro tone-gender with unequal steps. In regard to this, *vide* also p. 65 above, and **200**, p. 334/5.

In Batavia and South-Banten there exist at least another four different flute-forms, namely,

a. a bamboo flûte à bec, with either 6 or 7 finger-holes, and about 30 cm in length; this flute is called—in common with many Sumatran flutes of this type—*bangsing* (cf. Sanskrit, and ancient Jav., *bangsi*) [4];

b. a bamboo transverse flute of the same name, which forms part of the small "gambang-kromong" orchestra to be described further on; of this flute there are three different types, namely, one with 6 [5], one with 4 [6] and one with 2 [7] stops;

c. a "Kerbflöte", *i.e.* a flute whose mouthpiece is formed simply by a notch in the wall of the tube (cf. **275**, p. 81). The specimens inspected by me were all open at the bottom, and had 5 stops. The native name is *chalintu* [8];

---

1) Mus. Arch. Bat., No. 489.
2) Ind. Inst., No. 1029/4.
3) Ind. Inst., Nos. 1055/13–16.
4) In South-Banten, also *talèot.* (Mus. Arch. Bat., Nos. 426 and 427 (Banten); 433 and 434 (Batavia)). [*S 65]
5) Ind. Inst., Nos. 1030/3, 1045/18; Mus. Arch. Bat. No. 428.
6) Ind. Inst., No. 1030/2; Mus. Arch. Bat., No. 429.
7) Ind. Inst., No. 1045/2 and 6.
8) Ind. Inst. Nos. 1045/8, 9 and 10.

d. a slit stop flute (German: Spaltflöte), called *èlèt,* with either 4 [1]), 5 [2]), or 6 [3]) stops (cf. **311**, p. 148 *et seq.*).

Finally, I must say a few words about the **kolèchèr** [4]), the scarecrow whizzing instrument, consisting of a "propeller" with two blades made of wood and fitted loosely upon a horizontal axle, and which is fixed in some way or other in a tree. The wind causes the propeller to revolve rapidly and so to produce a softly humming sound.

The same instrument is also known from elsewhere in the archipelago *e.g.* from the Batak districts, the N.W. Toraja districts [5]), and—in combination with an ingenious construction, making use of small swinging-balls and creating a continuous roll on a bamboo slit drum owing to the rotation of the propeller—from the Tanimbar isles (*dedelak*) [6]).

c. Orchestras

The majority of the orchestras to be dealt with below may be found spread over quite a large area; in cases where they are found within a limited area only, the place or district where they occur will be specially mentioned. The composition of the orchestras often varies somewhat. The combinations given by me here are those which I have either been able to observe personally, or which were communicated to me by native civil servants, in documents usually illustrated by photographs. We need not go into further detail here—after what has been said on the subject in this and the preceding chapter when describing the instruments—concerning the respective functions of the various instruments within the different ensembles.

There are, in the Sunda districts, a large number of orchestras in which shake-angklungs take part. Of these, we mention here:

badut, consisting of 9 angklungs, 1–4 dogdogs, and a tarompèt. Whilst playing, this orchestra performs burlesque dances (ill. 149) [7]);

---

1) Mus. Arch. Bat. No. ?
2) Ind. Inst. No. 1045/17.
3) Ind. Inst. Nos. 1045/13 and 14.
4) Ind. Inst. No. 1045/20.
5) Mus. Arch. Bat. No. 358.
6) Ind. Inst. No. 1041/1.
7) A very good record, with a delightfully self-opiniated tarompèt-part, is Beka No. B 15723. [*S65]

ogèl, consisting of 4 (sometimes 6) angklungs of fairly large format (the so-called *angklung ubrug*), with 4 dogdogs. This orchestra provides the accompaniment to the performance of buffoons (*bodoran*) (**320**). In the regency of Lebak, the same combination, serving the same purpose, but augmented by a blown gong and a few more dogdogs, is called *doblang*. In regard to the magic background of the ogèl performances I refer the reader to **114**, p. 98.

It is said that, for the *topèng-* (= masked) dances, an ensemble was used in ancient times, all over West Java, composed of angklungs and 2 dogdogs. In the larger places, however, this combination is often replaced nowadays by a small gamelan, composed—at any rate in the regency of Batavia—of the following: kromong, 3 ketuk, rebab, blown gong, goöng gedè, kendang and kendang leutik.

Then there is the small orchestra called *bunchis*, from an abbreviation of the name of the popular song *Kachang bunchis* (the last syllabe to be pronounced with a long-drawn *chiiiiis*, the exact equivalent of the English "huuh") (**188**, Table I No. 1). This bunchis-ensemble is of the same composition as the badut-orchestra, but augmented either by a kendang or a jidor. The players —in so far as they manipulate angklungs—also perform simple dances, generally moving around in a circle.

Still more numerous than the angklung-orchestras are these combinations which include one or more terbangs.

To the sound of the *terbang salawat* (4 terbangs, and 1 kendang), and of the *terbang mumuludan* (5 terbangs and 1 bajidor), religious hymns are chanted.

An orchestra of from 6 to 10 *terbang ketimpring* (*genjring*), or *terbang gembrung*, or of a few *terbang besar* (*T. benjangan*), either with or without a kendang, accompanies the—mostly corrupted Arabian—songs, which are sung during circumcision- and wedding-festivities, and on the birthday of the Prophet (ill. 153). The last-named ensemble occasionally provides the musical background to the action of a wayang dancer. The most numerous and complete of these orchestras are found in good-Mohammedan Banten, and in the neighbourhood of Tasikmalaya.

During slametans in the Tasik districts, one may also frequently hear a number of *terbang batok* being beaten. In addition to this one finds, in this region, the terbang-ensemble *pichung lingkup*, consisting of five, unequally large, *terbang gembrung*.

A terbang may also be met with in the Sukabumi *ubrug*-orchestra [1]), the other instruments being the tarompet, kendang, kolantèr, and kekechrèk; this combination serves as accompaniment to a troupe of *bodoran*. Elsewhere, such an orchestra is sometimes called *longsèr*. In Lebak, its composition is somewhat different: tarompèt, rebab, kromong, 2 bedug, and 2 gongs, whilst in Sérang it consists of: rebab, 3 kenong, 2 bedug, and 1 gong.

Finally, the terbang is also to be found in the *bètok*-orchestra, a combination of two such instruments with a large and a small kendang, a tarompèt and a kechrèk, to the accompaniment of which the *kuda lumping* (**190**, p. 30/31; **114**, p. 97)—the equivalent of the Javanese *réog*, or *kuda képang*—perform their sham fights and trance-dances. This, however, is also done sometimes to the music of the *gamelan rèntèng*, at any rate in Indramayu.

Ronggèngs, usually accompanied by *ketuk tilu* [2]) (rebab or tarompèt, 3 ketuk, kendang, and gong), or by *banjèt* (*i.e.* the same combination, but *minus* the rebab) are to be seen, in the Sukabumi district, being danced and sung to the music of a somewhat more extensive ensemble, comprising rebab, 2 sarons, 3 ketuk, kendang, kendang leutik, 2 gongs, and kekechrèk. Such a ronggèng-band is called, in these parts, *ambèn* [3]).

---

[1]) Cf. **338**, p. 226, where mention is made of a gamelan *utuk-ubruk* being used, in Kebumèn, for the accompaniment of the wayang purwa, which gamelan consisted of 2 bonangs, 1 gendèr, 1 gong, 1 kempul, 1 kenchèr(? = kechèr), and 1 kenḍang, and, further, of the gamelan *utuk-ubrul* used in Magelang—*vide* our Appendix *57b*—(in sléndro), also serving as accompaniment to the wayang (both kulit and kliṭik), but also topèng, and consisting of saron, (ke)demung, gong suwukan, kenong, keṭuk, kempul and kenḍang.

[2]) Good illustration in VAN EERDE, "De Volken van Nederlandsch-Indië", vol. II, p. 259. [*S65]

[3]) Dr. PURBACHARAKA has pointed out to me the interrelation between this and the ancient Javanese music- and dance-play *amèn*, or *mèn-mèn*, mentioned, *e.g.* in the Tantu Pangelaran (edition PIGEAUD, pp. 104 and 170), in the combination *bhandagina mènmèn*, *i.e.* the executants of the *mènmèn*-play (Cf. also **194**, p. 8, note 6, and p. 39/40).

Amèn, for that matter, is nowadays (*vide* above, p. 174), in the north of Central East Java, also one of the names used for a small orchestra characterized by the absence of any gendèrs, and which, therefore, was probably used, in the beginning, more especially for this mènmèn-play.

The players are called *panjak* [1]; another name for them (*e.g.* in the district of Cheribon) is *kemprongan* = itinerant theatre; the songs that are sung belong to the class of *lagu jalan gedè* (= street-songs).

Roundabout Banjar, a kind of orchestra may be found, called *ronggèng gunung*, and consisting of 3 ketuk, kendang and gong; it supplies the accompanying music to a series of narrative songs, frequently relating to events that happened in ancient times in the Rawah Lakbok, a vast swampy territory between the inhabited regions of Tasik and Banyumas.

A dance with great sensual excitement is the *ronggèng dogèr*, practised more especially in the Tasik district. To the accompaniment of the ordinary ketuk tilu orchestra, a number of ronggèngs sing songs with an erotic flavour (*sisindiran bobogohan*) [2].

When the spectators are sufficiently keyed-up the ronggèngs throw a kerchief at the man of their choice, which means an invitation to join them in the dance. After this the dance changes to a common *tayuban* or *nayuban* of a more or less sensual nature.

The dress of the ronggèng dogèr is a curious one. They wear either black or red trousers, with a sarong wrapped around them, which, however, reaches only half-way down the thighs, so that the trousers stick out. The sarong is held up by a waistband, the so-called *ampok*, made of velvet and embroidered with gold and silver thread. The upper part of the body is covered by a shirt with short sleeves, preferably in glaring colours, and with flashy decorations. The head is wrapped round with a flowered cloth.

The dance called *penchak*—the cat-like, agile fencing-dance, also known elsewhere in Java (*vide* the exhaustive description by BRANDTS BUYS, in **43**, p. 22 *et seq.*)—is accompanied in the Sunda districts by the *kendang penchak*, played by 2 kendangs, tarompèt, and kempul. [*S[42,65]]

In the Garut district an ensemble exists which, after the instrument characteristic of it, is called *chalung* (ill. 154). It consists of one or more chalungs, usually of the type immovably tied together, and with only

---

1) Cf. Above, p. 138.
2) About this *sisindiran vide* **114**, p. 110 (116 *et seq.*).

few keys; tarompèt, goöng and **ketuk** awi, and dogdog, and may be heard more especially during circumcision festivities. The goöng awi is sometimes replaced by a goöng buyung.

The *gamelan Lilingong*, composed of two gambang kayu, kendang, and blown gong, is used as accompaniment to the shadow-wayang of the same name, which is dragging on a languishing existence, exclusively in the désa Seuseupan, in the Chianjur district. It is said that Balinese influences play a certain part in it. The tales that are staged are derived from the Damar Wulan cycle, the ḍalang giving them a strongly burlesque flavour.

According to another communication, the gamelan Lilingong exists also in the kampong Pasir Gombong. The kampong-chief ARMAWI is said to be the present ḍalang. In addition to the instruments named, there is also, it is stated, a rebab in the accompanying orchestra. The names given of the lakons played by this ensemble are: *Tambankan, Dermada, Wanagiri, Mupu Kembang, Tigasan, Sinduraja*, and *Perbu alengka*; the genḍings accompanying these: *Balapéka, Angkatan, Manggungkeun, Murua, Balanganjur* and *Papalayon.*

The *chelempung*-orchestra (ill. 131) is fortunate in being widely-spread. The name is derived from the idiochord bamboo instruments, which are found in it in two different functions, *i.e.* as kendang and as ketuk. The other instruments in this combination—another essential element of which seems to be a female voice—are: rebab, suling, goöng awi, and—not always, however,—a kachapi.

By *gamelan tiruan* is meant, in the regency of Tasikmalaya, a sort of substitute for the gamelan (*tiruan* = pseudo, from *niru* = to imitate, to follow); it consists of a goöng buyung gedè, and a goöng buyung leutik both with a single bamboo key; a rebab, a saron beusi (*i.e.* a saron with iron keys; Sund., *beusi* = Mal. *besi* = Jav. *wesi*); a gambang, and a kechrèk. The ensemble is used both during wayang performances and at dance-parties (*tayuban*).

Another, very popular, combination in West-Java is the cooperation between a solo voice and the suling, accompanied either by a kachapi or a siter (ill. 145). The repertoire is partly identical with that of the gamelan degung, and partly with that of the ordinary gamelan (although the latter in many cases has a slightly different scale). Apart from this, there are a large number of songs, based on the *nyorog*-scale (already mentioned p. 371), which do not directly originate from the repertoire of the other orchestras. The majority of records of Sundanese vocal music, made by the large gramophone companies are taken from such songs, accompanied by the kachapi and paraphrased by the suling. An excellent specimen of this is contained in the collection put together by Professor VON HORNBORSTEL ,"Musik des Orients", *i.e.* the Odeon record *Udan mas* (A 39651*b* = O 4491b), a *nyorog*-song. The lagu *Embat-embat* (App. *5*) is also in *nyorog* [1]). A good, if simple example of *mèlog*-song is the lagu *Mupu kembang* (H. M. V. No. 1873), the score of which is reproduced here as Appendix *53*. *Vide* also below, p. 398 *et seq*.

After hearing some of these records, which I had sent him, Mr. K. V. RAMACHANDRAN, B.A., the Indian musicologist, wrote to me as follows: "Your Sundanese records are very interesting. Indonesia has had no contact with India during the past 1000 years, and it is marvellous that classic Hindu melodies of great antiquity are to be heard in the Sunda islands today, in very nearly the same form".

The same combination of kachapi and suling, only augmented by a tarawangsa (which, however, is already being replaced by a rebab in many cases nowadays), is to be found under the name of *tarawangsa* (ill. 157). This combination also serves very often to accompany vocal music (especially pantun) (**188**, p. 238/9); sometimes, however, *e.g.* in Purwakarta, it constitutes the orchestra for the wayang golèk, *i.e.* the wayang with wooden dolls. Usually, it is the ordinary gamelan that serves to accompany this wayang golèk.

In the Garut district it is usual to enlarge the tarawangsa orchestra (with the original tarawangsa) by adding a blown gong, a ketuk, a kekechrèk, a kendang, and, sometimes, a rebab.

---

[1]) We must remind the reader to the fact that we here refer exclusively to the so-called nyorog-scale of the *kachapi*, which scale constitutes a tone-*gender*, either in pèlog (in that case, actually = transposed *miring*) or in salèndro (S. madenda). The *real* nyorog (*vide* App. *54*) is a tonal "key" belonging to the tone-gender *mèlog* of the pèlog system.

The play called *ujungan* [1]) used to enjoy a fair measure of popularity, especially in the south-eastern part of the Regency of Tasikmalaya (dèsa's Chijulang and Parigi). In latter years, however, it has gone into disuse through the interference of the civil service. The following description of this play will make it clear why the government interfered.

Ujungan was a sham fight between two persons. Both the fighters' bodies were wrapped round with cloths and *ijuk* (*arèn* fibres), and their heads and faces enclosed in a hood (*bala kutak*) made of cotton (*kapas*) and coconut fibres (*tepes*). Their otherwise unprotected legs were encased in short trousers (*chelana sontak*). There would be two seconds, one for each fighter, who, if it was a friendly game, were to put a timely end to it. It was no play for hyper-sensitive people: each of the "players" was armed with a rotan stick of between $1^1/_2$ and 2 m in length, which had been rubbed in with dried *ketan* (sticking rice). With these sticks they would try to touch the non-protected parts (hands and legs) of their opponent, in such a way that the skin would be torn open.

Not in every case was such a meeting held in a spirit of friendly sport; occasionally serious feuds were fought out by it. There have been instances when the fighters did not stop until one of them had been killed; it is said that the sticks were sometimes rubbed in with poison obtained from corpses.

The entire duel was fought out to the time and under the stimulation of a small orchestra composed of a kendang, small gong and tarompèt.

Duels such as this ujungan appear to be ancient Indonesian: kindred forms have come to our knowledge from various parts of the archipelago: in Java itself, in the Banyuwangi district, under the name of *gitikan* (**40**, p. 211); in Panaraga and Blitar, under that of *gebugan*; in Banyumas, as in Tasik, under that of *ujungan*; in Tegal, also under the name of *ujung(an)*, or, maybe, *lameng* [2]); in Bali, under the name of *karé* [3]) or *endé* [4]); in the Manggaray (West-Flores) (**221**, p. 95 *et seq.*), as *main chachi(k)*, or *parisé* [5]). We should also mention in this connexion the form of duel in vogue at the Mataram court in the 17th century, of which Van Goens writes: "to the playing of larges goms (*i.e.* gongs), two male

---

1) the noun derived from *ujung* (used side-by-side with *bujung*) = to chase after.

2) J. W. van Dapperen, Volkskunde van Java III ("Djawa" XV, p. 170), 1935. — *Lameng* = sword.

3) *Vide* N.I. Oudheidkundig Verslag 1930, p. 46.

4) Cf. Philip Hanson Hiss, Bali (1941), pl. 44. — Perhaps named after the Florinese place Endé? 5) from *paris* = schild?

persons, one with a pike, and the other with a shield and sword, each doing his duty in beating or thrusting at the other party" (**91**, p. 328).

The gambang-kromong orchestra takes us, in the first place, to Batavia, and to an environment subject to Chinese influences. Here, an orchestra composed of gambang kayu, kromong, ohyan, gihyan, bangsing, kenong and kendang plays the accompaniments to songs reciting highly emotional events which used to happen in years gone by (the so-called *shairs*), as, for instance, the *cherita Pitung rampok Betawi* (the story of P., the robber of Batavia); *cherita Angkri digantung di Betawi* (the story of A., who was hanged at B.); *cherita Delep kelebu dilaut* (the story of D., who was wrecked at sea). These songs are sung to different melodies, such as *Jalijali, Persi, Suriang, Lenggang-kangkung, Kramat Karam*, etc. A good example of this orchestra's playing, in which a strong Chinese element is noticeable, is given by Od. 91012 (lagu *Pobin Jinka Hwe Ke*) and Od. 91215 (lagu *Pobin Lian Hoa Tee*). Cf. also **140**, **238**, p. 87, and **265**. [*S71]

Another form of art showing Chinese influences is *lenggo*, a Batavian song- and dance-play, in which Malay songs are to be heard accompanied by 3 robana (= terbang), one or two rebab (usually replaced by violins), and a Chinese moon-guitar (ill. 156).

A third, specifically Batavian musical expression-form is the *wayang chokèk*, a song- and dance-play performed by women (originally slaves). In this they have their hair in plaits, and wear a *baju kurung* (*i.e.* a bag-shaped jacket without buttons, which the players pull on over their heads; *kurung* is really the cover of bamboo wicker-work, under which fighting cocks are kept). The orchestra consists of gambang kayu, rebab, suling and kempul, to which are sometimes added kenong, ketuk, kechrèk and kendang. A phrase often recurring in the text is: "Si Nonna disayang", or "Si Babah disayang" [1]), *i.e.* "our poor mistress", or "our poor master".

The remaining ensembles, which follows hereunder, may be classed—one in a greater, another in a lesser degree—with the gamelans proper.

---

1) According to the Regent of Batavia, *babah* is derived from an Arabic word *baba* = master; this word, it is supposed, was originally *hababa*, and signified "apple of the eye".

The **rèntèng** (ill. 158) is the Sundanese dèsa-gamelan. The nucleus is formed, as the name already indicates, by the kolènang rèntèng. Besides this there are present a goöng gedè and, generally, a kendang. To it may further belong a gambang gangsa, a kempul, a bèri without beating knob, and/or a set of chechemprès. The scale of the kolènang (as well as that of the gambang gangsa when present) is pentatonic in unequal steps. It is uncertain as yet whether its scale should be placed under the heading of the pélog tonal gender, or whether it is a more or less separate and independent form of its own. Sometimes there is a sixth key (in this case, an exchange tone), at any rate for the higher octaves. In the Kanoman (the seat of the wakil-Sultan Anom), at Cheribon, there is a gamelan rèntèng called *balè bandung*.

Here follow a few of the rèntèng scales measured:

Rèntèng from													
Chileunyi (dis-	330		360		395		494		538				660
trict Tg. Sari)	I	*150*	II	*161*	III	*387*	IV	*148*	V		*354*		I'
ditto from													
Chikebo (dis-	360		405		429		545		586				720
trict Tg. Sari)	I	*204*	II	*100*	III	*414*	IV	*125*	V		*357*		I'
ditto from													
Lebakwangi	377		402		451		547		590		671		754
(district	I	*111*	II	*199*	III	*334*	IV	*131*	V	*233*	VI	*192*	I'
Pameungpeuk)											*425*		
Balè bandung													
Kanoman	338		383		403		513		548				676
(Cheribon)	I	*216*	II	*88*	III	*418*	IV	*114*	V		*364*		I'

The **gamelan ajèng**, as it occurs, for example, in the kampong Pamijahan, dèsa Meganglaya, district Panjalu, and in the kampong Chikapas, dèsa Jalatrang, district Kawali (both situated in the Regency of Chiamis), is also closely akin to the ordinary rèntèng, from which it differs only—as compared to the majority of rèntèng ensembles—by a slightly greater variety of instruments and by a slightly deviating scale, comprising the intervals of the *ajèng* tonal gender, which belongs to the pélog system (cf. above, p. 60). Theoretically, this s˛ale is as follows:

I *150* II *120* III *390* IV *150* V *390* I'

The composition of the gamelan ajèng is as follows: a rènt èng of 14 kettles, 5 of which belong to the kachibong, and 9 to the rèntèng proper; a gambang gangsa, called saron, with 14 keys; two ketuk on a single underframe; kendang; goöng gedè; goöng leutik, and kekechrèk. Its repertoire is extremely limited, containing only six lagu's. These are unsuited to the dance, which is said to be the reason why this orchestra has gone into disuse.

In Chiamis there further exists a **gamelan Bali**, constituted like the Rèntèng, with this difference that it lacks the normal kolènang rèntèng, which has been replaced by a kolènang—also in one row—of only five kettles. The repertoire consists only of the gending Charabali. No dances are performed to this lagu, either, and neither are there any songs recited to it. We cannot say whether there is any connexion between this gamelan and the island Bali (cf. above, p. 264 *et seq.*).

The **gamelan degung** (ill. 159) has been, from ancient times, the gamelan of the highest in the land in West Java; specimens of it may be found in the kratons in Cheribon, and in practically all West Javanese kabupatèns, but only very rarely in the dèsa. Its composition is not quite constant; it often lacks the saron-like instrument, which, in the low register, is called panerus, in the middle, saron, and in the high register, titil; often, too, the goöng gedè and the suling are absent; in very rare cases even the kolènang is missing; one may—also rarely—find, in addition to the kolènang, a second instrument of that form, but tuned an octave higher, and called gembyang, as well as that other bonang-instrument with three kettles, called kepyak; the kendang, too, is sometimes absent; the only essential thing is the degung, *i.e.* the instrument after which the combination is called. With this degung, however, there *must* be an instrument playing the melody; hence the saron and kolènang are never *both* missing at the same time; one of them is always there. With regard to the function of the degung, the principal details have already been given (p. 366). Either the kolènang or the saron plays the melody, which is embroidered with variations by the suling (when present); when both the kolènang and the saron are present it is the former which plays the actual melody, which the saron doubles rhythmically or syncopates. When there is a kendang it has an agogic function; when there is no kendang then this task falls to the lot of one of the kolènang players (the kolènang—and this applies also to the kolènang rèntèng—is beaten by more than one player).

With regard to the scale—which, it appears, is a variety of sléndro resembling a pélog-scale: the so-called salèndro degung—this was discussed above (p. 65 and 370/371; *vide* also **197** and **200**). Here follow a few measurements:

Kabupatèn	363		397		443		542		584		726
Sukabumi	I	*155*	II	*190*	III	*349*	IV	*129*	V	*377*	I'
Kabupatèn	252		266½		314		376		400		504
Bandung	I	*97*	II	*284*	III	*312*	IV	*107*	V	*400*	I'
Kabupatèn	388½		420		476		584		634		777
Sumedang	I	*135*	II	*216*	III	*354*	IV	*142*	V	*352*	I'
Kasepuhan	250		272		305		363		397		500
Cheribon	I	*146*	II	*202*	III	*298*	IV	*155*	V	*400*	I'
Kanoman	428		465		520		636		704		856
Cheribon	I	*143*	II	*198*	III	*345*	IV	*176*	V	*338*	I'
Kacherbonan	426		445		486		618		666		852
Cheribon	I	*76*	II	*152*	III	*416*	IV	*129*	V	*427*	I'

The repertoire, although usually more extensive than that of the Rèntèng, is still rather limited. Some beautiful gramophone records of degung-music are put on the market both by Odeon and Ultraphone; *e.g.* Odeon No. A 39578 (the lagu's *Papalayon degung* and *Palimdungan*), and Ultraphone Nos. A 60010 (*Paron* and *Maninten*) and A 60026 (*Babar layar* and *Lalayaran*). [*S69]

The **gamelan miring**, as used in West Java, denotes *a.* a gamelan pélog with a scale derived from the miring tone-gender [1]), and *b.* a gamelan

[1]) In so far as it is played on a gamelan, the miring scale—at any rate in *this* meaning of the term—is a transposition, to the customary register of the gamelan pélog, of a scale obtained by incorporating the two "vocal" intermediary tones (*panangis* and *pamiring*; *vide* p. 53), and taking the tone *nem* (Sund. *barang*) as

pélog which, in contrast with the majority of orchestras of that name, possesses sarons with only 5 instead of 7 tones, *i.e.* only the 5 main tones of the mèlog-gender (theoretically consisting of tone-sequences with the intervals: 120–150–390–120–420) (**200**).

a. The purest example of a gamelan miring of the former type, which I have ever come across, was a gamelan in Serdang wètan (residency of Batavia, district Tangerang):

309½		337½		364		458		498		619
I	*150*	II	*131*	III	*397*	IV	*145*	V	*377*	I'

b. A good example of a gamelan miring of the second type is given in the following scale of another gamelan, also in Serdang wètan:

310		331		361		455½		489		620
I	*113*	II	*150*	III	*402*	IV	*123*	V	*411*	I'

The West Javanese miring scales belonging to the pélog system, therefore, have nothing to do with the *laras barang miring* of the Principalities (*vide* above p. 327), which is a sléndro scale tending towards pélog, and conforms to the Sundanese *salèndro degung* scale (*vide* above, p. 65); neither are they related in any way to the scale of the East Javanese gamelans miring, which, as previously stated (pp. 12, 33, and 74), embodies either more ancient forms of sléndro in its pure form, or the pélog-barang scale.

The large **gamelan pèlog** and **salèndro** in use in West Java (ill. 163) are more or less of the same composition as the Central Javanese orchestras, with this difference, however, that they often lack the metallophones with floating keys, and also the chelempung (with metal strings) and that the other instruments are generally represented by one specimen only. Only the ketuk—represented, in Central Java, by only one specimen—is often found double in the Sundanese gamelan, when they are tuned, respectively, to *barang* (Jav. *nem*) and *bem* (Jav. *gulu*). Usually there are also two kenongs, tuned to *barang* (Jav. *nem*) and *kenong* (Jav. *lima*).

---

penunggul (Sund. *singgul*); the tone *barang* (Sund. *sorog*) as *gulu* (Sund. *galimer*); the tone *pamiring* (Sund. *panelu*) as *ḍaḍa*, etc. etc.—a scale which, as stated before, may be expressed theoretically in *cents* by the numbers 150 – 120 – 420 – 120 – 390.

Frequently one also finds a *jengglong* in these large gamelans—an instrument never found in Central Javanese orchestras.

Now although the component parts of the Sundanese gamelan are practically the same as those in the Principalities, and fulfil the same functions within the ensemble, the style of playing in West Java is so utterly different from that in Central Java that the untrained ear will hardly be able to recognize the material similarity between the respective ensembles. Something that will at once strike the listener used to the orchestras in the Principalities, when hearing Sundanese orchestral playing, is the much greater prominence of the rebab [1]), and the different nature of the melodics, owing to their conciser structure and to the fact that they generally run along more smoothly, catch the European ear sooner than do the melodics of the Principalities, although the general beauty of sound produced by the Javanese manner of playing will, at the same time, be praised above that of the Sundanese orchestras. One should try to get hold of, and hear in immediate succession, the very good Sundanese gamelan record Odeon A 39501b (*Sulanjana*) and a record from the Principalities such as No. 10 of the collection "Musik des Orients" (Odeon O 1936) (*Kinanṭi madumurti*) or Beka B 150007–I(*) (*Sriharchana*), when the difference should be as clear as daylight. [**343**A]

In the Sunda districts, too, the gamelans are differentiated according to the pitch of their scales. In Sumedang the distinction, from high to low, is as follows: *Sekar tong(g)èrèt* [2]), *S. gadung* [3]), *S.* (*r*)*onèng* [3]), and *S. ropoh* [4]). Of these four different registers, the *S. gadung* and *S. ronèng* are by far the most widespread.

Other differentiations heard occasionally are: a threefold one, *laras leutik, L. tengah* (*sedeng, biasa*), *L. gedè*, and a fivefold one (also from high to low), *laras ding, L. dèng, L. dang, L. dong, L. dung* (in sléndro), or *laras ning, L. nèng, L. nang, L. nong, L. nung* (in pèlog). The pitches in the last-named 5-part differentiations are at a distance of one step from each other.

---

[1]) Thus, it is also the rebab—and not, as generally in the Principalities, the gendèr—which enables the ḍalang to get the right pitch and keep to it, in singing the suluks.

[2]) tong(g)èrèt is the name of an insect, a cicada, which produces a shrill, deafening sound.

[3]) a species of flower.

[4]) *poh* = weak.

(*) [*S[38]]

Special mention is due to the two orchestras of the Regent of Tasikmalaya: the sléndro, called "Layem" (ill. 161 and 162), because it is said to be a present from the Sultan Ageng (1613–1645) to one of the Regents' ancestors, and because its tone-series is still being copied for preference by newly-built ensembles;—the pélog one, called "Munggang" (ill. 160), because the instruments respectively fulfilling the functions of panerus (= Jav. demung), saron and titil (= Jav. peking) do not possess the usual metal keys, but are composed of series of kenong-like beating *kettles* mounted in jengglong formation (*vide* above, p. 367). This also applies to the kolènang and the rinchik (= Jav. bonang panerus).

In the Sunda districts, too, one comes across gamelans whose keys and kettles are made of iron instead of bronze. In Indramayu, Cheribon, Majalenka, Kuningan and Sumedang such orchestras are called either *gamelan kempling, dempling*, or *kedempling*; in Sumedang they also talk of (*gamelan*) *toplèk*. The general Sundanese term is *gamelan beusi*, or *tatabeuhan beusi* (beusi = iron).

It was customary in former times—not only in West-, but also in Central- and East-Java—for the nobility to install a gamelan in the upper storey of the portal giving access to their dalem. The chiefs of the East India Company adopted this custom too, as is evident from the description, mentioned before, of Mr. Kasteleyn's estate at Meester Cornelis (**56**, p. 368b): "In the centre, above the gateway, one may see the players sitting; sometimes making themselves heard ten, twelve or fourteen at a time; beating upon different sorts of cymbals, and small drums, and playing upon flutes made of reed, and attached together in the manner of the ancient shepherds. They also have a kind of zither, underneath which either the bass or the upper part is played on a large drum, which happens only now and then, and, to the best of my memory, with a stick, which is not disagreeable to the ear" [1]).

In those days (beginning of the 18th century), therefore, it seems to have been customary in West-Java to combine the instruments into en-

[1]) The great landlords of Batavia—at any rate in the 18th and 19th centuries—used to keep, at their country seats, European orchestras as well as gamelans, a (sometimes large) number of slaves playing instruments of western origin. Dr. V. J. VAN DE WALL (**393**, p. 85 and 92; **394**, p. 90) mentions various examples of this custom.

sembles of a slightly different character; for, according to the above description, it would appear that the hatong was played in the gamelan, and that the kachapi would make itself heard in conjunction with a bedug or a (ba)jidor.

d. Forms of composition, and their use

Sundanese musicians distinguish instrumental music (*gending, tabeuh*) and vocal music (*kawih*). Very often the pieces played consist of a combination of the two.

This distinction is crossed by another one having its criterion in the rhythm: *tembang* is the name for melodies recited in *free* rhythm, and either with or without instrumental accompaniment; *lagu tandak*, or also—less correctly—*lagu gamelan* or *gending*, for those strictly "quadratic" compositions serving principally as accompaniment to the dance. Added to these there is a special category, the children's songs (*kakawihan barudak*).

Of the *tembang*, there are two main classes:

I. *tembang buhun, i.e.* old-fashioned, "classical" singing, and

II. *tembang kaäyeunaän*, or "modern" vocal music.

Tembang buhun is usually performed without accompaniment. It is sung from a book, written in Arabic characters.

The content of these chants (*wawachan*) is either of an epic or of a religious character.

There are three main forms of this "classic" vocal music:

a. tembang ranchag;

b. tembang raèkan, and

c. beluk.

Tembang ranchag is a style of singing with hardly any ornamentation. Here, the singer's chief concern is the content of the story; hence the singer pronounces the words as distinctly as possible, and there is no necessity for him to possess a conspicuously fine voice. Apart from all kinds of *religious* tales relating to the hereafter, to the birth or ascension of the Prophet, one may hear, sung in this manner, such *epic* stories as *wawachan Amir Hamzah, W. Selarasa, W. Garib, W. Nalakasura Boma*, etc.

The recitation of this tembang ranchak is never alternated by choral singing (*alok*).

Tembang raèkan is festal singing *par excellence*. Here, not the text but the singing is all-important. The musicality and beauty of tone of the voice are, therefore, at a premium. Nevertheless, the texts are not chosen at random for this type of singing either; preference is given to those wawachan that are in some way connected with the occasion of the festivity; thus, for example, at wedding feasts, for preference the *wawachan Rengganis* and the *W. Danumaya*, both of which contain a good deal of amorous adventure. This raèkan singing is chiefly heard in the evening. One of the singers (the one who can read best) opens the wawachan-book in the light of a lamp, and starts reciting some stanzas as nicely as he possibly can. After this the chant is "*dijual*" (= sold) by him; this means that he *reads* the continuation of the text aloud, line by line [1]), and one of those present *sings* it after him, also line by line. In this way each participant gets his turn. Sometimes the others join in all together, either in chorus (*alok*), or with a single ejaculation (*senggak*) of some syllabic combination rich in sound, *e.g. aheng*!

By the time that 20 or 25 stanzas of the same metre have been safely gone through in this way [2]), the precentor proceeds to another form of verse, starting again by reciting a few stanzas as beautifully as he can.

The scales sung are the following: *salèndro lempang* or *jawar*, *salèndro madenda*, and *mèlog jawar*. There is no definite order of sequence prescribed in the use of these; it all depends upon the content of the story which mode is selected.

This raèkan-singing is kept up until about three o'clock in the morning After this it makes room for

beluk, in which the same modes are used. This time, the precentor does not sing himself. He provides, in a clear voice, the text, line after line, that the others are to sing. Each of the participants in turn then undertakes, each time, to sing one of the lines. One should hardly be expected, for that matter, to produce more than one line at a time, it being obligatory

---

[1]) This reading is called, in Sumedang, *ngechapan* = to pronounce words for somebody else, to prompt. In Bandung it is called *ngiloan* = to read attentively.

[2]) Such a group of similarly-formed stanzas is called *pupuh*.

to sing as loud and as high as possible. After each stanza follows either *alok* or *senggak*.

All this time both the singers and the audience eat and drink to their heart's content. Not until sunrise do the company disperse.

Old-fashioned people far prefer tembang buhun to the modern style of singing, which they call, deridingly, *kakawihan*, *i.e.* imitation singing.

Tembang kaäyeunaän is also differentiated into three kinds, or, rather, styles:

a. lagam kulon [1]) (*kakulonkeun, Chianjuran*);
b. lagam Bandung, and
c. lagam wètan [2]) (*kawètankeun, Chiawian*).

The cradle of *lagam kulon* is Chianjur. Thence, it has spread over the whole of West-Priangan, and a large part of Central Priangan. [*S33,37,38,42]

As we mentioned already, the two different tunings in vogue for lagam kulon are called *mèlog* and *nyorog* [4]). About the character of these two systems of tuning musicologists differ (**200**, p. 334/5) (*vide* also p. 65, note 3, and p. 370/371). The players call them by two names derived from the pélog system; it should be remarked, however, that it might be better to call the latter scale *miring* rather than nyorog, in view of its relation to the mèlog-scale. Both the mèlog- and the nyorog-scale, however, show small, but unmistakable deviations from scales of the same names in the complete system, whereas, according to some, amongst whom is also R. MACHYAR KUSUMADINATA, they may be derived quite purely and without any modification from the salèndro system, in which case they would represent, of that system, a scale of the *degung*- and one of the *madenda*-genus, respectively. In latter times these lagam kulon scales have become more and more westernized, under the influence of European music and musical instruments [3]).

---

[1]) = west(erly).

[2]) = east(erly).

[3]) In May, 1933, RADEN MACHYAR KUSUMADINATA (ill. 164) was requested by the Director of Education and Religion to make an attempt to raise Sundanese vocal music from its decline. The result of KUSUMADINATA's activities was surprising: within the space of twelve months, this apostle of music succeeded in winning over a large number of school-teachers to his ideal, and in thoroughly instructing them. Many of these educationalists, in their turn, started courses in singing, with the result that the native songs are now being sung once again all over the place, free from western stains; new vocal plays are being got up; the almost

[4]) [p. 370-1]

I give below a survey of the scale-structure, first of the mèlog- and then of the nyorog-system. Under 1, 2 and 3, three different forms of tuning will be found, all observed in actual practice (and all three already corrupted); under 4, the theoretically pure mèlog-, resp. nyorog-(miring-)scale; under 5, a theoretically pure degung- resp. madenda-scale, and under 6, an approximation to these scales in the European tonal system.

Mèlog [1])

	singgul (Jav.: *bem*)		*bem* (Jav. *gulu*)		*panelu* (Jav. *ḍaḍa*)		*kenong* (Jav, *lima*)		*barang* (Jav. *nem*)		*singgul leutik* (Jav. *bem alit*)
1. Nyi Eha	I	*87*	II	*178*	III	*432*	V	*62*	VI	*440*	I'
2. Nyi Mursih	I	*96*	II	*190*	III	*402*	V	*94*	VI	*398*	I'
3. Nyi Resna	I	*101*	II	*216*	III	*391*	V	*97*	VI	*395*	I'
4. theor. mèlog	I	*120*	II	*150*	III	*390*	V	*120*	VI	*420*	I'
5. theor. degung	I [2])	*120*	II	*240*	III	*360*	IV	*120*	V	*360*	I'
6. Europ. scale	C	*100*	D♭	*200*	E♭	*400*	G	*100*	A♭	*400*	C'

Nyorog [1])

	singgul (Jav. *bem*)		*bem* (Jav. *gulu*)		*bunggur* (Jav. *pélog*)		*kenong* (Jav. *lima*		*barang* (Jav. *nem*		*singgul leutik* (Jav. *bem alit*)
1. Nyi Eha	I	*87*	II	*412*	IV	*198*	V	*62*	VI	*440*	I'
2. Nyi Mursih	I	*96*	II	*402*	IV	*210*	V	*94*	VI	*398*	I'
3. Nyi Resna	I	*101*	II	*403*	IV	*204*	V	*97*	VI	*395*	I'
4. theor. miring	I	*120*	II	*390*	IV	*150*	V	*120*	VI	*420*	I'
5. theor. madenda	I [2])	*120*	II	*360*	III	*240*	IV	*120*	V	*360*	I'
6. Europ. scale	C	*100*	D♭	*400*	F	*200*	G	*100*	A♭	*400*	C'

forgotten, ancient playditties are being taught the children again at a number of schools; briefly, Sundanese popular vocal music has, humanly speaking, been saved from perdition for at least another generation.

[1]) The intervals VI/V and II/I, I suspect, have grown so small because of the fact that the tones VI and II function as "leading tones".

[2]) Actually the 2nd degree of the sléndro tonal sequence (cf. p. 65, note 3).

It may be said with respect to the mèlog songs that—expressing it in Western terminology—of the five tones of the scale, the *papetet* (*singgul*) may be regarded as the tonic (T_1), and the *kenong* as the dominant (D_1). This, at any rate, is the rule; but there are exceptions. One of these exceptions (at any rate in the *Nyi Eha* version) is the one which was heard in the lagu *Jemplang*. In this song, no pronounced tonality could be ascertained; to the European ear, it hung more or less in the air; it seemed to hesitate between the tonality determined by the fifth G/C and that determined by the fifth A♭/D♭. The melody finished on the (string-)combination A♭/D♭.

Further, in almost every case the tonic is at the same time the final note. It is probably for this reason that this tone bears the name of *papatet*, a word which might here be translated by "that which limits, determines position". On two occasions, however, a song ended on the dominant (*kenong*) (F_3). This was in the lagu's *Polos* and *Bubaran*. According to NYI EHA these were exceptional cases [1]).

Taking the above into consideration, therefore, the mèlog scale looks something like this:

The nyorog-scale presents a different picture altogether. It is obtained, starting from the mèlog-scale, by exchanging the third tone (*panelu*) for another one about a whole to $^5/_4$ tone higher (in the case of NYI RESNA the difference was 187; with NYI EHA, 234, and with NYI MURSI, 212 C). Hence, perhaps, the name of this new tone: *sorog gedé*, *i.e.* the "principal exchange-tone" [2]). To the European ear, this tone now sounds as the tonic (T).

These two changes—replacement of the third tone by another one, and shifting of the tonic—are, however, not the only ones. Pieces rendered in

[1]) The lagu *Polos*, moreover, has the peculiarity that its two melodic supports are not placed—as in all other cases known to me—at a distance of a fifth or fourth, but at that of a diminished fifth or augmented fourth: that is: in addition to the G (*kenong*), *the* D♭ (*singgul*) is the prominent tone.

[2]) Other unexplained names are the *sorog bungur*, *i.e.* "violet exchange tone", and the *sorog liwung*, *i.e.* the tone which "causes one to faint", or "turns one's head".

the nyorog tuning do not, as a rule, finish on the tonic, as do the mèlog songs, but usually have the dominant (in this case, C) as their *finalis* (F_1). In nyorog, too, therefore, this tone quite rightly retains the name of *papatet*. It may also happen, however, that the tonic is actually the *finalis* (F_2). The lagu's *Embat-embat* (app. 50) and *Sinom pangapungan* [1]) are examples of this. In these cases the "habitus" of the piece in question approximates somewhat to that of the mèlog songs; but owing to the notable difference in absolute pitch, and to the difference in the size of the succeeding intervals: *panelu-singgul* and *singgul-papatet*, on the one hand, and *barang-kenong* and *kenong-sorog gedè* on the other hand:

Mèlog: Pt' *440* B *62* K *432* P *178* S *87* PT
Nyorog: S.G.' *412* S *87* Pt *440* B *62* K *198* S.G.,
an appreciable difference still remains.

As a result of all this the nyorog-scale may be approximately represented in western notation as follows:

Whilst, further, both the singing voice and the suling player usually confine themselves, in mèlog, to the use of the tones contained in the accompanying string instrument [2]), they also make use, in the nyorog songs, of the tone or tones of the complete scale which are missing from the kachapi tone-sequence.

The songs of the lagam kulon are always accompanied instrumentally; originally, by the kachapi and the suling. In latter times, the kachapi is frequently replaced by its degenerate descendant, the siter, and occasionally a guitar and a mandoline are added to the combination.

The repertoire is a five-fold one, consisting of:

I. *pantun*-songs, such as *Mupu kembang* (App. 53), *Pamiring, Jemplang* [3]), etc.;

II. *tembang asal*, or *lalaguan tembang buhun*, i.e. classical tembang,

---

[1]) H.M.V. No. 2936 (singer: Ajum).

[2]) The exceptions (*e.g.* the lagu's *Papatet* (Odeon A 39524a) and *Pangapungan*, as regards the *sorog gedè*), confirm the rule.

[3]) H.M.V. 1879.

in a refined, embellished and modern form, such as *Dangdang gula kèntar* [1]), *Sinom pangrawit* [2]), *Bayubud* [3]), and others;

III. modified, "Sundanized" Javanese lagu's such as *Sinom Tegal* [4]), *Dangdang gula Batang* (it will be seen that, in such cases, the place of origin is incorporated in the title);

IV. songs derived from "quadratic" tandak-compositions, these having been re-shaped to such an extent that all rhythmic strictness is lost, in other words, that their character has become entirely *tembang*. Examples are *Kulu-kulu, Banjar Sinom, Udan mas* (App. 49), *Rènggong*.

With this group should also be classified the different *patetan* and *suluk*, as well as many *kakawèn*, such as *Waringin sungsang, Gedong duwur, Gunung keliran, Arjuna manangis*, etc.

V. In addition to the above there are, as fifth group, a number of genuine salèndro songs, which have penetrated from more eastern parts of the island; *e.g. Sinom loloran, Sinom sanga*, and a few *kakawèn.*

However simplistic this Chianjur vocal music may be, it emanates great charm. As an example we may take the just mentioned lagu *Mupu kembang* (i.e. "Picking flowers") (App. 53). This song was sung in 1926, in the form here reproduced, by the celebrated woman singer NYI ANAH [5]).

With the aid of means so simple that they could hardly be reduced still further, it possesses the choicest rhythmic refinements. Upon a perfectly solid instrumental foundation of quadratic structure, and with unfaltering adherence to the tonality, both the female voice and that of the suling move with the sureness of a somnambulist in unrestrained freedom. The fair bird of melody hovers in what seems complete independence over the well-cultivated, regularly plotted, dark earth of the accompaniment. The singing voice leads; the suling embellishes it and sometimes doubles it in a higher octave. And yet, there is a binding, a unity, an organic whole; now and then that light-winged melody just touches firm ground, drawing from it, as it were, new energy for further flight. But the tie uniting melody and accompaniment—tonally so strong, because of its simplicity—is stretched, rhythmically, almost to the point of brittleness; to that extreme which only an infallible instinct dares to go up to, and is

1) H.M.V. 1873.
2) H.M.V. 1875.
3) H.M.V. 1876; Odeon A 204007a and A 39588a.
4) H.M.V. 1875.
5) H.M.V. 1873.

able to reach without the risk of rupture. It is the triumph of freedom combined with lawfulness. This is natural hetero-rhythmics, non-intellectual, unconscious; and the soul of a people that generated such songs as these gives thereby evidence of an intuitive awareness of rhythm, no worthy counterpart of which exists, to my knowledge, in West-European folk-music. Nay, this melodic and rhythmic tissue is often so subtle that even the musically trained Westerner has the greatest difficulty in not getting lost in it.

Now if we analyse the lagu *Mupu kembang* more closely, we are struck—apart from what has already been said—among other things, with its partiality to syncopation in the kachapi part. This kachapi part was already referred to in the preceding paragraphs. Its structure is of the simplest, but not without charm. The introduction starts with small, fidgety syncopated figures, gradually going into another *motif* (14th bar *et seq.*), which provides a harmonic base for the melody. The rhythmic shift half-way down the bar, appearing in bar 27, and the counterpart of which is introduced in bar 33, leading back to the old rhythm, brings a welcome change. At those places where the connexion between the rhythm of the accompaniment and that of the voice is at its vaguest (bar 35 *et seq.*) only the second half of the rhythmic pattern is played, in a slightly modified form. Bars 42 and 43 bring the return to the introductory motif.

The vocal melody, too, is fairly simple as regards structure. Actually it consists of six small phrases, the sixth of which might be regarded as a less elaborate, if more emphatic, repetition of the fifth.

Phrase II (bars 18 to 20 incl.) is an abbreviated repetition of phrase I (bars 14 to 17 incl.). Both phrases—which do not manage to rise permanently above the dominant, and also close on it—get their repetition, but charged with greater energy, in phrase III (bars 21 to 29 incl.), when the melody is brought up to a higher plan, where it can deploy itself to the full. This phrase closes on the octave of the tonic. Not until then does the melody begin to spread its wings unhindered. From this moment it looks very much as if the accompaniment exists for it merely as a general harmonic basis, whose particular form of articulation is henceforth a matter of indifference to it [1]); all rhythmic contact between the two seems to have

[1]) This is also evident from the stanzas 2 and 3 —not reproduced in Appendix 53—of NYI ANAH's rendering, in which the singing voice starts, respectively, one bar earlier and one bar later.

been broken off. By means of a *tenuto* tone at the end of phrases IV (dominant), V and VI (tonic), however, a periodic effect of confluence is obtained; it is probably superfluous to point to the feeling of aesthetic gratification, which this parting and coming together again of the two rhythms creates in the listener [1]).

Not a trace of the quadrature of the accompaniment, or of any regular return of tonic accents is to be found in the vocal melody. Its centres of gravity lie at very unequal distances. Whereas, further, the accompaniment is a pure example of "*analytical*" rhythmics (based upon the ***divisible*** unit), the song- and suling-melodics is—especially in the second half of the lagu—an equally pure example of its opposite: "*synthetic*" rhythmics (starting from the smallest note-value, a given amount of which form together one "bar"). Hardly any two "bars" of this song- and suling-melody have the same length and/or subdivision. Notwithstanding this there is no question of any licentiousness or affectation, on the contrary, the compelling force and perfectly natural vitality of this vocal melodics is unmistakable.

We might call attention to an occasional difference in tempo as between the vocal part and the kachapi part: in phrase V (bars 35 to 39 incl.) this difference is most striking. I need not elaborate the point that the no-

---

[1]) Until quite recently there existed no equivalent of this in western music. In 1946, however, the Dutch composer Koos VAN DER GRIEND has obtained an analogous effect in the score written by him for a sound film. WOUTER PAAP, in "Mensch en Melodie" (Vol. I, p. 329), made the following remarks about this score: "... The composer has here made use of the possibility of mixing together three different musical records. He played three separate piano parts, which were successively recorded on the sound reel, and subsequently unified into a single sound-effect. As each of the three parts has its own metre and ryhthm, adapted to the speed of the film-action, [f.i. in score No. I one beat to 12, in score No. II one beat to 14 and in score No. 3 one beat to 16 film-pictures], the result was quite a new polymetrical and polyrhythmic effect, which can be obtained only (*sic*!) by these means."

Personally, I should have preferred, in this case, the terms *hetero*metrical and *hetero*rhythmic, reserving the terms *poly*metrical and *poly*rhythmic for those forms in which the hearer can discern in the simultaneously sounding voices their metrical and rhythmical correlation, as in the following instances (perhaps there are more):

(a) in combinations of different metra, but with simultaneous periodical accents;

(b) in combinations of bars of equal type, but whose accents lie apart by one or more beats ("shifting" of the bars in respect of one another, for example in a fugue where often the subject in some of its later entries starts on another beat than the first time); this frequently does not find expression in the notation;

(c) in combinations of bars of different type, but whose periodical accents coincide;

tation of a hetero-rhythmic duet of this kind is a rather ticklish bit of work, the result of which does not pretend to be more than an—admittedly precise—*approximation* and not a *perfect rendering* by any means. It is a labour of patience, which could never be accomplished without the assistance of a gramophone record. For, notation direct from the players' and singers' rendering itself can be accomplished with satisfactory precision only when the rhythmic constructions are not too complicated. And even if the executants should be prepared and able to repeat certain parts the desired number of times, they neither would nor could give an exactly similar rendering twice running. This is also quite evident from the record from which the score of *Mupu kembang* was transcribed: the song is there repeated three times, and all three stanzas differ from each other in small details of execution. Again, on the Odeon record A 39575b, taken some time later, NYI ANAH sings the same song, and again differently in trifling detail. The task of the Indonesian singer, in contrast to that of the European executant musician, is a *creative* one. Each time a lagu is sung the song flowers again from the traditional melodic groundwork, the unalterable melodic nucleus; often to the delight of those who have learned to esteem the native—in this case, the Sundanese—style of performance. [*S42]

How dignified, too, is the somewhat melancholy simplicity of the lagu *Embat-embat* (App. 50), when it is rendered the way I was privileged to hear it, recited by the singer BAKRI.

This lagu, although in nyorog, finishes—at any rate as sung by BAKRI [1])—

(d) in combinations of bars of different type, in which the accents coincide periodically after every few bars.

Examples of such polymetrics and polyrhythmics may be found in the western music of the last few centuries. Those defined under (a) are the most numerous; we find such formations in a great many orchestral and chamber music movements;

as an example of (b) I refer to BACH's "Well-tempered Clavier", Part I, the fugue in E (the third entry of the subject);

examples of (c) are the opening of the violin sonata by GABRIEL PIERNÉ (6/8, later 2/4 against 10/16); the opening of the Scherzo from RAVEL's string quartet (6/8 against 3/4) and DE FALLA, Pieces espagnoles, II. Cubana (6/8 against 3/4);

examples of (d): the middle part of the Pantoun from the pianotrio by RAVEL (3/4 against 4/2); p. 164 *et seq.* of the score of MOZART's Don Juan, where three orchestras play simultaneously in 3/8, 2/4 and 3/4 time, respectively (in this case, however, one 3/8 bar is equal to a single beat of either of the two other types of bar); a few pasages in WILLEM PIJPER's 2nd sonatine for piano (3/8 plus 4/8 against 4/8 plus 3/8), and in the sonata for flute of the same composer, 3rd movement at No. 26 (4/8 against 3/4).

[1]) RADEN SANUSI, however, gives the lagu according to the rule; *i.e.* with the dominant as *finalis* (H.M.V. 1881).

on the melodic tonic, and not, like the great majority of these nyorog melodies, on the dominant.

As far as its structure is concerned, it shows a less elaborate form than *Mupu kembang*. It possesses only three melodic phrases, of which the first, phrase I (in its first form), ends on the leading tone [1]) of the tonic (the fifth of the dominant); phrase II finishes on the dominant, and phrase III leads us back to the tonic again. The second half of this lagu is nothing but a repetition of the first half, on a somewhat broader basis; phrase Ia is a more emphatic repetition of phrase I, in a more elaborate form, which—ignoring the leading note used the first time as point of rest—moves towards the dominant; phrase IIa is a replica, slightly spun out, of phrase II, and phrase III comes back in exactly the same guise.

A thing which strikes one about *Embat-embat* even more strongly than in the melodics of *Mupu kambang*, is the frequent use made of triplet-formations. It should further be remarked that the register of the melody, which, in *Mupu kembang*, does not exceed a minor tenth, amounts, in *Embat-embat*, an octave and a fourth, *i.e.* the same compass span as that of, *e.g.*, the lagu *Udan mas* [2]). Very occasionally it is smaller, for example in the lagu *Cheurik Rahwana* [3]), which has a compass of only one octave. Generally, however, it is greater: *Papatet tengah* [4]) has a compass of an octave + a diminished fifth; the lagu's *Pamuragan* [5]) and *Polos* [6]) move over an octave + a pure fifth; the lagu's *Bayubud* [7]) and *Udan liris* [8]) extend over an octave + a minor sixth, *Dangdang gula kèntar* [9]) and *Lorloran* [10]) over an octave + a major sixth, whilst the lagu's *Kulu-kulu barat* [11]) and *Chirebonan* [12]) bear the palm in this respect, with a compass of no less than an octave + a minor seventh and a major seventh, respectively.

---

[1]) This lies *above* the tonic, since we are dealing here with a scale which, in common with the ancient Greek scales, are felt to run from high to low.

[2]) H.M.V. 1881: RADEN SANUSI; Odeon A 39651b: NYI RESNA.

[3]) Odeon A 204013a: NYI RESNA.

[4]) Beka B 15752I: NYI MURSIH. [*S[42]]

[5]) Odeon A 39576b: NYI RESNA.

[6]) H.M.V. 1874 and Odeon A 39588b: NYI ANAH.

[7]) Odeon A 204007a.

[8]) Beka B 15750^{II}: NYI MURSIH. [*S[38]]

[9]) H.M.V. 1873: RADEN SANUSI.

[10]) H.M.V. 1877: R. SANUSI; Odeon A 39576a: NYI ANAH.

[11]) H.M.V. 1880: R. SANUSI; Odeon A 39575a: NYI RESNA.

[12]) Beka B 15750^{I}: NYI MURSIH.

The *lagam Bandung* forms the transition between lagam kulon and lagam wètan; it is, however, closer to the lagam kulon, with which she shares the repertoire. Only the style of singing is different (another manner of ornamentation and more *portamenti*), whilst the number of lagu salèndro is larger. The rebab, moreover, in addition to the kachapi and the suling, is invariably among the accompanying ensemble. [**157**A]

The procedure at a Bandung singing-party—usually held in the evening and into the night—is as follows:

The opening of the concert is in the mèlog-mode with a few lagu tandak, modified (made "free") in the manner described above; *e.g. Rènggong manis, Rènggong ganchang*, etc., the majority of which are in patet barang (Jav. nem), the rebab or the suling leading. Following this, the principal singer sings a few kakawèn, *e.g. Sebrakan, Anglilir*, etc., with *karatagan*-(i.e. srepegan-) accompaniment on the kachapi, in order that the particular atmosphere of the prevailing mode may be unequivocably determined. In this, the rebab follows exactly in the footsteps of the singing voice, whilst the suling embellishes the melody with jaunty melisms. After this, but preceded by an introduction on the rebab, he sings either the lagu *Pamuragan* [1]) or *Rènggong*; the other singers take over the melody from him. After a few stanzas the performers proceed to another lagu. Invariably they are melodies, taken from the tandak repertoire, for example *Bubaran* [2]), *Liwung* [3]), or *Chirebonan* [4]).

Only then has the moment come to start real tembang. Now one will hear, in succession, for instance *Sinom Tegal* [5]), and various forms of *Dangdang gula* (amongst others, *Kèntar, Kèntar ajun, Bayubud*) [6]).

At about midnight, a change is made from the mèlog- to the nyorog-mode. As was stated above, this is obtained by replacing the tone *panelu* by the tone *bungur* (Jav. *pélog*). If, with R. MACHYAR KUSUMADINATA, we regard the kachapi-modes as belonging to *salèndro*, then we should say that the tone *sorog panangis* is raised up to and replaced by the tone *kenong*.

After this, melodies are sung and played such as *Dangdang gula kèntar*

---

1) Odeon A 39576b; Beka B 15752^{II}.
2) Odeon A 204003a.
3) H.M.V. 1876.
4) Beka B 15750^{I}.
5) H.M.V. 1875.
6) Odeon A 204007a.

nyorog [1]; *Sinom pangrawit* [2]; *Bantenan*; *Dangdang gula Batang*; *Asmarandana*; *Embat-embat* [3], etc. etc., which belong to the original tembang, and, in addition to these, lagu tandak such as *Kulu-kulu, Kulu kulu barat* [4], *Suntik dahi, Banjaran sorog, Udan mas* [5], *Udan liris* [6], etc.; these lagu's are sometimes rendered in the "tembangized", free form, and sometimes in their original, purely "quadratic" style.

The kachapi player now strikes up a *papapet* (Jav. *lagon* or *paṭetan*)(*) in order to let the singers know the paṭet; at the same time he sings the following stanzas (*sisindiran*) [7]:

Gunung Galunggung kapungkur
Gunung Sumedang katunjang
Talaga Sukawayahna
Rangechik di tengah leuweung
Ulah pundung ku disungkun
Ngopepang ku teu ditèang
Tarima raga wayahna
Nganchik di nagara deungeun.

Gunung Gedè siga nu nandè
Nandèan ka badan kuring
Gunung Pangrango ngajogo
Ngadagoan kuring wangsul
Wangsul ti pangumbaraän
Kebo mulih pakandangan
Nya munchang labuh ka puhu
Pulangkeun ka Pajajaran.

Freely translated, this amounts to the following:

Against the gunung Galunggung as background
There lies the gunung Sumedang, bordering on

---

1) H.M.V. 1873.
2) H.M.V. 1875.
3) H.M.V. 1881; Ultraphone A 60023, and our Appendix *50*.
4) H.M.V. 1880, Odeon A 39575a. [*S37]
5) H.M.V. 1881; Odeon A 39651b.
6) Beka B 15750^II.
7) Further details regarding *sisindiran* may be found in HIDDING (**114**, p. 110 (116 *et seq.*)).
(*) [S42]

The lake Sukawayahna;
The rangechik grows in the thick of the forest.
Please don't be annoyed when people treat you unkindly;
Don't be peevish because they don't come and see you.
Reconcile yourself to this, resign yourself,
For you are living in a foreign country.

(It almost looks as if) the gunung Gedè
Will envelop my body,
As if the gunung Pangrango sits
Waiting for me to return homeward,
Back from my wanderings.
The buffalo saunters stableward;
The kemiri nut falls at the foot of the tree-trunk;
Oh, take me back (home, too,) to Pajajaran.

Following this recitation, a large number of pantun-songs are sung, e.g. *Randangan*, *Jemplang*, *Pangapungan*, etc., alternated by different lagu tandak, such as *Paron*, *Sinyur*, *Puraganta*. In these, the rebab remains silent; the suling leads the melody.

At about 2 or 3 in the morning a change is made to salèndro. It is now the turn of the suling to be silent, and the rebab takes its place. Again, "emancipated" tandak songs open the performance. After this, the precentor sings a few kakawèn, *e.g. Gedong duwur* (also used occasionally as papatet), *Sendo(n)*, *Arjuna manangis*, *Sebrakan*, again with *karatagan*-accompaniment; this is followed—as in the first period—by a second series of modified tandak songs, such as *Dangdang gula pachig*, *Sinom loloran*, *Sinom Chiawian* [1]), *Solontongan*, *Rènggong sanga*, *Rènggong Garutan*, *R. Choyor*, *R. Entog*, etc. etc. These are often alternated by lagu in surupan madenda, as *Sinom pangrawit*, *Embat-embat* (App. 50), etc. (as a consequence of this, discrepancies arise between certain tones of the kachapi, which is tuned to salèndro lempang (= S. jawar), and the singing voice), and also, now and then, by tandak songs, both in salèndro jawar and in S. madenda.

At break of day the company disperses, satiated with song and conviviality, and perfectly contented.

[1]) Odeon A 204013b.

The songs of the *lagam Chiawian* (or *L. wètan*) are, with a few exceptions, in salèndro, namely, for the most part in surupan jawar, but some of them in S. madenda [1]).

The repertoire is threefold: it comprises (I) original tembang; (II) melodies adapted from Central Java, and (III) lagu tandak.

The three groups of songs have this in common that they are sung in free rhythm; the first two inherently so, and the third one through modification.

They are always accompanied instrumentally, by a combination consisting of rebab, gambang kayu, ketuk, kenong, kempul, goöng, kendang, and sometimes a kendang leutik (ketipung). Nowadays the gambang kayu is occasionally replaced by a kachapi.

Whereas the lagam kulon and the lagam Bandung are sung *sotto voce*, the Chiawian style requires a full, strong sound. Maybe because of this the absolute pitch of the lagam Chiawian is appreciably higher than that of the lagam Bandung and the kakulonkeun. Finally the lagam wètan is distinguished by the fact that many of its melodies are followed by an *alok*.

In former times the influence of the lagam Chiawian spread over the whole of Eastern and Central Priangan; in later years this style has gradually made way for the lagam Chianjuran.

In conclusion, a few observations with respect to Sundanese children's songs (*kakawihan barudak*), the data for which I also owe to R. M. A. KUSUMADINATA. These children's songs are generally in the ringkung-scale (cf. above p. 37 *et seq.*), covering an extent of, at most, one octave; usually, however, not more than two or three tones. An example is the lagu *Ngala papatong* (App. *51*, *sub D*). [*S65]

In addition to the ringkung-songs, there are also some in the mèlog- and degung-scales. These are evidently at a higher stage of development, and date from a later period. For, the scales in question, as compared to ringkung, represent a probably younger phase of evolution, and their range of tones is usually more than one octave [in those songs].

The notation of the children's songs placed on record by VON DEWALL

---

1) The reader is once again reminded of the fact that it is not quite certain that the madenda scales should be reckoned to belong to the salèndro system (cf. above, p. 370/371).

(**74**) give the impression of being a rendering, partly of salèndro- and partly of ringkung-melodies.

Some names of well-known children's songs from the Sumedang district are: *Prangpring*; *Tutunjulan-tetenjelan*; *Ayang-ayanggung* (a walking-song); *Eundeuk-eundeuk chang*; *Èyong-èyong* (a lullaby); *Unggut-unggut ngala iwung* (a swing song); *Chokchang*, and the one just mentioned, *Ngala papatong*. [*S65]

Inventive and handy as they are—like all little Indonesians—the Sundanese children, too, delight in putting together all sorts of small instruments from bamboo, clay and coconut leaf, on which they either accompany their little songs or mark the rhythm. [*S30]

More or less in opposition to ***tembang***, with its "free" synthetic time-measure, are the ***lagu tandak***, which, as we said before, are characterized by their rigorously quadratic structure and analytic time-division. As we saw before (pp. 404 and 406), they are occasionally sung alternately with songs in free rhythm. Their proper field, however, is that of orchestral music.

In contrast to Central Javanese orchestral compositions, in which the entire nuclear theme is thoroughly fixed, the Sundanese gamelan pieces possess a somewhat greater freedom in this way that only those tones which correspond to the ones that, in Central Java, are reinforced by the ***slenṭem*** in the lower octave, are emphasized; ***i.e.*** that only the fourth tones (though sometimes also other tones, lying closer together, or—in the larger compositions—maybe, farther apart) are usually "fixed" each time in this way. Since the function of the slenṭem is, in West Java, taken over by the jengglong, we may therefore say that the actual ***cantus firmus*** is formed by the jengglong-tones. As regards the remaining theme-tones there is usually a certain amount of freedom; the player is allowed to replace them by others at his pleasure. Only in the group of the ***lagu gedè***, the "great" compositions, the nuclear theme tones falling on the intermediary ***keteg*** (= ***takol*** = ***dami***) are also usually fixed by tradition. (In this case, especially, the distance between the jengglong tones is often greater than 4: it may be 8, 16, 32, and even 64 keteg-distances). It further happens sometimes that the jengglong tones are only one wilet from each other; in this case the jengglong part and the nuclear theme naturally cover each other, and the latter possesses the cantus firmus character to the full.

According to R. M. A. KUSUMADINATA the following groups of compositions must be distinguished in West Javanese music:

a. lagu gedè;

b. lagu sedeng, or *tengah*;

c. lagu leutik (*Rerènggongan*) [1].

In addition to these, and as a separate group, he also mentions the *lagu jalan gedè*, or *lagu ketuk tilu*, which, being played by a different ensemble, cannot be classified under any of the headings applying to the other compositions [2].

As in Java proper, the different groups of orchestral compositions in the Sunda districts are also distinguished according to their colotomic structure.

The **lagu gedè** possess gongan of 4 or 8 (more rarely, 16) kenongan; a kempul-beat is sounded half-way down each kenongan. Each kenongan comprises 4—very rarely 8—wiletan; half-way down every wiletan we hear a *panchèr* beat (on the instrument playing the nuclear theme; *i.e.* in most cases the saron) (cf. above, p. 168). The lagu gedè are more tied down by tradition than the other types of composition; there are no changes of tempo allowed, apart from those that have been customary since ancient times; the rebab keeps pretty strictly to the nuclear theme; the kendang player is not allowed to take any liberties or produce any fanciful rhythms. As an example we may mention the lagu *Sungsang* (App. *47*).

The **lagu tengah** differ from the lagu gedè, amongst other things, in that their gongan usually contain fewer wiletan—12 at most—and that these gongan are generally of unequal length. Broadly speaking, one may say that, in respect of structure, they are closer akin to the rerènggongan than to the lagu gedè, which latter, however, they resemble again more closely as regards melodics and tempo.

Finally, the **lagu leutik**, or **rerènggongan** are characterized by gongan whose length is, usually and at most, 4 wiletan; in other words, the length of one kenongan in a lagu gedè; there are some, however, with gongan of

---

[1]) In so far as *orchestral* music is concerned the terms *tabeuh* gedè, tengah, and leutik are also used.

[2]) Thus, the lagu *Erang sorong* has kenongan of *three wiletan*.

only 2 wiletan. The wiletan, in their turn, are peculiar in their "elasticity"; they may be taken, at will, in lengths of either 4, 8 or 16 keteg. As examples we may mention the lagu's *Sekar manah* (*Waled*) and *Udan Mas* (App. *48* and *49*).

It is in these rerènggongan that the rebab part—reproduced only summarily in the Appendices—is able to deploy itself most richly and vividly, and least hampered by tradition. Every now and then one may hear lovely, involved ornamental phrases (*lèlol*). The rerènggongan are more in favour as accompaniment to the dance than the lagu gedè and tengah. Led by the rebab, and its Grand Vizier, the kendang, the nayaga's abandon themselves to the full to changes of tempo and rhythm, passing to other paṭets and tonalities; in brief, one may say that it is only in rerènggongan-playing that the players appear to the best advantage and really show what they can do.

The wiletan, too—and this applies to all the composition-forms mentioned—are colotomically "articulated". Schematically a wiletan of, say, 16 wilet may be represented as follows (N = kenong; T = ketuk bem; t = ketuk barang; o = rest (Jav. wela), and ch = panchèr):

t T t o t T t ch t T t o t T t N;

a wiletan of 8 wilet as follows:

t T t ch t T t N,

and one of 4 wilet by;

T ch T N.

In the wiletan of 2 or 1 wilet, in order to avoid monotony, the jengglong takes the place of the kenong(s), which are then either silent altogether or heard only at regular intervals.

We already mentioned changes in *tempo*. Sundanese gamelan musicians distinguish at least seven different tempi (*wirahma*), which are called, from slow to quick—according to R. M. A. Kusumadinata's nomenclature:

1. *ngalamba* (extremely slow, as slow as possible);
2. *le(n)yepan* (very slow);
3. *rangkep* (= double) (slow);
4. *lanchar* (*poco andante*, fairly slow);
5. *dodoan* (moderately quick);

6. *kering* (quick), and
7. *genchlèk*, or *rusuh* (very fast).

Acceleration of tempo (Jav. *seseg, sesegan*) is called, in the Sunda districts, *naek*; retardation (Jav. *suwuk*), *mundur*, or *turun*.

Gamelan compositions are also classified according to their characteristic mood or atmosphere. Thus, the following distinctions are made:

lagu *gagah* (vigorous); *leuleuy* (soft); *nalangsa*, or *sedih* (melancholic); *peurih* (painful), and *sèwot* (angry, irate).

Structurally, the Sundanese gamelan compositions are on a lower plane of development than those of Java proper. They lack the articulation into mérong and munggah as customary in the Principalities. Frequently, however, pieces are strung together into a continuous whole; *i.e.* without each succeeding piece being preceded by an introduction (*pangkat*).

The artistic terminology of Western Java, tho' being, as may be gathered from what has been said above, fairly extensive, yet appears to be somewhat more limited than that of Central Java. The terminology stated above is largely derived from the Sumedang idiom. The unity of nomenclature, as we said before, is not so general in Western Java as in the Principalities; it is therefore probable that many a musical term, although properly Sundanese, but, maybe, in common use elsewhere, *e.g.* in the Chianjur, Chiawi or Banten districts, will be looked for in vain in the present treatise. I have long ago given up trying to learn them all, and, *a fortiori*, I have renounced the ambition of introducing every one of them in the course of these discussions.

During the last years, R. M. A. Kusumadinata has been at pains to come to a definite and general Sundanese terminology (**152, 170–174**c). The future will reveal to what extent he has succeeded in this task.

ADDENDUM

ad p. 140

The sad news reached me — too late for its inclusion in the text — that there is not now a single gong-smithy left in Semarang. As a result, owners of gamelans in both Java and Bali, knowing the replacement of their gongs to have become impossible, are giving greater care than ever to their maintainance.

This information was given me orally by His Excellency ANAK AGUNG, Prime Minister of the Republic East Indonesia.

Thus, an unrivalled craft was lost before our very eyes in a single generation. For shame!

[*S31]